select
editions

Reader's
Digest

Reader's Digest

The names, characters and incidents portrayed in the novels in this volume are the work of the authors' imaginations. Any resemblance to actual persons, living or dead, events or localities is entirely coincidental.

www.readersdigest.co.uk

Published in the United Kingdom by Vivat Direct Limited (t/a Reader's Digest), 157 Edgware Road, London W2 2HR

For information as to ownership of copyright in the material of this book, and acknowledgments, see last page.

Printed in Germany
ISBN 978 1 78020 107 8

select
editions

THE READER'S DIGEST ASSOCIATION, INC.

contents

Will Robie is an assassin. He works alone and doesn't allow anyone to get close to him. But that changes when an assignment goes wrong and the hunter becomes the hunted . . . with an innocent teenager in tow. A first-rate action thriller.

A senseless murder leaves a stunned, grieving husband and two motherless girls. This true story—full of tears, love and redemption—tells how the family of Open University lecturer, Lizzie Howe, coped after her death on 25 July, 1992.

trust your eyes
linwood barclay

277

A chance sighting of an image of a woman being strangled on a website called Whirl360, pulls two brothers into a frightening vortex of power, murder and deadly conspiracy. Barclay brings a classic Hitchcock premise into the internet age.

the snow child
eowyn ivey

441

A magical tale of heartbreak set in 1920s Alaska. When a childless couple build a child out of snow, the sculpture holds all their hopes and dreams. Next day the snow child is gone but a young girl appears in the woods. Is she real?

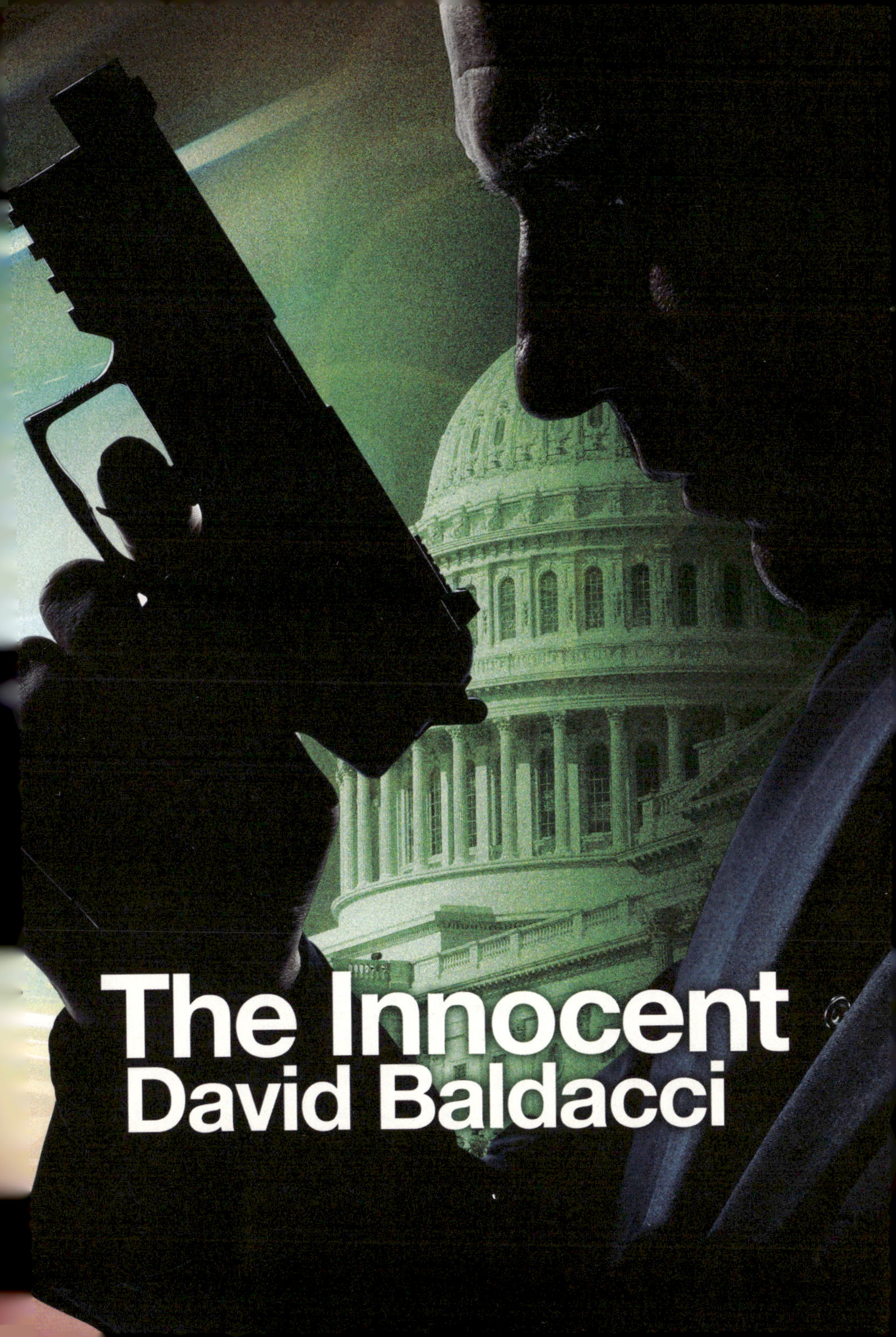
The Innocent
David Baldacci

America has ruthless enemies—people unstoppable by the police, the FBI, or even the military. That's why the government sometimes has to turn to men like Will Robie, a stone-cold hitman who never questions orders and always nails the target.

But Robie is about to make the first major mistake of his career, and it will change things entirely.

Suddenly, the professional assassin turns protector—and his protégée is just fourteen years old . . .

Chapter 1

Will Robie had closely observed every one of the passengers on the flight from Dublin to Edinburgh and confidently deduced that sixteen were returning Scots and fifty-three were tourists.

Robie was neither a Scot nor a tourist.

The flight took forty-seven minutes and the cab ride in from the airport took fifteen. He was not staying at the Balmoral Hotel or the Scotsman or any of the other illustrious accommodations in the ancient city. He had a room on the third floor of a dirty-faced building that was a nine-minute uphill walk to the city centre. He paid in cash for one night. He carried his small bag up to the room and sat on the bed. It squeaked under his weight and sank nearly three inches. Squeaking and sinking were what one got for so low a price.

Robie was an inch over six feet and a rock-solid 180 pounds. He possessed a compact musculature that relied more on quickness and endurance than sheer strength. His nose had been broken once, due to a mistake he had made. He had never had it reset because he'd never wanted to forget the mistake. His hair was naturally dark and Robie kept it half an inch longer than a Marine buzz cut. His features were sharply defined, but he made them forgettable by almost never making eye contact with anyone.

He had tats on one arm and also on his back. One tattoo was of a large tooth from a great white. The other was a red slash that looked like lightening on fire. They effectively covered up old scars that had never healed properly.

Robie had come to Scotland to work. Of the 365 days in a year, he was working, or travelling to do his job, on about half of them.

He checked his watch. Eight hours to go.

His internal clock woke him hours later. He left his room and walked up toward Princes Street. He ordered a light meal and had tap water to drink. Afterwards, he walked towards Edinburgh Castle and climbed to the top, peering over the gloom of the Scottish capital. He turned to his left and took in the full breadth of the sea that had made Edinburgh such an important port centuries ago. He stretched tight limbs, felt a creak. He would turn forty tomorrow. But first he had to make it to tomorrow.

He left the castle and headed down a side street, passing a sign for the ghost tour of Underground Edinburgh, adults only and after full darkness had set in. It was almost time. Robie had memorised every step, every turn, every move he would have to make. To live.

As he did every time, he had to hope it would be enough.

A bit later, he passed a man who nodded at him. It was just a slight dip of the head, nothing more. Then the man was gone and Robie went through the doorway the man had vacated. He locked it behind him and moved forward. His rubber-soled shoes made no sound on the stone floor. Some way in, he saw a door on the right side. He took it. A monk's cloak hung on a peg. He donned it and put the hood up. There were other things there for him, too. All necessary. Gloves. Night-vision goggles. A recorder. A Glock pistol with suppressor attached. And a knife.

He waited, checking his watch every five minutes. His watch was synched to the very second with someone else's.

He opened another door and reached a grate in the floor, lifted it, and skittered down a set of iron handrails set into the stone. He hit the floor silently, counting off his paces. He was in Underground Edinburgh now, home to several ghost- and walking-tours. He glided down the dark brick-and-stone passages, his powered goggles letting him see everything in crisp definition.

He checked his watch. Ten minutes to go. He moved more slowly, adjusting his pace so that he would arrive seconds before he was supposed to.

Just in case.

He heard them before he saw them. There were five, not counting the guide. The man and the peripherals. They would be armed. They would be ready. The peripherals would think this was the perfect place for an ambush. They would be right.

It was stupid for the man to come down here. The carrot had to be especially big. It was as big as it was total bullshit.

Robie rounded one final bend. He heard the guide talking, delivering the memorised spiel in a mysterious, ghostlike voice. *Melodrama sells*, thought Robie.

The tour was heading for the right-angle turn. So was Robie, just from the opposite way. The timing was so tight that there was no margin of error.

Robie counted the paces. He knew the guide was doing the same. They had even practised the length of their strides, to get them perfectly choreographed. Seven seconds later the guide, who was the same height and build as Robie, and wearing an identical cloak to his, came round the bend a mere five paces ahead of his party. He held a flashlight. That was the one thing Robie could not duplicate. Both of his hands had to be free. The guide turned left and disappeared into a cleft cut into the rock that led into another room with another exit.

Robie pivoted, putting his back to the group of men who would round the corner a few moments later. One hand slipped down to the recorder on his belt under the cloak and turned it on. The guide's dramatic voice boomed out, continuing the tale that he had momentarily halted to take the turn.

Robie did not like having his back to anyone, but there was no other way for the plan to work. The men had lights. They would see that he was not the guide. That he was not doing the talking. That he was wearing goggles. The voice droned on. He started to walk forward.

They caught up to him. He heard their collective breaths. Their smells. Sweat, cologne, the garlic they'd had in their last meals.

Or mine, depending on how it goes.

He turned. A deep knife-strike took out the point man and he dropped to the floor. Robie shot the second man in the face. The others were reacting now. But they were not truly professionals. They preyed on the weak and the poorly skilled. Robie was neither. There were three left but only two would be any trouble.

Robie hurled the knife and its point ended up in the third man's chest. The man behind him fired, but Robie had already moved, using the third man as a shield. The bullet hit the rock wall. The man executed a desperation spray and pray, emptying his mag. Bullets bounced off hard rock.

Robie dropped to the floor and fired one shot into the forehead of man number four. Man number five was now the only one left. Five was the reason Robie had flown to Edinburgh. The others were just collateral.

Five had no weapon. He had seen no need to carry one. Weapons were beneath him. He was no doubt rethinking that decision. He begged. He pleaded. He would pay. Then, when the pistol was pointed at him, he turned to threats.

Robie had heard it all before. He fired twice.

Number five kissed the stone floor.

ROBIE SLEPT SOUNDLY after killing five men.

He awoke at six and ate breakfast at a café round the corner from where he was staying. Later, he walked to Waverley Station and boarded a train to London. He arrived after four hours and took a cab to Heathrow. The British Airways 777 lifted off later that afternoon and touched down seven hours later at Dulles Airport. It had been cloudy and chilly in Scotland. It was hot and dry in Virginia.

A car was waiting for him outside the airport terminal. Black SUV. Government plates. He got in and lifted the *Washington Post* that sat on the seat. He gave the driver no instructions. He knew where to go.

Robie's phone vibrated. He looked at the screen. One word: Congratulations.

'Congratulations' was the wrong word, he believed. 'Thanks' would be the wrong word, too. He was not sure what the right one would be for killing five people.

He arrived at a building off Chain Bridge Road in northern Virginia. There would be no debriefing. No record of anything was better. If an investigation ensued, no one could discover a record that didn't exist.

But if things went wrong, Robie would have no official cover.

He walked to an office he sometimes used. Even though it was late there were people working. They did not talk to Robie. He knew they had no idea what he did, but they also knew not to interact with him. He sat at a desk and sent a few emails, and stared out of a window that wasn't really a window. It was merely a box of simulated sunlight, because an actual window was just a hole that others could get through.

An hour later, a chubby man in a wrinkled suit walked in. They didn't greet each other. Chubby placed a flash drive on the desk in front of Robie. Then he pivoted and left. Robie stared down at the silver object. The next assignment was already prepared. They had been coming at an increasing clip these last few years.

Robie pocketed the flash drive and left in an Audi parked in the adjacent garage. When he slid into the seat he felt comfortable. The Audi had been his for four years. Once he hit the public road he shifted gears and accelerated.

Robie thought of the underground tunnel in Edinburgh. Four of the dead men had been bodyguards. They were hard, desperate men who had allegedly murdered at least fifty people over the last five years, some of them children. The fifth man was Carlos Rivera, a trafficker of heroin and youngsters for prostitution. Though ostensibly visiting Scotland on holiday, Rivera had actually been in Edinburgh to meet a criminal czar from Russia in an effort to merge their business interests. Robie had been ordered to kill Rivera, not because of his human and drug trafficking businesses but because he was planning a coup with the aid of several high-ranking generals in the Mexican army. The resulting government would have been no friend of America, so this could not have been allowed to happen. The meeting with the Russian crime czar had been the carrot. There was no czar. The offending generals were also dead, killed by men like Robie.

IT WAS 3 A.M. Will Robie had been awake for two hours. The mission on the flash drive would cause him to travel well past Edinburgh. The target was yet another well-protected man with more money than morals. Robie had been working on the task for nearly a month. The details were numerous, the margin of error even less than with Rivera. The preparation was arduous and had taken its toll on Robie. He could not sleep.

He was sitting in the small kitchen of his apartment which was located in an affluent area with many magnificent dwellings. Robie's building was not one of them. It was utilitarian in design, with noisy pipes, odd smells and tacky carpet. Its occupants were diverse and hardworking: they left early every morning to take their place at law firms, accounting practices and investment concerns spread over the city. Robie did not know any of them, though he had been briefed on them all.

He had travelled the world for a dozen years now. And everywhere he went, someone died. The man who had previously held Robie's position had operated during a particularly busy time for Robie's clandestine agency. Shane Connors had terminated nearly thirty per cent more targets than Robie had in the same amount of time. He had been a mentor to Robie and there were few men he respected more. After his 'retirement', Connors had been assigned to a desk job.

Thinking about Connors made Robie dwell on his own retirement. His line of work was a young man's game. He couldn't do it another dozen years. His skills would erode. One of his targets would be better than he was. He would die.

His thoughts came back to Shane Connors sitting behind his desk. Robie supposed that was death by another name.

THE COSTA DEL SOL had lived up to its name so far. Robie wore a white T-shirt, a blue jacket, faded jeans and sandals. He looked to be on holiday. He boarded the high-speed ferry across the Strait of Gibraltar to Morocco.

He walked off the ferry in Tangier. Buses, taxis and tour guides awaited the masses. Robie bypassed them all and left the port on foot. He entered the main street of the town and was instantly besieged by peddlers, beggars and shopkeepers. He directed his gaze down and kept walking.

His destination was a room over a restaurant promising authentic local food. It was a tourist trap, he knew. The food was generic, the beer warm and the service indifferent. The bus guides led unsuspecting folks there and then hurried elsewhere to eat a better meal.

He headed up the stairs, unlocked the door to the room with the key he had previously been given, and locked the door behind him. He looked around. Bed, chair, window. All he needed. It was 11 a.m. local time.

The flash drive had long since been destroyed. The plan was in place and the movements practised at a mock facility back in the States that was the exact duplicate of his target. Now he simply had to wait.

This time, the target was no idiot like Rivera. This one would be harder. Robie had brought nothing with him from Spain because he had to pass through customs to get on the ferry, but everything he needed would be in Tangier.

He lay on the bed, and let the heat make him drowsy. When he woke, nearly four hours had passed and it was the hottest part of the day. He wiped sweat from his face and went to the window, looked out. He watched big tour buses navigate streets never built for anything so large or cumbersome. The sidewalks were full of people, both locals and visitors.

He waited another hour and then left his room. On the street, he turned east and double-timed it. In a few seconds, he was lost in the hustle and bustle of the old city. He would collect what he needed and move on.

All these items would be for the mission. He had travelled to thirty-seven countries and had never purchased a single souvenir.

SEVEN HOURS LATER, it was quite dark. Robie approached the large, stark facility from the west. Over his back was slung a hard case and a knapsack with water, a pee jar and provisions. He did not plan on leaving there for the next three days.

He checked his watch and heard it approach. He ducked down behind a cluster of barrels. The truck passed by him and stopped. Three strides later he was under it, holding on to its underside. It drove on and then stopped. There was a long, wrenching sound of metal on metal. The truck started up again with a jolt that nearly caused Robie to lose his grip.

Fifty feet later, the truck stopped once more. Its doors opened, feet touched the ground. Doors clunked shut. Footsteps headed off. The wrenching sound came again. Then hardened locks were clicked into place. There was quiet, except for the footfalls of the perimeter patrol that would be there 24/7 for at least the next three days.

Robie timed it so he was out from under the truck and racing away just as the wrenching sounds stopped. The facility technically had been cleared and put in lockdown. This had been the only opportunity Robie had had to get in. Mission accomplished, at least this part.

He took the steps of a nearby metal staircase three at a time, the hard-sided case hitting him in the back.

Next came the race against the clock. He reached the top, grabbed the girder, and did a monkey crawl to the targeted spot. He swung to the left and then made his leap. He landed nearly silently on metal and skittered to a spot eighty feet distant, in one of the darkest corners of the space. He did so with five seconds to spare.

The lights clicked off and the alarms came on. The interior space was instantly crisscrossed with beams of energy invisible to the naked eye. If anything touched them sirens would go off. All intruders would be executed. It was that sort of place.

Robie turned over on his back, his face to the ceiling. Seventy-two hours to go. It seemed his entire existence was one uninterrupted countdown.

THE TWO DOZEN MEN travelled in a four-Hummer motorcade. The Hummers were armoured to American military standards and would defeat all bullets and most missile strikes. The main man rode in the third Hummer.

The man's name was Khalid bin Talal. He was a Saudi prince. He did not come to Tangier often. He was there to do business, after which he was scheduled to leave during the early hours of the morning in his private jet.

The Saudis were close allies of the West in general, and the Americans specifically. A stable flow of petroleum made for good friendships. However, Talal hated the West, the Americans most of all.

It was a dangerous position to openly take against the world's remaining superpower. Talal was suspected of the kidnapping, torture and murder of four US servicemen, abducted from a nightclub in London. He was also suspected of bankrolling three terrorist attacks, resulting in the deaths of over 100 people, a dozen of them Americans. Nothing could be proven, but those actions had put Talal on a list. And the payment for being on that list was about to come due.

The people Talal had come to Tangier to meet did not much like the West or the Americans, either. They envisioned a world that did not have the Stars and Stripes leading the way. The gathering was to discuss how to make such a world happen. This caucus was a closely guarded secret.

Their mistake was letting the closely guarded secret no longer remain a secret.

The club was entered through a six-inch-thick hydraulic-powered door. There were blast walls set up at strategic points. The interior perimeter was ringed by armed guards. This was serious security for the few people who could afford it.

Talal had discarded his robes before going there. He wore a custom-made suit—carefully tailored to disguise his rapidly spreading waistline—that cost £10,000. He had fifty such suits and couldn't remember where they all were, since they were spread over his many properties around the world. He was worth well north of twelve billion dollars, making him the sixty-first richest person in the world, according to *Forbes* magazine.

The prince and his group sat at a large round table in a roped-off area that was hidden behind drapes and set atop an elevated teak-wood platform. As he sipped his Bombay Sapphire gin and tonic, the prince's eyes continually moved, sizing up the environment around him. He had survived two assassination attempts, one by a cousin of his. Talal trusted no one. His guards were vetted and loyal. He was armed. He was a good shot. He was prepared for every contingency.

He walked from the table with his guards organised in a hard-diamond pattern around him. He had copied this tactic from the American Secret Service. His personal physician travelled with him, just like the US president. And, in his mind, he was just as important as the American president. In fact, he would have liked to replace him as the de facto leader of the free world. Although the world would not be nearly as free with him in charge.

They moved on to their evening meal at a restaurant that had been completely rented out so that the prince could dine in peace. After that, he changed back into his robes and returned to his jet, housed in a secure hangar outside the city.

The Hummers pulled past the open doors of the hangar and stopped in front of the massive jet. The hangar doors closed before he got out of the Hummer. There would be no targets for long-range rifle shots between open hangar doors.

The meeting would be held on the plane, while it was on the ground. It would last for one hour. The prince would control the meeting. He was used to controlling situations.

That was about to end.

THE PRINCE SAT at the centre of the table in the main cabin. He gazed around the table. There were two visitors. One was Russian, the other Palestinian. An unlikely partnership, but it intrigued the prince. They had promised that for the right price, they could accomplish the impossible.

The prince cleared his throat. 'You're sure you can do this?'

The Russian nodded slowly but firmly.

The prince said, 'I have been told that it is pointless even to try.'

'The strongest chain is defeated by its weakest link.' This came from the Palestinian. It was clear that he was the leader of the partnership.

'And what is the weakest link?'

'One person placed next to the one you want. We own that person. This is a fact.'

'But even so, access to weapons?'

'The person's job will allow access to the necessary weapon.'

'This person must be willing to die, then.'

The Palestinian nodded. 'That condition is met.'

'Westerners do not do that.'

'I did not say that the person is a westerner.'

'A plant?'

'Decades in the making.'

The prince sat back. He looked intrigued.

The Palestinian said, 'The plans are in place. But significant funds are required for something like this. Much of it in the aftermath.'

The prince glanced out of the window. The windows were extra large, because he enjoyed the views from his high perch.

The subsonic round hit him squarely in the forehead, exploding his brain. Blood, bone and tissue covered the plane's once beautiful interior.

The Russian leapt up but had no weapon. It had been confiscated at the door. The Palestinian just sat there, paralysed.

The guards reacted. One pointed to the shattered plane window. Two guards outside the plane had drawn their weapons and were firing at the source of the fatal shot.

Shots pinged around Robie's position. He fired back. The first sentry fell with a shot to the head. The second collapsed with a bullet wedged in his heart.

Robie sent five shots right through the door of the plane, destroying the opening mechanism. He took out the cockpit window and with it the plane's controls. The big bird would be grounded for a while.

Now came the hardest part. The exit.

He tightrope-walked down the girder until he reached the wall on the far side of the hanger. He pushed open the window, attached a cable to a support ring and rappelled down the wall. His feet touched asphalt and he ran due east away from the hanger. He scaled a fence, dropped to the other side. He heard shouts behind him.

A car raced up. He threw his gear in the back seat, jumped in, and it drove off before his door was even shut. Robie did not look at the driver and the driver did not look at him. Fifteen minutes later, the car stopped at the port. Robie got out, popped the boot and pulled out a small bag packed with clothes and other essentials, including travel documents and local currency. He boarded not the high-speed ferry back to Spain, but instead the slow ferry from Tangier to Barcelona. No one would expect an assassin to escape via a boat that took over a full day to get to its destination. They would check the airports, the high-speed ferries, the highways and the train stations. But not the lumbering old bathtub that would take twenty-seven hours to go a few hundred miles up the Med.

Robie had had with him a long-range surveillance cone that had allowed him to hear the conversation on the plane. *Access to weapons. Decades in the making. Significant funds for the aftermath.* It would have to be followed up. But that was not his job. He had completed his task. He would make his report and others would now take over.

It had been a clean operation. Robie had had the prince in his cross hairs from the moment he had got out of his SUV. He could have taken him out then, but wanted to wait until the prince and his guards were on the plane. He had lost sight of the prince for about half a minute right after he had entered the plane, but had reacquired him as he sat at the table.

Robie had aimed for Talal's head—even though it was a tougher shot—because, when the prince had leaned forward, he had seen the straps underneath the man's robes. He had been wearing body armour.

Robie had spent three days and nights of his life, peeing into a jar and eating power bars while waiting for his target. Now the prince was dead, and his plans would die with him.

Will Robie closed his eyes and slept as the ferry gently swayed on its slow ride over the calm waters of the Med.

Chapter 2

This one was different. It was close to home. So close that it *was* home—right there in Washington DC.

Nearly three months had passed since the death of Khalid bin Talal. Robie had not killed anyone during that time; an unusually long period for him to be inactive, but he did not mind. He took walks, he read books, he ate out. In other words, he acted normal.

But then the flash drive had appeared and Robie had had to stop being normal and pick up his gun again. The mission had come to him two days ago. Not much time to prepare, but the mission was a priority, the flash drive told him. And when the flash spoke, Robie acted.

He sat in a chair in his living room, a cup of coffee in hand. It was early in the morning and he had been up for several hours. As the next mission grew closer, it grew difficult for him to sleep. It had always been that way with him—not so much nervousness, as a desire for heightened preparation.

During his downtime, Robie had adhered to his plan of socialising more. He had even accepted an invitation to an informal party held by one of his neighbours, who had introduced Robie to his friends. However, Robie's attention had quickly focused on one young woman who also lived in the building. She was a recent renter who made the trek to the White House—where she worked as early as 4 a.m.—on her bike. Robie knew where she worked because he had received a briefing on her. He knew she left that early for work, because he had often seen her through the peephole in his front door.

She was younger than Robie, lovely and intelligent, at least from what he had observed. At the party, she had worn a short, black skirt and a white blouse, her hair swept back into a ponytail. Every so often she would glance in Robie's direction and he had thought about approaching her. Yet he had left the party without doing so. It was probably better that way. What would have been the point?

Robie had done his recon for the mission in the abbreviated time allotted. The run-throughs, logistically harder in this situation, had still been performed. And he still didn't like it. But it was not his call. The location would not involve stepping on a plane or train. But the target was different as well. And not in a good way.

Sometimes he went after people intent on global menace, or sometimes he simply went after a problem. His employers decided who would qualify as a target. It made the world better; that was the justification.

The agency Robie worked for had a clear policy on operatives who were caught during a mission. There would be no acknowledgement that Robie even worked for the United States. There would be no steps taken to save him. Thus, on every mission, Robie had employed an exit plan known only to him, in case the operation went awry. He had never needed to employ his personal back-up plan. Yet.

Robie surveyed his apartment. He'd been there four years, liked it for the most part. There were restaurants within walking distance. Robie ate out a lot. He liked to sit at tables and watch people go by. He was a student of humanity in a way. That was why he was still alive. He could read people, often after observing them for only a few seconds.

He heard a door open in the hall. He stepped to his peephole and watched the woman who worked at the White House walk her bike down the hall. *A. Lambert* was the name on the mailbox. The 'A' stood for Anne. He had started referring to her in his mind as 'A'. She was in her late twenties, tall, long blonde hair, thin.

Robie moved to a window overlooking the street. A minute later she left the building, swung onto her bike, and was off. It was four-thirty in the morning.

He lay down in bed. He needed to sleep. The coming night would be busy. And *different*.

ROBIE WAS IN THE BASEMENT gymnasium of his building. It was nearly 9 p.m., but the place was open 24/7 for the residents. He hung upside down on the pull-up bar. He did stomach crunches and then worked his oblique muscles while holding a medicine ball. Robie was chiselled but never took his shirt off. No one would ever see him strolling along displaying his six-pack.

He was on the pull-up bar when the door opened. A. Lambert stared over at him. She didn't smile or acknowledge him. She went over to the corner and sat down crosslegged on an exercise mat.

Robie dropped lightly to the floor. He snagged his towel and wiped off his face.

'I think you're the only one who uses this room,' she said.

She was wearing tight jeans and a T-shirt. No place to conceal a weapon. Robie always checked that first.

'You're here,' he said.

'Not to work out,' she replied.

'What then?'

'Tough day at the office. Just chilling.'

He looked around the small, ill-lit room. It smelled of sweat and mould.

'Must be nicer places to chill than this,' he said.

'I didn't expect to find anyone else here,' she answered.

'Except me, maybe. From what you said, you knew I used this room.'

She said, 'I just said that because I saw you here tonight. I've never seen you down here before; or anyone else, for that matter.'

He knew the answer already, but asked: 'So, tough day at the office. Where do you work?'

'The White House. What about you?'

'Investments.'

She rose and said, 'I'm Annie. Annie Lambert.'

They shook hands. Her fingers were long and supple.

'You have a name?' she asked.

'Will Robie. Maybe we can go out for a drink sometime.' Robie had no idea why that offer had come out of his mouth.

'OK,' she said, casually. 'Sounds good.'

'Good night,' said Robie. 'Have a nice chill.'

He closed the door behind him and took the elevator back up to his floor. He immediately made a phone call. Any contact like that had to be reported. Robie didn't think there was anything to be worried about with Annie Lambert, but the rules were clear. Someone being friendly was a potential threat. A woman 'chilling' and saying hello had to be called in.

I live in a world that isn't remotely normal any more. But there's no agency rule against having a drink with someone.

He left his building and walked across the street. The high-rise there had a perfect view of his. Robie had a key for an apartment on the fourth floor. In the corner of the front room was a surveillance scope rated as one of the best in the world. Robie powered it up and turned its muzzle towards his building.

His floor, down the hall three doors. The lights were on, the shades raised three-quarters. He waited. Annie Lambert's front door opened. She stopped at the kitchen, opened the fridge and took out a Diet Coke. She walked down the hall. Before she got to her bedroom she slipped off her jeans and tossed them into a laundry basket.

Robie turned off his surveillance device. The scope cost nearly fifty grand. He was not going to use it for pathetic voyeurism.

He returned to his building, showered and changed into fresh clothes. Then he gunned up. It was time to go to work.

ANOTHER FOSTER HOME she did not want to be in. How many now? Five? Six? Ten? She supposed it didn't really matter.

She listened to the man and woman downstairs yelling at each other. Her foster parents. *Which is more than a joke*, she thought. It was criminal. They had a string of kids through their home and made them pickpocket people and deal drugs.

So tonight would be her last night there. There were two other kids in the one bedroom with her, both younger, and she was loath to leave them.

She sat them on the bed. 'I'm going to let Social Services know what's going on here. OK? They're going to come and get you guys out of this place. Soon.'

'Can't you take us with you, Julie?' asked the girl, tearfully.

'I wish I could, but I can't. But I'm going to get you out of here, I promise.'

The boy said, 'They won't believe you.'

'Yes, they will. I've got proof.'

She gave them each a hug, opened the window, climbed out and ran off into the darkness. *I'm going home.*

Home was a duplex even smaller than the one she had just left. She took the subway, then a bus, and then she walked. Along the way she walked up the steps of a government building, and pushed an envelope through the mail slot addressed to the woman who was handling the foster care placement. She was a nice lady, she meant well, but she was completely swamped with children no one seemed to want. In the envelope was a photo card with pictures capturing her foster parents sitting stoned-out on the couch, with crack pipes and piles of pills in full view. *If that doesn't do the trick*, she thought, *nothing will.*

She reached the house an hour later. She used a key she kept in her shoe to go in via the back door. She tried to turn on a light, but nothing happened. This did not surprise her. It meant that the utility bill had not been paid. She used the moonlight coming in through the windows to reach her bedroom on the second floor.

Her room was unchanged. A guitar, sheets of music, books, clothes, magazines were piled everywhere. She rationalised that her parents had not cleaned up her room because they knew she would be back.

They had problems. They would be regarded by most people as pathetic, drugged-out losers. But they were her parents. They loved her. And she loved them. She wanted to take care of them. At the age of fourteen, she was often the mom and dad. But that was OK. Plus, things were looking up. Her father was working on a loading dock and her mother laboured as a waitress in a diner. It was true that her mom and dad were recovering addicts, but they got up every day and went to work. It was just that the drug problems had led the city to deem them unfit to have custody of her.

But not any more. Now she was home.

She fingered the note from her mom that had been sent to her school. Her parents had plans to move away and start over, and they wanted their only child to go with them. Julie hadn't been this excited in a long time. She read it again. The only thing that bothered her was the contingency plan her mom had put in, if for some reason they didn't hook up with their daughter. There had also been cash along with the note for the contingency plan. Well, there was no reason now that her parents wouldn't be able to meet up with her.

She started to pack up her belongings and then stopped. There were noises. Her parents must just be getting home.

The next sound she heard erased all other thoughts. A man's voice. Angry. It was asking her father what he knew. How much he had been told.

She heard her father whimpering, as though he were hurt. Then Julie heard her mother asking the person to leave them alone.

Julie crept down the stairs, her body shaking. She had no cellphone or else she would have called the police.

When she heard the gunshot she started running down the stairs. She saw her father slumped against the wall. A man held a gun pointed at him. There was a dark patch on her father's chest growing bigger. He fell to the floor.

The man with the gun saw her. He pointed the pistol at her.

'No!' her mother shrieked. 'She doesn't know anything.' She hit the man in the back of the legs and he collapsed, his gun spinning out of reach.

'Run, honey, run!' screamed her mother.

'Mom!' she called back. 'Mom, what's—'

Her mother screamed again, 'Run! Now!'

She turned and ran back up the stairs even as the man spun round and landed a crushing blow to the top of her mother's head. She grabbed her backpack, sprinted to the window and climbed down so quickly that she lost her grip and fell the last six feet. She got up and ran off as the sound of a second shot came from the house.

When the gunman ran outside, the teenager was out of sight. But he stopped, listened. The sounds of footfalls reached him. He set out west, moving deliberately.

ROBIE STARED UP at the apartment building. There was no doorman. The outer entrance was locked and one needed a pass card to get in. He had that.

The dossier on tonight's target was light. Black woman, aged thirty-five. He had her picture and her address. He had not been told the specific reason why she must die other than she had ties to a terrorist organisation. Terrorist cell members were trained to blend in. She apparently was one of them. In any event, the reason she had to die was above his pay grade.

Robie had no problem killing cartel trash or megalomaniac sheikhs. But tonight he had a problem. He reached a gloved hand inside his pocket and felt the gun there. Usually it was reassuring for him to touch his weapon.

Tonight it was not.

She would be in bed. Her apartment was dark. At this hour she would be sleeping. At least she would feel nothing. He would make certain his strike caused instant death. Life would go on without her. Rich or poor, important or not, life just did.

Robie swiped the card and the door clicked open. He was wearing a hoodie and pulled it tighter around his head. He headed up the stairwell. On the fourth floor he exited the stairwell and closed the door behind him. Number 404 was the apartment he wanted. The lock was a deadbolt, yet it took him all of thirty seconds to defeat it using two slender pieces of metal.

He closed the door behind him and put on his night-vision goggles. His gaze swept the small living room. In one corner was a collapsible playpen. On two walls were pieces of paper. In childish script was the word 'I' and the word 'Mom' separated by a crude drawing of a heart. There were toys piled in one corner. This gave Robie pause. *I'm here to kill a young mother.*

Then in his headset came the voice: 'You should be in the bedroom.'

This was also what was different about tonight. He wore a pinhole camera that conveyed live video feedback, and an earwig through which a handler could prompt him.

Robie stopped at the closed door to the bedroom and heard low breathing. He pushed the door open and stepped through.

The bed was set against the window. It was dark but he could see her lying in bed. He lifted the Glock from his pocket and moved forward. Robie had opted tonight to make the kill shot from a few feet away. He would fire into the heart, and then for insurance he would place a second shot there, too. The bleed-out would be lightning fast. Quick, clean.

She was lying flat on her back. He lined up her heart in his gun sight. And—

Robie saw the small hump next to her. The head with the wiry hair sticking out. It had been hidden under the covers.

In his ear the voice said, 'Shoot.'

Robie did not shoot but he must have made some sound. The wiry head moved. Then the little hump sat up. The boy stared directly at Robie standing there, his pistol pointed at his mother.

'Mommy,' said the boy, in a fearful tone.

'Shoot,' said the voice. 'Shoot the kid, too. Now.'

Robie could fire and be gone.

The woman began to stir. 'You're safe, baby,' she said, in a sleepy voice. 'You're safe with Mommy. Nothing to be scared of.'

She saw Robie. And froze, but only for an instant. Then she pulled her child behind her. She screamed.

Robie said to her, 'Be quiet or I shoot.'

She didn't stop screaming.

He fired a round into the pillow next to her. The round deflected off the mattress springs and drilled into the floor.

She stopped screaming.

'Kill her,' the handler roared in Robie's ear.

She hugged her son. 'Please, mister, please, don't hurt us.'

'Just stay quiet,' said Robie. The handler was still screaming.

'Take what you want,' mumbled the woman, 'but please don't hurt us.' She turned, hugged her son. Lifted him up so they were face to face.

Robie realised something and his gut tightened. The handler was no longer screaming. His earwig held nothing except silence. He should have picked up on that before.

The window glass shattered. Robie watched as the rifle round passed through the boy's head and then drove through his mother's, killing them both. The woman's eyes were on Robie when her life ended. Mother and son fell sideways, together.

Robie looked out of the window. The fail-safe was out there with a fine sight line, obviously. Then his instincts took over and Robie ducked down and rolled away from the window.

On the floor he saw something else he had not expected to see.

Next to the bed was a baby carrier. In the carrier, sound asleep, was a second kid.

His earwig came alive. 'Get out of the apartment,' his handler ordered him. 'By the fire escape.'

'Go to hell,' Robie said. He ripped the pinhole and earwig off, powered them down, and stuffed them in his pocket.

He snagged the carrier, slid it towards him. He was waiting for a second shot. But he did not intend to give the shooter a viable target. He moved clear of the window and stood, holding the baby carrier behind him. He carried the child out of the bedroom and scanned the living room with a penlight. He spied the woman's purse and took out her driver's licence. He snapped a picture of it with his phone. Next he photographed her ID card. Her government ID card. *What the—? That fact wasn't on the flash drive.*

Finally, he spied a blue item partially hidden under a stack of papers. He grabbed it. A US passport. He snapped photos of all the pages, showing the places to which she'd travelled. Then he put the licence, ID card and passport back and grabbed the carrier again.

He opened the front door of the apartment and stepped out. He raced down the stairwell one flight, the layout of the building whirring through his mind. He had memorised every apartment, every resident, every possibility. Number 307. A mother of three, he recalled. Miraculously, the little one slept on. Robie set the carrier down in front of 307 and knocked three times. He heard someone coming to the door and then he was gone.

Robie had two options. The rear of the building was out. The fact that his handler had wanted him to leave by the fire escape told Robie all he wanted to know: a bullet in the head would be his reward for being stupid enough to try to get out that way. The front of the building was out for a similar reason. Well lit, one entry—he might as well paint a bull's-eye on his head. That left the two sides of the building.

He sprinted down the hall. Number 201 was empty. Ten seconds later, he was inside. The apartments all had the same layout. He reached the back bedroom, opened the window and climbed out. He looked down, gauged the drop and let go.

He hit and rolled, cushioning the fall. He waited for a shot to hit him. None did. He ran at an angle away from the building, hid behind a Dumpster for a few moments, recalibrating his senses to the new surroundings. Then he was up and over a fence and sprinting up the street. They probably hadn't seen him leave the building or else he'd be dead. But they had to know by now that he'd got away. A response team would be searching for him. Grid by grid. Robie knew the drill. Only now he had to defeat it.

For as long as he'd been doing this, Robie had known that what had just happened was a possibility. Not a distinct possibility, but one he had to account for. Like for all his other missions, he had a contingency exit plan in place. Now it was time to execute the plan. Shane Connors's advice to him had finally come into play. 'You're the only one out there who really has your back, Will.'

He walked ten more blocks. His destination was up ahead. He checked his watch. Twenty minutes to spare if the schedule hadn't changed.

He had used a fake name to reserve a ticket on a bus leaving in twenty minutes, destination New York City. Once he got to New York, he would execute the second step in his plan, which would entail leaving the country. He planned to put as much space between him and his own people as he could.

He paid for the ticket in cash and waited outside the terminal. Its location was not all that safe, especially at two in the morning. But it was far safer than the situation Robie had just left. He passed the time looking at the other people awaiting the arrival of the bus, counting thirty-five passengers, including himself. Most were poor, working-class; or otherwise down on their luck. They had bags, pillows and knapsacks. Robie had nothing except his night-vision goggles, his pinhole camera and his Glock pistol in an inside zippered compartment of his hoodie.

The bus pulled into the parking lot and came to a stop near them with a screech of brakes. They all lined up. That was when Robie noticed her. She was young. Maybe barely a teenager. She was dressed in faded jeans with holes in the knees and her dark, stringy hair was pulled back into a tight ponytail. She carried a backpack in one hand and seemed to be breathing hard. Robie noticed that both her hands and knees had traces of dirt on them. He looked around, but saw no one who could be her parents.

He edged forward in the line. It was not out of the realm of possibility that they would find him here before the bus departed. He gripped his pistol in his pocket and kept his gaze down.

On board the bus, he shuffled towards the back and sat in the last row. He sat next to the window. From here, he could remain invisible while still seeing anyone coming, through the gap in the two seats in front of him. The windows were tinted. That would foul any attempted shot from outside.

The teenage girl sat three rows up from him, on the opposite side of the narrow aisle.

Robie looked up as a man hustled onto the bus right before the driver shut the door. He moved towards the back. As he neared the girl he looked the other way. This was passenger number thirty-six, and the very last to board.

Robie sank lower in his seat and pulled his hoodie closer around his face. He gripped his Glock in his pocket and edged the muzzle up and forwards so that it was aimed at a spot the man had to cross if he continued to head his way. Robie had to assume that they somehow had found out about his contingency plan and had sent this man to finish the job.

But the fellow stopped one row beyond the teenage girl and sat in the seat directly behind her. Robie's hand relaxed slightly round his pistol, but he continued to watch the man through the gap.

The bus pulled off and Robie's gaze moved over the man. He was Robie's size and age. He had no bag. Robie's gaze went to the man's hands. They were gloved. Robie looked down at his own gloved hands. It was not that cold. Robie's instincts told him this man was not on the bus simply to travel to New York.

Professional killers are a unique lot, Robie thought, as the bus motored along. He stared through the gap, watching, waiting. When you were on a mission you looked for things that other people would never focus on. Like entry and exit points. Gunsight angles, positions from which others can strike back at you. Sizing up opponents without seeming to do so. Trying to ferret out intent by reading body cues alone. Never letting anyone notice you noticing him.

Robie was undertaking all of these tasks. And it was totally unconnected with his plight. He had people after him, clearly. But, just as clearly, the girl had someone after *her*.

Robie knew that he was not the only professional killer on board the bus. He was looking at the second one. He slipped the Glock from his pocket.

The girl was reading a paperback. That was not good. Young people made easy targets, glued to their phones, thumbs ramming keys, headphones on with music roaring. Easy prey.

The other man leaned forwards in his seat. Robie knew how he would do it. Head and neck. Pull right, pull left, the same method the US Marines teach. No weapon would be required. Most people died silently. People close by were clueless. Particularly those in this bus. Most people had settled down to sleep, though they'd barely gone half a mile as yet.

The man tensed.

Robie checked his gun. He had watched two people tonight lose their lives, one a little boy. He did not intend to make it three.

The man lifted his hands. *Pull-pull*, thought Robie. *Snap. Dead girl.*

But not tonight.

What happened next was not something Robie had anticipated at all. The man screamed.

Robie would have, too. Pepper spray stung like hell when it hit the eyes.

The girl had not even turned in her seat. She had just fired the spray backwards, over her head, nailing her attacker in the face. However, even as the man screamed and clawed at his eyes with one of his hands, the other hand found purchase on the girl's neck.

Robie's pistol collided with the man's skull, sending him crashing down to the floor of the bus.

The girl looked round at Robie as most of the other passengers, awakened now, stared at them. Then their gazes drifted to the fallen man.

The driver stopped the bus, turned to look at Robie and yelled, 'Hey!' He rose and started down the aisle. When he saw Robie's gun, he stopped. 'What the hell do you want?' he asked.

Robie said, 'The guy was attacking the girl. I stopped him.'

He looked at the girl for support. She said nothing.

'Would you like to tell them?' Robie prompted.

She said nothing.

'He was trying to kill you. You nailed him with pepper spray.'

Robie reached over and, before she could stop him, he'd ripped the canister from her hand and held it up.

'Pepper spray,' he said, in a confirmatory tone.

The other passengers' attention now turned to the girl.

She looked back at them, unfazed by their scrutiny.

'What's going on?' asked the driver.

Robie said, 'The guy was attacking the girl. She pepper-sprayed him and I finished him off when he didn't back down.'

'And why do you have a gun?'

'I've got a permit for it.'

In the distance Robie heard sirens. Was it for the two bodies back at the building he had just left?

The man on the floor started to stir. Robie put a foot on his back. 'Stay down,' he ordered. He looked at the driver. 'You had better call the cops.'

The girl grabbed her backpack and walked down the aisle.

The driver put up his hands. 'You can't leave, miss.'

She drew something from her jacket and held it in front of the man. From where he was standing behind the girl, Robie was blocked from seeing what it was. The driver immediately retreated, looking terrified. A woman screamed.

Robie used the fallen man's belt to tie his hands and ankles together behind his back, completely immobilising him. Then he followed the girl and caught up with her just as she reached the end of the street.

'What did you show him?' he asked.

She turned and held up the grenade.

Robie didn't blink. 'It's plastic.'

'Well, he didn't seem to know that.' Her voice was lower than Robie would have expected. She kept walking.

'Why did that guy want to kill you?'

She picked up her pace and slipped between two parked cars. Robie did the same. She hustled down the road. He grabbed her arm. 'Hey, I'm talking to you.'

He didn't get an answer. The explosion knocked them both off their feet.

ROBIE CAME TO FIRST. He had no idea how long he'd been out, but it couldn't have been long. There were no cops, just him and a bus that was no longer there. He gazed over at the skeleton of burning metal. There could be no survivors.

This area of DC was deserted at this late hour and there were no residences nearby. The only people wandering out to see what had happened were obviously homeless. Robie watched as one old man dressed in ragged jeans and a shirt turned black by living on the street stumbled out onto the sidewalk from his home of cardboard and plastic trash bags inside a doorway. He looked at the bonfire that had once been a bus with passengers inside and called out between rotted teeth, 'Damn, anybody got something good to grill?'

Robie slowly rose. He looked around for the girl and found her next to a parked Saturn. Robie felt for a pulse, found it and breathed a sigh of relief. A few moments later, her eyes opened.

Robie eyed the grenade that she still clutched in her hand.

'Did you leave a real one of those on the bus?'

She sat up slowly, looked towards the demolished bus. Robie expected the sight to evoke a reaction from her, but she said nothing.

'Somebody really wants you dead,' he said. 'Any idea why?'

She got to her feet, retrieving her knapsack. She looked up at Robie. 'Where's your gun?' she asked.

This caught him off guard. He didn't know. He looked under a few cars. There was a storm drain: it might have fallen in there when he'd been blasted off his feet. She was watching him. 'I'd find it if I were you. You're probably going to need it.'

'Why?' he asked.

'Because you've been seen with me.'

He could hear sirens getting louder. The responders were heading their way. The homeless guy was now dancing around the bonfire, yelling about wanting some 'damn marshmallows'.

Robie said, 'And why is that significant?'

She glanced at the destroyed bus. 'What? Are you stupid?'

Robie gave up the search for his gun and came over to her. 'You need to go to the police,' he said. 'They can protect you.'

'Yeah, right.'

'You don't think they can?'

'If I were you, I'd get out of here.'

Robie said, 'There's no one left alive on that bus to tell the cops what happened.'

'What do you think happened?' she asked.

'Over thirty people just lost their lives on that bus, including a guy who was trying to kill you.'

'That's your theory. Where's your proof?'

She started to walk off.

'You can't do this alone, you know,' Robie said. 'You've already screwed up, or got ratted out.'

She turned back. 'What do you mean?' For the first time, she sounded interested in what he had to say.

'They followed you to the bus or they were waiting for you. So either you screwed up and let them follow you, or else someone you trusted turned on you. How did you spot the guy on the bus?'

'Reflection in my window. I saw the guy sit down behind me. He passed by three empty rows. Made me think, you know?'

'I was behind you, too.'

'Too far behind to do you any good.'

'So you spotted me, too?'

She shrugged. 'You just get used to checking stuff out.'

Robie said, 'But you still can't do this alone. If you won't go to the police, you can come with me.'

She took a step back. 'You?'

He stared at her and listened to the sirens drawing close. 'You want to go it alone, go. I'm sure you'll be able to hold them off for a few more hours. But then it'll all be over for you.'

She looked once more over his shoulder at the burning mass.

'I didn't want anybody else to die,' she said.

'Anybody *else*? Who else has died?'

Robie had the feeling that she wanted to dissolve into tears, but she said, 'Who are you?'

'Someone who stumbled on to something and doesn't want to leave it.'

'I don't trust you or anyone else.'

'I don't blame you. I wouldn't, either.'

'Where do you want to go?'

'Someplace safe.'

'I'm not sure there is such a place,' she said in a voice that, for the first time, sounded like a kid's. Scared.

ROBIE DIDN'T JUST HAVE an escape plan in case something went wrong on one of his missions. He had a safe house, too. Now, with someone else in tow, he had opted for Plan C. Unfortunately, Plan C was already getting complicated.

His gaze swept from the end of the alley they had reached. He had put his goggles on. It was only a glimpse, but he clung to it, because he knew it was important: reflected light off a gun scope.

He removed the goggles, slipped back into the shadows and looked down at the girl.

'What's your name?'

She hesitated. 'Julie.'

'OK, Julie. You can call me Will.'

She looked past him, out into the darkness. They had covered about ten blocks; so far, in fact, that the sound of the sirens had receded. She had not committed to go with him. They had silently agreed to leave the scene of the explosion by simply turning and walking away together.

'There's someone out there,' he told Julie, in a low voice, pointing over his shoulder. 'Any chance you have a tracking device on you? How about your cell?'

'I don't have a cellphone,' she replied.

'Don't all kids have cellphones?'

'I guess not,' she said stiffly. 'And I'm not a kid.'

'How old are you?'

'How old are *you*?'

'Forty.'

'That's really old.'

'Trust me, I'm feeling it. How old?'

'Fourteen.'

He looked the way they had come. Something in his gut very clearly told him not to go back that way.

'What did you see?' she asked.

'Reflection of light off a rifle scope.'

Robie studied the walls on either side of them. Then he hustled to a construction Dumpster parked in the alley and searched through it. He finally pulled out several lengths of rope and quickly knotted them together. There was a length of plywood in the Dumpster, too. He positioned it so that it rested on top of the Dumpster's rim, giving them a platform on which to stand. He lifted her up and placed her on top of the plywood and hoisted himself on top of it.

'What now?'

'We climb.' He pointed up. 'We're aiming for that.'

It was a fire escape ladder that, in its locked position, ended well above street level. Robie tossed the rope over the bottom rung of the ladder. He took one end, fashioned a loop, and pulled the other end through it. He gripped the rope and quickly climbed up to the ladder, then freed the rope and passed one end back down to her.

'Tie the rope around your backpack straps and cross your arms. That'll keep the backpack from slipping.'

She did so, and he started pulling her up.

As soon as she reached him, Robie knew they were in trouble. Running feet were never a good sound.

'Climb as high as you can,' he said.

She struggled up the fire escape ladder while Robie turned back and focused on what was coming.

A man turned into the alleyway and moved forward, his rifle swinging in controlled arcs. He was good, but not good enough, because he hadn't yet looked up. When he finally did, it was just in time to see the bottom of Robie's feet rushing at him.

Robie's size twelves smashed into the man's face and drove him violently to the asphalt. Robie kicked the rifle away. The man was unconscious. Robie took a few seconds to search him. No ID. No phone. But no official credentials, either.

He did find an electronic device with a blinking blue light in the man's pocket. He crushed it underfoot and threw it into the Dumpster. He felt near the man's ankle and pulled out a .38 Smith & Wesson throwaway. He slipped it into his jacket pocket.

Julie was near the top of the building when he reached her.

'Is he dead?' she asked.

'I didn't check. Let's go.' He pointed upwards to the roof. He found a handhold on a windowsill and climbed. A minute later he stood on the roof. He lay on his stomach and fed the rope down to her. 'Tie it to your backpack straps like before.'

'Don't drop me,' she said, her voice panicky.

'I've already lifted you once. You weigh nothing.'

A minute later she was beside him on the roof.

Robie led her across the flat terrain, reached the opposite side. There was another fire escape on this side. He used the rope to lower Julie down, then slipped over the side, hung from the building for a few seconds, and let himself drop. He hit the metal of the fire escape, grabbed her hand, and they started down.

'Won't we have the same problem if someone is out there?' said Julie.

'We would if we were going all the way down.'

They reached the third floor of the building and Robie stopped. He used a knife to defeat a simple locking mechanism and lifted a window.

'What if someone lives here?' hissed Julie.

'Then we'll politely leave,' whispered Robie.

The apartment was empty. They ran down the hallway to the interior stairwell. A minute later they hustled down the street in the opposite direction from where they had come.

Robie said, 'They were tracking you. Which means you must have a bug on you somewhere.'

'How do you know that?'

'Piece of equipment I found on the guy. I busted it up, but we have to cut off the source. Open your bag.'

Robie quickly went through it but found nothing.

'Maybe you've got a bug on you,' she said.

'That's not possible,' Robie said, but then stopped and pulled out the pinhole camera he'd thrown into his pocket. He popped the cover and underneath was a second blinking blue light.

'See, it *was* you. I was right,' Julie said, triumphantly.

He tossed it and the earwig and power pack in a garbage can.

ROBIE BROKE INTO and then sparked the ignition of an ancient pickup truck parked in front of a gas station. Julie did not get in.

'You decide to go it alone?' he asked.

She didn't answer. He reached into his pocket, pulled out something and handed it to her. It was the pepper spray. 'You might need this, then.'

She took it but then climbed in the truck.

He drove off. 'Why the change of heart?'

'Bad guys don't give weapons back.' She paused. 'And you saved my life back there. Twice.'

'Fair enough.'

'So people are after me. Who's after you?' she asked.

'I won't tell you. It would not be good for your future.'

'I'm not sure I have much of that, anyway.'

She grew silent, staring ahead.

'You thinking about somebody?' asked Robie, quietly.

Julie blinked back tears. 'No. And don't ask me again, Will.'

She settled back in her seat and Robie drove fast. He made one stop, at an all-night convenience store to get some groceries. Half an hour after that, the truck lights flickered across the face of a small farmhouse. Robie pulled the truck to a stop.

'What is this place?' Julie asked, looking around.

They had driven down a gravel road. Woods starting to turn colour bracketed the drive which ended at the front of a white clapboard house. In the back, a barn rose high above the apex of the house.

'Safe,' he said. 'Or as safe as possible under the circumstances.'

She stared at the barn. 'Was this, like, a farm or something?'

'Long time ago. Woods have reclaimed the fields.'

This was Robie's fail-safe. His employer provided other safe houses for Robie and people like him. But this place was his alone. Ownership under a shell company. No way to trace back to him.

Robie drove the truck inside the barn. He grabbed the sack of groceries and Julie followed him to the house. Robie put in the code for the alarm system, careful not to let her see the numbers he punched in.

She looked around. 'Where do I go?'

He pointed up the stairs. 'Spare bedroom, second door on the right. Bathroom across the hall. You hungry?'

'I'd rather sleep.'

'OK,' said Robie. 'Goodnight.'

'Goodnight.'

'And make sure you don't shoot yourself with the pepper spray. It really stings the skin.'

She looked down at her hand where the small canister was hidden.

'How did you know?'

'I saw you had it pointed at me the whole drive over. Don't blame you. Get some sleep.'

She set off. He watched her trudge up the stairs. He heard the bedroom door open and close and then the lock engage. Smart girl.

He went into the kitchen. He sat down at the table and took out his cellphone. No GPS chip was in there. Company policy, because a chip could work both ways. But he had screwed up on the pinhole.

And they must have suspected he wouldn't fire on the woman tonight. They had the tracker on him in case he gave them the slip.

A set-up from the get-go. Nice. And now he needed to figure out why.

He looked at the photos he'd taken at the dead woman's apartment. Her driver's licence stated that her name was Jane Wind, aged thirty-five. He enlarged the screen on his phone so he could make out the ports of entry on her passport pages. There were several European countries, then Robie saw Iraq, Afghanistan and Kuwait. Unusual. He next looked at her government ID card. *Office of the Inspector General, US Department of Defense.*

Robie stared at the screen. *I'm screwed. I'm totally screwed.*

He used his phone to access the Internet. There was nothing on Wind, but the bus blowing up had already attracted attention. According to the news accounts, the authorities were not ruling out a mechanical cause for the explosion. *And that's where it might remain*, he thought, *unless they find evidence to the contrary.*

His handler had not tried to contact him. Robie was not surprised. He was safe here for now. Tomorrow? Who knew? He glanced in the direction of the stairs. He was on the run, and he was not alone. Alone he might have a chance. But now?

Now he had Julie. She was fourteen, maybe. She didn't trust him or anyone else. And she was running from something, too.

Is it guilt over letting a little kid die right in front of me? Am I making amends this way, by saving Julie from whatever and whoever is after her?

His mind and body tired, Robie could think of nothing else to do right then. So he did what made sense. He went upstairs to the bedroom across the hall from hers, locked the door behind him, laid the .38 on his chest and closed his eyes. Sleep was important. He wasn't sure when he would get another chance to do it.

Chapter 3

Early next morning, Robie showered, dressed and headed to the stairs. It was still partially dark outside. He heard gentle snores coming from the guest bedroom. He thought about knocking but decided to let her sleep. He glided down the steps and into the kitchen.

When Julie came downstairs twenty minutes later, the meal prep was far advanced.

'Coffee or tea?' he asked.

'Coffee, black,' she answered.

'It's over there,' he said. 'Help yourself.' He swished eggs in a bowl and glanced up at the small TV sitting on top of the fridge. He said, 'Check it out.'

Julie glanced up as she sipped her coffee. In the light of the kitchen, she looked younger and scrawnier than she had last night.

The sound on the TV was turned down low, but the scene on the screen was self-explanatory. The still-smoking bus, burned to a shell of metal. It had had a full tank of gas for the trip up to New York and had burned like an inferno.

The TV newscaster stared into the camera: 'The FBI is not ruling out a terrorist attack, though it doesn't seem clear at this point why the bus would have been targeted.'

'How do you think it happened?' Julie asked.

'Guy who was after you might have set it off.'

'What, like a suicide bomber? Wouldn't you have seen a bomb on him?'

'Probably. And I tied him up, so it would have been impossible for him to set anything off.'

'So it couldn't have been him.'

'Not necessarily. It could have been concealed on him and set off remotely. About half the suicide bombers in the Middle East never pull the trigger themselves. Their handlers detonate from a safe distance away.'

'But if the guy wasn't the source of the explosion—'

'Then something else hit that bus. An incendiary round into the gas tank is one possibility. Ignites the vapour, and boom. How do you think the guy found you on the bus?'

'Well, he came on fast and last . . .' she said, adopting an analytical tone.

Robie appreciated that tone. He used it often. 'So he either had just got the assignment at the last minute and was playing catch-up, or, more likely, they lost you but then reacquired you. Which do you think it is?'

'No idea. How about the guy in the alley with the rifle?'

'He was after me.'

'I know. You had the tracking device. But why?'

'Not something I can talk about.'

'Then that's my answer, too,' Julie shot back. 'So what now?'

They sat staring at each other.

'Where are your parents?' Robie asked.

'Who says I have any?'

'Everybody has parents.'

'I meant parents that were *living*.'

'So yours are dead.'

She looked away, fiddled with the handle of her mug. 'This arrangement is probably not going to work out.'

'If you tell me what's going on, I can maybe help you.'

'You've already helped me, and I appreciate that. But I'm not sure what else you can do, realistically.'

He glanced at the TV. Two sheeted bodies on gurneys were being wheeled out of a building. One body was big, one very small.

A spokeswoman from the DC Metropolitan Police said, 'The victims, a mother and her young son, have been identified, but we're withholding their names until next of kin are notified.'

'And the FBI is heading up the investigation?' asked a reporter.

'The deceased woman was a federal employee. The Bureau's involvement is standard operating procedure in those situations.'

No, it really isn't, thought Robie. He kept staring at the screen, hungry for more information.

'And there was another child?' asked the reporter.

'Yes. He was unharmed. That's all we can say right now.'

Robie turned back to find Julie staring at him. Her eyes were like acid, eating through any façade he could muster.

'Was that you?'

He said nothing.

'Mother and kid, huh? You help me to make up for that?'

'You want anything else to eat?'

'No. What I want is to leave.'

'I can drive you.'

'I'd prefer to walk.'

She went up to her room and was back down a minute later with her backpack.

As he opened the front door for her, he said, 'I didn't kill those people.'

'I don't believe you,' she said, simply. 'But thanks for not killing me. I've got enough shit to deal with as it is.'

He watched her hurry down the gravel drive.

Robie went to get his coat.

ROBIE PUT ON A HELMET, slid the leather cover off the Honda street bike and drove it out of the barn. He reached the road in time to see Julie climb into the front seat of an ancient Mercury driven by an old woman. Robie fell in behind. When the big car turned into the gas station, he cut down a side road and doubled back. He watched through a gap in the hedge by the road as Julie got out and went over to the pay phone.

She studied some cards in the booth, put some coins in the slot and dialled. Cab company, he deduced. When she'd hung up, she went into the store. She'd have to wait for the cab, and so would Robie.

His phone rang. He glanced at the screen and drew a quick breath. The number on the ID was known as a 'blue' call. It came right from the top of his agency. Robie had never gotten one of those before. He would have to answer it. But that didn't mean he had to be particularly cooperative.

He said, 'You can't trace this call. You know that.'

'We need to meet,' the man said.

It wasn't his handler. Robie knew it wouldn't be. Blue calls did not come from handlers in the field.

'I had a "meeting" last night. I don't think I can survive another.'

'There will be no repercussions. Your handler was wrong.'

'Good to know. I still didn't complete the assignment.'

'The intel was also wrong,' said the man. 'It was unfortunate.'

'Unfortunate? The woman was *supposed* to die. She was also an American citizen.'

Now it was the other man's turn to say nothing.

'Inspector General's office,' said Robie. 'I was told the woman was part of a terrorist cell.'

'Your job is to execute the order. If it's wrong, it's not your job to deal with it. It's mine.'

'And who the hell are you?'

'You know this is a blue call. It's above your handler. Well above. Let's leave it at that until we can meet.'

Robie watched as Julie came back outside.

'Listen, Robie, we don't want to lose you. You are a valuable asset.'

'Thanks. Where's my handler?'

'Reassigned. We're in damage control, Robie. We need to work together.'

'Did you send someone to kill me last night? Guy with a rifle in an alley? Has my shoe prints on his face? Might still be lying there, unconscious?'

'He was not one of ours, I can promise you that. Give me the exact location and we'll check it out.'

Robie didn't believe him, but it didn't really matter. He told the guy where it had happened and left it at that. 'What do you want from me? I'm not in the mood for more missions.'

'The FBI is heading an investigation in connection with the death of Jane Wind. We want you to act as an agency interface with the Bureau.'

As many scenarios as Robie had thought through, that had not been one of them. 'You can't be serious.'

'We need you to be the liaison. And we need you to play it the way we want you to. That is essential.'

'Why would we need a liaison to this case in the first place?'

'Because Jane Wind was working for us.'

THE MEETING PLACE and time was arranged, and Robie put away his phone. He watched as a cab rolled into the gas station parking lot. Julie climbed in and the cab drove off. Robie took up a tracking position roughly fifty yards back in traffic. He was not concerned about losing her. He had slipped a digestible bio transmitter into her scrambled eggs. It would be good for twenty-four hours and then it would wash out of her system. His tracking monitor was strapped to his wrist.

The cab turned onto Interstate 66 and headed east towards DC. It crossed the Roosevelt Bridge, and hung a right. The cab stopped at an intersection where a number of old duplexes were located. She got out, hesitated, then climbed back in the cab. Robie made note of the address and took up his tail once more.

About ten minutes later, Robie realised she was heading back to the location of the bus explosion. The cab had to let her out a couple of blocks from her destination because roads were closed off by police barricades. Robie saw cops and Feds everywhere. He parked his bike and took up his pursuit on foot. Julie was a full block ahead of him. Robie could see what was left of the bus, even though the police were in the process of shielding this sight from the public.

Robie looked at the spot where he had landed after the blast. He still had no idea where his gun was. That was troubling. He looked up at the corners of buildings. Were there surveillance cameras posted here? Right now, no one knew that they were the sole survivors of the explosion.

He spied a woman in her late thirties wearing an FBI windbreaker. Dark hair, pretty face. She was about five-six and slender. Her badge and gun rode on her belt. Both special agents and uniformed cops were talking to her and he noted their air of deference. She might be the special agent in charge of this thing.

He pulled back into the shadow of a doorway as Julie walked down the street away from the bus's remains. Robie followed her to a cut-rate hotel wedged between two vacant buildings and watched through a window as she checked in using a credit card. He wondered whose name was on it. If hers, it could send a marker through the system that would inform whoever was after her where she was.

A minute later she stepped onto the elevator. Robie went up to the front desk and said to the old man behind it, 'My daughter just checked in. I dropped her off for an internship on the Hill. I wanted her to use her

American Express card because the card I gave her was corrupted, but I think she forgot. I tried calling her, but I guess she turned her phone off. What room is she in?'

The old fellow smiled. 'I can't give out that information.'

Robie sighed heavily and pulled out his wallet. He slipped out a twenty. 'Look, the last thing I need is for some cyber creep to screw up my credit by my kid using the wrong card.'

The man looked at the records in front of him. 'Credit card used was a Visa. Name on the account was Gerald Dixon.'

'I know that. I *am* Gerald Dixon. I've got two Visa cards. Can I please see the numbers?'

'You can for another twenty.'

After exhibiting deep exasperation, Robie complied. He looked at the card and memorised the numbers.

'Great,' said Robie. 'That's the corrupted card.'

'Already ran it through, sport. Nothing I can do.'

Robie turned and left. He would find out who Gerald Dixon was. But he had to assume that Julie was safe for the moment.

He rode back to his apartment and checked out the front and back of his building before going inside. He took the stairwell instead of the elevator, passing no one. At this hour of the day, everyone was at work. He opened the door of his apartment and poked his head inside. It was all as he had left it.

It took him five minutes to make sure the place was empty. He employed little traps—a piece of paper wedged into a door track, a thread that would be broken when a drawer was opened—to alert him if someone had broken in and searched his place. None of them was tripped.

He changed into slacks, sport coat and white collared shirt and opened a wall safe. He hadn't used his cred pack—his badge and ID card—in a long time. He slipped it inside his jacket and set off.

The meeting was in a public place at Robie's insistence.

The Hay-Adams Hotel was located across the street from Lafayette Park, across Pennsylvania Avenue from the White House. The most protected ground on earth. Robie figured even his agency would have a hard time killing him here and getting away with it.

One minute before the allotted time, a man in his sixties walked into the Jefferson Room, an eating area off the hotel lobby. Modestly priced suit, polished off-the-rack shoes, the bearing of a lifelong public servant who had accumulated far more power than wealth. Two tall young men were with him. Muscle. They followed him into the room but did not sit with him. They took up positions on the perimeter of the room, their gazes sweeping for threats. One of them set a slender device on the piano in one corner. It emitted a humming sound. *White noise with a scrambler*, Robie knew. *If there are electronic surveillance devices in here, the recording will come out undecipherable.*

The room was empty even though it was lunchtime. Robie knew this was not a coincidence. The wait staff was not in evidence, either.

Robie sat diagonally to the man, his back to a wall.

'Glad you could make it,' said the man.

'You have a name?'

'Blue Man will do.'

He reached into his pocket and let Robie see the badge, the picture and the position stated on the ID card, but not the name. This fellow was high up in the agency. Far higher than Robie had expected.

'OK, let's talk,' said Robie. 'You said Jane Wind was one of ours. I checked her ID. She's DCIS. Defense Criminal Investigative Service.'

'Did you also see her passport?'

'Middle East trips, Germany. But DCIS has offices in all those places,' Robie said.

'That's why it made perfect cover.'

'So was she a lawyer?'

'Yes. But she was more than that.'

'What exactly did she do for you?'

'First, I need to know what happened last night.'

Robie told him. He figured keeping anything back was a stupid idea. However, he said nothing about Julie or the bus. In his mind, that was a separate matter entirely.

Blue Man took in the information. 'Agent Wind worked in the field for years. After she had children she was reassigned, but she still worked closely with DCIS and she continued to work for us.'

'How did that get her assigned to a hit list she wasn't supposed to be on? And how can something like this happen, anyway? I know we are clandestine, but we're also part of an organisation with checks and balances.'

'If one person, or more likely a small group of people, are determined enough, they can accomplish the impossible.'

'What did Wind stumble on that got her killed?'

Blue Man looked curious. 'How do you know she stumbled on to anything? What makes you think that?'

'She lived in a crappy apartment with two little kids. There were legal docs on her table in the living room so her work wasn't classified. According to her passport, her last trip out of the States was two years ago. She wasn't a field agent, at least not any longer. But she was back working on something, probably considered routine. She found something. That's why she was targeted. I doubt it was directly related to her work.'

Blue Man took this in, his head nodding approvingly. 'You analyse well, Robie. I'm impressed.'

'And I'm full of questions. Do you know what she had stumbled on to?'

'We don't. But, like you, we don't think it was tied to her official duties.'

'Why do you want me to act as the liaison with the Bureau? That's a big risk, particularly if they find out what I've been doing the last dozen years.'

'They won't.' Blue Man looked at Robie. 'Now give me your theory.'

'Someone found out what she had discovered and they ratted her. They weren't sure I would pull the trigger so they had a back-up. And you said my handler has been reassigned. That was a lie. I don't need lies from you.'

'How do you figure it was a lie?'

'He ordered me to kill Wind. You said that wasn't authorised. So the guy's a traitor. You don't reassign traitors. If you had him in custody, you wouldn't need me telling you what happened. That means the handler has disappeared along with whoever else he was working with. How many are we talking?'

Blue Man sighed. 'We think at least three other people in the chain, but there might be more. It's not good, certainly.'

Robie just stared at him. 'Understatement of the year. What exactly do you want me to do?'

'We have to keep tabs on the investigation without seeming to. So, officially, you will be a special agent with DCIS, but you will be reporting to me. We'll provide you with all the cover and creds you need. They're being placed at your apartment as we speak.'

Robie's face darkened. 'You've got at least four traitors. What if you have more? And what if one of them is at my apartment right now?'

'These agents were pulled from an entirely separate division. They've had no contact with your handler. Their loyalty is above question.'

Robie nodded, slowly. 'Why me?'

'Because you didn't pull the trigger. We trust you to do the right thing. There aren't many I can say that about right now.'

Robie had thought of another possible reason why they wanted him involved. *I was there. Which means I'll make the perfect fall guy if this goes to hell.*

But he said, 'All right.' He would prefer to work the case himself rather than wait for someone else to do it, and maybe screw it and him beyond repair. *If I go down, I go down by my own hand.*

Blue Man rose and put out his hand. 'Good luck.'

Robie didn't shake his hand. 'It's rarely about luck. We both know that.'

EVERYTHING WAS WAITING for Robie when he got back to his apartment. He looked over the file, the creds and his background information.

He had to come up to speed on this case as fast as possible. But fast-tracking something like this meant that mistakes could be made. *And probably will be.*

Then it became a case of how fast his support from Blue Man would fade away. *Faster than the party and financial support of a candidate with plummeting poll numbers.*

It was just how the town worked.

The name Will Robie stared back at him. Ironically, his real name was the safest one to use for this sort of assignment. Also waiting for him was a fresh Glock G20 and a shoulder holster. He strapped it on and buttoned his jacket.

As he headed out, Robie saw Annie Lambert. She was in a black business suit and sneakers.

'Don't usually see you here in the middle of the day,' he said.

'I forgot something.'

The enquiries into Lambert triggered by her contact with Robie in the gym had turned up nothing. Not surprising. To work at the White House, one had to be squeaky clean.

She hesitated and then said, 'Maybe we can have a drink sometime.'

'Yeah, maybe we can,' said Robie, who was thinking of all that lay ahead of him.

'OK,' she said, uncertainly.

He started to walk off and then stopped, realising that he'd been abrupt with her. He turned. 'I appreciate the offer. And I really do want to have a drink with you, Annie.'

She brightened. 'OK, Will. You know where I live.'

He walked off and wondered why he was suddenly so taken with the young woman. She was lovely and obviously smart, but in the past that had not mattered to Robie. He smiled at the image of her standing there in the tennis shoes and the business suit.

ROBIE DROVE HIS AUDI to the Jane Wind crime scene. On the way, he looked at his tracking device as he passed the hotel where Julie was staying. She was still there.

He walked to the apartment building's entrance feeling enormously uncomfortable. He was going to help investigate a murder at which he was an eyewitness. There was a pack of cops and suits huddled in the lobby of the building. The huddle broke up as he approached and out stepped the same female FBI special agent he had seen at the bus bombing.

She came forward, looking at him inquisitively. He pulled his cred pack, flashed the badge and then ID card. She reciprocated. She was FBI Special Agent Nicole Vance.

'Agent Robie, welcome to the show. Got some questions for you,' she said.

'I look forward to working on this case with you, Agent Vance.'

She said, 'I got a call from my supervisor about you. We're to associate you with the case, but purely for background information. The FBI has the lead, meaning *I* have the lead.'

'I didn't mean to imply otherwise,' Robie said, smoothly.

Vance seemed to study him more closely. 'OK,' she said, cautiously. 'Just so long as we understand the ground rules.'

'What would you like my help on?'

'Any background you can give us on the victim.'

Robie pulled a flash drive from his jacket pocket. 'Her official background file is on here.'

This earned him a smile. She took the drive and handed it to one of her associates. 'Get it read and summarised ASAP.' Vance turned back to Robie. 'We were about to go over the crime scene. Care to join us?'

'I'd appreciate that.'

As they headed to the elevator, Vance said, 'I guess you heard about the bus explosion, as well?'

'I saw it on the news. I understand the FBI is investigating that, too.'

'More specifically, I am. And I'm thinking of merging the investigations.'

'Why is that?'

'We found a gun at the scene of the bus explosion.'

Robie kept his gaze straight ahead even as his heartbeat quickened. 'Gun?'

'Yeah. And we've already run ballistics. The Glock we found matches a slug we took from the floor of the apartment the deceased lived in. So in my mind, the two cases are definitely connected. Now we just have to find out how.'

'The killer might have thrown the gun away during his escape. Might be a coincidence it was found near the bus.'

'I don't believe in coincidences. At least, not ones like that.'

As they stepped off the elevator and headed to the condo where two people had been murdered right in front of him, Robie wicked a drop of sweat off his forehead. He would take a hundred megalomaniacal Saudi princes and bloodthirsty cartel chieftains over this.

THE APARTMENT had changed since Robie had last been there. The cops were doing a thorough forensics search. He eyed a sealed evidence box on the table.

'Is that Agent Wind's work papers? Laptop?'

Vance nodded. 'We've sealed it pending your agency's review. But if there's something in those docs and files that got her killed, the Bureau needs to know.'

'Understood. I can have the review done today and you can be read in directly after.'

Vance's smile was guarded. 'I never met a more cooperative agency liaison. You're going to spoil me.'

'I'll do my best,' Robie said.

They walked into the bedroom. The bodies had been removed, but in Robie's mind he still saw them, their heads pulverised.

'Wind and her son, Jacob, were found on the bed. One shot killed them both.' She pointed to the shattered window. 'Shot came from that high-rise building, three hundred metres away. We're pinpointing the exact room. If we're lucky, the shooter left something behind.'

You won't be that lucky, thought Robie.

'But you said you found a Glock round in the floor. How does that tie into a shot at that distance? It wasn't a pistol round that killed them. Had to be a rifle round.'

'I know. That's what's so puzzling. If I have to speculate, there were two people involved. The person in this room last night fired a shot into the mattress that lodged in the floor. That slug matched the gun we found next to the bus explosion. But the kill shot came through the window.'

Robie stood in front of the bed, in nearly the exact spot from which he'd fired the night before. 'So the shooter in the apartment fired into the bed. Where was the slug found?'

Vance motioned for one of her techs to move aside the bed. Robie saw the evidence marker next to a hole in the wooden floor.

'The round fired into the mattress didn't hit them?'

'Negative. No other wounds on the victims.'

'So he fired a shot into the mattress—why? To get their attention, or maybe to get them to be quiet.'

'Maybe.'

'Were they awake when they were shot?'

'Looked to be. The position where they fell on the bed leads me to believe they were awake when they were killed.'

'So he fires, but doesn't hit them. Anyone report hearing any screams?'

Vance sighed. 'The only person who was here last night is an old woman who's both deaf and blind. She, of course, heard nothing. The apartments above and below this one are vacant.'

Robie went over to the broken window and examined it. There were other buildings separating the two high-rise structures, but they were all one-storey. The shooter would have had a clean shot.

'OK, gunman inside. Shooter outside. Gunman fires into the bed. Shooter outside kills Agent Wind and her son.' He turned back to Vance. 'Wind had two sons?'

'That's the other really puzzling piece. Her other son, Tyler, is less than a year old. He was found by a woman on the third floor. Someone knocked on her door shortly after the Winds were killed. The woman opened the door and there was Tyler in his car carrier, sound asleep. She recognised him and tried phoning Wind, then went to her apartment. No one answered so she called the cops. That's when the bodies were discovered.'

'You have a theory for that?'

'How's this? Intruder comes in, just a standard burglary. He somehow awakens Wind and her son. He fires a shot into the bed to keep them quiet. At the same time, a shooter is targeting her from that other building. He fires, killing her and her son. The intruder is stunned. He could have ducked down, thinking that he might be shot next. He sees the other kid in the carrier and, during his escape, drops him off at another apartment. Then he gets away.' She smiled weakly. 'I know. It's like the mother of all coincidences, isn't it?'

It's also exactly what happened, thought Robie.

ROBIE AND VANCE were in the other building, from where the kill shot had come. It was abandoned and full of junk. They had looked through several rooms that could have served as the shooter's sanctuary. When they entered the fifth, Robie said, 'This is it.'

He walked over to one of the windows. 'Window is open a notch. The sight line is dead on.' He pointed at the windowsill. 'And the dust has been disturbed. Check the pattern. Muzzle mark.' He pointed at a dark stain the size of a dime further along on the sill. He looked down at the concrete floor. 'Knee imprints in the dirt. He used the sill as his centre of support, lined up his shot and took it.'

He knelt down, slipped out his gun and took aim, lining up his sights with the window with the hole in it across the way. 'The angle is perfect.'

Vance looked impressed. 'You have special forces in your background?'

'If I did I couldn't tell you.'

'Come on. I know lots of former Delts and SEALs.'

'I'm sure you do.'

She looked out of the window. 'I also know some people at DCIS. I texted them about you. None of them has heard of you.'

'I just came back into the country. If you want to check me out, I can give you my superior's contact info.'

'OK, I will,' she said. 'So, my burglar and separate shooter theory looks sound. I can't see how the guy in the apartment last night could have known about the shooter over here.'

You're right, I didn't, thought Robie.

Vance continued. 'But now the question becomes, why kill Wind? What was she working on for your people?'

'I'll check, but it could be something she stumbled on to.'

'Stumbled on to? How does that make sense?'

'Not saying it does. Only that because she worked for DCIS, doesn't mean that was the reason she was killed.'

'OK, but forgive me if I take as my working hypothesis that her death was related to her work.'

Robie said, 'That's your prerogative. Has her partner been notified?'

'In the process. He's her ex. Her son is with Social Services for now.'

'What's her former husband do?'

'Rick Wind is retired military but he has another job. We're in the process of tracking him down now.'

'In the process of tracking him down? He'd have to have seen the news. He should've called you by now.'

'Believe me, Robie, I thought of that.'

'You have his home address?'

'Maryland. My agents have already been there. It's empty.'

Robie said, 'Where does he work?'

'He owns a place called the Premium Pawnshop in northeast DC. All locked up, and his home address is empty.'

'If he's not at home, and he's not at work, and he hasn't called the police, then there are only a few possibilities.'

'He either doesn't watch TV or listen to the radio, or he killed his ex-wife and kid and is on the run. Or else he's dead, too.'

'You really think the guy killed his ex and kid using a sniper rifle? Domestic issues like that are usually face to face.'

'Well, he was former military.'

Robie said, 'Have you searched his home and the pawnshop?'

'Home, yes. Pawnshop next. Care to tag along?'

THERE WERE BARS across the front door and windows of the pawnshop. The door had three serious locks. Vance sent the two other agents to check the rear while she and Robie approached the front. She peered inside. 'Can't see anything.'

'Can you knock down the door, or do you need a warrant?' Robie joined her at the front of the shop and peered between the bars into the darkened interior. 'He could be inside, hurt or dead. That should be enough.'

'And if we find evidence he committed the crime, and his defence lawyer gets it thrown out because our search was determined to be unlawful under the Fourth Amendment, what then?'

'I guess that's why you FBI agents get the big bucks. How about *I* kick open the door and search the place?'

'Still have the same evidentiary problem.'

Robie examined the door and the framing round it. 'Steel on steel. Tough stuff. But there's always a way. I'll tell them I did it all on my own, against your express instructions.'

'What kind of Fed are you?' she asked, her eyebrows hiked.

'Not the career-kissing type, obviously. Stay there.'

'Robie, you can't just—'

He drew his pistol, fired three times, and the trio of locks fell out onto the sidewalk. He opened the door and stepped inside.

Robie kept his gun out, felt for the light switch and the pawnshop was quickly draped in weak light. Watches, lamps, rings and an assortment of other items were stacked neatly in bins or inside glass cabinets. All had tags with numbers written on them. Robie moved forward, doing visual sweeps. When he heard footsteps behind him he turned to see Vance, her expression seriously pissed off.

'You're an idiot,' she hissed.

Robie put a finger to his lips. He'd heard it before her. A squeak. And then another. He pointed to the back of the shop. She nodded.

Robie led the way to a pair of swinging doors with a gap between. He kicked one of the doors open and bulled inside, his gun ready to fire as he stepped to the left. Vance followed on the right.

She grimaced as a grey critter skittered into a darkened corner.

'Rats.'

'I don't think rats squeak like that,' said Robie.

'Then what?' she asked.

He pointed to one darkened corner of the room. The man was hanging upside down from an exposed rafter. His body was swinging slightly and the rope was squeaking against the wooden beam.

Vance looked at the dead man.

'Is that Rick Wind?' asked Robie.

'Who the hell can tell? He's been dead a while.'

'Didn't kill himself. Hands are bound. And he didn't kill his wife and kid. Condition of the body means he was dead before they were. Rigor's long since passed.' Robie bent over and looked at the man's open mouth. 'And there's something else. It seems they cut out his tongue.'

ROBIE HAD LEFT AGENT VANCE to deal with the body in the pawnshop. They had confirmed it was Rick Wind. They had checked the shop's surveillance camera. Someone had taken the DVD.

Robie was now sitting in his apartment typing on his computer. He typed the name 'Gerald Dixon' into Google. He got too many hits and switched to a more exclusive database to which he had access. The hits that came back were more manageable. He refined his search and it narrowed to one name. One line on the man's record caught his attention. Foster care provider.

Gerald Dixon lived in a two-storey duplex in a lousy neighbourhood. When Robie knocked on the door it took a long time to get a response, and he heard noises inside that spoke of frenzied activity. The guy finally opened the door and Robie noted the crimson patches on his cheeks, the bloodshot eyes and the smell of breath freshener.

'Gerald Dixon?' Robie flashed his badge. 'I'm with DC Internal Affairs.'

Dixon took a step back. 'Ain't that for cops?'

'It's for a lot of things,' said Robie. 'May I come in?'

'Why?'

'To talk about Julie.'

Dixon's face screwed up. 'If you find her you tell her she better get her butt back here. If she ain't here I don't get paid.'

'So she's gone missing?'

'That's right.' Dixon let Robie pass through.

The inside of the house looked no better than the outside. They sat on tattered chairs. Robie noted papers and the end of a beer can sticking out from under a chair. He wondered what else was under there. His seat was very hard. He didn't think it was the cushion.

A small, curvy woman wearing tight jeans and an even tighter blouse came out of the back. She had the air of someone who was totally disconnected from reality. She eyed Robie.

'Who's he?'

'Some dude from Internal Affairs,' growled Dixon.

Robie flipped open his badge. 'I'm here to talk about Julie.'

The woman snapped, 'She's gone. Run off. Little shit never appreciated what we gave her.'

Robie opened a notebook he drew from his jacket. 'Tell me about Julie. Full name, background, how she came to be here.'

Gerald said, 'Her name is Julie Getty. She got here about three weeks ago.'

'Why was she placed in foster care?'

'Her parents couldn't take care of her.'

'Why? Were they dead?'

'No, don't think so. The agency people just give you kids and you take care of them.'

'And Julie's not here any more?'

'Run off in the middle of the night.'

'When did you discover her missing?'

'This morning when she didn't come down.'

'So you don't check on your wards at night?'

'She was very private,' said Gerald. 'We didn't like to butt in.'

Robie pulled the empty beer can out from under the chair. 'I can see that. You might want to open some windows. Get the reefer smell out.'

'We don't do drugs,' said Gerald, feigning astonishment.

'Have you heard from Julie since she left?'

They both shook their heads.

'Anybody come here who you didn't know? Suspicious cars?'

Gerald said, 'No. What the hell has she got herself involved in? Gangs? Do you think we might be in danger?'

Robie closed his notebook. 'I certainly wouldn't rule out the possibility.' He had to fight back a smile.

He lifted up the seat cushion and pulled out a baggie of coke, some vials containing a brown liquid and two capped syringes.

'Next time try locating your pharmacy somewhere private.'

As Robie left the duplex, he saw a woman holding an envelope striding towards him, two police officers in tow.

'You heading to the Dixons?' he asked, as the woman neared.

'Yes. Who are you?'

'Someone who wants you to make sure they never get foster kids again.'

The woman waved the envelope. 'Well, your wish has just been granted.' She steamed on with the officers right behind.

Robie's wrist beeped. He looked down at the tracker. Julie was finally on the move. And Robie was pretty sure where.

JULIE CLAMBERED UP the vine and slipped inside her bedroom window. She squatted on the floor listening. All she could hear were her own heartbeats. Her legs shaky, she moved down the stairs, holding on to the wall for support.

She rounded the bend, closed her eyes and then opened them. It was all she could do not to scream.

Robie stared back at her. 'You get around,' he said.

She looked quickly around the room. There was nothing there except for the furniture.

'Expect to find something else?' he said, moving towards her.

She backed up a step.

'How did you get here?' she asked.

'Followed you. This is your home, right?'

She just stared at him, more in curiosity than fear.

He looked at a picture on a side table. 'Your mom and dad were nice-looking. And there you are, right in the centre. Happy times.'

'You don't know anything,' snapped Julie.

'Correction, I know some things. Like you're in danger. People are looking for you. People who have a lot of money, muscle and connections.'

'How do you know that?'

'Because they covered up two murders right here.'

Julie's eyes widened as Robie motioned to the wall. 'Fresh paint. But only in that spot. It was put there to cover something up.' He pointed to the floor. 'Used to be a square of carpet here. You can see where the wood is lighter. Again, covering something up. You paint walls and remove rugs to take away blood, tissue, other bodily fluids. And they missed a spot of blood on the baseboard over there. Did you expect to find their bodies here?'

'You spend a lot of time around dead bodies?' she said, warily.

'Ever since I hooked up with you.'

'We're not hooked up in any way at all.'

'I know about your foster parents. The city busted them,' he said. 'Now tell me what happened here.'

'Why?'

'Call me a Good Samaritan.'

'There aren't any of those left,' she replied.

'Not even your parents?'

'You leave my parents out of this,' she said, sharply.

'Did you see how they died? Is that why you were on the run?'

For a moment Robie thought she was going to run for it. 'Were they mixed up in something over their heads?'

'My mom and dad wouldn't hurt anyone.'

'So they were killed? Just a simple nod will do.'

She moved her head forwards a notch.

'You saw that happen?'

Another nod.

'The guy on the bus, he was the one?'

'I think so.'

'Julie, tell me exactly what happened. It's the only way I can help you. If last night showed you nothing else, it's that I'm someone who can get things done.'

'What about those people on the TV? Did you kill them? A mom and her kid? You said you didn't do it, but I need to know the truth.'

'Well, if I did kill them there's no way in the world I would admit it. But if I did do it, why would I be here trying to help you? Give me a reason.'

She let out a long breath, played with the straps on her backpack.

'Do you swear you didn't kill them?'

'I swear. I'm working with the FBI right now to figure out who did.' He showed her his badge.

Julie said, 'OK. I came here last night. I heard someone come in. I thought it was my parents, but someone else was with them. He was yelling at them. Asking them stuff.'

'Asking them what? Try to be as precise as you can.'

'He said, "How much do you know? What have you been told?" Stuff like that. And then, and then . . .'

'He hurt one of them?'

Tears trickled down her face. 'I heard a gunshot. I ran down the stairs. My dad was against the wall over there, all bloody. The guy pointed the gun at me, but my mom hit him and he fell down. I wanted to stay and help her. But she told me to run.' Julie shut her eyes, but the tears eased out from under her eyelids. 'I climbed out of the window. Then I heard another shot. And I ran hard. I knew that shot meant my mom was dead. But I just ran. I was a coward. I just left her to die.'

'And if you hadn't run, you'd be dead,' Robie said. 'Your mom sacrificed her life for yours. So you did what your mom wanted you to do. Stayed alive.'

She dried her tears. 'So what now?'

'Do you think anyone around here heard the shots?'

'I doubt it. The place next door is empty. This used to be an OK neighbourhood, but then everybody lost their jobs.'

'Including your parents?'

'They worked at whatever they could find. My mom went to college. My dad was a good guy.'

'What were their names?'

'Curtis and Sara Getty.'

'No relation to the Getty Oil folks, I guess?'

'If so, nobody ever told us.'

He said, 'OK, here's my plan. We find out who killed your parents and why they did it.'

'But if it was the guy on the bus, he's clearly dead.'

'Did you leave last night and go directly to the bus stop?'

'Yes.'

'Then the guy wasn't alone. He couldn't have policed this place, gotten rid of two bodies, and made it to the bus.'

'But why my parents? It's not like they were important.'

'Where did they work?'

'Dad worked at a warehouse in southeast. Mom at a diner a few blocks from here. Why?'

'Just digging for info.'

'I want to leave. This isn't my home any more.'

'OK. Where do you want to go?'

'I got a place I'm staying.'

'Yeah, I tracked you down there. It was stupid to steal Dixon's credit card. They'll bust you and people can track you. I've got another place. Why don't you pack some things and come on.'

ROBIE DROVE JULIE to his neighbourhood. Only he didn't take her to his building but to the observation post across the street. He showed her how to use the alarm system and then let her pick out her bedroom from the two there. She dropped her backpack on the bed and wandered around the apartment.

'What's the telescope for?' she asked.

'Stargazing.'

'That's not an astronomical telescope. And there's not really an angle here to point it skyward.'

'You know about telescopes?'

'I go to school.'

'I like to watch things,' he said. 'And to see if people are watching me.'

'So are we going to be, like, staying here together?' She looked nervous at this prospect.

'No. I'm staying somewhere else. But it's close by.' He took a cellphone out of his pocket. 'This has my number loaded on speed dial. It's untraceable. You should have everything you need. I stocked up the kitchen last week. Anything else, give me a call.'

'What about school?'

This caught Robie off guard. 'Where do you go to school?' he asked.

'At a G and T programme in northeast DC.'

'G and T? That's a cocktail.'

'Not gin and tonic. Gifted and talented.'

'Pretty smart, then.'

'In some things.'

Robie looked at her. 'Considering what happened to your parents, I'm not sure I want you going back to school. Whoever killed them will know where you go. Or it'll be easy enough to find out.'

'I can use the cellphone to text my programme coordinator and feed her some bullshit.'

'You think you're smarter than all adults?'

'No. But I'm smart enough to know how to lie and make it sound like the truth.' She looked at him closely. 'I think you're probably really good at that, too.'

'The foster care people will be looking for you.'

'I know. Won't be the first time. They'll go to my parents' house. They'll think they skipped town and took me with them. Then they'll go to the school, find out I texted my coordinator, assume I'm OK, and that'll be a dead end. They've got too many kids in the pipeline a lot worse off to spend any more time on me.'

'Thinking several moves ahead. That's good.'

'I'm not just going to sit in this place and do nothing. I'm going to help you find the people who got my parents killed.'

Robie stared at her. 'Let's get something really straight. You're a smart kid. But the people who are after you will kill anyone who gets in their way.'

'Sounds like you know the type real well,' she shot back. 'You've got safe houses and guns and untraceable phones and telescopes pointed at who knows what. You kill people too, I bet.'

Robie said nothing.

Julie looked out of the window. 'My parents were all I had. Now they're dead. I know I'm young, but I can help you. If you just give me a chance.'

'OK. We'll do this together. You have paper and a pen in your bag?'

'Yes. And I have a laptop my school gave me.'

'Write down everything you can remember about the last couple of weeks. Try and recall anything you saw, heard or suspected. Anything your parents said. And anyone else around who they knew or were talking to.'

'I'll start tonight. I'll make a good partner, you'll see.'

'I have no doubt, Julie.'

But his gut was ice. He much preferred to work alone. He didn't like having another life riding on him.

'ROBIE, GOT TIME for a cup of coffee?' It was Nicole Vance on the phone.

Robie had answered the call on his way down in the elevator after leaving Julie. He'd given the teenager a key to the apartment but asked her not to leave it without checking with him first. And he had told her to set the alarm.

'Anything break on the case?' he asked the FBI agent.

'There's a place open late near First and D southeast called Donnelly's. I can be there in ten minutes.'

'Give me ten more than that.'

'Hope I'm not interrupting anything.'

'I'll see you there.'

Robie grabbed his car from the street. The traffic across town was light at this hour. He parked on First. Donnelly's was busy for the lateness of the hour. When Robie hit the doorway, Vance caught his eye from the back of the main room.

He sat across from her. Her clothes were off-duty ones because she'd been home. Slacks, flats, light blue sweater, corduroy jacket. Her hair was down around her shoulders. It had been tied back earlier. Long hair and crime scenes were sometimes problematic.

Her cup of coffee was parked in front of her. With a wave of his hand Robie got the waitress's attention and pointed at Vance's cup and then at himself.

Vance waited until the woman came with a fresh cup and departed before she pulled out a manila folder from the bag sitting next to her. 'Background on Rick Wind.'

Robie leafed through the photos and written materials. 'Army, huh?'

'Career enlisted. Went in at eighteen. Did his full time and then he was out. He was forty-three.'

'Their kids were little. Did they start late?'

'Jane and Rick Wind were married ten years. Lots of failed attempts at getting pregnant. They hit the jackpot twice in three years. Then they decide to end the marriage. Go figure.'

'You find a cause of death?'

'The medical examiner's still working on that. No obvious wounds other than his tongue being cut out.' She paused. 'Isn't that what the Mob would do to snitches?'

'Did Wind have ties to the Mob?'

'Not that we know of. But he runs a pawnshop in a bad part of town. Maybe he was laundering dirty money and got his fingers caught in the cookie jar.'

'Time of death?' he asked.

'About three days, the ME said.' Vance took a sip of her coffee. 'The kill round for Wind and her son looks to be military-grade ammo.'

'What was the specific round?'

She looked at her notes. 'It was a 175-grain Sierra MatchKing Hollow Point Boat Tail. Our gun expert speculated it was US military. Sound right to you?'

'Our guys use that ammo. But so do the Hungarians, the Israelis, the Japanese and the Lebanese.'

'You're just full of gun facts. I'm impressed.'

'The Sierra ordnance is also available to the public. Too bad we don't have the casing.'

'Oh, but we do. The shooter didn't police his brass. Or at least if he did, he wasn't successful. The casing rolled right into a crack in the baseboard.'

'OK. Was the casing shiny or dull?'

'I don't know. But one phone call can answer that.'

She made the call. 'Dull, not shiny. Tell me why it's significant.'

'The manufacturers charge extra to buff up the casing to make it look shiny for civilians. The army buys millions of rounds, so it saves them a ton of money to go without the extra buffing.'

'So then we're definitely looking at military-grade ammo?'

'And that makes things more complicated.'

'Is that all you can say?' she said, in an incredulous tone.

'What do you want me to say?' he replied, evenly.

'If this is a US military hit on a government employee then this is not just complicated. This is a shitstorm. That's what I want you to say.'

'OK, this is a *potential* shitstorm. Satisfied?'

'By the way, my boss was royally pissed that you shot your way into that pawnshop. He said he was going to be talking to DCIS.'

'Good. Maybe they'll pull me from the case.'

'Where the hell are you coming from, Robie? Do you even want to be an investigator?'

'Are we done here?' He started to get up.

She looked up at him. 'I don't know, are we?'

He left.

She followed him outside. 'Actually, I'm not done with you.'

Robie grabbed her arm, pulled hard and they both fell behind some trash cans. An instant later, a barrage of bullets shattered the front window of Donnelly's.

ROBIE LIFTED HIS GUN and aimed through a crevice between the toppled trash cans. His target was a black SUV. The muzzle of an MP-5 submachine gun was currently spewing out a hail of bullets from the rear side window. The bullets shredded the outdoor tables and chairs and pinged off the building's brick façade.

People inside Donnelly's screamed and ran for cover. Robie kept his calm and fired. He hit tyre rubber to disable the vehicle, the front and rear passenger windows to knock out the shooter and the driver, and the front-side metal of the SUV to kill the engine.

And nothing happened. The SUV roared off.

Robie was up in an instant, chasing the SUV down the street, firing at its backside. He nailed the rear tyres. Nothing.

But then Robie saw the windows of a Honda parked at the kerb explode and the branch of a tree fall down, and he stopped firing. The SUV turned the corner and was gone.

Robie looked at the Honda's shattered glass, heard the car's alarm going off. He was about to run to his Audi, then he saw the shot-out tyres on his car.

He heard running feet and turned to see Vance approaching.

'What the hell was that?' she exclaimed.

'Call it in. We need to get that SUV.'

'I already did. Did you get a plate number?'

'They had it blacked out.'

Sirens had started up. Robie looked back at the restaurant. He heard screams and people sobbing. There were casualties.

'How many?' asked Robie.

'I'm not sure. Two outside are dead. Three wounded. Maybe more inside.' She looked at the Honda. 'Did you do that?'

'Ricochet from my weapon,' said Robie.

'Ricochet? Off the SUV?'

'I hit it a total of seventeen times,' said Robie. 'Tyres, windows, body. Ricochets, all of them. The SUV was armoured and had run-flat tyres.'

She looked at him. 'Those sorts of vehicles aren't that plentiful outside certain circles.'

'Mostly our own government's,' he said.

'So were they aiming to kill you, me or both of us?'

'Shooter had an MP-5 set on full auto. That's an indiscriminate weapon. Designed to kill everything in the zone.'

She looked at his arm and flinched. 'Robie, you're shot.'

He looked down at the blood on his arm. 'It didn't go in. Just a graze.'

They went back to the restaurant. Robie went from one wounded person to the next, quickly triaging and stopping the bleeding with whatever was handy, while Vance assisted.

When ambulances showed up, he went to check out his Audi. He saw the holes in the body. MP-5 rounds. Not ricochets from his pistol. That meant they knew his vehicle. Had they followed him here? If so . . .

'Vance, can I borrow your wheels? It's important.'

She pulled out her keys. 'Parked around the corner. Silver BMW convertible. But how am I going to get home?'

'I'll come back and get you. I shouldn't be long.'

As Robie drove he called the phone he had left Julie. She didn't answer. *Shit!* He floored the accelerator. Driving this fast in town, even at this late hour, was problematic. Traffic and lots of cops. Then he saw the box under the steering column. *I love you, Agent Vance.*

He hit the switch and blue grille lights were activated while a siren started blaring. He ran four red lights and within minutes found himself tearing down the street where his apartment was located.

He parked on a side street, jumped out and zigzagged his way on foot to the building where he'd left Julie. He took the stairs two at a time and raced down the hall. He'd texted her twice on the way over and had gotten no response. He eyed the door. No forced entry. He pulled his gun, quietly unlocked the door and eased it open. He did not hear the beep of the alarm. *Not good*. He heard a noise and moved quietly into the shadows. He pointed his gun, ready to fire.

The light came on. He stepped out.

Julie screamed. 'What the hell?' she gasped. 'Are you trying to give me a freaking heart attack?'

She was dressed in pyjamas and her hair was wet.

'I called and texted.'

'I couldn't exactly take the phone in the shower.'

'Next time, at least take it to the bathroom. Why wasn't the alarm on?'

'I went down to the lobby to get a newspaper. I was going to set it before I went to sleep.'

'All right, but I want you to keep the alarm on all the time.'

She glanced at his arm. 'You're bleeding.'

He rubbed the spot. 'I cut myself.'

'Through your jacket? Tell me what happened, Will.'

'I think I was followed. But I don't know from what point. If it's from here, it's not good, for obvious reasons.'

'I saw or heard nothing suspicious. If someone wanted to get me, they had their chance.'

Robie holstered his gun. 'Everything OK? You need anything?'

'I did my homework, ate a healthy dinner and brushed my teeth' she said sarcastically. She handed him a piece of paper. 'The assignment you gave me. Anything weird in the last couple weeks? I put down the places where my mom and dad worked and friends they had. Things they used to do. I thought it might be useful.'

Robie gazed down at the precise handwriting. 'It will be useful.'

'Who shot you? Is it to do with that woman and her kid getting killed?'

'Probably, yeah.'

'You're still going to help me find out who killed my mom and dad, right?'

'I said I would.'

'OK,' she said. 'Can I go to bed now?'

'Yeah. I've got some things to do tonight. I'll set the alarm on my way out.'

ROBIE WAS PISSED OFF. He was getting played. That he knew. He just didn't know who was doing it. He pulled to the kerb and watched Vance finish up with the local cops. Ambulances were everywhere. Finally she walked over and got into the passenger seat.

'What was the final count?' he asked, quietly.

She exhaled a long breath. 'Four dead. Seven wounded, three of them critically, so the death count could go higher.'

'The black SUV?'

'Disappeared without the proverbial trace.' She sat back against the seat as the car moved off. 'Where did you go that was so important?'

'I needed to check on something.'

'Need-to-know and I don't?' She opened her eyes and stared at him. He didn't answer. 'Who are you really?'

'Will Robie. DCIS. Just like the badge and ID card says.'

'You handled yourself well back there. I was still fumbling for my gun while you emptied your mag at the shooters. That was basically a war zone and it didn't seem to have any effect on you.'

He made a left. He had no idea where he was going. He just kept driving.

'And you triaged those people really effectively. Where did you learn to do that?'

'I just picked up some tricks over the years.'

She glanced down at his arm. 'Damn, Robie, you didn't even clean your wound. You're going to get gangrene.'

'Where are we going?'

'First stop, WFO,' she said, referring to the Washington Field Office. 'Then hospital for you.'

'No.'

'OK,' she said. 'After WFO we can go to my place. You can get cleaned up there. And if you want, you're welcome to the couch.'

'I appreciate the offer but—'

'Careful. I'm not usually this nice, Robie. Don't blow it.'

He was about to decline again, but he didn't.

THEY PULLED INTO Vance's condo building and took the elevator up to her place. It was small, but Robie immediately liked it. Clean lines, no clutter and everything seemed to have a purpose. He assumed that matched the owner's personality.

He sat on a long couch in the living room while she unpacked some medical supplies she'd taken from WFO.

'Off with the jacket and the shirt,' she ordered.

When she saw the tats, her eyebrows hiked. She looked more closely and her eyes widened as she saw the old wounds the tats were obscuring.

'You've got to be former special forces, right? Ranger, Delt, SEAL. They all have builds like you.'

He didn't answer her.

She cleaned the wound, applied some antibiotics and then wound gauze round it, taping it securely down.

'I brought some painkillers. Pill or syringe?'

'No.'

'Come on, Robie, you don't have to play all macho with me.'

'Knowing your pain tolerance is important. Pills and needles mask it. I could be slipping and I'd never know it.'

'Guess I never thought of that.'

'Thanks for patching me up. I appreciate it.'

He slipped his shirt back on, wincing a bit as he did so.

'Nice to know you're human,' she said, watching him.

'I thought you could tell that from my ability to bleed. This the couch?'

'Yes. I've only got the one bedroom.'

'I've slept in a lot worse conditions, trust me.'

'Can I?'

'Can you what?'

'Trust you?'

'You invited me here.'

'That's not what I'm talking about and you know it.'

He walked to a window. To the north he could see the lights of DC. The Lincoln, Jefferson and Washington monuments were plainly visible. And, rising above them, the dome of the Capitol.

'I like getting up in the morning and seeing that,' she said. 'It's what I work for. Defending what those buildings represent.'

'It's good to have a reason,' said Robie.

'What's your reason?' she asked.

'Some days I know, some days I don't.'

She paused, then said, 'I know we only just met today, but it feels like I've known you for years. Why is that?'

He looked at her. From her expression it wasn't an idle question. She wanted an answer.

'Looking for a killer bonds people pretty quickly. Almost dying together bonds you even more.'

'I guess that's probably right,' she said, though her tone spoke of disappointment with his answer.

'You can, you know,' he said.

'I can what?'

'Trust me.'

Robie couldn't look at her as the lie rolled off his tongue.

Chapter 4

The next morning, Robie rented a Volvo. The agent told him that Volvos were very safe cars. *Not around me, they're not*, thought Robie, as he sped out of the rental garage.

What had scared him the most about the night before was not nearly being killed or seeing others die. It was the feeling in his gut when he'd thought something had happened to Julie. He didn't like someone else having that much power over him.

His phone buzzed. He glanced at the screen. Blue Man needed to meet with him again. Right now.

I bet you do, thought Robie.

No public place this time; no hotel with lots of witnesses. Robie didn't have much of a choice. There were rules one had to play by or one was out of the game.

The building was in a part of DC that tourists would never tread. Robie had to part with his cellphone before entering the secure room, but he would not give up his gun.

Blue Man sat across from him. Nice suit, neatly combed hair. He could be somebody's grandfather.

'First, Robie, we have not found your handler. Second, there was no man with a rifle found in the alley you identified.'

'OK.'

'Next,' said Blue Man. 'The attempt on your life last night?'

'The shooter was in a vehicle that looked a lot like a US government ride.'

'I don't think that is likely.'

Robie pointedly tapped the tabletop. 'You can't find my handler or a shooter I knocked out in an alley, but you think somebody gunning for me in a set of federal wheels is unlikely?'

'Who's the girl?' asked Blue Man.

Robie had known Julie's presence in all of this might come out.

'She's the linchpin. Anything happens to her, we're screwed. So if you're telling me that my handler found her out, you'd better be prepared to do something about her safety.'

The older man sat up straighter, adjusted his tie and then his cuffs. 'You'll need to explain that to me, Robie. The linchpin for what?'

'It won't take long, because I don't understand it all.' Robie took only a few minutes to describe the murders of Julie's parents, her escape attempt on the bus, the man attempting to kill her there and the bus exploding.

'That's when you lost your gun? The one you had at Wind's apartment?'

'I didn't "lose" it. The bus exploding knocked me fifteen feet. I tried to find it before the cops showed up, but I was unsuccessful.'

'But the FBI *did* find it. And now they believe there's a connection between the two cases.'

'Is there a connection?' asked Robie.

'Actually, we don't know for sure. We'd like to talk to the girl.'

'You go through me. No direct contact.'

'I'm not sure you're clear who's running this show, Robie.'

Grandpa was showing some balls now. Robie was impressed. Just a little.

'You have a mole on the inside. Even if my handler is gone, he might not have been acting alone. You go pulling the girl in here, the mole gets wind of it, we lose her.'

'I think we can protect her.'

'You thought you could protect Jane Wind too, didn't you?'

Blue Man adjusted his cuffs again. 'OK, for now status quo,' he said, stiffly. 'But I want a fuller debrief from you soon, and follow-up reports. Now talk to me about Vance. You spent the night at her place.'

'I didn't have many options, did I?'

'Your place is safe.'

'Is it?'

'Robie, we're not leaving you out there by yourself. We have to find out what's going on. It's nearly impossible to turn one of our people. The pay off must be immense and the target has to be of similar importance.'

'That's the most sensible thing you've said so far.'

Blue Man leaned forward. 'There are two possible reasons why Agent Wind and her husband were murdered. It either had to do with her, or it had to do with him.'

'You know Jane Wind's work. Could it be related to her?'

'I can't say definitively that it's not. Let's just say that I'm more interested in what you find out on Rick Wind's background.'

'Former military. Retired. Owned a pawnshop in a bad section of DC. Was hung upside down and his tongue cut out.'

'The last part has me concerned.'

Robie leaned back. 'Vance wondered if it was Mob-related. Guy was a snitch and they symbolically cut his tongue out.'

'Is that what you think?'

'No. I'm thinking what you're probably thinking.'

'You cut off the hands of a thief.'

'And the tongue of a traitor.'

'If it involves the world of Islamic terrorists.'

'If,' said Robie. 'But the guy was retired. What could he be involved in?'

'Terrorist cells are rarely obvious. At least the effective ones.'

'Did he spend time in the Middle East? Could he have been turned and sent here as a ticking bomb?'

'A time bomb that had a change of heart? Maybe, and, yes, he did spend time in both Iraq and Afghanistan.'

'Then why don't I hit that angle while you work the other side?'

'Robie, if anything occurs to you or you find out something while working with Vance that has to do with Agent Wind—'

'You'll get it.'

'Then we understand each other.'

The two men rose.

Robie looked at him and said, 'Is my place really safe? Because I could use a change of clothes.'

Blue Man managed a rare smile. 'Go and change your clothes, Robie. The ones you have on are looking pretty ragged.'

'Well, I'm feeling pretty ragged,' admitted Robie.

ROBIE BUMPED INTO Annie Lambert as she was coming out of her apartment with her bike.

'Late to work?' asked Robie.

She smiled. 'Doctor's appointment. Just routine. Even White House staffers have to take them.'

'Still up for that drink sometime?' he asked. Robie seemed surprised by his own question. *I'm learning a lot about myself this week*, he thought.

'How about tonight?'

'Will the president let you off?'

She grinned. 'How about eight? W Hotel rooftop bar?'

'See you then.'

Robie walked to his apartment. He had no idea why he had said that. Ordinarily, Robie disliked distractions while he was working. But somehow he was welcoming this one.

He changed into fresh clothes and made up a small bag with other items he might need if he didn't go back there for a while. Then he had the urge to check on Julie.

He backtracked his way to the other apartment, looking for elements of Blue Man's security force but didn't see any. *Maybe that's good*, he thought. *Maybe*.

She unlocked the door only after checking through the peephole. He was also gratified to hear her turning off the security system.

'Saw you talking to the bike chick,' she said, pointing to the telescope. 'That thing is powerful. So your other place is across the street?'

'Yeah.'

'Normally people like to spread out their residences. You know, Paris, London, Hong Kong.'

'I'm not normal.'

'Yeah, that one I figured out on my own. So what have you found out? I've been watching the TV. Sounds like it was a real war zone down there last night. You're lucky you weren't killed. At least I'm assuming that's where you got shot. You never got round to telling me about your arm.'

'Luck always plays a part,' he said, vaguely.

'So, when are we going to get going?'

He stared at her.

'Partners, remember. We find out who killed my parents?'

'I remember and I'm working on it.'

'I know you are. But I want to work on it, too. I gave you that list. What have you done with it so far?'

'Going to run it down.'

'Good,' she said, pulling on her hoodie. 'I'm ready to go.'

'I don't think that's a good idea.'

'Either I go with you or I go on my own. Either way, I'm going.'

Robie sighed and opened the door for her. 'But you let me handle the questions,' he said.

'I wouldn't have it any other way,' she answered.

Liar, thought Robie.

THEY SAT IN ROBIE'S RENTAL and watched her parents' duplex.

Julie squirmed a bit and said, 'Exactly how is this getting us anywhere? You're trying to make me so bored I'll quit and go back and sit at the apartment, right?'

'We're seeing if anyone interesting shows up. I'll give it another half an hour and we'll move on.'

'I just remembered something,' Julie said. 'When the guy with the gun started to come after me, my mom said, "She doesn't know anything".'

Robie sat up straighter and his grip tightened on the wheel. 'Which implies that your mom *did* know something. And before you said the guy asked your dad what he knew.'

'So now somebody thinks I know it, too, despite what my mom said. But if the guy who was after me died in the explosion—'

'Doesn't matter. He would have communicated to whomever he was working for—he wasn't a loner. Someone removed your parents' bodies and blew up that bus. And it wasn't him. He simply wouldn't have had time or the opportunity.'

'Why would they blow up the bus? If they were trying to kill me, I wasn't on it.'

'But they might not have known that,' Robie said. 'The windows on the bus were tinted. Let's say someone fired an incendiary round into the tank on the side opposite from the door. They might not have known we had got off.'

'Do you think they still believe I'm dead?'

'Doubtful. These people apparently have a lot of resources. We have to assume they know you're alive.'

'What could my parents have gotten into?'

'Let's track their days a little bit and see if anything comes up. Give me directions to the diner where your mom worked.'

It was only a short distance away and Robie stopped on the other side of the street. He cut the engine.

'They know you here, right?'

'Yeah, sure.'

'I'm not sure it's smart for you to be seen here, then.'

'So I just sit in the car by myself?'

He pulled out the bag he'd taken from his apartment and slid out a pair of binoculars. 'Here's the plan. I go in and ask questions. You keep a look out.' He pulled out two power packs, an earwig and a headset. 'You're command central. You speak into that, I'll be able to hear you but no one else will, OK? And you'll be able to hear everything from in there clearly.'

Julie smiled. 'Cool.'

He put on his earwig, powered up his pack and clipped it onto his belt, where it was covered by his jacket.

'Anything looks weird, you feel bad vibes, just say, "Come", and I'll be here in five seconds.'

'OK.'

ROBIE DROPPED ONTO a free stool and ordered coffee from a waitress in a frayed blue uniform. She was about fifty, with grey roots running through her blonde hair.

In Robie's ear, Julie said, 'That's Cheryl Kosmann. She's my mom's friend.'

Cheryl brought his cup of coffee. 'If you're looking to eat, our meatloaf is really good. Lord knows I've had enough of it.' She laughed.

'You're Cheryl Kosmann?'

The laugh caught in her throat. 'Who wants to know?'

Robie pulled out his cred pack, flashed the badge and then the ID card.

Cheryl stiffened. 'Am I in trouble?'

'No, you're not in trouble, Ms Kosmann.'

'Just make it Cheryl.'

Robie pulled out a photo of Julie and her parents. 'What can you tell me about these folks?'

Kosmann glanced at the photo. 'You're interested in the Gettys? They're good people. That little girl of theirs is something, smart as a whip. I love that girl.'

'But she's in foster care.'

'Well, she is and she isn't. Sara, that's her mom, does all she can to get her back each time.'

'And her dad?'

'Curtis loves her too, but that man is a mess.'

'When was the last time you saw any of them?'

'Funny you should ask that. Sara was supposed to work today, but she never came in. Never called. Not like her.'

'So the last time she was here?'

'Day before yesterday. She had yesterday off. Her shift was over at six. Curtis came to walk her home.'

'From his job?'

'Right. He walked her home a lot. I thought it was sweet. He really loved her and she really loved him. They had absolutely nothing. Lived in a dump. No car. No savings. Well, they did have Julie. They wanted the best for her. Didn't want her to end up like them. Paid every last penny they had and then some to get her into a gifted and talented programme at a really good school. Sara worked extra hours here all the time to help pay for the tuition. And Curtis pulled extra hours at the warehouse. He was a druggie, but he could work hard when he wanted to. And for his little girl, he wanted to.'

In his ear, Robie heard Julie breathing fast and hard.

'You see anybody hanging around here the last few weeks you didn't recognise?'

Kosmann frowned. 'Look, has something happened to them?'

'I'm just here collecting information. Did either of them seem edgy or concerned when you saw them lately?'

'Now that you mention it, yeah. At least Sara.'

'Did you ever ask Sara what was bothering her?'

'No. I figured it was Curtis or maybe losing Julie to foster care again. There was nothing I could do about any of it.'

'Her last day here—did anything unusual happen?'

'No, but the night before they had some friends in here for dinner. Leo and Ida Broome.'

Robie took a sip of his coffee and then wrote this down.

'Tell me about them.'

'They're in their late forties, nice couple. I think Ida works in a hair salon. And Leo does something with the city.'

'You have an address or phone number for them?'

'No.'

In his ear Julie said, 'I do. Both.'

Robie said, 'Cheryl, did you notice anything unusual while they were together that night?'

'Well, I just caught snatches of conversation, nothing important. But they all looked . . .'

Robie waited until she found the words she was looking for.

'Well, they looked like they'd seen a ghost.'

'And you didn't ask them what was bothering them?'

'No. If people want to talk, I'll listen, but I'm not into poking around things that don't concern me.'

'You got any time off coming up?'

She was clearly surprised. 'Got a week of vacation left.'

'You have family out of town?'

'In Tallahassee.'

'I'd go and see your family in Tallahassee.'

Kosmann stared at him as Robie's meaning sank in. 'Do you, do you think that I'm . . .?'

'Just take the vacation, Cheryl. Take it now.'

ROBIE CLIMBED BACK in the car and looked over at Julie.

'You OK?'

'I'm OK.' She stared over at the diner. 'That place was almost more of a home for me than my real home. I liked to do my homework there. My mom would get me pie and let me drink coffee. I felt really grown up.'

'And I guess it was nice being with her.'

'I liked to watch her work. She was good at it. Juggled all these orders. She never wrote anything down. She had a great memory.'

'Maybe your brains are genetic.'

'Maybe they are.'

'The night your parents were killed, they left the diner at around six. But they didn't show up at their house until hours later, and with the gunman. I wonder where they were in the meantime?'

'I don't know.'

'OK, how about the Broomes?'

'They live in an apartment in northeast.'

Robie put the car in drive. 'What can you tell me about them?'

'My parents have known them for years. Ida would cut my hair for free and my mom would bake stuff for her.'

'And her husband?'

'He was Dad's friend. I'm not sure what the connection was.'

'You think they could have anything to do with what happened to your parents?'

'I wouldn't think so. I mean, she works in a hair salon. It's not like they're international spies or anything.'

'Not that you know.'

'Are you kidding?'

'Spies don't usually look like spies. That's sort of the point.'

'You look like a spy.'

'That's good, because I'm not.'

'So you say.'

The apartment building had been built in the sixties but had been renovated. Robie could tell this from the new awning out front, the cleansed brick and the fresh paint on the trim.

They found apartment 410. Robie knocked on the door three times without an answer. He scanned the hall for a surveillance camera but found none.

'Turn around and face out into the hall,' he told Julie.

'Are you going to pick the lock?'

'Just turn around.'

It took Robie all of five seconds. The lock was not a deadbolt. One slender piece of metal did the trick.

They stepped inside and he closed the door behind them. The place was furnished sparingly, the rooms were few, and there was no one there. Robie surveyed the area.

'It's a little too clean, don't you think?'

'Maybe they're neatniks.'

He shook his head. 'This place has been scrubbed.'

Julie swallowed, then looked up at him. 'You mean—'

'Maybe the Broomes are OK, but someone has wiped this place down. We need to find out what Leo Broome did.'

'We can go to the hair salon and ask around.'

'I have a better idea. *You* can go to the hair salon and ask around. They know you, right?'

WHILE ROBIE WAITED OUTSIDE in the car, Julie entered the hair salon. It was full of customers and Julie's gaze darted around, noting the stylists working today. Ida Broome was not among them.

'Julie, right?' said the young woman behind the counter.

'Yep. Is Ida in? I was hoping to get my bangs trimmed.'

The woman shook her head. 'She was supposed to be in at ten, but she never showed. I called her place, but no one answered. Really put us behind. Maybe some emergency came up.'

'Maybe it did,' said Julie, slowly.

'Maria has an open slot after the lady she's working on now.'

'That would be great.'

Maria greeted Julie with a toothy smile. 'No school today?'

'Teacher conference.'

'How's your mom?'

Julie didn't blink—she had been expecting this question. 'She's fine.'

She settled in the chair and Maria swept a black smock over her and tightened it down round her neck.

'Have you seen Ida lately?' Julie asked. 'The girl at the front told me she didn't come in today.'

'I know. Surprised me. She never misses and she had a full slate today. But she was acting kind of funny the day before yesterday. She messed up a lady's perm and then took two inches off a client instead of one. I asked her what was up, but she wouldn't say much. Just that it had to do with Leo.'

'Her husband? Did he lose his job or something?'

'I doubt it. He works for the government. Ida told me that his job was pretty important. Down on Capitol Hill somewhere.'

'So Ida wasn't in yesterday, either?'

'It was her day off. But today is a whole different story.'

Maria had been working this whole time and said, 'OK, we are done and looking sharp.'

Julie admired her hair in the mirror. 'Thanks, Maria.'

'SO WE STILL DON'T KNOW exactly what Leo does,' said Robie, after Julie had spent a few minutes filling him in.

'If Mr Broome has some important job in the government, do you think he's the reason for all this?'

'It's certainly a possibility.'

'But why would that involve my parents?'

'They were friends. He might have let something slip.'

'Great,' she said, her voice catching slightly. 'My parents might have been killed because they had dinner with the guy?'

'Stranger things have happened.'

'What now?' she asked.

'I drop you back off. I have to get going.'

'Does this mean I go back to the apartment and die of boredom?'

'Don't you have homework to do?'

'Calculus, wow.'

'You're only fourteen and you're already doing calculus?'

'I actually don't like math very much. But I'm good at it.'

'Education is the key to success.'

'You sound like somebody's grandfather.'

'You disagree?'

'I'm just taking it one day at a time.'

'Not a bad philosophy.'

'My classmates' parents have their whole lives planned out for them. Wall Street, medical school, law firms. The next Steve Jobs, the next Warren Buffett. Makes me want to gag.'

'Then do something else. Something that helps people.'

She gave him a sideways look. 'You mean like you?'

He glanced away. *No, not like me*, he thought.

AFTER DROPPING JULIE OFF, Robie navigated the traffic until he arrived at Donnelly's, about twenty-five minutes later. Federal techs and FBI agents were working the crime scene hard. Vance met him out front. She seemed hassled and harried.

'What's the latest?' Robie asked her.

'Two more of the victims died last night. That makes the total count six. And chances are we might lose more.'

'Any clues?'

'Black SUV was found abandoned about a mile from here. It had bullet pocks on it and was heavily armoured.'

'Who was the owner?'

'The US government. Secret Service,' Vance said. 'It went missing from one of their motor pools.'

So I was right, thought Robie. *And Blue Man was wrong*. This did not make him feel any better. In fact, it made him feel worse.

'How? Those places are monitored around the clock.'

'We're running that down now.'

'Anything else?'

'MP-5 casings all over the street. Just hope we find a gun we can match them to.'

'No one saw anything? No faces?' Robie asked.

'Nothing so far.'

'Are we sure we were the targets?'

'We're profiling all victims and all persons who were in the restaurant last night. Maybe we get lucky and one of them provides a motive for this level of carnage.'

'But if we *were* the target?' said Robie. *If* I *was the target.*

Vance shook her head. 'Why would they waste time taking us out? Just because we were investigating the bus blowing up or Jane Wind's murder? They kill us, other investigators take our place.'

'Latest on Rick Wind?'

'They're doing the posts today. I asked for a rush on the results.'

'The bus?'

'Just going through the bodies—or body parts, rather—will take a long time. We're transporting the remains to an FBI evidence facility. We'll comb it to see if we can find what caused the blast.'

Robie asked the question that had been hammering in his gut. 'Any surveillance cameras in the area?'

'There were some. They might give us something to go on.'

'Where are you collecting them?' he asked.

'The mobile command post outside.'

Robie nodded, thinking how he was going to phrase his next question. 'I know that technically I'm not deployed on the bus case, but since it seems the two cases might be connected, you mind if I go over it, too?'

'Never turn down a fresh pair of eyes.'

Robie glanced at the portable command centre. *And if I show up on one of those videos? Or Julie does?*

He turned to see Vance watching him.

'So what can I do to help?' he said.

'You can follow a few leads down. Wind's employment at DCIS, for one.

And then there's her husband. Was there something in her background that led to his death?'

'From the condition of the body, he was killed before her.'

'Which leads me to believe the reason might lie with Rick Wind,' said Vance. 'Anything else you know about him?'

'He was deployed to both Iraq and Afghanistan.'

'So was everybody in uniform in the last ten years,' Vance said.

'He left the military with a clean record. His wife also visited Iraq and Afghanistan on several occasions.'

'You said Wind left the army clean, but could there have been something else? How long was Wind in the Middle East? Was he wounded or captured? Or did he have a change of heart?'

'You want to know if he was turned somehow? Became an enemy of his own country?'

'Yeah, I would.'

'I don't know the answer, Vance.'

'Tongues cut out, a bus blown up. This is starting to look like international terrorism, Robie.'

'Why the bus?'

'Mass casualties. Throws the country into a tizzy.'

'Maybe.'

'Rick Wind was somehow involved. He got cold feet. They took care of him. And then killed his wife because they were afraid he might have told her something.'

'His ex-wife. And she works for DCIS. If he had told her something she would have told us. And I can tell you that she didn't.'

'Maybe she never had the chance.'

'Maybe she didn't.'

'It's a workable theory.'

Robie scratched his cheek. 'I guess.'

'You don't sound convinced.'

'That's because I'm not.'

ROBIE WALKED OUTSIDE an hour later, after going over the details of the mass shooting. He mulled over what Vance had told him. A Secret Service SUV had been the shooter's platform. It had gone missing. Things did not go missing from the Secret Service.

He glanced to his left and saw the FBI mobile command post. He approached, flashed his creds and was allowed in. There were four other people present: special agents and tech support.

Robie said, 'Vance told me about collecting surveillance camera footage from the scene of the bus explosion. You got any surveillance camera footage uploaded yet?'

The agent who had let him in nodded. 'Hang on a sec.'

He texted something on his phone.

He's getting the OK from Vance to show me the pictures.

Robie heard the sound of a text shooting back to the agent. 'Over here, Agent Robie.' The agent indicated a blank screen. 'Here's what we have so far.' He punched some keys and a file uploaded.

'Have you looked at it yet?' Robie asked.

'First time for me, too.'

Robie felt his pulse quicken.

The door opened and Vance walked in.

'Am I in time for the show?' she asked.

On the screen the bus came into view. Robie was relieved to see that the camera shot was not on the side with the door. A few seconds later it exploded. Robie tensed. With the bus destroyed, there would be nothing to block the camera's view across the street, where Robie and Julie were coming to rest. The screen went black.

Robie looked at the agent. 'What happened?'

'Blast must've knocked out the camera.'

Robie sat through two more video feeds like the first. Opposite end of the bus, and the cameras went down after the explosion.

'Any cameras around the bus depot showing the passengers getting on?' asked Robie.

'Not that we can find right now,' said Vance. 'But we're trying to locate more footage. Particularly from the other side of the street. I'm going to have my guys go check this afternoon.'

Which means I have to find it first, Robie thought.

ROBIE STOOD NEAR what was, for him, ground zero. The remains of the bus were being sifted through by a dozen forensic techs. He looked left and right, up and down the street. Vance was correct; nothing obvious that he could see. Robie had walked to the end of the street when he saw the homeless guy from the night the bus had exploded, the one who'd been yelling about wanting some marshmallows to grill. He and two fellow homeless people were huddled on the other side of the police barriers.

Robie could see that the reporters were giving the three a wide berth. He wondered if it had occurred to any of the journalists that the people of the streets might have seen something that night. And then he wondered if the FBI had attempted to interview them.

Robie cleared the police barrier and was immediately engulfed by reporters. He pushed mikes out of his face and kept going until he reached the three street people.

'You hungry?' he asked.

The marshmallows fellow nodded. 'Always hungry.'

At least he can understand me, thought Robie. He eyed the two women. One was small, bloated, blackened by the street. She might have been twenty, she might have been fifty; Robie couldn't tell under the layers of grime. He glanced at the second woman. She did not have years on the street grafted onto her. And there was both intelligence and terror behind her eyes. 'Can I get you something to eat?'

She shook her head. Robie understood her trepidation. He took out his badge and held it up. 'I'm a federal agent.'

The woman stepped closer to him, looked relieved. Marshmallows' grin faded. The other woman just stood there. Recent homeless still respected authority. People long on the streets did not.

To Marshmallows, Robie said, 'There's a café down this way. I'm going to get you some food. For her, too,' he added, indicating the silent woman. 'Will you wait until I get back?'

'Yeah,' said Marshmallows.

Robie turned to the second woman. 'Will you come with me?'

'Am I in trouble?' she asked.

'No, not at all. Were you here the night that bus blew up?'

'We all were,' she said. 'But we left after it happened. I don't think the police are aware that we saw anything.'

Robie focused on her. 'What's your name?'

'Diana Jordison.'

Robie escorted Jordison to the café and seated her at a table in the rear. 'Order anything you want,' he said, handing her a menu from a stack on the next table.

He walked up to the counter and said, 'I need some food to go,' and listed some things. While it was being prepared, he sat down across from Jordison. A young waitress came over to take their orders.

Robie said, 'Just coffee.' He glanced at Jordison.

She flushed and looked unsure of herself. Robie wondered how long it had been since she had ordered anything in a restaurant. He pointed to an item on the menu. 'The American has just about everything: eggs, toast, bacon, grits, coffee, juice.'

Jordison nodded meekly and Robie ordered from the waitress. Then he said, 'I'm going to take the food to the other two, then I'll be right back, OK?'

Jordison nodded but wouldn't meet his eye.

When Robie got back to Marshmallows and the other woman, a male reporter he'd seen earlier was circling the pair like a shark.

The reporter looked at Robie. 'Playing the Good Samaritan?' he asked, eyeing the bags and beverages Robie was carrying.

'Your tax dollars at work,' replied Robie.

Robie handed one bag and coffee each to Marshmallows and the woman. The latter snagged her food and coffee, grabbed her plastic bags, and disappeared down the street. Robie let her go because he didn't think she would be able to tell him anything.

Robie hooked Marshmallows by the arm and walked away from the reporter. 'Tell me what you saw the night the bus blew up.'

Marshmallows took a bite of sandwich. 'Boom,' he said. 'Fire. Holy shit.'

'Anything more detailed than that?' Robie asked, slowly. 'Did you see anyone around the bus? Maybe get off or on?'

Marshmallows chomped. 'Boom,' he said again. 'Grilling out.'

Robie decided that Marshmallows wasn't sane. He left him there and walked back to the café. Jordison was eating her food slowly. Robie sat down across from her. 'How long you been out there?'

'Too long,' she said, 'I had a house and a job and a husband.'

'I'm sorry.'

'Me, too. Surprised me how fast it all went to hell. No job, no house, no husband. Nothing but bills I can't pay. I went to college. Got my degree. Worked hard. The American dream. Right.'

'That's rough. Where did you work?'

'Admin support for a construction company. I was one of the first to go, even though I'd been there twelve years.'

Robie was afraid she'd start crying but she took a quick sip of coffee and said, 'What do you want to know?'

'The night the bus blew up. What can you tell me?'

She took a few moments to collect her thoughts. 'I saw the bus come down the street and stop. I remember wondering why.'

'What side of the bus were you on? Facing the door?'

'The door was on the other side.'

'OK, go on.'

'Well, it just blew up. It was horrible.'

'Did you see anything that might have caused it to explode?'

'I just assumed it was a bomb. You mean it wasn't?'

'We're still working it out,' said Robie. 'But if you saw anything impact the bus, that could be important. A shot fired into the gas tank, maybe?'

Jordison shook her head. 'I know I didn't hear a shot.'

'Did you see anyone?'

'After the bus blew up, I saw two people on the other side of the street. Before, the bus was blocking my view. But then it wasn't. A man and what looked to be a girl, maybe a teenager.'

Robie sat back but kept staring at her. 'Can you describe them?'

Better it come out now, he thought.

'The blast must've knocked them both down. The guy came to first and then he helped the girl up. Then the guy started looking around the parked cars. That's when the old guy back there started dancing around. Then the guy and girl took off.'

'What did the guy look like?'

She stared at him pointedly. 'He actually looked a lot like you.'

Robie smiled. 'I guess I look like a lot of people.'

'I couldn't pick him out of a line-up, if that's what you mean. But the fire really turned night to day.'

'But my height, build, age roughly?'

'Yeah.'

'Thanks, Diana. If I need to get back in touch with you, will you be around here?'

'I really don't have any other place to go,' she said.

Robie handed her a card. 'I'll see what I can do to get you off the streets.'

Jordison's voice shook. 'Whatever you can do, mister, I'd really appreciate it.'

Robie drove back to Donnelly's and was getting out of his car when Vance spotted him.

'We got a break. ATF guys found the source of the detonation on the bus. Wheel well of the bus, left side. Had a motion sensor. Bus starts going, engages the timer. A few minutes later, boom.'

Robie stared at her, his mind racing. The guy after Julie certainly wouldn't have gotten on a bus he had just rigged to explode. That left only one explanation. *I was the target.*

Chapter 5

Robie spent an hour with Vance going over the ATF findings, then he slipped away and made a call to Blue Man.

'Her name is Diana Jordison.' Robie described her. 'She'll be hanging around the area where the bus was detonated. She was very helpful and I think she might be more helpful down the road. But she needs to get off the streets. Too risky otherwise.'

Blue Man said he would take care of it, and Robie had to trust that he would. He planned to check, later. Robie could not trust anyone.

'I also want whatever you can find on a Leo Broome. Works somewhere on Capitol Hill.'

'How does he figure into this?' asked Blue Man.

'I don't know if he does. But I have to cover that angle.'

'That briefing, Robie. I want it soon.' Blue Man clicked off.

I want a lot of things, thought Robie. *I want a way out of this nightmare.*

Back at his apartment, Robie took a shower and changed his clothes ahead of his eight o'clock date with Annie Lambert. He texted Julie and received a response a few seconds later confirming that she was OK.

He entered the W hotel and rode the elevator up to the rooftop bar. He took a seat at a table next to the railings and ordered a ginger ale. Lambert arrived fifteen minutes later.

'I am so sorry,' she said. 'I got caught up in something right at five to eight. Had to get it done. And I did.'

'Then that deserves a reward.'

Lambert ordered a vodka tonic and the waiter brought it, along with a bowl of nuts. Lambert gobbled a handful of the snack mix.

'No time for lunch today,' she explained.

'You want to order off the menu?'

She ordered a cheeseburger while he went with some spring rolls.

'My diet is not the healthiest in the world,' she said.

Robie settled further back in his chair and prepared himself to engage in small talk. He had wanted to have a drink with Lambert, but now he was here with her it seemed crazy, given all that he was confronting right then.

I can't be normal, no matter how much I want to be.

'I can understand that. You do much travelling in your job?' he said, trying to sound excited to hear her answer.

'No. I'm not officially high enough in the pecking order to travel on Air Force One or even in any of the secondary planes. But I'm working hard and making a name for myself, and maybe one day, who knows, right?'

'Right. So you enjoy politics?' he said.

'I enjoy *policy*,' she replied. 'Energy is my specialty and I help write speeches for the administration in those areas.'

Their food came and she bit eagerly into her burger.

She said, 'How'd you end up in DC? Or are you from here?'

'I came from the Midwest. How about you?'

'Connecticut. My parents were from England. I'm actually adopted. Only child. Do you have any brothers or sisters?'

'No.' He glanced over her shoulder after he heard a siren.

She looked at him resignedly. 'It feels like we're just going through the motions, doesn't it?'

Robie didn't process this right away. 'What?' he said.

'I'm not sure you're really here, if you know what I mean. I mean, I'm just a policy geek. You've made a lot of money, probably travelled the world. I must seem pretty boring to you.' She nervously picked up another fry but didn't eat it.

Robie hunched forward, coming out of his protective shell in more ways than one. He took the fry from her and bit off half.

'I wanted to have a drink with you. If I didn't want to, I wouldn't. And if I was going through the motions, I apologise. I don't find you boring.'

She smiled. 'Did you like the fry?'

'Yeah. You want some of my spring roll?'

'I thought you'd never ask.'

As they ate from each other's plates, Robie took in the view of the city.

Lambert followed his gaze and said, 'Even though I work there, it's still weird to see the snipers on the roof of the White House.'

'Countersnipers,' said Robie automatically, and then regretted the slip. He smiled. 'I watch a lot of *NCIS*. That's where I learned that word.'

'I DVR it,' said Lambert. 'Great show.'

They lapsed into silence again.

Robie finally broke it. 'I'm sorry, I'm not a good conversationalist. Has nothing to do with intent. Just tends to ebb and flow.'

'Neither am I, so maybe we're very compatible.'

'Maybe we are,' said Robie. He watched her as she finished her meal. 'So, what's next for you after the White House?'

She shrugged. 'Frankly, I never thought I'd ever get this far.'

'You must have done something right. Ivy League? Connections?'

'Guilty on both counts. My parents are pretty well-off and they're active politically, so I know they pulled strings.'

'I think to get to the White House you have to do it mostly on your own, because everybody at that level has strings to pull.'

'Thanks for saying that. So what's next for you?'

'Maybe a change in direction.'

'Change is good.'

'Maybe we can talk about it some more another time.'

She beamed. 'Are you asking me out?'

'Can't I go from drinks to date?'

'That's OK in my rulebook,' she said.

He walked her back to the White House. She'd explained that she needed to retrieve her bike. Along the way, Lambert slipped her arm through his.

When they arrived, she held out a card. 'All my relevant info is on here.' Robie gave her his cellphone number, which she keyed into her phone. She leaned forward and kissed him on the cheek.

'Thanks for a really nice time. Let's work on that "date" thing together.'

'Count on it,' said Robie.

A few moments later she hurried through the White House gate.

Robie walked off, trying to put aside their encounter, yet feeling the warmth of her lips on his face.

ROBIE STOOD IN FRONT of the terminal from where the doomed bus had left. He thought over the events of that night: he had failed to kill Jane Wind and the back-up shooter had done the job for him; he had executed his escape plan and come to this terminal to catch a ride out of the city. He had told no one. He had left no trail of any kind. *But I reserved a ticket for that bus using an alias that only I was supposed to know existed. But someone else knew. And they were willing to kill all those people just to get me.*

He glanced around. There was no way anyone could have planted the wheel-well bomb in the terminal. He walked to the maintenance yard two blocks away. The gate was shut but Robie got the attention of a security guard. The guy was suspicious until Robie flashed his card.

'Had some FBI agents in here already. What can I do for you?'

'Walk me through the prep for the buses.'

'I don't really know much about it. You need to talk to Willie.' The guy pointed to a brick building. 'He works until 2 a.m.'

'Thanks.'

Robie swung a door open and looked around at a cavernous space with high ceilings, rows of tube lighting, five parked buses and rolling toolboxes. Everything was drenched with the odour of oil, grease and fuel.

He called out, 'Anybody here?'

A tall, thin, black man dressed in work overalls walked the front of a bus rubbing his hands on a dirty cloth.

Robie held up his cred pack. 'I need to ask you some questions.'

'Cops already been by.'

'I'm just one more cop coming by,' replied Robie. 'So, can you run me through how the buses are processed?'

The man stuffed the oily cloth in the back pocket of his overalls. 'They come in maybe six hours before they're scheduled to head out. We go over them in here. Then we gas them up at the fuelling station near the front gate and they sit until the drivers check in.'

'Could you show me where?'

Willie led him out of the building and pointed to a spot near the fence. 'They're parked right there until the driver shows up.'

'How many buses were sitting here the night the one blew up?'

'Two. The 112 to New York. The 97 to Miami.'

Robie eyed the fence. The bomber could have hopped over and planted the bomb in less than a minute.

He looked at Willie. 'That night, how long was the 112 bus sitting out here before the driver showed?'

Willie thought about this. 'Maybe two, three hours.'

Robie eyeballed the spot the 112 bus had been in. Bomber did the bus. Robie got on the bus. Robie got off the bus. Bus blew up. They sent a shooter into the alley to finish the job. Someone really wanted him bad.

Another thought occurred to him. *But maybe not that bad.*

'Doing some private sleuthing on your off time?'

He turned and looked through the chain-link fence. Nicole Vance was staring back at him.

Robie walked back through the open gate.

'Where have you been all this time?' Vance asked.

'Let's go back to Donnelly's,' said Robie.

'Why?'

'I want to check something I should have already checked.'

FIFTEEN MINUTES LATER, Robie stood in the same spot he had on the night an MP-5 had tried to rip his life away. Vance was watching.

'We're not dead,' said Robie.

'A somewhat obvious deduction,' Vance said, dryly.

'Eleven people shot and yet the shooter misses us? We were the closest target, right out in the open.'

'You're saying the shooter missed us on purpose?'

'The guy missed us at basically point-blank range with a weapon designed for mass destruction. Look at the shot pattern. He was firing *around* us.'

'Then you're saying they killed all those people for what? A warning? Something to do with the Wind case? The bus bombing?'

Robie didn't answer her. His thoughts were racing ahead, taking him in a direction he had never expected to go.

'Robie?'

He turned to her.

Vance said slowly, 'I guess looking at it that way, what you're saying makes sense. We should be dead. So it has to relate to the Winds or the bus, or maybe both.'

'No, it doesn't.'

Someone is playing mind games with me.

'Robie, do you have any other enemies?' asked Vance.

'None that I can think of,' he said, absently. *Other than a few hundred.*

'Is there something you're not telling me?'

He broke off his thoughts and rubbed the back of his neck. 'Do you tell me everything?'

There was a pause. 'I guess not.'

'Then you have your answer.'

'But you told me I could trust you.'

'You can, but you have your agency and I have mine. I'm assuming you'll tell me everything you can and I'll do the same. I've got people to report to and so do you. It all has limits. But that doesn't mean we can't work together to get the job done.'

Vance glanced down at her feet. 'So, did you find anything over at the bus maintenance shop that you *can* tell me?'

'The bus was parked there long enough for someone to plant the bomb.'

'So the bomber knew the target was going to be on the bus.'

'Do we have a passenger list?' he asked.

'Only partially. For those who paid with a credit card; not for those who paid with cash.'

'So how many people on the bus?'

'Thirty-six, plus the driver. We're doing background checks on all known persons, which leaves eight unaccounted for. They were probably walk-ups that night, who paid cash.'

She showed him the list of names on her phone. Julie wasn't on it. And neither was Gerald Dixon, which meant Julie had not used his credit card to buy her ticket. No other name meant anything to him, other than the alias he had reserved his own ticket under.

He had been the target, not Julie. But why try and kill him on the bus and then miss him on purpose?

The plan changed, that's why. They wanted me dead. Now they want me alive. But why?

'I don't recognise anyone on that list.' His lies to Vance were piling up. 'Anything new on Rick Wind?'

'Cause of death was suffocation. They forced his severed tongue down his throat and wedged it there,' she said. 'Look, Robie, if the killing of Jane Wind and her husband and the bus exploding are connected, there have to be some common denominators.'

'The only reason you think they're connected is because of the gun. Whoever was in Jane Wind's apartment could have just flung it away. It could have nothing to do with the bus exploding.'

'Or it could.'

'Just don't have tunnel vision on this. If the cases aren't connected, then trying to hook them together is not smart. You make assumptions and decisions based on assumptions that you otherwise wouldn't make.'

'What would you do?'

'Work both cases, but in parallel. You don't cross the streams unless you have solid evidence of a connection. And that means something more than a gun near the scene.'

'OK, that makes sense, actually.'

Robie checked his watch. 'I'm going to grab a few hours' sleep.'

'You have a place to sleep? If not, you're welcome to crash at my place.'

'I've got a place. That changes, I'll let you know. Thanks.'

He walked to his car. Time to check on Julie.

ROBIE UNLOCKED THE DOOR and turned off the alarm system.

'Julie?'

He moved down the hall, his hand on the butt of his gun.

'Julie?'

He cleared three rooms before reaching her bedroom. He eased the door open. She was asleep in the bed. Robie closed the door and walked down the hall to his bedroom.

His phone rang. The Blue Man.

'Leo Broome's a Fed. Works as a public liaison officer for the DOA.'

'The Agriculture Department?' exclaimed Robie. 'You're kidding me.'

'I'm not. His background is being emailed to you right now. Take a read. And see what hits you.'

'There has to be something there,' said Robie.

'Then find it.' Blue Man hung up.

Robie's email inbox buzzed and he brought up the story of Leo Broome's professional life. He read it over carefully.

'What are you doing up?' he said, without looking at her.

Julie stood there in sweatpants, looking sleepy. 'Find out anything?'

'I think I was the target of the bomb, not you.'

'That's comforting'

'Leo Broome works for the Department of Agriculture. He was also in the army. Gulf One.'

'So?'

'The woman and child who were killed? Her ex-husband was also murdered. He was in the military as well. Maybe he and Broome knew each other.'

'And if they did, what would they know that would get them killed? And how does that tie into my parents being murdered?'

'I don't know. I'm still working on the possible theories.'

'And whoever blew up the bus, why did they want to kill you?'

'For things I can't talk about.'

She said, 'Could it be that this Wind guy told something to the Broomes, who told something to my parents?'

'Yes, it could. That's my most promising line of investigation.'

'I want to be part of it, too.'

'You are. You've been helping me.'

She stood there looking at him, then asked, 'What do you think they did with my parent's bodies?'

'Probably in a place we'll never find,' said Robie. 'Remember them as you knew them. Don't think about where they are now, OK? It won't do you any good.'

'Easy to say.'

'Yes, it is easy to say, but I think it needed to be said.'

Robie waited for her to break down and cry. Kids were supposed to do that, or so he'd been told. He had never done it when he was a child. But his childhood had not been normal in any possible way.

But Julie did not break down. She did not sniffle. She did not cry. She glanced at him and the look on her face was cold.

'I want to kill whoever did this.'

'Killing someone is not as simple as it sounds.'

'Will you help me kill them? I know you can.'

He said slowly, 'This is not a game, Julie. You want to kill them. Fine, I get that. But you won't be able to kill them when it comes to it. Just keep one thing in mind.'

'What's that?' she asked, in a strained voice.

'They want you dead. And when they get the chance, they won't hesitate for a second.'

It was two a.m. and Robie had been asleep for exactly one hour when his eyes opened. He padded into the living room and put his eye to the telescope. Annie Lambert was on the move. Robie watched as she walked from her bedroom to the kitchen. She was dressed in black tights and a blue football jersey.

She pulled out a book and sat down to read, spooning yogurt into her mouth. He was not the only one tonight with insomnia.

He pulled out her business card and called her cellphone. 'It's Will.' He watched as she sat up straighter. 'Can't sleep. Hope I didn't wake you.'

'I wasn't asleep. I'm just sitting here, eating yogurt.'

He said, 'You know, there's a nice view from the top of our building. Ever been up there?'

'I didn't think you could get up there. Isn't it locked?'

'No problems with locks if you have a key. How about I meet you at the stairwell in ten minutes?'

'Really? You're serious?'

'I don't call people at 2 a.m. unless I'm serious.'

'You're on.'

She clicked off and Robie watched in amusement as she raced down the hall, presumably to change her clothes.

Nine minutes later, he was standing at the entrance to the stairwell. She had changed into a knee-length skirt and blouse. He led her up the stairs. When they came to the locked roof door he pulled out his pick tools and in a short time it swung open.

'That wasn't a key,' she said, smiling in admiration at his skill. 'You just picked the lock.'

'A pick is a key by another name. That's as close to poetic as I'll ever get.'

She followed him up a short flight of stairs. The rooftop was flat and radiated a slight warmth.

Robie pulled out a bottle of wine from under his jacket. 'Hope you like red.' From his pocket he produced two plastic wineglasses.

They stood by the edge of the roof and rested their glasses on the chest-high wall of the building. The wind blew gently across them as they sipped their wine and talked. The conversation was innocuous and yet helped to deliver a bit of a respite to Robie.

'I've never done anything like this before,' said Lambert.

'I've come up here before, but not with anyone else.'

'I feel honoured, then,' she said.

Robie looked at his watch. 'Well, I guess we should call it a night.'

He walked her back to her apartment.

She turned and kissed him gently on the lips, letting her fingers linger on his chest.

'Good night,' she said.

After she went inside Robie stood there. He wasn't sure what he was feeling. Well, maybe he just hadn't felt it in a really long time.

ROBIE GOT BACK to the other building a few minutes later. He checked on Julie and found her asleep. He showered, dressed and left, setting the alarm.

He drove through the empty streets, his first stop Julie's home.

He parked a block away and a minute later he was in the duplex. He navigated with a penlight through the dark interior. He stooped and studied the mark on the wall. Blood, to his eye, but the police might not even notice it. But that little smudge was telling Robie something.

Blood spatter. They got all of it except this spot, in plain view.

Robie straightened. That mark was a message. But who for?

Was it for one of the Gettys' friends? Who might want to talk to the police, but wouldn't if they knew they'd been killed? *That's a stretch*, thought Robie. The friend might never see this mark or know what it was. *But I would know.*

He searched the rest of the house, ending in Julie's bedroom. He saw a stuffed bear in a corner, lying on its side. He put it and a photo of Julie and her parents in his knapsack. He'd give them to Julie when he saw her again.

His phone buzzed. It was Blue Man.

'We found your handler. Come and see what's left of him.'

ROBIE LOOKED DOWN at the mass of blackened bone and then stared at Blue Man. His white shirt was crisply starched, his tie point dropped right at six o'clock. He smelled of cologne. It was a little after five o'clock in the morning and he looked ready to make a presentation to a Fortune 500 board.

Blue Man was staring down at the black husk of the man who had ordered Robie to kill a woman and child. They were standing in the middle of a park in Fairfax County, Virginia. To Robie's left was a Little League baseball diamond.

'What do we know?' said Robie.

'His name, position and employment history. We do not know his recent whereabouts, why he was turned or who killed him.'

'We sure it's the guy? You can't get DNA off charred bone.'

'They covered a finger with fire-retardant material. We made the match off that, both prints and DNA. It's him.'

'They're taking care of loose ends,' said Robie. 'How'd you find out about the body?'

'We received an anonymous phone call.' Blue Man pointed to an SUV parked at the kerb. 'I think it's time for that briefing.'

'I don't have much to tell you.'

'I'm awake. There's fresh coffee in there. Whatever you tell me will be more than I know right now.'

Robie eased into the back seat of the SUV. He should tell the man everything but he had a natural disinclination to tell anyone anything.

'My handler is lying out there barbecued,' he began.

'I wouldn't trust anyone either,' replied Blue Man, reading Robie's thoughts. 'I can't force you to tell me what you know.'

Robie let the statement sit there. 'Heightened interrogation techniques?'

'Don't believe in them.'

'Is that the agency's official position now?'

'It's my personal one.'

Robie mulled things over for a few seconds then said, 'The girl on the bus is Julie Getty. A guy on there tried to kill her. I took him out. We got off, and the bus blew up. I lost my gun in the blast. We got away from the shooter in the alley, and she's staying at my other place.'

'Ties to Leo Broome?'

'A friend of Julie's parents, Curtis and Sara. The guy on the bus killed them; maybe they knew something and had to be silenced. We need to check out their backgrounds. Julie gave me the names of friends of her parents. The Broomes were on that list. I went to their apartment. They were gone. And the place had been scrubbed.'

'So they're on the run or dead, too,' said Blue Man. 'Broome was with the DOA. Not exactly the epicentre of espionage.'

'He was also in the military, in Gulf One,' replied Robie.

'Which does open up some possibilities.'

'There's something else,' said Robie. 'I thought Julie was the target on the bus. Now I believe that I was.'

'Why?'

'I had reserved a seat using an alias, an alias someone knew who shouldn't have known. They couldn't have known Julie would be on the bus. But they knew I would be. And that bomb had to be placed on the bus before I even got to the Wind apartment.'

'But why kill you? What do you know that can hurt them?'

Robie shook his head. 'I can't figure that one out.'

Blue Man said, 'You should be dead from the shooting at Donnelly's.'

'I know. They let me live.'

'So they wanted to kill you before, but now they want to let you live.'

'Change in plan.'

'Why? Do they need you for something?'

The way Blue Man said it made Robie look at him. 'You think I've been turned, too?'

Blue Man stared over Robie's shoulder towards the remains of what had once been a man.

'Well, if you have been, you can see there's no future in it.'

RICK WIND HAD LIVED on a narrow street in a working-class neighbourhood. There was a police presence there, though no crime had been committed. Blue Man had had his people call ahead, and the officer on duty let Robie pass after he showed his cred pack.

Robie put on latex gloves and shoe covers before entering the house. He turned on the lights and gazed around. The furniture was old and shabby, the rugs stained and worn.

There was a shelf against one wall. On it were a few books and a number of framed photographs. Robie picked them up one by one and saw Rick and Jane Wind and the couple's two sons. The family looked happy, and Robie wondered what had caused the marriage to break down. He put down the photo. Affairs of the heart were beyond his expertise.

He worked his way from the basement to the top floor. And found nothing. This had been a wasted trip. He called Vance.

'Got time for some coffee?' asked Robie. 'I'll buy.'

'And what exactly do you want for that?'

'How about the medical examiner's report on Rick Wind?'

He heard her sigh. 'Where and when?'

Vance was already there when he arrived at the café on King Street. She had ordered a coffee for him. After he had taken a sip, she slid a file out of her bag filled with photos of Wind's body and a detailed analysis of his cause of death.

Robie studied the pages. 'So, Wind wasn't in the greatest shape. Heart disease and a bad kidney; liver and lungs suspect.'

'My older brother fought in the First Gulf War. He died at forty-six. His brain looked like Swiss cheese.'

'Gulf War syndrome?'

'Yep. Never got much traction in the news. Too many defence dollars stacked against it. Truth could never get out.'

Robie put the file down. 'Interesting tattoo on his left forearm.' He slid out the photo of the arm and showed it to her.

'I know. I wondered what that was,' said Vance.

'It's a Spartan warrior, like in the movie *300*. Makes sense for Wind to have a tattoo like that. He was in the infantry. You mind if I keep this file?'

'Go ahead. I have copies.'

Her phone buzzed. She listened to the caller and Robie noted her eyes widen. She clicked off. 'An eyewitness to the bus blowing up has come forward. Her name is Michele Cohen. She saw everything.'

'That's great,' said Robie, a sliding feeling in his stomach.

'You want to follow me over?' Vance asked, rising from the table.

Robie looked up at her. 'I've got a meeting at DCIS I have to get to. Where are you going to be questioning the woman. WFO?'

'Yes.'

'I can hook up with you there later.'

They parted company at the door. Robie hustled back to his car and drove off. He got on the phone to Blue Man and filled him in.

'I would stay away from this eyewitness if I were you.'

'I think I had that one covered on my own. But find out what you can about her. Do you have Jordison?'

'She's cleaned up and has new clothes. Does our help include finding her suitable employment?'

'It does, and preferably with a nice bump in salary over what she was making before.'

Robie clicked off and sped up. He needed to talk to Julie.

She was waiting for him wearing jeans, a sweatshirt and an exasperated expression.

'I'm not sure how much longer I can sit and do nothing, Will.'

'I've got a question for you. Depending on how you answer might change the complexity of everything.'

'What is it?'

'Why the bus? There are lots of ways you could've got out of town. Why did you choose that way?'

'My mom sent a note to my school. She wasn't allowed to talk to me because I was in foster care. The note said to come home that night. That my mom and dad were going to get a fresh start.'

'But what about the bus?'

'That was in the note. Mom said if they weren't home, I was to go to the bus station and take the 112 bus to New York City. They would meet me the next morning. They put cash in the envelope.'

'Did you recognise your mom's handwriting?'

'It was typed.'

'Did she often send you typed notes?'

'Sometimes. She used the computer at the diner. They have a printer, too.' She stared at him. 'You think my mom didn't write that note?'

'I think the odds are very high she didn't. Someone else wanted you on that bus. They were counting on the fact that I would have intervened when the guy made his move against you. Then the most likely result is we both get off the bus.'

'You say "we" as though we were paired together.'

Robie said, 'I think we were supposed to team up.'

'But why? Wouldn't they want us dead?'

'Apparently not.'

'That makes no sense.'

'If I'm right, it makes sense to someone.'

Robie unzipped his knapsack and pulled out her stuffed bear and the photo he'd taken from her home. He handed them to her.

'Why did you go back there?' she asked, looking down at the objects.

'To see if I missed anything.'

'Did you?'

'Yeah. They wanted me to spot the blood. They also want me to know I'm being played.'

'What about that guy in the alley with the rifle? If they wanted us to get away, why send him after us?'

'I think their plan all along was for me to walk away. But they knew I'd get suspicious if they made it look too easy. They had to send someone else after me. It was probably the shooter from the Winds' apartment.'

'But if they wanted you to live and me too, that means they need us for some reason,' Julie said slowly.

'Exactly. Nobody puts this much effort into something, kills that many people, without a damn important reason.'

ROBIE WAS ON THE MOVE with Julie. He'd had her pack up most of her stuff in her knapsack without really giving any explanations as to why.

He glanced at her from time to time as he steered the car through the traffic. She caught him doing it more than once and said, 'Why do you keep staring at me?'

The answer was actually easy, if unwelcome, Robie thought. *I have somebody other than myself I'm responsible for and it's driving me nuts.*

His phone buzzed. It was Vance.

'The eyewitness saw a man and a teenage girl get off the bus right before it blew up. She also said the man's gun landed under a car. That's the gun we found that ties into the Wind killing. So there is a definite connection.'

'Where was she while all of this was going down? And why is she only coming forward now?'

'She was leaving a hotel in the area after spending some time with a man other than her husband. We're having one of our techs put together a digital image based on her description of the man and girl. Just get down here. I want you to hear her story.'

'I've got a meeting but I'll be there as soon as I can.'

'Problems?' asked Julie, when he clicked off.

'A few.'

Julie picked up a file that lay on the dashboard. 'What's this?'

'An autopsy report on a guy. Not something you want to look at.'

She flipped it open anyway and looked at the glossies. 'Gross.'

'What did you expect? The guy's dead.'

Julie's hands began to shake. She held up a photo of Rick Wind's right arm and said, 'It's a Spartan warrior.'

He looked at her in amazement. 'How'd you know that?'

'Because my dad had a tattoo exactly like it.'

Robie pulled the car to the kerb and turned to stare at her.

'His name is Rick Wind. That ring any bells with you?'

'No.'

'Was your dad in the military?'

'I don't think so.'

'But he has that tattoo. Did you ever ask him where he got it?'

'He said he was into ancient Greek history and mythology. That's where it came from.'

'It might be that he served with Rick Wind. Lots of grunts from the same unit did similar body art.'

'If my dad was in the military, why wouldn't he have talked about it?'

'Lots of people don't talk about their military service.'

'I bet heroes do.'

'A pretty accurate rule of thumb is the people who did the most, talk about it the least.'

'If my dad was in the military, do you think he was maybe a hero or something?' Julie asked, quietly.

Robie knew the answer she wanted by her wistful tone.

'Maybe he was,' Robie said.

Julie said, 'Can you find out?'

'Shouldn't be a problem.' He slid his phone out and relayed his request to Blue Man.

'We'll know soon enough,' Robie told Julie.

Robie's phone buzzed again. He glanced at the screen. Vance again.

Julie saw it, too. 'Sounds like Agent Vance really wants you.'

'Well, Agent Vance will have to wait,' replied Robie.

'An eyewitness to the bus explosion?'

Robie shot her a questioning glance.

'Agent Vance has a loud voice—I heard her. Did the eyewitness see us?'

'Would seem so.'

'If the person sees you? Big problem.'

'That's right,' replied Robie.

'Will, where are we going?'

They had driven across Memorial Bridge and were in northern Virginia. He turned off the road and reached a gate.

'Change of location for you.'

'Why?'

'Never a good idea to stay in one place too long.'

A man in uniform holding an MP-5 strode towards the car. Robie rolled down his window and held out his cred pack.

'I'm on the list.' The guard checked on his cellphone. Two other armed men searched the car. The gate rose. Robie pulled forward and slipped into an empty parking lot.

'What is this place?' Julie asked.

'Safe. For you. That's all you need to know. '

'Is this, like, the CIA?'

'No. I wouldn't have brought you to Langley. This place is a couple of steps down, but it's secure.'

'So you're just going to drop me here?'

'Come on,' he said. 'We need to do this, Julie.'

She followed him across the parking lot. They were buzzed through the doors of a two-storey building, and then led to a narrow conference room.

Julie sat while Robie paced. 'Are you nervous?' she asked, finally.

Robie looked at Julie and realised she was scared. Why wouldn't she be? This was a lot to deal with.

He sat down next to her. 'It's better for you to be here. We need to keep you safe.'

The door opened and Blue Man entered, carrying a manila file.

Robie said, 'This is Julie Getty.'

Blue Man nodded. 'I deduced as much.'

'Do you two work together?' asked Julie.

'No,' said Robie.

'Sometimes,' amended Blue Man.

She looked around the room. 'Am I supposed to stay here somewhere? This isn't, like, a house or anything.'

Blue Man turned to Julie. 'We can accommodate you comfortably. We have certain quarters for, uh, guests.'

Robie said, 'Anything on my queries?'

'Quite a lot, actually. Do you want to hear it now?'

Robie glanced at Julie and then back at Blue Man with an enquiring look.

Blue Man cleared his throat. 'I see no reason why she can't hear this. It's not classified.' He opened the file. 'Miss Getty, your father had a very distinguished military career in the army.'

Julie sat up straighter. 'He did?'

'A Bronze Star with valour, a Purple Heart and several other impressive commendations. He was honourably discharged, leaving the service with the rank of sergeant.'

'He never talked about it.'

'Where did he serve that he got the Bronze?' asked Robie.

'Gulf One,' answered Blue Man.

'Was his discharge based on anything other than him not re-upping?'

'There were some medical issues. PTSD,' replied Blue Man.

'That's post-traumatic stress disorder,' noted Julie.

'Yes, it is,' said Blue Man.

'Anything else?' asked Robie.

Blue Man glanced down at the file. 'Some cognitive issues. It was alleged that he had exposure to some materials that might have adversely affected him.'

'DU?' said Robie.

Julie shot him a glance. 'DU? What's that?'

'DU stands for depleted uranium,' said Robie. 'It's used in artillery shells and also on tank armour.'

'Uranium? Isn't that bad for you?' asked Julie.

'There have never been any conclusive studies done that demonstrated the truth of that statement,' Blue Man said.

'Did they run any tests on him?' asked Robie. 'To see what the cognitive issues stemmed from?'

'No.'

'They probably didn't want to prove that this DU crap messed with his mind,' said Julie, glowering at Blue Man.

Robie pulled out the glossy of Rick Wind that showed the tattoo.

'Julie said that her dad had a tat just like this one. Can we find out if they ever served together?'

Blue Man made a call. 'We'll have an answer shortly.'

'Anything on this eyewitness?' asked Robie.

'Michele Cohen? Not yet. She's in FBI custody.'

'If she can ID me and Julie—'

'That would be catastrophic,' Blue Man said.

'Maybe she's lying,' said Julie.

'If so, we need to find out her motivation,' said Robie.

Blue Man said, 'How will you handle this with Vance? You can't keep ducking her.'

'I'll figure something out.' But right then, Robie had no idea what.

His phone buzzed. Vance.

'I told you I was in a meeting,' he said.

'Cohen gave us enough to get a description out on the two people from the bus. Might be a father and his daughter.'

'OK,' said Robie. 'You said the girl was a teenager?'

'Light-skinned. The guy was much darker.'

'Come again?'

'African American, Robie. Can you get your butt over here?'

Chapter 6

Robie and Vance sat across from Michele Cohen in a small conference room. She was in her late thirties, and seemed nervous. Robie would have been surprised if she weren't.

Cohen had told her story in detail. Coming out of the hotel seconds before the explosion. Seeing the man and young woman get off the bus. Running down an alley to her car.

The hotel had confirmed that Cohen had come in at the time she said she had. The man's story had also checked out. There was no reason why either he or Cohen would lie about this. And yet, of course, Robie knew they had. But he couldn't tell Vance that without revealing his own secret.

Robie wondered where they had found Cohen. Maybe she was a former actress who needed some fast money. Yet she knew she was lying to the FBI. That would not be done lightly. There had to be a very large incentive.

'Could you pick the guy and teen out of a line-up?' he asked.

'I'm not sure. There was so much going on.'

'But you're sure they were African American?'

'Definitely,' she said.

'Initially you didn't go to the police.'

'I was worried about being exposed.'

'You mean your affair being exposed?' amended Robie.

'Yes. I'm not proud of what I did,' Cohen said, stiffly. 'But I did come forward. I'm trying to help.'

'And it's much appreciated,' cut in Vance.

As soon as Cohen had departed, Robie said, 'For the record, I think she's lying.'

'What possible motivation would she have?'

'If I knew that, the case would be solved.'

Vance said, 'There were at least six black men on the bus and three black teenage girls. Cohen's story fits the facts.'

'You've never gone with your instincts?' he asked.

'Not when they're trumped by cold, hard facts.'

Robie rose.

'Where are you going?' she asked.

'To find some cold, hard facts.'

MICHELE COHEN poured herself a cup of coffee and carried it into the family room where the TV was on. She changed the channel.

'I preferred the other programme, actually.'

She screamed.

Robie sat down in the chair opposite her. It had not been difficult to track her down. Her home address was in the file Vance had let him read.

'You should lock your doors, even while you're home,' he said.

'I'm calling the police. I don't have to stand for this.'

Robie held up a flat, square box. 'Know what this is, Michele?'

'I'm not going to sit here and play stupid games with you.'

'It's a DVD. From a security camera pointed right at the spot where the bus exploded.'

'If that's the case, why didn't the police know about it?'

'Because it was from a webcam a guy set up overlooking the street. He had problems with burglars. I found it because I went door-to-door before the cops did. It didn't see you, Michele, or your boyfriend.'

'That's ridiculous. Why would we lie about something like that? And the hotel clerk backed up our story.'

'I'm not saying you weren't at the hotel. I'm just saying you're lying about what you saw. You saw nothing.'

'You're wrong!'

'You said you saw the bus explode and the guy's gun fly off and land under a car?'

'That's right.'

'The explosion would have blown thousands of pieces of debris into the air. And you saw one little gun land under a car?'

She jumped up and raced to the phone. 'I want you out of here. Now. Or I will call the police.'

'We both know that you didn't see two black people get off that bus, Michele. And the DVD will confirm that. So you lied to the FBI. That will get you at least five years in a federal prison on about three different felonies.'

'You're just trying to scare me.'

'No, I'm trying to enlighten you on just how serious your situation is. Now, why don't we talk about this and maybe come up with a way out of it for you.'

'Why would you do that?'

'Because I'm a nice guy. If I believed for one second that you weren't just a patsy in this whole thing I would've already arrested you. But if I can use you to get to the people I really want, then that's valuable. That's something you can negotiate with, Michele.'

Cohen sat on the sofa, her gaze downcast.

Robie sat back, studied her. 'Who told you to lie?'

'I can't talk to you about this. They'll kill my husband.'

'What's he got to do with this?'

'Gambling debts. But someone approached him and told us there was a way out. All debts forgiven if we did this.'

'What does your husband do?'

'He's a partner in a law firm. He's a good man but he has a problem with betting. He used client funds to make up a shortfall. He'll be ruined if it comes out.'

'Who were the people who got you to do this?'

'I never met them. My husband was taken to a room, sat in the dark. They told us everything we needed to do.'

'Why were you chosen to do it instead of your husband?'

'I guess I'm cooler under pressure than he is. We didn't think he would be able to lie to the FBI.'

'Who was the guy you were with?'

'They supplied him. We just sat in the hotel bedroom staring at the floor. Then we left at the time we'd been given. I didn't actually see the bus explode. I was told to say it was a black man and black teenager who got off the bus.'

'Where is your husband now?'

'Confirming that his gambling debts have been taken care of.'

'You really think it's that easy? You're a liability to these folks, Michele.'

Her face flushed. 'But we don't know anything.'

'What you just told me disproves that. What time is your husband supposed to be back?'

She looked at her watch. 'About twenty minutes ago.' She grabbed her phone and punched in a number. 'It went right to voicemail.'

'Text him.'

They waited for five minutes and no text came back.

'Where was he going to confirm that the debts were cancelled?'

'At a bar over in Bethesda.'

'Let's go. We might be in time to save his life.'

ON THE WAY, ROBIE CALLED Blue Man and requested back-up. They would meet him at the bar.

Cohen's face was tear-streaked. 'You think he's dead, don't you? It seems so stupid now. Of course they wouldn't just let him walk away. But we were desperate.'

'Which made you the perfect people to approach.' Robie pulled the car to the kerb. 'That the place?' he asked, indicating a bar with the sign 'Lucky's' above it.

She nodded. 'Yes. That's Mark's car over there.' She pointed to a grey Lexus sedan parked half a block down.

Robie looked around for his back-up. He texted Blue Man. The reply came almost immediately. Sixty seconds away.

A few moments later, an SUV pulled up behind Robie. He signalled to the driver. The man signalled back. Robie got out and escorted Cohen to the SUV. There were three men inside. Cohen got in the back seat.

'Stay put,' he told her. 'These men will take care of you.'

Robie looked at the man in the passenger seat. 'You want to come in with me?'

The man nodded and the pair moved down the street, looking for anything threatening. The bar was closed.

'How do you want to do this?' asked the other man.

'Give me two minutes to access the back. Then hit the front. We'll meet in the middle.'

Robie skirted down an alley and found the back entrance. He used his pick tools to beat the lock, pulled his gun and slowly pushed the door open. It was totally dark inside. He let his eyes adjust to the low level of light and moved forwards. His partner should be coming through the front door right about now.

Only his guy wasn't there. But someone else was. Robie approached the man sitting in the booth to the left of the front door. There was enough light coming in from the front windows for Robie to see what he needed. Single gunshot wound to the head. Robie touched his hand. Cold. He'd been dead a while.

Robie snaked his hand inside the man's jacket and pulled out his wallet. The name on the licence was Mark Cohen. He put the wallet back, looked at the front door. *Shit.*

He raced to the door, unlocked it and stepped outside. His Volvo was there but the black SUV was not.

He got on the phone to Blue Man. 'Mark Cohen is dead and your guys took off with Michele Cohen. Want to explain that?'

Blue Man said, 'I don't understand. They're two of my best men. My most trusted people. They were supposed to follow your orders.'

Robie said, 'There were *three* guys in the SUV.'

'I only sent two.'

'Then one of them tagged along, and I guess now we know why.'

'This is unprecedented, Robie.'

'I'll be there in twenty minutes. Go and check on Julie. Take a bunch of guys with you. They can't have bought off all of them.'

'Robie, are you saying—'

'Just do it!'

WHEN ROBIE RACED INTO the secure building, the first person he saw was Blue Man. The second person was Julie.

Blue Man said tersely, 'Follow me, both of you.' They walked quickly down the hall into a room. Blue Man locked the door behind them. He motioned for Robie and Julie to sit.

'Michele Cohen?' Robie asked.

'Dead. Along with two of my men. The two I officially sent. They just found the bodies in the SUV.'

'Who was the third guy?'

'Malcolm Strait. Worked here for ten years. Impeccable record.'

'Describe him.' Blue Man did so. Robie said, 'He was the guy who was supposed to come through the front door of the bar.'

'What are we talking about?' asked Julie.

Robie took a few minutes to fill her in. She looked puzzled.

'Why would they get this lady to tell an obvious lie?'

Blue Man said, 'Exactly. What did they gain by it?'

'Who else did this Malcolm Strait work with here?' said Robie.

'Lots of people.'

'You need to talk to all of them. We need to learn if he left behind anybody.'

'So this guy might have somebody else here?' said Julie. She looked straight at Blue Man. 'Not so safe a place.'

Robie said, 'We can't stay here now. We have to move.'

Blue Man said, 'Where are you going?'

'Someplace safer than this,' said Robie.

ROBIE PILOTED THE VOLVO through the gate and turned left.

'Where are we going?' Julie asked.

'The only place left is the house in the woods.'

'Pretty isolated if someone wants to ambush us.'

'And far easier to see someone coming at us. Trade-off.'

'They might send a lot of guys.'

'They might. And, then again, they might not send anybody.'

'But why wouldn't they?'

'Think about it, Julie. What's their endgame? This Malcolm Strait guy was inside that facility with you. He could've killed you there. And they could've popped me a couple of times already, but conveniently missed.'

Julie sat back, thinking, then said, 'Will, this isn't the way to your place.'

'Slight change in plan.'

'Why?'

'Getting a little needed help and making a big confession.'

Robie had made an unusual decision for him. He did not normally seek help from others, yet he had finally realised that he could not do this alone.

He pulled into the condominium complex and Julie trailed him inside the building. Robie knocked on the door of 701.

The door opened. Vance stared first at Robie, and then her gaze fell on Julie.

'What the hell is going on? Who's the kid?'

'That's why I'm here,' said Robie.

Vance stepped back and let them pass through.

'Michele Cohen and her husband are dead,' said Robie.

'What?' exclaimed Vance. 'How?'

He sat on the sofa and motioned to Julie to take a seat. Vance stood in front of him, hands on hips.

'She was lying, like I said. Her husband had gambling debts. This was a way out, or so they thought. I saw him with a third eye at a bar in Bethesda. She died later, along with two federal officers.'

Vance gaped. 'What in the hell is going on?'

'Got any coffee? This might take a while'

'I just put some on.'

'I like mine black,' said Julie.

'Oh, really?' said a bemused Vance.

Robie walked into the kitchen.

Vance was right on his butt. 'You better start talking, Robie.'

'OK. First, I don't technically work for DCIS.'

'Big surprise. What else?'

'This needs to be off the record.'

'The hell it is.'

'You want that coffee now?'

'What I want are straight answers from you.'

Robie poured out two cups of coffee and handed one to her. He looked out of the window at the monuments in DC. He pointed to them. 'What's it worth to you to keep that place safe?'

'What's it worth? Hell, it's worth everything.'

'Now, what's it worth to keep that girl in there safe?'

'You haven't even told me who she is.'

'Julie Getty. She was on the bus but got off before it blew up.'

'How the hell do you know that?' Vance asked, sharply.

'Because I got off with her. That's why I knew Cohen was lying. As you can see, Julie and I aren't black.'

Vance stood there trying to process this stunning revelation. '*You* were on that bus? Why? And why am I just finding out now?'

Julie said, 'Because it was a need-to-know and you didn't need to know. At least back then.'

They both turned to see Julie standing in the doorway.

Vance looked from her to Robie. 'Need-to-know? So you're in intelligence? I swear to God, Robie, you have a ton of explaining to do. Who blew up the bus?'

'I don't know. But it had to be done remotely. Not a timer because they didn't want to kill either of us.'

'Why?'

'Don't know. I just know that they want one or both of us alive, for some reason.'

Vance turned to Julie. 'What were you doing on the bus?'

'Can I have my coffee first?'

'Jesus, here.' Vance handed Julie a cup. 'Now, what were you doing on that bus?'

'Some guy murdered my parents. My mom sent a note to me, at least I thought it was from my mom. It told me to get on that bus and meet them in New York. When I did, the same guy who killed my parents got on and attacked me. Will helped stop him. We got off the bus. And that's when it blew up.'

Vance turned to Robie and snapped, 'It was *your* gun we found near the bus. You were in Jane Wind's apartment. You were going to kill her!'

'Just listen to him, Agent Vance,' pleaded Julie. 'Will saved my life. He's a good guy.'

Vance calmed and glanced at Robie. 'You've put me in an awkward situation. I should report this.'

'Agreed. I did with my people, only to find out we had a traitor in the ranks. I wonder what the odds are of there being more?'

She hiked her eyebrows. 'You mean at the Bureau?'

'You never had any bad apples?'

'Not many,' she said, defensively.

'It only takes one,' said Robie.

Vance sighed. 'What do you want me to do?'

ROBIE TURNED THE VOLVO in at Dulles Airport and bought a ticket for Chicago, went through security, and hit the restroom. He came out later wearing a tracksuit, glasses and a baseball cap. He rode the bus back to the car rental outlets, leased an Audi using a credit card under an alias and sped west on the toll road.

An hour later, he pulled into his hideaway in the woods. He drove the car into the barn and closed the doors. He removed a hatch from the floor and hoisted himself down through the opening. He flicked a switch and old fluorescent tube lighting blinked on. Robie moved down a short hallway and stopped. In front of him was a wall of firepower, including pistols, rifles, shotguns, and even a surface-to-air missile launcher. He took down what he needed and spent another ten minutes picking out various other items. He packed everything in a large duffle bag, and put it in the trunk of the Audi.

Five minutes later, he was speeding back east. He checked in at an extended-stay motel and called Julie, who was in the care of Vance and the FBI. Vance had only told her superiors that Julie was a possible witness and needed protection. Two agents from out of town had been called in to assist with the protection detail. Robie didn't trust anyone in DC.

Julie sounded excited. 'I called the Broomes on the phone you gave me, and I got a text back,' she said. 'They want to meet.'

'You know it's probably *not* the Broomes, right?' said Robie, in a calming tone. 'If it were the Broomes, they probably would have simply called.'

'Do you always have to be a downer?' asked Julie.

'Where and when?'

She told him.

'This is most likely a set-up. You're not going. I'll handle it.'

'That sucks.'

'It's the smart thing to do.'

Robie put the phone back into his pocket and mentally prepared for the upcoming meeting. At some point, whoever was behind this would no longer be interested in keeping him alive. He called Vance and filled her in.

ROBIE SPOKE QUIETLY into his headset as he eyed the Martin Luther King memorial. 'You in place?'

Vance's voice came into his ear. 'Roger that.'

'See anyone?'

'No.'

Robie kept moving and kept looking. He had on night-vision goggles, but they couldn't see what wasn't there.

'Julie?' The voice was to Robie's left, near the memorial.

It was a man. Robie tightened his grip on his pistol and spoke into his headset again. 'Did you hear that?'

Vance said, 'Yes, but I don't have a visual on the source yet.'

A second later, Robie did. A man stepped clear of the memorial. With the aid of his goggles, Robie could see that it was Leo Broome. He recognised him from a photo he had seen in the man's apartment.

Vance's voice came into his ear. 'Is that Broome?'

'Yes, sit tight and cover my back.'

Robie moved forwards. 'Mr Broome?'

The man immediately ducked back behind the memorial.

'Mr Broome,' Robie said again.

'Where's Julie?' Broome said.

'We didn't let her come. We thought it might be an ambush.'

'That's what I'm thinking,' said Broome. 'Just so you know, I've got a gun.'

Vance came out into the open and held up her weapon and badge. 'I am with the FBI, Mr Broome. We just want to talk.'

Robie said, 'Julie's parents are dead, Mr Broome. I've been trying to help her find their killers.'

'Curtis and Sara are dead?'

'So are Rick Wind and his ex-wife. Both murdered.'

Broome appeared round the edge of the memorial. 'We've got to put a stop to all this.'

'Couldn't agree with you more,' said Vance. 'First we need to get you to a safe location. And your wife.'

'She's dead.'

Robie said quickly, 'Were you with her when it happened?'

'Yes, I barely got out in—'

Robie was already running full tilt towards Broome. 'Get down now! Down!'

But he was too late. He heard the crack of the shot. Broome hit the dirt hard and lay still.

Robie ducked down and surveyed the area. He realised this had been a set-up. He was never intended to get any information from Leo Broome. They were still just playing him.

Vance knelt down next to Robie. 'Is he dead?'

'Round blew right through his head.'

'You were telling him to get down before the shot. How did you know?'

'They killed his wife, but he got away? I don't think so. They don't let people just get away.'

'So why let him come here at all?'

'This seems to be a game to them.'

'People are dying here, Robie. Some game.'

ROBIE SAT IN HIS APARTMENT in the dark. Vance and a quartet of FBI agents were keeping watch over Julie. He had told her about the Broomes' murders. She had taken it stoically, apparently accepting it as just a fact of life. *But maybe that's worse*, thought Robie. It didn't seem right that a fourteen-year-old should have her emotions so hardened that violent death didn't shock any more.

He had come back to his apartment because he needed to be on his own. He wasn't concerned about killers coming for him, at least not yet.

They want me alive, for something. Then they'll want me dead.

He had strained his mind going back over missions he'd performed. In his line of work, there would be many who would want revenge against him.

He looked out of the window. It was 2 a.m. There were a few cars on the street, no people. But then he caught sight of Annie Lambert bringing her bike to a stop outside the apartment. When she got off on her floor he was waiting for her. She looked surprised to see him. Then she smiled as she struggled with her bag. Robie took it from her.

'Thanks, I'm tired,' she said. 'I had to work overtime.'

'Here, I'll help you to your door and you can get some sleep.'

As they walked down the hall, she said, 'When I said I was tired, I didn't mean I needed to go to sleep. Would you like to come in for a beer?'

'OK.'

They went inside her apartment. She put her bike away and pointed Robie to the kitchen, where he got out two beers and came back into the living room. When she came out of her bedroom, she wore jeans and a long-sleeved T-shirt, and her hair was pulled back in a ponytail. She plopped down in a chair and curled her feet up under her.

'I actually have the day off tomorrow,' she said. 'The president is out of town. When he gets back, there's a big White House dinner. I have to work the event. So I'm going to enjoy my day off.' She clinked his beer with hers, then looked at him. 'So is this officially our first date?'

'Technically, I wouldn't think so,' replied Robie. 'It was more spontaneous. But we can make it anything we want. It's a free country.'

'I like you, Will. I like you a lot.'

'You don't really know me yet.'

'I'm a good and quick judge of people. Always have been.' She paused. 'You make me feel, I don't know, good about myself.'

'You have a lot of reasons to feel good about yourself, Annie.'

She rose and sat down next to him. She touched Robie's hand with hers. 'I've had a couple of bad experiences with guys.'

'I promise you won't have one with me.' Robie had no way to guarantee this, but he believed it to be the truth.

At the same moment they each leaned towards the other. Their lips touched gently. Then they drew apart.

'Did you not like that?' she asked.

'No, I liked it a lot, actually.'

They kissed again.

'I'm a lot older than you,' he said. 'Maybe we shouldn't do this.'

'Maybe we should do exactly what we both obviously want to do,' she murmured in his ear.

IT WAS SIX IN THE MORNING and Robie was on the move again, leaving Annie Lambert lying in bed. His rental glided down the dark street.

He called Vance. Despite the early hour, she picked up on the second ring.

'What happened to you last night?' she said. 'You sort of disappeared after we got Julie squared away.'

'I just had to step back for a bit, get my head straight.'

'Is it straight now? Because we have a case to work.'

'Yeah.'

'I haven't had breakfast. There's a twenty-four-hour place around the corner from WFO. You know it?'

He beat her there and had already ordered them coffee when she walked in.

She took a sip and said, 'You don't look good.'

'Should I look good?' he shot back. He wondered for a moment if she could tell he had been with another woman.

They sat in awkward silence until Robie said, 'How's Julie?'

'Fidgety, depressed. I think she believes you've abandoned her.'

'How did you explain things to your boss about all this?'

'I skirted the line. Told him some things, didn't tell him others.'

'You don't have to cover for me, Vance.'

'If I don't cover for you, the FBI will come down like a ton of bricks. And, quite frankly, I'm not just doing it for you. If everything does come out, my butt is probably off this investigation and it'll get so muddled we'll probably never figure it out. And I obviously have a problem with that happening.'

'Just so we understand each other,' said Robie.

'I'm not sure I completely get you, but that's neither here nor there. I'm just working with you to see if we can put away some killers.'

'Leo Broome,' he said. 'Anything found on him?'

'He had nothing on him. But we did find a tattoo on his forearm identical to the one on Rick Wind's arm. It has to match the one Julie said her dad had.'

'So they must've known each other in the army,' said Robie.

'You said they *let* him escape after they killed his wife. Part of the game, you said. If this is a contest between you and them, there must be something in your past to account for it. What line of work *were* you in, Robie?'

He said nothing, because there was nothing he could say.

'Fine,' said Vance. 'You don't have to answer, but hear me out, OK?'

Robie nodded.

'I think you were at Jane Wind's apartment to kill her as some sort of sanctioned hit. Only someone else pulled the trigger from long range. You took her youngest child to safety and then got out of there. Then you got roped into investigating a crime you were present at under the cover of a DCIS badge. How am I doing?'

'You're an FBI agent, I would've expected no less.'

'Tell me about the hit on Wind.'

'It wasn't really sanctioned. I should never have been dialled up, but I was. Person who did it is now a burnt pile of bone.'

'Cleaning up loose ends.'

'How I see it, yeah.'

'Seems like the start of it was your going after Wind. Her hubby was already dead. So the Winds are out of the way. Point one.'

Robie finished his coffee. 'Keep going.'

'Point two. Julie's parents are killed. They were friends with the Broomes. And Rick Wind and Curtis Getty had the same tattoo as him on their arms. It must be from them serving together in the military.'

'Have your people connected them yet?'

'Still working on it. Point three. Getty, Broome and Wind, including their spouses, are all dead.'

Robie nodded. 'I try and make my escape on that bus. They knew that

I would. Julie gets routed to the same bus. We get off, the bus blows up.'

'The attack outside Donnelly's where you and I should have been killed?'

'More window dressing, more playing with my mind.'

'Some playing. A lot of innocent people were killed,' Vance said. 'How do you want to attack this?'

'Priority one is keeping Julie safe. We obviously had a mole in our operation, and I have to count on the Bureau.'

'We will do all we can to make sure no harm comes to her, Robie. What's the second priority?'

'I have to find out who in my past wants me this bad.'

ROBIE SAT IN THE SMALL ROOM he had used as an office for the last five years, staring at the computer screen. Staring back at him were the reports on his last five missions. The two most recent captured his attention for they involved targets with long arms and many friends.

An image of Carlos Rivera appeared on the screen. Robie had killed Rivera in Edinburgh and made what he thought had been an undetected escape. Rivera's younger brother, Donato, was every bit as ruthless as his brother but content to run his drug empire without involving himself in politics. Still, he might want to avenge Carlos's death.

Do I fly to Mexico and attempt to kill Donato? Something deep in his gut told Robie that little brother was doing very well without big brother around.

So Robie moved on to the next target of interest. Khalid bin Talal, one of the Saudi princes, richer even than Rivera. Robie's shot had hit the man dead centre in the head. No possibility of survival. Robie had gunned down his bodyguards, disabled the plane and been on the slow ferry to Barcelona within the hour. Clean kill, clean exit. And, the truth was, Talal was not popular in the Muslim world. His ideas were too radical and it was largely at the Saudi ruling family's behest that Robie had been sent out on the mission.

He sat back in his chair and rubbed his temples. If he had still smoked, he would have lit up right then. He needed something to take his mind off a deep sense of failure. Something was staring him in the face. Perhaps it was the answer he needed. But it wouldn't come.

He went back through the three missions previous to Rivera and Talal. Every step, like he had with the Latino and the Muslim. Clean executions, clean exits, all of them.

And yet, if not one of them, who?

His phone started buzzing. It was Blue Man.

They had tracked down the military ties between Curtis Getty, Rick Wind and Leo Broome. They had all served together.

'I'm on my way,' said Robie.

'SAME SQUAD,' said Blue Man.

He and Robie were sitting together in Blue Man's office.

'They fought together for the entire campaign, along with other assignments post-Gulf One.'

'No wonder Julie didn't know. She wasn't born.'

'And her father was tightlipped about his service,' said Blue Man. 'Maybe he didn't even tell his wife.'

'Anything in his records to warrant such secrecy?'

'Maybe.' Blue Man pulled out a folder. 'Kuwait is one of the richest Gulf states. Cash, gold, precious jewels, that sort of thing. Getty, Wind and Broome might have had sticky fingers when they were there. They were each given general discharges.'

'You told Julie that her dad got an *honourable* discharge based on medical reasons.'

'That's right. I did.'

'Why?'

'I have granddaughters.'

'I can understand that,' said Robie. 'But if these three were involved in thefts, none of them showed any signs of wealth.'

'Curtis Getty probably put most of it up his nose. Rick Wind owned a pawnbroker's business. We could find no record of how he was able to buy it.'

'But he stayed in for the full ride. How would that be possible if he was believed to be a thief?'

'Lack of evidence, I suppose. But the general discharge speaks volumes. He didn't contest it. If he did steal the stuff and still got his pension, Wind probably thought he got a great deal.'

'And Leo Broome?'

'Hit the jackpot there. They had an oceanfront home in Boca Raton and we tracked down an investment portfolio under another name. Had about four million in it.'

'OK, at least it seems he stole. You think someone's coming for them after all this time? Why stick me in the middle of it?'

'The three ex-soldiers maybe fit a pattern. You don't.' Blue Man closed the file. 'You went back over your recent missions?'

'No clear reason why someone would want to come after me.' Robie brooded for a few moments. 'They want me involved in this somehow, whatever it is. I need to make them try a little harder to engage my attention.'

'What do you mean?'

'I'm going to make them push harder. When people push harder, they make mistakes.'

Robie walked out of the room. He was convinced that whatever the three soldiers had done twenty years ago was irrelevant.

This started with me, thought Robie. *It has to end with me.*

'SO, MR BROOME and Rick Wind served with my dad in the army?' said Julie.

Robie was sitting with her in the FBI safe house. How safe it was Robie wasn't sure, but he had few options left.

'Apparently, a number of soldiers in their squad got that tattoo.'

'Did you find out anything else?'

'Not really,' said Robie.

Julie eyed Robie closely. 'OK, Will, why do I think you're not telling me everything?'

'Because you're naturally suspicious, just like me.'

'So you haven't figured out what's going on, then, have you?'

'Not really. Your mother said that you didn't know anything, right? When she was talking to the guy in your house. That implies that your mother probably knew why the guy was there. Why he wanted to kill them.'

'We've already covered this ground, Will.'

'And Leo Broome implied that he knew something, too. Now, Cheryl Kosmann said that the day before your parents were killed, they had dinner with the Broomes at the diner. She said they looked like they had seen a ghost. When was the last time you talked to your parents before you went back to your house that night?'

'Just before I was put back in foster care.'

'And how did your mom seem?'

'Fine. Normal. We just talked about stuff.'

'And then later a guy is at their home looking to kill them, and your mother is not surprised by it. Something had to happen between you seeing her last and your parents having dinner with the Broomes.'

'But we don't know what that something is.'

'The way I see it, either your parents found out something and told the Broomes, or the Broomes found out something and told your parents.'

'Do you think it has something to do with their time in the military?'

'My gut tells me that it should. But all the facts don't point to that. Namely, my involvement in all this. If I'm the reason why this whole thing has been orchestrated, why involve your parents, the Broomes and the Winds? I didn't know any of them.'

'So you really think all of this is tied to you, somehow?'

'Yes, I think it is. Too many coincidences, otherwise.'

Julie pondered this. 'So either the Winds, my parents or the Broomes found something out. Because they were in the military together, the guys might have told each other about it. The bad guys found out and they had to kill them.'

'That makes sense.'

'Yeah, I guess it does,' Julie said, looking away from Robie.

He let a few tense moments pass. 'Julie, if this is really all about me, and your parents and the others were caught up in it, I'm sorry.'

'I'm not blaming you, Will,' she said. 'Blaming you isn't going to bring them back. I want to get whoever did this. *All* of them.'

'I think whatever got your parents killed was communicated among Wind, Broome and your dad. If we can trace any type of communication among that group, we might be able to get a better handle on all this.'

'Can you do that?'

'We can at least give it a hell of a shot. The problem is, so far nothing suggests they were involved in anything that could have been the catalyst for this.'

'Well, they weren't the only ones in the squad, right? A squad consists of nine or ten soldiers, with a staff sergeant in command.'

'How do you know that?'

'American history class. So my dad, Wind and Broome are three guys. That means you have six or seven more to track down.'

Robie shook his head, wondering how he'd missed something that obvious. Then he looked down at Julie's chest.

The laser dot was centred right over her heart.

Chapter 7

Robie made no visible reaction to the laser dot. He knew it was from a sniper rifle. He didn't look to the window, where he knew the blinds must be partially open. The rifle and the shooter were out there somewhere. He put his hands under the table separating him and her. He smiled.

'What's so funny,' she said, quizzically.

'I was just thinking about something that happened to me a long time ago—'

He felt along the underside of the table. Solid wood, about an inch thick. That might be good enough. He flipped up the table with one hand so it was shielding Julie from the sniper, and drew his Glock with his other hand.

Julie screamed as Robie fired, killing the overhead light. The rifle shot shattered the window but the table threw off the line of fire. It struck the wall to the left of Julie.

'Get down,' snapped Robie. He moved behind the table. He turned to Julie who lay flat on the floor with her hands over her head. 'Are you OK?'

'Yes,' she said, in a trembling voice.

'Did you open the window blinds?'

She peered up at him. 'No, they were like that when I got here.'

The door started to open. A voice called out, 'Robie, you OK?'

Robie called out, 'Put your gun down on the floor and slide it in the room with your foot.'

'What the hell is going on, Robie?'

'Just what I was about to ask you. Who opened the blinds in this room?'

'The blinds?'

'Yeah, because a sniper just took a shot right through that opening. So unless you have an answer, I'll shoot the first person that comes through the door. I don't care if it's you or anybody else.'

'Robie, we're the FBI.'

'Yeah, and I'm one seriously pissed off guy with a Glock. Where does that get us?'

'There's a sniper outside?'

'That's what I said. Didn't you hear the shot?'

'Hang tight.'

He heard feet running away.

Robie pulled out his phone, thumbed Vance's number. She answered. He said, 'Sniper at the safe house. Mole somewhere. Need back-up. Now.'

He clicked off and took Julie's hand. 'Keep low,' he warned her.

'Are we going to die?'

'Just keep down and follow me.' He led her out of the room, cleared the hall and they ran. Robie had no idea if the guy who had told him to hang tight was an ally or foe, and he didn't think it was a good idea to wait and find out for certain.

They would be expecting them to go out of either the back door or the window on the side opposite from the sniper fire. So Robie planned to go out at the front. But first they had to get there.

When Robie looked round the corner into the front room, he saw the body of one of the agents lying there, blood around his neck. Not a bullet wound—they would have heard the shot. Had to have been a knife. Hand over the mouth, knife slash to the neck, not much sound. Killer would've had to get real close for that.

Another traitor in the ranks.

Robie thumbed his phone keypad again. Vance picked up. Robie could hear the sound of her engine.

'Got one dead agent with an up-close wound,' he said, softly but clearly. 'Whoever nailed him, he thought was a friend. Don't know where the others are. How far away are you?'

'Three minutes.' She clicked off.

Robie turned to Julie, keeping his voice low. 'We're going to go out of the front door, but we need to draw attention somewhere else.'

'OK,' she said. 'How?'

Robie cleared the chamber on his pistol and inserted two rounds he'd taken from his jacket pocket. He edged to the front door and used his foot to move it open. 'Cover your ears and look away from the door.'

He aimed and fired. The first round hit the gas tank on the car parked in the driveway. The incendiary round ignited the gasoline vapour and the explosion lifted the sedan right off the asphalt. His second shot was aimed at the second car. A second later, it joined the fireball of the first.

Robie grabbed Julie's hand and they sprinted through the doorway.

Keeping the wall of flames and smoke between them and, hopefully, whoever had just tried to kill Julie, they ran. A car turned onto the street and Robie flagged Vance down. The Beemer skidded to a stop and Robie pushed Julie into the back, then jumped into the passenger seat.

Vance put the car in reverse and smoked her tyre tread backing down the street. She hit a U-turn and gunned it.

'So tell me what the hell happened.'

Robie said, 'Just keep driving.'

ROBIE RODE SHOTGUN and he kept rotating his gaze to look behind and then over at Vance. His gaze was suspicious and his hand gripped the butt of his Glock. That had been unbelievably close. If he hadn't looked down and seen the dot, Julie would have joined her parents among the dead. It was apparent to Robie that the other side no longer required either or both of them to continue living.

Vance kept her gaze on the road. They had travelled about two miles when she finally spoke. 'You have a reason for keeping your gun pointed in my direction? I didn't rat you out, Robie.'

'Good to know.' His voice was flat.

'Where do you want to go?'

'Why don't you pick a place? We'll see how it goes.'

'Is this a test?'

'Someone just set us up while in FBI custody,' said Robie. 'So pick a place, Agent Vance.'

'Robie, I'm on your side!'

He glanced out of the window. 'The guys you called in?'

'I don't know them specifically. I put in a request for agents from out of town. At your insistence.'

'Someone left the blinds open in the room where Julie was placed.' He looked at her. 'Which agent sent you back there?'

Julie said, 'The one who came to the door after the shot was fired. I recognised his voice.'

'The one that never came back. The one that killed his partner,' added Robie. He sat back in his seat and rubbed his face. 'So, I've got traitors in my own organisation. Traitors in the FBI. A puzzle I'm not close to solving. And time is running out.'

'So what are you going to do?' Vance asked, nervously.

'Regroup and rethink. The three of us are going to stick together. But we need new transportation.'

'What's wrong with my car?'

'Principally, that people know it's your car,' he said, before suddenly bringing his gun up and hitting the button to bring his window down. 'We have an SUV on our six and it's coming fast.'

Vance looked in the rearview mirror. An SUV, black, big and gaining on them way too fast. She punched the gas and the Beemer leapt forward. A shot shattered the rear glass. Julie shrieked as the bullet passed between Vance and Robie and cracked the windshield.

'Get in the footwell,' Robie shouted to Julie. She dropped into the space between the front and rear seats.

Robie took aim with his Glock and fired through the shattered back window. His shot hit the front of the SUV and pinged off.

'Armoured,' he said to Vance.

He fired next into the left front tyre. The rubber should have shredded. It didn't.

'Run-flat tyres again,' said Robie. 'Cute. Really cute.'

'If they're armoured, we should be able to outrun them.'

Robie saw the gun appear from the passenger-side window. It wasn't just any gun. If it hit them it would be over. He grabbed the wheel from Vance and slammed the car into a hard right turn that took it off the road and into someone's front yard.

A split second later the gun pointing from the SUV roared a dozen times. The rounds missed the Beemer but, behind them, a parked car exploded. The SUV couldn't make the turn and continued to speed down the road. Then came the screech of brakes.

Robie worked the wheel and the Beemer jumped the kerb and landed back on the road

'What the hell was that?' demanded Vance.

'It's called a Sledgehammer,' said Robie. 'Assault combat shotgun. It must've ignited the fuel tank on that car back there. Take the next left and then a right and then hit the gas hard. By the time they get back on our tail we'll be gone.'

Vance did as he instructed, and they were soon alone on a road leading away from all the shooting.

Vance said, 'They didn't want to kill us before, just scare the shit out of us or intimidate us or who the hell knows what. But now it seems pretty clear they want us gone. So what changed?'

Robie didn't answer. He just stared straight ahead. But finally, *finally*, he might have something.

ROBIE DIRECTED VANCE to his hideaway farmhouse. At his demand, she had turned off the GPS chip in her phone.

'You have to go off grid,' said Robie. 'You OK with that?'

'I have no problem going off grid so long as there's a plan.'

'What changed was Julie came up with the right answer.'

'What answer?' Julie asked.

'As soon as you said it, the red dot appeared on your chest. That's when we both might've become expendable.'

Vance looked at Julie. 'What did you say?'

'That my dad and Mr Broome and Rick Wind were part of a squad. And a squad has nine or ten soldiers in it. So maybe they talked to someone else in the squad. I mean, if the three of them kept in touch, maybe some others did, too.'

Robie nodded and looked at Vance. 'So the safe house wasn't just unsafe. It was also bugged. The second Julie said that, the dot appeared.'

Vance said, 'You think that might be it? The other members of the squad?'

Robie nodded. 'I think we need to find out fast.'

'You can get that info pretty quickly from DCIS.'

'I could. But DCIS has been infiltrated.'

Vance thought about this. 'And the Bureau was infiltrated, too.'

'I know someone who might be able to help,' Robie said. 'An old friend. But I have to leave you to go and see him,'

'Do you think it's a good idea to split up?' asked Vance.

'No,' he replied. 'But it's the only way this will work.'

ROBIE GOT THEM SETTLED in the house, showed Vance where things were, set the alarm and perimeter security, then strode out to the barn. He climbed on his motorcycle.

The building he arrived at nearly thirty minutes later had a high fence running round it. There was a guard in uniform posted out front. Robie had called ahead. He was on the list. He had his proper creds. The guard let him pass through after doing a thorough search.

A few minutes later, he was walking down the only hall the building had. Doors on the left and right led off from this main artery. They were all closed. The hour was late. There wouldn't be many people here.

But there was at least one. The one he wanted. The man who had held Robie's position before Robie had.

He stopped at one door, knocked. A man in his mid-fifties with white, close-cropped hair stood before him. He ushered Robie in. The room was small, efficiently laid out. The man sat behind his desk, on which was a small laptop.

'It's been a while, Will,' said Shane Connors.

'I've been kind of busy, Shane.'

Robie took ten minutes to walk him through the recent developments. When he was done, the other man leaned back in his chair.

'I can get the squad make-up right now. But once you get that, what are your plans?'

'To follow it up. There's a maximum of seven of them left. Local ones will be the focus, of course.'

Connors leaned towards his laptop, hit some keys, and then sat back. 'Give it ten minutes.' He continued to look at Robie. 'It's been twelve years for you.'

'I know. I've been counting, too.'

Connors said, 'Looked down the road yet?'

'I've been looking down the road since the first day.'

'And?'

'And there are certain possibilities, but nothing more than that.'

Connors looked disappointed by this, but he said nothing.

When the email fell into the electronic mailbox, Connors printed the papers out. He passed them to Robie.

'I need a car. Untraceable,' said Robie. 'I can leave my bike as collateral.'

Connors nodded. 'It'll take two minutes.' He made a call. Two minutes passed. The computer dinged. Connors nodded. 'Done.'

'I appreciate this, Shane.'

As Robie turned to leave, Connors said, 'Will, when you look down the road, look further than a place like this.'

Robie glanced around the office, settled his gaze back on the man and gave a slight nod. Then he was walking down the hall, the papers clutched in his hand.

BEFORE STARTING UP THE CAR, a tan Chevy, Robie looked at the pieces of paper. There were three names, the only surviving members of the squad. All lived locally. That made Robie's job a little easier. Also included were their current addresses and a brief military history of each. The military kept impeccable records.

As he retraced his route back to Virginia, he thought about Connors in his little cage. Connors had taught Robie pretty much everything he knew: the man was a legend in the field of sanctioned assassinations. There were a few men who could not be bought under any circumstances. Shane Connors was one of them.

Robie got back to the farmhouse early in the morning. Vance had seen the car pull up. 'Where'd you get it?' she asked, motioning to the car.

He held up the pieces of paper. 'Same place I got these.'

They sat, looked over the names and addresses.

'Two guys and one woman,' said Vance. 'How do you want to do this? Split up again?'

'Don't think so. They've been warned by Julie's comments.'

'So they'll anticipate we'll go after these folks, and they'll be waiting?'

'Maybe something a little more efficient. Maybe they'll make all three disappear, except if they need one of them to do something.'

'Like what?'

'If I knew that, I wouldn't be sitting here trying to figure it out.'

'What do we do with Julie? We can't leave her here. And it would be really stupid to take her on something like this.'

'It might be stupid, but I'm going anyway.'

They glanced over to see Julie standing in the doorway.

Vance said, 'Boy, you're really good at eavesdropping.'

Julie retorted, 'It's the only way I find out anything with you two.'

Robie said, 'It's dangerous.'

'What else is new?' Julie replied in an even tone. She sat at the table. 'I've been shot at, nearly blown up, seen my parents killed, chased on foot, chased by car. So really, your "dangerous" argument falls pretty flat.'

'So the logic is, since you've nearly been killed a few times, the smart thing is to put you in another situation where you'll probably get killed?' said Robie.

'I want to find out why my parents were murdered. That's all. Anything more than that, I don't care.' She looked at Vance and then at Robie. 'So don't feel you have to care about what happens to me. Because you don't.'

'We're trying to help you, Julie,' exclaimed Vance.

'I'm not your little do-gooder project, OK? Foster kid off the street you want to make all well and good. Forget it.'

'You're stuck with us, Julie, whether you want to be or not. And if it weren't for us, you'd be dead,' said Robie.

'I feel like I'm already dead. Why should I trust anybody?'

'I think we've earned your trust,' Robie snapped.

'Well, think again,' Julie shot back, and left the room.

Robie said to Vance, 'Can you believe that crap?'

Vance stared across the table at him. 'She's just a kid, Robie. She's lost her parents and she's scared.'

Robie immediately calmed. 'I know.'

'We have to stick together to get through this.'

'Might be easier said than done. Your loyalty should be to the FBI, Vance. Not me.'

'Why don't you let me decide that for myself?' She put a hand over his. 'And me being here shows exactly where my loyalties lie.'

Robie stared at her for a moment and then got up and walked out, leaving a surprised Vance staring after him. He went into the barn, uncovered a box on the workbench, and took out a pack of cigarettes. He lit up and put the filter to his mouth.

Lung cancer slow or bullet fast. What's the real difference?

He left the barn and stared up at the farmhouse. There were two lights on inside. One room where Julie was. One room where Vance was. He was separated from them by fifty feet.

He was separated from them by about fifty light-years.

I am a killer. I end lives.

He turned and pulled his gun so fast Vance threw up her hands.

He eased down his gun. 'I thought you were in the house.'

'I decided to check on you.'

He holstered his weapon but said nothing.

She moved closer. 'You know, I understand guys who keep it all bottled up inside. The silent, stoic warrior. The FBI sure as hell has enough of them. But it does get old after a while. And a little grating, particularly at times like these.'

Robie looked away. 'I'm not like anybody at the FBI, Vance. I kill people.

I'm ordered to do it. But I carry out those orders. No remorse. No nothing.'

She said, 'So why didn't you kill Jane Wind and her son? Why did you take the time to get her other child to safety? And you did it while people were trying to kill you. Explain that to me.'

'Why do you care?'

'It just seems that I do. I swore an oath of loyalty to you back there. But it didn't seem to register. I wasn't expecting you to jump up and cheer when I put you above the FBI and my professional career, but I did expect some type of positive reaction. Instead, you walked out.'

Robie turned and started to walk back towards the house.

'Do you always walk away when the questions get tough?' she snapped. 'I expected better from you.'

He turned back round, settled his hands in his pockets and took several shallow breaths.

Vance walked towards him. 'I thought I came here to be part of something. Please don't tell me I was wrong about that.'

Robie glanced at the house. 'Julie's only a kid. She's in way over her head. She shouldn't be involved in this at all.'

Vance said, 'But you're a killer, Robie. So why do you care what happens to her? It's just another job.'

'But she shouldn't die. She deserves to have a life.'

'Pretty weird statement for a cold-blooded killer to make.'

'OK, Vance, I get your point.'

She pointed at the house. 'Let's go and work on the plan. All of us.'

Robie started to walk towards the house again. He said, 'Whatever happens, Julie is going to survive this.'

Vance said, 'For what it's worth, I'll do all I can to make sure you do, too.'

ROBIE STARED at the three names as he drank his coffee at the kitchen table. Jerome Cassidy. Gabriel Siegel. Elizabeth Claire Van Beuren—she had incorporated her maiden name, Claire, into her married name, Van Beuren.

He could hear the shower running upstairs and figured Vance had just stepped into it. Julie was in the back room, brooding.

Fifteen minutes later, Vance and Julie were seated across from him. He pushed the pieces of paper at Julie. 'Recognise any of these names?'

She took her time looking at the list. 'No. My parents never mentioned any of them.'

Robie eyed the list. 'Siegel is closest. We'll go there first.'

'OK,' said Vance. 'What does his military history tell us?'

'He was the staff sergeant. The leader of the squad. Fifty years old now. Out of the service for years.'

Julie pulled out the phone Robie had given her. 'Let me see if Google can tell us anything.'

She waited for the data to load. 'Mr Siegel has a Facebook page. It says he was in the army during Gulf One, and he's even listed the name of the squad he was in. According to his profile, he works at SunTrust Bank as a branch manager.'

'Lots of SunTrust branches around here,' said Vance.

'What about Cassidy?' said Robie.

Julie hit some keys. 'Quite a few Jerome Cassidys. I don't see any that list military service or the address that's given for him.'

'Try Van Beuren. That's not such a common name,' said Vance.

Julie did so. The page loaded. 'A lot more than one would think,' she said. 'It'll take a while to go through these.'

'We don't have a while,' said Robie. 'We need to hit this now.'

He had pulled the car into the barn. Earlier, he had loaded it with gear he thought they might need from the bunker underneath the barn. He showed Vance the firepower in the back seat. She touched an MP-5, and gazed at a Barrett rifle that could punch a hole in an armoured Hummer.

'Where'd you get stuff like that?' she asked. 'Never mind, I don't want to know,' she added, quickly.

Robie took out three armoured vests and put one on Julie.

'It's heavy,' she said.

'Better than taking the bullet it'll stop,' replied Vance.

They got in the car, Robie gunned the engine and, after closing the big barn door behind them, drove towards the road.

IT WAS A QUIET, tree-lined street with modest-sized houses. Robie slowed his car and checked the addresses. Vance saw it first.

'Third one on the right,' she said. 'There's a van in the driveway. Hopefully, someone's home.'

Robie eased over to the kerb and surveyed the area.

'We're way out in the open here,' he said.

'No surprise,' replied Vance. 'I'll go. You cover me.'

Robie and Julie watched as Vance rang the doorbell. The front door opened and Robie fixed his gaze on the woman standing there. Vance showed her creds, they spoke for about a minute, and then Vance walked quickly back to the car.

'Gabriel Siegel works at a SunTrust branch about ten minutes from here. Got the address from his wife. She's probably calling her husband as we speak. So let's get going.'

They reached the bank branch in less than ten minutes. Robie asked for Gabriel Siegel and was shown back to a glass-enclosed cubicle about ten feet square.

Siegel was about five-eight, stocky and pale. He rose from the chair behind his desk and asked, 'What's this about?'

His wife had obviously called him.

Robie said, 'You were in an army squad in Gulf One?'

'Yeah, so?'

'I'm interested in the people you served with. You keep in touch with any of them?'

'*Exactly* what is this about?'

'It's a national security issue. It might be tied to the bus explosion and the deaths of people at a restaurant on Capitol Hill.'

Siegel turned pale. 'Jesus. Somebody from my old squad was involved in that? I can't believe it.'

'Which of them have you kept in touch with?'

Siegel said slowly, 'Doug Biddle, Fred Alvarez, Bill Thompson and Ricky Jones died. Years back. We would call each other. Fred got killed in a car accident. Billy put a gun in his mouth, and Doug and Ricky both had cancer.'

'Any of your old buddies locally that you hang with?'

'I saw Leo Broome a few times. That was ten years ago. In the Middle East, I was closest to Curtis Getty. But I haven't seen him since we got back stateside.'

'Anyone else? Rick Wind, for instance?'

'I read that he had been murdered. Is that what this is about?'

'Had you been in contact with Wind?'

'Not for years. Used to see him. But he'd gotten strange. Bought a pawn-shop in a crummy neighbourhood. I don't know. It was just different.'

'How about Jerome Cassidy?'

'Nope. Haven't heard from him since we left the army.'

'Elizabeth Van Beuren? Her maiden name was—'

'Elizabeth Claire. I know. Lizzie was a better soldier than I was, I can tell you that.'

'But she's no longer in the army,' said Robie.

'Well, there's a good reason for that,' replied Siegel. 'Cancer. Started in her breasts and then it spread. She's terminal. She's at a hospice centre in Gainesville.'

'You've seen her?'

'Went regularly until about a month ago. She was in and out of it. Mostly out. Morphine. I'm not even sure if she's still alive. I should have kept up, but it was just too hard to see her like that.'

'What's the name of the place?'

'Central Hospice Care. It's off Route 29. I'm telling you, it's all the crap we breathed in over there. Depleted uranium, toxic cocktails from all the artillery blasts. And there we were, just sucking it in.'

'Thanks for your help.' Robie handed Siegel a card. 'Anything else occurs to you, give me a call.'

THEY PULLED INTO the parking lot of the hospice twenty minutes later. Robie pulled into a space and looked at Vance.

'You want to do this one or should I?'

Julie said, 'I want to go in. Maybe she knew something about my dad.'

'She's probably not in much condition to talk,' said Vance.

'Then why are we even here?' asked Julie.

Robie said to Vance, 'I'll take her in with me. You keep watch.'

The hospice building was a two-storey brick structure with lots of windows and a cheery atmosphere. It did not look like a place where people came to die.

The flash of Robie's creds got them escorted to Elizabeth Van Beuren's room. There were flowers on the windowsill and light was streaming in. A nurse was checking on Van Beuren.

The critically ill woman looked like a skeleton and was on a ventilator, the machine inflating her lungs via a tube inserted down her throat. There was a feeding tube inserted into her abdomen, and multiple IV lines running to her.

The nurse turned to them. 'Can I help you?'

'We came to ask Ms Van Beuren some questions,' said Robie. 'But it doesn't look like that's possible.'

'She was put on the ventilator six days ago. She's on heavy painkillers.'

'I'm with the DOD. We were making some enquiries into a military matter and her name came up as a possible source.'

'Well, I don't think she'll be of much help. She's in the last stages of her disease.'

Julie had wandered over to the windowsill and picked up a photo. She said to the nurse, 'My dad was in the same army squad as Mrs Van Beuren. I was hoping to find out some things about his past from her.'

'Oh, I see, sweetie. I didn't realise. That's her and her family.'

Robie took the photo. It showed Van Beuren in healthier days in her dress greens, her chest awash with medals. A man was beside her, presumably her husband, and a girl about Julie's age.

'So that's her husband?' asked Robie.

'Yes. George Van Beuren. And that's their daughter, Brooke. She's in college now. They come here regularly.'

'Anybody else come to see her?'

'A few people.'

'You have a guest log?'

'It's out front by the receptionist. But not everyone signs in.'

'Why not?'

'People who come here to visit friends and family are usually very upset. Sometimes they forget to sign in, or one person signs in for the group. As you can imagine, we're a bit flexible on that.'

'Understood. How long has she been here?'

'Four months.'

'Isn't that a long time to be in hospice?'

'We have people here for longer and shorter periods. And, until a couple of weeks or so ago, Ms Van Beuren wasn't like she is now.'

'But the ventilator will keep her alive so long as it's on, right? I mean, even if she can't breathe on her own?'

The nurse seemed uncomfortable. 'Normally the use of a ventilator would decertify a person for hospice care. We're not a place where someone goes to be cured of her disease, or to artificially sustain life.'

'So the use of the ventilator in a situation like this is unusual?'

'It could be grounds for decertification and the transfer of the patient back to a hospital or other care facility,' said the nurse, carefully.

'So why the ventilator?' asked Robie. 'Does she have a chance of pulling through?'

'Even if I knew, I couldn't tell you. Federal and state law prohibits me from doing so. What I can tell you is that sometimes families reach a point where they have false hope.' The nurse looked at Julie. 'I'm sorry that she couldn't tell you anything about your father.'

Julie reached over and touched Van Beuren's hand. 'I'm sorry,' she said to the dying woman.

Then she turned and left. Robie handed his card to the nurse. 'If her husband comes in, can you have him give me a call?'

IT TOOK OVER AN HOUR to get to Jerome Cassidy's place in Arlington because traffic was bad. It was nearly lunchtime when Robie found a parking space and pulled into it. He turned to Vance.

'You sure this is the place?'

She held up the page and he read it off. All three of them turned to look at the building.

'It's a bar and grill,' said Julie.

Robie looked up. 'But there seem to be rooms above it. Maybe Cassidy lives in one of them.'

Vance undid her seat belt. 'My turn,' she said.

'Let's all go in on this one,' said Robie.

'What about the car?' Vance asked.

'I got this car from a special source, which means it has some special defensive devices.'

'Like what?'

'Like if someone tries to break into it or booby-trap it, it will not be a fun time for them. And we will most certainly know about it.'

The name of the bar was the Texas Hold 'Em Saloon. It was decorated in a western theme. At the far end of the space was an enormous bar that spanned the entire width of the interior. Behind the bar, a large Texas flag hung on the wall. All around the flag were stacked hundreds of libations designed to wet the whistle, lighten the wallet and dull the senses.

'Somebody spent a lot of cash on this place,' commented Robie.

A young woman in a cowboy hat approached them. 'Hi, I'm Tina,' she said. 'Party of three?'

'We were given this address for a friend of ours. Jerome Cassidy. You know him?'

'Mr Cassidy is the owner.'

Vance held out her cred pack. 'FBI. Could you take us to where he is?'

The woman looked at them nervously. 'Is Mr Cassidy in some sort of trouble? He's a great boss.'

'We just want to talk to him,' said Robie. 'Lead the way.'

She walked past the bar and down a short hallway. She stopped at a door marked 'Office' and timidly knocked.

'Mr Cassidy? I have some people who want to talk to you.'

'Then tell them to make an appointment.'

Robie moved past Tina and tried to open the door. It was locked. He pounded on the door. 'It's the FBI. Open the door. Now!'

He heard shuffling and a drawer slamming. He moved back and then drilled his right foot against the door knob. The door flew inwards. Robie moved into the room first, with Vance covering him.

Cassidy was standing behind his desk. He was about Robie's height, with broad shoulders. He said, 'You want to tell me why you broke my door and are pointing a gun at me?'

'You want to tell me why you didn't open it?'

Cassidy glanced at Robie's gun. Then he stared over at Vance as she moved into the room. 'Let me see your creds, right now.'

Robie and Vance held them out.

Cassidy read them carefully and picked up a pen and wrote their names and badge numbers down on the white blotter on his desk. 'Just want to get the info right for my lawyers when they sue your asses.'

'You didn't open the door, Mr Cassidy,' pointed out Vance.

'I was just fixing to when you broke it open.' Cassidy looked at Robie. 'You're DCIS.'

'You know DCIS?'

'I was in the army. So what?' He sat down behind his desk.

Robie looked around the office. It was high-dollar decorated. And there was a shelf full of business awards against one wall.

'You look to be pretty successful. Bar must do well.'

'This bar is one of twenty businesses I own. All of them are highly profitable, and I don't have one dime of debt.'

'Good for you,' said Robie. 'We're here about your old army squad.'

Cassidy looked genuinely surprised. 'What the hell for?'

'You keep in touch with any of them?'

Cassidy saw Julie peering round the corner of the doorway. He slowly rose. 'Come on in here, girl.'

She stepped into the office.

'Closer,' said Cassidy. 'Damn. You're Julie, aren't you? I knew your parents real well. How they doing?'

Robie said, 'How do you know them?'

'Like you said, the squad. Curtis Getty and me served together. Saved my ass a couple times in Gulf One.'

'How did you know I was Julie? I don't think we've ever met.'

'Because you look just like your mother. Same eyes, same dimple, everything. And we *have* met. Only you were just a baby.'

'So you kept in touch with them?' asked Robie.

'Not for a long time. I haven't seen them since Julie turned one.'

'What happened?'

'Folks drift apart.' He eyed Julie. 'Your mom doing OK?'

'No, she's dead.'

'What?'

Robie said, 'She and Curtis were murdered.'

Cassidy dropped into his chair. 'Why? How? Who did it?'

'We were hoping you could help us answer those questions.'

'I haven't seen the Gettys in a long time.'

'Didn't you know they lived in DC?' asked Robie.

'No. They were in Pennsylvania last time I saw them. Near Pittsburgh. I lived with them for a while, trying to get back on my feet.' He turned to Julie. 'I actually knew your mom before she met your dad. They got married while he was still in uniform. I was at the wedding.'

Robie noted Julie's wide-eyed look at all this new information.

Cassidy continued. 'After Gulf One, I got into some bad stuff. They helped me out.'

'Drugs?' asked Robie.

'I wasn't the one into drugs,' said Cassidy, quietly, looking away from Julie.

'I know my parents had drug problems,' said Julie. 'Especially my dad.'

'He was a good man, Julie,' said Cassidy. 'Like I said, he saved my butt over in the desert. Earned himself the Bronze with valour. A Purple, too. When we were in uniform, he never touched even a drop of liquor. But after we came back we were all changed. The war wasn't that long, but we saw some serious stuff over there. Lots of deaths, mostly civilians, women, kids. And lots of guys came back messed up or sick. Anyway, your daddy started using. Your mom tried to get him straight, but never could. And then she fell into that crap, too. Hard as hell to get out of that hole once you're in it.'

'And what was your vice?' Vance asked.

'I was a drunk,' said Cassidy, frankly.

'And yet you own a bar?' said Robie.

'Best way to test yourself on a daily basis. I'm surrounded by the stuff, and I haven't touched a drop of it in over a decade.'

'Julie's fourteen. So about thirteen years ago was the last time you saw the Gettys?' asked Vance.

Robie looked around the office. 'The Gettys were down on their luck. Might've been good if you'd helped them out.'

Cassidy said, 'Would've been glad to. If I could've found them.' He opened a safe and pulled out a stack of letters. 'I wrote to your parents, Julie, over the years. All returned unopened, addressee unknown. I spent a lot of time and money trying to find you all.'

Robie looked at the letters. 'Lot of effort went into those.'

'They were my friends. Curtis saved my life.'

'Do you remember Gabriel Siegel and Elizabeth Claire?'

'Yeah, I do. How are they doing?'

'Not so great, actually. How about Rick Wind?'

'He was a good guy. Fine soldier.'

'He's dead now, too. So is Leo Broome.'

Cassidy stood and slapped his desktop. 'All these people from my old squad have been killed?'

'The mortality rate is higher than we'd like to see,' said Vance.

'Should I be worried?' asked Cassidy.

'I think everyone should be worried,' replied Robie.

TRAFFIC WAS BAD again heading west, and it was over ninety minutes later when they were seated at the table in the farmhouse kitchen.

'Let's go through it again.' Robie looked at Vance. 'Your turn.'

'OK, let's start by ruling some people out. I don't see how Van Beuren can be involved in any of this. She's been in hospice for months and she's got a machine breathing for her.'

Robie nodded. 'Siegel seems to be just as clueless. He seemed genuinely surprised when I told him why I wanted to talk to him.'

'Maybe you were wrong, Robie,' remarked Vance. 'You said it was what Julie mentioned about the other squad members that caused them to try and kill her. It doesn't appear to be the case.'

Robie said, 'But what about Cassidy? I don't personally buy the fact that he couldn't find the Gettys. Or that he didn't know that any of his other squad members were around. The guy has cash, and cash gets you results. And while he seemed genuinely surprised that Curtis and Sara were dead, it just seems pretty odd.'

Julie said, 'Mom and Dad never mentioned him. That's odd, too, considering how close he said they were. Why didn't they answer his letters?'

Vance was about to say something when her phone buzzed. 'Hello?'

The person on the other end of the line started speaking fast. Vance pulled out a notepad. 'OK, I'll be right over.'

She clicked off. 'That was Gabriel Siegel's wife. I left my contact info with her. Her husband got a phone call just after you left him. He walked out of the bank right afterwards and never came back. He's disappeared.'

SIEGEL'S WIFE WAS WAITING at her door as they pulled into the driveway. The woman looked at Robie strangely until she saw Vance behind him.

'We're partners,' Vance said. 'Robie, this is Alice Siegel.'

'Mrs Siegel, we're here to help find your husband.'

Alice Siegel nodded, her eyes brimming with tears. When she caught sight of Julie, she looked confused. 'Who is she?'

'It's not something we can go into right now, ma'am. Can we go inside?'

Alice let them pass through into the house. They settled in chairs around the living room.

Vance opened the conversation. 'So, you said your husband received a phone call and then walked out. Did it come to his line at the bank or his cellphone?'

'His office line.'

'Didn't someone at the bank ask who was calling?'

'I guess the person who answered just assumed Gabe would want the call. It was a man.'

'Have you tried calling his cellphone?' said Robie.

'Twenty times. I texted him, too. Nothing. I'm very worried.'

'Can you think of any reason why your husband would just up and walk off like that?' asked Vance.

She eyed Vance suspiciously. 'Well, *you* came to talk to him. And then he disappeared. Maybe you can tell me the reason.'

'Your husband was in the army during Gulf One. We wanted to ask if he'd been in touch with anyone from his old squad,' said Robie.

'He kept in touch with Elizabeth Van Beuren. She's dying.'

'We know that,' said Vance. 'Anybody else he mentioned?'

'Leo Broome? Rick Wind? Curtis Getty?' prompted Robie.

'Getty, yes. Gabe said they had been close, but he hadn't seen him since he'd come back. The thing is, Gabe didn't talk much about his military time. He was terrified that he was going to die because of the toxic conditions they fought in. After Elizabeth got sick, he went into depression. He was convinced he would be next.'

Julie said, 'You mentioned he and Curtis Getty were friends. Did he have any pictures of them together?'

Robie and Vance looked at Julie. Robie felt immediate guilt. He had never stopped to consider how all of this talk must have been affecting the teenager.

Alice looked momentarily flustered. 'I believe he does. Hold on for a moment.' She left the room and a couple of minutes later came back holding an envelope of photos.

Julie said, 'There's my dad!'

The group was standing in front of a burned-out Iraqi tank. Curtis Getty was on the far right, dressed in combat fatigues, a pistol clenched in his right hand. He looked young and happy. Next to him was Jerome Cassidy. His shirt was off and he looked tanned, lean and muscular. Elizabeth Claire looked tougher than all of them. She stared at the camera with a serious expression.

Alice said, 'That's Gabe on the far left there.'

Siegel seemed confident, even cocky. *These days, he's a shell of the man in the photo*, thought Robie.

'I don't know why my husband's military service would come up now, after all these years.'

'Does he have anything else connected to his time in the army?'

'Not that I know of. He brought some things back. His helmet, boots and other things. But he got rid of them.'

'Why?' asked Vance.

Alice looked surprised by the question. 'He thought they were toxic, of course.'

WHEN THEY RETURNED to the farmhouse, Vance called in to the FBI and got an earful for going off grid. After her superior finished his tirade, Vance asked him to trace the phone call Gabriel Siegel had received at the bank. He called back twenty minutes later. Disposable phone, dead end. He ordered Vance to come in to the office.

Robie overheard this part of the conversation. When Vance started to refuse, he grabbed her arm, his gaze going upwards to where Julie had gone to use the bathroom. He said, 'Go, and take Julie with you. Take her to WFO and surround her with firepower. Then you can come back and hook up with me.'

Vance studied him warily, distrust in her eyes.

The voice squawked from the phone.

'I'll be in directly,' she said into the phone. 'I'll be bringing Julie Getty with me. I hope we can do a better job of protecting her than we did last time.'

She clicked off and gazed at Robie with a searching look. 'If you're screwing with me . . .'

'Get Julie settled and then come back here.'

'And you'll just be here, waiting for me?' she asked, sceptically.

'If I'm not here, you have my phone number.'

'I don't believe this, Robie. You're shutting me out—'

'What's going on?' Julie peered over the stair rail at them.

Vance sighed. 'Come on, Julie. We need to get out of here.'

Robie watched as the Beemer careened down the road away from him. He was better alone than with a team. It was just how he was built. He felt an immediate freedom.

He drove from his mind the promise that he had made to Julie to let her help in finding out what had happened to her parents. Fulfilling it, he told himself, would only end up getting the girl killed.

It didn't really matter one way or another to Robie. He kept telling himself that as he prepared to finish what he had started.

This is about me. And it's also about something bigger.

Now he had to find out what that was.

Chapter 8

The first stop was to the bank. Robie talked to the employees but they had no helpful information. Gabriel Siegel had left his briefcase, which indicated that his hasty exit had been unplanned and not related to business. His car was still in the parking lot. Robie searched it but found nothing useful.

Next stop was the hospice. He had forgotten something when he was there before. The guestbook.

The receptionist let him look at it. While she was attending to something else, he took photos of the pages for the last month or so.

Nothing much had changed in Elizabeth Van Beuren's room. She was still in bed with a pipe down her throat, hanging on to life.

Robie picked up the family photo on the windowsill and stared at it. At some point in his life, Robie had supposed he could have had a family like this. Annie Lambert's face appeared in his thoughts. He shook his head clear. He just didn't see how something like that was possible.

He set off for Jerome Cassidy's bar and ordered a beer. He asked for Cassidy. The man came out a few minutes later and approached Robie, an uncertain look on his face.

He eyed the beer like it was a stick of TNT about to go off.

'Like to talk to you about Julie,' said Robie.

'What about her?'

'You planning on telling her you're her father?'

'Let's go sit.'

Cassidy led him over to a booth in a corner. They settled in their seats as Cassidy said, 'How the hell did you know?'

'Guys don't write bundles of letters to "friends", especially guy friends. You don't spend time and money tracking them down. And I saw how your face lit up when Julie walked in. You hadn't seen her since she was a baby, but you instantly knew. Not that hard to figure out, actually. There may be a lot of her mother in Julie, but there's some of you, too.'

Cassidy blew out a long breath and nodded. 'Think she knows?'

'No, I don't. Why don't you tell me what happened?'

'Not much to tell. I cared for Sara before she was married to Curtis. Then Curtis came along. Love at first sight. I didn't feel bitter about it. I didn't love Sara like Curtis did. And, like I said, he saved my life. He was a good guy.'

'But Julie?'

'Stupid last roll in the bed. Curtis thought Julie was his. Sara knew better. I knew better. But I never said a word. There was no way I could take care of a kid. It was an easy out for me, you see.'

Cassidy eyed the full beer.

Robie said, 'You want it?'

'I do want it, but no.'

'Not so easy now?'

'Older you get, the more regrets pile on you. I wanted to see what sort of person Julie had become. By then I'd left Pennsylvania. By the time I got around to trying to find them, they'd left, too. Looked everywhere except right here.' He paused. 'What's going on here? Feds involved. People getting killed. Julie in the middle of it.'

'Can't tell you. What I can tell you is that Julie will need a friend after this is over.'

'I want to help. You think I should tell her?'

'I'm not sure I'm the best person to advise you on that. Never been married. Never had any kids.'

'Well, let's assume you are the best person. What would you advise?'

'She loved her parents. She wanted their lives to be better than they were. She wants to find out why they were killed. She wants to avenge them.'

'So you're saying not to tell her?'

'You're the only one who can really make the call.' Robie stood and eyed the beer. 'And you're going to make it.'

Cassidy stared at him. 'Why?'

'You turn down a perfectly good beer under these circumstances, you can turn it down under any circumstances.'

ROBIE DIDN'T KNOW WHY he had gone back there. It was the apartment across the street. After leaving Cassidy, he'd ridden to the scene of the bus explosion, then over to Donnelly's, which was still closed. Now he was here, and he wasn't sure why.

He looked through the telescope and his condo building came into focus.

He shifted the viewing angle to Annie Lambert's place. She was padding down the hall in her work gear. Robie lost her but picked her back up again about a minute later. She'd taken her blouse off and replaced it with a sweatshirt. Part of him wanted to go over and see her. Then he saw her lift up a long black dress on a hanger which had been draped over a chair. It was a strapless gown. Annie was going out on the town tonight, it seemed. Part of him felt jealous. It was an odd emotion for him.

He sat down and drew out his phone. He brought up the photos he'd taken of the guest register at the hospice and scrolled from screen to screen, not expecting to find much of interest. The only name he recognised was Gabriel Siegel from about a month before. Then something caught his eye. There was an entire day missing. He enlarged the screen and spied the remains of a page that had been ripped out of the book.

Why would someone have taken a page? There could only be one answer. They wanted to cover up whoever's name had been written there. What if Broome or Getty or Wind had visited Van Beuren while she was still lucid? And she had let slip something that had led to all three of them having to be silenced?

Robie looked at the dates. Eight days ago. That would fit with the timeline. Wind had been the first to die—he might have been killed shortly after he had visited Van Beuren.

And that would explain the heated discussion that the waitress at the diner had witnessed. Broome had told Getty. He then might've told Wind. Or it could have been the other way around. Robie couldn't know for sure without seeing which of them had visited. No chance had been taken. Husbands, wives and an ex-wife—who was also a potentially dangerous government lawyer—had had to be killed.

Robie's mind next drew to the ventilator. It kept a terminally ill woman alive but it also prevented her from saying anything. They had put the tube in her to shut the poor woman up. But whatever she had told her former squad members had been the reason they had been killed.

Robie raced out of his apartment.

VISITING HOURS WERE OVER, but Robie's repeated, urgent raps on the glass door brought an attendant. He flashed his badge. 'I need to see Elizabeth Van Beuren.'

'That's not possible,' said the attendant.

The nurse Robie had spoken to before came forward. 'So you're back?' She was clearly not pleased. 'Ms Van Beuren passed about three hours ago. The ventilator tube was removed.'

'Who ordered the tube removed?'

'Her doctor.'

'I'll need his name and number, right now.'

Robie called the doctor who said, 'Mr Van Beuren had the medical power of attorney.'

'So he told you to remove it. Was it by phone or did he come here in person?'

'By phone.'

'Strange that he didn't want to be here when his wife died.'

'Frankly, Agent Robie, I thought the same thing.'

Robie called Vance but got her voicemail. He next called Blue Man but he didn't answer, either.

Robie raced down the hall to Van Beuren's room. He picked up the photo and looked at George Van Beuren. Short hair, muscular physique. Robie wondered if he was maybe military.

The nurse had followed him. 'Is this really necessary?'

'Did you ever see George Van Beuren wearing a uniform?'

'No. He just dressed normally.'

'I'll need his home address.'

'We can't give out that information.'

Robie took a long stride until he was within a couple of inches of her. 'If you have information that might be able to stop an attack against this country and you don't provide it to a federal officer who has requested it, you're going to prison, for a long time.'

The woman gasped, then said, 'Follow me.'

THE VAN BEURENS lived about twenty minutes from the hospice. Robie made it there in fifteen.

The house was dark but one vehicle was parked in the driveway. Robie stopped his car at the kerb, pulled out his pistol and crept towards the house. He hurried round to the back. Putting his elbow carefully through the glass in the back door, he reached through and turned the lock. He pulled out a flashlight and made his way through the house. He ended up in the front room and shined his light around. It hit on various objects on walls and shelves. He picked up a photo of the Van Beurens. Mother, daughter and father.

George Van Beuren was in uniform, a very distinctive one. White shirt, dark pants, dark cap. The uniform of the United States Secret Service Uniformed Division. George Van Beuren helped to guard the President of the United States.

And then, in a flash of synapses, Robie finally made the connection. He was watching Annie Lambert walking down the hall. He had lost her for about thirty seconds. But then regained her. She had changed clothes in those few seconds. Robie took his mind back to that airplane hangar in Morocco. Through his scope, he had watched Khalid bin Talal climb the steps to his jet. After that he had lost sight of the prince for a brief period. And then he had regained him as the Saudi walked down the aisle of the plane.

That's when Robie had noticed the straps round the prince's middle holding on his body armour. But the prince had not been wearing body armour before he got on the plane: Robie would have seen the outline of the armoured vest under the robes. And it took longer than a few moments to put on, especially if one was wearing a long robe and was heavy in the belly.

What had happened was now clear. Talal had been warned about a possible hit. He had employed a double to take his place at the meeting. Maybe he thought the Russian and the Palestinian would try to kill him. Maybe he suspected a traitor in his inner circle or a sniper like Robie waiting to take his shot. He had outsmarted them all. He had had his double die in his place.

Robie thought back to the conversation he had overheard that night. *Something that everyone assumed was pointless to try. The weakest link. Willing to die.* There could only be one possible target. The President of the United States.

Now the theft of the Secret Service SUV made sense. They had someone on the inside. They had George Van Beuren. And the fact that they had let Elizabeth Van Beuren die told Robie that the time to make the attempt was right now.

Then Robie remembered something Annie Lambert had told him. When the president got back to DC, there was going to be a big event at the White House.

He pulled out his phone, did a quick Internet search. Tonight, the president would be entertaining the crown prince of Saudi Arabia.

Talal was multi-tasking tonight. He was going for both men.

ROBIE WAS HALFWAY TO DC when he finally reached Blue Man on his cellphone. In terse sentences, he told him about his latest deductions. Blue Man's response was equally terse. He would meet Robie at the White House with back-up.

Twenty minutes later, Robie slid his car to the kerb, jumped out and ran. He was on Pennsylvania Avenue heading to the front gates of the White House. He looked at his watch. Nearly eleven. He imagined the party would be winding down by now. And, if the attempt hadn't occurred yet, it would have to shortly.

He spied Blue Man and a group of men, a mixture of FBI, Secret Service and the Department of Homeland Security. He ran up to them. 'Do they know where Van Beuren is?'

Blue Man said, 'They're hunting for him now, but we don't want to show that we're suspicious. Van Beuren may not be the only asset they have in there.'

A grey-haired, tall man in a suit stared over at Robie. Robie recognised him as the director of the Secret Service.

'You're the one who called this in? I sure as hell hope you're right. Because if you're not . . .'

'If I'm wrong, nothing bad happens.'

The director looked at Blue Man. 'We'll move in through the visitors' entrance. Hopefully, though, they'll snag Van Beuren before we even get in the place.'

'And the president?' asked Robie.

'If Van Beuren is involved he'll know our protocol and may have set an ambush somehow, so we decided to sequester the president in an atypical place—the Family Dining Room—along with the crown prince, the president's staff and some select VIPs. No uniforms are part of the security detail. Van Beuren can't get near him. We did it subtly. Now we just have to find Van Beuren.'

They raced to the visitors' entrance and through the security checkpoint. All uniformed Secret Service had been pulled off interior guard duty and massed in a hallway. Each of them had been questioned. None of them knew where Van Beuren was. He had been assigned to a security perimeter on the lower level. He wasn't there. All rooms on the lower level had been checked.

Robie and the others ran up the stairs to the main level of the White House. As they were walking towards the Family Dining Room, one of the agents with them received a message. 'They found Van Beuren in a storage room,' he said.

They changed direction and quickly reached the room. Van Beuren was on the floor, eyes closed and trussed up. A patch of shiny blood was mixed in with his hair. One of the agents felt for a pulse. 'He's alive, but somebody hit him hard.'

Blue Man said, 'Why knock out and tie up your assassin?'

Robie was the first to spot it. 'His gun is missing.'

All eyes went to the man's holster. The 9-millimetre that should have been there wasn't.

Robie said, 'They just needed his weapon. That way, they didn't have to sneak one past security.' Robie remembered the overheard conversation from Morocco. *Access to weapons. Decades in the making. Willing to die.*

He said, 'The shooter has his gun. They have to be in with the president and the crown prince.'

The director paled. 'You mean part of his staff? Or a guest?'

Robie didn't answer.

THE GROUP MARSHALLED OUTSIDE the door to the State Dining Room, which adjoined the Family Dining Room.

The director said, 'We're going to alert agents inside the room that the shooter is probably in there. They've already formed a hard wall around the president and are awaiting my order to get him out of the room.'

Blue Man said, 'If they do that or start searching people, the assassin will fire. In such close quarters and despite the wall around the president, the bullet might hit its target.'

'We can't just wait and see if the person acts or not,' countered the director. 'Protocol says to move fast. I should have already given the order.'

Robie said, 'How many people in that room total?'

'About fifty,' said one of the agents.

'This could turn into a bloodbath,' said Blue Man.

The director said curtly, 'No one wants that, but my focus is only on the president. We plan to take him out through the chief usher's office and from there to the Entrance Hall.'

Another agent said, 'And the longer we wait, the less chance we have of getting him out of there safely.'

Blue Man said, 'What if there's more than one shooter? You could be leading him directly into an ambush.'

Robie said, 'Van Beuren was found in the West Wing. Did one of the prince's staffers have access to the West Wing tonight? Because Van Beuren's head injury was recent.'

'None of the prince's staffers was near the West Wing.'

Robie said, 'Then the shooter must be someone who works here. The person behind this has lots of money. No one is off-limits. For all we know, he might have bought off a Secret Service agent in there.'

'So what do we do?' asked the director.

Robie said, 'A staffer will know the interior security agents but they won't know me. Let me go in dressed as a waiter under the pretence of bringing in coffee.'

'And then what?' demanded the director.

'I identify the shooter or shooters and take them out.'

'How will you identify the assassin?' snapped the director.

Blue Man spoke up. 'Agent Robie is very adept at spotting assassins, Director.' He drew closer and whispered into the man's ear.

When he had finished, the director gazed at Robie. 'If you fail, the president dies.'

'Yes, sir. But I am prepared to die making sure he doesn't.'

'If I can't alert the agents in there about our plan and you pull your gun, they will shoot you.'

'It's always in the timing, sir.'

The director and Robie locked gazes for a long moment. Then the director said, 'Get him a waiter's uniform and a cart of damn coffee.'

ROBIE WHEELED THE CART into the room. The waiter's uniform they had got for him was for a bigger man. Robie had insisted on this. He couldn't allow a gun bump. He had two pistols, one in his holster, one hidden under the cloth covering the coffee cart. The director had his walkie-talkie ready to order his agents not to fire at Robie if he pulled his gun. Yet he knew that would be an impossible order to give in time. As far as the director was concerned, Robie was a dead man from the moment he walked into the room.

The agents inside had been told that the danger was over but to still maintain the wall around the president. The crown prince and his staff were standing in a corner diagonally across from the president, surrounded by other agents. The thirty-odd White House staffers and other guests were in the middle of the room.

The door was shut behind Robie and he continued to push the cart along. He gridded the room without seeming to do so.

Robie's thoughts went back to the overheard conversation at the plane hangar. *Not a westerner. Decades in the making.* That obviously couldn't be George Van Beuren. He should have realised there had to be a second person.

Robie could see the president in the middle of a wall of agents. But even with that, there were clean shooting lines right to the man if one was close enough. Each agent was looking outward, at possible threats.

He rolled the cart further into the room. He checked the crown prince's corner one more time. If the threat came from there, it would be a difficult shot to hit the president.

He turned his attention to the last group. The staffers stood in the middle of the room. They were all formally dressed. Some of the women carried tiny purses, all too small for Van Beuren's sidearm. The men huddled together. Suits with pockets and maybe a stolen 9-millimetre in one of them. The majority of them appeared to be westerners, but of that Robie couldn't be certain. But there were about a dozen who looked to be from distant places.

Robie fixed his sights on this middle group, equidistant between the two national leaders. This positioning made the most sense if the plan was to kill both men. It was not impossible for someone who knew what he was doing.

I could do it, thought Robie.

It was difficult to fire a gun in close quarters and go unnoticed. Agents would rush forward. People would grab at the person. But the shooter might get off another shot. It was certainly feasible.

And with that thought Robie came to understand the order of targets. *President first. Prince second.*

As people came forward to get their coffees, a group of guests and staffers hung back. Mostly women, Robie noted. Three-inch-heel syndrome. Their feet were probably killing them.

Robie took in the people one by one. And then he stopped. Annie

Lambert was looking back at him. She had a jacket over her strapless dress. Her hair was up. She looked beautiful.

So, this was the reason for the black dress. She had told Robie she would be working an event, but he had failed to make the connection.

He promised himself that whatever happened, he would save her from harm. She would not die tonight.

Her lips were set in a firm line. She obviously recognised Robie. But she did not smile. *She's probably scared*, he thought. For a terrible second, he wondered if she would raise the alarm about him. To her, Robie was an investment banker. Why would he be there, dressed as a waiter? He just had to hope she would not panic from seeing him.

Yet there was a calmness about her that Robie found enviable under the circumstances. His respect for her grew even more. Her eyes were wide and seemed to take in every bit of him in one glance.

Then he saw that her pupils were also dilated. And then she smiled at him in a way she never had before. And, in that moment, Robie saw a side of Annie Lambert he had never suspected even existed.

There was a split second where Robie's mind shut down, as though he'd been struck by lightening. Then his brain fired back up.

He shouted, 'Shooter!' He drew his gun.

With astonishing speed, Lambert pulled the gun from her jacket, aimed and fired, seemingly all in one smooth motion.

The president was only a few feet away. Her shot hit him in the arm instead of the chest. An agent had grabbed him when Robie had shouted. If the president hadn't moved, then his heart would have been pierced by the round instead of his limb.

As Lambert started to point her gun at the prince, Robie's shot hit her directly in the head, the slug embedding in the wall behind her. She fell backwards, hit a table and slid to the floor.

The Secret Service removed the president from the room so fast his blood barely had time to touch the floor.

Robie heard screams, sensed people rushing in and out. But he simply stood there, his gun pointed down, staring silently at Annie Lambert's body.

ROBIE WAS IN A ROOM at the White House. He had been led there and told to wait. He heard people talking in the halls. Occasionally the sound of a siren. None of it made an impression. He only saw Annie Lambert's face, her eyes seemingly too large to be contained in such limited space. He saw the round from his Glock hit her head and end her life. He saw this a hundred times. He could not make his mind turn off the image.

'Agent Robie?'

He saw the director of the Secret Service. Behind him was Blue Man.

'The president would like to personally thank you.'

'How is he?'

'Fine. The hospital released him. Thank God the bullet went clean through his arm. More blood than damage. He'll be fine in no time.'

'That's good,' said Robie. 'But there's no need to thank me. Just doing my job.'

'Robie,' said Blue Man. 'The president is expecting you.'

The president sat behind his desk, his left arm in a sling. He looked shaken, but there was firm resolve in his grip as he shook hands with Robie.

'You saved my life tonight, Agent Robie.'

'I'm just glad you're OK, Mr President.'

'I can't believe that one of my staff was involved. Ms Lambert, I believe. They tell me there was nothing in her background that would have hinted at this.'

'I'm sure it was a surprise to everyone,' replied Robie, dumbly.

Especially me.

'How did you recognise so quickly that it was her?'

'She had taken a drug, to calm her nerves. Suicide bombers often do this. Her pupils were dilated from the drug's action.'

'She was drugged, but could still shoot straight?'

'There are chemicals that relax the nerves, sir, without dulling the other senses. It actually makes you a better shot. Nerves kill the aim faster than anything. And I would assume that even the most gifted assassin would have been nervous tonight.'

'Because they would know they would die,' said the president.

'Yes, sir. And she was close to you, only a few feet away. Her accuracy, of course, was important, but not as critical as her speed.'

'They tell me that if I hadn't been moved I would be dead. And I wouldn't have been moved except for your warning.'

'I wish I could have stopped her before she fired.'

The president smiled and held up his wounded arm. 'I'll take this any day over being dead, Agent Robie.'

As if on cue the president's wife walked in, the night's terror still in her eyes. She swept over to Robie and took his hand in hers.

'Thank you, Agent Robie. Neither of us will ever be able to repay the debt we owe you.'

'You don't owe me anything, ma'am. I wish you both the best.'

A minute later, Robie was walking fast down the hall. It had been as though he couldn't breathe in there. He had reached the front entrance lobby before Blue Man caught up with him.

'Well, at least it's over,' said Blue Man.

'It's not over,' said Robie. 'In fact, in some ways it's just beginning.'

'What are you talking about?'

'It will be in my next report.'

Robie walked out of the front door of the White House and kept going.

It isn't over yet.

IT WAS STILL EARLY in the morning. Robie stared through the telescope to where Annie Lambert had lived. The place would be swarming soon with federal personnel. They would go through every inch of her life. They would find out why she had tried to kill the president. They would discover why she was doing the bidding of a fanatic from the desert world who possessed limitless petrodollars.

Again the words of the Palestinian came back to him: *We own that person. Decades in the making.*

Did they own you, Annie Lambert?

I slept with her right across the street. I had drinks with her. I liked her. I felt sorry for her. I could have maybe come to love her.

Robie knew that Annie Lambert living in the same building as he did was not a coincidence.

This is still about me. She came to live here because of me. Talal wants his revenge. He wanted to mess with my mind. And he'll want it even more since I destroyed his plan.

The phone rang. Nicole Vance's cellphone.

He hit the answer button. He knew what was coming.

'The package will be delivered to your door in thirty seconds. You will follow the instructions completely.'

The connection went dead.

Blue Man had told him, although Robie had figured it out for himself already. Vance and Julie had never made it to the WFO. They had been taken. This was Talal's fail-safe.

He walked slowly to the door and picked up the envelope. He took out the pages. The first ten were photos. Him having drinks with Lambert. Him being kissed by Lambert. Finally, him having sex with Lambert in her bed. He wondered where the camera had been placed for that shot.

Robie dropped the photos on the coffee table and looked at the other pages. He sifted through them. There was nothing surprising here. He had anticipated most, if not all, of it.

It is still very much about me. And Talal wants me back where it all started. The offer was crystal clear. Him for Julie and Vance. He considered it a fair trade. If Talal could be trusted. Which he could not, of course.

Yet Robie would still have to accept it. Much as Talal wanted to end his life, Robie wanted to end Talal's even more. Using Annie Lambert as a vicious tool, Talal had taken something precious from Robie.

He's taken away my ability to ever really trust myself again.

He looked at the photos again. Annie Lambert looked like a beautiful woman with a bright future ahead of her. A nice person, wanting to do some good in the world. She had not been born a killer. She had been raised to become one.

I was not born to be a killer, either, he thought. *But I am one now.*

Robie started to pack. He intended to follow the instructions. At least most of them. For certain key elements, he intended to create his own rules.

Talal had beaten Robie in Morocco.

Robie had bested him in Washington.

The next two days would determine who would be the winner of the third and final round.

WHEN THE FERRY DOCKED in Tangier, Robie boarded one of the tour buses along with a group of other passengers. The bus ride took about twenty minutes and by the time the doors hissed open, rain had begun to fall. While the tour guide took charge of the group, Robie walked off in the opposite direction. There was supposed to be someone waiting for him.

The man was young, but his features carried the weariness of someone much older. He wore a white robe and a turban.

'Robie?' the young man said.

Robie nodded.

'You come here to die,' said the man, matter-of-factly.

'Or something,' replied Robie.

'This way,' the man said.

They entered an alley where there was a van. There were five men in the van, all larger than Robie and just as fit and strong. Two searched him in every possible way.

'You came without weapons,' said the young man, in an incredulous tone.

'What would have been the point?' replied Robie.

He was hustled into the van and driven out of the city.

About thirty minutes later, the van stopped and passed through a security checkpoint. It was not the same private airport. The doors to the hangar opened and the van drove straight in. A different jet was parked there.

Robie was pushed roughly out of the van. The kick in his back that knocked him to the cement was not wholly unexpected.

The young man said something in Farsi to the man who'd kicked him.

Robie picked himself up. 'Tell him he hits about as hard as my sister.'

The young man said, 'I will not tell Abdullah you said that. Otherwise he will kill you.'

Robie turned to see Prince Khalid bin Talal walk down the stairs from his jet. Rain pinged loudly off the metal roof of the hangar. Talal came to a stop about ten feet from Robie. He wore a stylish suit that somehow managed to make his portly form look sleeker.

'You're not quite as fat as your body double, Talal,' said Robie.

'You will refer to me as Prince Talal.'

'Where are Vance and Julie, *Prince* Talal?'

The two women were led out of a far corner of the hangar. Vance's face was purple and black. She walked stiffly, as though every step was killing her. Julie had two swollen eyes, she carried her right arm at an awkward angle, and her left leg dragged a little. Their condition made Robie's anger rise, but he willed himself to remain calm. He would need to be, for what was coming.

'I'm sorry for all this,' said Robie, to them.

They stared back at him without speaking.

Robie turned to Talal. 'But at least the only one who died was your person. The president is safe.'

'The only one to die just yet,' said Talal. He smiled. 'But you knew her, didn't you? You knew her quite intimately, if the photos are any indication.'

'I know it was a game to you, Talal,' said Robie. 'But it's never been a game to me.'

Talal wagged a finger at Robie. 'My name is *Prince* Talal.'

The blow hit Robie from behind, knocking him to the floor.

'My friend here, Abdullah, also does not like your disrespect.'

'I can tell,' said Robie. He looked over at Vance and Julie. 'Now you have me, you can let them go. I expect you to honour our agreement.'

'Then you are an idiot.'

'You don't keep your word?' Robie looked at the others. 'So how can they trust you, Talal? You tell them one thing and do another. If a leader doesn't keep his word, then what's he worth? Nothing. He's worth nothing.'

Talal was unfazed by this. And his men did not seem to even understand what Robie was saying.

Robie said, 'I'm going to offer you a chance to surrender. I'm only going to offer it once.'

'You speak gibberish. I expected better from you. You are obviously paralysed with fear.'

'Trust me, it would take a lot more than your fat ass to make me afraid. Do you refuse?'

'What I think I will do is watch all three of you die, right now.'

'I'll take that as a no,' said Robie.

'Abdullah, kill him,' said Talal.

Abdullah drew two guns. It only took a moment, but he flipped one pistol to Robie, who used it to shoot three of the men closest to him. Abdullah fired twice, killing two other guards.

When the other men drew their weapons, Robie emptied his mag at them, grabbed Vance and Julie, and pulled them behind the front landing gear of the jet.

'Cover your ears,' said Robie to them. 'Abdullah!' he shouted, and the big man slid behind the van.

An instant later, the right-side window of the hangar blew open, shattered by massive rounds from a 30-millimetre chain gun. Next, rifle rounds fired through this opening slammed into the remaining guards. One by one they dropped until the only one left standing was Talal.

Outside the window, a chopper hovered. It was a stealth aircraft; the rain had covered any sounds it had made. Shane Connors slid his self-loading sniper rifle off the metal support and kissed the hot barrel, his longtime ritual. He gave Robie a salute and then signalled to the pilot. The chopper slowly moved off.

Robie approached Talal. Abdullah walked out from behind the van and joined him.

Talal gazed at Abdullah in disbelief. 'You betrayed me?'

'How do you think we got on to you in the first place, Talal?' said Robie. 'If you can buy our people, we can buy yours.'

Robie lifted his gun. Talal stared at him. 'So you kill me now?'

The hangar door opened and a gold SUV pulled in. Inside were five men, all in robes. All armed. They got out of the car, lifted Talal up and carried him to the vehicle. He screamed.

'You're going back to Saudi Arabia, Talal,' said Robie. 'The Americans have officially turned you over to your countrymen. I think you would have preferred the bullet.'

The SUV drove off and Robie beckoned to Vance and Julie. 'There's a chopper outside that will take us to our ride home,' he said quietly. 'And there's a medical crew on board.'

Vance hugged him and said, 'I don't know how you managed all this, Robie, but I'm sure as hell glad you did.'

Robie put one arm round Vance and held his other out to Julie, who took it. They walked out to the waiting helicopter.

Chapter 9

Blue Man and Shane Connors were sitting at a small table in the conference room when Robie walked in. Connors and Robie made eye contact, exchanged a brief nod and then Robie sat next to him. Blue Man said, 'I've just congratulated Agent Connors on a job well done.'

'Got me out from behind a desk,' said Connors.

Robie eyed Blue Man. 'What did Van Beuren tell us?'

'He turned on his country for money and morals.'

'The money I get. Explain the morals.'

'Well, the money was not exactly what you might have imagined. It was going to pay for medical bills, with plenty left over for Van Beuren to retire on. Even though they had insurance, it didn't cover some of the experimental treatments that they used to try and save Elizabeth Van Beuren.'

'And the morals?'

'Van Beuren blamed the government for his wife's cancer. He said it was exposure to the toxins in the battlefield that led to her illness. He wanted revenge. And the president and one of the leaders of Saudi Arabia were excellent targets.'

'And Van Beuren's daughter?'

'Knew nothing about any of it, her father said. And we believe him. Nothing will happen to her.'

'Why was Van Beuren knocked out?'

'The original plan had been to leave him completely blameless. You discovering what you did made this impossible, of course, but they didn't know that. So Lambert knocks him out and steals his gun. Van Beuren was going to retire and live somewhere else.'

'But I guess George Van Beuren screwed up,' Robie said. 'He told his wife what he was planning. Maybe he didn't even think she was listening or lucid. But she heard him and, being the patriot she was, the lady was disgusted. When she was visited by Broome or Wind or Getty, she told them. Van Beuren found out and action had to be taken. Scorched earth. Killed them all.'

'It was actually Leo Broome who visited her,' said Blue Man. 'Talal's people had Broome under surveillance. Broome told both Rick Wind and the Gettys. That signed their death certificates. They dialled you up to kill Jane Wind because they were terrified her ex had told her something. And it was also the catalyst to set you in motion along the course Talal had planned for you.'

'And they put the tube down his wife's throat so she couldn't talk again,' noted Robie.

'They actually wanted to kill her, but Van Beuren said he wouldn't go through with it if they did. When the plan was set and about to go off, he took her off the ventilator, and she died naturally.'

'What about Gabriel Siegel?' asked Robie.

'They wanted us to think he was involved. They called him at work, told him his wife would be killed if he didn't meet them. I'm not sure we'll ever find his remains. They had no reason to keep him alive.'

'The attack at Donnelly's?' Robie said.

'The Saudis have interrogated Talal. Apparently, he wanted you to suffer. Wanted you to blame yourself for what happened. He was certain you would figure out that you were the real target.'

'Broome's money?'

'Stolen Kuwaiti antiquities. He and Rick Wind were involved. Broome invested well, Wind did not. Curtis Getty was clean.'

Blue Man studied Robie. 'But even though the president and the crown prince were the actual targets, you were at the centre of this.'

'I didn't kill Talal, and he decides to find out who I was and to come after me. When Elizabeth Van Beuren talked, Talal saw a way to involve me in all of it. My handler orders the hit on Jane Wind, and I'm off and running from one orchestrated event to another.'

Connors said, 'It was a win-win for them. If you killed Wind and her son and later found out she was innocent, they figured that would screw you up. And if you didn't pull the trigger on a mother and son, they had the back-up shooter. They'd learned of your exit plan on the bus. And they made sure Julie would be there, too.'

Robie said, 'And they probably figured whether I pulled the trigger or not, I'd most likely get on the bus with Julie after I figured out who Jane Wind really was.'

Blue Man added, 'But when they learned that Julie came up with the idea of questioning other squad members, the game suddenly became too risky. That could lead to Van Beuren. They would kill Julie, and you, too, if necessary. Nothing could jeopardise the assassination attempt.'

'Guess it all makes sense,' said Robie, slowly.

Blue Man said, 'And Annie Lambert was an even earlier plant. After Talal escaped the attempt on his life in Tangier and found out you were the shooter, he had her move into your building. Talal evidently had plans for the two of you.'

Robie had not thought about Lambert since the night he had killed her. 'She was better than me,' he said at last. 'Faster, steadier. Never seen anyone that calm in a situation like that.'

'She was also drugged,' Blue Man pointed out. 'The Saudis were able to get some information from Talal. Her adoptive father was English, the mother Iranian. They had emigrated to Iran while the shah was still in power. Apparently, they were brutalised by members of the shah's regime and even lost family members during the course of it. Back then, the shah could do no wrong and, as you know, we helped keep him in power. The Lamberts hated the West, obviously, and apparently America in particular. They returned to England, adopted Annie, moved to America, and raised her as their daughter.'

'But they were brainwashing her, programming her the whole time?' said Connors. 'For something like this?'

'Apparently for all of her life. There was no guarantee, of course, that she would get a position at the White House. But one can attempt to kill the president in other places as well. Her parents were wealthy and politically active. She was a brilliant student and she was clearly a superb actress. We haven't interviewed one person who had any inkling she was a ticking time bomb. She led the perfect life. Was able to interact socially, perform outstandingly at work. There was no flaw, no warning sign. It was as though she was two different people residing in the same body.'

She was, thought Robie. *She had to be.*

Blue Man paused and looked over at Robie. 'She fooled the best we had.' He continued, 'And we're all terrified because she didn't fit any profile. What if there are more Annie Lamberts out there?'

Robie smacked the table. 'She was a puppet, her life taken from her by her parents. She's dead and they get to live. Tell me, what's wrong with that picture?'

Blue Man said nothing for a few moments. 'If it makes you feel better, Khalid bin Talal is no longer among the living.'

Robie said nothing.

'Then there is the matter of Julie,' said Blue Man.

'I've got that covered,' said Robie. He rose and looked at Connors. 'I owe you, Shane. More than I'll ever have in the bank.'

'We're square. Like I said, got me out from behind the desk.'

'Robie?' Blue Man held up a manilla folder. 'This was delivered to us by messenger. I believe you received a set, too. I think you should take this and do what you want with it. It's of no use or concern to us.'

Robie took the package, opened it and glanced at the photos inside. The first one was of him and Lambert on the rooftop bar. The next was of her kissing him in front of the White House. He didn't look at the rest.

'Thanks.'

He walked out of the door.

ROBIE DROVE. This time Julie was shotgun. Vance was in the back.

They had mostly recovered from their injuries, though Julie still limped a bit and Vance's face was still puffy.

'Where are we going?' asked Julie.

'Somewhere you've already been,' Robie replied.

He had explained what he could to Julie about her parents' deaths. He had watched her sob, given her tissues. He'd talked with her quietly as her anger grew, peaked and then faded to more tears. The fourteen-year-old, street-hardened kid had finally unravelled in the face of overwhelming misery and grief. But at least she'd had some closure.

He parked the car and the three of them got out and walked into the bar.

Jerome Cassidy was waiting, dressed in what looked to be a new suit with shiny black shoes.

'What are we doing here, Will?' asked Julie.

Cassidy said, 'He brought you here so I could tell you the truth.'

'What truth?'

'I wasn't just friends with your parents, I was your mom's half-brother. That means I'm sort of your uncle.'

'We're related?' said Julie.

'Yes, and I seem to be the only relation you have left. Now, I know you don't know me or anything, but I have a proposition.'

Julie looked at him suspiciously. 'Like what?'

'Like we take some time getting to know each other. See, the reason I was trying to track you all down was because your dad and my sister loaned me money when I was down. I owed them big. Never got a chance to repay that debt.'

'I see where this is going,' said Julie. 'You don't owe me anything.'

'No, Julie, it's a real debt. They loaned me money. I signed a note. That note was transferable into stock in a company I started with the loan. You're a forty per cent owner in my business, Julie. Your parents earned the right to share in the rewards. Well, since they can't, you should.'

He stopped talking and looked at her uncomfortably.

Julie glanced at Robie. 'Is this on the up-and-up?'

'We checked out his story. It's all true. You'll be able to go to any college you want. You'll be able to do anything you want.'

Julie looked at Cassidy. 'What does that mean for you and me?'

'It means you can live with me. I can legally adopt you. Or, if you prefer, you have the financial means now to have a guardian appointed and live in your own place.'

'Live with you?'

'It would be flexible. I keep pretty busy, but I've got a housekeeper who's been with me a long time. She's got a daughter about your age. I think it would work out. But it's up to you.'

'I'll need time to think about it,' said Julie.

'Absolutely. Take all the time you need,' said Cassidy, quickly.

Robie said, 'Why don't you start trying to get to know each other right now? I can come back and pick you up later.'

'I guess that would be OK.'

Robie looked at Cassidy and smiled. 'Have a good time.'

'Thank you, Agent Robie. From the bottom of my heart.'

Julie caught up with Robie and Vance before they had even reached the car. 'That story was total bullshit. What's really going on here?'

Robie said, 'You *are* related to him. He cared for your parents. He will care for you. He's rich. Life will not suck.'

A smile crept across Julie's face. 'Pick me up in two hours.'

Robie put the car in drive and pulled away from the kerb.

Vance looked at him. 'You ever going to tell me the real story about Cassidy?'

'No.'

'OK.' Vance touched him on the shoulder. 'You doing all right?'

'I'm fine.'

Robie slowed the car and looked at her.

She glanced away. 'I don't understand you completely, Robie, but I want to understand you. Does that make sense?'

He looked at her, a smile edging across his lips. 'I think you'll have the opportunity, Nikki.'

'I'll hold you to that.'

HE PICKED UP JULIE at the appointed time and drove her back to an apartment the Feds had temporarily got for her. Before she got out of the car, she said, 'Is this goodbye, like, for ever?'

'Do you want it to be?'

'Do *you* want it to be?'

'No, not really,' he said.

'But you're not sure.'

'I don't want you to ever be hurt again because of me.'

'Life is what it is, Will. You take it as it comes.'

'That's always been my philosophy.'

'Where do you think I learned it from?' She playfully punched him in the arm. 'Thanks. I mean it. For everything.'

She reached over and hugged him. Robie was tentative at first, but finally he hugged her back. She got out of the car and slowly walked up to her apartment. She waved at him, and then, despite her still-gimpy leg, Julie skipped up the last few steps. *Like a kid.*

Robie smiled. Her injuries would fully heal. At least her physical ones. And her emotional ones might too, given her age.

Robie could not say the same for himself. The image of Annie Lambert came bursting into his mind. She had been a killer. Just like he was a killer. His had been by choice. She had had no real choice in the matter. So who was the guiltier?

It was like Julie had said. *You have to take life as it comes*.

He was who he was. He could not change that. He was not an innocent. And the people he hunted certainly weren't innocent.

Maybe the best Robie could do was protect those who were.

david **baldacci**

Profile

Born:
August 5, 1960.
Family:
Wife, Michelle; teenage son and daughter.
Education:
BA in Political Science from Virginia Commonwealth University. Law degree from the University of Virginia School of Law.
Most exciting moment:
Births of his children.
Favourite drink:
Full-bodied Italian red wine.
Pets:
Two not-so-well-behaved Labradoodles.

The urban Washington, DC landscape that serves as a backdrop to *The Innocent* is home turf to David Baldacci. A Virginian born and bred, he grew up in the city of Richmond and later studied in two state universities before training as a lawyer and working with a DC firm for nine years. Today, he lives in a Washington suburb with his wife, Michelle, and their two teenage children.

Baldacci first hit the big time in 1996 with a thriller called *Absolute Power*, now a movie starring and directed by Clint Eastwood. Since then, he has produced a chart-topping blockbuster every year. What is his method? 'It takes me, from start to finish, about eighteen months to produce a book,' he states. 'I know some writers can write a novel in six months. But it takes me six months just to adequately perform research for a novel. I will never sacrifice quality for quantity.' As Baldacci's fame has grown, that research has become easier because he is able to get access to senior people in the government organisations that he writes about—the FBI, CIA and DEA to name but three.

After the research, comes the plot. 'In coming up with plots,' he explains, 'I look for classical dilemmas, interesting confrontations, ordinary people close to powerful epicentres. Political situations, lawyers, Washington, all allow for those creative elements. I try also to have at least one character represent the "every person". It's a way for readers to relate to the events taking place in the novel, and also to have someone to root for (or against) as the case may be. Most stories need a moral linchpin as well, and there's always one of those, in the form of a character, in my stories.'

Baldacci works out every plot line in his head before he types out the narrative.

Meantime, he jots down ideas in notebooks where he stores character details and 'backstory'. That doesn't mean characters are set in stone, however. 'Spontaneity is not a bad thing,' he emphasises. 'You shouldn't be afraid to go off the road because if you surprise yourself, you'll surprise the reader.'

The origins of his talent seem to lie in a natural way with words. He remembers talking so much as a kid of around eight or nine that his mother had to take steps to stem the flow. 'She got me a book with blank pages to write on, mostly to keep me quiet.' In high school and then in college, he wrote short stories, but it soon became clear that his forte was for extended narratives. On a larger canvas, with books such as *The Simple Truth*, *Split Second* and *The Winner*, he really got into his stride.

Now that he has achieved many of his writing goals, David Baldacci is doing his very best to put the tools of literacy—family literacy, in particular—into as many deserving hands as he can. With his wife, Michelle, he has set up a charity called the Wish You Well Foundation (wishyouwellfoundation.org). In 2010, the Foundation partnered with Feeding America to launch a programme that explored the links between literacy, poverty and hunger. The united force of the two charities eventually collected and distributed one million new and used books through local food banks.

In addition, David and Michelle Baldacci have enjoyed creating scholarships to give less-well-off children the chance to follow writing and other creative careers. 'I'm interested in areas of life that will have a heavy impact on what kind of world we can expect to have fifty years from now. With two children of my own, I've found that I have to think about "life" conditions beyond my own lifetime. As all parents know, that can be a humbling, troubling and sobering revelation.'

Does the philanthropic work inspire or motivate him to write in any way? 'Helping others is an obligation we all share, or should share. I have been very blessed in my life, and it is only right to share the wealth. I like to go into a situation and make it better. When you see all the need out there, it's a hard-hearted person who could turn away. It keeps you humble. Emotion makes for powerful fiction, too. I charge my characters with a spirit that real human beings all possess, but show in varying levels. My experiences in philanthropy have given me insights into the human condition that have influenced my writing and helped me to make my characters as real as possible.'

What tips does this mega-star have for would-be writers? 'Never turn off your passion for the written word and love of a great story. Watch life, listen intently, and absorb your environment. When you're naturally curious, you uncover storylines everywhere. Write about what interests you. Sustain the passion as you work. Writing is hard. It's easy to give up. Set yourself up for success instead of failure by building on that passion.'

Mummy
Daddy

Jeremy Howe

Everyone's worst nightmare is a knock on the door in the middle of the night from the police. For Jeremy Howe, that moment changed the course of both his and his two daughters' lives as he learned that his beloved wife, Lizzie, had been murdered.

Twenty years on, Jeremy and his girls are not the people they might have become had Lizzie not been killed. They are different, but not damaged. This is the candid, heart-rending story of how they got there: how Daddy became MummyDaddy and dealt with the aftermath of tragedy.

PROLOGUE

On the evening of 25 July the students for the 1992 English Literature Open University Summer School gathered in a junior common room in the University of York to hear a lecture on the poetry of Stevie Smith from one of their teachers.

The only thing missing was the academic who was supposed to be delivering the lecture—Dr Elizabeth Howe, BA (Oxon), MPhil (London), DPhil (London). She had been spotted soon after her arrival at the campus just after lunch and the course convener thought her non-appearance was strange. Eventually he and a college porter went up to her room, and after repeated knocking on her door they decided to enter.

What they found was her mutilated naked body. There was blood everywhere. There was little doubt that she had been murdered. Dr Elizabeth Howe—Lizzie—was my wife and the mother of our two children, Jessica (aged six) and Lucy (aged four).

This is our story.

1

Do you find that birthdays and anniversaries come in waves? Imagine what the early summer is like for me: Lucy was born on 18 May, her older sister, Jessica, on 9 June and their mother—Lizzie—on 28 June. It is a kind of bomb alley for my poor bank balance.

The summer of 1992 is worse than usual because we have decided to have the kitchen in our small Oxford terraced house doubled in size. The work is due to start after Lucy's birthday and finish a couple of weeks after Lizzie's.

Lucy is looking forward to her birthday party big time. The day is beautiful, but both Lizzie and I are edgy. Will the games (my responsibility) be up to the mark? Will the cake (Lizzie's) pass muster? Are our parsimonious party bags going to elicit raised eyebrows from the mums?

After a ridiculously early lunch, the children are sent upstairs to get ready. The house is vacuumed by me (God knows why, considering the maelstrom that is about to be meted on it by children and builders), Lizzie frets over the food. 'Why bother with sandwiches when all they want is cake and chocolate biscuits?' I say. Lizzie, who is a food puritan, is cutting up carrot sticks and gives me a contemptuous stare. As a concession, she has permitted me to buy two bottles of Coke, which are to be handled as if they were vintage champagne.

The birthday cake is more problematic. The year before, Lucy had set her heart on a cottage but the cake was a disaster, at least in Lizzie's eyes. Her charmingly rustic sponge cottage would not stand up and had to be supported by flying buttresses made of chocolate swiss rolls. Lucy was delighted but the public unveiling in front of the mothers was humiliating for Lizzie. So this year it is a one-layer sponge, decorated to look like a pond adorned with four marzipan ducks, one for each of Lucy's years. It is more naive art than neorealism and I reckon the ducks look quite ducklike. The idea has been ripped off from a neighbour (a fine artist) who six months previously delivered a table-sized cake mapping out Treasure Island for her toddler son. Eating this work of art was almost sacrilege. Lizzie can't wait for Lucy's friends to make her far less accomplished work of art disappear for ever. Between us we can muster four degrees and a full deck of highly graded A levels, but we both dropped art before GCSEs because we were plain rubbish at drawing. No one told us that to be a good parent you needed to be able to bake a cake or, even worse, design one.

And then disaster strikes. Lucy has decided it is time she learned how to slide down the stairs on her stomach and manages to give herself a nasty carpet burn on her cheek. She is inconsolable because it hurts; we are inconsolable because it looks like we've walloped her across the face. My abiding memory of the party is of Lucy dressed in all her party finery, clutching her *Little Mermaid* toy, Flounder, watching a video with a big red mark on her cheekbone.

Of course the party is a breeze. The cake goes down a storm; the children love the games; no one cares that the party bags are cheap because the ten pence worth of sweets in paper bags are masked by the ingenious trick of getting the children to decorate their own bags after tea; and NO ONE is sick before the mums arrive.

After that, we collapse—but not until Lizzie and I have thrown away industrial quantities of half-eaten sandwiches and discarded carrot sticks, and then blitzed the wreckage that was our sitting room.

And then, because both Lizzie and I have been working so hard (me at my job at the BBC, Lizzie masterminding the completion of her about-to-be-published book), we tell the children that tomorrow we are going to the seaside. We get up at the crack of dawn and drive to Swanage, where we have booked a hotel on top of a cliff with steps right down to a sandy beach. Given that the sun shines constantly and that we spend most of the day building sandcastles, Jessica and Lucy have a whale of a time. So do I. I have not been to Swanage since my parents took me when I was four years old. It was the best holiday ever and I thought the Isle of Purbeck, with its sandy beaches, its high cliffs, and the fingerlike ruin of Corfe Castle perched on its hill, was just holiday heaven. And when I return with Lizzie, Jessica and Lucy, I find I know my way round Swanage as if I had visited it only a year before.

Having been to the National Trust shop, where Jessica, Lucy and I secretly buy Mummy a white and blue birthday mug with a drawing of a cat on it—we have just acquired a kitten—Lizzie and I sit in a tea garden overlooking Corfe Castle while the girls play. We chat and I remark how much of an impact Swanage made on me and I wonder how much of this little holiday will stay with our two. As we drive home, the dramatic ruin of the castle comes into sight once more and I tell the girls to wave it goodbye through the back window of the car. I am consciously trying to create memories for them in the same way that the Swanage holiday was like a Super 8 film recording my incredibly happy childhood. And as I try to piece together what happens to us next, that moment has stayed with me.

What actually happens next is that the builders move in, which gives us a get-out clause for Jessica's birthday party three weeks later. We decide—sod the expense—to hold her party on a local farm. Apart from writing the cheque, all we have to worry about is the weather and the day living up to Jessica's mounting sense of excitement.

Well, the weather is iffy but once we have assembled the posse of a dozen children and a few hanger-on mums, for all Jessica cares it could rain locusts: she is going to have a great time. We start with a treasure hunt round the farmyard, which involves the children meeting the cows, the chickens, the sheep and the pigs. This is followed by a ride in a hay trailer pulled by a tractor. This may not sound exciting, but clinging on for dear life as the tractor roars its way along at about 10 mph up impossibly steep hills and back down again is about as exciting as it gets when you are six, especially as the farm dog chooses to sit by Jessica for the whole trip.

On the way home Jessica wearily sighs, 'That was the Best Party EVER!'

'What was the best bit?'

'All of it!'

'Mummy, when can I have my party at the farm?'

'Next year perhaps, Luce.'

'Can't it be sooner?'

'Not really, darling, no. You've just had your birthday party.'

'Oh yes. I forgot.'

TWO DOWN, one to go. The weekend before Lizzie's birthday we go for a family picnic on a punt with two friends from college. It is idyllic. It is also the week before Lizzie's book is published. She has turned her doctoral thesis into a narrative history of the impact of the introduction of actresses on the English theatre at the time of the Restoration. The fairy godmother to both the thesis and the book, and the surrogate godmother to both our girls, is the superstar academic Inga-Stina Ewbank, and for Lizzie's actual birthday we decide to invite her and her husband Roger to supper.

Because we can't cook (I should confide that Lizzie was not a great cook and I was plain lousy), we take them out for dinner. It is one of those perfect summer evenings—celebrating a birthday and a momentous life-changing event. Lizzie is the only person among all our combined families, friends and peers who has written a book that is to be published. I am so proud of her. Things couldn't really be any better for us that summer of 1992.

SO WHO WERE the Howes—Jeremy, Lizzie, Jessica and Lucy?

Lizzie was born in Bradford on Avon in Wiltshire in 1958. Her younger sister Louise was born in 1961. Their parents, Ethel and Mirko Milicevic, known as Maka and Deda (Serb for grandma and grandpa), married in

Belgrade, where Maka, straight from school in Wiltshire, was working for the Foreign Office. Because she didn't enjoy living there and he, as a middle-class Serb, was struggling to get on in Tito's communist state, they came to England. Begrudgingly, Maka's father got Deda a job sweeping floors at Bowyers Sausage Factory, there not being much call for Serb-trained lawyers in Great Britain. A few months into the job his supervisor told him that if he played his cards right he would make foreman in five years. By the time I met Lizzie, both the girls had been through private education at Bath High School, they had a grand house, and Deda was the International Development Director for the company that had bought out the company that had bought out Bowyers.

I was born in 1956 in Bexleyheath, the middle one of three children—Jonathan, Jeremy and Philippa. My father—who died in the late autumn of 1991—ran a small cloth merchandising company that had gone belly up during Edward Heath's three-day week, which left us in penury for much of the seventies. The situation was not helped by my mother walking out on my father (he was a nice man, but was also a workaholic, absentee father who never said much—I could see her point) and for four years he lived with his mother in Teddington, the rest of us in Bromley with my mother's mother in a vast house that we rattled around in because we didn't have any furniture.

Growing up in a single-parent family was an adventure—all the rules of family life changed. I learned to be a very self-sufficient child and I learned a lot, unconsciously, about single parenting. I also worried constantly on my mother's behalf about money, because we never had any. We were middle-class poor.

But my father was a dogged individual and he put the marriage back together. Suddenly, the no-money life was over. One weekend he bought a new fridge, so we didn't have to use one shelf in my grandmother's refrigerator. Never had the purchase of a domestic appliance brought such joy to a thirteen-year-old boy—it was a sign that we were destined to be a family again.

Four years previously, at the start of the summer holidays, my mother had said, 'We are going away for a week in Norfolk and then we are going to move house. Your father is not going to come with us.' Now, as casually as they had appeared to separate, they came together again.

'Your father is coming to stay.'

'For the whole weekend?'

'No. For good.'

LIZZIE AND I met at Oxford. We both studied English, were in the same year, and shared a love of theatre. We met properly when she stage-managed a production of Samuel Beckett's *Endgame* that I was directing, rehearsing all through the Easter vacation of our second year. As stage manager, she was totally reliable, well organised and unfailingly nice to work with.

After the show had finished, the cast and crew all went their separate ways. Except one afternoon I dropped by the workshop where my designer, Jim, was building a set for another show. Lizzie was there. I kind of knew she would be. I remember her standing with her back to me, one leg crooked in her skin-tight jeans, one hand on her hip, the other holding a paintbrush. Her long chestnut hair cascaded down her back. When I said hello, she smiled, said she had to go and left.

'I saw the way you were looking at her,' Jim said. 'You just want to get inside her pants, Mr Howe!'

I went bright red. Jim was right.

It was the spring of 1978 and we started going out together a couple of weeks later, and living together about a month after that. I think we knew this was the one from that moment. Lizzie worked hard for finals, but never panicked. I just panicked. We both got a viva for a first—the moment I opened my mouth I am sure the examiners realised I was a sham, so I didn't get a first. But nor did Lizzie, who was so obviously a first-class student. It rankled with her for ever. Her cause wasn't helped by the fact that when she got nervous or excited her brain would work faster than her mouth and she stammered, which I found endearing, and she hated.

We graduated and moved to London, where I tried and failed to get work as a theatre director and she puzzled over what to do next. In retrospect, it was blindingly obvious she should be an academic, but at the time she was unsure. She did a masters degree in Restoration theatre, then worked in publishing in Brighton, before setting up a social research journal at York University that led her into hospital administration. When we moved to Colchester she was offered a similar job, but she threw it all in to do her doctorate and paid her way by teaching. When we moved to Belfast she started teaching for the Open University, most interestingly at the Maze Prison, where she taught a former hunger striker who was the most gifted student she had ever come across.

After we went back to England and settled in Oxford, she got down to turning her thesis into a book. *The First English Actresses* was published by

Cambridge University Press just six weeks after Lucy's birthday party. It immediately got a rotten review in the *Sunday Times*, but then, months later, all the academic journals started reviewing it—fulsomely. It won an award in the States, was turned into a stage play and later was the source book for a not very good movie. And it is still making money.

You might be wondering why Lizzie's short life reads like a round-Britain road movie. The answer is because she was following me. After a year of doing nothing in London, I got my break as a theatre director at York Theatre Royal. One morning in February 1981, just before I left for York, while I was shaving and she was getting dressed in our tiny flat in Bayswater, I suddenly called out: 'Why don't we get married?'

So we did, in September 1981, from her parents' house in Bath—a beautiful celebration on a wonderful Indian summer day. And the honeymoon in Venice wasn't bad either.

Lizzie Milicevic was now Lizzie Howe—she hated her Serb name, which made her stand out when all she ever wanted to do was to blend in. Her foreignness fascinated me, but to her it was an irritant. A conversation in our early courtship went something like this:

'Hello, I am Lizzie Milicevic.'

'Hi, I'm Jeremy Howe.'

'That's a nice name.'

'Jeremy?'

'No, Howe. Will you marry me so I can change my name?' She grinned.

And on 5 September 1981 we were both grinning with sheer happiness.

But Lizzie had to stay in London for her research and I was in York. Most of our quality time was spent at the buffet in King's Cross station. We were not happy. When Lizzie got the publishing job in Brighton, I moved there to be with her. But no sooner had I done that than my work dragged me back up north. So she chucked in her job and we moved into a beautiful house in Fulford Road in York.

After York, I got a job in Colchester, where we bought our first house. Then my career went pear-shaped—the theatre there nearly went bust and I was laid off. We had been trying for a baby without success and for a year Lizzie was taking fertility drugs. 'I think we should bring in your husband for a sperm count,' said the consultant. A few weeks later Lizzie had arranged to meet me in town after her latest appointment with the doctor. She came up from behind and whispered in my ear, 'No need for the sperm test, sweetie.' Jessica was on the way. Only problem—I was a freelance theatre director, which is an arty euphemism for being unemployed. 'You need to get a proper job, Jeremy,' Lizzie said forcefully. I had under nine months to find one.

In January 1986, with less than five months to go, I was interviewed by the BBC to work as a radio drama producer in Belfast and was offered the job. 'Oh fuck,' said Lizzie. The Troubles were still at their height, so her reaction was perhaps not that surprising.

A fortnight after the move, at five in the morning, Lizzie woke me up. 'Jeremy, I'm bleeding.'

'I'm sure it's nothing serious. Go back to sleep, darling.'

'No, I'm bleeding. Look it up in Penelope Leach. Now.'

The ambulance arrived ten anxious minutes later, and Lizzie spent the next month in hospital suffering from placenta praevia. The consultant reassuringly told me that 'If it's between saving the mother's life or the baby's, we save the baby's.'

Jessica was born two weeks prematurely by emergency Caesarean section on 9 June 1986. We had no problems conceiving Lucy, who was born naturally on 18 May 1988. Even more astonishingly, Lizzie had researched most of her doctorate while she was pregnant with Jessica and wrote it between Jessica's birth and Lucy's. Supermum.

A year later, I got a job at Film 4. Not wanting to live in Twickenham, we moved to Oxford and I commuted to London every day. Our lovely little four-bedroomed terraced house was less than a mile from the city centre and the libraries Lizzie needed for her research, within walking distance of two state nurseries, and 400 yards from the River Thames. It was brilliant. 'I never, ever want to move again,' said Lizzie, and she didn't.

After a couple of years I rejoined the BBC, as Editor of Drama on Radio 3, where I was working in the summer of 1992. Life seemed pretty good. We had our ups and downs, but I think we both knew in our hearts that we had found the right person with whom to share our journey through life.

Not far from where we lived was a place called Wittenham Clumps, a group of hills topped with trees, commanding a view across the Thames flatlands towards the spires of Oxford. Lizzie and I were like two trees on Wittenham Clumps—one faced east, one west, each protecting and supporting the other. As a couple, we were greater than the sum of our parts.

And Lucy and Jessica? Two beautiful, lovable girls.

Jessica, now six, was quite tall for her age, boisterous, loud and brimming with innocent confidence. The first time I saw her as a newborn baby she fixed me with a steely, blue-eyed stare which rather implied, 'Who are you, exactly?' She has maintained that gaze ever since, enquiring and accusatory. Although inclined to be bossy, she doted on Lucy. They were the very best of friends and playmates.

Lucy was little and four. It's odd to think that this slightly chubby, small individual has grown into a taller woman than her sister. She was the exact counter to Jessica, with whom she got on wonderfully, but boy, could they quarrel, especially when Jessica's tendency to be overbearing got to her. Lucy was shy, quiet (well, silent), biddable, and had a sweet nature that masked a quiet determination: Lucy always knew her own mind, it's just that she didn't feel the need to share it with anyone else.

Three birthdays done, one book successfully published and a new kitchen—we Howes were ready for the summer holidays. All we had to do was negotiate Lizzie's week away at the Open University Summer School.

ON SATURDAY 25 July 1992 we all got up to start the summer holidays.

The girls had broken up from school a couple of days before. As an end-of-term treat, they had all been asked to turn up in Victorian costume to celebrate the hundredth anniversary of the school buildings. It was a day of intense excitement, and the pictures that a neighbour took of Jessica and Lucy in their Victorian bonnets and long frocks (two of their mum's dresses hemmed up) are incredibly cute.

For Lizzie, the Friday had been a day of anxiously putting the finishing touches to the lecture she was giving the next day to kick off the Open University Summer School at York.

I had had a day from hell at work—clearing my desk for a week's holiday is always a nightmare, but it was compounded by an unhappy event. The previous evening an elderly actress had dropped dead during a play recording, leaving the production team in a state of shock, and I was trying to dispense some much-needed TLC. Almost as bad, the recorded rushes of a programme had disappeared; I had to find out what had happened. It was a long day and, for a bit of light relief, I took out for lunch a producer whose last day it was in the BBC, after a career of forty years.

John was a Greek anglophile who had grown up under English rule in Egypt; he was one of the most cultured men I had ever met in the BBC.

Over coffee, I asked him what was the best play he had produced. Without hesitation, he said, 'The one I have just completed. Yeats's version of *Oedipus* has more wisdom than any play I have encountered.'

'Why?' I only vaguely knew it.

'The last two lines are extraordinary. "Call no man fortunate that is not dead. The dead are free from pain." In other words, no man is happy until he dies.'

'That's pretty bleak, John.'

'I think what he means is that we just don't know what is round the corner. That you cannot rest on your laurels until the moment you die. Very sobering, don't you think? After all, none of us knows what lies ahead.'

'Oh, I know what lies ahead. My bloody in-tray.'

SATURDAY DAWNED as a classic first-day-of-the-holidays morning—sunny and cool, but with a promise of hot weather to come.

We were in a tearing hurry—Lizzie had to be on a train to York first thing, then I had to do the packing and take our kitten, Milly Molly Mandy, to the cattery before Jessica, Lucy and I hit the road for a week. We were driving to York to meet up with Lizzie via my mother's house in Suffolk and my sister's in Norfolk, all rounded off with a weekend on the beach in Scarborough. Because I was anxious about what to do with the children when in sole charge, I had concocted a timetable that would keep us on the move until we hooked up with their mummy on the Friday afternoon.

We raced to the station, just a little bit late. As the train drew in, Lizzie arranged to phone me at about six. We said our farewells and, with the train drawing off, waved goodbye as if our lives depended on it, until the train disappeared round a bend. Our family. Lizzie, Jeremy, Jessica and Lucy.

I shepherded the girls off the platform, acutely aware of a sense of anti-climax: while Mummy was off to do her glamorous job, we had the prospect only of a day of domestic tasks. I felt myself to be faintly heroic in my herculean task for the week—sole carer for the children. What a saintly husband I was. God knew how I would get through the week.

It was a frantic day, as I simultaneously packed, looked after the children, supervised the electrician who had come to finish off our kitchen and drove the kitten to the cattery. This involved a mere thirty-mile drive with a screeching animal. Lizzie didn't phone at six, but what with feeding and bathing the children, I didn't notice until I was halfway to Suffolk, with the children dozing in their pyjamas in the back of the car. As I thundered along the motorway I watched a plane take off from Stansted Airport and wished we were on it, going on holiday to some beach. Then I thought of Lizzie and felt vaguely annoyed—there she was, having a good time at the summer school and forgetting us, and here was I, en route to see my mum on a boot camp of a holiday.

We arrived in Sudbury, and though I managed to greet my mother, recently widowed and in her late sixties, I just brushed her aside as I raced into the house and went up to the attic bedrooms with sleeping children in my arms. I stood them up to take off their dressing gowns and slippers, then lay them down and pulled the blankets round them. Jessica said, 'Daddy, I love you,' and then, like Lucy, she was fast asleep once more.

I raced back downstairs, unloaded the car and at last gave my mother a hug. 'Has Lizzie phoned?'

'No, darling. Only Philippa.' My sister.

'That's not like Lizzie. I wonder if she has forgotten to take your number with her to York.'

'She's probably having a good time and has forgotten.' Lizzie was so punctilious about such things that I thought it unlikely, but we sat and chatted and before long I had forgotten about the missed call. Knackered, I went early to bed.

I AM AWARE that I am having an anxious dream when I wake to find my mother in her dressing gown standing over me, shaking me. It is pitch-dark.

'Darling, there is someone banging on the front door and shouting that he is the police looking for you. It's one o'clock.'

I wake instantly and pad downstairs as fast as I can, my mother following me like a shadow.

I open the front door a crack.

'Are you Mr Jeremy Howe?' A young police constable. Looks about twelve.

'I'm Jeremy Howe. What's the problem?' I wonder if he wants me to move my car as I think I might have parked it on a yellow line.

'It's about your wife.'

'Is she OK?'

'I'm afraid she's been injured. Can I come in, please?'

He comes in. I shut the door.

'How badly injured?' A whole sequence of scenarios about nursing her back to wellness race through my mind, which is abruptly halted by—

'She's dead, sir. You need to phone this number. It's a direct line to the officer handling the case at York police station.'

I can't have heard him correctly.

'Lizzie dead? That's not possible.'

'I am afraid she is dead, sir.'

I wasn't expecting that. I WAS NOT EXPECTING THAT.

Call no man fortunate that is not dead.

Suddenly I am very awake.

'She was attacked. You'd better phone this number, Mr Howe.'

I speak to a very matter-of-fact Yorkshireman, who tells me that my wife was found dead in her room on campus at about six o'clock on Saturday evening, that her throat had been slit, and that they have apprehended a student on the campus who they will charge with killing her later today. It appears to have been a random attack by a man who had never met Lizzie before. She was the wrong person in the wrong place at the wrong time.

Lizzie was one of the most blameless people I'd ever met. And now she was dead. Not dead—murdered. Shit. This was BLOODY HOPELESS, and there was no one to bargain with, no one to retrieve our lives, no one to wind the clock back. As I listened to him, I found myself thinking, *So this is how it was meant to happen.*

As if what had just occurred was inevitable.

'So what should I do now?' I ask.

'We would like you to come to York to identify her body as soon as possible. We really are very sorry, Mr Howe.'

I put the phone down. I don't know how to react. What are you supposed to do at the moment when your life implodes?

I say to no one in particular, 'Lizzie—has—been—murdered.' I see the policeman standing there embarrassed, my mother looking helpless.

I collapse onto the floor and sob. I can feel the hard stone floor beneath the rug which is getting damp as I weep. I hear my mother asking the constable if he would like a cup of tea.

'No thanks. I'd best be off.'

I feel a bit silly, so I stand up, wipe away the snot, blow my nose and apologise for my behaviour. We shake hands and he takes his leave.

I think of Lucy and Jessica innocently asleep up in the attic.

I don't know what to do.

After a cup of hot sweet tea, my mother and I make a plan. Even though it is nearly two in the morning I phone my sister who tells us to come to Norfolk once the girls are up. She sounds like she knows what to do, so her plan becomes our plan. I try ringing Lizzie's parents, but the call goes straight to an answerphone.

It is the middle of the night but I can't sleep. I go to my mother's bedroom and lie on her bed. She hugs me and we talk about Lizzie and me, how falling in love changed me as a person, our crazy lives apart in York and Brighton, our struggle to have children, and so on and so on, but my mind is in turmoil. I can't focus and eventually my mother goes back to sleep and I try to doze beside her. It is as if I am a child again.

Shortly after four I get dressed and creep out of the house to go for a walk across the water meadow on the other side of the street. A drizzly mist hangs over the river banks, cattle graze, their snorting breaths breaking the silence, but that apart, nothing is stirring. The world may just be waking up, but I am wide-WIDE awake. I feel giddy with emotion, I can feel the loss of Lizzie like a sharp pain in my stomach. I feel smashed up. I want to take Lizzie in my arms and tell her I love her. I want to kill the man who has done this to her, to us. I feel terrible thinking about what I am going to have to tell the children. I want to talk it through with Lizzie more than anything.

I am alone in a new and frightening world.

I walk fast, because I am thinking fast, as if my life depends on it. *Do I stay in Oxford? Do I relocate to London to be nearer to my job? Do I ditch my job and bring up the children? Or do I just bury myself in work and get one of my family to bring them up? Or do I look for a new mother for the children? Or do I just run away?*

As I walk, I come to the footbridge across the Stour, a river made famous by the paintings of John Constable. Nine months earlier I had stood here on a cold starlit night trying to digest the news that my father had just died. That night I thought his death, upsetting though it was, was just a part of the order of things. I felt sad, but there was a natural justice in his death, his life had been of the right span. But not Lizzie's. Her death is an outrage against nature. All I can feel is hurt, anger. The injustice is a physical pain—my heart is beating fast, my breathing shallow. My stomach is in knots. I rub my brow trying to relieve the stress, trying to think clearly. And the river flows on, for ever and ever.

I walk on. There is a fork in the path. I hesitate. Turn left and I return directly to my mother's house, turn right and I loop round the meadow, over the river. *If I go left I sink, if I go right I swim. Left or right? Sink or swim? Do I let this destroy me? I am so frightened.*

What would Lizzie have wanted me to do? With each second her life is coursing away from me like the water in the river.

I take the right fork.

I will do what I think Lizzie would want me to do—bring up the children as best I can, keep my job, maintain our lives, move forward.

I stand up straight, breathe deeply and stride forward.

I will swim.

IN THAT HALF-HOUR WALK, I made most of the decisions about how to lead my life, our lives, which is the story of this book. For years, if I have needed to clarify what I am doing and why I am doing it, I have tried to get back to the state of mind on my walk through the Sudbury water meadow. It is my Mount Sinai, and Jessica and Lucy are the tribe that I will lead out of the wilderness.

The first step was to go to my sister's; she had offered to look after Jessica and Lucy while her husband Malcolm drove me to York.

I crept back into the house. My mother was standing in the kitchen with her back to me, lost in thought. She turned round and I saw her face change from anxiety to warmth, as if she had put on a mask. She gave me a hug.

'What shall I say to the girls?'

'I just don't know, darling.'

I poured two glasses of juice—just as Lizzie and I had done every morning. I went upstairs and woke them up.

'Darlings, there has been a change of plan. We're going to get up now and drive to Auntie Philippa's before breakfast.'

'Why, Daddy?'

'Er . . . Daddy has to go to the office. With Uncle Malcolm.'

Not one of my best fibs, but they were excited about seeing their Auntie Philippa and their cousins and the dog. They accepted their Daddy's gloss on the day. But I had bottled out.

I just wasn't ready to tell them, so we began to live a lie.

We arrived at my sister's sometime around eight o'clock; under heavy grey skies everything felt muted, as if I was wrapped in cotton wool. We had breakfast and I made the phone call I was dreading.

Still Maka and Deda's phone went straight to a machine. I phoned directory enquiries and got the phone number of Maka's best friend and neighbour. I knew her, but not well.

'Sue, it's Jeremy Howe, Lizzie's husband. I am so sorry to disturb you but I have to get hold of Lizzie's mum and dad. It's urgent. Would you get them to ring me on this number immediately? It's not good news.'

'Of course. Right away.'

Five unendurable minutes later the phone rang.

'Maka. Thank God. I have been trying to get hold of you all night.'

'Bloody Deda put the phone on answerphone. Wretched man.'

'I have some terrible news. Lizzie has been killed.'

Pause.

'How did it happen?' she said calmly. I told her and she responded as if she had been expecting this to happen. 'I see . . . yes . . . of course.'

I put down the phone. Silence. I tried to imagine what Lizzie's mother was doing at that moment. In my mind, I heard an anguished howl, saw a face cracked open with sobbing, her husband unable to console her tears, then or ever.

I made calls to Lizzie's sister Louise, to my brother Jonathan and to the police to tell them I was leaving, and then I breezily said goodbye to the girls, who were busy admiring my sister's doll's house with their cousins, and set off with Malcolm on my awful odyssey to identify Lizzie's body.

2

We drove in silence. Malcolm—twelve or so years older than me, a research engineer for the Lotus car company, hardworking, clever but not a talker—suggested, 'It might not be Lizzie. You won't know until you have identified the body.'

Malcolm was right: there was still a scintilla of hope.

As we got closer to York a knot tightened in my stomach. I was on a different planet to the one inhabited by everybody else. Planet Grief is an alien place, smashed up, desolate, savage. I was trying to make sense of the mess, but there was no sense to be made. All I could do was embrace the storm, not fight it, nor reason with it. It must not destroy me. I was in the first phase of grief—shock and disbelief.

We stopped at a Little Chef ten miles or so short of our destination for a pee. I didn't want a pee, but I did want to delay having to confront the truth. There was still hope. Once I had identified the body, there would be no hope. I felt sick.

We arrived in York and parked in the hospital car park, all too familiar from meeting Lizzie when she had worked there as an NHS administrator. We walked over to reception, empty and shut up for the weekend. The Assistant Coroner greeted us—'I am sorry to meet you under such terrible circumstances.' He was in his fifties, charming, softly spoken and very apologetic.

He led us down spotless white corridors into the centre of a deserted maze, until we reached a large room divided in two by a long, diaphanous white curtain covering a glass partition.

'This way, Mr Howe,' and he took me behind the curtain.

THERE IS A GURNEY covered in a shroud. There is a body beneath.

'Are you ready, Mr Howe?'

Am I ready to confront the unconfrontable? No, but none of us is ever ready: I can't believe this is happening to me.

He pulls back the cover.

There is Lizzie, the woman I had kissed goodbye barely twenty-four hours ago, but lifeless, and not Lizzie at all. She doesn't even look like Lizzie sleeping. Apart from a livid red mark on her throat she doesn't look like she had been hurt.

'Mr Howe, is that your wife, Elizabeth Howe?'

'Yes. It is. It's Lizzie. It is Elizabeth Howe.'

'Would you like a few moments alone to say goodbye to your wife?'

I hesitated. Yes, I supposed I should. But I was not sure why.

'OK.'

'Please don't move the sheet covering your wife's body, Mr Howe.'

He closes the curtain to give me privacy.

I stand and gaze at Lizzie. I don't know what to do. I dare not touch her. I feel giddy. I think my heart is about to explode.

And then I start to weep. I kiss her gently on the forehead, I tell her that I love her, that I promise to look after the children, I thank her for our lives together, for our love, our girls, our happiness. It is like some ghastly film, but this is real and I can't believe this is happening to me. I still can't believe this waxy cold body, looking so calm and at such peace, is the violated body of the person I love with all my heart.

I say a prayer I have said every night now for nearly twenty years. 'Dear Lord, thank you for Lizzie, please let her know that I love her and that I promise promise promise I will look after the children.'

And then I pull myself together, say goodbye to her, and walk through the curtain into an uncertain future, knowing only that I will never see Lizzie Milicevic, my heart's best treasure, again.

We follow the Assistant Coroner to the police station. I know the way because our last house in York had been bang opposite. It was now a b. & b., and I had booked in to stay there at the end of the week with the family.

We park, and as Malcolm and I walk towards the entrance the Detective Chief Superintendent ambles past and we are introduced.

'I am so sorry, Mr Howe, that you are having to visit this beautiful city under such awful circumstances,' he says.

'We used to live here. It is a horrible homecoming.'

'Oh, I didn't realise. Thank God we have apprehended the man we think did this terrible thing.'

'Yes.'

'If there is anything you need us to do—like book a hotel or anything like that—do let us know.'

Thinking about it afterwards, I reckon that the Superintendent had probably been waiting in the car park for us to arrive. I feel like some toxic celebrity and I envy him as he gets in his car and drives off back to a life of normality.

We go into the police station, a large, drab 1970s building, buzzing with activity, and the Assistant Coroner leads us into the bowels of the station. We walk past a table and laid out there is the dress that Lizzie had been wearing when she left home yesterday and my briefcase that Lizzie always used. I try to linger, but I'm hastily ushered into an airless cupboard of an office. The Assistant Coroner eventually unearths the correct form, gets me to certify that I have identified Lizzie's body, and then disappears.

I sit with Malcolm in silence. Fifteen minutes later, the Assistant Coroner reappears. 'The officers running the enquiry have asked me to get you to write something a little more detailed. Just write down where you were and what you were doing yesterday from the time you last saw your wife until the time the police contacted you at . . . when was it?'

'About one o'clock this morning.' Pause. 'Where is the man who they think killed Lizzie?'

'In one of the cells down the corridor, I believe.'

'Has he been charged with her murder?'

'Not yet. By law they need to give him some rest before they are allowed to question him.'

Sitting within a few yards of the person who killed Lizzie is surreal. I want to kick the shit out of him. I want to retrieve her things sitting outside on the table, to touch them, smell them. I take a breath and ask if I could have them back, or at least go and look at them.

The Assistant Coroner gets defensive. 'No. I am afraid the police will need to use them as evidence. They shouldn't really have been there when you came through . . . Look, I'll see if I can rustle you up a sandwich. I fear all this may take time.'

I start to write on their form—a diary of what felt like my last day before we entered hell. I get to the bit about taking Milly Molly Mandy to the cattery, which Lizzie had booked not realising it was halfway to Swindon, and I had cursed her for it. That had been at about four o'clock, about the time they thought she had been murdered. Apparently, people along the corridor had heard screaming, had called out, but it had stopped so they had assumed everything was all right. She had lain there dead for over two hours. I had been cursing Lizzie at roughly the time that she had died.

As I write the statement, I realise that Milly Molly Mandy is my alibi, and that if I need an alibi, then I might be a suspect. Do they really think that I might have been involved in the murder of Lizzie?

I finish the statement. The Assistant Coroner thanks me. 'Can you hang on? I just need to show it to one of the officers.'

We wait an age, in silence, and then a police officer pokes his head round the door. 'The Detective Inspector running the case wants a few words with you. Would you come upstairs with me please, Mr Howe?'

'Can my brother-in-law come with me?'

'Yes.'

We are led into a very large room, which looks more like a study than a detective's office. Two burly policemen in plain clothes offer condolences and I sit in a chair facing the desk. My back is to the window which overlooks the house where Lizzie and I used to live. It had been our first home together. We had been very happy there.

They question me, taking it in turns—soft cop, hard cop, treating me as a suspect. They ask me to talk my way through my statement. When they get to my trip to the cattery they slow down, they want a minute by minute breakdown of what I did, where I was, who could verify this information.

'Do you have the number of the owner?'

'Not on me, no. Sorry.'

This is serious. The Detective makes a note on his pad.

'And do you know a Robin Pask?' asks his colleague.

'No. Who is he?'

'Did he know your late wife?'

'Why?'

'We think he killed your wife.'

The police told me that he had been arrested, dressed in her clothes, when trying to drive off from the campus in his car just as it was getting dark. They had apprehended 'her' because 'she' was behaving so strangely.

'I have no idea if she knew him. Lizzie might have taught him at the summer school before, I suppose. I wouldn't know.'

'He is a science student from Bolton, Mr Howe.'

'Lizzie taught English. Neither of us have ever been to Bolton.'

'Would he have any motive for killing her?'

'NO! Lizzie was blameless. Why would anyone want to kill Lizzie!?'

'Any money problems at home, Mr Howe?'

'No. Why?'

'People get their nearest and dearest killed to claim on the insurance.'

'My life is insured, not Lizzie's.'

'How was your relationship with your late wife? Did you quarrel?'

'We get on fine. We got on just fine.'

'How was your sex life, Mr Howe?'

'Er . . . fine. We have two children.'

'I mean, were either of you having an affair, Mr Howe?'

'What do you mean? No. NO!'

And on and on, twisting me into knots. I want to tell them to fuck off. What right do they have to do this to me? Meanwhile, the man who killed Lizzie is sleeping in a cell so he is refreshed enough for police questioning, whereas I have been up since one o'bloody clock.

Finally: 'We would like to search your house in Oxford. Do you have a key on you?'

Bloody hell. I have the front-door key in my pocket. I am sure there will be one in Lizzie's purse. We have a mate—Henry—staying there, house-sitting for us. But I don't want them ransacking my house without me being there.

'No.' It is a lie. They must know it is a lie.

There is silence while the Detective Inspector thinks. 'No matter, Mr Howe. It would just be a routine search. Do you have any questions?'

'Yes. Who is he, Robin Pask?'

'Well . . . he's in his thirties, some kind of lab technician on his first summer school. He has a previous police caution for threatening violence towards women and a history of mental illness. We think he got to York sometime around yesterday lunchtime. Got tanked up on booze and pills and he appears to have randomly attacked your late wife. More than that, we don't know.'

The Detective Inspector says, 'What would you like us to put in the press release?'

'Er . . .?'

'Would you like a press conference?'

'Should I have a press conference? I'm not sure—why would I?'

The two officers share a look. 'We generally only suggest the victim's relatives hold a press conference if we think they have something to hide. It flushes them out, if you see what I mean.'

As they are speaking I suddenly recall a recent news story. A dead girl's boyfriend had made a passionate appeal for her killer to give himself up at a police press conference. The next day he was arrested and charged with her murder.

'And . . . do you think I have something to hide?' I asked.

'No, we don't.'

So we drafted a press release, and then they said that they would stay in contact with me about the progress of the case.

I couldn't wait to get out, to get some air, to escape from this nightmare. But before we started our journey home, I had one more task to perform.

I crossed the road and walked up the familiar garden path to the house where Lizzie and I had lived. I knocked on the door and, after an age, it opened. A man looked at us quizzically.

'Hello. My name is Jeremy Howe. We have a booking for my family for next Saturday evening. Which I would like to cancel.'

'I see.'

'My wife has been killed.'

Silence.

'I am so sorry.'

And with that, we left for Norfolk, to pick up the pieces of my life.

WE WERE the last item of the three o'clock Radio 4 bulletin. 'Police have arrested a man in York suspected of killing an unnamed Open University teacher . . .' We retuned to Radio York . . . 'of killing a Doctor Elizabeth Howe . . .' and they read out verbatim the press release I'd co-written not half an hour ago.

Using one of those first-generation mobile phones the size of a brick, Malcolm called home to let Philippa know we were on our way. I briefly chatted with her. 'We've just got back from the summer fête. Jessica and Lucy had a lovely time. Do you want to have a word with them?'

'No. Just send them my love. But please don't turn on the radio. The news is just breaking. I really don't want them to hear.'

'OK. When are you going to tell the girls?'

'I don't know, Philippa, I just don't know.'

I felt a million miles from the events she was describing in Norfolk—lunches and trips out and ice lollies. I so wanted a lifeline to that world, and here I was returning with a toxic virus: coming to blast the world that I hoped would look after me.

I desperately wanted to be home, but what was home now? Home had been Lizzie and me, we had built that loving home. Home was now me and God knows what. Going home should mean going home to share with Lizzie what had happened. Now I had no one to share the awfulness with and, now that the news was out, I could not put off telling the girls. But how? It would wreck their lives.

I wanted to blot out the future, to curl up and hide. I was exhausted. I wanted to sleep for ever.

'You can take a sleeping pill,' suggested Malcolm.

'I've never had a sleeping pill,' I snapped. But the idea took hold of me.

Malcolm phoned home again. 'Does anyone have a sleeping pill?'

Philippa ransacked the medicine cabinet. 'No, we don't, sorry.'

It became an *idée fixe* with me. Malcolm suggested we try a doctor. Good idea. But on a Sunday? Malcolm phoned home and got the number of a friend of a friend who had the home number of a doctor, whom he then phoned. The doctor suggested trying a casualty department. OK.

Lizzie's death was now the lead item on the Radio 4 four o'clock news.

The phone rang. It was my sister saying that Henry our house sitter needed to talk to me because there were about a million journalists camped outside our front door who wanted a comment from him and a photograph of Lizzie. Oh God.

I spoke to Henry, and he managed to convey to me that if he could give a photograph of Lizzie to the press outside they had promised to leave us alone.

This was horrible. I sent him off to hunt out the photographs that Lizzie's publisher had had taken of her a few weeks previously. She'd hated nearly all of them, but I knew that there was one that she had liked. He found the photos in her study and we talked through them.

'There is a nice one of her in the garden smiling. A lovely likeness.'

'No. Not that one. She hates that one.'

I rejected photograph after photograph as he described them to me. I finally agreed on the image of Lizzie that I thought was the one that she liked. And I got it wrong. Plastered across every newspaper over the next few days was a grainy image of Lizzie smiling that I knew she hated—I can tell that the smile is more of a rictus grin than an expression of her natural warmth. Even now, I still feel wretched about agreeing to use that image. As I rang off, I felt like I had achieved something. But Malcolm saw how distressed I was.

'I'll phone that doctor again.'

The doctor was reluctant, but Malcolm would not take a no from him. He agreed to meet us at the surgery but, because Malcolm never went to the doctor, he had no idea where the surgery was. We finally arrived after six at a purpose-built health centre in the middle of nowhere. The GP, a tall man in his late forties, was clearly pissed off at having his Sunday interrupted.

He hadn't really believed what Malcolm had told him on the phone and asked me to tell him in my own words why I was distressed. As I relayed what had happened, I could see that if we had been in a sitcom his jaw would have dropped. I had never told a story before that had had such impact. He was appalled by each twist and turn of my terrible day and quickly granted me my wish—he fished out of the desk drawer a blister pack of twelve tiny blue bombs. He split the pack in two. I only ever took half of one pill at a time, and somewhere squats a spare half pill.

It is easy for me to see my story from my point of view. Almost impossible to understand the collateral damage I was inflicting on others. I came into people's lives like some plague, like some inverted Midas, polluting everything I touched without even being aware of it.

WHEN WE ARRIVED BACK at my sister's the children were in their pyjamas and Grandma was reading them a bedtime story.

'Daddy, Daddy, look at what I got at the fête,' and Jessica showed me one of the bracelets that Auntie Philippa had bought all four of the girls.

'Look mine is green, Daddy,' chimed in Lucy.

'So you had a good day?'

'Oh yes! We had the best day EVER!' And Jessica gabbled away but I was not really hearing her. All I could think of was that I couldn't tell them now. Not before bedtime. I just couldn't.

'I shall tell them tomorrow,' I said to myself.

But, alas, tomorrow came all too soon. After a night of drug-induced sleep, I crept downstairs at about seven o'clock. My mother and sister were in the kitchen, talking in hushed voices, struggling to come to terms with our new shared nightmare lives.

Philippa wondered if I might do it when I woke them up, because she was sure that Jennifer—the oldest of her three children—had sussed that something was up. But I didn't think it was a terribly good idea. It was an excuse, of course. I wondered how long I could go on living this weird make-believe. Days? Weeks? Years? But the worry of it was making me ill. I had to act PDQ.

I poured out two glasses of juice and took them upstairs. I woke them up like Lizzie and I did every day.

'Did you sleep well?'

'Mmmmmm. Yes. Very. I was having lovely dreams about dancing in a ballet.' Jessica always wakes up wide awake and chirrupy.

'And you, Lucy?'

'I'm tired.' Lucy never wakes up wide awake and is never chirrupy.

'Did you talk to Mummy last night, Daddy?' asked Jessica.

An agonising pause. It felt like I had been kicked in the stomach.

'I miss Mummy,' said Lucy.

A pause which felt ten years long.

I ruffled her hair. 'She sends lots and lots and LOTS of love.'

'When can we talk with Mummy?'

'Well, it's tricky because she isn't on the phone.'

I diverted them into thinking about what to wear and then I slipped downstairs, feeling like a soldier who had just been relieved from frontline duty in a dangerous trench.

My mother, sister and I decided on a plan. Immediately after breakfast, I would take the girls into the garden and tell them. My mother would follow after to help pick up the pieces, while my sister told her three in the sitting room.

Telling the girls was so painful that I am struggling to remember what happened next. I have blanked it out.

I can remember saying to them that there was something I wanted to tell them and asking them to come into the garden.

'Are we going to the seaside today?' Jessica bounced.

If only.

I remember that getting to the garden took for ever, and I can remember exactly where we stood. I remember how grey the sky was, how still the air, how humid. I remember crouching down to be on their level and putting my arms round their shoulders, but I have no memory of telling Jessica and Lucy that their Mummy was dead.

My mother said she could hear the low rumble of my voice, then silence, then an awful cry from Jessica. My sister later said that wail was like the end of Jessica's childhood.

Jessica says that she remembers thinking, 'I wonder how long it will take the trees to grow tall enough to reach Mummy in heaven.'

I don't really remember anything, except that when I said I would look after them just like Mummy, Lucy wailed, 'But, Daddy, you can't cook.'

'Yes he can. He cooked us pizza on Saturday,' Jessica blubbed.

'But that was from a packet.'

'And he cooked us fish fingers last week.'

Jessica then proceeded to list things that Daddy could cook. It wasn't an impressive list. Lucy had a point. She'd rumbled that I was underskilled in the mother department.

3

That time in Norfolk with my sister was the strangest of weeks. I moved from denial, the second phase of grief, to the third: pain and guilt. We grown-ups sat around, mostly silent, while the children played happily together. Every so often, Jessica or Lucy would come to me just for a hug, and then would resolutely scurry off, while one of us would go and make a cup of tea or flick through a newspaper.

At the beginning of the school summer holidays, a couple of weeks after the horrific killing of Rachel Nickell on Wimbledon Common, Lizzie's death was headline news. On the Monday morning Lizzie's photograph was plastered across the front pages of all the tabloids. I didn't really recognise the family paraded across the front pages as us—the coverage was so inaccurate and sketchy. People whom I had never heard of in our street said nice things about us, and the Open University—for whom Lizzie had worked for four years—clearly had no idea who she was. My boss was quoted as saying that I had had a glittering career in front of me. 'Had', note, not 'has'. On Friday I had been one of those upwardly mobile, thirty-something execs in the BBC with a promising future; by Monday, because of personal circumstances, I was a has-been.

I phoned my boss to explain why I wouldn't be coming to work. He said that I shouldn't even consider returning until things had settled down and offered me all the support and love he could muster, etc. It was obvious from our conversation that he still thought of my job as in the present and not in the past, which was a consolation.

I called Inga-Stina Ewbank. She was inconsolable. She said it brought to mind King Lear's dying speech. 'Never never never never never,' he cries over the body of the dead Cordelia.

When I put the phone down, I realised I was in that play, not as a bit-part player, but at the centre of the storm. It was as if the gods had plucked me from my humdrum happy life to test me.

Two university friends of ours visited on the Tuesday afternoon. While their girls played with my two, we sat in the garden. Karen—a journalist—said the only way to put the press disinformation right was for me to do an interview: she knew someone at the *Daily Telegraph*. I called him later that day and he was very nice to me. Just as he was ringing off, he innocently asked me where I was staying. I paused, and then demurred from telling him anything other than 'East Anglia'. My sister's house in the middle of nowhere in Norfolk was like a refuge from a storm. In this oasis of calm, I felt I could protect Jessica and Lucy and me from being exposed.

And yet, I confess, all this publicity made me feel good. It made me feel that the awfulness of what we were going through was somehow validated by the outrage of the rest of the world. But I lived in fear of being doorstopped.

As other news stories of the August silly season kicked in, Lizzie's death moved from page one to page three and then, by the end of the week, disappeared altogether. I was gratified when the *Independent* ran an obituary of Lizzie, making the cherished life that I had lost feel as significant as her death. OK, so it was written by Karen, but it helped me realise what an extraordinary person I had married.

Sitting in the sun-drenched Norfolk garden, Karen, her husband Andy and I had talked about damage. 'You and the girls will be different, but you don't need to be damaged.'

I think Karen was right. I have taken enormous comfort from what she said. We have led a different life to the one we might have led if Lizzie had not been killed. Some things are less good, some things are better—we have had more adventures, and my relationship with Jessica and Lucy is bound with hoops of tempered steel. The broken bone, a colleague said, is stronger once mended, and our bones are strong for having been broken and expertly reset. The only person who came out of it with nothing—and as I write this I am angry and upset as I ponder the pointless waste—is, of course, Lizzie herself.

Family came and family went—Maka, Deda, Louise, Jonathan—all of us paralysed into inactivity, not knowing how to react. We would sit in my sister's garden, fuelled by endless cups of tea, pushed together but not united by grief. Just mentioning Lizzie's name reduced her father to tears, to the annoyance of her mother and to the Howes' English embarrassment. It was important to be together, but what was there to be done or said?

And so, not really knowing what to do with, or for, the children, I decided we would go to the seaside as promised. And their cousins, Jennifer and Katherine, wanted to come too—which left no room in the car for any grown-ups apart from me.

So the five of us set out for Great Yarmouth. I discovered that if you keep moving you don't get depressed. So we kept moving—a picnic lunch on the beach, a walk along the promenade, ice creams with chocolate flakes ('Really, Daddy, with a flake?' 'Yes, really, Lucy.' 'Wowwww!!!! Thank you, Daddy.'), twenty-five pence each for the slot machines, and then a visit to the funfair.

The girls wanted to go on the Big Wheel and I had to wait and wave at them while they went round and round. I felt so alone, a solitary middle-aged man lost in a children's funfair. I couldn't wait for the ride to finish so I could grasp Jessica and Lucy by the hand; being separated from them was physically painful.

I then suggested that instead of slogging back along the front to the car, we would take a pony and trap. Sod the fact that it was a rip-off and that Lizzie and I would have run a mile from such an extravagance: it was a real treat to round off a day of treats. The children loved it. Mostly, we had a wonderful day out, during which we forgot our troubles and just had fun.

Early that evening the phone rang.

'Mr Howe. It's the Detective Superintendent looking after the case of your late wife.'

Did they want to search our house? Did they want to question me again? Did they still see me as a suspect, even though Robin Pask had been charged with Lizzie's death in court the day before?

'My commanding officer has given the all-clear for you to go ahead with your late wife's funeral. Were you thinking of a burial or a cremation?'

'Er . . . ?'

'We would like you to bury her in case we need to exhume her body at some point. And Mr Howe . . .'

'Yes?'

'There'll be a lot of press interest and that will attract all sorts of weird people. Keep it low-key is my advice, Mr Howe.'

I was more than happy for Lizzie's parents to arrange the funeral. We agreed that Lizzie should be buried in Bath, in the same plot as her aunt who had died the year Lucy was born. Her parents said they would pay for it all and wanted it to be family only. I disagreed—I wanted our friends to be there too. Maka conceded, but she had another anxiety.

'Who will look after the children?'

'I had assumed that I would. They'll come with me.'

'They're too little. They would find it too upsetting.'

My instinct was that Lucy and Jessica were inseparable from me and that they should accompany me to the funeral. Of course, it would be upsetting for them, but weren't they upset anyway? Surely they should come?

I sought advice. By some miracle, my sister managed to get me an appointment with the head of the Children's Psychiatry Department in Norwich (waiting time approximately six months) *later that same morning*.

As I sat in the waiting room with Philippa, I felt like a fraud. Surely all I had to do was ask, 'Do I take the children to their mother's funeral?' She would then answer yes or no. I could have done it by phone.

My sister and I were with her for over an hour. Although she knew my story (she too had read the papers), she wanted me to tell it in my own words. As we sat in her cool, darkened room, time stopped. I had the space to breathe, to relax, to reason. We hardly touched on the subject of the funeral but when I left a) I wanted to hug her and b) I was beginning to know my own mind. I had, it seems, discovered the first law of coping: trust your instincts. Don't let the heart rule your head, go lower down. Trust your gut. By the end of the day, the answer was clear. Of course the children should come to the funeral.

If this wasn't miracle-working, I don't know what is.

'If you need any more help,' she said as we shook hands, 'I know a colleague in Oxford. I will write to her and your GP and let them know you are coming.'

She was as good as her word. But that is another story.

WE LEFT NORFOLK, briefly touched base in Oxford to pick up clean clothes, and moved on to Bath for Lizzie's funeral. One thing I had to do before we went was to collect our hapless kitten from the cattery. I dumped the children with Julia across the road—she was Lizzie's best friend in Oxford—and raced off. It was the first time I had really been by myself since my walk across the water meadows. I felt bereft. Each corner, each turning, each signpost on the familiar Oxford to Swindon road seemed to trigger a memory of Lizzie. I started to weep, shouting Lizzie's name. I felt miserable beyond words, helpless, hopeless, sobbing. I was driving so fast that I realised I was in danger of losing control. I got a grip and pulled into a layby. I sat there hunched. 'Oh, Lizzie, Lizzie, Lizzie. I CANNOT bear it.'

I got out of the car, walked down the road for a hundred yards, taking deep breaths, got back in and began to drive sanely.

The lady at the cattery was very understanding: she knew what had happened because the police in York had phoned her. The cat, however, was not the least bit pleased to see me and howled all the way home, where she was nearly squeezed to death by the girls. I arranged for a neighbour to feed her, and then we packed up and went off to Bath, leaving Milly Molly Mandy to guard the house.

We arrived at the house where Lizzie had grown up, a large, honey-coloured Regency villa, which the girls treated as a second home. Getting ready for the funeral reminded me so much of our wedding day, only Lizzie wasn't there to worry and get into a strop because there wasn't enough hot water for her to wash her hair. And, like our wedding, I had almost nothing to do with planning it: Maka had organised everything and my brother Jonathan had invited people.

The morning was one of bathing and hair-washing and brushing, ironing and laying out our clothes in readiness. I had arranged to go to the church with the children to see the coffin. I didn't want it to be a shock when they arrived at the service and saw the box with their mother inside for the first time. And this way we had a private moment to say goodbye.

Jessica and Lucy had each decorated a plate with sea shells, which we were going to place on the coffin with a posy of garden flowers. Bearing our plates and posies, we crept into the empty church, rain rattling on the roof tiles. Laid out on a trestle at the head of the nave was the coffin. The girls were excited and curious rather than daunted, and wanted to be lifted up to inspect their Mummy's coffin.

'I didn't know Mummy's middle name was Mary, like mine,' piped up Jessica, peering at the brass name plaque.

'Mummy never had a middle name!' said Lucy. That Lizzie had never been given a middle name had been a bone of contention with her. That Jessica had been saddled with Mary (in memory of my grandmother, who had died before she was born) was a bone of contention with *her*—'Mary's a horrible name'—whereas Lucy was incredibly proud of her middle name, Elizabeth.

I felt physically sick—why had I let someone else organise things and screw them up? But, for the girls, it changed the mood.

'How come the funeral people don't know Mummy's name?'

'Maybe it's not Mummy in there. Maybe she's not really dead.'

'I'm afraid she is dead, my sweet,' I told her. 'It's definitely Mummy in the coffin.'

'Can we have a look, Daddy, just to make sure?'

'No, darling, you can't. It is screwed down ready for the funeral.'

'Please. I want to look at Mummy.'

'No, Lucy my sweet. I am afraid you can't. I'm sorry.'

On the advice of the police, the undertakers and just about everybody, the coffin had been nailed down securely. Lizzie's injuries were too horrible to witness (which was why the Assistant Coroner wouldn't let me touch the sheets when I had to identify her body), and so I am the only one of the family who saw poor Lizzie's dead body.

'I guess Maka just made a mistake,' I said.

'She does keep calling me Lizzie all the time. It's quite funny.'

For the rest of her life, Maka invariably called Jessica Lizzie.

I lifted each girl in turn and they carefully placed their plates and their flowers on the coffin. I said a simple prayer—'Dear Lord, please look after our Mummy. Please let her know that we love her, now and always. Amen.'

Maka was genuinely surprised about the error and phoned the undertakers immediately. She really had thought that Lizzie's middle name was Mary. I realised that, beneath her no-nonsense exterior, she had lost it. I don't think she ever refound it.

After a desultory early lunch, every mouthful of which stuck in my throat, we got ready. Then suddenly the funeral director arrived and we were whisked off to the church in the pouring rain.

We assembled under umbrellas, Lucy, Jessica and I at the front. The undertaker peeked into the church and then pushed open the heavy door with a clatter and, to the sound of the organ, we processed into the church.

I don't know what I was expecting, but as we entered, Jessica and Lucy tightly clutching a hand each, several hundred faces in an absolutely packed church turned round to look at us. I was buoyed up on a sea of love, hugely relieved.

'Daddy,' Jessica whispered, 'are we sitting at the front because we're special?' She made it sound like a treat.

We sat by the coffin. I noticed that 'Mary' had been crudely excised from the brass plaque and the girls' plates and posies had been fixed to the lid, making it look faintly like a table laid for dinner. I couldn't believe that

Lizzie was inside. I don't suppose that anyone at any funeral can believe it is their beloved in that box. Death and disbelief travel hand in hand.

'Why is everybody looking at us, Daddy?' said Lucy loudly. It broke the ice. Some people laughed, some began to sob.

The service went by in a daze. My boss read from Milton's 'Lycidas', Lizzie's favourite poem, Inga-Stina Ewbank read from Ecclesiastes, another friend from Wordsworth's 'There Was a Boy'. The priest gave a beautiful address, we sang Lizzie's favourite hymns and said prayers. And then it was all over.

Jessica, Lucy and I filed out first behind the coffin and then, like at a wedding, we shook hands with the entire congregation. I don't think I've ever been hugged by so many people in my life, but each hug restored just a little piece of the love I had had ripped away from me.

Then came the committal at the grave. The rain had stopped and the sun was breaking out. I had compromised with Maka and Deda, and the committal was to be private. Not even the girls were to be there; I had arranged for my mother and sister to look after Jessica and Lucy back at the house. I had promised them that I would put some flowers from Jessica and from Lucy a fresh fig—the fruit Lizzie loved above all others—into the grave for them. But it was as if I were umbilically attached to them, and there was no way that we were going to go our separate ways. Nor was I going to stop all those wonderful people attending the actual burial, which took place in a cemetery high on a hill that seemed to overlook the rest of the world. All I can recall is streams of people hurrying over the downs towards the grave, which was surrounded with more flowers than I have ever seen in my life.

As the coffin was lowered into the grave, Jessica threw in her flowers and Lucy was about to throw in her fig, but instead tried to jump in herself.

'I want my Mummy,' she wailed. 'I want to be with my Mummy.' And, sobbing, she was scooped up by my mother.

And Lizzie, my heart's best treasure, was buried at the age of thirty-four.

THE DAY AFTER the funeral, I took the girls to see the Walt Disney film, *Peter Pan*. I held Jessica's hand most of the way through, as she and Lucy stuffed their faces with popcorn (a special treat; I mean, why not just spoil them for the rest of our lives?). Once the popcorn was finished, Lucy clambered onto my lap.

Peter Pan is a mother-fixated story. When Peter sat on Wendy's lap and asked her to be his mother I had tears streaming down my face. I had forgotten how unsuitable it was for two girls who had just buried their own mother. 'What are you thinking, Lucy?' I asked a rapt child. I wondered if she was in a state of trauma and needed to leave.

'I was thinking what a beautiful dress Wendy is wearing.'

OUR RETURN TO NORMALITY was prompted by Jessica's best friend Katie's birthday party.

We arrived back in Oxford before lunch on a Saturday. On the new worktops were two *Little Mermaid* beakers, with a note: 'To Jessica and Lucy. I hope you enjoy your new kitchen. Love Paul.' He was our builder. Catherine, our childminder, had decorated the kitchen with flowers. I was incredibly touched. But the house didn't feel like our home.

While the girls got changed for the party, I went looking for something. My mother had said that she could feel my father's presence in their house long after his death. I searched for Lizzie everywhere, but she had vanished utterly. There was no lingering smell of her in her bathrobe hanging by the shower, no imprint of her in our bed, no surprising notes or reminders left on her desk. Just a lot of freshly washed clothes and neat files of paperwork, her everyday objects devoid of their purpose—her nightie under the pillow, her lists of things to do pinned on the noticeboard in her study, her wardrobe, her books. Everything was exactly as she had left it, but there was no trace of her. I felt cheated. With increasing anxiety, I pulled open drawers, opened jewellery boxes, smelled her clothes. Where was she? I'd been certain that I would find her once we got home but she had bloody well vanished.

I remembered a car that we had passed on the way from Bath: a crumpled wreck left on a verge, the bonnet wrenched open, the radiator like a toothless grin, the roof crumpled, the sides stoved in. Smashed to bits. Lizzie's death was that car crash. I saw Jessica, Lucy and me as survivors, me standing with my arms round them on the side of the road, forlorn, stunned, but alive. All our worldly belongings scattered round us, blowing in the wind.

I was reminded of the Wittenham Clumps, of the two trees. Partners for life—like Lizzie and me. But what happens when one tree dies? Two trees, now one, alone and defenceless, facing the wrong way. Next to it is a gaping hole. I was standing next to that hole. I was scared that we would be sucked into it and drown in grief—

'Daddy, Jessica wants to know where you put Katie's present,' Lucy interrupted. 'Why have you thrown all Mummy's jumpers on the floor?'

'I was looking for something. Lucy, you look lovely. Is that the dress Maka gave you for your birthday?' It was her only dress. Lucy didn't do dresses. 'The present's downstairs in the pretty paper with elephants on.'

'Daddy!' Jessica called up. 'I can't find my hairbrush.'

I suddenly realised that, in the girls' eyes, I was now their mummy as well as their daddy. Presents and hairbrushes were what mummies did. As a dad, I saw myself as the Minister of Fun—'Let's go to the fair!'—and Lizzie was the Minister of Work—'Time for bed girls!' In gaining a new mother, I wondered if they had lost a father, because I wasn't much good at being fun any more. And I was certainly a different type of mother, mostly because a) I was a man, b) I was a working mum and c) I was inept. Whenever Lizzie had gone away I had played at being mum and had been interestingly different from their real Mummy, but, let's be honest, not much good. This was now for real, and was for ever.

'Come on, girls. Here's the present. Have you written the card, Jessica?'

'We were going to make one, remember, Daddy?'

'Oh.'

'Shall we do one now?'

'No, darling. Katie will have to go without a card or we'll be late. She'll understand.'

Off we set. As I was about to slam shut the front door—

'Daddy, have you remembered the door key?'

'Shit. Oops. Poo, I mean.' They giggled. 'Lucky you reminded me.'

For the next two years, practically everyone on our street had a door key to number ten, just in case I forgot.

Off we trooped across the park, me feeling as if I had lost several layers of skin. We reached the door of the church hall. It was dark and it took all my courage to go inside. I stopped and gave them both a cuddle—I could see they were both as anxious as I was.

'Aren't you coming in with us, Daddy?'

'No, I'm . . . OK, just for a few minutes.'

What happened next was surreal. All the mums—almost none of whom I recognised—were standing around talking, and all the children were clustered round Katie as she opened her presents. When we went in, everyone went quiet. Jessica, Lucy and I stood there, stranded.

Katie broke the silence by coming up to Jessica and giving her a hug. And then she hugged Lucy and smiled at me.

'I am glad you could come,' her mother whispered to me. 'Katie was so worried that Jessica wouldn't make it.'

'Jessica wouldn't have missed Katie's party for the world.'

'We are so sorry about your news.'

'Yes, it's awful.'

'I know.' She wasn't a woman of many words. We stood in silence, then she asked, 'You don't know any party games do you? Dave was going to do that bit, but he's had to go to work.'

Ah, I thought, one smart dad.

And so, for the next hour, I organised party games—rather manically. All the mothers drifted off back to their Saturday afternoons. I had nowhere to drift off to, so playing games was probably good therapy. But of this I was assured—our little community of south Oxford was in shock.

THE FOLLOWING MONDAY, I began an unscheduled maternity leave which would last the duration of the girls' summer holiday. My job was instantly displaced while I learned to be a mother. Well, kind of learned.

Anger is the fourth phase of grief, so I don't need to tell you what my reaction was when the washing machine flooded the utility room. A couple of months before, I had promised Lizzie that the next time it went wrong we would get rid of it, so Jessica, Lucy and I mopped the floor and trooped off to buy a new one. It's only money, after all.

Late one morning, we heard terrified mewing outside from Milly Molly Mandy. We all rushed out into the garden and there she was, stuck on the roof, up by the attic-bedroom window. It was all my fault, I should not have left the window open; Lizzie wouldn't have done so. Because I owed the cat one for being my alibi, I decided to rescue her. I don't know who was more terrified, the hapless cat or the children down below or me, risking life, limb and dignity as I half-clambered out of the window to grab her.

I got letters of condolence and support from work—people like the head of radio, the Director General and his deputy (John Birt—heard of him?). Blimey, I thought, I'm famous. For all the wrong reasons. And every so often my boss phoned me to tell me not to come in to work.

Personnel phoned to reassure me that there was no expectation of my returning to the office before I was ready. This shadowy bit of the BBC, in charge of hiring, firing and other dark deeds, became a security blanket and then a friend. It was they who had arranged for flowers in the house on my return from the funeral, and now they sorted out how I should gradually return to work. In fact, 'they' was one woman, Kate Poulton. She was amazing, but behind her I could see the paternal hand of my boss.

My secretary was dispatched to Oxford to see if she could help sort out the bits of my work that had been left hanging. She was lovely, but, like a lot of people, I think she was overwhelmed by witnessing the awfulness of what we were going through. And all the questions she asked me about work were met with a blank look of incomprehension. My overloaded brain had deleted the answers.

One day two colleagues descended on me like ministering angels. The rain put paid to their plan to take me out for a picnic, so we sat round the kitchen table, which heaved under the heaps of M&S finger food they had brought, and we chewed the fat. They came unannounced (having checked that I would be there) and left just as unceremoniously in the late afternoon. It was an act of simple human warmth. I felt connected, as if I had had a holiday that afternoon.

A week later, I took delivery of a pile of boxes from the BBC—a fax machine, a modem, a printer, an answerphone, etc. with a note that read: 'Hope this helps. Clive.' My closest colleague at work had seen to it that, if I chose, I need never come to the office. Which was great. But it still left me with a Massive Dilemma.

Massive Dilemma, Part One: how could I go on with my job? I was an executive for the BBC, I worked hard and put in long hours for my living.

Massive Dilemma, Part Two: my domestic accounts.

July 1992:

my income

+ Lizzie's income

– the cost of bringing up two children

– paying a mortgage

– a small amount of child care

= break even.

August 1992:

my income

~~Lizzie's income~~

– the cost of bringing up two children

– paying a mortgage

– shed loads of child care

= oh shit.

I could have given up my job, but I enjoyed my work. It also gave me an identity. I worked with some great people, too—they were my friends; and it paid me a decent wage. Giving up my job was never a serious option.

Perhaps I should move closer to work? But how on earth could I move to London? I didn't have any network of support there. I would sink.

Should I look for a job in Oxford? All I knew about was broadcasting, and the university didn't even have a media studies department.

Deda tried to persuade me to live with them in Bath. My in-laws wanted to furnish their basement for me so that I could use it as my pad and the girls could live with them upstairs. It was a generous offer—except that their basement was as dingy as hell and 110 miles from my office. Just thinking about it made me think of being incarcerated in a world of single-man hell, while my family scampered around above me. Like being in a Borrowers movie directed by Roman Polanski.

I know that what Maka and Deda really wanted to do was to scoop up Jessica and Lucy and bring them up as their own children. Who can blame them? They desperately wanted to cuddle up to their bereft granddaughters, and they fully expected me to find another partner and go off into the sunset. Deda hinted at this several times.

It didn't happen. I chose to bring up the children, for good or for ill, and to remain in Oxford in the house we called home.

So I needed tons of child care. Our fabulous childminder, Catherine, had looked after the girls for about five hours a week. I calculated I now needed someone who could take them to and from school and look after them until I got back home. That was . . . *sixty hours a week*, starting at breakfast time, finishing at bedtime. She would need to live in. It would cost a bomb, but what could I do?

I went to a nanny agency based in a poky little office up some grim back stairs in central Oxford. It was staffed by two thirty-something women who were too busy to take much notice of me, despite my having an appointment. Eventually, I was permitted to explain what I was looking for.

'I'm afraid I really don't think we can help you. We would never find a nanny who would live in with a single-parent father.'

I hastily came up with a Plan B: if I abandoned the idea of the nanny taking them to school, she would start at three in the afternoon and sixty hours miraculously shrank to twenty-five. I put an advert in the local paper. How would I manage the early morning school run? People might just notice if I never got to the office before eleven in the morning. But I was desperate.

I decided to at least try the other city-centre agency—just for luck. They were a lot posher and a lot more expensive. Their office was more like a sitting room than a place of work. The lady who ran it had a cup of tea waiting for me when I arrived, and she was sympathetic: she knew my story and she wanted to help me. She suggested that I see what came of the newspaper ad. If it didn't work, come back to her. There was a way out of this mess! As I drove back home I felt elated.

I passed a cyclist coming in the opposite direction and, for one moment, I thought it was Lizzie! My heart raced. I stopped the car. I wanted to tell her that I loved her, that the girls were fine, that I was missing her like mad, that, well, Lizzie, you can come home now. But the girl on the bike rode past and she wasn't the least bit like Lizzie. Bitterly disappointed, I drove back home. But for days afterwards I felt as if I had been so close to Lizzie that I had touched her.

That, of course, would have been the solution to my problem. Have Lizzie back. I needed a wife and a mother. And a lover.

Of course, Jessica also had a child-care plan: 'Daddy, why don't we go round to Jane's for tea? I like playing with Clara.'

Clara was Jane's daughter, a couple of years older than Jessica.

'Yes. That's a nice idea.'

'Daddy, didn't Clara's dad die?'

'I know, darling. How sad. She must be very sad.'

'And Jane must be sad. She must be lonely. Like you, Daddy.'

Jane lived a few doors down, with her two girls and a boy. Her husband had died about five years ago. From where I sat, her life looked like chaos, like ours. We duly went for tea. I liked Jane. She was feisty and fun, and surviving just fine. Unlike me.

'Why don't you marry Jane, Daddy?'

'Because . . .' You could see the sense in Jessica's argument. Jane is single and a mum. Daddy is single and a dad. Ergo, they should get married and we can be one big happy family. Onwards.

Or rather, back to the nanny. People had rung about the ad. I would have to check them out. My sister Philippa helped me. We would do the introductions and then the girls would take them up to show them their bedroom. After about ten or fifteen minutes, I would go up and fetch the prospective nanny down so we could 'have a chat'.

A succession of six young women came to visit, the ones whose CVs looked promising—as in, they didn't immediately suggest alcohol dependency or certified insanity—and who had some experience of looking after children. All were smartly turned out. It was an exhausting afternoon, but the task was enormously simplified by Lucy.

There was only one girl Lucy didn't rush up to and hit, saying, 'I don't want you. I want my Mummy back.' In retrospect, it may have been because by the time she saw Linda, Lucy was tired. I gave Linda the job.

Linda was to start the week the girls went back to school. The arrangement was that I would drop the girls off at Catherine the childminder's before school and either Linda or Catherine would pick them up each afternoon. It meant that I could go back to work. Bit by bit, I was rebuilding the edifice that had been Family Howe.

4

The rest of that summer holidays was pretty odd. It rained nearly every day. I developed a kind of agoraphobia. I also developed a furrow in my forehead, the world's deepest worry line.

One morning, my mother, who was staying with us to help, had a stroke. It was very minor and the hospital assured us she was fine, but it showed the strain we were all under.

Well-wishers trooped through the house on a regular basis, all of whom wanted to hear my story. Recounting Lizzie's death became like replaying a cracked record, but the record was damaging the stylus—me. A friend suggested I get a T-shirt saying, 'Read the press release'. I was visited by friends I had not seen in an age. They would drop in for an hour, and then leave. Many of them never got in touch again.

One neighbour just knocked on the door one Saturday. 'I think you did the right thing by taking your daughters to their mother's funeral.'

'Thank you.'

'It's just that my mother died when I was six and I was not allowed to go to her funeral. It still rankles with me, you know.'

Another was a man in a very similar position to mine. His wife had been pregnant with their third child and both she and the baby had died in childbirth, leaving him to bring up their two young children. He had moved to live almost next door to his late wife's parents and had got enough child care to allow him to go back to work. Now, his in-laws were trying to take over the care of his children and he was having an affair with the nanny. I felt sorry for him but I couldn't wait to get him out of the house. In case he infected me.

By and large, I was grateful not to be left alone, but at the same time, I felt that my life was public property. I desperately wanted any distraction from our situation but, no matter how tricky it was, I did need to get on with real life.

Every morning I would wake up feeling acute anxiety. I just wanted to escape back into the oblivion of sleep. Then I would hear a call from the girls: 'Daddy! Can we have our juice now, please?' I would spring into action. If it wasn't for the girls, I don't suppose I would ever have got out of bed. I'd pad downstairs, feed the cat, take the girls their juice, and then sit in our new kitchen and open the mail.

I got hundreds of cards of condolence, which somehow made me feel wanted. I would get withdrawal symptoms if I came downstairs and there were no cards waiting for me on the doormat.

Once I had given the children breakfast, the structure of my days became horribly random. I had precious little idea what to do with the time. One afternoon I was lying on the sitting-room floor while Lucy, curled in the crook of my leg, was busy drawing.

'If Jesus came back from being dead, why can't Mummy?' she said.

'Well, Jesus was the son of God. It's different from Mummy.'

She carried on scribbling. 'Daddy, Snow White came back from the dead—why can't Mummy?'

'Well, darling, she was never really dead like Mummy is.'

More scribbling. 'Daddy—what about the Sleeping Beauty?'

I lifted Lucy onto my lap and told her that her Mummy was never coming back, but that she was still alive in our memories and our hearts, that half of what made up Lucy was Mummy, and she would never, ever lose that. I don't know if she understood, but the cuddle made her feel a bit better.

A couple of evenings later, Jessica piped up. 'Daddy, you know the bad man who killed Mummy?'

'Yes, darling.'

'Where did he hit Mummy?' I had told the girls a half-truth—that a bad man had hit their mummy and that she had died. This clearly did not satisfy Jessica. 'How did she die?' She relentlessly used this line of questioning most days. When she saw me pause, she continued to probe. 'How exactly did Mummy die?'

I decided to bite the bullet. Somewhere, I'd read that more soldiers died in the Great War of infections caused by the filth that got into their wounds than from the shrapnel that caused the wounds. I saw the truth as some kind of astringent that would keep Jessica and Lucy's wounds clean.

My uncle had died in a car crash when I was a little boy. We were told what had happened and it made a huge impression. I can still remember sitting in the bath when my mother told us. Driving home from the office too fast, after a few drinks, my uncle lost concentration and ended up wrapped round a lamppost a mile from home. He died instantly. For some reason, his daughter, my cousin Liz who was the same age as me, had been told a different story—that he had crashed the car, but had come home and had a heart attack in the kitchen and died in the small hours. We were told never to talk about her father's death with Liz—we surmised this was because the two versions of the story didn't match. Of course, all we wanted to do after that was speculate about my uncle's death. The version told to Liz doesn't ring true. Why hadn't Liz been woken by the arrival of an ambulance? Why was her mother up in the middle of the night to witness his heart attack? Twenty years later, Liz's mother—a heavy drinker who smoked forty cigarettes a day—died of a heart attack. Liz was distraught. Her father had died of a heart attack in his thirties, her mother in her late forties. What hope had she? My mother had to take her to one side and tell her the truth.

Lies are messy, the truth is clean and simple. Clean wounds heal, dirty wounds do not.

'I mean, if you hit someone, you don't die, do you? I hit Lucy yesterday and she's not dead.'

I sat down and told Jessica and Lucy that I would tell them exactly how Mummy had died, that they were not to be frightened, that it would never happen to them, that it was a horrible, freak occurrence.

'Mummy was in her room at the college in the middle of the afternoon. I bet she was working at her desk . . .'

'Did she have a cup of coffee?'

'I expect so.'

'And some dried figs?'

It was like telling them a ghastly inverted fairy story.

'Anyway, a man knocked at the door and barged in and stabbed her with a knife for no reason at all other than he had gone mad. Now he is safely locked away and cannot hurt anyone ever again. Mummy died almost instantly. I don't suppose she felt any pain.'

On the death certificate, one of the causes was heart failure due to shock. Those last few seconds must have been . . . well, words don't take you there. In A. S. Byatt's *Still Life*, a novel that had made a huge impression on Lizzie, the heroine is electrocuted by faulty wiring in a fridge. In the nanosecond between the moment of shock and her death, all that goes through her mind is: 'Who will look after the children now?' I think that is probably how Lizzie died, and why my duty of care to Jessica and Lucy has been so important, above and beyond the fact that I love them unconditionally. But I don't think that her death was painless.

'Was there any blood, Daddy?'

'Yes, my sweet.'

'How much blood, Daddy?'

'A lot, I think. It was like a very, very, very bad cut that wouldn't stop bleeding. And if that happens, your heart runs out of blood and you die. Like Mummy did. But it happens very fast.'

Pause.

'I see.'

There was a silence. I could see by the look on Jessica's face that I had put her worries and fears about her mother's death to rest. She never asked about it again, not because she couldn't, but because she didn't need to.

I gathered them both up in my arms and wept, and they wept, and we lay on Lucy's bottom bunk for an age until they were dozing. I lifted Jessica up into her bunk, and sleepily she said, 'I love you. Thank you for being such a good Daddy.' Then I put little Lucy, who had uttered not a word during the whole episode, under her duvet and cuddled her. What does it feel like to be four and not have a mummy? It was an unbearable thought. Her eyes fluttered open and she smiled at me and fell back to sleep.

I crept downstairs and howled my eyes out. I had no one to share it with; most of all, I wanted to share it with Lizzie. But I had told the girls the truth about what had happened to their mother. I had left their wounds clean, so that they had the best chance possible of healing strongly—and I think they have done so—but doing so left me wrung out.

OVER THE NEXT few weeks, I got used to going round to Jessica and Lucy's friends' houses and chatting with their mothers while the children played.

'Polly, I think I might have had a stroke like my mother. I don't seem to be able to think straight.'

'Oh dear.'

'All I can think about is what meal I need to prepare next.'

'That's not a stroke, Jeremy. That's called child care, the next best thing to having a lobotomy. Ask any mother.'

Then, one morning that August, the phone rang.

'It's the BBC here. We were expecting you for a job interview this morning and you haven't turned up. The interview board is pretty pissed off.'

Months ago, long before Lizzie died, I had applied for a job in television drama. I had completely forgotten.

'I am sorry, but if someone had told me about the interview, you never know, I might have turned up.'

'We sent you an email.'

'But I've been out of the office for over a month.'

'Well, look, can you come for the interview after lunch?'

'I'm in Oxford and I have to look after my two girls this afternoon. Do you know anything about me and my situation?'

'No.'

'Brace yourself, it isn't a pretty story. My wife was killed earlier in the summer, I am on compassionate leave, and I'm not really in any state for a job interview.'

'I see. But if I can rearrange the interview for this afternoon . . . They do want to see you.'

'Who's they?'

'The Head of Television Drama and the Head of Drama Series.'

So nobody important then. They only look after about half a billion pounds' worth of programmes. 'Well, you had better tell them about my situation. Oh, and I haven't watched any television for two months and I'm not sure I could do the job any more.'

'Hmm, I see.' He sounded affronted. And that, so I thought, was that.

After lunch, the phone went again. 'Jeremy, it's about your interview.' His tone of voice was gentler, as if I were an invalid. 'The two heads still want to see you. Shall we say four? And I will get you a parking space at TVC.'

Being offered a parking space at Television Centre was a bit like being offered a bag of gold. They must be serious, I thought. They had fixed for me to park in the Director General's space.

I had about half an hour to prepare for the job of Senior Development Executive for TV Drama Series and sort out who would look after the children. A friend across the road was dead impressed. 'They must want you. Of course, I'd love to look after the girls. What will you wear?'

'I might change my shirt, if I can find a clean one.'

So my preparation for the interview consisted of ironing a shirt.

The main thing I remember about the interview was the delicious chocolate biscuits with Earl Grey tea, served in a china cup. My interviewers were on their best behaviour. That might have been because as I sat down I asked them to be nice, otherwise I might burst into tears.

We talked as much about child care as about television and, just before I left, I said, 'Look, in the unlikely event of you offering me the job, it's inconceivable that I would be able to take it.'

'Of course. But thank you for coming. And good luck.'

Personnel phoned the next day. 'They were very impressed with you.'

'How come? I displayed no knowledge of television and we talked mostly about what a crap mum I was being.'

'They think you're a crap mum who's got balls,' she laughed.

The story has a happy ending: they didn't offer me the job, but for about six weeks they couldn't decide between me and my best friend in my department who finally got the job. All I can say is, the rest of the field must have been truly shit, but it did my sense of self-worth a power of good.

THE BUREAUCRACY OF DEATH is horrible. Read Kafka to get the gist of what you need to go through.

Before we had been allowed to bury Lizzie's body, we had to wait for the coroners' court verdict. The death certificate that was issued was horribly graphic. Requesting multiple copies of this document in order to change bank accounts, house deeds, mortgages and so on left me reeling.

Then there was child allowance. If a husband dies, the widow gets a one-off lump-sum payment and increased child support, but if the wife dies, the widower gets nothing. According to the Secretary of State for Pensions, who replied to my distraught letter on the subject, there are statistically so few single-parent fathers it just isn't worth the cost of the administrative machinery to set it up. At least it wasn't in 1992.

And so on and so on. I tried seeking advice. I went to a single-parent support group, but it felt like a dating agency and I felt like an intruder. The man at the Citizens' Advice Bureau had no advice for me at all. He seemed to imply that my problem was beyond their remit, that there was no citizens' advice on coping with my particular car crash of a situation.

We were not helped by my mortgage company. One August morning, a letter landed on my doormat addressed to Mr J. P. Howe and Dr E. Howe (deceased). I opened it—'Dear Mr J. P. Howe and Dr E. Howe (deceased)' Did they not think it a bit strange to be writing to a dead person? But the contents of the letter were chilling: because I had not been paying my mortgage, they were taking steps to foreclose on our house. WHAT THE ****!? I phoned my bank. 'Unless you have asked us to cancel them, all your direct debits and standing orders should still be working, Mr Howe.'

Ten minutes later they called back and said that, actually, my standing order for the mortgage had been cancelled—by the mortgage company. Bloody hellfire!

I rang the mortgage company.

'Mr Howe, it is company practice to cancel all mortgage repayments on the death of our clients, because most of our mortgages are insured.'

Because our mortgage was so expensive, Lizzie and I had decided to insure it on my death only, as I was the main earner.

'Cancel without informing me?'

'Yes.'

'And then threaten me with foreclosure?'

'That was an error on our part. Please accept our apologies.'

'And you think the best way of informing me is to write to me and Dr E. Howe (deceased)?'

'Well, obviously someone made a mistake. We would like to apologise for that too. If you wish to make a complaint—'

I am sure you get the gist of the conversation. And so the repayments began to drain my bank account once more. If only we had paid that little bit more to insure Lizzie's life.

I HAD CANCELLED a trip to Portugal we had planned to take after Lizzie's return from York, and that put the lid on a summer holiday. I was in no fit state to organise another one. Then my friend Clive insisted I accompany him on a trip to the west of Ireland. He had taken a cottage in remotest Donegal for a week, while his wife was off in the States. He had care of Joe, aged ten months. His parenting skills were on a par with mine. He needed a companion, so he chose me. Was he nuts? I agreed.

I had absolutely no idea what to pack, so I packed everything the children owned. Apart from their underwear, which I left behind in our new tumble drier.

While I was ransacking the wardrobe, there was a knock at the door. On the doorstep was a familiar figure.

'Jessica, Lucy, Mr Townsend's here to see you.'

'Who, Daddy?' came screaming from upstairs. There was a lot of thumping and giggling.

'Mr Townsend. You know, your Headmaster.'

The thumping and giggling stopped instantly.

Mr Townsend was a sweet man, bearded, smiley, faintly chaotic, whose school was the focal point of our little community.

'Hello, Jessica. Hello, Lucy,' he called out, considerably less bellicosely than me. 'I just popped round to see how you are.'

Two solemn-looking girls marched slowly down the stairs. They looked worried—what on earth could they have done that merited the Headmaster coming round *in the middle of the summer holidays*?

Once they realised he had simply come to say how sorry he was about Mummy, my two warmed up and we quickly settled down to play the National Trust Animal Game, which someone had just given us. It was a rubbish game that would keep a brain-dead two-year-old entertained for less than five minutes, but even with Lucy patiently and sweetly explaining the rules to Mr Townsend, he didn't seem to grasp its subtleties. But he made instant friends of the children and they were quickly at ease.

He had really come round to ask how I thought we should handle the announcement of Lizzie's death to the rest of the school. It was decided that the girls would perform some 'important errand' with one of their teachers while the announcement was made at midmorning assembly on the first day back, and that they would slip into the hall surreptitiously afterwards with Mrs Naumann, who had been Jessica's form teacher and whom both girls adored.

As a sneak preview of the coming term, he told them that Jessica was to be in Mr Standish's class, a new member of staff, while Lucy was to remain in Michelle's nursery class, where Elizabeth, her favourite teacher, was the classroom assistant. The girls treated this as Extra Privileged Information and couldn't wait to rush off to tell their friends.

'I wonder if Mr Standish will be strict?' mused Jessica after her headmaster was safely out of the door.

'He's a man teacher, he is bound to be strict,' cooed Lucy, smug in the knowledge that Elizabeth was the Best Teacher in the Whole Wide World.

My holiday packing continued and I got in a panic over just about everything. My major panic was what would happen to the children if the plane crashed and I died (well, they'd probably die too—but I wasn't being rational). I needed to make a will. A solicitor friend in London said she didn't do wills and that I should speak to someone locally. Getting nowhere on a bank holiday Friday evening, I just typed one out on a piece of A4 paper, leaving everything to the children, with Phillipa having custody of them.

When I asked a neighbour to witness it, she told me, 'A lot of people in the street have been writing their wills since your wife died.'

I also rang the Open University: I was nursing a grudge about their silence. Lizzie had been contracted to do a week's work and, through no fault of her own, she had been unable to do it. The university had agreed to pay all her travel expenses and I was running short of cash. I eventually got through to the summer school director, who bizarrely said that they had been trying to get in touch with me—'Well, you could try phoning my home number, which you have on Lizzie's contact details,' I replied tartly.

He meekly offered the Open University's condolences and said he could not pay Lizzie's outstanding wages. 'We need proof of her death and proof of who the beneficiary is.'

'If you need proof of her death,' I retorted, 'just read a newspaper. It happened, in case you were unaware, while she was working for you. And, as her husband, I am her beneficiary.'

'There is no need for you to lose your temper, Mr Howe.'

We parted company with me slamming down the phone. The bloody man even wanted receipts to cover Lizzie's train fare. 'They are with the police,' I snarled at him.

I wrote a letter to the vice-chancellor and faxed it through. On our return from Ireland, there were about six messages on the answerphone, a letter, a cheque and a lot of humble pie, which resulted in the establishment of an Open University trust fund in Lizzie's name.

Next morning, Lucy's godfather, Eoin, drove us to Heathrow and flew with us to Belfast, where we stayed overnight with our friend Aine and her family.

The next day we were to set off to join Clive. Going on holiday as a threesome felt very strange. Surveying our loaded car, Aine suggested, 'Wouldn't you prefer to stay here? I'll cook you meals, you can go for days out and we'll spoil you rotten.'

'What about Clive?'

'He's mad. He can look after himself.'

I so nearly hoiked the children out of the car, but instead we drove off, heading westwards. It was an adventure, after all.

The car we had borrowed from friends had a sunroof and the girls begged me to have it open. Fine. Then it started raining and I couldn't get it to close, so we put our cagoules on and drove through the rain as if we were in an open-top bus.

Some miles later, there was a voice from the back. 'Daddy, I need a wee.'

'I do too, Daddy. And I'm thirsty,' chorused Jessica.

Miles later, no toilets.

This was a new experience—the three of us alone in the car with no Lizzie to minister to their needs. Eventually we found a layby with a public toilet, where a new problem confronted me: Lucy was only four and had never been to the toilet by herself in a public place. No way was I was going to take her to the gents nor was I going into the ladies. What to do?

On this occasion, I just shepherded them into the ladies and waited outside and several ages later they came out, merry as crickets, Lucy wearing only one shoe.

'Lucy dropped her sock in the toilet, so we had to fish it out. A nice lady helped us dry it off on the hand-dryer but it's still a bit wet.'

'Silly billy.' Lucy just grinned at me.

I didn't ask why Lucy was taking off her shoes and socks to go to the toilet. Some things are best left unasked.

We arrived in Donegal, where the cottage overlooked the sea, which was grey like the sky, and a gentle drizzle was coming in off the Atlantic. Joe had kept Clive up all night, but off to the beach we went. Lunch consisted mostly of biscuits, with a few packets of M&Ms to liven it up, and then we went shopping. For kites and jigsaw puzzles. Oh, and a packet of bacon, a tin of beans, Nutella (strictly forbidden by Lizzie) and a bottle of Paddy's, of course.

Despite the weather, our stay was a great success—mostly because Jessica and Lucy took endless pleasure in mothering Joe ('Clive, I think Joe has done a poo. Do you want us to change the nappy for you?') amusing him and singing him to sleep, while Clive and I got on with the humungous jigsaw we had bought. It struck me as a brilliant arrangement.

Every so often we would go on a jaunt. Rock-pooling, kite-flying, jumping the Atlantic breakers as they surged over our castle, that kind of thing. I discovered that my girls were good travellers, but no one could accuse them of being curious ones. On car journeys they just listened to tapes or read. I don't think they ever looked out of the window.

'Look, darlings,' I said, having stopped at the top of a pass in Donegal, looking down to a sweeping sandy bay. 'Isn't that view beautiful?'

'I can't see it, Daddy.'

'Why not, Lucy?'

'I've got my eyes shut,' she said.

Late one afternoon I went off alone with the girls and we ended up on a narrow jetty in a harbour, with the car facing the wrong way.

'If I'm not careful I'll drive off into the sea,' I laughed nervously.

'Good,' said Lucy. 'Then we'll all drown and we can join Mummy in heaven.' She meant it.

Perhaps the high/low point of the holiday was when we were packing to leave. We were tidying up the wreckage we had created (doing washing-up for the first time in a week, you know the kind of thing) when Clive, being a bit vigorous with the cold-water tap, wrenched it off. Water gushed over the kitchen floor in a rather satisfying arc.

We panicked. While Clive tried to mop up the kitchen floor, I searched for the cold-water stopcock. No luck. We swapped places. Clive had no luck. Heads were scratched.

'Ooh, look, Lucy, there's a fountain in the kitchen.'

'Daddy, why don't you just turn off the tap?'

'Daddy, water's seeping onto the living-room carpet.'

'Bloody hell!'

'Can we help mop it up?'

'Good idea.'

While the girls mopped, Clive and I decided that we needed a plumber. But we were in the middle of nowhere. The nearest plumber was probably in Boston, Massachusetts.

'I'll phone for one.' Clive, flash git, had a mobile phone. Only there was no signal. Ireland didn't do mobile phones back then.

'I'll drive until I find a phone box. See if I can raise a plumber.'

As I was unlocking the car, an elderly man cycled past.

'Lovely day!' he called. It was raining.

'Hi! I don't suppose you could help us? Our kitchen tap is spouting water and we need a plumber. Do you know where we can find one?'

'Which house would that be?'

'Over there.'

'Ah, I built that house, d'you know. I'll fix it for you, no problem.'

So there is a God.

We entered the house, to see Jessica and Lucy ferociously mopping and Clive struggling with a bawling baby.

'That's a fine mess you've got there. I'll see if I can fix it.'

It took him a couple of minutes. We offered him money.

'Sure, I wouldn't dream of it.'

We offered him half a bottle of whiskey we hadn't managed to drink.

'Well, I'll be thanking you kindly.' He put it in his jacket pocket, put his cycle clips back on, and pedalled off.

When we got back to Belfast, Aine said that she had prepared supper for us all every night because she expected us back early. There's confidence in our child-care skills.

I had survived my first holiday! Clive even said that I wasn't as miserable as he had feared. It was then that I realised what an incredibly heroic thing he had done—offering to spend a week alone with the most miserable man in the universe. And every year for the next ten years Clive and his wife Elaine took us on holiday with them—Dingle in Co. Kerry, France, Italy, Spain, Blackpool. They arranged it, we turned up. It was the best gift anyone could have given us.

TURNING THE KEY in the front door on our return from Donegal left me with a sinking feeling: the silent, empty house, the unpaid bills, unopened post, the struggle to keep going. It was the beginning of the rest of our lives, and it wasn't going to be easy. I was terrified that we might sink—unless I made things happen.

In fact, the pace of things changed dramatically. It was as if we had escaped from limbo, but the road ahead was uncertain. The fifth phase of grief is the rebuilding of normality.

On the last day of the holidays, our nanny Linda started. Then came the new term at school. Hand in hand, we crossed the park. Other mums with children waved at us. We waved back, but I felt very tense. Although I had taken the girls to school from time to time, it was a rarity. Now I would have to go in through the school gates myself. It was like *my* first day back, not least because I realised that I didn't really know what to do. I was only an honorary mum.

But Jessica knew. She took control, showed me where they should hang their coats, where Lucy's classroom was and led us to her own room. We walked past Mr Standish, mobbed by flirting six-year-old girls and their equally flirting mums. Jessica said, 'You can go now, Daddy,' half telling me 'You've done what mums need to do, well done,' and half 'Get lost, please.' As I left with Lucy, Mr Standish caught my eye and smiled. It made me feel less like an interloper.

I took Lucy to the nursery. Though she knew Michelle and Elizabeth, I wasn't sure I would recognise them. But of course they knew me because we were celebrities. The moment we entered they both swept Lucy up. I was assured that she was indeed in safe hands.

It turned out that Jessica loved Mr Standish and settled back into school quickly. It was helped by the fact that someone told her that her Mummy had met Mr Standish on the last day of the summer term and had liked him. At the end-of-term parents' evening, Mr Standish told me that she was one of the most well-balanced children in the class, as bright as a button. I came out of the meeting with a spring in my step.

I then went to see Michelle. She told a different story.

'All I can say, Mr Howe, is that Lucy got through the term. Let's say she has been treading water.'

'What do you mean, treading water?'

'She spends most of the day sitting on Elizabeth's lap. She doesn't play with the other children, she doesn't join in. She just wants to be cuddled. I'd say she was depressed.'

I was heartbroken and angry. My poor Lucy. I felt helpless.

I always understood Jessica. For all her mood swings and tantrums, she was articulate about what had happened and transparent in her behaviour. I was out walking with them one day, Jessica holding my hand, talking nineteen to the dozen, Lucy silent on my shoulders. We were talking about Mummy.

'Do you mind talking about Mummy, darlings?'

'No, Daddy,' said Lucy.

'No. Mummy was special,' and Jessica chirruped on about how sesame snaps and plain scones were Mummy's favourite food.

We talked about Mummy a lot, almost always as if she were present. We would talk about how nice she was, what a good Mummy she was, about how cross she got when they were bad girls. 'Mummy could be very shouty couldn't she, Daddy?' (Understatement!) 'Mummy didn't like mess did she, Daddy? You don't seem to mind.' (Even my girls had noticed what a tip the house had become.) 'Mummy wasn't a very good driver was she, Daddy?' I never wanted to turn her into a beatified mother figure. I wanted her to be real to them.

'I do like talking about Mummy, but I don't like it so much when you get sad and begin to cry. Like you are about to now.'

Jessica was right. I could feel the tears welling up; it was like a pain barrier that I had to get through, so I soldiered on, and wept and talked. They got used to seeing their Daddy cry, but I figured if their Dad had licence to cry, then so did they.

I could see that Jessica sometimes tried to be the mummy in the house. 'I turned out all the lights after you because I didn't want us to waste electricity.' 'I think Lucy is running out of clean knickers, Daddy.' 'Daddy, have you packed the toothbrushes? You forgot them last time.'

In spite of this, I tried really hard not to let her be anything other than a child. I didn't want her to grow up too fast, but she was very watchful. Not long ago, she told me why Lucy always sat behind me in the car and she on the other side. 'I was always worried that you drove too fast and I wanted to be able to see the speedometer. And when you went too fast, I would say something like, "Daddy, I feel a bit sick. Do you think you could slow down a bit?"'

And she had terrible mood swings.

'Daddy, I can't decide what to do,' was always the prelude to a tantrum. Once I was standing in a playground with my friend Maddie, watching the girls play with her two when Jessica started behaving awfully, shouting at me and blubbing about something or other. I tried comforting her and then getting cross with her, to no avail. So I just sent her packing with the stern admonishment that if she didn't pull herself together we'd go straight home, right this minute. She stormed off in a terrible sulk.

On the way home, driving down the motorway (therefore when I was in no position to bite back), with Lucy out like a light, Jessica said very quietly, 'I wish you had died and not Mummy.'

There followed a Very Long Pause while I considered my response. Then, sweetly, 'That's not a very nice thing to say, is it, darling?' And then I let her stew in it.

When we got home she gave me a huge cuddle. 'I am sorry I was nasty, Daddy. I don't know why I was so horrible. I love you, Daddy.' She was brilliant at making up. But, boy, did she have demons inside her. She has the same fiery Serb temperament as her mother.

One Sunday evening, just before bedtime, she was being horrible to Lucy. I put her to bed without her usual bedtime story, which showed her that I was dead cross with her. Predictably, she couldn't get to sleep. Eventually, I took her out into the hall and had a Grown-up Talk with her.

'Jessica, what exactly is wrong?'

She thought for a moment. 'Well, Daddy, you remember when Maka gave us a tube of Smarties last week? And you shared them out between Lucy and me?'

'Yes.'

'Lucy got the extra one. And you promised that the next time, I'd get the extra one. And when we had some yesterday, you ate it.'

Do you laugh or do you cry? Well, I laughed. There was a wonderful transparency about Jessica, and deep down I knew how to handle her, probably better than Lizzie.

But it troubles me that I could never get on Lucy's wavelength. Even now, when I try to imagine what it is like to lose your mother at the age of four, my mind hits a blank and forbidding wall.

My image of Lucy before Lizzie's death was of a little girl sitting on her mother's lap, just happy to sit there. She would go off on little expeditions, always knowing Mummy's lap was there to come back to. She never talked much, rarely lost her temper and was quick to laugh. Jessica was wiry and demanding; Lucy was sweet and self-contained.

It is a family joke that whereas Jessica had about a million cuddly toys, each one named after either foodstuffs (the most famous being the gibbon Banana Custard) or colours (Blue Duck), Lucy only had two she really liked, and both were called Dennis.

'If you had children, what would you call them, Lucy?'

'Dennis, of course. I like the name Dennis.'

'And if it's a girl? Denise?'

'Don't be silly. That's a horrible name.'

When we talked about where Mummy was now, Jessica would say that Mummy was sitting in heaven, sunbathing on a deck chair, eating figs, drinking scalding-hot coffee and reading a detective novel. Lucy never told me about what she imagined. The only way she could articulate seemed to be through silence.

Some years later, she made friends with a girl called Bea, whose mother had just recently died of cancer.

'Daddy, I can't decide if it's better for your mummy to die like Bea's, which was so slow, or like Mummy, which was so quick.'

'No, nor can I, darling.'

'I think it is better the way Mummy died.'

I am not sure I agree, even though you are left with happy memories of a fit mum rather than one who was terminally ill, but that was what Lucy was used to. It had become normal in a way.

In the end, I decided that the only way I could really help her was by being the best dad I could possibly be, by making life as normal as possible and giving her lots of cuddles, letting her know I was always there for her.

Two incidents from primary school stand out.

Every morning, once we got to the nursery classroom, Lucy would choose a book for me to read to her—either *Topsy and Tim* or Janet and Allan Ahlberg's *Bye Bye Baby*. I would read while she looked at the pictures, but, that apart, Lucy showed little interest in reading. Then, the following year, she went up to big school (an easy transition—she went from one playground to another) and had a new set of books to choose from.

I settled down with her to read.

'No. I'll read to you.'

'Er, but, Lucy, you can't read.'

'I can now I am in the Big School.'

And, word perfect, sight unseen, she read me the book. That is so typical of Lucy—don't appear to be able to do something until you have mastered the skill in private, and only then present it to the world.

Jessica told me about the other one years later.

At break time Lucy would walk round the playground wearing her anorak the wrong way round, with the hood down under her chin like a pouch, and her friends would put crisps in the hood for her to eat.

'Well, you never gave us money for crisps and people felt sorry for me.'

Lucy might well have been appearing to tread water, but all the time she was deceiving us all. Even so, Michelle's image of her wrapped round Elizabeth while classroom life went on still breaks my heart.

NOW THE GIRLS were at school, I began to ease myself back into work. After nearly two months away, it was a strange, unfamiliar world in which I felt I never really fitted. Now I was leading two lives: Jeremy at home was very different from Jeremy at work.

Work was only possible because we had a nanny. I had high expectations of Linda, but she never really lived up to them. She was good on paper, and not much use off it. I think my expectations of a twenty-year-old having to deal with a family mired in grief were wholly unrealistic. It turned out there were many days she couldn't do because of other commitments; she seemed to have no energy; and sometimes she just didn't turn up, which meant Catherine and other friends had to fill the breach. Although she was very nice and kind to the girls, they ran rings round her when she was there.

So many people brought us sweets that I stored them in an old ice-cream tub, which Jessica and Lucy could open only on pain of death. One night I came home late feeling peckish and opened it—to find it empty. Next morning, over breakfast, I quizzed the girls.

'Linda let us eat them because Lucy was sad,' said Jessica.

'I started to feel sick, so I couldn't eat them all,' chimed in Lucy.

'So Linda and I finished them off between us.'

As I was now back at work almost full-time, there then began the juggling act all working mothers are familiar with. On the three days she looked after the girls, Linda would pick them up from school. She would cook them supper (Jessica and Lucy liked her cooking), give them a bath, then get them ready for bed and read them a story. I got the feeling they spent quite a lot of time parked in front of the television watching *The Jungle Book* while she sorted out her social life on our phone.

I would catch the 6.15 p.m. train from Paddington, which got me home just before 7.30 p.m. At twenty to six I would leave the office (it didn't matter if I was in the middle of a meeting) and, as I pressed the lift button, suddenly all the worries and anxieties about home would hit me.

I would get home and go straight upstairs. Lucy would be in the bottom bunk, Jessica on the top. I would kiss them and do a handover with Linda while they told me, in a torrent, all the day's news.

'Really . . . well done . . . full marks! . . . did she? . . . did he? . . . that was naughty of him . . . ugh, spinach.' And so on.

Linda would call out from downstairs, 'Bye! See you tomorrow.' And the front door would slam and they would wave her down the street from the bedroom window.

I would then read the girls a bedtime story. I ransacked all Lizzie's children's books, broken-backed, much-read Puffins—*The Little House on the Prairie*, *The Railway Children*, *Ballet Shoes* and, of course, *Milly Molly Mandy*. Jessica drank them up. Lucy just gazed into space. What on earth was she thinking?

Then Jessica would say, 'Daddy, tell me a story about when you were a little boy.' And I would oblige.

There was the story about when we went to Swanage with my grandparents when I was four, wearing my first ever pair of black lace-up shoes. We had arrived at the hotel, having travelled in a first-class carriage in a train hauled by a steam engine, in time for a late lunch, where tomato soup was served as a starter. I had never had tomato soup before and it was delicious (this was a miraculous discovery, as I disliked nearly all food apart from mashed-up banana and raspberry or blackcurrant jam on sliced white bread), but my shoelace was undone and I asked my granddad to do it for me, because I hadn't yet learned to tie my own. While I was distracted, the waitress took away my half-finished bowl of soup. I was devastated. All week they served different soups, all uniformly horrible. Thereafter, my mother bought every conceivable type of tomato soup on the market but none was as delicious as that first ever tomato soup. Not since that day have I ever had such tasty soup—and they took it away from me.

'Daddy, tell us the one about you and the swing.'

'Well, when I was a little boy we had a swing in the garden, which Uncle Jonathan and I used to love playing on. Because he was bigger than me—he was nearly seven, so I was nearly four—he was always telling me to swing higher and higher, and I always did. One day he said wouldn't it be exciting to jump off the swing while it was really high. Because he was my older brother and he was always right, I decided to try—and off I jumped and landed in a crumpled heap on the lawn. As I stood up, the swing came back and hit me bang on the head and I fell over again. I just lay there, and all I remember was Uncle Jonathan running indoors shouting, "Mummy! Mummy! I've killed Jeremy!"'

'Were you really dead, Daddy?'

'Of course not, silly, otherwise I wouldn't be here, would I? But I had knocked myself out, so Grandma dumped me in Auntie Philippa's pushchair—she was still a baby then—and rushed me round to the doctor's. I felt terrible—because only babies go round in pushchairs.'

I quickly ran out of new stories to tell. What I never quite sussed was that Jessica loved hearing the same ones over and over. Or ones about Mummy as a little girl, which were more difficult because, of course, I hadn't grown up with her.

After the stories, I would draw the curtains and they would turn on their bedside lamps. Then it was time for prayers. I can't remember where Jessica got the idea of prayers from, but it was certainly after Lizzie's death. She would kneel on her bunk and squeeze her eyes tight shut with Banana Custard or Bobba (a teddy bear) clamped under her arm.

'Dear Lord, thank you for the nice day I have had today and thank you for looking after Lucy and me and Daddy and Maka and Deda and Grandma and Auntie Louise and Auntie Philippa and the cousins, and please look after them tomorrow and always. Can I speak to Mummy now? Hello Mummy, I had a nice day today, I hope you did too. Catherine took me and Lucy to school, and she got cross with Joe because he wanted to take a squashed frog to show Mr Standish. We had a spelling test today and I got full marks. For lunch we had cottage pie and cabbage and I sat next to

Becca. Linda picked us up from school and we went round to Suzy's, where we made animals from clay. I made a bumble bee, but it wouldn't come out right, so I got cross. We had sausages for tea, I had three and Lucy only had one and then we watched a bit of *Beauty and the Beast*. I am going to write my Christmas list soon. I want a Thumper Rabbit like Lucy's. Look after yourself and speak to you tomorrow. I love you lots, Mummy. Amen.'

It was an agonising ritual we performed every night for years. And every night it wrung my heart. Lucy would never join in. 'I don't need to speak to Mummy—she can see me through a window in heaven, so she knows what I have done today.'

Which is more than I knew, as she would never tell anyone. For example:

'Did you have a nice day at school today, darling?'

'Yes.'

'What did you do?'

'I can't remember.'

'Who did you sit next to in class?'

'Esther.'

'Is she your best friend?'

'Sometimes. Can I go and watch television now?'

After the goodnight ritual, all I was fit for was a drink. But usually Lucy needed a wee and Jessica remembered she had not cleaned her teeth. Jessica would only go to sleep if she knew I was downstairs, so the deal was that I would take Banana Custard downstairs with me and tuck it under her duvet next to her once she was asleep. This involved creeping upstairs every ten minutes to see if she was asleep, but, of course, if I disturbed her as I put the floppy gibbon next to her, her eyes would spring open and the whole process had to begin again. Sometimes I would come up three or four times before she was settled. Or, even worse, I would FORGET and a tearful Jessica would appear downstairs weeping, and the whole palaver would begin again.

Sometime around eight-thirty, I would start cooking supper. Around eight thirty-five, I would sit down for supper (my cooking was that good) with a glass of wine. Radio 4 became my constant companion. I had no idea what I was listening to; it just made the house less silent.

My diet became a dull litany of the children's reheated leftovers: microwaveable pasta bake, a steak pie or pasta with pesto. Sometimes I would grill myself a pork chop. I existed on those incredibly expensive bags of pre-washed lettuce and Müller Fruit Corner Black Cherry Yoghurt (for years they were three for the price of two). The taste of any of those things will instantly bring back the silence of the house in Oxford: lights burning everywhere to make the house feel less lonely, the creeping about so I didn't disturb the girls whose lives I shared for an hour and a half every day. I felt like an interloper.

The only room I liked was the girls' bedroom. It was the only room that felt lived in. Our house had had the life sucked out of it.

At about nine o'clock, I would settle down to some work or I would play chess against myself. And kill time.

One night the phone rang. It was Maka. This was unusual. Unfailingly, she would phone the girls every evening after supper and if I was at home I would talk to her, but if she phoned me, it was usually about when she should next come to Oxford. She didn't really do small talk.

She immediately launched into some obscure stuff about inheritance and the children. I found I was struggling to understand. Then she rang off. I pondered the import of what she'd said. Then picked up the phone.

'Maka? I was thinking about what you just said.'

'Yes.'

'Correct me if I am wrong, but you have written me out of your will.'

'That's right. Sorry if I wasn't very clear.'

'So not only have I just lost my wife, but you have taken away any financial safety net that being married to her gave me.'

'Yes. I suppose that is true. But our priority is to provide for the grandchildren.'

'Is that very fair on me? Is it that you don't trust me?'

Pause. 'That is what we have decided.'

'I feel hurt. Obviously it is your money and you need to do with it what you think fit, but let me just say how hurt I feel.'

'If that's the way you see it . . .'

'I do.'

Phone conversations don't come much more painful than that, to either party. I was upset. But who should I tell I was upset? The cat?

Naively, I had always seen myself as being as much their son as their son-in-law, an extension of their beloved daughter. Not only was this a body blow, but so too was the fact that another safety net had been swiped away from me at a point when I needed all the security I could grab. Looked at rationally, it was a completely obvious thing for them to do—why on earth would they leave half of their estate to an outsider?—but we were not in a rational world. Nor did they really need to tell me. They could have written me out of their will and I need never have known. In telling me, they had undermined our relationship. Yes, it was the decent, honest thing to do but it was insensitively handled. I felt as if a bond had been broken. I had been deceiving myself that I was a son to them; now I knew that I was not. If only Maka had kept silent. By telling me, our relationship had been damaged irreparably.

All that said, Maka and Deda were still extremely generous: they paid for the girls' piano lessons, they bought them clothes. More significantly, they paid for the nanny, and Maka would come and stay to look after the children at the drop of a hat. But nothing was the same as it had been before Lizzie died.

Lizzie and her mother had been close. They'd speak nearly every day, and when the children were first born, Maka would come over and stay with us in Belfast for a week or two at a time. I liked her and we got on. She was fiercely intelligent, brisk to the point of rudeness and, like a lot of women of her generation, had lived her life vicariously through her daughter's achievements, never having had the same opportunities herself.

She never recovered from her daughter's death. For nearly fifteen years, she got on with life as before, phoning the girls every day, doing *The Times* crossword and playing chess with herself. She read a crime novel a day, drank too much and smoked too many fags. She was outwardly content, but to me it seemed she was wearing a mask. After I gave her the news about Lizzie, I only ever saw her really happy once, when she was lying on her deathbed after a massive stroke. She looked contented. She had wanted to be with her beloved daughter since the day Lizzie died, and now she was about to join her.

It seems to me that, just as there are distinct phases of grief, there are also three immutable, almost Newtonian laws of grief:

The First Law: I loved Lizzie with all my heart, but there was always the possibility that I would find another partner. But Maka . . . At sixty-five, you cannot have another daughter. It is a loss you can never recover from.

The Second Law: people grow and change at different rates, dependent on age. Lucy was four and Jessica six when their mother died. Six years later, both girls had lived half of their lives without her. They had moved on simply by growing. Maka and Deda had lived less than a tenth of their lives in those six years and were still the same people they had been when Lizzie died. They were mired in grief.

And the Third Law: grief can pull people apart. Show me a family who has suffered a public bereavement (the Lawrences, the Paynes, for example) and five years on, the chances are that the mother and father have separated. In order to survive a tragedy, which is going to test you until you are at breaking point, you need very firm foundations.

Mostly I would go to bed at about eleven. I had moved downstairs to the spare room, which only had space for a small double bed and me. The walls were bare except for a print from Blake's illustrations of the Book of Job (Job was a man with whom I empathised). It was my cell. Comfortless but for the bottle of whisky beside a pile of unread books.

Another day survived. Thank God. I too said my prayers—a grown-up version of Jessica's, repeated like a protective mantra: 'Dear Lord, thank you for looking after us, and please let tomorrow be another good day. Let Lizzie know that I love her, and look after her. For Jesus Christ's sake, Amen.' I would list everybody who I wanted looked after and slow down—and mouth the words—for the bit about Lizzie, just to feel her in my heart for as long as possible. It was all the emotion I allowed myself and so painful that I would get it over as early before bed as possible. After what had happened to us I wasn't even sure I believed in God, but it was a kind of insurance policy. Then it would be a slug of whisky and lights out.

Damn! Banana Custard was still bloody well downstairs.

5

We struggled on but it was tough going. We needed a miracle. To our relief, a miracle came, in the shape of Dr Forrest. Good as her word, the head of child psychiatry in Norwich put us in touch with her opposite number in Oxford.

Dr Forrest was petite, with an intense, warm gaze, a few years older than me. In a movie, she'd be played by Helen Mirren. The children loved visiting her and she always made me feel good about my role as a parent.

First thing every Friday morning for over a year, we would leave the car in front of the Park Children's Hospital, a rambling Victorian house, and climb the stairs to the attic space. We would sit on a padded bench and wait; the ritual was to sit Jessica on one knee and Lucy on the other and play 'This is the way the lady rides, trot trot trot trot', joggling them gently up and down, getting more and more vigorous until: 'This is the way the kangaroo jumps, boing boing boing boing', which would all but throw them off my knees.

Then Dr Forrest would greet us and we would troop into her consulting room built into the eaves. The girls would again sit on my lap, so I was almost hidden behind them, and Dr Forrest would ask them how they were.

'Fine, thank you, Dr Forrest,' they chorused.

'Actually, you haven't been sleeping too well, have you, Jessica?' I added.

'No. Lucy talks in her sleep and keeps me awake.'

'I don't, Daddy, do I!?'

'No, darling, Jessica is talking rubbish.' And Jessica would giggle. She always has been the world's most pathetic fibber.

Then Dr Forrest would shift the squabble into why Jessica was having problems getting to sleep—because she was worried that I might disappear like Mummy did, and so on. It was Dr Forrest who had come up with the nightly ritual with Banana Custard; it was Dr Forrest with whom I discussed whether or not we needed to continue with her prayers.

'Now, girls, why don't you draw me a picture? You know where the crayons are.' They would scurry off and find pens.

I had been worried that before Lizzie's death Jessica used to write stories and now she would not. Instead, she lay on the floor writing rows and rows of numbers. She didn't want to draw pictures any more.

Lucy, on the other hand, drew all the time: Mummy standing on the grass in the sunshine with a big smile on her face. Next to her was a huge rabbit-like monster with arrows shooting out of it saying 'Lucy'; or a spindly Mummy picking flowers in a beautiful garden. She then changed the picture by placing Mummy in a massive, scribbled black frame, as if Mummy was in a Mark Rothko-like box.

I was disturbed by these.

'Don't be, Mr Howe. Obviously the black box represents Lucy's Mummy's death. But she has drawn Mummy in a lovely garden—aren't these flowers pretty, Lucy? Did your Mummy like picking flowers?'

Lucy nodded. Lizzie was a fervent picker of flowers.

'And are you sad that your Mummy is dead? Is that why you have drawn these big black lines round her?'

'Yes,' she said very quietly and gave me a cuddle.

'Everybody is very sad that your Mummy is dead.'

'At Mummy's funeral EVERYBODY was crying,' chimed in Jessica.

'Well, she was a very special and lovely Mummy. You are right to feel sad, Lucy.' Pause. 'Do you want to play with the Playmobil?'

Lucy slipped off my knee and, with Jessica's help, got out the biggest, most wonderful Playmobil set ever, with schools and farms and families with children and firemen. If you are not a Playmobil aficionado, you will have no idea what I am talking about, but my two loved the bendy plastic figures who slotted neatly into furniture. Dr Forrest had the Playmobil set to end all Playmobil sets, and she would play it as her trump card. Lucy was instantly happy as she and Jessica clucked and cooed over setting up a Playmobil hospital while Dr Forrest and I continued to discuss the pictures.

'A lot of children who come to see me just cannot bear to draw a picture of their dead parent. That Lucy is drawing pictures of her mother in such a lovely space is an incredibly good sign. Her memories are good ones and she can express them freely.'

Too quickly our precious hour would be up. I remember once, when I was feeling particularly hopeless about my parenting skills, as we left the room, Dr Forrest whispered to me, 'Mr Howe, you are doing just brilliantly.' No one has ever given me greater praise. It utterly transformed how I felt about myself as a parent.

'In child psychiatry, we always say that the first four years of good parenting are worth money in the bank and, Mr Howe, your two girls have gold in their bank.'

For that, I loved Lizzie more than ever. I think it is the valediction she would have prized above everything else: that as a mother she had put gold in her children's bank.

Session over, we would race downstairs to the hospital lobby, where stood two of the largest rocking horses ever made. Jessica would clamber up onto hers (on the left) and I would lift little Lucy onto the one on the right and they would gallop away on them for ten minutes, riding all the cares of the world away.

'Time to get to school, girls.'

'Just one more minute, Daddy, please,' and they would gallop away over the last furlong of their imaginary race course. Then I would take them into class and go to work myself, very, very late.

On one occasion I wanted Jessica to see Dr Forrest by herself—she had such anxieties about being apart from me and I felt that with me in the room she would never talk to Dr Forrest.

'Maybe the next time you come,' Dr Forrest suggested, 'how about if your Daddy was to sit outside while you and I have a little chat?' Jessica clearly thought this was a pants idea, but she was so in thrall to Dr Forrest that she grudgingly agreed.

Next Friday, we took Lucy to school and then Jessica and I drove up to the hospital. While we waited, she sat silently on my lap, as if clamped to me. When Dr Forrest welcomed us, Jessica held my hand as tightly as she could and all but dragged me into the consulting room. It was obvious that she was not going to be parted from me, so the deal was that she would sit on my lap while she and Dr Forrest chatted.

When I say chatted, I mean Jessica remained silent while Dr Forrest and I talked. Apart from the occasional mumbled grunt, Jessica didn't really join in, despite Dr Forrest's best endeavours.

'Do you know what I think, Jessica?' she said as the session drew to a close. 'I think your coming to see me works best when you and Lucy and Daddy are here all together. Next time, why don't all three of you come?'

Game, set and match to Jessica Howe. She chatted all the way to school.

'I THINK YOU ARE underskilled in the washing, ironing and cooking departments,' was what the next miracle who came into my life, Dr John Hall, told me on our first meeting. I needed counselling, not just for my family, but for myself. I was not coping. My GP, who was very sympathetic, suggested I try a bereavement counsellor. 'I can tell one thing, Mr Howe,' the counsellor said, after I had blubbed through my one and only session, 'that you are sad. Very sad.'

'I did wonder if they might find you a bit of a challenge,' said my GP. 'Ask Dr Forrest if there is anyone she knows. I will happily refer you.'

I asked her. She was hesitant. But my sister Philippa, who was staying with us, told me I had missed a call from a John Hall, who had said that he might be able to help me.

'I told him you didn't need any old help. I asked him if he had any experience in counselling people in your situation. He said he had. He told me he was the head of the Clinical Psychology Department at the Warneford Hospital.'

'Blimey. I'd better phone him then.'

At our first meeting he kind of auditioned me, and for half an hour seemed pretty reluctant to commit to seeing me even to the end of the appointed session. But finally he agreed to see me on a regular basis. I felt pleased with myself that I was clinically mad enough to have passed my interview.

'I think I can be of some help,' he told me before going on to give me his low opinion of my domestic skills. I had visions of him teaching me how to iron shirt collars, but in fact he was fabulously helpful.

John told me that I had lost my map, that his job was to help me re-find my bearings and the path that I had mislaid. He was dead right—I lived day by day, and could no longer even conceive of a future. Six months after I began seeing him, I woke up one morning and realised how much I was looking forward to Lucy's godfather Eoin taking us to Spain at Easter. It was an amazing breakthrough. John was gradually guiding me towards seeing that there was a future.

When I first saw him, I was sleeping badly. He thought for a few moments. 'How old is your duvet?'

'I dunno. About ten years, I guess.'

'I think you should buy a new one, a thicker one. Two bodies sleeping together create a lot more heat than one. Now you are sleeping alone, you need a decent duvet.'

He was right. I started to sleep through the night because I was warm.

I told him about how badly I thought I had been treated by the police, how I felt that the Open University had been neglectful and careless of my feelings.

'These are sins of omission, they are people not meeting the standard of behaviour you are entitled to, but in comparison with the sin of commission—the murder of Lizzie—they are inconsequential. Treat them as such.'

Or, to put it another way: get a grip, man, and save your anger for the person who most deserves it, the man who murdered Lizzie.

He was right. It calmed me down.

It was he who—by deduction—told me why Robin Pask had killed Lizzie: he was a schizophrenic for whom there was no cure.

I told him that my grief felt like an infinite black hole which was swallowing up my whole life. 'Let's define the hole,' he told me, 'work out how big it is. Then you may wish to look into it or put a fence round it and ignore it.' He was right—if you try to get the measure of something, it becomes easier to deal with. He taught me how to cope.

'I sense that you fear going back to York,' he told me.

'I'm never going there again if I can help it.'

'You have to put returning to York on your agenda. Right now I don't think you can, but one day you might be called on to go. Don't let that ambush you. Besides, this year it's York you can't visit, next year Yorkshire, then the north of England, until eventually you will become trapped in your house.'

He developed strategies with me so that I could handle birthdays, Christmas, the impending trial, the anniversary of Lizzie's death and all the other traps that the calendar presents to the bereaved. He eased me back into the real world and helped rub out the chalk circle that was isolating me.

Initially we met two, sometimes even three, times a week. Then I was eased off our meetings. After two years, it was time to part.

'Jeremy, what you have been through is acute post-traumatic stress.'

I felt a bit cheated. Why hadn't he told me this when we first met? As I was wading through grief, unable to work out why I was feeling so inadequate, telling me this might have helped me find my compass. But I realised that when we started, I was so far from the mountaintop that any information that he might have given me on how to get there would not have helped. I couldn't see the road ahead. It is a commonplace that time is a healer. Time certainly helped to heal me, but with a lot of assistance from men of medicine.

THIS IS THE STORY of a typical weekend with the Howes.

It was November 1992. A Saturday. I was up and dressed and fearfully crotchety by about a quarter to eight. I was nagging the children to get ready, because—Saturday is the day we go to Sainsbury's. And if we didn't get there by nine o'clock it would be full of people, and much as I dislike supermarkets, I am phobic about supermarkets with people in them.

Jessica was quite amenable; Lucy was just grumpy and uncooperative. God knows why, because they would get to choose a cake each. And if they were really good, I would let them push the trolley.

The supermarket was empty.

I didn't have a list. That would be too anally retentive. I am a man. When I arrived I felt quite upbeat, but by the time I'd got through the barrier of fruit and veg at the entrance, I had lost the will to live. Sensing this, the children scurried off to choose a breakfast cereal.

Every week, I got them Weetabix, because I naively thought that it didn't have any added sugar. Lucy hated Weetabix.

'So what do you want?'

'Coco Pops.'

'But you can't have Coco Pops. What do you want if you can't have Coco Pops?'

'Coco Pops.'

'Lucy, why don't you choose Cheerios. Daddy won't let you have Coco Pops,' mediated Jessica.

'But I like Coco Pops.'

'But you do like Cheerios.'

I went off to hunt for tea bags and let them fight it out. I returned to find Coco Pops in the trolley and the girls hopping about on either foot, hoping I wouldn't notice.

'You can't have Coco Pops, Lucy.' I put them back.

'But I like Coco Pops.'

I chucked in a box of Rice Krispies, thus deferring the row until Monday morning. By then I was exhausted, pushing a trolley full of inedible garbage that no one liked, except for two gingerbread men, which we always got.

'That one please, not that one,' said Lucy, who I was holding up to the glass counter.

'This one?' asked the man serving us.

'No, that one. That one there.' She pointed rather vaguely.

'I think she means this one, with red, yellow and blue Smarties for buttons, not the one with the three orange ones.' Whoever heard of a child wanting matching colours when they could have lots of different ones? Clearly the man behind the counter had never met a child. Pah.

'Thank you, Daddy.' And she held my hand tightly and flushed pink. The way to a child's heart is through coloured Smarties.

After about a hundred years lost in the aisles of the supermarket, we reached the checkout. The thought of having to unpack all this stuff onto the checkout belt, only to repack it into the trolley, only to load it into the car, only to unload it and then unpack it at home was dispiriting, especially as I could now see what I had forgotten.

I had become a useless shopper. Which I didn't understand, because I used to do the Saturday shop when Lizzie was alive. I actually used to quite enjoy it. Now I seemed to spend huge amounts of money on food that no one liked.

I flopped down at home with a cup of coffee and a sticky bun. It was not yet ten o'clock, but I was knackered. I wished it was bedtime already.

I had my regular Saturday migraine coming on. Before Lizzie died, I didn't know what migraines were. Now, every Saturday, I would get a pain like someone was screwing a vice onto my temples. My brain would slow down so that I slurred my speech and I would feel tired, irritated and nauseous. My body was willing me to lie down.

The doorbell rang. It was Julia wondering if the girls would like to come over to do some cooking. Thank God. Maybe I would like to pop round for some lunch later, say in a couple of hours. Jessica and Lucy thought this was a brilliant idea, so I took half a sleeping tablet, set the alarm and tried to sleep off my headache.

My alarm went off. The pain in my head having receded, I wandered over to Julia's, where family life was in full swing. Jessica and Lucy were baking, as at home there as they were in our house. Lucy came and snuggled on my lap to draw a picture while Julia cooked lunch and her husband Ollie pottered around.

'That's really nice, darling. What is it?' A huge head filled the paper. It had tiny features and a large, smiling mouth.

'It's a picture of you.'

'Why have I got such a big head and two tiny bodies?'

'Because you are my mummydaddy,' and she laughed and turned pink.

I've still got that drawing. Lucy had summed up my challenge and qualities as a parent succinctly. I wasn't Mummy (how could I be?) and I wasn't just Daddy any more. I was, simultaneously, Mummydaddy.

We lunched as a family, then the girls went off to play while Julia, Ollie and I chatted over coffee. I was always clock-watching. I always felt like an imposition, never wanting to outstay my welcome, but always keen to stay, to feel a part of normal family life. I found a lot of surrogate families that year, they were a lifeline. They helped me feel like part of the human race.

And, boy, did I learn the meaning of 'singing for your supper'—I would tell funny stories, entertain them as best I could and never unburden my multiple woes. I so hope that all those generous people didn't feel I leeched off them.

After being fed, watered and generally looked after, we'd go home and the children would settle down for a good long play of the Anna game.

The origins of the Anna game are lost. I have no idea who Anna is or was, but it absorbed the children. My observations revealed that it could only really be enacted in their bedroom, that it was a make-believe game, and that it consisted of getting a lot of props together and playing out any one of about a million scenarios (for example, after returning home from a holiday abroad, it would consist of the girls playing at air hostesses; when a friend of ours took them to the ballet, the Anna game became a dance class, and so on). Dressing up in their mother's clothes was mandatory.

If I ventured into their room they would stop and Jessica would say, 'We're busy with the Anna game, Daddy. We can't be disturbed because we are busy stamping library books. Unless you would like to borrow some?'

'That's a good idea. I need some new books to read.'

Then I would discover that the rules for borrowing books were so stringent and complicated that Lucy would have to choose them for me and Jessica, as the bossy librarian, would have to tell me off.

After a couple of hours of this, they would come down and watch the video of *The Little Mermaid*, exhausted, while I made an attempt at cooking supper, usually involving a grill or the microwave and always served up with raw sliced red pepper and carrots. I was eventually rescued from cooking hell by my sister giving me Delia Smith; at least with Delia I kind of knew what I was supposed to be doing. There must be one or two other dishes I learnt to cook apart from spaghetti Bolognese, but I am blowed if I can remember what.

I'd wash up, they'd put away, and then we would settle down for a game—Frustration or Sorry or Uno.

Supper at six, game at six-thirty, bath at seven, lights out at a quarter to eight. A structure and a timetable somehow kept me going—and then the rest of the evening was mine, in which to feel like a spare part. Without the girls or my work, I just did not exist.

Sunday was different. Sunday is a family day, and we weren't really a family, more a husk of one. Families spend Sundays together, so there were rarely any casual drop-ins by friends or neighbours to while away our time. I was on my own, unless I'd had the wit to organise something or some kind-hearted person had invited us somewhere. Sundays could be the best of days if we had an outing, or the worst if we didn't, and I became acutely aware of what, as a family, we had lost.

But Sundays were also a lie-in day. So, at about half past seven, Jessica would pad into my bedroom and ask if she and Lucy could watch television. I would settle them down in front of the telly and go back to bed to snooze for half an hour or so.

To give the morning focus, I invented a new ritual. We'd have breakfast and go to the Didcot Wave. As a child, I remember being taken swimming to Woolwich Baths most Sunday mornings, and I loved the journey because we were driven by a friend: at that time we didn't have a car, so this was a big treat. On the way home we would drive across the Abbey Wood marshes, an eerie and fascinating wasteland. An even bigger treat was that after swimming, we would troop into a sweet shop by Abbey Wood station and my mother allowed us to choose a sixpence worth of sweets each, which for some reason were called fairy sweets. Heaven indeed!

I kind of replicated those swimming expeditions for us three. Compared with Oxford, Didcot is the arse end of the world, our version of Abbey Wood. The whole swimming experience seemed to be one of coldness and chlorine, just like my childhood.

The first time we went to the baths a problem presented itself—where should we get changed? I started off by taking the girls to the men's changing rooms, but somehow them getting undressed in front of loads of hairy men didn't feel right, so once Lucy could dress herself, the girls would troop off to the ladies' changing rooms. I could see that it made them feel terribly grown up, whereas I just felt wretched. I was still so unsure of their safety (why? How many child abductions take place in ladies' changing rooms in municipal baths in the UK? Mind you, how many women are stabbed to death on British university campuses in broad daylight?). I'd get changed in about thirty seconds, whereas it seemed to take Jessica (chatting, as ever) and Lucy (slowcoach) about thirty minutes before they would appear by the poolside and scamper up to me, Lucy replete with armbands, Jessica, a proud swimmer, without.

I would try to smile and be nice, but inside I was a bundle of irritation, anxiety and boredom—and then, of course, we had to go swimming. I got my twenty yards certificate at school aged ten, and that was that. I have the natural buoyancy of concrete and water is not my natural habitat. The good thing about going to the baths with a non-swimmer (like Lucy) is that you have to stay in the shallow end. I do like my feet to be able to touch the bottom. We would play tag and have races (I am a fast swimmer over six or seven feet) and mess about and wait for the wave machine, which was fun, and then I would start to get cold and grumpy and be angling to go, and the girls would be angling to stay. Eventually I would win, and we would part at the communal footbath. I would get showered and changed in about thirty seconds, feeling even more like a spare part as I watched fathers and sons get changed. The girls would take for ever, and after several epochs of hanging about in the entrance lobby, my two would appear, chattering away like teenagers, not a care in the world.

We would stop for Sunday Sweets—something that would never have happened under the former regime, as their mum was an E-number/sugar fascist. I would stop the car, lock them in, dash into the shop, always keeping them in my eyeline, buy the *Sunday Times*, a bar of chocolate for me (adult size) and one each for them (child size) and dash back. Amazingly, they were still safe. I just didn't have the patience to spend half an hour unbuckling them, shepherding them into the shop and then leisurely reading the Sundays while they agonised over how to spend their fifteen pence, so I did it for them.

The first time, I felt dreadfully guilty about buying them sweets at all. And the look on their faces when I handed the booty over was one of astonishment.

'Jessica, Lucy—look what I have got you.' Through the car window, I waved two micro-sized chocolate Animal Bars, Lucy's with an elephant (her favourite animal) on the wrapper, Jessica's with a giraffe (they don't do bees—she loved bees, possibly because they were the only animal she could draw).

'Are they for us?'

'Yes. A treat.'

'Really? Thank you, Daddy! Thank you!'

They clutched them as if they were gold ingots.

'Eat them now if you want,' I said, as I bit off a chunk of Mars Bar (I was allowed to eat sweets without permission from anyone, they weren't—isn't that the best thing about being grown up?).

I have no idea how children can make such a small bar of chocolate last for so long, or how Lucy could get so much of it smeared round her mouth. I soon began to realise why mothers have so many paper hankies stashed up their sleeves, why they have handbags filled with wet wipes and Calpol and sticking plasters. If you were to go through my old jackets, you would be guaranteed to find them stuffed with screwed up paper hankies, plastic medicine spoons and broken hair clips.

After the sweet shop, we'd head home down the dual carriageway at breakneck speed, as if I were in a race against time. I set targets for everything—back by ten-thirty, when we didn't leave until twenty past ten, that kind of thing. Although I was driving, it was as if I were driven.

Sweets, drive, home—if possible in time for the second half of *The Archers*, because, as managing editor, it was my job—flop with the papers while the children played.

Then, almost inevitably, I'd remember an errand we needed to do. This particular weekend it was a birthday present for Jessica's friend Charlotte. We had an early lunch and then drove up to town. We had one hour's parking in which to buy Charlotte a present—we headed straight for the Early Learning Centre, chose a drawing kit and were out in about seven minutes. Then we went to the card shop (two minutes) and then the Nosebag café, where I had a coffee and the girls had juice and we shared a Bakewell tart.

We were chatting away about how much Mummy liked to come here and pretend to read a book and just people-watch, when an elderly Indian man leant over towards us and said to the girls, 'I remember your mother. She used to sit and read on a Sunday afternoon. She was a lovely lady.'

We talked to him, and it really was Lizzie he was talking about. Here was a random stranger who had a link to our past, a man who knew about us. It was a magical ten minutes. Lizzie was suddenly real and, as he spoke, the girls' eyes got bigger and bigger.

Our parking was about to run out, so we said our farewells and left. As they clambered down the café stairs, the girls were full of him: 'Daddy! Daddy! He knew Mummy! Was Mummy famous, Daddy?'

'No, my sweets, she was just Mummy.'

'But people know all about our Mummy! She wasn't just an ordinary Mummy, was she, Daddy?'

'No, she wasn't.'

As we walked back Lucy suddenly exclaimed, 'Look! There's Mummy!'

I stopped, stunned. 'Where, darling?!' I searched the street. For a moment I believed Lucy.

Harry from across the road had once found twenty pence in a gutter. Ever since, Lucy's eyes had been trained at her feet, looking for treasure—and now she had found some, of a kind. Lying in the gutter was a copy of Friday's *Oxford Mail* and on the front page was a photograph of Lizzie side by side with one of her killer being led into court. His trial date had been announced the day before.

That image summed it all up—Lizzie lying discarded, her destiny yoked to an anonymous stranger whom I never wanted to have anything to do with. Since she'd died, I had desperately tried to separate Lizzie and her life from the manner of her death. It was a superhuman task, and here they were, randomly paired in a gutter, Lizzie and her murderer. It felt horribly public and horribly careless.

Years later, I searched the cuttings archive high and low for that edition of the paper, but could never find it. I sometimes wonder if we all imagined it.

In the end, the waves on the beach will wash away everything.

'So Mummy *is* famous, Daddy!'

I was giddy with emotion. 'Not really, darling.' I could barely talk. Jessica squeezed my hand as we walked on in silence, but Lucy was skipping because she had found her Mummy, who was famous.

Then, just like all our Sundays, we went home, took a walk in the park, with the girls on their bicycles, and a play on the swings. And then a supper of chicken drumsticks and baked potatoes and bed—for them.

The bit of the weekend I looked forward to most was nine o'clock on a Sunday evening, with the children fast asleep and me spark out on the sofa. I would then hear a knock at the door. It was Catherine Unia, our childminder. On Sunday evenings I would pay her wages and we would spend an hour or so reviewing the week just gone and previewing the week ahead.

When we had moved to Oxford, Jessica and Lucy had been the first two children Catherine had taken on as a childminder and she had continued to look after them since. I'd drop the girls off at her house after breakfast and either she or Linda would pick them up after school. She was a godsend, not a word I use carelessly. Oh, and did I mention that she was a qualified doctor, who had taken a break from doctoring to bring up her family of six children, one of whom was adopted, and that on Saturdays she ran a family-planning clinic? She was married to Pram, who was a senior manager in the Overseas Department of Oxfam. Her son Joe was in Jessica's class at school. He was a cheeky monkey.

The Unias were an extraordinary family. Each one of them, in their way, held out a lifeline for us. But chief among them was Catherine. She was a year or two older than me, tall, floor-length earth-mother skirts, long hair that hid her smiley eyes. She was fabulously judgmental, gossipy, fiercely principled and fundamentally atheist. Yet she is the closest I have come to meeting a saint.

Catherine sat down on the sofa in our sitting room, calendar in hand, to organise my life for the next seven days.

'Well, how has it been this week?'

'I got through it.'

'I thought the girls had a good week. Jessica is really getting on with Katie.'

'Just because she can boss her around! But why does Jessica have to be so clingy every morning and Lucy so grumpy?'

Weekday mornings were not our best time. Breakfast chez Howe would go like this: Jessica would munch her way through her Weetabix talking nineteen to the dozen, probably about Katie, 'who is my best friend and I hate her' or Becca, 'who is a pain'. Lucy sat stirring her Rice Krispies idly with a spoon, daydreaming.

'Lucy, eat up, sweetie, we have to go to Catherine's in a minute.'

'I don't like Rice Krispies.'

'Lucy, you had better eat them up or Daddy will get cross with you,' her sister chipped in unhelpfully.

'But I don't like them.'

'Eat five more big spoonfuls and then we'll call it quits. OK?'

'But I'm not hungry.'

I picked up Lucy's spoon and filled it to the brim with Rice Krispies. 'Come on, Lucy. I won't let you leave here without eating some breakfast.' Breakfast was the holy of holies for me. You can't go to work on an empty stomach, and it was the only meal over which I had any control.

'Come on, Lucy.' She moved her head to one side. The spoon followed her tightly pursed mouth and she swung her head round and spilt milk all over her sweatshirt.

'Lucy! Look what you've done,' I shouted. 'Go and wipe down your sweatshirt. You can't go to school unless you have had some breakfast. How about I make you a peanut butter sandwich?'

Brian Redhead gave another *Today* time-check, which meant I had about six minutes to get out of the house.

Lucy knew that if she played for time she would not have to eat breakfast because I needed to leave the house at twenty-five past eight and by now it was nearly half past. I wheeled my bike down the road, Jessica holding my hand. Lucy walked beside me with a big wet stain in the middle of her sweatshirt.

So far, so good. Then it began to get tricky.

We crossed the road to Catherine's and I could feel Jessica holding my hand tighter and tighter. We knocked on Catherine's door and Jessica mumbled, 'I don't want you to go to work, Daddy.' Joe opened the door and I dragged Jessica into the kitchen, where Catherine was feeding yoghurt to baby Leila, whose mouth was open like a fledgling. I wished Lucy would exhibit a similar attitude.

'Can I have some toast please, Catherine?' said Lucy, as if the breakfast episode had never happened.

'Help yourself. Plastic bread or brown bread?'

'Plastic bread please.'

'There's some white already in the toaster. Don't let your dad see!'

'We had a row over Rice Krispies,' I said lamely, as I tried to unwrap Jessica's clenched fingers from my hand.

'I don't want you to go, Daddy!' she mumbled.

'Come now, Jessica,' said Catherine. 'Daddy has to go to work and we have to go to school. Joe can't wait for science lesson today. Apparently, Mr Standish is going to do some experiments. Do you remember last time he set the desk on fire?'

Jessica wrapped herself round my legs. 'Daddy, don't go to work. I don't want you to go to work!' she sobbed.

'Now, now, darling. I have to go. If I don't work, we can't eat. You don't want to starve, do you?'

'I don't care. I DON'T WANT YOU TO GO!'

Lucy was busy spreading Nutella on her toast.

Catherine came over to untangle us. 'Now, Jessica, after school I thought we could have fairy cakes, like your Mum used to bake. What flavour icing should we make?' And under her breath to me, 'You go.'

'Chocolate,' muttered Jessica.

'Bye, darlings. I'll see you after supper. Be good.' I kissed Lucy on top of her head and Jessica on the cheek. She looked imploringly at me through tears. 'I don't . . . want . . . Daddy . . . to . . . go.'

I caught the train, just. I would always catch the train, just. I've been setting my watch fast by five minutes for the last twenty years. I have always, always been in a rush.

When I got to my office I would phone Catherine. 'She's fine, Jeremy. The moment you left, she stopped crying and helped Lucy feed Leila. She chatted all the way to school as if nothing had happened.'

I used to dread crossing the road to Catherine's, because that was always when Jessica started acting like a limpet, with me as the rock.

Back to our Sunday evening briefing.

'Friday, I'll take them to school, as we're seeing Dr Forrest, and I think Julia will pick them up and give them tea, but I'll have to check. Anyway, I'm probably working from home that day.'

'Do you want me to do some of your ironing?'

A guilty pause. 'That would be great. Thank you so much. I'm getting better at ironing, but what with the cleaning and cooking . . .'

'I've had an idea about the cleaning.'

'Do tell.' I looked around our front room despairingly. Lizzie had been not so much house proud as messaphobic, whereas me . . .

'Do you know Ruth Lee?' She described one of the school dinner ladies. 'I'm sure she'd be very happy to help.'

So she arranged for Ruth to come in once or twice a week and clean the house. In fact, Catherine organised a rota of all the school dinner ladies who came and blitzed our house. From then on it was always clean. It also meant that the girls always got big helpings of their favourite puddings.

'I noticed the other day when I was looking for a biscuit for the girls that the top cupboard in the kitchen was full of half-mouldy cakes in tins. I threw them away. I hope you don't mind.' Catherine had rumbled me. At least once or twice a week, a neighbour—generally someone I only vaguely knew—would knock on our door and thrust a cake tin into my hand and say, 'I was doing a bit of baking, so I made an extra one for you.' I would thank them profusely and then store it in what became known as the cake cupboard. Catherine let it be known at the school that the Howes were growing fat on cake and our cake mountain disappeared.

Catherine organised me and the girls in various other discreet, subtle ways, reliable as a rock. In child-care crises, she was always there.

'Catherine? Bit of a problem. Lucy has just eaten some cherries—stones and all. Should I go to casualty?'

'How many did she eat?'

'Six, I guess.'

'You counted them in, so count them out. If they all come out in her poo, then no harm done. Nothing to worry about, honestly.'

That was Catherine. The patron saint of child-rearing.

After we'd gone through the week's appointments, Catherine would kiss me on the cheek and say, 'I'll see myself out. You're doing OK. Honestly. The girls are fine.'

And the weekend was over.

As I came out of the tube and walked to my office one grey November Monday, I imagined I was at the wheel of an ocean-going yacht on tempestuous seas with the girls huddled either side of me. The wind was a cacophony, the waves mountainous and I had no certainty of a safe passage. I was scared. I was hanging on, but only just.

We had been clinging to that boat for nearly four months, and surviving was a matter of getting on with the awfulness of our bereft state. The one huge saving grace was that, although I had changed, work had not. It was a lifeline of normality for me. But lying ahead was a series of events that we had to confront as a family of three.

Every year since we had come to Oxford, we had thrown a party for Bonfire Night. It had been fun. This year, though, I just couldn't face it. Neighbours had a few fireworks and jacket potatoes, but it was a pale imitation of our bonfire fest, and everyone knew it. I felt a heel.

Two weeks later was my birthday, which I tried hard to ignore. What was there to celebrate? I remember I was recording a play in west London (Hugh Grant was playing the lead—he wasn't famous then), but because I had changed jobs from running the drama on Radio 3 to looking after drama series and serials on Radio 4, I was summoned in my lunch break to a meeting with the controller of Radio 4 in his office at the top of Regent Street—a bit of a drag. I got there late and everyone else was waiting. I offered my apologies, then one of my colleagues produced a birthday cake. I was overwhelmed. Later I bought champagne for the cast, but felt utterly hollow attempting to celebrate a day I felt was best left unmarked.

Christmas, however, was a really thorny one—the girls would never have forgiven me if I'd buried it, like I had my birthday.

My plan was simple. I would take as little time off work as was possible and I wouldn't stand still long enough for depression to overwhelm me.

It mapped out like this. Christmas Eve: we went shopping in town, saw a morning matinée of a Christmas show at the Oxford Playhouse and then dropped off huge tins of chocolates to various families in the street who had saved our bacon. We had supper with friends and then we came home. Playing Father Christmas alone, stuffing their stockings and wrapping their presents, was a melancholy affair.

Christmas Day: our stockings were opened fiendishly early. Father Christmas had made sure that they contained Mummy's specialities as well as the goodies Daddy had invariably bought in past Christmases. We breakfasted on Coco Pops and other assorted treats. Jessica and Lucy then opened their presents from Daddy—the chief of which was an enormous wicker dressing-up basket, which Lizzie and I had promised them.

We packed up and drove to Maka and Deda's. The car broke down in the middle of nowhere. I called the AA, and we arrived late for lunch.

Once lunch and the Queen's speech had been dispatched, we opened more presents—Jessica and Lucy were given the fairy ballerina outfits they so coveted. We then drove through the dark to see Karin and David, old bosses of mine, in Somerset. More gifts. I finally inveigled the girls to shed their fairy ballerina outfits for bedtime and the adults played Risk.

On Boxing Day we went kite-flying and then we drove to my brother's. The car broke down. Again. We called the AA. Again.

We arrived flustered. There were more presents. Then we went on to my mother's, a difficult call for me, as it was the first time I had been back to Sudbury since Lizzie's death. I went for a walk by myself across the water meadow. It felt weird—I couldn't reach the emotional heights of that morning after Lizzie's death. I just felt numb and miserable.

After yet more presents we went to the pantomime at the theatre in Colchester where I used to be a director. In the birthdays section at the end, the dame—a mate of mine—read out, 'And a very happy birthday to Mr Jeremy Howe, who is one hundred and four and a half today.' I felt cherished. I took Jessica and Lucy backstage to meet the cast, which they thought was utter magic, but I felt terribly lonely standing there holding their hands while we waited to be buzzed through the stage door.

And so continued our round-England tour of friends, relatives and whoever would have us. By the time we reached home, we practically needed a trailer to ferry the excess of presents the children had been given. We opened the last of them on Twelfth Night and finished the Christmas chocolates sometime near Good Friday.

Easter, by contrast, was easy to manage—and fantastic. Eoin whisked us away to spend the holiday in the south of Spain with two friends of his, Willy and Alison, who had a house overlooking a huge empty beach. A succession of their friends dropped by and spoilt us all rotten, Alison mothered the girls, I relaxed properly for the first time since Lizzie had died and we gorged on more chocolate. It set the pattern for our future holidays.

I got good at holidays as a single parent, on my own terms—lots of excursions and not very much lazing round the pool or sunbathing. We always took them with another family, something we had never done before Lizzie's death. I am not sure I could have borne taking the girls away by myself. They always enjoyed the company of other children and having a surrogate mum on hand who did all the mumsy kind of things that I was so crap at. I enjoyed it too. Having a mother on tap 24/7 was lovely for me as much as for the girls. As was the company, especially in the evenings, which for a single parent can seem like a vast desert of time to kill. Holidays were a way of creating some kind of family normality in my own head, and we took lots of them. Basically, if someone was kind enough to suggest, 'Would you think of coming on holiday with us?' it was firmed up within minutes. As any working mother knows, trying to stitch together a line through the six-week school summer break is like trying to solve the most fiendish equation.

The year after Lizzie's death, after a week in the Dordogne with Clive and Elaine, we arrived back late on Saturday night only to drive to Bath first thing on Sunday morning for the girls to go on holiday with Maka and Deda in Devon.

A couple of years later, we had two and a half weeks in Greece booked, and then Clive asked me if we would like to share a villa with them in the south of France just a fortnight later. Unhesitatingly, I said yes. They were offers I felt I couldn't refuse in case they were never made again. I closed my eyes to the state of my bank account and disregarded the amount of leave I was taking. On holiday I was able to relax and really enjoy the company of

Jessica and Lucy. I felt none of these things at home. I was in a permanent state of anxiety.

However, one particular holiday was not a success. Karin and David invited me out for a long weekend to Norway, just me, without the girls—'To give you a break,' they said. I was so looking forward to it and I had a terrible time, even though Karin and David were excellent company and generous to a fault.

The hotel we stayed in overlooked a beautiful lake, with an island in the middle, which we rowed out to, and there were epic views of the mountains beyond. At noon a raven flew over the lake. It cawed. That was the only sign of life all day. The emptiness of the landscape was overwhelming enough, but the real problem was that I missed the children. I realised that without them I was just a lonely middle-aged man killing time in a beautiful place. I couldn't get back to them quickly enough.

But you know what children are like. You arrive home and they affect not to notice you have been away. After ten minutes of being quite nice, they start to squabble. And they are not the teeniest bit interested in hearing about where you have been and what you have done.

'That's nice, Daddy,' said Jessica, sighing. 'I am trying to watch *Pingu* and it's getting to the good bit.'

And I loved them for it.

After our Easter in Spain, we were faced with the tricky last furlong of the calendar—Lucy's birthday in May, Jessica's in early June and Lizzie's at the end of the month, and the anniversary of her death a month later in July.

Lizzie and I had promised Lucy that she could have her next birthday party at the farm where Jessica had had hers. I booked it with a heavy heart. Returning would bring back such painful memories. I needn't have worried. Lucy loved the fact that it was exactly the same as Jessica's party last year—'Only much better, Daddy!'

A couple of days later we celebrated her proper birthday with the tradition Lizzie and I had started, opening presents on my bed before breakfast.

For Jessica's birthday, my brother and I drove ten children up to Cadbury World. And brought back all ten, stuffed with freebie chocolate, without one of them being sick.

I had somehow managed to establish a new fun regime for birthdays, and by making them big treats and spoiling my two rotten, I had dispelled the aura of sadness that surrounded them.

I was determined to keep the sadness at bay on Lizzie's birthday too. That first year I bought a tiny cake with one candle and a present for the house. And that's what we've done ever since.

The anniversary of her death is a different matter. It creeps up on me and ambushes me. And then I go into an awful depression. I just want the day to be obliterated and it never is. But the first anniversary of her death was especially awful—it coincided with the week of the trial.

6

Robin Pask had been arrested and charged within hours of the incident. There was no doubt that he had killed Lizzie. It took nearly four years to bring him to justice.

Justice is a very important part of healing, something I had never before realised. If Pask had been found not guilty, I know deep down I would not have been accountable for my actions. It was an ugly feeling, mostly involving a double-barrelled shotgun.

Whenever I began thinking about the man responsible for Lizzie's death, I became angry and irrational. I spent a lot of time trying to blot him out of my life. I wanted to get back to an image of Lizzie that didn't involve her violent death. Like Jessica and Lucy, I wanted the wound to be clean, and Pask's impending trial was getting in the way of that process.

Then there were the police to contend with. My relationship with the police hadn't really recovered from my experiences at York Police Station. I was wary of them. Whenever they called, I could feel my heart rate go up.

One Thursday morning, in the spring of 1993, they phoned me at the office. 'Mr Howe, something has come up and we wondered if we could see you.'

'Why can't you just tell me now?'

'We would like to meet you tomorrow at your home in Oxford.'

'But I'm at work tomorrow. Why don't you come to the office?' I was anxious. I reasoned that they wouldn't dare do anything untoward on BBC premises.

'How about Saturday?'

'Well, I'm busy,' I lied. I had no plans for the weekend.

'You name a time on Saturday and we will be there. Any time.'

I calculated that it was about a three-hour drive from York. I wanted to make it as inconvenient for them as I could without seeming unreasonable. I did not want the police in my house.

'Can you be there by nine?'

'No problem.'

'You might have to wait outside. I've got to do the week's shopping first.'

'Fine.'

'How will I know it's you?'

'You'll know who we are. Goodbye, Mr Howe. And thank you.'

I was convinced they were going to arrest me. Irrational, I know, but I phoned my sister and told her how worried I was. Much to her husband's annoyance, she pandered to my paranoia and agreed to be in Oxford the next morning. I wanted a witness and somebody to look after the children if I was carted away.

I woke the girls up especially early on the Saturday morning and they rather grumpily came with me to Sainsbury's before eight o'clock. Philippa was due to arrive at nine, to coincide with the police. I bought enough provisions to withstand a siege—in case I had to go away. I even bought the police officers a cake each: how could they arrest me if I'd bought them a cake?

As we drove down our street, we saw a red Ford Sierra with an enormous aerial on the roof. As I parked the car and the children helped me unload the entire stock of Sainsbury's, two burly guys got out of the Sierra and started helping with the shopping. In their leather bomber jackets, they were like a parody of extras from *The Bill*. They had been right, though—I did know who they were.

As I unpacked the shopping, they prowled round the kitchen and chatted to me. One of them picked up a photograph of the four of us. It was taken in the States; it was boiling hot, we were all wearing shorts.

'I can tell this is a holiday snap,' one of them said.

'How?' I said.

'I am a detective.' He grinned.

That is the only scrap of conversation I can remember. Nor can my sister recall what they talked about. It felt like a PR exercise, to show how caring the police can be. I wrote a piece for the *Sunday Times* a few years later and used this story as the centrepiece of the article—and the North Yorkshire Police threatened legal action against me.

They stayed about half an hour and then went. They didn't even eat the cakes I'd bought. Once they had gone, I felt sick. Which perhaps says more about my state of mind in the spring of 1993 than about the way the police behaved.

One of the things gnawing at me was that I wanted Lizzie's things back. I could understand that some of them might be required as evidence, but not her lecture notes, her wedding ring, the watch I had given her. Most of all, I wanted back the kitten mug the girls had given her for her birthday four weeks before her death and which she had made a point of taking with her to York. Surely they were of no use in the case?

'But we require all of it for evidence and we can't return anything until after the trial, Mr Howe.'

'When will that be?'

'It could be anything up to a year.'

'I see. But I want everything returned.'

'Sorry, Mr Howe, I'm afraid we will destroy most of your late wife's effects.'

'You can't do that! I want them back. They are precious. Why?'

'Well, sir, a lot of her things are covered in her blood. They would be a health risk. We will have to incinerate them, sir.'

'But can't I at least see them to find out what is important? If I come up to York?' This was a big step for me.

'You cannot tamper with evidence. I'm sure you understand, sir.'

'I don't know what is there . . . Is there at least an inventory of her things?'

'I will certainly look into it, sir.'

A week or two later, an inventory arrived in the post. It was vague and meaningless—'papers', 'sundry items', 'clothes, some bloodstained'. The list meant nothing. What was particularly painful was that I had such a strong image of all Lizzie's stuff laid out on a table in a corridor in York Police Station the day after her death—so close then and now utterly unreachable.

I phoned them. It took for ever to speak to the right person. We wrangled and reached a compromise, and he agreed to send down a few of the more precious things. A couple of weeks later I picked up a package from Oxford Police Station. They handed over a small Jiffy bag. Once outside, I tore it open: Lizzie's wedding ring and her watch in a small plastic bag. The leather strap was stained in places with her blood. I was both elated and terribly cast down—so much and so little. I wore her watch until it gave up the ghost a year later. It made me feel just a little bit closer to Lizzie.

The wedding ring was a different matter. On Lizzie's finger it had meant so much, but in my hand it was just a cheap band of gold from H. Samuel. I squirrelled it away.

Months later, a random package of Lizzie's papers arrived in the post, including the Stevie Smith lecture she was due to deliver. I have never been able to read it. The notes are bloodstained. I can imagine them on her desk in her room in York, and then my mind shuts down. I can't go there.

The reality of Lizzie's trial, however, was still hanging over me. Just days after her death, Pask appeared at a magistrate's court, where he was charged and was denied bail. Then he was referred to the High Court. He entered a plea of not guilty of murder, but guilty of manslaughter with diminished responsibility. I got accustomed to the glacial progress the case was making through the legal system, about which I realised I knew absolutely nothing.

The trial would not take place for almost a year. Why? I learned that Pask was in the hospital wing of a prison in Hull, awaiting psychological reports, that there was a shortage of High Court judges, and then that the trial slated for May had been put back while the defence prepared their case. What case? Although Pask never admitted to murdering Lizzie, he did admit to being the only person in the room when she died.

One morning after Christmas, a letter arrived informing me that the trial had been delayed. Because I was working at home that day, I took the children to school. As I walked back through the park, on that grey day, pregnant with rain, I thought of Pask and was overcome with grief and self-pity. I stood in the empty park and shouted out, 'You bastard! Look what you have done to us! I HATE YOU!' Even as I stood there I was aware that I was acting like a character in an Ingmar Bergman film. But I was utterly bereft.

When I arrived home, Maka, who was staying with us, got up from doing her crossword. She too had been fretting over the news of the trial. We hugged.

'I am so sorry. Poor, poor Lizzie. That wretched bloody man.'

I pulled myself together and wiped my nose. I cried my way through so many handkerchiefs that year.

'I am going to have a stiff whisky. Will you join me?' she asked.

It was ten past nine in the morning and I opted for coffee and a Penguin biscuit; even that felt a bit decadent. I would never dull the pain with alcohol. That was Maka's problem—she tried to drink away her sorrows, but drink never flushed them away.

I received a notice of summons from the High Court saying that I might be called upon to give evidence at the trial of Regina vs Pask, and failure to do so might result in prosecution. Attached to the summons was a line drawing of what a court looks like, from which it was all too clear that when I gave evidence I would be standing right next to the man who had killed my wife. I phoned the police.

'It's a form letter, sir, and you shouldn't have been sent it. You will not be required to give evidence. We apologise.'

It was an endurance test during which I learnt that the victim's relatives had no place in the criminal justice system. I was a nuisance.

A new date was set for the trial. The anniversary of Lizzie's death.

The police wanted to know if I would attend.

'What provision is made for the victim's family?'

'Well, sir, you sit in the public gallery.'

'Do we have special seating?'

'Well, no, sir, seating is on a first come, first served basis, sir.'

'So I might not even get in.'

'That's a possibility, sir.'

'And I might be sitting next to *his* family?'

'That too is a possibility, sir. Also, I should warn you that the press will be on the lookout for you.'

The prosecution barrister got in touch. He wondered if we might meet up the week before the trial. I met him in a suitably Dickensian wine bar opposite the Royal Courts of Justice. A slightly overweight Yorkshireman, dressed in a very expensive suit, he exuded both the good life and immense capability. I liked him.

'I don't know what your plans are, but I would strongly advise that you don't come to the trial.'

'I think I have already made up my mind. As I see it, I have a lot to lose from going and nothing to gain.'

'Sensible chap. You see, I think you might be expecting the truth to emerge in a trial, and you'll get nothing like it. It's a game between me and the defence barrister. I will do anything to get a result, and so will he. And in that situation, I'm afraid, the truth is invariably a victim.'

He was the first person who explained how the justice system works and talked to me like an equal. I left the bar feeling immensely grateful.

THE WEEK of the trial was high summer at its hottest. I now understand why trials are so called: it was like waiting for an operation to remove my heart. The pressure made me feel as if I were being shaken until I broke, and all the while I tried to conduct myself as if everything was normal. I took meetings at work, I read scripts, I smiled on the way to school. But it was a mask.

The police had agreed to keep me informed of the trial's progress, my wonderful personnel officer arranged a rota of friends and colleagues to take me out to lunch every day, and Lizzie's sister Louise travelled north to Leeds Crown Court with her new husband to witness proceedings.

On day one, Pask entered a plea of not guilty.

'But he killed her,' I told the police when they phoned.

'Yes, but he is hoping to get convicted of manslaughter with diminished responsibility.'

'What does that mean?'

'That he is admitting he is insane.'

'What's the difference between manslaughter and murder?'

'Well, if it was murder he would get a life sentence and serve fourteen or so years in prison, but with diminished responsibility he will be sent to a prison hospital and probably remain there for life.'

'Why would he choose to do that?'

'My guess, Mr Howe, is that he can't face up to his crime. He would rather hide behind a verdict of insanity than face up to murder.'

Louise phoned me to tell me that in court Pask looked like a worm. 'Jeremy, I am so glad you didn't come here. There are hordes of photographers waiting on the steps of the court, all with photographs of you so they can identify you.'

On day two, Pask's sister and his mother gave evidence *against* him.

'Mr Howe, in my experience, murder trials rarely go to plan, and with that evidence I can't see the trial lasting the week. Something strange is going to happen, mark my words.'

On day three, the evidence about what Pask actually did came out in court. What he did to Lizzie after she was dead was unspeakable.

I was sitting in my office just before lunch the next day, when my phone rang. It was the police.

'Mr Howe, the trial has collapsed.'

'What!?'

'Pask collapsed in court and the trial has been adjourned while doctors make an assessment of his health.'

'Till when?'

'Indefinitely. The judge instructed that Pask should be submitted for psychiatric testing to establish his suitability to stand trial.'

I felt cheated.

Louise called me on a payphone from the court lobby.

'I told you he was a worm. He was being led from the court and deliberately tripped over a chair. I saw it. He is faking it.'

I made my apologies to my secretary and went home, shattered. The story was in the early edition of the *London Evening Standard*. It was on the news on telly.

I didn't know what to do with myself. A friend of Lizzie's from university came to see how I was and we went for a walk round the park. I remember her giving me a hug. I can still feel the warmth of her body pressed to mine. It was such a familiar feeling, such a lost feeling. I so wanted Lizzie back, and I don't think I ever felt further from her in my life.

That weekend, we marked the anniversary of Lizzie's death by having a short service to bless the gravestone in the cemetery above Bath. I had fretted over what kind of stone, what shape, what inscription? I wanted everything to be as simple as possible—just as Lizzie was a simple and straightforward person. So her grave was in plain Bath stone with the inscription 'My heart's best treasure'. Wordsworth again. I felt I had done the right thing by her.

From then on, Lucy and I would visit the grave every Mother's Day with a bunch of daffodils. Jessica has never been since that day.

NEARLY THREE YEARS LATER, Robin Pask was brought to a retrial. He entered a plea of guilty to manslaughter with diminished responsibility and was sentenced to detention at Her Majesty's pleasure in a prison hospital. The trial lasted half a day. 'It means life, Mr Howe. And Ashworth isn't a pleasant place. I am sorry it has taken so long.' A few papers gave the story a paragraph. I felt mightily relieved. Justice had been served. End of story.

Nearly. The day after the verdict I phoned York Police Station to enquire about getting Lizzie's things back.

'Of course we will send them, Mr Howe, once we have received a cheque for seven pounds and thirty pence to cover postage and packing.'

'I can't believe you are saying this to me.'

'It's the rules. Please make it payable to North Yorkshire Constabulary.'

'How about if I charge you seven pounds thirty for the use of my wife's things for four years? Then we are quits.'

'Don't get sarcastic with me, Mr Howe.'

I was in the office. I put down the phone. 'I can't believe what I have just been told.'

My PA, who had heard the conversation, was appalled. 'Why don't you phone the Chief Constable? Do it now, while you are still angry.'

Amazingly, I got through. He heard me out, apologised and said the parcel would be sent right away. Forget about the cheque.

When it arrived—a big brown paper parcel—it sat threateningly in the kitchen like an unexploded bomb. I couldn't touch it.

After several days of it sitting there untouched, I sat down with Louise and opened it. There was my briefcase, Lizzie's wallet, the birthday mug with the kitten, her return rail ticket to Oxford, lists scrawled in her large, restless handwriting, pictures of the girls, her biros, a couple of dresses, some moisturiser. The detritus of the living, only old, like exhibits in a museum.

For a second I got my Lizzie back and then she vanished.

It was unbelievably painful. But there was some closure, as they say.

THE ORIGINAL TRIAL finished the day before the girls broke up, the day that Linda handed in her notice. I can only imagine that the strain of dealing with a family in meltdown must have been awful. For a twenty-year-old, a year was enough. I don't think we ever heard from Linda again. I was both relieved—it had never really worked—and in a blind panic: the whole edifice of child care had collapsed. A year on from Lizzie's death, I was in bits on account of the trial. I had no idea how I was going to get through the holidays, but I knew I couldn't take six weeks off work.

'I know just the person you need.' The wonderfully capable woman who ran the nanny agency remembered me when I phoned her, and she came up trumps. We appointed Annette, loud, bottle-blonde and bubbly, she was almost as bad a cook as me, but she loved the children, the children loved her and she was a brilliant nanny.

'I thought you might get on with Annette,' said the agency lady.

She made the children prize-winning costumes for fancy-dress parties, played singing games, made them toffee apples with dolly mixtures stuck in them and put their hair up in every shape and form imaginable. She read them stories, got them fixated on TV game shows, got them to tidy up, to brush their teeth, comb their hair, change their knickers—and made it all feel like fun. And she was strict to boot.

'Why is Jessica in her pyjamas at the table?' I said one evening when I got home from work.

'Daddy, Annette won't let me get down until I eat all of this soup. Look, it's all cabbage.'

She slopped bits of cabbagey gruel off her spoon. She had a point.

'You'll get a cuddle when you eat three more mouthfuls.'

'Hmph. I hate you too.'

She also introduced the girls to *The Sound of Music* (the story where the nanny gets the widowed dad), which they have now seen a zillion times and I have never watched in its entirety. On the grounds that it might have been a dangerous influence on me.

The high point of my children's lives was almost certainly watching Annette appear on *The Crystal Maze* on telly. Every friend Jessica and Lucy have ever had has been made to watch the tape of it.

The year Annette was with us, it seemed that the sun was always shining.

I OFTEN WONDERED if I was the world's worst mum. Sometimes it felt like a near-run thing.

Love, warmth, tenderness, creating a home that is stable and caring. I guess these are the key attributes of being a good parent. I think that, on the whole, I was pretty good at supplying these in the broader sense. But being a good mum is also about the detail. Clean clothes, brushed hair, good food and so on. What are all those skills that make women so effortlessly good at child-rearing? What qualities would I need to develop to enable me to become a domestic goddess?

Patience. I found it very hard to help them to learn to read or ride a bicycle for hours on end.

Clean clothes and all those kinds of things? I was OK at that sporadically. Once a month or so I could be a very enthusiastic tidier-upper but doing it on a daily basis seemed to be beyond me.

I learned to put the girls' hair into ponytails and, once in a blue moon, I had the patience to put it into bunches, but plaits were a grade above me. I would brush their hair, but not without them yelping. My suggestion that they got their hair cut short was treated with scorn. In fact, I never once managed to get their hair cut. The haircut fairy must have done that. I never really mastered the nit comb and lived in perpetual fear of finding a head louse. They probably had nits for years, but I failed to notice.

I also lived in fear of their first periods. I did try to explain the facts of life to Jessica once, but she said, 'I know all that, Daddy. Maka told me.'

I got pretty good at packing swimming costumes. However, on one occasion I did forget to pack towels and the girls had to walk around the outside of the pool until they dried off. Also, I never seemed to be able to pack spare clothes. I could get the girls out of the door efficiently, but never with the right clothes for the weather.

I never quite mastered the art of sorting washing. I was pretty good at separating whites from coloureds but I invariably failed to spot those tissues lodged in pockets that ruin any wash. And watching me iron was a pitiful sight.

However, my children learned how to throw good, firm snowballs, were utterly fearless about the scariest fairground rides and became ferocious card players who played to win—things I can be very proud of. Mind you, despite my best endeavours, they were pretty crap at football.

By now you are well acquainted with my culinary philosophy—that cooking is hell. If it came out of a packet, I could cook it, although not well. I have never knowingly roasted a chicken—it is way beyond my powers of time coordination. Two bubbling pans I can cope with, but combine them with having to watch an oven and it is just too much. In fact, ovens can be added to the list of household appliances of which I am wary (power drills, lawn mowers, washing machines, etc.). At least with a grill you know where you are.

Waste management was also a bit of an issue. I've never been convinced that bins need frequent emptying—I find the forceful use of a foot on top of the rubbish creates plenty of space.

Food waste was worse. Before I could fill the fridge with the week's shopping, I needed to empty it of pasta hardened to a crisp, fossilised bacon rashers and curdled milk. And the bread bin seemed to need washing weekly to get rid of the aroma of mould. For ages we drove around with a festering cooked chicken in the car boot because I couldn't find it (stuck in a wellington boot, I seem to recall), but we kind of got used to the smell.

In one way I was supremely feminine—if something went wrong, I called a man to help me, as in: 'Julia, I've got a problem. Any chance of Ollie coming over?'

In four years, the children almost never had a day off school, not because they weren't sickly, but because I just pretended not to notice or gave them Calpol. They never complained. Well, not to me.

And the children were always hopelessly in arrears with their pocket money, so there would be endless bargaining, usually in the toy shop in Oxford on a Saturday, along the lines of: 'If I give you this eighty-seven pence'—always in coppers—'and you pay for the rest with the four weeks' pocket money you owe me and my pocket money for the next fortnight, then you will owe me twenty-eight pence in three Saturdays' time.' It meant that Lucy was fiendishly good at mental arithmetic.

In short, nothing ever seemed to be under control and I spent most of my life worrying about the things I hadn't done, rather than actually doing them. But, in the end, we were a happy family and a loving one, albeit a family wearing odd socks and with holes in our jeans.

And I always got the children to the dentist for their check-ups.

So, to sum up, the Jeremy Howe rules of mothering are:

Where at all possible, delegate. By profession, I was an executive producer. Execs don't actually do anything; they tell/persuade/inveigle other people to do things for them. Amazingly, some people like darning tights.

If you can't do it, don't even try. I would list baking, nit-combing, roasting and plaiting as way beyond me. So I never tried.

Let your children get on with it. The girls became self-sufficient very fast. I once said to Jessica that bringing them up is the achievement I am most proud of in my life. 'Bringing you up, Daddy, was Lucy's and my proudest achievement.'

And, finally, when the house becomes too messy, move.

I wasn't the world's worst mum. I was one of the world's better mummydaddys.

THIS BIT IS all about sex and the single parent. But don't think you are about to read a steamy account of my sex life. There wasn't one.

How odd to have shared a a bed and all those intimacies and intricacies of life with someone you love who then disappears. Which left me with an interesting challenge. I was a free agent, could play the field. Well, Jessica, Lucy and I could play the field.

What I soon discovered is that single dads are not like single mums. Both are sexual outcasts, but in completely different ways. No man will go near a single mum for fear, I guess, of being burdened with kids. By contrast, I was inundated by women who wanted to help me. And, boy, did I need help. I can think of a dozen or more women who just scooped up Jessica, Lucy and me and made sure we were clothed, washed and fed. They were my lifeline. They welcomed me in and I became an Honorary Mother.

But I wanted to be Hugh Grant in *Four Weddings and a Funeral*. That was a bit more tricky. I found myself sitting on trains looking at women in a totally new way—might they be the kind of person I could fall in love with?

There was a woman who used to commute from Oxford on my train. She was about my age, Australian, gregarious, smartly turned out. I was fascinated by her and discovered she caught the same tube as me, got out at Oxford Circus and, lo and behold, one morning she went into Broadcasting House like me!

The next time we were on the same train, I summoned up the courage: 'I see you work at BH like me.'

'Yeah, I freelance for *Newsbeat* sometimes.'

'Oh, I'm in the drama department. I'm Jeremy.'

'Hi, I'm Megan.'

It was the first time in fifteen years that I had introduced myself to a woman as a single man. I felt exhilarated.

After that, Megan and I met on the train a number of times. She was married to a lecturer at an Oxford college and knew who I was (after all, she was a journalist who sometimes worked for the BBC, where Lizzie's death had been a big issue). We would go round to her house for tea; she doted on Jessica and Lucy. She was lovely. But she was a friend, not a romantic attachment.

A year after Lizzie's death Libby Purves asked to interview me for *Good Housekeeping*. I was trying to raise money for the Open University trust fund in Lizzie's name, so I agreed. Libby was very engaging and I enjoyed her company—no wonder she was a chat-show host, I thought. But I felt like I had sat mute for a couple of hours while she entertained me and wondered if she had enough material.

A couple of days later she faxed through her copy for the article. It was as if she had taken an X-ray photograph of me and my emotions. It was devastatingly accurate.

She phoned me that evening. 'Jeremy, I just wanted to clarify one thing you said about *The Winter's Tale*.'

'Well, the last thing Lizzie and I saw together at the theatre was an extraordinary production that has haunted me ever since. It is the most moving statement about how love survives a tragedy like ours. Leontes banishes Hermione in a fit of jealousy, but when he hears of her death he is inconsolable. At the end of the play, when he is presented with a life-sized statue of Hermione, he gazes on it in love and grief "which sixteen winters cannot blow away". And then the statue comes to life. Hermione and Leontes have been reunited. It is a tale of love surviving catastrophe. And that statue coming to life is my fantasy. For me, that last scene of *The Winter's Tale* is what I want my life to be.'

She had asked me about remarriage. 'Of course, I have had that thought,' I told her, 'but, you see, what I desperately want is to fall in love again. With Lizzie. Again. And to have another child with her.'

She made this the basis of her closing paragraph, and when the article was published my boss phoned me.

'I saw Libby's piece—she has caught you to a tee. Was it sponsored by a dating agency? I'm sure you will get several offers of marriage from it!' And he laughed.

I was embarrassed—but he was right, of course. I might just as well have put my contact details and 'eligible middle-aged man with two adorable kids seeks kind, loving woman with a GSOH' at the bottom. It even had the most lovely photograph of the three of us. And the adorable man is doing it all for charity! If only they had published it on Valentine's Day.

I did get a couple of the barmiest letters from women who thought I sounded like a very special person and would I like to share my troubles with them—with phone numbers attached. I showed them to a friend and she and I laughed and I threw them away. But secretly I was sorry I didn't get more letters.

Then, quite late one Sunday evening, came a knock at the door. It was

Sam, a neighbour. She was a bit older than me, quite attractive, resolutely single and . . . very 'alternative'—I am sure she ate macrobiotic rice and burned joss sticks. Alternative is a word that always makes me go into spasm.

After Lizzie's death Sam would call by occasionally. She was desperate to alleviate my suffering with reiki. I was desperate for her not to. But there she stood on my doorstep.

'Hi, Jeremy. Sorry to disturb you so late, but my boiler has broken and I wondered if could use your bath?'

What do you say when a single woman of a certain age asks a question like that?

'Er . . .' was what I said.

'I know it's late. But I've got no hot water.'

'Sure,' I said. I was sure it was a lie. She didn't want just a bath. She wanted a bath and . . . well, I shan't go there.

'OK. But you'll need to be quick, as I am about to turn in. But OK.'

'I'll be back in five minutes.'

Had I just invited her in for sex? Or rather, did she think I had just invited her in for sex? Because I certainly hadn't.

What she didn't know was that I was with Rachel and her husband Chris, two neighbours who had dropped by.

I went back into the sitting room. Rachel had her hand over her mouth to stop herself from shrieking with giggles. 'Jeremy, what was that all about? She comes round here asking for a bath!?'

'Er . . . she may well have been asking for a bath, but I can't help feeling she wanted something else!'

'And?'

'Well, I said she could come round. For a bath.'

'Are you having an affair with her?'

'NO WAY!'

'There's you, a single man, and her, a single woman. Why ever not?' And she and her husband burst out laughing.

There was a knock at the door. There, in a bathrobe was a single woman of a certain age Coming to My House for a Bath. I assume she had nothing on underneath her robe. I assume she didn't just want a bath.

I introduced her to Rachel and Chris. I wasn't quite sure how I should handle this, but I am sure I handled it better because they were there. I took her up to the bathroom and padded downstairs.

I wonder what she was thinking while she took her bath?

Sam came downstairs shortly afterwards, washed and scrubbed. The four of us chatted for about one minute and then she went off into the night, with Rachel and Chris leaving shortly after.

I knew it would be all round the street by the time the school bell rang tomorrow. I was living under a microscope, my every move watched by half the neighbourhood.

I had to get out.

7

'That man behaves as if he has a red-hot chilli up his bum,' a friend once quipped. I have never been a restful person, but after Lizzie's death it was as if I was on some adrenaline kick. Four months after I had returned to work full-time, I switched jobs within my department, so I had a completely new brief to master. Within a few weeks of that, I was seconded onto some BBC think tank, which, for three months, was virtually a full-time job on top of the day job. Once we'd produced our report, doing just the day job seemed a bit humdrum. I began to sniff around for something new. Then, in the spring of 1994, my dream job came up, running *10x10*, a BBC Two series of short films for new directors, produced out of Bristol, less than a dozen miles from Maka and Deda in Bath. It looked like it had been heaven-sent.

Miraculously, I got it, even though the children had taped *Fireman Sam* over half of the video showreel they had asked me to watch for the interview. So I blagged about films I hadn't seen. Nothing changes.

The sixth phase of grief is called the upward turn. This was my new start. I told the children over breakfast.

'Girls, Daddy's got a new job. It's based in Bristol, so we'll need to move to Bath, near to Maka and Deda.'

'That's nice. You do that, Daddy, and Luce and I will stay here,' said Jessica matter-of-factly, munching her Rice Krispies.

'I agree,' chimed in Lucy.

Good start, I thought.

I handed in my notice, put the Oxford house on the market and every weekend we went to Bath looking for a new home.

Eventually, we found one just down the hill from what was supposed to be the best primary school in town. The owners accepted my offer, but as they were in no hurry to move we put everything on hold. Then came two big snags: the best primary school in town seemed not to want Jessica and Lucy and I couldn't sell the Oxford house.

Meanwhile, I started the new job, which meant driving from Oxford to Bristol and back nearly every day. One morning, as I turned right out of our street, I collided with a motorcyclist. It was as much his fault as mine, but it was unnerving. I decided this couldn't go on, so I found the girls a school even though it wasn't terribly close to the new house, and I took out a humungous loan so we could move to Bath full-time, regardless of whether or not we sold the Oxford house. I had mortgages worth over five times my salary, but who's counting?

We decamped to Bath for the summer holidays and returned to Oxford every weekend. Once term began we lived with Maka and Deda until we could move into the Bath house at half-term. And having said the fondest of farewells to Annette, I found another nanny—a slightly scary, half-Chilean divorcee called Adriana, who had brought up two children of her own, so she obviously knew what she was doing. Or so I reasoned. Unfortunately, Maka and Deda both seemed to treat her like a servant. And even I had to upbraid her because she had allowed Jessica—now eight years old—to cook pancakes unsupervised. I gave her one more chance, but it was rocky.

Then I got a call from Maka while I was at work. Adriana had poured water all over Lucy and had made her cry, and now Adriana was under the kitchen table refusing to come out and hugging Lucy, who was not at all happy. Well, traumatised actually.

I asked to speak to Adriana. Eventually, after much off-line squawking, she came to the phone.

'What's going on?'

'You don't understand, Mr Howe.'

'From what I hear, you have poured water all over Lucy and now you are terrorising her under the kitchen table. I'm coming home right now. If you don't have a good explanation by the time I get back, you don't have a job.'

By the time I got back, Adriana had left. The children were chattering away. 'Daddy, she poured water all over Lucy!'

'We were playing with our buckets in the bathroom and she just poured a whole bucket of cold water over me, Daddy.'

'Were you very upset, sweetie?'

'I was a bit. I didn't like it when she took me under the table.'

'Maka said it was Adriana's pills, Daddy.'

The next day, I went round to her flat and paid her.

'You have a lot to learn, Mr Howe.' And she handed me a book called *Learning to Forgive*. It sat accusingly on my bedside table for a couple of weeks, then I threw it away.

So much for Nanny Number Three. On to Number Four.

When Kerry came for her second interview, we were just moving into the new house in Bath, a move that felt like one bloody big gamble. New job (where no one knew me), new life (where no one knew me) and new mortgage (they certainly knew me). Looking back, moving us to Bath was a turning point in our return to normality. But as I doggedly unpacked all our stuff, it just felt like I had bitten off rather more than I could chew.

Kerry and I chatted and then she went upstairs to find the children. She later confided to one of my friends that she had found Jessica and Lucy aimlessly moving a pile of soft toys from one bed to the other. 'I could be of some use here,' she thought, and she took the job.

Milly Molly Mandy, however, had one final test for Kerry. She had been shut in the house because she was new to it, and on the Sunday evening before Kerry started, I was putting out the rubbish and the cat darted between my legs into the back garden. I tried to cajole her back in with food, but instead she ran off into the night. Bloody cat.

Next morning, there was still no sign of the cat, only a plaintive mewing coming from somewhere outside. We were walking (actually, we raced, because I was always late) along the street to the car when Lucy spotted her.

'Look!' And there she was, stuck up the tree at the end of our terrace and looking deeply miserable. She couldn't get down.

We stood at the bottom of the tree calling her, but all she did was mew.

'Look, I'll have to take you to school and see if I can get her down before I go to work.'

'But, Daddy . . .'

I left the distressed cat and took two weeping girls to school. When I got back I rang the fire brigade—'Sorry, mate, that's an RSPCA job'—then the RSPCA.

'How long has she been up there?'

'All last night.'

'Sorry, sir, we don't come out on cat rescues until they've been up there forty-eight hours.'

So I left a hastily scrawled note for Kerry. 'Slight problem. Cat up tree. Can you fix please. J.' And went off.

When I got back at about 7 p.m. I was greeted by said bloody cat, two children hopping with glee and Kerry.

'Daddy, Kerry was ever so clever. She rescued Milly Molly Mandy!'

'How on earth?'

'I hailed a passing BT van with a ladder on its roof and offered him ten quid to get her down. She didn't half struggle though,' she said, matter-of-factly. We had found our Mary Poppins, and all for ten quid extra. Kerry was unflappable.

I made it a point of principle that the girls would visit me at work once every half-term and once in the school holidays. Firstly, because they enjoyed it (what child wouldn't? I worked as part of the unit that madc the Wallace and Gromit films and we had a viewing room lined floor to ceiling with cartoons) and secondly, to make sure my boss knew what I was up against.

I would take them and Kerry would come to my office to pick them up. My secretary said of Kerry, as she left with the children, 'Blimey, I wouldn't get on the wrong side of her.' Six foot tall, leather bomber jacket, long dark-brown hair, built like a streetfighter's gal and very direct, when Kerry said, 'Come on, girls. Time to go,' the children would obey. Instantly.

You didn't mess with Kerry. But the children doted on her, Maka and Deda called her 'our angel' and she was such a brilliant nanny that she survived with us until after the birth of her first child, and it was only when she was pregnant with her second and Jessica was about to sit her GCSEs that we parted company. She was, as she said, 'of some use'.

The great advantage of my new job was that I could take the girls to school nearly every day, pick them up regularly and eat supper with them once or twice a week. I would feel lonely waiting at the school gate with the other mums, who were all strangers to me. There was one man who regularly picked up a girl from Lucy's class. I found it a bit odd. A man at the school gate! Was he a perv, or a gay dad, or what? I realised that I was beginning to see myself as a mother. I had travelled a long way in two years.

JESSICA WOULD NEVER do sleepovers. Lucy was as happy as a cricket to go and sleep with friends. Jessica absolutely would not. She was happy to sleep anywhere at all, as long as it was with me, Maka or one of a short list of babysitters.

Her younger sister would go off with her sleeping-bag without a murmur, but Jessica would stay put. Her no-sleepover rule was as immutable as one of the Ten Commandments: the sky is blue, day follows night and Jessica doesn't do sleepovers. Oh, and nobody was to know. Because she was embarrassed about it.

'Does Lucy want to come over for a sleepover on Saturday night?'

'Yes, I'm sure she'd love to.'

'Jessica can come too.'

'Er. Sorry. No can do. She's climbing Everest and I'm not expecting her back till late.' I had run out of plausible excuses.

Once, when we were still in Oxford, I tried to get her to go. A birthday party was on the horizon which involved An Adventure—a walk along the Berkshire Downs with an overnight in a youth hostel. In March. Sounded more like a penance to me. And Jessica—who was Becca's special friend—was most definitely invited. I broached this with her, dressing it up as enormous fun, but of course she WOULD NOT GO.

With six weeks' notice, I gently told Becca's mum that we would be going away that weekend. 'Not to worry, we'll change the date to suit you.' The whole thing seemed to revolve round Jessica. I even resorted to telling the truth to her mum, but not even that cut any ice. 'We'll look after her. All children get a bit nervous about going away, don't they?'

But then Jessica changed her mind. I don't recall her changing her mind either before or since. But now she told Becca she would come along.

The week before the trek was a tad tense, but although she wavered a little every night, Jessica seemed determined to go ahead with it.

On the day—grey and wet—I walked round to Becca's with her, silent, like a hero from a Greek tragedy. *Jessica auf Naxos*—that kind of thing.

Lucy and I had a quiet day that Saturday. I was expecting a phone call to rush to Berkshire to pick up a traumatised child.

Sunday was the same. The only sound was the clock ticking.

And then, midafternoon, she returned, wet, tired and grumpy.

'I don't ever want to do that again. Ever.'

I have no idea what the trip had been like—'I don't want to talk about it.'

Nor did anyone else. Becca and her mother and the fellow sufferers all seemed to have signed a pact of silence.

Jessica never did a sleepover again. Which was a looming problem. I had visions of me as an old man shackled to Jessica, going to live with her at university because she didn't do sleepovers.

Then, in her final year at primary school in Bath, the big treat was a week-long stay at an activity centre on the Isle of Wight. Exactly the kind of thing my physically fearless older daughter would relish if only she could overcome her inner demons.

Ten months before the dreaded trip, I got in touch with Dr Forrest. Would she be able to help? She couldn't see us because we had moved out of her area, but she quickly referred me to a child psychiatrist in Bath.

So, once every three weeks, from the beginning of the autumn term in September, we would visit this poor man. Jessica would only go if Lucy went. A typical session would go like this:

I sat opposite the doctor in his spacious office. Lucy would be drawing endlessly on a large blackboard. Huddled in a corner was her sister, pretending to be deeply absorbed in her book. The doctor and I would talk. Occasionally he would throw a direct question to Jessica, like, 'What do you enjoy most about school, Jessica?'

Long pause punctuated only by the scratch of Lucy's chalk on the board. Somebody mumbled something and Lucy then said, 'Jessica says she enjoys reading and writing most of all.'

'Lucy, why do you think Jessica won't talk to the doctor?' I asked.

She said, 'You know why,' and went back to her drawing.

This went on for seven torturous months.

And do you know what? Jessica did go to her adventure camp. Saying farewell to her as she boarded the school bus was painful and the week she was away an eternity. At mealtimes Lucy and I sat in silence. 'I think it is Jessica who does all the talking, don't you, Daddy?'

The bus home arrived bang on time and there was Jessica, calmly walking towards me, expressionless. At the very last moment she flung her arms round me. 'I did it, Daddy,' she whispered. I felt so proud of her.

Three years later she went on a school trip to China. When her best friend dropped out she still went. She went off to uni—not happily, I have to admit—but she went, and I didn't have to live with her there. Miracle-workers come in many guises: that poor doctor must have done something!

EIGHTEEN MONTHS AFTER we moved to Bath I made a film about Lizzie's death. It was like walking up to Medusa and looking at her full in the face. It didn't break me. But it did change me.

Out of the blue, the series I was running for BBC Bristol was decommissioned. I was summoned to see my boss. Instead of curtains, which is what I was expecting, he said, 'I want you to work alongside Peter Symes and coproduce *Picture This*. Are you interested?' *Picture This* was the most prestigious series BBC Bristol was then making for BBC Two, a run of authored thirty-minute documentaries.

You bet, I thought. 'Yes. Sounds good to me,' I said.

'Oh, and you'd have to direct a film for the series.' Was this Christmas? Was I hallucinating, or what?

'OK. Fine.'

'Have you directed for telly before?'

'Er . . . No. I've mainly produced.'

'Here's your chance. How do you feel?'

'Excited. Nervous . . .'

'It'll be nerve-wracking, but you'll learn a lot. Good luck.'

Not quite the meeting I was expecting.

I spent the weekend coming up with ideas and on Monday afternoon I met Peter for 'a chat'. I had spoken with him but I hardly knew him. His reputation was pretty extraordinary: 'legend' kind of sums it up. Peter Symes, the patron saint of serious documentary television. He asked me what film I would like to make for his series. I pitched various ideas, but I could sense his complete lack of interest.

'Any other ideas floating around?'

I paused. 'Do you know Shakespeare's *The Winter's Tale*?'

I told him of the last production I had seen with Lizzie and how I thought the transformation scene with the statue, which is, for me, one of Shakespeare's greatest achievements, just hadn't worked.

'Yes?' he questioned, in a tone that suggested that he thought this drama luvvie had lost the plot. 'And why do you want to make this?'

And then I told him my story, the story of this book, and his piercing blue eyes lit up. He leaned forward, and, like the doctor in that surgery in Norfolk nearly four years before, I could see that his jaw was about to drop.

'I want to bring Lizzie back to life.'

'But how?'

I told him about *La Jetée*, a cult French short made in the sixties, which I had seen the year before. It tells of how a man who survives a nuclear holocaust is trained by fellow survivors to travel into the future to get help, but first he needs to learn to travel into the past. It is a film about memory, the memory of a love affair he once had. Uniquely for a movie, it is all shot in black and white stills. Two thirds of the way through, the hero remembers one afternoon when he and his girlfriend made love and there are shots of her lying on her side, her head propped up by her elbow. She is looking straight at the camera. And then she blinks. *She blinks.* In a film made entirely from still photographs, she comes to life. This, the only moving image, is about a second long. As I sat in the cinema, it blew my mind. That one device had brought the past into the present. Just as I wanted to make Lizzie a part of my present. The film haunted me. And now I wanted to remake it about Lizzie.

'I see,' he said. 'That's clever.'

It became an obsession. Film-making is an obsession—making a good film is so hard that unless you are obsessed it is just not worth doing. For four months I was in the grip of it, my mission to bring Lizzie back to me.

I scoured the south of England for the remotest, most desolate locations, cast doubles to play me and Jessica and Lucy. We filmed the image I had been carrying in my head since Lizzie died—of a smashed-up car with all of our belongings strewn across a fog-bound landscape. We filmed Wittenham Clumps, we filmed mist-shrouded, uprooted trees, we filmed the actors playing the three of us waving off the train from Oxford Station, Jessica's double saying her prayers. In nearly every shot there were photographs of Lizzie: scattered in fields, on car seats, against train windows, reflected in windscreens.

I went to Oxford to interview Catherine Unia, Dr Hall and my sister Philippa. All of them were very tense about the ordeal they'd signed up for.

I asked Philippa how she remembered Lizzie and me.

'I remember one Christmas when we were all opening our presents at our mother's house and you had given Lizzie a clock, and as she opened it I remember the look between you across the crowded room. Nobody else existed. When you two were together everyone felt a bit locked out.'

I felt my chest tighten. I don't know if I remembered the moment or if, in that instant that my sister spoke, I reconstructed it, but I could see Lizzie opening my present and I could see and feel across that noisy room the smile in her eyes that bonded us. Lizzie and Jeremy. That is who we were, who I was, who I should be. Together I always felt that Lizzie and I could conquer the world. One word defines what gave us that strength. Love. We had lost so much. And at that moment the pain of that loss made me feel as if my heart was about to burst.

'. . . and in agreeing to be in the film,' Philippa continued, 'you've made me remember things I wanted to forget. I've had to open a drawer full of memories of the time that Lizzie was killed and to look at them again, and to be honest I can't wait to get home and repack them and close the drawer and lock it shut . . .'

I felt envious. As Philippa said it I realised that I had a mess of wreckage blocking my view of the past and my path into the future, fouling up the present, polluting everything.

I was interviewed for the film, too. I could hardly interview myself, so I asked another Philippa (not my sister, but a mate) who happens to be the best documentary interviewer I have ever come across. When she said, 'Yes, of course, I'd be honoured,' I felt I might have a film on my hands.

She interviewed me in the cold gloom of my house in Bath (the boiler was making so much noise the sound recordist had insisted we turn it off, even though it was January). It was like being in a confessional, reliving the misery of what happened to us in front of the six earnest people who were my crew. It was horribly public.

'If it hurts, it's real,' I said, 'the only way I have felt real since Lizzie died is if I hurt. I think something of me was murdered that day.'

I was weeping now, but I didn't care.

'Essentially, Lizzie and I were the same person, so losing her was like having my arm ripped out, and the damage that causes is massive. Grief is a black hole that sucks everything into it. It's not a pleasant place to be in, but it's also fascinating. You see the whole world through a different set of spectacles. I am sure I am a stronger person for what I have been through. You see other people suffering grief, and then I think, thank God, I am not still in that awful place.'

After three hours of this, we walked to a pub round the corner.

'Jeremy,' Philippa asked, 'why on earth are you making this film?'

'I thought it would be cathartic.'

'Catharsis happens in Greek tragedy, not in lives like yours or mine, you chump.'

I was chastened, but it was too late to turn back. I was climbing a treacherous rock face with my team. I had to get to the summit.

You might recall that John Hall had suggested that I needed to put going back to York on the agenda. So, I decided to go to the room where Lizzie had been killed. It would be the climax of the film.

When I interviewed him, I mentioned this to John. 'Hm. When I said to go back to York, I didn't quite anticipate you going there with a film crew and visiting the room where Lizzie died.' I think his subtext was, 'Have you lost your mind, mate?'

'I see.'

'It's a bit extreme.'

It was a bit extreme for the University of York too. They flatly refused permission to film. I resorted to coercion, not far short of blackmail. Peter Symes was a friend of the vice-chancellor's wife, and he leant on her. I, meanwhile, wrote a stinker of a letter to the press office stating that if they refused me permission I would include that refusal in the finished film and use footage from the local BBC TV archive to drag the university through the mud.

Not nice but it worked. They gave permission to film in the room on condition that I did not reveal its exact identity and location.

We hastily assembled the crew and set out for York. As we approached, I got more and more morose. John Hall had been right—what in God's name was I doing this for?

The next day, we spent the morning filming at York Station. Then we went to the university, where we were met by a hapless press officer outside the block where Lizzie died. It was the vacation and the place was utterly deserted.

This was always going to be a one-hit wonder—you can film a man going to the scene of his wife's death for the first time only once. There can be no retakes. My researcher and the cameraman went up to the room with the press officer to check it out, while I sat trying to blank out what I was about to do. Suddenly I was on the runway ready for takeoff. It was as if I were acting, that I was only pretending this was happening to me. I knew I needed to look sombre, so I thought sombre, and we were off. I wasn't really thinking about what I was going through. I was protecting myself by thinking about how I looked on film.

We reached the top of the stairs, walked along the corridor and then

I pushed open the door and walked into the room where Lizzie had been murdered.

It was just a plain, freshly painted, empty university study bedroom on the top floor of a 1970s student block and not at all how I had imagined it. At first it was just a room, but as I stood there and thought about what I was doing, it became the bleakest place in the universe, even with three of us and a camera crowded into a small space.

Lizzie was not there. I tried to enact in my head the events of her death. I could imagine her sitting at her desk working, I could imagine the knock on the door. Then my mind just stopped. And I started to weep.

I wanted to leave, but instead I sat at her desk and buried my face in my hands and wept, dimly aware of the two people unsure of quite how to cope with the wretched scene they were trying to film. I wanted to be with Lizzie, but Lizzie just wasn't there.

I stood up, wiped the tears away and said, 'Let's go.' I took one last look at this meaningless, existential space and before I knew it I was outside being hugged by my PA and my researcher.

I was speechless. In shock.

I didn't find Lizzie there, but I could at least imagine her death in a way that I had never been able to do before then. In that small room I encountered the deepest misery I have ever had to confront. I got closer to her death. Her murder. The evil done to her. I'd thought that if I could confront her death, I could bring back her life. That didn't happen, but I had survived an ordeal.

I have never returned to York since.

THEN I HAD to edit the damn thing. I had four weeks, which was generous. Week one was fun: we gave it a loose structure. The editor reduced the room sequence from twelve minutes (which is how long my awful visit had taken) to about ten. Watching seals being clubbed to death would have been more edifying. We sliced our way into it, cutting it down to about two horribly raw minutes of programme.

Week two was difficult, but lightened by the fact that it was half-term and every day the girls came with me to the edit suite and busied themselves making their own films, which they loved.

Week three was tougher—the girls were back at school and we had narrowed down our options—but week four was unbelievably hard, because we needed to show this private weep-fest to my various bosses. Editing the film to a fine cut forced me to make order out of the chaos caused by Lizzie's death. It took me as close to breaking point as I had ever been before, but at eight o'clock on Friday of week four, the film was completed.

A couple of evenings later, at our house, I showed the finished film to Maka. It is full of still images of Lizzie and it keeps returning to one photograph in which she is looking away from the camera. At the point where I am marooned in The Room, the film cuts to that image and Lizzie turns and looks directly into the camera. It is a video grab from the only footage I have of Lizzie, and I had designed the whole film—called *A Moving Image*—round that closing four-second clip. The statue comes to life.

As she watched the closing moments, Maka just murmured, 'Oh my Lizzie' and hugged me.

There in our cosy sitting room, surrounded by Lizzie's books, with our children safely asleep upstairs, our cat dozing on the sofa, Lizzie turns and looks at us through the artifice of film. Her fine, dark-chestnut hair, her warm, loving brown eyes, a smile of love and affection, my darling Lizzie was there with us. I could smell her soft, flawless skin, recall her stammering, rapid speech, her fierce, restless intelligence. The Lizzieness of her is with me. I am so happy that I cry, and Maka just repeats and repeats, 'My darling, darling girl,' and then the moment is gone, but I shall have it in my heart for ever.

EXHAUSTED, I took the best part of a month off work and pottered. I felt like I was recovering from shellshock. It gave me the chance to reflect on what had happened to us. Were we damaged by Lizzie's death? I looked at my cousin, whose father had died, whose mother had fallen apart. Was her mother damaged by her husband's death? I think she was.

I looked at a former colleague. He had been having an affair, was driving home to his family late one night along a dual carriageway when a man ran out in front of him. He hit him and killed him instantly. My colleague's life fell to pieces. I remember him sitting in my office: 'What happened to you was far worse, but I'm a wreck and you are not. Why?'

Is it luck? Yes and no. I had two children to bring up. I had a reason to get up every morning and I had to earn a living—there was no other way to support our lives. While his life was perhaps built on sand, I had secure foundations. That said, I still don't really know the answer to his question.

And the girls? A few months after Lizzie's death, Karin and David came round to lunch and Jessica and Lucy had two friends, sisters the same age as my two, round to play. As I made the lunch, Karin was watching the four of them out in the garden. Jessica was busy telling everyone what to do and Lucy was being her able lieutenant.

'Do you know, Jeremy, if I didn't know otherwise, I would say that it was not your two who had been through a tragedy. Jessica and Lucy are very sure of themselves and their place in the world.'

Karin was right. When I look at the girls now and see the well-adjusted young women they have become, I touch wood, for it might have been so different.

And Lizzie? I have dreamt of Lizzie only three times since she died, but those dreams have stayed with me for months, as if she had just walked back into my life. We still use the blue and white kitten mug the girls gave her. She is an invisible part of our lives. I see her in the way that Lucy wipes her nose, and when she sits down to play the cello, when she concentrates, I could be looking at Lizzie. I have a photograph by my desk of Lizzie aged seven—every time I look at it I do a double-take because I think it is Jessica. And it is weird when Jessica behaves in a way that is emotionally identical to her mother: when she was studying for her GCSEs, it was like having Lizzie in the house.

Every single day since Lizzie died I have thought of her, and sometimes I have a ridiculous worry that if she came back she wouldn't know where to find us because we have moved, that she wouldn't recognise Jessica and Lucy because they have changed. If Lizzie were still alive what would we all be doing now? It would be different, I am sure, but I am convinced that it would be neither worse nor better.

But although Lizzie lives on in my heart and in our memories, she will never come back, and our life together feels as if it happened to another person. I am not damaged, but I am changed. Lizzie wasn't just damaged, she was destroyed.

A few months after we made the final cut, the film was broadcast. It had a mixed reaction. Deda hated it. Some of the reviewers thought it was dreadful, but most admired it for its searing honesty. I also got the largest postbag I have ever received for a programme. One did call it self-indulgent and excremental, but the rest thanked me for sharing my story.

I never showed my film to the girls. I had edited a copy without any of the really graphic bits about the murder, in case they wanted to see it, but they never asked. And my interviewer, Philippa, was wrong. It *was* cathartic. I was a changed person. I packed my baggage away and shut the drawer and, lighter, I moved on. I really did.

THE SEVENTH PHASE of grief is about acceptance and hope. My story has a happy ending.

Once upon a time, I used to be a theatre director and, out of the blue, my old boss from the theatre called me.

'Jeremy, I am looking for a Scottish woman to direct a show for me, so I thought of you,' and he laughed.

So a couple of months after *A Moving Image* was aired, I took unpaid leave from the BBC and went to Perth in Scotland to direct Terrence Rattigan's *In Praise of Love*, a beautiful play about a middle-aged couple faced with the wife's terminal illness, a play about trying to cope with loss before it happens. I wonder why I was the Scottish woman director he was looking for!

My three-week stay in Perth was the longest I had been apart from the girls. My fortieth birthday fell while I was away, so Jessica and Lucy, accompanied by Kerry, came up for my birthday weekend. I arranged for them to be off school for three days and gave them a small fortune for sweets and comics for their epic train journey. Early on Thursday evening, tired but excited, they arrived in Scotland for the first time.

On Friday they pottered while I rehearsed. On Saturday morning they came with me to work and tried on all the costumes being made for the pantomime which was the theatre's next show. After lunch, with rehearsals over, we drove to Edinburgh, walked down Princes Street and gawped at the shops, went for a ride on the carousel by the National Gallery and had a slap-up supper at Pizza Hut on the Royal Mile. Tired but elated, we drove back to Perth—and Jessica, Lucy and Kerry went to bed. I stayed up and watched a film.

Sleepless in Seattle came out the year after Lizzie was killed. Friends would say, 'Jeremy, you have to see *Sleepless in Seattle*, it is so like you. On second thoughts, maybe you shouldn't see it.' So I hadn't until that November evening. It blew me away. As I wept over the closing credits, I rang Jennie.

Jennie?

Jennie and I had been introduced that spring by Karin and David at their cottage in Somerset. Jennie had been en route to her cottage in north Devon. She had been a film producer—real films, not poxy bits of TV like mine—had got fed up with the hassle and had retired to write and do a bit of teaching.

Jennie and I got on rather well. Later in the summer, when we were by coincidence on holiday in north Devon, she came over with two boxes of books (and some posh chocolates) for the children. They scampered off upstairs while Jennie and I chatted. We certainly did get on.

A couple of weeks later we had supper. The following week we arranged for her to pick me up from London after a morning screening and drive me back to Bath, where she was staying with her brother. We met at the cutting room at 11 a.m. that Friday morning. What I didn't tell her was that my screening had been cancelled the evening before—'Film's in no state to be seen, Jeremy mate. Sorry'—so I had travelled down to London early, simply to get a lift back home with her. It was during the journey that it all happened between us and then almost instantly I was off to Perth.

'Were you watching *Sleepless in Seattle*?' I now asked her.

'Of course,' she sobbed. And for the next two hours we talked and talked. And I fell in love on the day before my fortieth birthday.

This wasn't an affair, this was the real thing. Jennie was beautiful, witty, charming and, for all her exotic past—she'd been married to a jazz trumpeter, had worked in Hollywood and produced a string of classy movies—she was incredibly like me. We were both middle-class English graduates, who had somehow found themselves in the mad world of films. I know this sounds facetious, but sitting in the garden with Karin, David and Jennie that Sunday afternoon, with the children trying to do handstands against the garden wall, I kind of knew that Jennie was someone special. She is such good fun and we had so much in common.

A few weeks later we moved in together. It was the easiest decision of my life. For me, it was like coming home: our house became a home for the first time in four and a half years, my life became normal and we became a family, and all because of Jennie. Jeremy, Jessica, Lucy and Jennie: our family. I put my past in the drawer that Philippa had told me about, along with the wedding ring Lizzie had given me, and moved forward, no longer a widower but at last a normal person again. There will always be a part of my heart that is Lizzie's, but I was no longer locked into that past. What had seemed impossible just a few months before now seemed so natural and easy. Ordinary life beckoned. I just love ordinary life.

And the happy ending? I am writing now by the ocean in California, while Jennie, my wife of over ten years, is asleep across the room. I found love and companionship and a proper family when I thought all those things had been snatched from me for ever. Jennie has been a brilliant mother to Jessica and Lucy, who are women now. The reason I am in California is that Lucy is at university in San Diego and Jessica has taken a week out from her job as an assistant producer at a radio station to hang out with us. My life is back on track and I am contented in a way that I never thought would be possible after that dreadful day in July 1992. I hear the wind in the rigging of yachts as I walk by the harbour and I am reminded of the storm that blasted our lives. But it is just a memory now, and I have been allowed to move forward. I am not going to write about the present, my wonderful marriage, my grown-up, beautiful daughters, full of poise and grace. My story is of one long moment from the past and how it helped forge us, Jessica, Lucy and me. We were not damaged, just changed. To butcher Wordsworth, it is a story of how the father was mother to the women—my two beloved daughters.

JEREMY HOWE

Jeremy Howe was born in south London and now lives in north London having crossed the Thames after living in Bath, Oxford, Belfast, York and Colchester. He moved around because he used to be a theatre director but now is a senior executive at the BBC. He is married to Jennie and his two daughters, Jessica and Lucy, are now grown-up.

LINWOOD
BARCLAY
TRUST YOUR EYES

Whirl360.com is a very special website that enables anyone, anywhere, to view any street in the world from a home computer.

To thirty-seven-year-old Ray Kilbride, it's the lens through which his autistic brother Thomas indulges his obsession with mapping the world, street by street, memorising them all along the way. Right now, Thomas is exploring downtown Manhattan . . .

but he's about to see something he should never see. He's about to become a witness to murder.

Which means life will get very complicated indeed.

PROLOGUE

It was just by chance that he turned down Orchard Street and saw the window when he did. It could easily have been a week from now, or a month, even a year. But it turned out that this was going to be the day.

Sure, he would have wandered down here eventually. Sooner or later, when he got to a new city, he hit every street. He always started out intending to be methodical about it—follow one street from beginning to end, then head over a block and backtrack on a parallel street—but then he'd get to a cross street and something would catch his eye, and all good intentions would be abandoned.

That was how it turned out when he got to Manhattan, even though, of all the cities he'd visited, it was the one that most lent itself to being explored in an orderly fashion—at least those parts of the city north of 14th Street, laid out in that perfect grid of streets and avenues. South of that, once you got into the West Village and Greenwich Village and SoHo and Chinatown, well, it was chaos down there, but that didn't bother him. It certainly wasn't any worse than in London or Rome or Paris or even Boston's North End, and he'd loved exploring those cities.

He'd turned south onto Orchard from Delancey, but his actual starting point for this stroll had been Spring and Mulberry. He'd gone south to Grand, west to Crosby, north back to Prince, east to Elizabeth, south to Kenmare, then east, continuing along Delancey, then, when he got to Orchard, decided to hang a right.

It was a beautiful street. Not in the sense that there were gardens and lush trees lining the sidewalk, but it was a street rich in texture and steeped in history. Narrow, one-way, running north. Old brick tenement buildings, few more than five storeys, many only three or four, dating back a century and a half. The buildings, with their skeletal fire escapes clinging to the fronts, reflected the Italianate style popular in the mid- to late nineteenth century, with arches above the windows, stone lintels projecting outwards, ornate carved leaves in the trim work; but their ground floors housed everything from trendy cafés to designer dress shops. There were older, more conventional businesses, too. A uniform shop, a real-estate agent, a hair salon, a gallery, a place that sold luggage. Because the building blocks of a city were his primary concern—its architecture, its layout, its infrastructure—he paid little attention to the people he came across in his travels. He didn't strike up conversations.

He meandered down the centre of the street, not particularly worried about the traffic. It wasn't a problem right now. He always found you got the sense of a place by walking down the middle of the road. It offered the best vantage point. You could look ahead or from side to side, or whirl around 360 degrees and see where you'd been. It was good to know your surroundings and your options, in case you had to make a fast move.

When he got to Broome Street, he spotted an inviting-looking restaurant with small white tables and yellow plastic chairs set up on the sidewalk. But there was no one sitting outside. A sign in the window read, 'Come in and get warm.'

Reflected in the restaurant's window was that car he'd been seeing throughout his travels. Nondescript sedan. With the apparatus on the roof. If he didn't know better, he'd think it was following him. He put it out of his mind and looked through the glass, into the restaurant.

He wished it were possible for him to go inside and have a latte or a cappuccino. He could almost smell the coffee. But he had to keep going. So much of the world to see and so little time. Tomorrow he had plans to be in Montreal, and maybe Madrid the day after.

But he would remember this place. The sign in the window, the tables and chairs outside. The other businesses on Orchard. Plus everything that he had seen on Spring and Mulberry and Grand and Crosby and Prince and Elizabeth and Kenmare and Delancey.

He would remember it all.

He was about a third of the way down the block from the Broome cross street when he made that upward glance.

That was really where the element of chance entered into it. It was the fact that he looked above the storefronts. He didn't always do that. He scoped out the businesses and read the signs in their windows, made a mental note of the numbers above the doors, but he didn't always cast his eyes above the ground or first floors. He might easily have gone down this street and never glanced upon that particular window of that particular tenement building.

Then again, he thought, *chance might have had nothing to do with it.* Maybe, in some strange way, it was a test. To determine whether he was ready, even though he believed he was. But those who would make use of his talents—they might need some convincing before taking him on.

The window was on the second floor, above a place that sold cigarettes and newspapers—there was that car again, reflected in the window—and a second shop specialising in women's scarves. It was divided into two panes. An air-conditioning unit stuck out from the sill, taking up half of the lower pane. Something white, above the air conditioner, had caught his eye.

At first, it looked like one of those white Styrofoam heads department stores and hair salons use to display wigs. But the more he looked at it, the less sure he was. The surface appeared more shimmery. Perhaps plastic, like the bags the grocery stores used. He attempted to get a better look, zero in. The thing was, this white, almost circular object in the window still had the shape of a head. The plastic material strained against a protuberance that could only be a nose. It hugged tight across what appeared to be a brow near the top, a chin at the bottom. There was even a trace of mouth, the lips open as though gasping for air. Or screaming.

It was, he reckoned, as though a white stocking had been pulled down over someone's head. But the material's sheen still made him think it was plastic.

That wasn't a very smart thing for someone to do. To put a plastic bag over their head. You could suffocate doing something stupid like that. A person would have to be pulling on the plastic bag, twisting it from behind, to make it conform so tightly to the contours of their face. But he didn't see this person's arms or hands doing anything like that. Which made him wonder if someone else was doing it.

Oh. Oh, no. Was that what he was witnessing? Someone putting a bag over another person's head? Smothering them? Who was this happening to? A man? A woman? And who was doing it to them?

Suddenly he was thinking about the boy in the window. A different window. Many years ago.

But the person in this window, right now, was an adult. An adult whose life was coming to an end. That certainly was how it looked to him.

He'd seen things before on his travels. Things that weren't right. But never a murder. That's what he was sure this was.

He didn't shout out. All he did was reach out, tentatively, as though it were possible to touch the smothered face on the second floor, make some sort of assessment as to—

Knock knock.

Then, maybe then, he'd have a better idea of what was actually happening to this person in—

Knock knock.

He'd been so transfixed by what was happening at the window that he did not, at first, realise someone was at the door.

He spun round in his padded computer chair and said, 'Yes?'

The door opened. Someone said, 'Come down for dinner, Thomas.'

The man sitting in the computer chair said flatly, 'OK.'

He resumed looking at the frozen image of the window on his oversized computer monitor. The blurry, white, wrapped head suspended there. Had anyone seen this at the time? Had anyone looked up?

No one had seen the boy when he was in the window. No one had looked up. No one had helped him.

The man left the image on his screen so he could study it when he came back up after dinner. Then he'd make a decision about what to do.

ONE

Two weeks earlier

'Come on in, Ray.'

Harry Peyton shook my hand and led me into his law office, pointing me towards the red leather chair opposite his desk. About the same age as my father, he was six foot tall, trim, with a head smooth as a melon. Baldness aged some guys, but not Harry.

'Again, I'm so sorry,' Harry said. 'Adam Kilbride was a good man.'

I forced a smile. 'Thanks for coming to the service. It almost got us up to a dozen.'

Eleven people showed up for the funeral, counting the minister and myself. There was Harry, and three of Dad's coworkers from the company he'd worked for, including his one-time boss, Len Prentice, and Len's wife, Marie. Also, Alan, a friend of Dad's who had run the local hardware store; and a woman named Hannah who lived down the road from Dad. And there was a woman Thomas and I knew from high school, Julie McGill, who worked for the local paper, the *Promise Falls Standard*, and had written the story about Dad's accident. She hadn't come to report on the funeral—how Dad died had made him a small news item, but he wasn't citizen of the year or anything. Julie had come to pay her respects, simple as that.

The funeral home had a lot of egg salad sandwiches left over. They insisted I take some back to the house for my brother. I'd explained his absence by saying he wasn't feeling well, but no one, at least no one who knew my brother, believed it.

'I'd hoped your brother might have come,' Harry said. 'It's been some time since I've seen him.'

'Yeah, well, I gave it my best shot,' I said. 'He wasn't really sick.'

Peyton shook his head sympathetically. 'Your father, he tried to do his best by him. Just like when your mother—Rose, God bless her—was still with us. How long's it been?'

'She passed away in 2005.'

'After that, it must have been even more difficult for your dad.'

'He was still with P&L then,' I said. Prentice and Long, the printers. 'I think, maybe, after he took that early retirement, it got tougher. Being there, all the time. It got to him, but he wasn't the kind of man to run away from something.' I bit my lip. 'Mom, she found ways not to let it bother her, but it was tougher for Dad.'

'Adam was a young man, really,' Harry said. 'Sixty-two. I was stunned.'

'Yeah, well, me too,' I said. 'I don't know how many times Mom told him, over the years, that cutting grass on that steep hill, on the lawn tractor, was dangerous. But he always insisted he knew what he was doing.'

'How long do they think your father was out there before they found him, Ray?'

'He probably went out to cut the grass after lunch, and wasn't discovered until nearly six. When the tractor flipped over on him, the top edge of the steering wheel landed across his middle and crushed his insides.'

Harry winced. 'He was a year younger than me,' he said.

'He spoke highly of you,' I said. 'You were always a friend first, and his lawyer second.' They'd known each other at least twenty-five years, back to when Harry was going through a divorce and, after giving his house to his ex-wife, lived for a time above a store here in downtown Promise Falls, in upstate New York.

Harry's phone emitted a single chime.

'Last time I talked to Dad,' I said, nodding at the phone, 'he was thinking about getting one of those. He had a phone that would take pictures, but it didn't take very good ones.'

'This new high-tech stuff never scared Adam,' Harry said. 'You were saying, at the funeral, that you've still got the studio in Burlington?'

I lived across the state line, in Vermont. 'Yeah,' I said.

'I saw one of your drawings—is that what you call them?'

'Sure,' I said. 'Illustrations. Caricatures.'

'Saw one in the *New York Times Book Review* a few weeks back. I can always tell your style. The people all have really big noggins and the tiny bodies. I love how you shade their skin tones. How do you do that?'

'Airbrush,' I said.

'You do a lot of work for the *Times*?'

'Not as much as I used to. I'm doing more for web sites these days.'

'You design those things? Web sites?'

'No. I do artwork for them and hand it off to the web-site builders.'

When I said nothing else, Harry opened the file on his desk and studied the papers inside. 'Ray, I take it you've seen the will your father drew up.'

'Yes. I guess the way it is now,' I said, 'is fifty-fifty. Once the estate is liquidated, half goes to me and half goes to my brother.'

'Yes. Property, and investments.'

'About a hundred thousand there,' I said. 'What he and Mom had managed to scrape together for retirement. And I gather there's a life insurance policy that's fairly small.'

Harry Peyton nodded and leaned back in his chair. 'You'll have to decide what to do about the house. You've every right to put it up for sale, split the proceeds with your brother. There's no mortgage on the place, and I'm guessing you could get three, four hundred thou for it.'

'About that,' I said. 'There's nearly sixteen acres.'

'Which, if you got that, would leave each of you with about a quarter of a million, give or take. How old are you, Ray?'

'Thirty-seven.'

'And your brother, he's two years younger, that right?'

'Yes.'

'Invested wisely, it might be enough to last him quite a few years, but he's still a young man. And he's got a while before he hits Social Security. He's not really employable, from what your dad told me.'

I hesitated. 'That's fair.'

'For you, well, the money's a different thing. You could invest it, buy a bigger house for the time when you have . . . I know you're not married now, Ray, but some day, you meet someone, you have kids—'

'I know,' I said. I'd come close to getting married, a couple of times, in my twenties, but it never happened. 'I don't see any kids on the horizon.'

'None of my business, anyway, except in an unofficial capacity, because I think your dad hoped I'd look out for you boys.' He smiled.

'Appreciate it, Harry.'

'The point I'm making, Ray, is for you it's a minor windfall. But for your brother, this inheritance is all he'll ever have. He might need the money from the house to keep him afloat, provided he can find a place, some place suitable, where his rent's subsidised or something.'

'I've been thinking about that,' I said.

'Will you be able to get him out of the house? I mean, permanently?'

'I don't know. Dad managed to get him out, once in a while. Mostly for his doctor's appointments.' I found it hard to say the word 'psychiatrist', but Harry knew. 'It's not getting him outside that's the problem. It's prising him away from the keyboard.'

Harry said, 'Well, I'll get the ball rolling here. There'll be the occasional item I'll need your take on, and I'll have Alice give you a call.' He ruffled through his papers. 'I got all your numbers and email address here.'

'Yeah,' I said.

'And you probably knew—your dad had sent me a copy of the policy for his files—that there was an accidental death provision in his life insurance.'

'I didn't know that.'

'Another fifty thousand.' Harry paused. 'So, you're going to be hanging around for a while, then, before you head back to Burlington?'

'Until I sort things out.'

As Harry led me out of the office, he put his hand on my arm.

'Ray,' he said, 'do you think if your brother had noticed how long it had been since your dad had been in the house, if he'd gone out looking for him a little sooner, it would have made any difference?'

I'd asked myself the same question. There had to have been quite a racket when it happened. The tractor flipping over, the rotating blades roaring. Would any of the sounds have carried up over the hill to the house?

'I tell myself it wouldn't have made any difference,' I said.

Harry nodded. 'I guess that's the best way to look at it. What's done is done.' Then he said, 'He's really off in his own little world, isn't he?'

'You don't know the half of it,' I said.

I GOT INTO THE CAR and drove back to my father's house. With Dad dead less than a week, I knew it was going to take a while before I could think of it as anything but his place. But it wasn't. It was mine. And my brother's.

I'd never lived here. My parents had bought this place when I was twenty-one. I'd already moved out of our house in the heart of Promise Falls. My parents had hoped one of their sons would make something of himself, but put that dream on hold when I bailed on my university career in Albany and got a job at a Beekman Street art gallery in Saratoga Springs.

My parents were never farmers, but when they'd spotted this place, it fitted the bill. The place came with a barn, which Dad didn't have much need for, other than to store tools and park the lawn tractor. But they had both loved the look of the structure, with its dormer windows and wraparound porch.

There was a lot of land, but my parents maintained only about two acres of it. Behind the house, the yard stretched out flat for about sixty feet, then sloped down and out of sight to a creek that wound its way to the river that flowed into the centre of town and cascaded over Promise Falls.

I'd been down to the creek only once since I'd come home. A task awaited me there, when I finally felt up to it.

I nosed the car close to the steps that led up to the porch, parking my four-wheel-drive Audi Q5 next to Dad's Chrysler. I took the porch steps two at a time, unlocked the front door and went into the kitchen. The clock on the wall said it was nearly four thirty. Time to start thinking about dinner.

My father wasn't much of a cook, but he could boil water for pasta, or heat up an oven and throw a chicken in there. But for the days when he hadn't the energy for anything that fancy, he'd stuffed the freezer with hamburgers and fish fingers and french fries and frozen dinners. Tomorrow I was going to have to make a trip to the grocery store.

I opened the refrigerator. There were some cans of Bud in there. 'To you, Dad,' I said, raising a can, then taking a seat at the kitchen table. I sat there, drinking Dad's beer, working up the energy to defrost or nuke something. I cracked open another as I began pulling things out of the freezer.

When things were almost ready, I walked through the living room and rested my hand on the banister before heading upstairs. I cast my eye across the room: while the furniture was dated, Dad didn't skimp on the technology. There was the TV itself, a thirty-six-inch flat screen with HD that he'd bought a year ago to watch football and hockey. There was a DVD player, and one of those gadgets that allowed him to order up movies from the Internet. The living room looked like a million other living rooms. Normal. Nothing extraordinary.

That changed as you got to the top of the stairs.

My parents had tried to keep my brother's obsession contained to his own room, but it was a losing battle. The landing was totally papered over. Looking down the hallway, I thought of how a World War II underground war room might have looked, with oversized maps of enemy territories pinned to the walls of the bunker. But it seemed unlikely that any war planner worth his salt would tape a map of Poland next to one of Hawaii. Or have a street guide of Paris overlapping a gas station highway map of Kansas. There were written notations everywhere.

I don't know how Dad, on his own, tolerated it. When Mom was alive, she told him to get out of the house, go to a sports bar and watch a game with Lenny Prentice, or one of the others from work. Or Harry Peyton.

I went to the first bedroom door, which was, as usual, closed. I raised my hand to rap on it but, just before I touched my knuckles to the wood, I listened. I could hear talking on the other side of the door. A conversation, but only one voice. I knocked.

'Yeah?' Thomas said.

I opened the door, wondering if maybe he'd been on the phone, but there was no receiver in his hand. I told him it was time for dinner.

'*WELL, IT SURE IS NICE to hear from you.*'

'Thank you for taking my call.'

'*I don't give my private line to just anyone. You're a very special prospect. I got your latest email message. Sounds like things are coming along very well.*'

'Yes, they are. I'm still wondering . . . do you have any idea of the timing of the incident, sir?'

'*If only we did. It's like asking the exact moment when terrorists will hit next. We simply don't know. But we have to be prepared.*'

'Of course.'

'*And I know you'll be ready. You're going to be tremendously valuable to us. A wonderful resource.*'

'You can count on me, B—oh, I almost called you Bill.'

'*Hell, that's OK. Listen, I have to go. My wife gets back from a trip to the Mideast today. Anyway, carry on.*'

'Thank you, Mr President. It's—it's still proper to call you that, isn't it?'

'*Of course. You retain the title.*'

'I'll be in touch.'

'*I know you will.*'

'LET'S SAY you were staying at the Hotel Pont Royal and you wanted to get to the Louvre, how would you do that?' Thomas asked me.

'What?' I said. 'What city are you talking about?'

He sighed and looked at me sadly across the kitchen table. We looked a lot alike, Thomas and I. Both around five-eleven, thinning black hair, but Thomas had a few pounds on me. I was definitely healthier looking. When you hardly went outside and spent twenty-three hours a day in your bedroom, you developed an almost sickly pallor. He was probably suffering from a Vitamin D deficiency. He needed a week in Bermuda. And even though he'd never been there, he could probably name me all the hotels and tell me what streets they were on.

'I said *Louvre*. Louvre, *Louvre*, think about it.'

'Of course,' I said. 'Paris. You're talking about Paris.'

He nodded encouragingly. He'd already finished the frozen meatloaf dinner I'd heated up in the microwave. 'Right, so you want to get to the Louvre. Which way do you go?'

'I have no idea, Thomas,' I said, tiredly. 'I know where the Louvre is. I've been to the Louvre. But I have no idea where this hotel is.'

'The Pont Royal,' he said. 'On the rue de Montalembert. Come on. It's an old hotel, all grey stone, has a revolving door at the front. The building looks like it's eight storeys and on the left side there's a very expensive-looking restaurant with a black awning thing and—'

All this from memory. 'I'm tired, Thomas. I had to talk to Harry Peyton.'

'The Louvre is, like, the simplest place to get to from the hotel.'

'Do you not want to hear what happened at the lawyer's?'

He waved his hands. 'You go across the rue de Montalembert and then across a triangle of sidewalk, and then you're on the rue du Bac and—'

'Mr Peyton said Dad left the house to both of us.'

'Let's do a harder one. Name a hotel in any other part of Paris and I'll tell you how to get there. Shortest route.'

'Thomas, I need you to stop,' I said. 'We need to talk about Dad.'

'Dad's dead,' he said, looking at me like I was short of a few IQ points. Then, with something that looked like sorrow washing briefly over his face, he said, 'I found him. By the creek.'

'I know.'

'Dinner was late and I was getting really hungry so I came down to see what was going on. I went all over the house first. When I couldn't find him I went outside. I walked around and when I got to the top of the hill I saw him with the tractor on top of him.'

I'd heard all this before. 'I know, Thomas.'

'I pushed the tractor off him. It was really hard to do. But Dad didn't get up. So I ran back up here and called 911. They came and said he was dead.'

'I know,' I said again. 'That must have been pretty awful for you.'

'It's still down there.'

The tractor. I had to bring it back up and put it away in the barn. It had been sitting out there at the bottom of the hill since the accident.

'There are things that we have to get figured out,' I said. 'About what to do, now that Dad's, you know, passed away.'

Thomas nodded, thinking. 'I was wondering,' he said, 'whether it would be OK to put maps on the walls in his bedroom now. I'm running out of space. And with Mom already gone, no one's sleeping in there.'

That wasn't exactly true. I'd started off sleeping in the empty bedroom next to Thomas's, the one Mom had always kept ready for me when I came to visit. But last night I ended up moving down the hall into Dad's room because I could hear all the mouse-clicking through the wall.

'You can't live in this house all alone,' I said. 'I have to go back home.'

'You are home. This is home.'

'It's not *my* home, Thomas. I live in Burlington.'

'Burlington, Vermont. Burlington, Massachusetts. Burlington, Ontario—'

'Thomas.'

'I didn't know if you knew how many other Burlingtons there are. You need to be specific. Don't be angry with me,' he said.

'I'm not angry with you. But we do need to talk about some things. I'm going to be worried about leaving you here on your own.'

Thomas shook his head. 'I'll be fine.'

'Dad did everything,' I said. 'He made the meals, he cleaned the house, he paid the bills, he went into town to get the groceries, he made sure the furnace was working.'

'The furnace works fine,' he said.

'You don't have a driver's licence. How are you going to get food?'

'I'll have it delivered,' he said.

'We're out in the middle of nowhere. And who's going to actually go to the grocery store and pick out the things you like?'

'You can come back,' he said. 'Once a week, and get my food and pay the bills and see if the furnace is OK and then you can go back to Burlington.' He paused. 'Vermont.'

'Are you going to be OK making your own meals?'

Thomas looked away.

I touched his arm. 'Look at me,' I said. He turned back, reluctantly.

'Maybe,' I said, 'maybe you could take on some of these responsibilities yourself. Maybe you need to manage your time better.'

He adopted a puzzled expression. 'I manage my time very well.'

I took my hand away. 'Describe your day for me.'

'Well,' he said, 'I get up around nine o'clock, and I have a shower, and then Dad makes me breakfast around nine thirty, and then I get to work.'

'Work,' I said. 'Tell me about that.'

'You know,' he said. 'I go to work after breakfast, and I take a break for lunch, and then I go back to work until it's dinnertime, and then I do some more work before I go to bed.'

'And that's around, what, one, two, three in the morning?'

He nodded. 'Why are you doing this, Ray?'

'I guess I'm thinking if you spent a little less time on this work, as you call it, you'd be in a better position to look after yourself. Thomas, it's no secret you've got issues and I get that. Just like Dad and Mom did. And, compared to plenty of other people who aren't able to shut out the voices or deal with other symptoms, you manage very well.'

'I know,' Thomas said, somewhat indignantly. 'I'm perfectly normal.'

'But the amount of time you spend on your . . . work stands to interfere with your ability to live here by yourself, and if you're not able to do that, then we're going to have to look at some other arrangement.'

'What do you mean, another arrangement?'

I hesitated. 'Living somewhere else. Maybe some sort of housing where you'd be with other people with similar issues, where there are staff who look after the things you can't look after yourself.'

'Why do you keep saying "issues"? I don't have issues, Ray. I've had mental problems, which are very much under control.'

'I'm sorry. I was just . . .' I didn't know what to say.

'I can't leave,' Thomas said. 'All my stuff is here. My work is here.'

'Thomas, you spend all but an hour of your day on the computer, wandering all over the world. Day after day. It's not healthy.'

'It's only a more recent development,' he said. 'A few years ago, all I had were my maps and my atlases and my globe. There was no Whirl360. It's so much better now. I've been waiting my whole life for this.'

'You've always been obsessed with maps, but—'

'*Interested*. I've always been *interested* in maps.'

I sighed. 'This Whirl360 has not been healthy for your interest in maps. Are you hearing me? You don't go out. You don't see people. You don't read books or magazines. You don't even watch television. You never come down and watch a movie.'

'There's nothing good on,' he said. 'The movies are very poor.'

'All you do is sit at the computer and click your way down street after street after street. Listen, you want to see the world? Pick a city. I'll take you to Tokyo. I'll take you to Mumbai. You want to see Rome? We'll go.'

Thomas looked blankly at me. 'No, I wouldn't want to do that. I like it here just fine. And there's not time.'

'What do you mean, not time?'

'There's not time to get to every place in person. I can get it done here faster, get the work done.'

'Thomas, what work?'

'I can't tell you,' he said. 'I'll have to check if it's OK to tell you.'

I let out a long sigh. I was exhausted. I decided to change the subject.

'You remember Julie McGill? From school?'

'Yes,' Thomas said. 'What about her?'

'She came to the funeral. She asked about you. Asked me to say hi.'

Thomas looked at me, expectantly. 'Are you going to say it?'

'What?' Then I got it. '*Hi*. Was she in your class?'

'No,' he said. 'She was a year ahead of me, and a year behind you.' Thomas paused. 'She lived at 34 Arbor Street, which is a two-storey house with the door in the middle. She was always nice to me. Is she still pretty?'

I nodded. 'Yeah. Her hair's still black but it's short now. Did you guys ever date?'

'No,' he said.

I could have guessed. Thomas had never had a steady girlfriend. Back then, he was already amassing his huge map collection.

'But I liked her,' Thomas said. 'Is there going to be any dessert?'

'Uh, I think I saw the end of a container of ice cream in the freezer.'

'Could you bring it up to me? I've been down here longer than I planned and I need to get back.' He was already on his feet.

'Yeah, sure,' I said.

'I saw something,' Thomas said. 'On the computer. I think it would be OK for you to have a look at it. I don't think it would violate any security clearance or anything.'

'What is it?'

He said again, 'You should take a look at it.' He paused. 'When you bring up the ice cream.'

I WENT UP to Thomas's room five minutes later. There was a tub of vanilla in the freezer and I was just able to scrape out one small serving.

I should have known better than to think I could reason things out with Thomas about how he spent his days. My parents had tried for years without success. My brother was who he was.

The signs came early. At least some of them. The fascination with maps revealed itself when he was around six. At the time, he just seemed like a very gifted baby brother. Somewhat withdrawn, shy, but no indication that he was troubled in any serious way. That would come soon enough.

My parents were proud as could be of him. Me, not so much. At least not on family vacations, when we'd hit the road for Atlantic City or Florida.

Mom had a terrible time reading the road maps. So Dad would read the map. When people today talk about the dangers of sending text messages while driving, I want to laugh. He'd have Mom fold the map to a manageable size, drape it over the top of the steering wheel, and glance down every couple of seconds as we roamed across America.

Until Thomas got to be seven. 'I'll read the map, Dad,' he offered. He had only to glance at it for a few seconds before he said something like, 'Just stay on 90 for another ten miles, then get off and go east on 22.'

'Let me have a look at that,' Dad had said, taking the map back. 'I'll be damned,' he said. 'The kid's right.'

Thomas was always right when it came to reading maps.

There was a hint of things to come, where Thomas was concerned, during a summer trip to a lodge in southern Pennsylvania, when I was eleven and Thomas was nine. It was a fun week, but the most memorable part of the vacation was the drive home, when Dad decided to deviate from the route Thomas had prepared for him.

Thomas had spent several days—ignoring Mom's pleas that he come for a swim or play horseshoes—figuring out that we needed to take 99 north up through Altoona, and while we started out intending to go that way, Mom had then decided she wanted to go home by way of Harrisburg, just in case there was any good shopping there.

'You can't do that!' Thomas had said. 'We have to take 99!'

'Your mother wants to go to Harrisburg, Thomas,' Dad said.

'I spent all week planning the route!' He had started to cry.

'Listen, son, we're just going to—'

'No!' Thomas had undone his seat belt and had got up on his knees on his seat, and started to bang his head against the window.

'Thomas!' Mom shouted.

I had grabbed for him but he pushed me away. He kept banging his head against the window. A small smear of blood appeared on the glass.

Dad had swung the car over onto the shoulder. Mom jumped out and opened the back door. She wrapped her arms around my brother.

'It's OK,' she said. 'We're going to take 99. We're going to go home just the way you said.'

I DIDN'T LIKE going into Thomas's room. Entering his domain made me uncomfortable in the same way the decorated landing did, only more so. Maps were stuck to the wall everywhere and scattered across the floor.

Thomas was seated at his computer. He had one keyboard and three flat-screen monitors arrayed in front of him, each showing a different browser.

On the screens were three images of the same street—left-, middle- and right-side views. At the top of each screen was the web-site address: whirl360.com. I had to admit, it was a pretty amazing web site. You basically had the world at your fingertips. You picked a spot anywhere on the globe and initially viewed the location from above, either in a traditional map form, or in satellite mode, as though you were suspended in the sky.

Cool enough. But it got so much better.

You could click on a specific street, and see it. Like you were standing there, right in the middle of it. With each click of the mouse you progressed several yards ahead. When you clicked and held, you could move to the left or right, or all the way round for a 360-degree view. If something in a store window or a restaurant caught your eye, you could zoom in on it. Read the daily special: 'Liver and onions $5.99.'

I could understand how, for someone like Thomas, the arrival of this kind of technology was a dream come true. Like a *Star Trek* fan waking up one morning to find out he was actually living on the USS *Enterprise*.

The street Thomas was currently fixated on was unknown to me. It was narrow. I was guessing maybe some place in Europe.

I set the ice cream next to the phone. Thomas had his own line up here that our parents had put in, back when Internet hookup was over the phone. Now, with wi-fi in the house, Thomas didn't have much need for it.

'Where's this?'

'Salem Street. Boston. In the North End.'

'Oh, OK, yeah, of course.'

'You see anything weird?' he asked.

I looked. People, their faces blurred—that seemed to be a Whirl360 protocol, to blur faces that could be seen head-on, as well as licence plates—were walking along the street. There were cars.

'No,' I said.

'See this silver SUV here?' He pointed. It was visible on the right screen. 'Look what he's done. He's backed into this car, this blue one.'

'I think you might be right,' I said. 'So, just at the moment the Whirl360 people were driving around with their picture car, they got a shot of this guy backing into the blue car. They caught an accident in progress, and you just found it. That it?'

'I bet the SUV driver didn't even know he did it,' Thomas said, spooning some ice cream into his mouth. 'We need to report this.'

'Thomas, honestly. First of all, they blur all the licence plates, so there's no way you could ever find out who owns the SUV, or the blue car. And second, this picture has probably been up here for months, even a couple of years. This is not some live stream, you know. These are snapshots in time.'

'It's not right to stand by and do nothing,' he said.

'We're not—it's not like you just saw the SUV run some guy down. This is exactly what I'm talking about, Thomas. You're spending too much time up here. Come down and watch a movie. Dad got this great TV.'

'You go,' he said. 'You pick a movie and we'll watch it.'

I went downstairs and turned on the television. I came across a film, only a couple of years old, made in New Zealand, called *The Map Reader*.

'Hey, Thomas! There's a movie here you'll love.'

'Sure thing,' he said. 'I'll be down in a minute.'

He didn't come down. After waiting fifteen minutes, I turned off the TV, went into the kitchen, and drank Dad's very last beer.

TWO

Nine months earlier, Allison Fitch lifts her head off the pillow on her pullout couch and looks at the digital clock read-out on the DVD player on the other side of the small living room. Nearly noon.

She's pretty sure she's alone right now in the apartment she shares with Courtney Walmers, who has the bedroom. Unless you found some place that was rent-controlled, there was no way you could live in this city by yourself, certainly not on what a waitress made. Courtney has an office job, down on Wall Street, so she's out of the apartment by eight. Allison usually starts her shift around five. Sometimes, if Courtney's able to sneak home from work early, they'll actually see each other for five minutes.

Allison hopes this isn't one of those days. She knows Courtney wants to have a talk with her and it is a conversation Allison does not want to have. Because she knows exactly what it's about.

Money. It's always about money, ever since Allison hasn't been meeting her share of the rent, and other expenses, like the cable and Internet. She works her ass off waiting tables, dealing with customers, taking abuse from the kitchen who can't get a single order straight. She earns her money. She just doesn't have enough of it.

Things really escalated after Allison's call home a couple of months ago. Allison, talking to her mom back in Dayton, telling her the Big Apple wasn't quite everything she'd hoped it would be.

'Oh, sweetheart, you should come home,' her mother said.

'Mom, I'm not coming back.'

'Have you met anyone? I figured, you working in a restaurant, there'd be lots of opportunities to meet young men. You're thirty-one, you know.'

She needed to throw her mother a bone. 'I *have* met someone,' Allison said. It helped that it was actually true.

'Who?' her mother asked excitedly. 'Tell me all about him.'

'It's too early,' Allison said. 'I'm just going to see how it plays out. If this is the one, I'll let you know. OK? No third degree. Right now, I've got more serious things to worry about.' Setting the hook.

'Like what?'

'Well, the customers, they're just not tipping the way they used to. And business is down. And there was the whole thing with the chipped tooth.'

'Chipped tooth? What are you talking about?'

'Didn't I tell you about that?' There was no chipped tooth.

'You never said a word. How'd that happen?'

'OK, so, there's this girl I work with? She's coming through the crowd with a full tray of drinks, right? And she raises her tray up just as I'm coming from the other direction, and the edge of it smacks right into my mouth and when I look in the mirror I've got this chip in my front tooth. So, anyway, I went to this dentist up on Madison and he fixed it and I swear, if you looked at it with a magnifying glass you'd never be able to tell.'

'That must have cost you a fortune,' her mother said.

'Yeah, well, it's not like the waiting staff have a dental plan,' she said, and laughed. 'But don't worry about it, I'll manage somehow. Courtney'll understand, you know, if she has to wait a while for my share.'

'Oh, honey, you can't do that to your room-mate. That's just not fair.'

Her mother put a thousand dollars in the mail that day.

When the cheque arrived, Allison immediately deposited it in her account, bringing the balance to $1,421.87. But the longer Allison looked at the balance on her ATM slip, the less certain she was that she wanted to give any of that money to Courtney.

That 'someone' she had mentioned to her mother was going to Barbados in two weeks, and had invited Allison to come along. Allison had said sorry, can't afford it. All that had changed with the money to fix her chipped tooth.

So she had booked a week in Barbados.

Courtney, when she saw Allison packing her bags, said, 'Are you kidding me? You're into me for more than two grand and somehow you've got enough for a vacation? You want to explain that to me?'

'It's not *my* money,' Allison said. 'My mom gave me the money for it. I haven't saved up enough money from my job to pay you back yet. This money, from my mom, for my vacation, is totally separate.' It made perfect sense to Allison. 'I've gotta go. My flight leaves in, like, three hours.'

Courtney must have sent her at least a hundred texts and emails while she was in Barbados. Ranting about what a selfish, self-centred, self-consumed bitch Allison was. But it was still worth it.

When Allison had returned, Courtney had said she was going to kick her out, but Allison had put on a huge song and dance that she really, really was going to pay her back, that she was going to ask her mother for money.

That was a week ago. She hasn't called her mother yet. Allison thinks it's too soon after the tooth story. She figures, if she can come up with an equally compelling tale, she'll try it on her mother in another week or so.

Allison sits up in bed, reaches for the remote on the coffee table and clicks on the television. As NY1 comes on with the latest news round-up, she grabs her phone to see whether she has any emails or Facebook messages. Allison glances from the phone to the TV and back again.

Glances back at the TV. Is about to look away when she thinks she catches a glimpse of a face she recognises.

A reporter standing on the sidewalk outside some downtown office building says, 'Expected to be a formidable challenger to the incumbent governor, Morris Sawchuck, seen here with his wife, Bridget, is perceived as being much stronger on law and order issues, and has made no secret that he would like to see a return to more traditional values. He's said to have some very powerful people working behind the scenes for him, including the former Vice President of the United States. Back to you—'

She turns off the set and stares into space, trying to take it all in. She still has the image in her head: the couple getting out of the back of a car, waving to supporters, going into a building to give a speech or something.

'Sawchuck?' Allison whispers. 'The guy's a politician?'

She runs her fingers out through her shoulder-length black hair and lets out a very long breath. Allison is glad she hasn't already called her mother, because there may be another solution to her cash-flow problem.

'YOU'VE GOT AN APPOINTMENT today with Dr Grigorin,' I said, while Thomas poured some milk on his cereal. 'Dad set it up a few weeks ago.'

'If I had a reason to go, I would go, Ray. But there isn't one.'

'There is a reason, Thomas. We've lost our father. And as difficult as this is for me to get through, I suspect it's even more troubling for you. I mean, you guys lived under the same roof.'

'He got mad at me a lot,' Thomas said. 'He was always telling me to do things I didn't want to do.' He gave me a look. 'Kind of like you.'

'But Dad was never mean to you,' I said.

'I guess,' he said. 'He didn't like me staying in my room all day. He wanted me to go out. He didn't understand how busy I am.'

'It's not healthy,' I said. 'You need some air. Thomas, you have to know, in your heart, that there's a problem when you're so addicted to what you're doing that you don't even go to Dad's funeral.'

'I had to go to Melbourne that day,' Thomas said.

'Thomas, you did not *have* to go to Melbourne that day. You needed to go to our father's funeral.' I knew I wasn't being fair, blaming Thomas for this. I knew he most likely couldn't help himself. As soon as I'd said the words, I regretted them. 'I'm sorry,' I said.

He didn't say anything. Neither of us did, for the better part of a minute.

I broke the silence. 'I think it's important that while I'm trying to sort out a few things, you go and see Dr Grigorin. I'd also like to talk to her.'

Thomas eyed me. 'Are you having some issues, too? She could help.'

I blinked. 'Help me? Help me with what?'

'About your need to control other people. She might be able to give you something for that. She gives me something to help me with the voices.'

'Well, there's an idea,' I said. 'The appointment's at eleven.'

'Eleven, eleven, eleven,' he said, casting his eyes upwards, like he was trying to remember what he'd written down in his date book.

'I'm sure you're free,' I said. 'We'll need to leave around ten thirty.'

'I really have a lot to do,' he said, starting to walk out of the kitchen.

'You can fiddle around with the GPS in the car.'

That stopped him. 'OK, I'll be ready at ten thirty. But you have to promise to talk to the doctor about your behaviour.'

'I promise,' I said.

After Thomas had gone up to his room, and I'd finished cleaning up, I decided it was time. I headed out of the back door, walked across the yard, then came to a stop where the ground sloped down to the creek.

It was, as I'd told Harry Peyton, a steep hill. A lot of people would have been content to let the grass and weeds grow wild on the slope. But Dad liked the idea of a groomed yard that went right to the water.

I remember Mom asking me, during one of our phone chats about a year before she died, to talk my father out of his practice of riding the mower on this hill, from side to side, leaning into the slope to keep the machine from tipping over. 'He's going to get himself killed,' she'd said.

'He knows what he's doing, Mom.'

'Oh, you men,' she'd said, exasperatedly. 'I tried to get Harry and Len to talk some sense into him and they said the same thing.'

Turned out the men were wrong.

My understanding was, the tractor had rolled once and landed on Dad. When Thomas got there, it wasn't possible to roll the tractor back up the hill. So he'd given the tractor a shove downwards. It had landed on its wheels on level ground just before the creek. It had been there ever since.

I walked carefully down the hill, looking down at the place where my father had taken his last breath. I felt a lump forming in my throat. Then I went down the rest of the way to the machine.

I didn't know whether I'd be able to get it back to the barn. I swung a leg over and dropped my butt in the seat. The key was still in the ignition, set to 'off'. I went to raise the blade housing, which you put into the down position only when you are actually cutting grass, but it was already up.

I put the choke on full, slid the throttle all the way up, and turned the key. The damn thing roared to life. I dropped the machine into its lowest gear to get it back up the hill. Once I'd crested the hill, I drove the tractor into the barn, parked it, slid the door shut behind me, and went back into the house.

Thomas was downstairs at ten. 'I think we should go.'

'OK.' I grabbed my sports coat and slipped it on.

We stepped out onto the porch and I locked the front door behind me. Thomas made a beeline for the Audi. He got in, put on his seat belt, and watched me impatiently as I came around the car, got in, did up my own belt, and keyed the ignition. The dashboard screen that allowed the driver to monitor dozens of the vehicle's functions, including the GPS, came to life.

'OK, how it works is—'

'I can figure it out,' Thomas said. 'I got it. You put in the city first, right?' I watched him type in 'McLean'.

'What are you doing?' Dr Grigorin's office was in Promise Falls.

'I want to see what directions it gives for McLean, Virginia,' he said.

'Why the hell would we go to Virginia?' I asked.

'I don't actually want to go there. I wanted to see if it would give us the best route.' He studied the screen a moment longer, appeared to get frustrated and said, 'Fine, I'll enter in the coordinates for the doctor's office.'

He entered them, and waited a couple of seconds for the nav system to figure things out.

'*Proceed to the highlighted route*,' the car's computer said.

'That's Maria,' I said. 'That's what I call the lady in my dashboard.'

'Oh,' Thomas said. He was studying the screen as I drove down the road. 'We're just passing Miller's Lane,' he said.

'You could look out of the window and know that,' I said. 'Let me ask you something. About when you found Dad. You OK talking about that?'

'What do you want to know?'

'Either before or after you pushed the tractor off him, did you touch any of the controls on it? Like turn off the key, or lift up the blades?'

'No. I don't even know how to drive it. This computer is wrong.' He hadn't taken his eyes off the navigational screen.

'What about when the ambulance came, or the police. Did any of the paramedics touch it?'

'They only cared about Dad. And I never saw the police do anything with it, but I wasn't always there. Maybe later they came.'

'But it hasn't been moved all week,' I said.

'Did you hear what I said?' Thomas asked. 'Maria's wrong.' He was still staring at the screen. 'She's telling you the wrong way to go.'

'She does that sometimes. You can choose to take her advice, or not.'

'*In one hundred yards, make a right turn*.'

'No!' Thomas shouted at the screen. 'She'll take us down Saratoga Street. I don't want to go down Saratoga Street.'

'What difference does it make?'

'I don't want to go that way!' He was starting to sound frantic.

'Just tell me which way you want me to go,' I said. 'We can tell Maria to take a hike.'

Thomas said he wanted to go by way of Main. I said OK. I ignored Maria when, as we passed Saratoga, she implored me to turn round.

'I don't believe this,' Thomas said. He was becoming increasingly agitated. 'Make her stop. Make her stop talking.'

I reached over, fiddled with the settings, and shut her down.

Thomas sat back and took a few deep breaths. Finally, he looked at me and said, 'You should get rid of this car.'

I TOOK A SEAT in the waiting room while Thomas went in for his session with Dr Grigorin. I glanced at my watch, figured I had a bit of time, and stepped out into the hall. I took out my cellphone, looked up a number online, and tapped to connect.

'*Promise Falls Standard*,' a woman's recorded voice said. 'If you know the extension, enter it now. To use the company directory, press Two.'

I struggled through the process until an actual phone rang.

'Julie McGill.'

'Julie, hi, this is Ray Kilbride. Am I catching you at a bad time?'

'Just waiting on another call,' Julie said. 'What can I do for you?'

'I wanted, first of all, to thank you for coming to my dad's funeral.'

'No problem,' she said.

'I wondered if we could grab a coffee so I could ask you a couple of questions about my father. Since you did the piece for the paper.'

'I don't have a lot of detail, but sure. Why don't you come by around four, we'll grab a beer. Gotta go.' She hung up.

As I stepped back into the waiting room, the doctor and Thomas were emerging from her office. Thomas pointed to me. 'So you'll talk to him.'

'I will.'

Dr Grigorin—her first name turned out to be Laura—had fiery red hair spun up into a bun, and stood about five-four in her heels. She was a striking woman in her early sixties. She wore a red blouse and a straight black skirt that came to just below her knees.

'Mr Kilbride,' she said to me. 'Won't you come in.' She told Thomas to take a seat in the waiting room while we spoke.

'I'm supposed to prescribe you something,' she said, smiling and motioning for me to take a chair. She took a chair across from me.

'To keep my controlling nature in check,' I said.

'That's right.' I liked her smile. 'How does he seem to you?' she asked.

'It's hard to tell. I know my father's death has to have affected him.'

'I can tell he's upset, even though he keeps things bottled up,' Dr Grigorin said. 'Your father was very concerned about how much time Thomas's preoccupation was taking up. Thomas said he's cutting back, and watched a movie with you the other night.'

'That's not true. He didn't want to leave his *work*.'

'Has he explained it to you?'

'He likes to explore the world's cities online.' I grinned. 'Although he did mention that I needed security clearance to see what he was up to.'

Dr Grigorin nodded. 'Thomas said it would be OK if I told you what he's been doing. He believes he's working for the CIA.'

'I'm sorry. The what? The Central Intelligence Agency? Working how?'

'It's somewhat complicated. First of all, Thomas believes there's going to be a cataclysmic event, some kind of digital, electronic implosion or explosion. Perhaps a global computer glitch, or even something orchestrated by some foreign power—an ingenious computer virus—that will cripple this country's intelligence-gathering ability.'

'Oh, man.'

She continued. 'When this happens, the first thing that will go down will be online maps. They'll all vanish instantly. All the people in the intelligence community who depend on those will be scrambling, because they've been under orders from on high to save paper costs—' She must have noticed my eyebrows going up and she smiled. 'Anyway, the point is, the government no longer has any hard copies.'

Knowing Thomas as I did, it all made sense, in a bizarre kind of way.

'And when that happens,' she continued, 'who do you suppose the CIA is going to be turning to?'

'Let me guess.'

She nodded. 'He'll be able to draw for them, from memory, all the street plans of all the major cities in the world. He's got them all up here.' She tapped her temple with her index finger. She wore red nail polish.

'But hang on,' I said. 'There'd still be old maps around.'

'Now you're being logical,' Laura Grigorin chastised me. 'The way your brother visualises this apocalyptic event, those resources have already been destroyed. Libraries everywhere got rid of them and went digital. Every household has put their old maps out with the newspapers in the recycling and now relies solely on the computer. It'll be a world without maps, and the only person who will know how to reproduce them will be Thomas. And not just maps, but how each and every street in the world looks. Every storefront, every front yard, every intersection.'

I shook my head. 'So he's getting ready for if and when this happens.'

'Not if,' she said. 'It's coming. That's why he's spending every moment in his room travelling the world, memorising as many cities as he can before this event.'

Something occurred to me. 'McLean.'

'What?'

'Isn't that where the CIA has its headquarters? Thomas wanted to program a route into my car's GPS system to get there, then thought better of it. Maybe because I didn't yet have clearance.' I laughed.

'Your brother trusts you. That's a plus. People with schizophrenia often lose trust in those closest to them. They're fearful of everyone.' She took a breath. 'Now, I started off telling you there were different elements to this.'

'OK.'

'In the meantime, before this incident happens, Thomas believes the CIA may call on him for other help. Let's say they have an agent in jeopardy in Caracas. He's on the run, and he doesn't know which way to turn. The CIA will put in a call to Thomas, ask him for an escape route. He'll be able to give them one, faster than they could get it on a computer.' Grigorin continued, 'And governments might also want him for help in disasters. Rescuers could call Thomas, tell him that they're at such and such a corner, and he could tell them what they should be looking for.'

I rested my palms atop my thighs. 'So, where does this leave us?'

'I'm not sure. I understand, as a result of your father's death, there may be a need to change Thomas's living arrangements.'

I discussed my concerns about his living in the house alone.

'Your concerns are valid,' she said. 'He should be living in town, in an environment where he can be checked up on. Not in a repressive kind of way. I can recommend a place you might want to take a look at.'

'Do you think he'd go?'

She leaned back. 'I think, if you introduce him to the idea gradually, he might. He'd be able to keep his computer. But it's important you get him out of the house. The more he's out of his bedroom, the more comfortable he becomes, the easier it will be to move him into a new environment. I take it you don't want to move back and look after your brother.'

'I don't . . . I don't want you to think I don't care about him.'

She shook her head. 'Not at all. In fact, I'm not sure that would be the best thing for him. We need him to be more independent.'

'Do you think Thomas is worse? Since Dad died?'

'I don't know. I asked him if he still hears the voices—often associated with schizophrenia—and he says occasionally. He talks to former president Bill Clinton, who's acting as his liaison with the CIA. Thomas's medication keeps the voices to little more than a whisper, and I don't want to up his dose. He does take his medication every day, yes? You've seen him?'

'Yes.'

'I think, considering everything, Thomas is doing well. He has his troubles, some of which he won't talk to me about, but—'

'Like what troubles? What's he not talking about?'

'Well, if he'd talk about them I'd know,' she said. 'I know there's something, from his childhood, that haunts him, but he's never opened up about it.' She moved on. 'The good thing is, Thomas thinks the world of you. He's brought me clippings of your illustrations to show me.' She smiled. 'I think he's always been envious of your talent, of being able to take a picture that's in your head and put it on paper.'

'It's what he does with maps,' I said.

'You have similar gifts, but they manifest themselves in different ways,' Dr Grigorin said.

'Did you talk to my father when he came in with Thomas?'

'Yes,' she said. 'I never treated him. But he did seem . . . weary. I think the strain of looking after your brother, alone, was wearing on him.'

'He had an accidental death insurance policy,' I said. 'That, along with some other things, would be enough to set Thomas up for a while.'

Dr Grigorin's eyes were piercing. 'Are you suggesting something, Ray?'

'I don't know.' I waved my hand. 'Let's forget about it.'

Our time was up. I stood. 'Oh,' she said. 'I almost forgot. I'm supposed to give you something to deal with your bossiness.'

She reached into her desk and came out with an opaque prescription container filled with oversized pills in several different, brilliant colours.

'What are these?' I asked, as she put it into my hand.

'M&Ms,' she said.

STUNNED AFTER RECOGNISING her new lover on television, Allison Fitch fires up her laptop to do some research.

'Son of a bitch,' she keeps whispering, under her breath.

While Morris Sawchuck has his eye on the governor's mansion, he already wields plenty of power as the state's attorney general. He's fifty-seven and Bridget is his third wife. He married her three years ago, and it's still a subject of gossip, what with her being twenty-one years younger, and quite a looker, too. There's talk about the fact they take separate vacations, but Allison already knows that.

Sawchuck met his first wife, Kathleen Wolcott, while attending Harvard. Five years later, he divorced her for Geraldine Kennedy.

Geraldine committed suicide in 2001. Sits in her BMW with the garage door closed and the engine running and lets the carbon monoxide do its thing. She had, the stories said, been diagnosed manic depressive.

Sawchuck settled into an appropriate period of mourning, threw himself into his work as a prosecutor. He garnered a lot of attention, going after crooked union bosses, Russian mobsters, a gang of child pornographers.

A couple of years after Geraldine's death, he was spotted occasionally with a number of different, and very attractive, women. Some talking heads expressed concern that his eye for the ladies might prove a political liability. But then came Bridget. A one-time fashion model with jet-black hair who stands five-ten in her stockinged feet—she has a passing resemblance to Allison herself—she works for a prestigious public relations firm. They appeared to hit it off from the get-go. Three months later, they're married.

Sawchuck, Allison's research finds, has powerful friends from across the political spectrum. Oh, and there's something else that's of particular interest to Allison. The dude is loaded. Most of it inherited: you don't make that kind of money working for the state, unless you are very dirty, and there's nothing to suggest Morris Sawchuck is, even if his closest friend and adviser, Howard Talliman, has been known to cut a few corners here and there. Morris's father, Graham, had been a big-time real-estate developer and owned a couple of dozen skyscrapers in Manhattan. Sawchuck inherited the business when his father died, which is now run at arm's length to avoid any allegations of conflict of interest.

What he really craves is attention and influence and the high profile, and he's found the best way to get it is through the relentless pursuit of those who break the law.

Allison jumps from web page to web page, finding more information about how much money Sawchuck has. Millions, for sure, if not billions. Looks like she might be able to get what she needs to pay back Courtney, and buy herself a new pair of Manolo Blahniks, too.

She practises what she's going to say. She doesn't want it to sound like out-and-out blackmail. What she's really looking for is a loan. Payments stretched out over, say, the next couple of thousand years. So, OK, maybe it's more like a gift she's seeking. And Allison can show gratitude by keeping her mouth shut. That's her way of saying thank you. Because something like this coming out, well, that's not going to do help Mr I-Want-to-Be-Governor one little bit.

Allison picks up her cellphone. Her heart is pounding. This is what happens when a girl leaves Dayton for the big city.

'Hello?'

'It's Allison. Remember me?'

'Of course I—look, I really can't talk now.'

'I saw you on the news. I had no idea who you are. How'd you forget to mention something like that? First, that you're married, and second, that—'

'Look, Allison, there's a lot going on right now. If you saw the news, you know things are starting to heat up in the campaign and . . . there are other problems. A possible investigation of—'

'You remember where we first hooked up?'

'Yes, of course.'

'Be there at three.'

'I'm really sorry, but we can't be seen together.'

'Three o'clock.'

By half past two, Allison's at a Gramercy Park bar. Manages to get the same booth they shared on their first date.

She orders herself a gin and tonic, keeps an eye on the door.

At three o'clock, right on the dot, someone walks through the door. She doesn't look like the Bridget Sawchuck Allison saw on the news. She has her hair wrapped up in a scarf. She's wearing sunglasses that cover up half her face. But it's her, all right. The attorney general's hot little wife.

Bridget Sawchuck walks straight to the booth where Allison's sitting, slides onto the leather seat across from her. 'I have only a few minutes,' she says. 'Why the urgent meeting?'

'Like I said to you on the phone, we've got some things to talk about.'

THREE

Dad didn't worry about leaving Thomas on his own, and neither did I. While my brother had a number of odd notions and peculiar habits, there was nothing to suggest he was a threat to anyone, or himself. My father would leave Thomas when he drove into Promise Falls to buy groceries or run other errands. The one apparent benefit of spending all his time in his room was that he didn't get into any mischief.

So I didn't have any qualms, later that afternoon, telling Thomas I was going to be out for a while. 'I'll bring back dinner.'

I had the Audi parked in the *Promise Falls Standard* lot a couple of minutes after four. I was afraid I'd be keeping Julie McGill waiting, but she wasn't in the lobby when I went in. I'd have asked the person at reception to let her know I was there, but there was only a phone on the desk inviting me to dial an extension, a list of them taped to the desk beside it.

I heard a series of speedy clicks on a set of nearby stairs.

'Hey,' Julie said. 'I see you've met the receptionist.'

She said the closest place to get a beer was Grundy's. She was dressed in black boots, jeans, a man's white dress shirt with button-down collar, and a well-worn black leather jacket. An oversized black bag was hanging from one shoulder, making her walk slightly lopsidedly.

We grabbed a booth. Julie held up a hand to the waitress, caught her eye and smiled. 'Hey, Bee, my usual, and something for the lady.'

Bee looked at me. 'I'll have whatever she's having,' I said.

As the waitress walked away Julie said, 'Again, sorry about your dad. But it's good to see you. Long time.' She smiled.

'Yeah,' I said.

Her face broke into a grin. 'You don't remember. Sadie Hawkin's dance. You were six months from graduating, I was a year behind you. You got asked by Ann Paltrow, had been drinking before the dance. She got mad and ditched you, at which point you started putting the moves on me. Turns out I'd downed a few Buds myself and before you knew it, we're in the back of your dad's car making out for an hour. Tell me you've forgotten that.'

I smiled, swallowed. 'I have forgotten that.'

'Then I guess you've also forgotten that I left town a few months after that, and nine and a half months later—' She grinned again. 'I'm just messing with you. About the last part, anyway. I mean, I did leave town, but I just had to get out of this place. I never felt like I fitted in around here.' She looked at me. 'You always seemed a bit out of place, too.'

'I suppose,' I conceded. 'I didn't hang in here all that much longer.'

'And now we're both back,' she said, as the waitress delivered two Coronas. 'At least you've got an excuse. A death in the family.'

'What's yours?'

'I travelled around, got jobs at several small-town papers. And then they started downsizing, and I was out of a job. But, as it turned out, tough as times are, the *Standard* newsroom had openings. It pays a tenth of the bills till I find something else. And believe me, I'm looking.' She paused. 'You wanted to talk to me because of the story I wrote about your dad.'

'I wondered if there was anything more you knew about it.'

'Not really.'

'Do you know whether there was any kind of investigation afterwards?'

'Yup. The usual. Death-by-misadventure kind of thing. The facts were pretty straightforward. There was no inquest.'

'I shouldn't have troubled you with this.'

'It's OK,' Julie said. 'These things, I mean, you know, they're hard. Look, is there anything I can do for you, for Thomas?'

'No, it's—yeah, I mean, drop in some time. I know Thomas would be happy to see you. He's—I guess you know he's kind of different.'

She nodded, slowly. 'He always had a thing about maps. Still into those?'

'Yes.'

I worked on my Corona. Julie had nearly finished hers. 'You were a bit weird yourself. Always drawing things. You weren't exactly a jock.'

'I threw the javelin,' I said defensively. It was true. And I was damn good at it. That, and playing darts in our basement rec room.

'Really,' Julie said. 'I see the drawing thing paid off for you, though.'

'Thanks.'

'You get married along the way?'

'No. Came close a couple of times. You?'

'Lived a few months with a guy who does that relaxation music, you know, like they play when you're getting a massage? Then there was a thing with an NBA coach, a reality TV producer, and a guy who raised iguanas.'

She paused. 'But, hey, that's California. Maybe it's good to be back here.'

Out of nowhere, I had a flashback. 'Purple,' I said. 'Your underwear. It was purple.'

Julie smiled.

THE NEXT DAY, at breakfast, I said to Thomas, 'I liked Dr Grigorin.'

'She's OK,' he said, grabbing a banana. 'Did she tell you?'

'Tell me what?'

'What I'm doing. I told her you could know about it.' He bit into the banana. 'I figured, coming from her, you'd believe it.'

'You think Dr Grigorin believes it?' I asked him. 'What it is you're doing? Memorising maps and street plans so you can help secret agents on the run? And that one day, there won't be any maps at all and you'll have all the information stored up here?' I tapped my index finger just above my temple.

He put the banana down. 'If she didn't believe it, why would she ask so many questions about it? If she didn't believe it, she'd dismiss it out of hand.' Disappointment washed over his face. 'I guess you don't believe in what I'm doing. I was wrong, thinking Dr Grigorin could convince you.'

'Think about it, Thomas. You're just some guy, living in a house outside Promise Falls in upstate New York. You've never worked in law enforcement or for any government agency. You believe that you, with no actual qualifications and no connections, have attracted the attention of the Central Intelligence Agency, and they want you to be their map guy.'

Thomas nodded. 'I know. It's amazing, isn't it?'

'That it is,' I said. 'What I'm trying to do, Thomas, is point out to you how totally absurd this is. Dr Grigorin even told me that you've been in touch with former president Clinton.'

Standing at Thomas's partially open door, I'd heard him carry on a conversation with someone who wasn't there. The phone was on the hook. I'd heard him say, 'I almost called you Bill.'

'That's right,' Thomas said. 'But you can still call him Mr President. Former presidents are still called that.'

'I know.'

'I don't want to talk about this any more,' Thomas said. 'Those pills the doctor gave you aren't working. I thought they'd make you more tolerant and understanding. But you're just like Dad.'

He got up, went back up to his room, and slammed the door.

I WAS LOADING UP on frozen foods at Price Chopper when I ran into Len Prentice and his wife, Marie. Len and my father had maintained a friendship after Dad left the printing company. Len looked as though he'd got some sun lately. Marie, however, was pale. She'd had health problems as long as I'd known her. I couldn't remember what, exactly. Always tired. I'd known the two of them—admittedly, not well—for the better part of three decades.

'Hey, Ray,' said Len. 'How're you and Thomas doing?'

'Hi,' I said to both of them. 'We're good. Managing.'

'It was a lovely service,' Marie said earnestly.

'Yes,' I said. 'Thanks again for coming.' I looked at Len and smiled. 'I meant to ask you the other day whether you fell asleep under a sun lamp.'

Marie patted my arm playfully. 'Oh, you. Len got back from a vacation a couple of weeks ago.'

'Where'd you go?' I asked. 'Florida?'

Len shook his head. 'Thailand. Have you been there, Ray?'

'Never,' I said. 'People say it's wonderful. You didn't go, Marie?'

She sighed. 'I don't have the energy for travel. But just because I'm not up to gallivanting around the globe doesn't mean Len shouldn't head off with others who feel more up to travelling than I do.'

'Ray,' Len said, 'I've been meaning to come out and see you before you go back to Burlington.'

'Not sure when that will be,' I said. 'I have to decide what to do about the house. Thomas can't live there on his own.'

'Oh mercy, no,' Marie said. 'The boy needs looking after.'

I felt my back go up, but didn't show it. Thomas didn't deserve to be treated as though he were a child. And then I wondered if I'd been too hard on him, the way I'd been challenging him about his mission.

'Yeah, he does,' I said. 'But I'm going to see if I can make him a little more self-sufficient.'

It was something I'd been thinking about. I wanted to get him making his own meals, and helping out around the house. Maybe, if I started giving him responsibilities, it would keep him out of his room for longer intervals.

'Well, we should let you go,' Len said. 'Good to see you.'

'I keep meaning to drop by with a casserole for you boys,' Marie said. 'Or maybe you'd like to come over for dinner?'

'That's very kind,' I said. 'I'll talk to Thomas about that.' *Fat chance*,

I thought, although dinner out with people he knew might be worth a try.

'Thomas still memorising maps for when the big computer virus hits?' Len asked, a hint of a smile in the corner of his mouth.

I was caught off guard. 'You know about that?'

'Your dad told me. I guess he needed to talk to somebody about it.'

Slowly, I nodded. Marie said, 'Len, it's none of your business.'

'It was. Adam told me,' he snapped at her, and Marie blinked. To me, he said, 'Your dad was feeling the burden of it all, you know?'

So everyone seemed to be telling me.

I OPENED THOMAS'S DOOR. 'I'm back. And you're making dinner.'

That got him to turn around. 'What? I never make dinner.'

'Then all the more reason to start. I got some frozen stuff. I'll walk you through it. How to put the oven on, all that stuff. Come down around five.'

I treasured Thomas's shell-shocked expression as I closed the door.

Almost on cue, my cellphone rang. It was my agent, Jeremy Chandler.

'I've got three jobs here for you. Magazines and one web site, Ray, with deadlines. Looming deadlines. If you can't do the work, I need to know now so I can farm these jobs out to other artists.'

'I told you, I'm at my father's place.'

'Oh, yeah, I forgot. He died, right?'

'Yes, and so I have some stuff to deal with. I might have to set up a makeshift studio here temporarily.'

'Good idea. Did I tell you I heard from Vachon's people?'

Carlo Vachon, a noted Brooklyn crime family boss, was facing a slew of possible indictments on everything from murder to unpaid parking tickets. I'd been commissioned by a New York magazine to do a drawing of him in which I'd exaggerated all his physical features as he held a gun to the Statue of Liberty. In my version, she had both her arms in the air.

I was breaking out in an instant sweat. 'Is there a hit out on me?'

'No, no, nothing like that. Apparently he loved the illustration and he wants to buy the original.'

'Send it. No charge,' I said.

'Done. But that's not why I called. There's a new web site about to start up that's got backing from some very big people. They want to take on the Huffington Post, but they want something different, and I said to them, what about an animated political cartoon?'

'You mentioned me?'

'I didn't even have to. They came to me. This woman who's setting it up, her name's Kathleen Ford. Got financial backing like you wouldn't believe. Lots of media money. She wants to have a sit-down with you ASAP.'

There was a knock at the front door. A purposeful, somebody-means-business kind of knock. 'Someone's here,' I said. 'I'll get back to you.'

I left the phone on the kitchen table and went to the door.

There were two of them standing there on the porch, a black sedan parked behind my Audi. A man and a woman, both in their forties. Both in suits, although his came with a narrow, businesslike tie.

'Mr Kilbride?' the woman asked.

'Yes?'

'I'm Agent Parker, and this is Agent Driscoll. FBI,' she said sternly.

BRIDGET SAWCHUCK believes that if she's going to have to discuss her situation with her husband's closest friend and chief adviser, Howard Talliman, it had better be in a public place. Maybe he'll be able to resist the temptation to throttle her if there are witnesses. She has invited him to lunch at the Union Square Café, booking a table for one o'clock.

Talliman has been Morris Sawchuck's best friend since God was a boy. They went to Harvard together, got drunk together, practised law together, vacationed together. Howard, very early on, began working behind the scenes on political campaigns—Republican, Democrat, didn't matter. Only winning mattered. He's never wanted to be the candidate. He is short and paunchy, and says he has the sex appeal of a garden gnome; but he knows how to turn others into winners.

'You can take this as far as you want to go,' Howard told Morris more than a decade ago. 'The only thing that limits you is your own ambition. But you have to build in increments. A tough prosecutor, then an attorney general; you start drawing a line and see where it takes you. It takes you right to the top, that's where it takes you.'

All the hard work is paying off. Big time. Morris is surely headed to the governor's mansion, and who knows where the hell he'll go after that?

As proud as Howard is of shaping his best friend into a political star, it was finding him a new, beautiful young wife to stand at his side during victory speeches that really puffs him up. He'd encountered Bridget at the PR firm he had hired on behalf of another client. The moment Howard saw her, he knew she'd look perfect standing next to Morris at every campaign stop across New York. She was sexy in a Michelle Obama–Jackie O kind of way. Statuesque, long neck, nice figure but not too busty. Poise to spare.

Howard, Bridget realises now, manoeuvred Morris and her together without their even knowing it at the time. Howard made the introductions, whispered into each of their ears that the one was interested in the other.

But there was something there. Within a week, Bridget found herself sprawled across the back seat of Sawchuck's limo, belts unbuckling, snaps unsnapping. A lot of fun, even if Bridget has not always been, strictly speaking, exclusively heterosexual. But what the hell. Once she found out the kind of life she was looking at, hooking up with someone like Morris Sawchuck, she figured she could play on just the one team for ever.

Didn't turn out to be the case.

Not that Allison was her first time falling off the hetero wagon. But she was the first one Bridget had slipped away with for a few days. She didn't consider it serious, and Allison didn't appear to, either. Bridget hadn't used her real name—made sure Allison never saw her passport—and stuck with the oversized sunglasses and sun hat whenever they were out and about.

And now Bridget's in trouble.

She glances at the café menu and, when she looks up, there he is.

'Bridget,' he says. 'You look delicious, as always.'

Howard settles into his chair across from her. He knows something is up. He wouldn't be where he is now without being able to read people.

Although he hadn't read her right. Not when he met her. If he had, well, they wouldn't be where they are now, would they?

'We're going to need drinks, I suspect,' he says. 'What will you have?'

'Uh, white wine spritzer,' she says.

Howard's eyebrows go up. 'Things can't be that bad, then, can they?' He turns in his chair and catches the attention of a passing waiter. 'The lady will have a white wine spritzer. Scotch neat for me.' He turns back to Bridget. 'So, what's on your mind? I figure you didn't bring me here to start an affair.' Howard has never been married.

Bridget swallows. 'You know I would never do anything intentionally to cause trouble for Morris. I would never want to embarrass him. Never.'

Howard studies her. 'It's money, or it's sex,' he says. 'Or it's both. There's really nothing else.'

'It's both,' she says.

'I see,' Howard says. 'Just how bad is it?'

'Bad.' She collects herself. 'I'm being blackmailed, Howard.'

'So, there's the money part. And the leverage your blackmailer has over you, that will be the sex part. Unless, of course, I have this all totally wrong, and you've gone and killed someone.'

'I haven't killed anyone,' she says.

'Well,' Howard says, as the drinks are placed in front of them, 'there's a cause for celebration.' He takes a sip of his Scotch.

'I had an affair,' Bridget says.

Howard nods wisely. 'We're talking about something that has happened since you and Morris engaged in the bonds of holy matrimony.'

'Yes.'

'Is it over? This affair?'

'Yes.'

'Do I know him?'

Bridget pauses. 'No.'

'That was a troubling hesitation, Bridget. It means I may know him, and you're lying, or you're responding truthfully in a deliberately obtuse way.' His eyes bore into her. 'I think it's the latter.' He keeps his eyes on her another moment, then asks, 'Who is she?'

He really is something. 'Her name's Allison Fitch.'

Howard's eyelids flutter rapidly. It's what he does when he's searching through his mental database. 'You are right, I don't know her. Did you make it known to this Allison Fitch that you were the wife of a prospective governor, the state's current attorney general?'

'No. I gave her another name altogether. But she saw me on television, on the news, at a function with Morris.' Bridget gives him the Reader's Digest version of the story: where they'd met, how many times they'd seen each other, the time they'd gone away together.

'Are there any photos? Hidden camera, that kind of thing?'

'I don't think so. Allison never mentioned it. I don't see why she would have filmed me. She didn't know, at the time, who my husband was.'

'Then what proof has she? One possible strategy is to ride the thing out. It'd be ugly, but we stonewall, deny, suggest that your husband's opponents choreographed the entire episode. In the meantime, we dig into her past, find something good on her that destroys her credibility, and after the press has some fun with it for a while, everyone gets bored and—'

'There are texts,' Bridget says. 'Between us. Phone records, and texts.'

A pause. 'And what do these texts say, Bridget? What is their nature?'

'They're . . . I guess the word would be salacious.'

'And would you be the author of any of these salacious texts, or are they all written by Ms Fitch?'

'Fifty-fifty, I'd say.'

Howard runs his tongue over his teeth. 'How much is she looking for, and what does she intend to do should you not meet her demands?'

'One hundred thousand. Or she goes public.'

'Not very imaginative, is she? If I were her, I would have asked for at least a million. And how do we know she won't take the money and sell her story, anyway?'

'I know what you're thinking. That she'll come back again and again.'

'I think that's very likely, Bridget. But, perhaps, with the right degree of persuasion, she can be happy with one reasonable sum. And then she agrees to go away, and we never hear from her again.'

Bridget sighs. 'I knew you'd know how to handle this, Howard. I don't want Morris to know about this. You're not going to tell him, are you?'

'I love you both too much to do that. You have a beautiful future ahead of you if you learn to control your . . . impulses.'

'It was a slip,' she says. 'It's never going to happen again.'

'Of course not,' he says, patting her hand, 'because I will not—repeat, not—allow anyone to get in the way of Morris's destiny, and that includes you. Is that clear?'

Bridget nods. 'Perfectly.'

FOUR

'We'd like to come in and speak with you,' FBI Agent Parker said.

I asked to see their IDs, which they flashed at me, then stood back for the two of them to enter the house. I gestured towards the living room couch and chairs, but they chose to stand. I did the same.

'We need to see some identification,' Driscoll said.

'Do I need a lawyer or something?'

'We'd just like to establish exactly who we're talking with,' Parker said.

Fearing the consequences of being disagreeable, I reached around for my wallet and dug out my driver's licence. Parker took it in her hand.

'You're Mr Kilbride,' she said. 'Ray Kilbride.'

'Yes.'

'What do you do, Mr Kilbride?'

'I'm an artist. An illustrator.'

'And just what kind of things do you illustrate?' Agent Parker asked.

'My work's appeared in newspapers, magazines, web sites.'

'So, I guess you do a lot of your work on the computer.'

'Sure,' I said.

'And you live out here and do that?'

'I don't live here. I live in Burlington.'

Agent Driscoll stepped in. 'Then whose house is this?'

'It's my father's.' I cleared my throat. 'It *was* my father's.'

'What's that mean?' Agent Parker snapped.

'It means he's dead,' I snapped back. 'He died in an accident out back of the house a few days ago. His name was Adam Kilbride.'

Agent Driscoll said, 'Did your father have a computer?'

I was still wondering what this was about. 'What? Yes, he did. A laptop.'

Agent Parker had her notebook out. 'What day did your father die?'

'Friday, May 4th.'

She showed her notebook to her partner. 'Messages that day, and since.'

Now I was getting it.

'You're Ray and your father was Adam,' Agent Parker said. 'Is there a Thomas Kilbride who resides here?'

'Yes. He's my brother. He's upstairs.' What the hell had Thomas done to bring the FBI down on us? And how was he going to react when he learned they were here to see him? 'My brother stays in his room most of the day. I don't know what you want with him, but he's absolutely harmless.'

'What's he doing in his room?' Parker asked.

'He's on his computer. Look, my brother has certain psychiatric issues.'

'What sort of psychiatric issues?' Driscoll asked.

'Nothing that anyone else needs to worry about,' I said. 'He's got his problems, but he never bothers anyone.'

Driscoll asked, 'Are you aware that Thomas Kilbride has been emailing the Central Intelligence Agency on a regular basis? And that many of these email messages have been addressed to former president Bill Clinton?'

I felt my insides liquefying. 'Please tell me these were not threatening messages. That you're not here to arrest him or anything.'

The two glanced at each other. Parker said, 'No, not threatening. But . . . concerning. You want to call him down?'

I hung my head and shook it. 'Wait here.' I went upstairs, opened Thomas's door without knocking. 'I need you to come downstairs, Thomas,' I said. 'You have visitors. They're government people,' I warned him.

That stopped him. Then he nodded. 'Oh,' he said. 'That's great.'

'Thomas, it's not great. What the hell kind of messages have you been sending to the CIA?'

'Progress reports,' he said.

Once he hit the living room, he went straight for them, shaking hands. 'I'm Thomas Kilbride,' he said. 'It's a pleasure to meet you. The president never said anything about you dropping by for a visit.'

'The president?' Agent Parker said.

'Well, former president,' Thomas said. 'But Mr Clinton said you can call him that. But I hardly need to tell you, if he's the one who sent you.'

'Why would he have sent us?' Driscoll asked, stone-faced.

For the first time, Thomas looked concerned. 'Aren't you from the CIA?'

'No,' Parker said. 'Agent Driscoll and I are from the FBI.'

Thomas was unable to hide his disappointment. 'I thought you'd be from the CIA. They're the ones I've been in touch with.'

'Mr Kilbride,' Driscoll said, 'why don't we all have a seat.' The agents took the two chairs, and Thomas and I sat on the couch.

'Don't get the wrong idea,' Thomas said. 'The FBI does a good job.'

'Well, we all work together,' Driscoll said. 'All on the same side, right?'

I was detecting the slightest change in tone from the agent. Less edge. Now they could see—I hoped—that Thomas did not present a threat.

'You've been writing to the CIA about a computer virus that's coming,' Parker said.

Maybe Driscoll had lost his tone, but not Parker.

Thomas began, 'I've already explained this in my messages to the CIA, and President Clinton and I have talked about it. I don't actually have any inside information on the virus. I don't even know if it will be a virus. It might be a solar flare, or a kind of nuclear explosion.'

'Uh huh,' Parker said. 'So, what is it you think it's going to do?'

'Wipe out all the GPS systems and maps that are stored on computers.' Thomas then explained his role in helping the country through this catastrophe, how he was memorising the streets of all the major cities in the world. 'And, I'm at the ready, should any agents of the US government be on the run in a metropolitan area anywhere in the world, to offer guidance.'

'Uh huh,' Parker said again. 'Thomas, you wouldn't be trying to write some kind of virus yourself that would cripple the computer systems of the US government, would you?'

'No,' he said, not the slightest bit offended. 'I'm not really that good with computers. I know how to turn them on and do email and how to use Whirl360, but that's about it.'

'And what is it you want from the CIA, Thomas?' Parker asked.

Thomas sat up a little straighter. 'I don't want anything from them. I'm offering my services. You should already know this. When all the computer maps crash, I'll be able to assist the government.'

'And just how will you be able to do that?' she asked.

Thomas sighed. 'Because I have them in my head. All the maps. All the streets. What everything looks like. When all the computers fail I'll be able to draw the maps, or be a guide, if needed.'

Parker's tongue pushed her cheek out. 'OK. You ever been to Georgetown, Thomas?'

'Georgetown, Texas? Or Georgetown, Kentucky? Or—'

'Georgetown, in Washington, DC.'

Thomas nodded. 'No. Actually, I've never been to any of them.'

'So let's say I'm in Georgetown, and I'd like to buy a book, and—'

Thomas squeezed his eyes shut for a moment, and opened them. 'There's a Barnes & Noble bookstore, on M Street, NW, at Thomas Jefferson Street. And if you're hungry, there's a Vietnamese restaurant right across the street, although I don't know if it's any good or not. I've never eaten Vietnamese food. Is it like Chinese food? I like Chinese food.'

Agent Parker glanced at her partner.

'I know the government is trying to save money these days, so it's important you know that I'm not looking for any big salary,' my brother said. 'Just enough to cover my expenses.'

'Thomas, Agent Driscoll and I would like to see where you work.'

'Sure,' he said.

I followed everyone up the stairs. When they got to the first floor, the agents stopped and took in the wall of maps. Thomas opened the door to his bedroom. 'This is my work station,' he said. 'And I sleep here, too.'

'What's this?' Parker asked, pointing to the monitors. One of them showed an office building with the letters 'CIBC' running across the windows.

'Yonge Street, Toronto,' Thomas said. 'It runs north and south, starting at Lake Ontario, at Queen's Quay Boulevard.'

'So how much time do you spend doing this?' Parker asked.

'I sleep from around one at night to nine in the morning, and I take meal breaks, and I have a shower every morning, but all the other times I'm working. I had to see my psychiatrist yesterday so I lost some time there, but I'll make it up.'

I saw the agents exchange looks when Thomas said 'psychiatrist'. Parker said, 'Show us what you do.'

'OK.' Thomas sat, then moved the cursor around the street on the centre monitor. 'I keep clicking and I move up the street, and then I hold the button down and I can move around three hundred and sixty degrees like this and see all the stores. You usually can't see the people clearly and the licence plates on the cars are blurred, but everything else is really clear.'

'Can you open up your email program, Thomas?' Parker asked.

'OK.'

His inbox was empty.

'You delete all your mail right away?' Driscoll asked.

'I don't get any,' Thomas said. 'I don't have any regular friends that write to me. Sometimes, I get junk. I delete those immediately.'

I was thinking maybe I should raise an objection, that if they wanted to snoop around in my brother's emails, they should have a warrant. But it was my hope that once they saw how innocent his pursuit was, whatever it was that worried them about him would evaporate.

'Show us what's in your deleted file,' Driscoll said.

'I always forget to empty this,' Thomas said. 'There.'

The folder was, as Thomas had said, filled with junk emails.

'And now the folder with sent messages,' Parker said.

Thomas did a click with the mouse and there it was. The sent file. The messages filled the screen. Hundreds and hundreds of messages. Written by Thomas Kilbride. All of them directed to the same address.

The email address of the Central Intelligence Agency.

'I like to keep everyone apprised of what I'm doing,' Thomas said.

I was stunned. Agents Parker and Driscoll, not so much.

Seeing as how these emails had been sent to the CIA, I figured they'd seen them already. But, despite that, Driscoll asked, 'Why don't we open a couple of those emails at random. How about this one?' He pointed to the screen.

Thomas clicked on one that, like all the others, had been directed to the general enquiries email address of the CIA, which I was guessing was available on the Internet to anyone. Thomas had typed 'Whirl360 update' into the subject line. It read:

> Dear Former President Clinton: I'm sure you have lots of connections with all government agencies, not just the CIA, so I would urge you to have them start checking into what this catastrophic event is that is coming. Once it happens, it will be a lot harder to deal with. Because computers will be affected, I want to give you a phone number where you can reach me, and my address. Just call and tell me what to get to work on and I will get right to it. Sincerely, Thomas Kilbride

The contact details followed.

'Thomas,' Agent Parker said, 'have you ever been in trouble? Trouble with the police?'

'No, I've never been in any trouble with the police.'

Parker and Driscoll exchanged looks again. I'd lost count of how many times they'd done this. Parker said to Thomas, 'Why don't you get back to work and we'll let your brother show us out.'

'OK,' he said, turning back to his mouse and keyboard.

When the three of us got back downstairs, I asked Parker, 'What now?'

She said, 'We'll make our report. This visit was a threat assessment, Mr Kilbride. I don't believe Agent Driscoll sees one, and I would have to concur. The US government hears, on a daily basis, from a great many'—she paused—'individuals whose interpretations of the world around them are unique. Ninety-nine per cent of them present no discernible threat, but we spend a lot of time tracking down the one per cent that do.'

I had been holding my breath for an hour. I took what she had to say as good news, but my stress level was off the scale. On top of that, I was furious with Thomas. I knew I had to make certain allowances for him, but bringing the FBI to our door?

Parker continued, 'If your brother keeps communicating with government agencies with his tales of a computer infrastructure meltdown, you're going to be visited again. If not by us, then someone else.'

'I hear you.'

'It's a different world from twenty years ago,' she said. 'No one takes these things lightly. Thomas mentioned a psychiatrist.' She had out her notebook again. 'Name?'

I didn't want to give it to her, but how long would it have taken her to find out on her own? I gave Parker the name.

'Good day, Mr Kilbride,' she said. Driscoll nodded.

I watched them go down the porch steps and get into their government-issued wheels.

When I walked back into his room, Thomas said, 'I thought they were nice, but they should have sent the CIA.'

I reached over to where the power strip went into the wall outlet and yanked it out. The soft whirring of the computer stopped instantly.

Thomas screamed, 'Hey!'

Then I reached over another few inches, where the phone line went into the jack, and pulled that out as well. Thomas stared, dumbstruck, at the suddenly black monitors.

'Turn them on!' he shouted. 'Turn them back on!'

I shouted back, 'What the hell were you thinking? Can you tell me that? Getting in touch with the CIA? Are you crazy?' Even as I said it, I knew it was wrong. But I couldn't stop myself.

'Plug it back in, Ray!' Thomas was out of his chair now, dropping to his knees, scrambling for the cord that led out of the power strip.

I grabbed him by the shoulders and pulled him away. 'No! This is it, Thomas! The damn FBI at our door! I've had it! Enough!'

But Thomas scrambled ahead, getting himself under the table. I grabbed hold of his legs, dragged him out and pulled him to the middle of the room.

'I hate you!' he shouted, tears streaming down red, angry cheeks.

'You're done with this!' I said. 'Done! You're getting out of this room and going outside! You're going to start living like a normal person!'

I knew this was wrong. Yelling at Thomas, pulling the plug on his computer. I'd lost control of the situation, and I'd lost control of myself. Losing my father, coming back here, trying to figure out what to do with the house and Thomas, and now a couple of federal agents at the door—I'd snapped.

But there was no excuse for coming down on Thomas this hard.

Thomas looked at me and shook his head. 'No, no, no,' he said, and began to hit himself. He was driving the heels of his hands, alternating left and right, into his forehead. Hard. He made unintelligible grunting noises of frustration.

'Thomas!' I said. 'Stop it!' I tried to get my arms around his, but they were like pistons. He was pounding his head hard enough that it sounded like wood hitting wood. 'It's OK!' I said. 'Thomas, stop!' I hoped that by restricting his movements I'd calm him. 'It's OK,' I said again. 'I'm sorry.'

Like a switch had been flipped, he stopped. His forehead was red and beginning to bruise. He was crying.

I felt myself overwhelmed. My throat felt thick, my breathing quickened. I was crying, too. 'Thomas, I'm sorry. Promise me you won't hit yourself any more, OK?' I eased him up into a sitting position, ran my hand down his back.

'I won't,' he said.

'OK, that's good. We're good.'

He glanced over at the power strip. 'I'm going to plug it back in.'

'I'll get it, let me.' I shoved the plug into the outlet. The computer started to hum. 'But we need to establish some rules, OK? Before you start exploring again.'

He nodded slowly. 'What are the rules?'

'I just want you to check with me first before you send any emails or make any phone calls. Is that a deal?'

He thought about it. 'I don't know. I'm going back to work now.' His back to me, he said, 'Am I still making dinner tonight?'

I had forgotten. 'No,' I said. 'Don't worry about it.'

'THE FBI SENT SOME PEOPLE to talk to me, Mr President.'

'*Yes, of course, that makes sense. It's standard procedure.*'

'OK. Because they weren't friendly. They asked if I'd ever been in trouble. And I think they meant the kind of trouble where I was the one who did the bad thing. But it wasn't my fault. I don't like to talk about it. Dad wanted to talk about it just before he died, wanted me to talk about it. It was very confusing, because for years and years he wouldn't let me talk about it, to anyone. And I never did. Not even Dr Grigorin knows.'

'*I know.*'

'It's safe, telling you.'

'*What about your brother? Should you tell him?*'

'No. No. I don't think so.'

HOWARD TALLIMAN does not want to meet Allison Fitch where they can be seen together. So he books a suite for the day at the Roosevelt at Madison and 45th. He wants a room with a separate living area. He has instructed Bridget to contact Allison and invite her to the hotel for two in the afternoon. Allison does not know that Howard will be taking the meeting.

He orders coffee from room service with instructions that it be delivered ten minutes before Allison's scheduled arrival. He is guessing that when $100,000 is at stake, that's a good reason to be on time.

The china cups and saucers are set out on the coffee table when there is a soft rapping at the door at one minute before two. Howard opens the door.

Allison's mouth drops open. 'I'm sorry. I've knocked on the wrong—'

'Ms Fitch, a pleasure to meet you,' he says. 'You're right on time.'

She hesitates, then steps into the room. 'Where's Bridget?' she asks.

'I will be representing Bridget's interests here today,' he says. 'My name is Howard Talliman.' He doesn't see the point in using some sort of alias. 'I am a friend of the family.'

'Oh, yeah, I know who you are,' she says.

'Won't you sit down? I've ordered coffee.' Howard picks up the silver coffeepot and says, 'May I pour you a cup?'

'Yeah, sure.'

Steam rises from the coffee as it streams into the cups. Howard leans back comfortably in his chair, saucer in one hand and cup in the other.

'So, Ms Fitch, you've certainly stirred things up, haven't you?'

'Yeah, well, I don't know what exactly Bridget has told you.'

'She's told me that you two became very special friends, that you spent time together in Barbados, that you subsequently learned that she is married to Morris Sawchuck, and, having learned this, you saw an opportunity.'

Allison Fitch blushes. 'I would call it doing Bridget a favour.'

Howard's bushy eyebrows soar briefly. 'Explain that to me.'

'Well, I figured she wouldn't want it getting out that we had had a thing, and I was offering her a way to make sure that didn't happen.'

Howard nods. 'You're a very kindhearted person, aren't you? Just how were you hoping to ensure that this information did not become public?'

'Look, you already know the answer. I told her I've been having kind of a cash-flow problem lately, and that if she could help me out, I'd make sure nothing came out about her, something that could ruin her husband's chances of being governor or president or head of the glee club or whatever it is he wants to be when he grows up. I mean, what's a hundred grand for her and her husband? That's, like, what? Lunch money?'

Howard Talliman smiles. 'How do you know the police aren't listening in on this conversation in the other room?'

Allison tenses up. But then her muscles appear to relax.

'I don't think you'd do that. Because then it would all come out. That the governor's wife had been having a lesbian affair.'

'You think you could survive that kind of publicity?'

'Sure.'

'How do you think your mother in Dayton would handle it?'

That gets her. But she composes herself. 'I think Mom's been suspecting it. The real question is, could Bridget and her husband survive it?'

'They'd simply deny it,' Howard says. 'Your word against hers. She's married to an attorney general and you, my dear, are a barmaid.'

'A barmaid with proof.'

He's been waiting to see whether she'll play this card.

'Proof,' he says. 'And what proof would that be?'

'We had a lot of conversations. The kind that there's a record of.'

'Your phone. Let me see it.'

Allison shakes her head. 'Do I look stupid?'

'If you want the one hundred thousand, you will have to produce your phone at the time of delivery so that I can be certain those messages have been expunged.'

Allison appears to be thinking. 'I suppose that's OK,' she says.

'And what assurances does Bridget have that you won't come back and ask her for more money?'

'You'll just have to take my word on that,' Allison says.

'Yes, I'll just have to do that,' Howard says. He slaps the tops of his knees. 'Well, thanks so much for dropping by. We'll be in touch.'

'Don't you have my money?'

'Not at the moment,' Howard says, standing. 'I wanted to get a sense of the situation first. It will take time to get that kind of money together.'

'Is it all going to be *cash*?'

'Absolutely.'

Howard is thinking ahead. Suppose she does go to the press? It could be a tough go, no doubt about it. But Bridget is not the one running for office. If this scandal is to end up destroying her, so be it. Morris can probably survive it, even if it means cutting Bridget loose. The whole thing could conceivably garner the man some sympathy, once the hoopla dies down.

But paying her the hundred grand—how will that look if it gets out? Howard's mind races. He'll take the blame. Resign if he has to, at least publicly. While survivable, it'll set back the timetable a bit. They've already had to put things on hold because of that other matter but, as each day passes, things look more promising. And as for this woman, maybe, just maybe, once she has her money, she'll really go away.

And then Allison Fitch says, 'Just don't try anything funny. Because I know stuff.' She's heading for the door. 'Now that I know who Bridget is, you think back, stuff you saw, stuff you overheard; it all starts to come together.'

Howard feels a chill. 'What, exactly, are you talking about?'

The last thing she says as she goes into the hall is, 'You just come up with the hundred grand and you won't have to worry about it.'

Howard stares at the door as it closes.

He is going to have to have another chat with Bridget. And, before that, he would put in a call to Lewis. Whenever things looked as though they were going to escalate, he talked to Lewis.

BRIDGET IS COMING OUT of the building on 35th Street where the PR firm she works for is headquartered, when she sees him waiting for her.

He grabs her by the elbow and starts leading her down the sidewalk.

'Howard!' she says. 'Let go of my arm! You're hurting me.'

Howard Talliman says nothing. He swiftly moves her along and then steers her into the lobby of a building, the first place he's spotted where he can talk to her without anyone else listening in.

'What does she know?' Howard asks once they are inside. 'She says she heard things.' He is hissing, almost snakelike.

'Heard what? What did she say she heard?'

'She didn't say. But she intimated that it was something damaging. Things you'd said, things that made sense once she knew who you were.'

'Howard, I swear—'

'You talked to Morris when you were with Allison Fitch?'

'Yes, yes, I'm sure I did. I mean, she might have been in the other room. I talked to him when I was in the bathroom, or maybe when Allison was. I talked to him by the pool one day, when she went off to get us drinks.'

'So she might have heard any of these conversations?' Howard says.

'I suppose it's possible but, even if she did, I'm sure I never said anything that—'

'You know about Morris's situation,' Howard says grimly.

'How could I not know? Morris is going out of his mind about it, thinking it's going to come out, that Goldsmith will implicate him.'

So she did know.

Howard had never been able to persuade Morris not to discuss political liabilities with his wife. Morris had clearly told her how Barton Goldsmith, the CIA director, had involved Sawchuck in his plan to cut deals with a handful of terrorism suspects. Goldsmith had argued he was doing it to protect the people of the United States, but it turned out the people of the United States didn't quite see it that way after the *New York Times* did an exposé on how he had leaned on various prosecutors and law-enforcement agencies across the country to allow certain terror suspects to walk, in return for information. Like the two nut-jobs who were about to set off a bomb in a Florida theme park when they were nabbed. The moment he was notified of the arrests, Goldsmith had leaned on Florida's highest-ranking law-enforcement officials to hold the two men until his people arrived. Goldsmith's intelligence experts had said something much bigger was coming, and those clowns in Florida agreed to tell everything they knew in return for a couple of air tickets back to Yemen.

Goldsmith had credited the deal with thwarting the plans of another underwear/shoe-type bomber before the guy boarded a Washington-bound plane in Paris, but the *Times* story could find no definitive link between the two events. It suggested Goldsmith was inflating the value of the intel he'd received from the two theme park terrorists to justify sending them home.

Goldsmith was pilloried. He resigned. Florida's attorney general followed.

What the *Times* didn't know was that Florida was not the first incident. A Saudi illegal with al Qaeda sympathies had tried to set off a car filled with explosives round the corner from the Guggenheim. But a woman looking out of her window had wondered why he kept checking the truck's cargo bed, and called NYPD. Goldsmith had been in the loop from the beginning, scooped the suspect, found out the suspect had a bunch of similar-minded friends he was willing to roll on, all in return for a trip home.

Goldsmith had called Morris.

Morris had balked at first. He'd prosecute the son of a bitch. Told Goldsmith he wasn't interested in making deals with terrorists. Goldsmith had replied, 'You know, terror suspects aren't the only people we have a lot of background intel on, if you get my meaning.'

Morris Sawchuck could only have guessed what Goldsmith might have had on him. Knowledge of one or more dirty tricks Howard had performed on his behalf. Campaign donations that hadn't gone through channels. Sawchuck allowed himself to be overruled. The bomber went home.

When the *Times* story broke, Howard and Morris waited for the other shoe to drop. The *Times* would keep digging and find out Morris had caved. They could see the headlines: 'New York Attorney General Allows Guggenheim Bomber to Skip Country.' It would finish him.

It is all this, Howard fears, that Allison Fitch has heard Bridget talking about on the phone with Morris.

'Bridget, how stupid are you? How stupid is Morris?'

'He never talked about anything specific. Everything was in general terms. Just that he's worried. That he hopes all this will blow over soon.'

'That's the thing, Bridget. We think it's going to blow over soon'—his voice is very low—'but not if you start blabbing about it on the phone where some blackmailing lesbo bimbo can hear you. If this woman really heard something, she's got dynamite. You understand what I'm saying?'

'Howard, really, she's bluffing. And even if she heard every word, she never heard—'

'Enough,' he says. 'Not one word to Morris. Not one single word.'

Abruptly, he strides out of the lobby to the sidewalk and heads east.

MICHAEL LAMBTON wants some. This is a celebration, after all. He's pulled it off. The vote's this Sunday, and all indications are the dumb bastards are going to approve it. Narrowly, probably, but they're going to ratify a contract that gives them a zero pay increase, a clawback in benefits, and no job-security clauses.

But they still have jobs, and they don't want them moving to Mexico or China or Taiwan. They want to keep making automotive parts and shipping them off, not just here in the good ol' USA, but overseas, too.

That is what Lambton tells them when he presents the company's offer. He calls it 'a punch to the gut of each and every hard-working man and woman in this plant' but he also calls it 'our best hope of keeping our jobs'.

There's grumbling in the union hall, but they know, in their hearts, that Michael Lambton is right. They know Michael Lambton is looking out for them. They know Michael Lambton is a straight shooter. They know shit.

Weeks ago, the company bosses had him in for a little chat in the boardroom. Three of them on one side of a long, mahogany table.

The company president says, 'You are going to sell our offer to your people. You can badmouth it all you want. But, in the end, you're going to sell this offer, because it's the best they're going to get in the current climate. Tell them that if they're happy for someone named Juan or Felipe or Dong Hung Low to make these parts, then vote to reject.'

Michael Lambton calmly pushes back his chair, stands, unzips his jeans and sends a stream of urine across the mahogany tabletop.

The company people, seated on the other side of the table, push their chairs back a little as the puddle spreads.

Lambton zips up and says, 'That's what I think of your offer. The economy's coming back. GM's having a good year, so's Chrysler. You guys are making money and you can afford to continue to give my workers a decent wage.' He smiled. 'Are we done here?'

The president turns to the man next to him and says, 'Get some paper towels and blot that up.'

When the mess is cleaned up, the president places a satchel on the table.

'It's half a million,' he says. 'You can count it if you want. All you have to do is get your people to vote for this contract.'

Lambton says, 'That does change things.' He is a practical man.

'Half now, half after the vote, assuming it goes the way it's supposed to,' the company president says.

Now, driving home from the union meeting, Lambton's certain he'll be getting the other quarter mil. In a few days, the members will mark their ballots. They'll hold their noses when they vote, but they'll go for it.

He thinks, briefly, about hitting a bar, maybe lucking into somebody. He may end up paying for it, and he can damn well afford it, but feels that's beneath him. He considers himself a good-looking guy.

He's heading down a quiet two-lane highway, hitting the wipers every ten seconds or so to clear some light drizzle coming down, when he sees a car pulled over onto the shoulder about a hundred yards up ahead. Some Japanese import wagon, the back door swung open. Some chick's trying to wrestle a spare tyre out of the back. He can only see her from behind, but he likes what he sees. Blonde hair to the shoulders, black jacket, blue jeans, over-the-knee leather boots. Slim.

Lambton slows as he cruises past. He noses over onto the shoulder just ahead of her car, kills the engine and takes out the key as he opens his door.

'Trouble?' he shouts. Figures, *Help her out, change her tyre, then see if she wants to grab a coffee somewhere*. He'll be all wet by that time. She'll feel sorry for him, indebted. Maybe she'll suggest he come back to her place, dry off.

The woman peers out from behind her car. 'Oh, thanks for stopping!'

He's around the back of the car now, getting a good look at her. High cheekbones. Long legs, jeans fitting her tight like leggings, tucked into her boots. Leather gloves. Something athletic about her.

'I guess I'm lucky you were going by,' she says.

'What's your name?'

'Nicole.'

'I'm Frank,' he says. Why use his real name?

'Is there anything I can do?' Nicole asks. She takes out her cellphone. 'I've got this app—I can turn the phone into a flashlight.'

'You don't want to get that all wet,' he says. He has a grip on the tyre and is levering it over the back bumper, getting ready to drop it to the ground.

'Which tyre's flat, anyway?' he asks.

'Front passenger,' Nicole says.

As he peers around to the front of the car, Nicole bends down.

'Nicole, that tyre doesn't look flat to—'

The ice pick, swift and noiseless, feels hot going into his right side, just above his waist. Nicole withdraws it and thrusts it into him once again, this time higher, between his ribs. She withdraws again, then drives the ice pick in a third time. Hard.

Michael Lambton gasps and falls to the wet gravel.

Nicole kneels down and says to him, 'Your people, they wanted me to tell you, they know you sold them out. They know about the double-cross.' Then she runs the ice pick into him a fourth time, piercing his heart.

She stands and turns her face up to the rain. It feels good. Cleansing.

She rolls Michael Lambton down into the ditch by the side of the road and slips the spare tyre back into the hold below the hatchback floor.

Once she's behind the wheel and heading off down the two-lane blacktop, her phone rings.

'Yes.'

'It's me.' No hello, no introduction. It's Lewis.

'I'm calling about your availability. I mean, it's not like you're exclusive with Victor any more. I may have something for you.'

'I'm about to take some time off.'

'But if I had something, could you take it on? It'd be worth your while.'

'What do you mean, if?'

'I have to make the case to my boss. I think he'll go for it.'

She really wants some time off, but she hates to turn down work.

'What's the job?'

'Some chick works in a bar,' he says. 'Piece of cake.'

'Let me know when you've talked to your boss.' She ends the call.

There's something about his voice. It reminds her, just a little, of her father's, although she hasn't spoken with him for many years. The miserable son of a bitch. But he's always in her head, dear old Dad.

She can still hear him saying, '*Silver?* We came all the way to Australia so you could win *silver*? You know what they say? If you win bronze at the Olympics, you're just happy to go home with a medal. But when you win silver, it eats you up for the rest of your life. It's like being the second guy who walked on the moon. Who remembers him?'

She can still remember the slap she got when she said, 'Buzz Aldrin.'

FIVE

The following morning, it was as though it had never happened. Even though I hadn't stopped feeling guilty about how I'd handled things after the visit from the FBI, Thomas was going about things the way he always did, which is to say, he stayed in his room and travelled the world.

So many things about him puzzled me. I wished I could get inside his head. He'd always been a mystery to me, even when we were kids. There was this bubble around him, something that kept me from getting through, and him from reaching out.

There was no shortage of theories about why Thomas was schizophrenic. When we were kids, bad parenting—specifically, bad mothering—was often blamed, which didn't go over well with our mom, who was a patient, loving woman. A nurturing woman, she'd have been more likely to mitigate the effects of someone's mental distress rather than exacerbate it.

Over time, other theories came to the fore. It was genetic. Environmental. A chemical imbalance in the brain. Stress. A childhood trauma. Processed foods. A combination of all of those things.

Or maybe something else entirely.

The bottom line was, no one really knew. And, Thomas, while troubled, was also tremendously gifted. His ability to remember all the things he saw while on Whirl360 was beyond my ability to comprehend. I asked him once if he'd be happier without this so-called gift, and he threw it right back at me. Would I be happier if I had no artistic ability? What I judged to be his curse, he saw as his talent. This was what made him proud.

My parents did everything they could to help Thomas, and loved him unreservedly. They took him to specialists. They met with all his teachers. Often, I was drawn into the circle of anxiety. Once—I think I was fifteen at the time—Thomas had been missing for hours. He'd often get on his bike and wander Promise Falls, mapping it, learning every square inch of it. He'd return, his notebook filled with street plans, detailed right down to the placement of the stop signs and fire hydrants.

This particular day, he hadn't returned home for dinner.

'Go and see if you can find him,' Mom said.

I hopped on my bike and headed downtown. It struck me that that was where I'd find him. The crisscross of streets was more intricate downtown, and offered more entertainment value for someone with Thomas's interests.

I couldn't find him. But I found his bike. It was tucked in an alley off Saratoga, between a barbershop and the Promise Falls Bakery. I went up the street and back, checking into every business, asking if anyone had seen my brother. At one point, I stood on the sidewalk at the front of a shoe store, overcame my fear of drawing attention to myself, and shouted, 'Thomas!'

When I went back to where I'd found his bike, it was gone.

I pedalled home furiously, getting there about ten minutes after he'd returned. Thomas was sullen, never saying a word through dinner. But that night, I had heard them in the basement, Dad speaking angrily to him. I had figured Thomas was getting chewed out for going AWOL. Whatever he'd been up to never came up again.

I was sitting at the kitchen table, pondering this and watching Thomas eat his cereal, when I said, 'Instead of making dinner, I have something else for you to do.'

He looked up from his bowl. 'What?' He sounded alarmed.

'The house needs cleaning. I'll clean the bathrooms, you vacuum.'

'Dad did the cleaning,' he said. 'I've never used the vacuum.'

'Do you agree that the house needs to be cleaned?' I asked.

Slow to answer. Finally, 'I guess.'

'Well, if Dad's no longer here, how do you think we should solve that problem? It's the two of us living here, at least for now, and I want to include you in the problem solving around here.'

'I suppose,' he said thoughtfully, 'you could do it.'

'I'm already doing the grocery shopping. And I've been making the meals. And dealing with the lawyer. And, Thomas, I have a job.'

'Me, too,' he said.

'That's true. But, I figured, if I have to cut into my work time to get errands done, then it's only fair that you should, too.'

'When did you want me to do this for you?' he asked.

'You have to understand, Thomas, that you're not doing this for *me*. Pitching in, sharing chores, we do that for each other, and for ourselves.'

'I guess so. So when do you want me to do this?'

'What about now? You get it out of the way and you've got the rest of your day free. Go and haul out the vacuum, I'll show you the basics.'

He went to the closet and dragged out the machine with all the grace and familiarity of a yak handling a set of golf clubs.

I gave him a brief lesson. At my urging, he flipped the switch and the machine roared to life. I shouted, 'I've got some mail and stuff to deal with, so I'll leave you be.'

I'd come back to Promise Falls in such a rush that I hadn't packed a laptop; I was using the email program on my cellphone, and any correspondence that required a reply of more than a few words was a pain to type out on the phone's keypad. Plus, I knew I had a few bills that needed to be paid.

Dad had a laptop. I took it out with me onto the porch. I sat in one of the wicker chairs there, opened up the computer and hit the power button. I entered the password to get into my email program.

Inside, it sounded like the vacuum had just sucked up a squirrel. Thomas had undoubtedly caught the carpet fringe. He'd figure it out.

I opened up Safari. I wanted to look at the residence Laura Grigorin had suggested might be a good place for Thomas. I went up to the corner of the screen to enter some key words into Google.

As soon as I began to type, a list of previous searches popped up onto the screen. These would have been the things Dad was looking up the last time he used this computer. Before he died. I glanced at the list. Three items.

smartphones

depression

child prostitution

I stared at the list for a long time.

The door opened. 'I think the vacuum's broken,' Thomas said.

HOWARD TALLIMAN is sitting on a bench in Central Park, just north of the Arsenal, south of 65th, waiting for Lewis Blocker.

For years, Howard has employed the former New York police officer. It started as the occasional freelance job, but that meant there might be times when Lewis was busy doing work for someone else. That didn't work for Howard. So he had put Lewis on an annual salary so he could be confident that whenever Lewis's skills were required, he would be available.

Howard needs Lewis right now more than he ever has before.

Howard looks south, sees Lewis. The man is just under six foot, with broad shoulders and a nose that had been broken years ago. It let people know he'd been hurt, and survived, and didn't have any qualms about getting hurt again.

Lewis Blocker nods at Howard and sits next to him. 'You could give her the hundred grand,' he says, 'but that won't be the end of your problem.'

'Go on.'

'I asked around,' he says. Howard does not have to ask Lewis whether he has been discreet. That's what Howard pays him to be.

'Allison Fitch owes money. She bounces cheques. She borrows money and doesn't pay it back. She hasn't been paying her share of the rent and when she gets money, instead of paying back the people she owes, she blows it on herself. I think, if you give her that money, it'll blow her mind. She'll get her own place, lease a flashy car, open a charge account at Bloomie's.'

Howard nods thoughtfully. 'So she'll be back?'

'No question. And the way she's going to spend that money, it's going to attract attention.'

Howard says, 'Maybe what we do is give her the hundred, but you have a word with her, make her understand that if she flashes the money around, or comes back for more, it might not be in her interest.'

'Hurt her,' Lewis says. 'A little.'

Howard can't look the ex-cop in the eye. 'You're the expert.'

'Yeah. And that's why I think you should hear me out on what I think you need to do. Because we haven't even addressed your other problem.'

'About what she might know?'

Lewis nods.

'I spoke to Bridget,' Howard says. 'She thinks it's *possible* Fitch might have overheard one of her phone conversations with Morris. It's *possible* they may have discussed his problem.'

'But it's not the sort of thing you want to leave to chance.'

Howard rubs his hands together. 'If you had a chat with her, you could determine what she knows and what she doesn't.'

'I don't think that's a good idea, Howard. If she doesn't actually know anything, we'll be telling her we've got more to hide than the fact that Bridget swings both ways. Gives her even more leverage.'

'What a mess. Lewis, how the hell did you miss this about Bridget?'

'Maybe because you didn't ask me to do anything but a superficial check. She was so perfect for Morris, you didn't want to dig too deep.'

Howard knows this is true. But he can't stop himself from adding, 'Well, you should have done what you knew was most prudent.'

'Interesting you should say that,' Lewis says. 'I'm going to recommend what I think you need to do about Allison Fitch.'

Howard looks wary. 'What?'

'You have to make it so she won't be a recurring problem.' Lewis waits for Howard to figure it out.

Once he has, his face blanches. 'No, that's not—look, I've done some things in my time. Things I had to do. But, Lewis, we don't kill people.'

Lewis gives a measured nod. 'It wouldn't be us, Howard.'

'What?'

'It wouldn't be you, and it wouldn't be me. It wouldn't be connected to us.'

Howard's mouth is very dry. 'Then . . .'

'I've already had a preliminary discussion with someone about our situation,' Lewis says calmly. 'I know her work, and she can do this.'

Howard shakes his head. 'I don't know. I just don't know.'

'Ask yourself how long you want this problem to continue. If you're prepared to endure it indefinitely, then give her the hundred thousand now.'

Howard stares ahead, then says, 'Do what you have to do.'

'THE VACUUM SUCKED UP the edge,' Thomas said as I came into the house, leaving Dad's laptop on the porch. He pointed. The power head appeared to have digested half of a carpet runner that ran between the front door and the kitchen. The machine turned itself off when it jammed.

'Thomas, just pull the carpet back out of it.'

The phone rang. I picked up. 'Yeah?'

'Ray, it's Alice, at Harry Peyton's office? We were wondering if you had a moment to sign a few papers related to your father's estate.'

'Uh, yeah, sure,' I said, trying to collect my thoughts. 'Of course. When does Harry want me to come in?'

'Well, it's actually pretty quiet here right now.'

'Fine. I'll be there in a few minutes.'

I hung up. When I turned round, I nearly bumped into Thomas.

'What's going on?' he asked.

'I have to go to the lawyer's office and sign some papers.'

'I'm going to go back to work,' Thomas said, his eyes darting upwards.

'Fine. I'll be back in a bit.'

Driving into town, I couldn't stop thinking about why my father would be scouring the Internet for information on child prostitution. The first two search items I could get my head around: he'd been talking about getting a new phone, and, based on the snippets I had heard lately from Harry and Len, maybe Dad was depressed. But child prostitution?

I tried to think of some logical reasons why Dad would be doing such a search. Maybe he'd seen something on television about the sexual exploitation of children. Maybe he wanted to make a donation to a charity that was working to free children from this kind of servitude.

Did that sound like my father? No.

So what other reason? The one I couldn't bring myself to consider was that Dad was *interested* in the subject.

There was one other possibility: Dad never looked up child prostitution in the first place. Someone else had been using Dad's laptop.

'You OK, Ray?' Harry Peyton asked as I pulled my chair close to his desk to sign a few documents.

I scribbled my signature in the places he was indicating. 'I'm fine.'

'How about things at the house? How's Thomas?'

I put the pen down. 'The FBI paid us a visit,' I said.

'They what? Ray, you should have called me! Did they have a warrant?'

'They just showed me their IDs.' I told him all of it. How they asked questions of Thomas and me. Finding out Thomas had sent all those emails to the CIA, addressed to Bill Clinton. How I'd heard him having an imaginary conversation with the former president.

'Unbelievable. You've got a lot on your plate, Ray.'

'There's something else,' I said. 'Did Dad ever . . . did he ever talk about dating anyone? You ever see him with anyone?'

'No. But you know, a man his age, there's every reason to think he'd be, you know, sexually active. Do you mind my asking why this is an issue, Ray?'

'No, no, it's OK,' I said. 'Forget I even asked. It's nothing.'

Maybe that was what I should have done. Forgotten about it. Pretended I never saw those two words on my father's computer. But before I let this go, I was going to see what web pages that search had led him to.

When I got home, Thomas was where I expected him to be: in his room. Dad's laptop was sitting on the kitchen table, closed. He must have brought it in from the porch and turned it off.

I opened the lid, hit a button, waited for the computer to power up. Then I opened the web browser. I went to the search field and typed in a single letter to bring up the previous searches. There was nothing there.

'What the hell?' I said under my breath.

I moved the cursor up to 'History' and clicked. It was empty. The list of all the web sites that had been visited with this machine had been erased.

MANY NIGHTS, even after all these years, she dreams of being on the bars.

It's 2000. The Sydney Olympics. Nicole is fifteen. Performing her routine on the uneven bars before thousands of spectators, hundreds of cameras, her coach. She feels the chalk on her hands, then leaps for the lower bar, grasping it firmly, spinning around it twice before having enough momentum to propel herself to the higher bar. She is soaring. There's nothing like it.

The nights she does not dream about the bars, she dreams about the kills. They are, in their own way, equally graceful. Swooping in on one's prey as noiselessly and as swiftly as moving from the upper bar to the lower. A perfect execution. Whether her dreams are of uneven bar routines or assassinations, they are always gold-medal performances.

She is on Orchard Street.

Nicole has been briefed. She has a picture. Tall, with long, dark hair. The target will be there. Allison Fitch. She shares an apartment, but the friend works days. Allison works in a bar at night, so she sleeps through the day.

Nicole doesn't know who this Allison Fitch is, or what she has done. But given that it is Lewis who has engaged her, she can guess that this woman presents a threat to someone important. Fitch has something on someone, and it may be in her phone—Nicole has been told to make sure she recovers it.

She pulls her black baseball cap down low on her forehead as she crosses Orchard. She feels in her pocket for the plastic bag. It's a strong one. Even if the woman claws at it with her fingernails, it will not tear. Nicole does not like guns. A gun is heavy, difficult to conceal. And it makes little use of the body. Nicole likes physical involvement. Suffocation involves strength. So does thrusting with an ice pick. But today she will use a simple plastic bag.

She stands at the entrance to the building and, before entering, glances up and down the street. Sees no police cars, nothing to worry her. A block away, there is a car, with some odd contraption strapped to its roof, stuck in traffic, but it is of no concern to her.

Nicole steps into the lobby of the building, studies the directory of names and buzzers. She presses several at once, careful not to buzz the one for Allison Fitch. A voice crackles from the speaker. 'Hello?'

But another, less cautious tenant has actually hit the button to buzz someone in. Nicole opens the door and enters the building, then waits for a couple of minutes. She doesn't want anyone opening their apartment door to see who was hitting the buzzer.

This is a building without elevators. She climbs the two long flights of stairs and is relieved to encounter no one. She determines that the apartment overlooking Orchard is the one at the very end of the hall. She approaches the door to apartment 205, but before going to the trouble of picking the lock, she tries turning the doorknob with her gloved hand.

No joy. It's locked. She reaches into the inside pocket of her windbreaker and finds the tool she carries for just such an occasion.

She opens the door a fraction of an inch and listens. She can see a sliver of kitchen, and beyond that, a small living room. A foldout couch has been left open. If the target is not using the pullout, she must be in the bedroom.

Nicole opens the door, steps in and closes it behind her without a sound.

She stands frozen, listening. A window must be open, because the sounds of the street are distinct. Nicole listens for another person. Snoring, soft breathing. A shower running. She hears nothing, yet senses a presence. She takes a couple of steps towards the living room.

She edges past a table. Nicole can see the bedroom door, and into the room. It's a typically small New York apartment bedroom. Eight by ten, maybe. Just enough room for the unmade double bed. A window on the far wall. Raised.

There she is, standing at the window, her back to Nicole. Dark hair hanging to her shoulders. Her hands resting on top of the air-conditioning unit. Looking down at the street. She is dressed. Blue skirt, white blouse.

There's only twelve feet between them. Nicole's measuring the distance in her head. She'll be on her in half a second.

Nicole reaches into her pocket and quietly draws out the white plastic bag. Waves it lightly to open it up.

She leaps onto the bed, uses it as a springboard. By the time her prey realises she's not alone, it's too late. Nicole has the bag over her head.

She lets out a muffled scream and then, just as Nicole knew she would, she's clawing at the bag. But Nicole has drawn the bag so tight it is like a second skin.

The woman, in her final gasping seconds, collapses onto the air conditioner. She rests there for a second, then drops to the floor.

Once she is certain the woman is dead, Nicole removes the bag, wads it into a tight ball, and returns it to her jacket pocket. She grabs a handbag that's on the bed and finds the phone. She slips it into her pocket.

Then she gets out her own phone, unlocks it, presses twice.

'Done. Cleanup set to go?' This is a job where the client doesn't want a body left behind, and removals are not Nicole's area of expertise.

'Yes.' Lewis.

She ends the call without another word, puts her own phone away. A golden performance. No falls. No fumbling on the dismount.

She is getting ready to leave when she hears the apartment door opening.

It's too soon for the cleanup crew to be here.

SIX

I rapped on Thomas's door to tell him that dinner was nearly ready.

'What are we having?' he asked.

'Burgers on the barbecue,' I told him.

When dinner was over, and the dishes were in the sink, I put my hand on his arm so he wouldn't jump up from the table and head back upstairs.

'You brought Dad's laptop in off the porch.'

He nodded. 'Someone might have taken it. I put it in the kitchen and I turned it off.'

'Did you do anything with the history?'

Thomas nodded. 'I erased it,' he said. 'I always do that. Every night when I go to bed I erase the history on my computer.'

'When you erased the history, did you look at it first?'

Thomas shook his head. 'Why would I do that?'

'Thomas,' I said. 'Do you ever use Dad's laptop?'

He shook his head emphatically. 'No, never. I have my own computer.'

'Did Dad ever lend his computer to anyone?'

'I don't think so. Can I go now? I lost time this morning, vacuuming.'

'Thomas, please. If no one has used that computer since Dad died, why was there still some history on it this morning?'

'Because when Dad used it, he turned it off himself. I'd tell him to erase the history, but he didn't worry about it like I do.'

I rested my back against my chair. 'OK. Thanks.'

But instead of getting up, he stayed in his chair.

'What is it?' I asked him.

'I know you're still mad about when the FBI people came to the door. And I haven't sent any emails to the CIA or to President Clinton since.'

'Good to know.'

'But what if I saw something I thought the CIA really should know about, like a crime? Would it be OK if I sent them just one little email?'

'Thomas, I don't care if you saw someone putting a nuclear bomb on a school bus, you are not calling the CIA.'

I could see the frustration on his face.

'Thomas, what is it?'

He shook his head. 'It's about something that's happening in a window. Sometimes things happen in windows.'

'Thomas, look, whatever it is, just don't worry about it.'

Abruptly, he pushed back his chair and stood. 'Fine.' He marched towards the stairs.

'Thomas, do not send a message to the CIA. Are you listening?'

He stopped. 'You're the one who isn't listening, Ray. You don't want me to call the CIA so I ask you what I should do about what's happening in the window and you don't listen.'

'OK, OK. You want me to have a look?'

'Yes,' he said.

I followed him up the stairs. There was a folding chair in Dad's bedroom. I grabbed it, returned to Thomas's room, and opened it up next to him. Thomas had nudged his mouse to bring the monitors back to life.

'So where the hell are we tonight?' I asked.

'This is Orchard Street. In New York. In Lower Manhattan.'

'Okey doke,' I said. 'Show me what you've got.'

Thomas pointed to a window on the side of what appeared to be a five-storey structure. An old tenement building.

'You see that window?' he said. 'On the second floor?'

There was a white blob in the window's lower half. 'Yeah, I see it.'

'I'm going to zoom in on it,' Thomas said. He clicked twice on the image. That had the effect of making it larger, but slightly less distinct. But it was starting to look like something.

'It kind of looks like . . . it looks like a head,' I said. 'But with something wrapped around it.'

'Yeah,' Thomas said. 'You can see the shape of the nose and the mouth, and there's the chin, and up here's the forehead. It's a face.'

'I think you're right. It looks like someone with a bag over their face.'

Thomas nodded. 'Yes. But the bag has to be on really tight.'

'I guess,' I said. 'Maybe it's a mask or something.'

'But there are no holes for the eyes, or the mouth, or the nose. If that's a mask, how is the person supposed to breathe?'

I stared at the image. 'I don't know, Thomas. It is what it is. Someone goofing around with a bag on his head. Maybe someone knew the Whirl360 car was coming and thought they'd do something silly for the camera.'

'I think this person is being killed,' Thomas said. 'This is a murder. I want you to check it out. I want you to go there.'

'You want me to go to New York to check out this window?' I said. 'I don't think so.'

'Well then, I guess I'll have to make some calls,' Thomas said, 'and I have no choice but to email the CIA and ask them to look into it.'

'Thomas, listen very carefully to me. First of all, you are not making any calls to the CIA or Homeland Security, or the Promise Falls Fire Department, for that matter. And, as far as my going into the city to look at this stupid window, that's not happening either.' I went downstairs.

A few minutes later, Thomas came downstairs. He went to the closet by the front door, opened it, and grabbed a jacket. I asked, 'Where're you off to?'

'New York,' he said. 'I'm going to look at that window.'

'How're you getting there?'

'I'm going to walk,' he replied. 'I know the way. It's 192.3 miles. If I walk twenty miles a day, I'll be there in—'

'Oh, for Christ's sake,' I said.

IF THE TRAFFIC'S NOT BAD, you can drive from Promise Falls to New York in about three and a half hours. But that's a big *if*, certainly where the latter part of the drive is concerned. So I opted for the train. The plan was to catch it early in the morning, do what I'd promised to do, and catch one home the same day, so I wouldn't be leaving Thomas alone overnight.

He'd promised he wouldn't do anything that would upset me while I was gone, so long as I kept my part of the bargain.

If Thomas wanted to think I was making this trip into New York just for him, he was welcome to. But the moment he started pushing for me to go into the city, I thought of the woman Jeremy wanted me to meet. It meant future money for me, and from the sound of it, quite a bit.

I called Jeremy and asked whether he could set something up for the following day. An hour later, he reported that Kathleen Ford could meet us for a drink at the Tribeca Grand Hotel.

Jeremy and I arranged to meet at the Waverly Restaurant, on Sixth Avenue, for lunch, which would be handy enough to get to the hotel, and to run my little errand for Thomas.

I was up before the sun, and caught the train at Rensselaer. I had time to think about whether agreeing to go by Orchard Street was a stupid thing to do—whether it would just encourage Thomas. But if it kept him from sending another message to a federal agency and attracting more unwelcome attention, it was a smart thing to do.

The problem with giving in to Thomas on this particular occasion was, what if he saw something else, in another window, in another city, and that city just happened to be, say, Istanbul? I figured I'd deal with Thomas on a case-by-case basis. I'd been able to dissuade him from doing anything rash when he'd got himself in a lather about that possible minor traffic mishap in Boston, so it was possible to discourage him from pursuing frivolous matters. But there was something about this covered face in the window that had got to him.

'People don't look up enough,' he had said to me.

I'd left home with a print-out of the scene in the window, and took it out of my pocket as the train ran down alongside the Hudson. I had to admit, there was something intriguing about the image. I wasn't inclined to buy Thomas's theory that the passing Whirl360 camera car, while on its mission to video all the streets in Manhattan, had caught an actual murder in progress. That was pretty far-fetched. But the longer I looked at the image, I had to concede Thomas's interpretation was not entirely off the wall. It did kind of look like a person being suffocated, as though someone had come up behind and slipped a bag over his or her head and drawn it tight.

But I also knew it could be any number of other things.

Before embarking on this mission, I had suggested to Thomas we do some online research. When it came to searching the net for specific information, I was better. So I got Dad's history-cleared laptop and entered into the search field 'Orchard Street New York' and then added the word 'murder'.

My goal here, honestly, was to take the wind out of Thomas's sails. If our search produced no stories about people being suffocated in windows, I hoped Thomas would mellow out a bit.

And there were no stories about people being suffocated in windows. The only story that even remotely caught my interest was a short news item about a thirty-one-year-old waitress named Allison Fitch of Orchard Street (no specific address given), who had been reported missing the last week of the previous August. The story had run the first week of September, but I didn't see any follow-ups, so it seemed likely the matter had resolved itself.

I got off the train at Penn Station and headed first to Pearl Paint, the huge artist supply store. I ended up buying a dozen Paasche airbrush needles and a couple of air caps, as well as a box of fine-point black Sharpie pens. Then I grabbed a cab and got dropped off in front of the Waverly.

Jeremy was already in a booth by the front window, looking at the menu, when I came through the door. I slipped in opposite him.

We ordered lunch as Jeremy told me Kathleen Ford wanted one animated drawing a week and was willing to pay $1,500 for each one. That might sound like a lot, but it actually meant dozens of drawings to make it work.

'I'll bet there's a program that'd make it easier,' he said.

I knew of a couple that would make the job much less labour intensive. Once I had an idea, I could probably knock one off in a couple of days, which would still leave me time for other freelance jobs.

Jeremy paid the bill and then we caught a cab to the hotel. Ford was fifteen minutes late, but she looked like a woman who never had to apologise for her tardiness. Five-ten, slim, mid-fifties, brilliant blonde hair, discreet designer labels. She said she was a huge fan of my illustrations, and then talked almost nonstop about all the important New Yorkers she knew who were going to be contributors to her new web site. Then, just as she whisked off to her next engagement, she said I had the job. The site was to be up and running in three months. I accepted.

Once she was gone, it felt as though a tornado had just whipped through. Jeremy and I agreed that we'd be talking soon, and I left.

Outside the hotel, I hailed a cab. 'Houston and Orchard,' I said.

HOWARD TALLIMAN had not been sleeping well for nine months; he hadn't had a good night's rest since the end of August. He'd lost weight; if it weren't for the bags under his eyes and his grey pallor, he'd look good.

Talliman's appearance and his short temper, brought about by too little sleep, were sources of embarrassment. They sent a signal that something was troubling him, and he did not want anyone to think he was worried.

Howard made other people worry.

The action he'd approved back in August, the wheels he had allowed Lewis Blocker to set in motion—with the intention of protecting Morris Sawchuck—had the potential to destroy them all.

Sawchuck was Talliman's ticket to the Big Show. Once Sawchuck was Governor of New York, it was only a matter of time, Howard knew, before he moved up the ladder from there. Sawchuck had the personality, the showmanship—even the perfect teeth—to make it to the White House.

Howard had believed that Bridget's lesbian affair with Allison Fitch, and what that woman might know about Morris's political problems, could derail all that. He'd trusted Lewis's instincts about what had needed to be done.

Not that Howard hadn't expected there to be some fallout once the job had been executed, as it were.

There had been one story in the *Times*. Police had tried to track down Allison Fitch's whereabouts when she failed to show up for work. The article reported that she was originally from Dayton.

A missing person in Manhattan was not news for long. Unless someone stumbled upon a body. No one had stumbled upon a body.

Ordinarily, a body being stumbled upon would have put Howard Talliman at ease. Because even if the rest of the world did not know what had happened to Allison Fitch, he would know what had happened to Allison Fitch. But he did not. Lewis didn't know, either.

Shortly after Nicole had been sent to do the job, Lewis had placed a call to Howard. 'I heard from Nicole. There's a problem.'

'What sort of problem?'

Lewis had explained that Allison Fitch, who worked nights, would be home throughout the day while her room-mate would not. But on this particular day, Lewis had continued, there was an unforeseen development.

'The woman in the apartment was not Allison Fitch. The wrong target was taken out.'

Howard had struggled to remain calm. The room-mate? Dead? Sure, Howard had caused collateral damage in the past. But nothing like this.

'What about Fitch?' he had asked Lewis.

'Gone,' Lewis had said. 'She walked in on it. Saw what happened. Took off like a bat out of hell.' In the intervening months, Allison Fitch remained missing. As long as she was out there, she was a ticking bomb.

And then Lewis had said, 'It gets worse.'

I THOUGHT Thomas's confidence in me might have been misplaced. He'd seemed so certain I'd return from Manhattan with The Mystery of the Head in the Window all solved. I really wasn't all that keen about heading down to Orchard Street. I mean, once I was able to see the window in question, what was I supposed to do? My hope was that the head would still be there; that it was, in fact, one of those Styrofoam heads used for wig displays.

A couple of minutes later, I thought I was in the general area. Below the second-floor window I was looking for was supposed to be a store that specialised in scarves, and beside it, a shop selling newspapers. The entrance to the apartments was a lobby door between the two businesses. I was to find it on the west side of the street.

And then, suddenly, there it was. The window. I looked again at the image Thomas had printed out for me. Studied the arrangements of neighbouring windows, where the fire escape came down, the storefront below.

There was no white head in the window above the air conditioner.

I got out my phone, set it to camera, and took a shot of the building.

Would this picture be enough to satisfy Thomas? Doubtful. I had to admit, if I were him, I'd find my effort somewhat halfhearted. I supposed it wouldn't kill me to go up there, knock on a door, say hello to whoever lived there. Maybe, if I had a peek into the apartment, that Styrofoam head I was so desperate to see would be sitting on a kitchen table or something.

I studied the window so I'd have a chance of figuring out which apartment it was once I was inside. I entered the lobby, which was really nothing more than an alcove with mailboxes and a directory.

Judging by the directory, there appeared to be five apartments on the second floor, the last names indicated with thin strips of shiny black tape.

The tape strips all looked weathered with age, and the one for apartment 205 was half-missing, reading 'ch/Walmers'. Kazinski was in 204, Goldberg in 203, Reynolds in 202 and Michaels in 201. I took out my phone and snapped a picture. I also took a shot of a note posted next to the directory, with a number for rental enquiries.

What to do, what to do? As I pondered this, a man came charging out of the inside door. Without thinking, I grabbed the handle before it could close.

I climbed two flights of stairs. When I was on the second floor, I took a moment to get my bearings so I could figure out which apartment was most likely the one that faced the street above the scarves store. I settled on 205.

With the print-out in my left hand, I knocked on the door with my right, the Pearl Paint bag swinging clumsily with it. When no one came after three seconds, I tried again. And waited.

I was about to knock a third time when a door down the hall opened: 203. I turned and saw a heavyset woman, looking at me through black, heavy-framed glasses. 'No one lives there,' she said. 'The girls are gone.'

'Oh, OK, I didn't know.'

'Been gone for months,' she said.

'OK,' I said again, nodding. 'Thanks.'

She stepped back into her apartment and closed the door.

So that was that. I turned left as I walked out of the front of the building, heading north up Orchard, thinking about what I would tell Thomas when I got home. Not much, really. I had given it a shot, but the place was empty.

I was sitting on the train when something that had been troubling me at an unconscious level came bubbling up to the surface again: *Why* was *the blade housing up, and the ignition in the 'off' position, on Dad's mower?*

THOMAS KNEW he was going to have to make his own breakfast and lunch. Ray had told him it was going to be his responsibility. 'There's bread and jam and peanut butter and tuna. Look around.'

Ray didn't seem eager to check the window on Orchard Street, but Thomas was pleased he'd agreed to it. He wasn't sure he'd have sent another message to the CIA outlining his concerns about the face with the bag over it—he wanted to keep his relationship with the agency on a professional level.

In the kitchen, he stood a moment, staring at the cupboards. He was pretty sure the cereal was in that cupboard next to the fridge. He opened it tentatively, and there was the box of Cheerios he was hoping to find.

The milk was in the fridge. He got a bowl, poured cereal into it, added milk, ate it all, and returned to his room, leaving the dirty dish on the table and the cereal and container of milk on the counter. Ray had said nothing about cleaning up. Thomas figured Ray would want to do that when he got home, just to make sure it was done the way he liked. That was how it had been with their father. Adam Kilbride had never let Thomas do the dishes.

After breakfast, he continued his exploration of San Francisco.

He returned to the kitchen just before one. Thomas found the peanut butter and some bread, and was in the middle of making himself a sandwich when there was a knock at the door. He set down the knife and went to see who it was.

It was Len Prentice. 'Oh, hi, Mr Prentice.'

He stood like he was expecting to be invited in, but Thomas didn't want to do that. He had never liked Len Prentice.

'Your brother around?' he asked.

'He's in New York City today,' Thomas said. 'He's checking to see whether somebody was murdered by having a bag put over their head.'

That stopped Len for a second. Then, 'You really are crazy, aren't you, Thomas? Can I come in?'

He hesitated, then said, 'I guess it's OK.'

'I was driving by and thought I'd pop in and see how you boys were getting along. So whattya been doing to keep yourself busy, Thomas?'

'I work on the computer.'

Len nodded knowingly. 'Oh, yeah, right. Your dad used to talk to me,' he said. 'He and I, we were friends. And he said you were always finding pictures of things on the Internet that got you all riled up.'

Thomas wanted Len Prentice to leave so he could finish making his peanut butter sandwich and take it upstairs with him.

'It was Marie who suggested I drop by. She thinks it would be a nice thing if you and your brother came over to the house for dinner.'

'I'd have to talk to Ray,' Thomas said. He would get Ray to tell them they couldn't go.

'Your dad used to say he just didn't know why you're the way you are. Happy to be cooped up, sitting on your computer all day. The thing I can't believe is, you wouldn't even go to your own dad's funeral. Was your little computer fixation so great you couldn't even do that for him?'

Thomas blinked. 'Why are you saying these things to me, Mr Prentice?'

'I don't know. I guess I'm a simple man, Thomas. I thought I knew what this schizo thing is you have, that it means you have a split personality, but your dad told me that it's not like that at all. What I don't get is, if you know you've got a problem, why don't you do something about it?'

'I don't have a problem,' Thomas said. 'I have to make my lunch. I'm making a peanut butter sandwich.'

'I've got an idea,' Len said. 'Why don't I take you out for lunch?'

'I already started making the sandwich.' Thomas pointed to the counter.

'So what? You can eat it later for an afternoon snack. I insist.'

'I don't want to go.'

'I think that's where your dad made his mistake. He always let you get your way. He needed to introduce you to new experiences.'

Thomas took a step back.

'You know, from what I hear, you're going to have to get used to being out of this house. What about when your brother sells this place?'

Thomas said, 'Maybe he'll decide to live here. We could live together.' But even as he said it, Thomas wasn't sure this was what he wanted. He loved his brother, but he could be difficult. Like their father, he was critical.

'Well, whatever happens, I'm sure it'll work out for the best,' Len said. 'Now, you want to grab a jacket or something? I don't know about you, but I could go for some KFC. You like KFC?'

Thomas did like KFC, but he did not want to go anywhere with Len Prentice. He felt himself becoming increasingly anxious. He might have been willing to go out, briefly, with people he liked and trusted, but he did not like or trust Len Prentice.

And his father never really had, either. They'd had a friendship. But whenever Adam Kilbride returned home from spending time with Len, he'd say, 'That guy can really suck the life out of you.'

Len grabbed Thomas by the arm. 'Let's go, pardner.'

Thomas wrenched his arm free. He put more into it than he needed to, and his hand flew up accidentally and slapped Len across the cheek.

Len stopped and said, 'Well, Thomas, I sure wish you hadn't done that.'

SEVEN

Truth be told, Lewis Blocker wasn't sleeping all that well, either.

Allison Fitch was out there, somewhere, and not knowing where she was, or what she might do, had Lewis worried for all the same reasons it did Howard Talliman. If she decided to walk into a police station and tell everything she knew, it was all over for them.

They had to make sure that did not happen.

Several steps were being taken. First, Lewis had Nicole watching Fitch's mother in Ohio. He figured, sooner or later, the girl would attempt to get in touch with her. What daughter in trouble didn't want to talk to her mom?

Lewis had decidedly mixed feelings about keeping Nicole on this project after the way she'd screwed up. His initial impulse had been to make Nicole pay the ultimate price for her mistake. But, right now, he needed all the help he could get, so he would use her until this mess was resolved.

Lewis also wanted to maintain surveillance on the Fitch apartment. Although he thought it highly unlikely the woman would return there, he believed it was possible someone who knew her might show up at some point. Such a visitor might provide a clue to Allison Fitch's whereabouts.

Lewis couldn't post someone in the hallway 24–7. And though he'd spoken to the landlord and arranged to make sure the rent was paid for the foreseeable future, Lewis didn't have the manpower to have someone in the apartment at all hours in case a visitor showed up. Which was why he installed the camera.

A pinhole affair, motion-activated, mounted behind the door. Whenever a person came to within a few feet of the apartment, it came on. Every day Lewis reviewed any images, which were automatically sent to his computer. Usually, it was the superintendent. One day, a delivery guy at the wrong door.

Lewis was thinking it was time to abandon this idea. And then the guy with the Pearl Paint bag shows up.

Lewis sat in the study of his Lower East Side apartment, looking at the monitor of his computer. The man knocked with the hand holding the bag from the art store. Lewis, in his investigation of Allison Fitch, had never seen him before. Had no idea whether this visit was in any way significant.

Then Lewis caught a look at the piece of paper in the guy's other hand. There was a colour image in the upper-left quadrant of the page. It looked like a grouping of windows. There was a logo in the upper-left corner.

Lewis was pretty sure he knew what it was. The Whirl360 logo. For that web site that allowed you to look at the actual streets of cities all over the world. If this was, as he suspected, the logo for Whirl360, then it made sense that the image on the page had been printed off that web site.

Lewis magnified the blurry image. It did appear to be a series of windows, like the ones on the old tenement buildings in the neighbourhood where Allison Fitch's apartment was. But it was impossible to see anything with any clarity. Well, Lewis reasoned, if this guy could find the image online, then he could do it, too.

He went to the Whirl360 site and entered 'Orchard Street, New York City'. And almost instantly, he was there, clicking his way down the street. When he got to the block where Fitch lived, he dragged the mouse across the screen, allowing himself to whirl around Orchard.

He positioned the image so he was looking directly at Fitch's building, moved the mouse to the top of it, clicked, held and dragged down, which had the effect of craning one's neck upwards to the upper storeys.

'What?' he said under his breath. 'What . . . is . . . that?'

He was focused on one particular window.

THEY MET AGAIN on the same Central Park bench. Lewis Blocker handed Howard Talliman a sheet of paper, folded once.

Talliman unfolded the sheet and looked at it, puzzled. 'I have no idea what this is.' Howard had never been to the Orchard Street address.

'That window, that's the apartment. What you're holding there, that's a print-out from the Internet.'

Howard touched the head in the window. 'Is this what I think it is?'

'Yes. You familiar with Whirl360?' Lewis asked.

'I don't live in a cave, Lewis.'

'That picture was taken from the web site. Anyone in the world with a computer who happens to explore Orchard Street can see that. What has to have happened is, one of those Whirl360 cars with the panoramic cameras was going along Orchard Street at the same time that Nicole was doing her thing at the window.'

Howard blurted, 'How the hell did you discover this? You just found it?'

'Someone came to the apartment. A man, I'd say late thirties, early forties. Knocked on the door. The camera activated.' Lewis nodded to the print-out. 'He had a sheet, just like this, in his hand.'

Howard put a hand to his head. 'Who was he? How would he have that?'

'I don't know.'

'What the hell *do* you know, Lewis?'

Lewis remained unruffled. 'I know that we have a couple of problems, Howard. The first is this man. Who is he? Why does he have that print-out? Did he happen upon it, or did he know it was already there? Is he acting alone, or on someone's behalf? Does he know what that image represents? Is he with the police? What did he want? Who was he looking for?'

Howard looked at Lewis. 'What's the second problem?'

'The image,' he said. 'It's still up there. On that web site.'

IT WAS NEARLY TEN when I turned down the driveway. What struck me first was how dark the house looked. The front porch light, the one at the side of the house, and the one on the barn door are on timers, so they were on. But there was no light emanating from behind the windows.

The front door was locked. I let myself in, turned on some lights, then stopped and listened. No sounds. Not that Thomas was ordinarily noisy.

'Thomas?' I called out. I had expected him to be waiting up for me. I could see through to the kitchen. Dirty dishes littered the table.

I mounted the stairs and knocked on Thomas's door. When there was no response, I eased it open. The bed was empty.

I stepped out into the hall. 'Thomas!' I called. 'Thomas! I'm home!'

Unease washed over me. I hoped the FBI hadn't taken him away. I went back downstairs, made my way to the door to the basement that was off the kitchen. 'Thomas?'

No reply, but I descended the steps, anyway. I pulled the chain to turn on a bare bulb fixture. Thomas was not there.

I went out of the kitchen door and sprinted across the yard to the barn. Once inside, I turned on the lights. There wasn't much in there, aside from the lawn tractor that had killed our father.

'Thomas! Damn it, if you're hiding from me—'

I cut myself off, knowing how unlike Thomas it would be to play hide-and-seek. Displays of playfulness were rare from him. Struggling to think where he might be, I killed the barn lights and went back to the porch, looking out to the road. Who was there to call, other than the police? Thomas had no friends.

That was when a car started slowing on the highway, coming from the direction of town. About two car lengths from the end of our driveway, it edged off the road, turned and started approaching the house. I came down the porch steps, worried that this was not someone bringing Thomas home, but someone bringing me bad news about him.

The car pulled up just behind mine, so that when the passenger door opened, I could see Thomas getting out, but not the person behind the wheel.

'Thomas! Where the hell have you been?'

He was holding something in his hand, about half the size of a clipboard. I realised it was one of those high-tech tablets that allow you to do a hundred things, including surf the web. He didn't look the slightest bit concerned about the worry he'd caused me.

'I went out to get something to eat. KFC. This thing is way better than the GPS in your car. What did you find out in New York? I want to hear everything.'

He strolled right past me, up the steps and into the house.

I heard the driver's door open and close.

'Hey,' Julie said. 'We had a great time. And this thing about somebody's head in a bag? Man, that's some kind of story.'

I said to Julie, 'What's going on?'

'You said drop by. I dropped by. You were out. Thomas was home. I asked him if he wanted to go out and grab a bite and he said sure.' She looked at me. 'You asking me in for a drink or am I gonna have to drive home sober?'

'What did you find out?' Thomas shouted. He had come back out, still holding the tablet in his hand.

'Give me a second here,' I said to him. 'I'll be right in.' To Julie, I said, 'Where'd he get that thing?'

'I'm letting him borrow it,' she said. 'I showed him how he could look up maps on it anywhere. Doesn't have to be sitting at his desk all the time.'

'I want to get one of these, Ray,' Thomas said.

'Thomas,' I said, aggravation creeping into my voice, 'I'll be in, in a minute.' Thomas went back into the house.

'He's right,' Julie said. 'He said you're mean to him.'

'I'm not mean to him. I'm trying to do my best.'

She smiled. 'I'm sure you are.'

'You're patronising me.'

Her smile broadened. 'Yeah, I guess. Listen, I'll just head back and—'

'No, come on in. You can fill me in on what a terrible brother I am.' I said, 'I'm surprised you got him to leave the house.'

'The gadget helped. That, and offering to get him some KFC.'

'That would do it,' I said as we walked inside.

Thomas was clicking away upstairs. He called down, 'Come upstairs!'

'I'd better deal with this,' I said. 'You wanna come up?' She nodded. 'I kind of need to prepare you for what it looks like up here.'

'Thomas already showed me,' Julie said. 'No big deal. My brother used to have naked women all over his wall. I'll take maps.'

I looked at her for a second and shook my head. 'OK.'

'Well?' Thomas said as we came into his room. 'So what happened?'

'I found the address. Here.' I took out my phone, opened the camera app, and handed it to him. 'There's a picture of the place.'

Thomas studied the image, then compared it to a print-out similar to the one he had given me before I'd gone to Manhattan.

He nodded. 'That's the window. The brick patterns all match up.'

'And, as you can see,' I said, 'there's no head in the window.'

'You say that like it proves something,' Thomas said. 'If someone had a car accident at the end of our driveway a month ago, and you took a picture of it, taking another picture at the end of our driveway today wouldn't prove that the accident never happened.'

'He's got ya there,' Julie said.

'I did go up to the apartment,' I said. 'The place is empty. A woman down the hall told me. No one's lived there for months.'

'Did you ask her if anyone had been killed in the apartment?'

'No. I'm guessing that's the kind of thing she might have mentioned. She said the girls or whatever had moved out a long time ago.'

'And the apartment has been empty ever since?' he asked.

I shrugged. 'I guess.'

Thomas still had my phone, and had swiped his thumb across the screen to see the next picture. 'What's this?'

'Oh, that's the directory, in the lobby.'

'Is that the landlord's number? You talked to him?'

'No, I did not talk to him.'

'Why didn't you talk to the landlord? He would probably know if someone had been killed in one of his apartments.'

Julie asked, 'How hard would it have been to talk to the super? Or some of the other neighbours?'

I glared at her.

'Yeah,' Thomas agreed. 'This wasn't much of an investigation. It's certainly not up to the standards of the Central Intelligence Agency.'

'OK,' I said, raising my hands in defeat. 'I did what I could. Honestly. There's nothing online about anyone being killed at that address. Whatever you saw, it's pretty clear it was nothing. The best thing to do now would be to let this go.' I took the print-out from my pocket and tossed it into the trash.

What Thomas said next came out of left field. 'I don't like Mr Prentice.'

I blinked. 'What? Why don't you like Mr Prentice?'

'He wanted to take me out for lunch and I didn't want to go.'

'Today? He came by here?'

My brother nodded. 'He grabbed me to make me go and then I hit him.'

I put a hand on his shoulder. 'Thomas, you hit Len Prentice?'

Thomas nodded. 'Only a little.' He stood so he could demonstrate. 'He grabbed me like that and then I pulled away and then I hit his face.' He did it in slow motion, touching my cheek with the back of his hand.

'What did he do then?'

'He left.'

I sighed. Before I could sell this house and go back to Burlington, I was going to have to get Thomas settled in a place where he'd be supervised. The other thing that alarmed me was that Thomas had got physical. In his defence, he'd been provoked.

'Thomas,' I said, 'it's not like you to lose your temper.'

'I know,' he said, settling back into his chair. 'Usually I'm good.'

'Come on,' Julie said softly. 'I think we could both use that drink.'

'WHO'S LEN PRENTICE?' Julie asked, as I handed her a beer from the fridge.

I told her, and said she might remember him from the funeral. When I described him, she did. 'Thomas has never liked him,' I said. 'Thing with Len is, he doesn't quite grasp the concept that some people are different. He figures if Thomas hears voices he should just put in ear-plugs, and his ailing wife should be more energetic so she can travel with him. You know.'

'Yeah, I know the type.'

We stood there in the kitchen, sipping our beers.

Finally, I said, 'Thank you for being so nice to him—taking him out for dinner, letting him use your iPad.'

'You see, that's what he's talking about,' Julie said. 'You're thanking me for spending time with him. Like I was baby-sitting.'

'I never meant—'

'Thomas is a nice man,' Julie said. 'A decent, well-meaning guy. Yeah, he's got some issues. He told me how he got you to go to New York looking for this head-in-a-bag person. Did you really go to the city just to do that?'

'I had a meeting about a job, too.'

'Did you know he dreams about your dad every night?'

He'd never told me. 'I'm sure he misses him,' I said.

'And you remember Margaret Tursky?' Julie asked.

I had to think. 'Yeah, I do. Red hair? Braces?'

'Thomas had a real thing for her.'

'He and I, we don't really talk about stuff like that. There's kind of a lot going on around here, Julie, since our dad passed away.'

She said, 'Look, I know I'm speaking out of turn here. There's just more to Thomas than meets the eye.' She reached out and poked me in the chest. 'And you're not mean.'

'But he said I was.'

She nodded. 'He did. But after that, he said you're just trying to do the right thing. Ray, he loves you, he really does.'

I said, 'I guess I don't always look at the entire person.'

She took a step closer. 'You're just really close to the situation and, like you say, you've got a lot on your plate. Don't beat yourself up about it.'

'Let me just try again and say thanks, without it meaning anything derogatory about anyone.'

She smiled and nodded. 'You are welcome.' She gave me a peck on the cheek. 'All is forgiven.'

I set my beer on the counter and leaned in to kiss her, and not on the cheek, and she was showing no signs of trying to stop me from doing this, when Thomas started shouting from upstairs.

'Ray!'

I let go of Julie as I heard Thomas coming down the stairs. He said, 'I called the landlord.' I recalled that he'd lingered on the picture on my phone of the tenement building's directory. He'd memorised the number.

Thomas continued, 'He had some interesting things to say, which you would have found out if you'd taken the time to ask.'

Julie started heading for the door. 'G'night, guys,' she said.

EIGHT

There were times when Nicole wondered how it was that someone who'd beaten the odds to make it to the Olympic Games—who had returned home with a silver medal—could be that same person sitting there now, surrounded by electronic eavesdropping equipment, waiting for a break so she could find Allison Fitch and kill her?

Well, you had to do something*, right?*

Anyone else might have returned from the Games with their head held high. *OK, so maybe you didn't win gold, but bringing back a silver medal, doesn't that say you came pretty damn close?*

'Close only counts in horseshoes,' her father had always liked to say. And her coach wasn't much better. The two of them, those two impossible-to-please men, had put all their hopes and dreams on her.

She had started doing poorly in school. Her father wanted to know what the hell was wrong. Did she take a stupid pill in Australia?

Nicole—of course, that wasn't her name then—knew what the problem was. She could never make him happy, so why bother? If her mother hadn't had cancer when Nicole was twelve, things might have been different.

She didn't just let her grades slip. She partied. She slept around. She did drugs. Let her once perfectly toned body get out of shape.

When she was eighteen, she met a man thirty years older than she was, who worked for someone who ran a meth lab. His name was Chester and he had a Winnebago that he used to load up with product. Because Chester's boss was linked into a major distributor based in Las Vegas, it meant making plenty of trips to Nevada, so Chester hired Nicole to tag along with him. If he ever got pulled over by police, it looked less suspicious: he'd tell them she was his daughter, and he was taking her out west to be with her mother.

They made the trip from New Jersey to Vegas a dozen times. Always pulling the RV into the same warehouse on the outskirts of Vegas, making the exchange with the same people.

It was the thirteenth trip where things went off the rails.

Nicole knew something was up the moment the warehouse door began retracting. Usually, first thing they'd see would be the guys' Escalade sitting in there, the boys leaning up against the grille. Instead, there was a Ford Explorer. No one outside the car but two inside.

'I don't like this,' Nicole had said.

'Don't worry about it,' Chester replied. 'I got a call a couple of hours back, while you were sleeping. Said they'd have someone else receiving today.'

Nicole had taken a few steps back into the kitchen, slipped open a drawer, grabbed something. Chester pulled the RV up alongside the Explorer, and opened up the side door. The two men from the Explorer were out now, waiting near the door of the RV for Chester to hop out.

One had dirty blond hair, the other one didn't have any hair at all.

'Hey, fellas,' Chester said. 'Don't believe we've met before.'

The blond one reached behind his back with his right hand, pulled out a gun that had been tucked into his jeans, and shot Chester through the head.

Nicole had been standing to the side of Chester when the gun went off. Chester hadn't even hit the ground before Nicole had the knife out of her back pocket. A four-inch blade, solid handle. Very sharp.

Something happened in that moment. It was like she was back in Sydney.

Suddenly, her body had known instinctively how to move, how to spring, how to measure distances. And there wasn't that much distance to cover.

The knife went in his neck fast. Blondie went down on the cement floor.

The bald guy had jumped back when the blood spurted and had started running for the Explorer. She bolted after him, caught up just as he had the door to the car open and was half-inside. She threw all her weight against the door, slamming it against him, smashing his head up against the pillar.

He was seeing stars when she ran the knife into his side. She opened the door, allowing him to slide to the cement. She plunged the knife into him a second time to let him know she was serious. 'Who do you work for?' she had asked. 'Tell me and I'll get you an ambulance.'

'Higgins,' he gasped.

Then she had slit his throat.

THEY FOUND the boys' Escalade in the desert. They'd all been shot in the head, the SUV set ablaze. Their boss, a man named Victor Trent, offered Nicole a job. He was impressed, and grateful—not only that she had killed the two men who'd murdered his employees, but that she'd had the presence of mind to get the name 'Higgins' out of them.

If he'd known her a little longer, he'd have had her take care of Higgins herself. But he had one of his long-time employees do that. Higgins met his maker in the desert, too, but no one ever found him. Nor did anyone ever find the two men Nicole had killed in the warehouse.

Nicole had, Victor quickly determined, abilities that far exceeded other girls—and most guys—her age. She had control. She had discipline. She had a willingness to learn. There was always work for a woman like Nicole. She never told him who she used to be, and he never asked.

She spent five years working for Victor and was paid well. He introduced her to a former NYPD officer by the name of Lewis Blocker. Victor had hired Lewis to do some surveillance work for him, and in addition wanted him to teach Nicole the craft. She learned a great deal from him.

Finally, Nicole had reached a point where she did not want to work solely for Victor Trent any more. She had invited him for dinner at Picasso in the Bellagio. Told him what a wonderful mentor he had been to her, how much she'd valued his friendship and guidance, but she wanted to go it alone.

And Nicole had done pretty well, until now.

It was bad enough she'd killed the wrong person. But to have the intended target then show up, see what had happened, and get away? Nicole took her job seriously. She wasn't in this line of work because she took pleasure in ending someone's life, although there was the satisfaction of a job done well. Having screwed up a job, she had an obligation to make it right. Too bad it was taking so much longer than anticipated.

Nicole had been monitoring Allison Fitch's mother's residence for months now. She'd got into it within days of Allison's disappearance, while Doris Fitch was out meeting Dayton police to discuss what progress was being made in New York to find her daughter. Nicole had used that time to plant a listening device on Doris Fitch's phone, and another within the apartment itself, and to install a program on the woman's computer that would allow Nicole to monitor it from her own laptop. Nicole figured it was only a matter of time before the daughter got in touch.

Not that this system was foolproof. Allison could approach a third party to relay a message to her mother. But, if and when such a message was delivered, there'd likely be a change in Doris's routine. She'd book an airline ticket, for example. Nicole just hoped it wouldn't be too much longer. She hadn't made a dime in months. She was dipping into her reserves.

Maybe it was time to get out of this line of work before her luck ran out, if it hadn't already. She had a bad feeling about Lewis—that he was going to settle up with her for her mistake. She'd have to be ready.

Nicole had found a vacant apartment across the street that allowed her a view not only of Doris Fitch's apartment, but the lot where she parked her car, a black Nissan Versa. It wasn't possible to sit by the window and watch the woman's place twenty-four hours a day. But the surveillance equipment was voice activated. The moment it was engaged, the recording equipment began. If the Versa moved, a tiny beacon would alert Nicole.

Still, it was prudent to stay close. Nicole's cellphone rang. 'Yeah?'

'Hey,' Lewis said. 'You have to go to Chicago.'

The way this son of a bitch was talking to her lately. She didn't like it.

'Can't,' she said.

'Not up for debate. You got your laptop in front of you?'

'Hang on. OK, go ahead.'

'Go to the Whirl360 site, then go to New York. Orchard Street. I'm guessing you know the address.'

'OK, so I'm on the street,' she said. 'What's the deal?'

'Pan up.'

Nicole clicked and dragged her finger down across the laptop's track pad, altering the perspective on the image to the building's second floor. She saw the window.

'Tell me I'm not seeing this,' she said.

SHE COULD DRIVE to Chicago in four hours.

Lewis had given Nicole a name: Kyle Billings. Thirty-two years old. Had worked for Whirl360, at their Chicago head office, for three years. Kyle was responsible for, among other things, overseeing the program that deleted selected portions of the streetscapes when they were posted online.

Nicole needed Kyle to go into that program and delete an image on Orchard Street before anyone else found it. Some guy had shown up at the door, a Whirl360 print-out in hand. Lewis was on it, trying to figure out who the guy was.

What she had to do was find Kyle Billings, and use all her powers of persuasion to get him to go into the Whirl360 database of streetscapes, erase that image in that second-floor window, and purge it from the database for ever. She knew Kyle Billings would do exactly what she wanted.

Kyle Billings had a wife.

NINE

'Thomas?'

'Yes?'

'It's Bill Clinton.'

'Oh . . . hi. It's good to hear from you.'

'How are things going?'

'They are going very well. Have you been getting my updates?'

'Of course. Just terrific work. But, Thomas, there is something I'm a little worried about.'

'Yes?'

'I understand the FBI came to see you the other day.'

'That's right. Remember we talked about this? I think they were just making sure I was staying on task.'

'Sure. But you have to be very careful these days, Thomas. Never reveal anything very personal, or you might be perceived as being weak. This would be true for any traumatic incidents in your life. You keep them to yourself, and you move forward. Do you understand?'

'I believe so.'

'And cover your tracks. Like erase your computer history—'

'Sure. I do that, Bill.'

'I can't begin to tell you how proud I am of you, Thomas. Everyone at the agency is very impressed.'

'I won't let you down. Since you're on the line, I wanted to tell you something. When I was memorising the streets of New York, I saw—'

'Thomas, I have to go. Maybe next time, OK?'

THOMAS WOULDN'T TELL ME anything about his chat with the landlord after Julie left. He said he was still too annoyed with me. He went to his room and closed the door. I could hear him chatting with one of our former presidents.

So, the following morning, when he came down to the kitchen, I asked nothing. Except what kind of cereal he wanted.

Halfway through the bowl, as I was pouring myself a second cup of coffee, Thomas said, 'Don't you want to know about my conversation?'

'Who with?' I asked, figuring he meant Bill Clinton.

'With the landlord. Mr Papadapolous.'

'If you want to tell me. You didn't last night, so it's up to you.'

'I think I woke him up,' Thomas said. 'He seemed very angry. And I had some trouble understanding him. He had some kind of accent.'

'I'd bet Greek. Never mind. Carry on with your story.'

'I told him who I was, and that I am a consultant to the Central Intelligence Agency.'

I put down my coffee. 'Thomas, no.'

'I didn't want to lie. And I think identifying myself that way made him more agreeable to answering my questions.'

I figured it was only a matter of time before the FBI returned.

'I asked him who had lived there before,' Thomas said. 'Two women.'

'That's what the woman down the hall said,' I reminded him.

'I asked if they were sisters, or a mother and daughter, or just friends, and he said they were room-mates, but not very good friends, because sometimes one of them didn't always pay her rent on time.'

I nodded. 'Good questioning.'

'He said their names were Courtney and . . . the other one, I think he said was Olsen but it was hard to tell with his accent.'

'That's a first name and a last name.'

'"Olsen" was a first name. I have the last names. I wrote them down. He said as far as he knew, Olsen still hasn't been found.'

I perked up. 'What do you mean, hasn't been found?'

'He said Olsen disappeared. And I asked him who was living in the apartment now, and he said nobody. But,' Thomas said, 'the apartment is being rented.'

'Who's renting it?'

'Mr Blocker,' Thomas said. 'Why would someone rent an apartment but not use it?'

'Lots of reasons. Maybe he doesn't live in New York but has to come in all the time on business.'

'I don't know. But what I do think is, it's probably the Olsen woman who's in the window. She got killed, and that's why no one has seen her.'

'I see. And why was she killed?'

He thought a moment. 'So Mr Blocker could have her apartment when he came into Manhattan.'

I laughed. 'I was in the building. I don't think there's an apartment worth killing for.' I placed my palms on the table. 'Look, Thomas, all we know is, two women used to live there, and now they don't, and your landlord friend says Mr Blocker now pays the rent on it but doesn't actually live there. That little bit of information doesn't add up to a murder.'

'Except one of the women is missing.'

'According to the landlord, who is not exactly a detective for the New York Police Department. Maybe the woman's been found, but no one's bothered to tell this guy.'

'That's a good idea,' Thomas said. 'Calling the New York police.'

'I didn't say that was a good idea. I just said that the landlord might not be your best source for information.'

'Then we should go to the best source.'

'OK,' I said. 'Leave this with me. I'll put in a call to the New York police. Ask them about this missing woman, see if she turned up.'

'And tell them to go online, check out Orchard Street on Whirl360, and tell them to look at the face in the window.'

'Sure,' I said.

Thomas went back to eating his cereal. We were done with this. The odds of my picking up the phone to talk to the NYPD were about as good as anyone at the NYPD paying any attention to me.

I told Thomas I was driving into town and would be back in an hour. 'I'd like you to make lunch today,' I said. 'For both of us. And I'll do dinner.'

He stopped and spun round in his chair. 'Do I clean up, too?'

'Yes. Catch ya later,' I said.

I PULLED INTO THE DRIVEWAY of a single-storey ranch on Ridgeway Drive and rang the bell. It was Marie Prentice who answered.

'Why, Ray!' she said, holding open the screen door. She shouted into the house, 'Len! Ray's here!'

A door in the hallway opened and Len emerged from the basement. I knew he had a workshop, that he made furniture.

Len cracked a nervous smile. 'Hey there,' he said. 'You on your own?'

'Yeah,' I said.

'Why don't you come downstairs and I'll show you what I've been working on,' he said, giving me a look that told me he knew why I was there, and that he didn't want to talk about it in front of his wife.

'Sure,' I said.

He closed the door behind him as he followed me.

'Nice workshop,' I said. It looked as though Len had every tool a master craftsman might need. 'So, what are you working on?'

'I don't have any projects on the go,' Len said. 'I figured you'd want to talk privately.'

'Thomas told me there was an incident yesterday,' I said. 'I came over to find out more. I understand Thomas struck you. I'm sorry.'

'I guess he can't help it,' Len said. 'Being crazy and all.'

'He's not crazy,' I said. 'He has a mental illness. You know that. What happened, exactly? When you came out to the house.'

'I dropped by, just to see how you boys were doing—that's the kind of thing your dad would have wanted me to do. You weren't there, just Thomas. He said you were in New York.'

'And what happened?'

'I tried to do something nice, that's what happened.' Len cleared his throat and continued, 'I offered to take him out for lunch.'

'You know Thomas doesn't like to leave the house much.' I didn't add that he especially wouldn't have liked leaving it to go out with Len.

'Yeah, yeah, I know that, but I thought it would do him some good.'

'So when did Thomas hit you?'

Len shrugged. 'I guess I was kind of pressing the point. Trying to talk him into coming out. I took hold of his arm. He yanked it back and he caught me on the side of the face. If Thomas said it was anything more than that, if he said I hurt him or anything, that's totally not true.'

'He never said anything like that,' I said. 'Len, I suspect you meant well, and I know you were my father's friend, and I mean no disrespect, but I won't have you calling Thomas crazy. He's a good, gentle, decent person. I'm not going to try to argue that he's not a bit unusual. But if he doesn't want to take you up on your offer to go to lunch, you need to respect that.'

As I turned for the stairs, Len said, 'He's not so gentle, you know. Your dad told me. Thomas could get real angry. Did you know he tried to push your dad down the stairs one time? Oh, he made all kinds of excuses for your brother's behaviour, but if you want my honest opinion, he ought to be locked up in a loony bin.'

KYLE BILLINGS was in mid-whisper. 'Are you there? Hello?'

'I'm here,' Nicole said, putting the phone to her ear.

'It's done.'

'The image is gone?'

'Yes. The head's been blurred out, and now the window just looks dark.'

'Are there any previous versions that can still be accessed?'

'No. They're wiped. The database is clean.'

'That's excellent.' Nicole smiled at Rochelle Billings, who was smiling back and tearing up a little. 'OK, Kyle, I guess we're done. Thank you for this. You'll find your wife in the basement when you get home.'

'Is she OK?'

'She's fine. Rochelle, say hello.' Nicole held out the phone.

'Hi, honey! I love you!'

'You, too, babe. Everything's going to be OK.'

Nicole pulled back the phone. 'OK, Kyle. Goodbye.'

She ended the call, and tossed the phone, which was Rochelle's, onto the carpet. And then she just sat there, looking at the floor. Thinking.

'What?' Rochelle asked. 'Aren't you going to go? He did what you want, didn't he?'

'He did,' Nicole said. 'He did.' She took out a plastic bag from her pocket.

'What are you doing with that?' Rochelle asked.

It took much longer than she would have liked but, when it was done, Nicole settled back in her chair and waited for Kyle Billings to come home.

LEN PRENTICE'S ATTITUDE, and comments, had left me shaken.

Calling Thomas crazy had made me furious, but his revelation that Thomas had tried to push our father down the stairs had left me deeply troubled. Dad had never mentioned anything like this to me, but that didn't mean the incident never occurred. Whatever problems he'd had sharing a house with Thomas, he had kept from me.

Driving away from the Prentice house, I felt myself getting swallowed into some kind of vortex. I'd come to Promise Falls to deal with my father's estate, set my brother up some place and get rid of the house, but really hadn't made a dent in any of it. I kept finding myself sidetracked: strange and unsettling words on Dad's laptop, Thomas's preoccupation with that face in the window, an unfortunate encounter between Thomas and Len Prentice, and apparently another between Thomas and our father.

There was this other thing niggling away at my brain, too. The lawn tractor. The key in the 'off' position. The blade housing raised, which indicated Dad had stopped mowing the lawn. But the job hadn't been finished.

Was it possible someone had come down the hill to talk to him? It was almost impossible to carry on a conversation with the tractor running, so Dad would have turned off the ignition. And if he thought this interruption was going to be an extended one, he'd have brought up the blades.

It wasn't the best place for a conversation. It was a precarious spot, given how steep the slope was. Dad, sitting on the tractor, would have had to lean into the hill continually to keep the machine from tipping. Sitting straight up in the seat might have been all the leverage that was needed to topple the damn thing. Which was what happened. But if someone had wanted to talk to him, then who was that person, and why hadn't they called for help?

Thomas had been the one who finally dialled 911. After he'd found Dad, already dead, pinned by the machine. Unless Thomas was the one Dad had stopped for. To have that conversation. If it had turned into a heated argument, a simple shove would have been all Dad needed to go tumbling, taking the machine with him. No. That was unthinkable.

I steered the car over to the shoulder, stopped and put it in park. I got out my phone. A few seconds later, someone said, '*Standard*. Julie McGill here.'

'Why don't you come out to the house for dinner tonight?'

'Is this George Clooney?'

'Yes.'

'Sure.'

WHEN I WALKED into the kitchen, I saw a tuna sandwich sitting on a plate on my side of the table. There was a napkin folded at the side, and an opened bottle of beer that was now warm to the touch.

He made my lunch. I knew I'd asked him to, but I guess my expectations had been low. I felt bad.

I knocked on Thomas's door and stepped in. 'Thanks for making me a sandwich,' I said. 'Did you eat? I hope you weren't waiting for me.'

'I ate. And I put my plate and my glass and the bowl I mixed up the tuna and mayonnaise in into the dishwasher.'

'Thanks, man. We're going to have a guest for dinner. Julie.'

'OK.'

I sat on the edge of the bed, which put me at a ninety-degree angle to him as he stared at the screen. 'I want to ask you a few things about Dad.'

'What?'

'OK, first, the day Dad died, did you go out and talk to him when he was cutting grass on the side of the hill?'

'I was going to. I was looking for him.'

'You didn't go out, even to give him a phone message or anything? Something that made him turn off the machine and lift up the blades?'

'The only time I went out was to find him because I was hungry.'

'And he was trapped under the tractor?'

He nodded.

'The two of you, you got along pretty well most of the time, didn't you?'

'Sometimes he got angry with me,' Thomas said.

'Did you—did you try to push Dad down the stairs?'

Thomas nodded. 'Yes. Sort of. About a month ago.'

'Tell me about it.'

'He wanted to talk about something that happened a long time ago. I'm not supposed to talk about it. Dad told me not to.' He paused. 'At the time.'

'Thomas, what are you talking about? When was this?'

'When I was thirteen.'

'Dad did something to you when you were thirteen that he told you never to talk about?'

My brother hesitated. 'Not . . . no, not exactly.'

'Thomas, look, whatever happened, it was a long time ago, and Dad's gone. If there's something you need to tell me, then you can do it.'

'President Clinton says I'm not supposed to talk about this stuff. It makes me look weak.'

'OK, but, Thomas, can we just go back to the thing that happened a month ago. What was that about?'

'Dad wanted to talk about the thing that happened when I was thirteen.'

'Out of the blue, Dad wanted to talk about it again?' I was grasping here, trying to figure out what the hell Thomas was talking about, what this thing was that had happened twenty-two years ago.

'Yes. He said maybe he was wrong and that he was sorry about it. Dad was following me up the stairs, saying he wanted to talk to me about it, but I didn't want to talk. I'd tried really hard not to think about it for all those years and so I turned round and said I didn't want to talk about it and that if he didn't want to listen to me when I was thirteen why did he want to listen to me now and I put my hand out to stop him from following me and I didn't push hard but he tripped on the stair and he fell a little bit.'

'Fell a little bit?'

Thomas nodded. 'He was on the fourth step going up, so he didn't fall far. I was sad that he fell.'

'Did he go to the hospital? Or the doctor?'

'No. He took some extra-strength Advils. He said it was OK. He said I was entitled to be mad, and if I didn't forgive him, he'd live with that. And the pills started to work, but it hurt for about a week.'

Len must have noticed my father was in pain and asked what he'd done to himself.

But what was Dad sorry about? And why didn't Thomas want to talk about it? What did my dad think he wouldn't want to forgive him for?

'You need to tell me,' I implored. 'I need to know.'

'No, you don't. It doesn't matter. He's not going to hurt me again.'

'Dad? Dad can't hurt you any more?'

Thomas shook his head. I didn't know whether he was saying no, or dismissing me. 'Dad would have believed me if you'd looked up at the window,' he said, but when I asked him to explain, he looked away.

AT DINNER, it struck me that Julie was not digging into her fish fingers with much enthusiasm, although the same could not be said about her glass filled with pinot grigio.

'Sorry,' I said. 'When I went to the store the other day, I kind of loaded up on stuff that would be easy to throw together.'

'No, it's great,' Julie said. She looked at me. 'You've been quiet.'

'I guess I've got a few things on my mind.'

'Like calling the police?' Thomas asked. 'You said you were going to call the police in New York.'

'I haven't done that yet,' I said. 'I'll get right on that tomorrow.'

If Thomas suspected I was being less than sincere, he didn't show it. He took his plate to the sink, rinsed it off and said he was going to his room.

'Let me clean up,' Julie said.

'Leave it,' I said. 'Come on.' We took our glasses of wine into the living room and sat down on the couch.

'You're not going to call the police, are you?' she asked. I had filled her in on my pledge to get in touch with the NYPD.

I shook my head. 'No.'

Julie kicked off her shoes. 'I get that. I mean, it would be hard to get anyone to listen to you. A blurry white head in a window. I love Thomas, I do, but after what you told me about the FBI coming to visit, maybe keeping a low profile is a smart thing.'

She knocked back the rest of her wine, put our glasses on the table, and snuggled in to me. I put my arms around her and placed my mouth on hers. This went on for a while until Julie said, 'We don't have to stay on the couch.'

'Upstairs,' I said. 'Thomas won't be coming out of his room. Some time around midnight he'll pack it in. We're not going to see him before that.'

So we slipped upstairs. I steered Julie into the bedroom at the end of the hall, and over to the queen-sized bed my father had slept in.

I barely had the door closed when Julie started unbuttoning my shirt. I slid my hands under her sweater as we moved to the bed.

'I know some excellent stress-reduction techniques,' she said, as she slid off my jeans and boxers. She tossed them onto the floor and whisked her top off in one swift motion, exposing a lacy, purple bra.

'Purple?' I said. 'Is that the same—'

'*Ray!*' I could hear Thomas's door open. 'Ray! Come here! Ray?'

I went to call out, then stopped. I didn't want to bring him in here.

'Where are you?' he called. 'Ray? Are you in Dad's room?'

The door was flung open. Thomas walked in. Didn't even look at Julie as she grabbed the bedspread to cover herself.

'Ray!' he shouted. 'It's gone! The head's gone.'

'What?' I said, reaching down quickly to retrieve my boxers.

'You have to see this!' he said. He ran back down the hall.

I followed him, wearing nothing but my underwear. Julie had struggled back into her top and came along after me.

I saw that Thomas had all his monitors focused on the window on Orchard Street. It sure looked like the same window, except this time there was nothing in the frame. It was black. No more bag-wrapped head.

Thomas stood there, pointing. 'Where did it go? What happened to it?'

I stammered, 'They must, they must have updated it.'

'No!' he said. 'Everything's the same except the head is gone!'

Thomas grabbed a sheet of paper off the table and handed it to me. A print-out of the original image. 'It's exactly the same, right?'

I studied the print-out. 'It's the same, Thomas, it's the same.'

Thomas asked, 'Why is it gone, right after you went to check it out?'

I couldn't make any sense of it. I felt a chill.

Julie touched my brother gently on the arm. 'OK, you know what, Thomas? Tell me all about what you've seen, and what you think it means.'

LEWIS BLOCKER called Howard Talliman on Monday morning.

'It's done. Go to your computer.'

Howard said, 'Hold on.' He put the cellphone on the granite counter in the kitchen of his Upper East Side brownstone. This was the call he was waiting for. He opened the laptop on the raised stretch of counter, entered the Whirl360 address into the web browser and found his way to that Orchard Street window. The head was gone.

He picked up the cell again. 'I looked. It's gone. Any complications?'

'Some.'

'Any that could blow back and hurt us?'

'No.'

'It's nice to have a little bit of good news for once,' Howard said.

'Yes.' Lewis paused. 'I'll keep you posted.'

Howard hung up. He needed a drink and it was only eight. He had an appointment with Morris Sawchuck that morning. The man wanted to announce formally, after delaying for nine months, that he would seek the office of Governor of the State of New York.

It had made sense, back in August, for Morris to put his ambitions on hold. One very personal reason that had become very public, and another—his complicity in the CIA director's deal with terrorists—that he'd prayed would never become public at all.

And a third he knew nothing about.

Oblivious, Morris believed there was no longer a reason to put his career on the back burner. Had he known Allison Fitch was still out there—and that she could destroy him—he might well have felt differently.

Every day, Talliman lived with the fear that the woman would surface. Imagined Wolf Blitzer saying, 'And now, in a CNN exclusive, we talk to a woman who's come out of hiding to accuse Morris Sawchuck and the people around him of trying to have her killed. Not only is she accusing the New York attorney general of attempted murder, but of being complicit in the disgraced former CIA director's plan not to pursue charges against—'

That was when Howard imagined turning off the TV, getting his hands on a gun, and blowing his brains out.

Not unlike what Barton Goldsmith had ultimately decided to do.

While Howard and Morris had fretted that the attorney general's involvement in the CIA director's deal with terrorists would become known, Goldsmith had been called to testify before a congressional committee. Everything would have come out. So Barton Goldsmith had walked into his garden, put the barrel of a pistol in his mouth, and pulled the trigger.

With Goldsmith out of the picture, Morris felt that threat had been neutralised. But Fitch had intimated she knew something. And Howard knew that if she surfaced, and talked, everything would start spilling out. He could not allow Morris to move forward while that remained a possibility. The trick was keeping the man in check without telling him why he needed to hold off. Howard could not, could *never* tell him the truth.

He was at his desk when the phone buzzed. It was his secretary, Agatha. 'He's here,' she said. The door opened and in strode The Man himself.

Howard was up and around his desk, hand extended.

'I had a very interesting conversation this morning,' Morris said, returning the handshake with a firm grip.

'Who with?' Howard said.

'Bridget.'

'Is that a fact,' Howard said.

Morris nodded. 'She said to go for it. She said I'd waited long enough. She told me she didn't want me waiting any more because of her. Because, honestly, she's the only reason I've still been waiting, Howard. This thing with Goldsmith, it's over. The man's secrets died with him.'

'We can't ever be certain of that.'

'So what are you saying? That we never move forward?'

'I'm not saying that. But we still need to proceed with caution. We can't lose sight of our long-term objectives. Morris, you can make it all the way. You can get there, right to Pennsylvania Avenue, I know it. But it can't happen if we take the short view.'

'Bridget said something else,' Morris said. 'She said she forgives me.'

'Well, that's good, Morris. And I've told you, you don't have anything to feel guilty about. You weren't the only one who didn't see the signs.'

'I still can't get my head around it. I asked her, I asked her why. Why didn't she just talk to me? We could have worked it out. She said not to blame myself.'

'Well, that's terrific. That really is.'

Morris gave his friend a sharp look. 'Don't be flip about this, Howard.'

'I'm sorry. Really, I am. But, Morris, we can't move forward based on—'

Morris seemed not to be listening. 'It's just, when you compare what Bridget is saying now, to what she told you on the phone—it's very different. She told you I was sucking the life out of her.'

'Morris!' Howard exploded. 'Enough. You can't keep doing this to yourself. You have to stop. You have to move on.'

'Haven't you been listening, Howard? That's exactly what I want to do, what Bridget wants. You're the one holding me back.'

'And you should thank God I am,' Howard snapped back. 'While you're having chats with ghosts, I'm dealing with political realities.'

Morris looked away. 'It would be hard enough for a man to have one wife kill herself. But two? What does that say about me? First Geraldine kills herself in the garage. And then Bridget.' He looked imploringly at Howard. 'Just what kind of monster am I?'

'You see?' Howard said. 'This proves you're not ready to get back into the game. You still need time to heal. Morris, trust me. I'm your friend.'

Yeah, I'm some friend, Howard thought. *I sent someone to kill your blackmailer, and ended up killing your wife instead.*

TEN

It is August. Allison Fitch has worked her usual shift, and would normally be sleeping now, at this time of day, but she's up early. She's had a phone call, and now she has to go downstairs to the scarf store. She had managed, the week before, to get them to accept a cheque for $123.76 for two silk scarves. 'I live on the block, practically above your shop,' she'd told them. She'd shown them her ID. The girl on the cash register had finally relented. The cheque bounced.

It was the manager that called. Told Allison that if she isn't there with $123.76 in cash in the next hour, she's going to call the police.

As it turns out, Allison has more than $500 in cash in her bag. A bunch of traders from a Wall Street firm had a party at the bar last night. Tipping big. And, earlier in the day, Allison had gone to the ATM and taken out a couple of hundred. With all that cash, she figures she could go on a shopping spree. A warm-up before the really big money comes. She figures Howard Talliman will be in touch any time now to set up a meeting.

Boy, she thinks, *the expression on his face when I let him believe I'd heard Bridget having some kind of top-secret chat with her husband*. She'd figured a man like Morris Sawchuck had secrets, and that he might discuss them with his wife. Hilarious thing is, she never heard a thing. But now she's more sure than ever that she's going to get that one hundred grand.

So she figures, what the hell, she'll pay for the scarves, then come home, go back to bed.

She is slipping on her jacket when she gets a buzz from the lobby.

Allison hits the button. 'Yeah?'

'It's me. We need to talk.'

Shit. *Bridget*.

Allison lets her in and, half a minute later, Bridget is at her door.

'Hey,' Allison says, closing the door as the woman goes into the kitchen.

'What did you tell Howard? What did you tell him you heard?'

'Look, we met, we came to an arrangement, and everything's OK.'

'Allison, listen. You're making a mistake, pushing Howard too far.'

'We got along fine. Everything's cool.'

'Whatever he's agreed to give you, you have to promise him you'll never, ever, hit him up for more. He'll do anything to protect my husband. If you're smart, you'll call it all off. You'll tell him that you never heard—'

'Look, I really have to go. I'll be five minutes. Stay here, we'll talk when I get back.' Allison heads out into the hall, closing the door behind her.

Bridget stands briefly in the kitchen, then, feeling restless, goes to the living room window, gazes down the street. There's a car down there with something funny on top of it. She wanders into the bedroom. She walks around the bed to the window. She berates herself, for at least the hundredth time, for putting everything at risk. *I'm such a fool*, she thinks. *Such an—*

Hears something behind her.

Everything goes white. She cannot breathe.

NICOLE IS FINISHED. She has retrieved the cellphone from the target's handbag. She is preparing to leave when she hears the door open.

It must be the room-mate. She's supposed to be at work. She's come back.

From the kitchen, a woman calls out, 'Bridget?'

Nicole's briefing for this job included two names: the target, Allison Fitch, and Courtney Walmers, the room-mate.

If the woman Nicole has just killed is Bridget, then the person entering the apartment could be the target. Or it could still be Walmers.

Before Nicole can make a move, the woman appears in the doorway.

Her eyes move from Nicole to the dead woman and back. In an instant.

That's all it takes for Nicole to see who she is. *This* is Allison Fitch. She's about the same size and height as the dead woman. Fitch screams, turns, runs.

Nicole knows she has to move quickly to shut the woman up. For ever. She leaps onto the bed, but her foot gets tangled in the rumpled bedspread. She untangles her foot from the spread, comes through the bedroom door. The door to the hall is open.

Nicole descends the two flights of stairs three steps at a time. Bursts onto the street. Stops, looks both ways. No sign of Allison Fitch.

Nicole calls Lewis. 'You're not going to like this,' she says.

LEWIS CALLS HOWARD. Tells him the wrong woman was killed. That Fitch got away. And that it's even worse than that. The dead woman is Bridget.

Howard says, 'What are you telling me? *Bridget?* She killed *Bridget*? Lewis, you said this was the way to handle it! I listened to you!'

'Howard, you can vent later. Right now, we have to think. Fast.'

Lewis is right. They have to move quickly. 'She can't be found there,' Howard says. 'But she has to be found. She can't just . . . disappear. That'll drag on for months.'

'I agree.'

'Is it possible to make this look like an accident, or better, self-inflicted?'

Lewis is quiet for three seconds. 'Maybe.' Then, 'Morris and Bridget have several residences in the city. We need the one that's easiest to get into.'

Howard forces himself to concentrate. 'Bridget's apartment, the one she had before she met Morris. Off Columbus. No doorman, and I remember her saying the surveillance cameras were for show. She hung on to the place for when friends came into town. The key should still be on her ring.'

'Address?'

Howard gives it to him.

'OK,' Lewis says. 'I have her phone. You'll get a call within the hour. From Bridget's phone. You'll take this call in front of Agatha. When you answer it, you'll pretend to talk to her. You ask her what's wrong, she's upset. Then she's going to hang up, and when Agatha asks what's going on, you say, "Bridget said, 'Howard, I'm so sorry, but he's sucking the life out of me. I can't take it any more.'" Does that work for you?'

'Yes.'

'Then call Morris. Tell him you got this strange call from her.'

'I've got it.' Howard's thinking of loose ends. 'A note,' he says.

'Way ahead of you,' Lewis says. 'Found a sample of her handwriting in her bag. Piece of cake. Done it before.'

'Go,' Howard says.

Lewis ends the call.

Howard takes a moment to attempt to decompress. Agatha, he suddenly remembers. He needs her here. She's his witness.

'Agatha,' he says, walking out to her desk, making sure he has his cell with him, 'I need you to pull together all the polling numbers we've done on Morris in the past six months.'

'Of course, Howard. I'll get right on it.'

He returns to his office but leaves the door open. Tries to look busy.

His cell rings. Howard grabs it, looks at the call display: BRIDGET.

'Hello?' he says, getting up, strolling out past Agatha's desk. 'Bridget, what's wrong?' he says.

Agatha looks up, clearly sensing something is amiss.

'Bridget, are you OK?' he says. Pauses. 'Where are you?'

Agatha's expression becomes increasingly concerned.

'Bridget?' Howard takes the phone from his ear. 'She hung up.'

'What's wrong?' Agatha asks.

'She wasn't making sense. She said she was sorry, and then how Morris was sucking the life out of her, and she couldn't take it any more.' He fumbles with his phone. 'I'm calling her back.'

He enters the number. 'She's not answering. I have to call Morris. Maybe he knows where she is.'

Of course, Morris does not. He tries to get her on her phone, too. He, Howard and Agatha start calling Bridget's friends.

Hours later, Howard comes up with the idea of checking her old apartment. He and Morris get there before the police.

IT IS DETERMINED to be a suicide. Bridget Sawchuck, the police conclude, chose an unorthodox, although not unheard of, technique.

First, she writes a note to her husband. Four words: 'Morris, forgive me. Bridget.' Investigators will conclude it looks like her handwriting. Maybe a little off in a couple of places, but the woman was about to end her life.

Once she has completed the note and placed it on the carpet just inside the apartment door, she takes a garment bag from the closet and pulls it over her head. She secures it around her neck with several turns of duct tape. Forensic investigators will find traces of tape adhesive on her fingers.

With what little air she has left, she lays on the bed and secures her wrists to the bedpost with a set of handcuffs, so that once she starts panicking about being unable to breathe, she won't stop what she has set in motion.

There is, admittedly, much about the death that is suspicious. But there are no other signs of violence or any kind of struggle. No indications that anyone else was there. There is the short note.

Most persuasive of all is the call from her cell to Howard's. The cellular provider is able to determine the call came from the area where Bridget was found. Agatha tells the police she was right there when Howard got the call. Howard tells the police it was definitely Bridget on the phone. And she did not sound coerced in any way. The call sounded entirely genuine.

Everyone involved knows this is a sensitive case. The dead woman is the wife of the attorney general. Morris Sawchuck, through Howard, exercises his influence. There will be a complete lid put on this, given that the evidence tips towards suicide. After a couple of days, a statement is released to the press that Bridget Sawchuck 'died suddenly'. Code for 'suicide'.

A distraught Morris Sawchuck puts his political ambitions on hold.

Meanwhile, police conduct a cursory investigation into the seemingly unrelated disappearance of Allison Fitch. Lots of people go missing, and she has, according to her mother, vanished for extended periods before, usually surfacing when she needed money.

Courtney Walmers, who assumes Fitch ran off to avoid paying off her debts, is approached by a man who identifies himself as an undercover policeman. He tells her Allison Fitch, during the day, had been selling crack out of the apartment and that it is still under surveillance. He wants to sublet her apartment, maintain the appearance that it is still a place where drugs are sold. He will pay her first month's rent in a new location, as well as any money Fitch owed.

Courtney is horrified. Courtney wants out. Courtney takes the deal.

Lewis sets up the motion-activated camera behind the apartment door.

Nicole goes to Dayton in her search for Allison.

Morris grieves.

Howard wonders every day whether he will have a heart attack.

And then, nine months later, a man comes knocking on the apartment door with a print-out of a murder that the entire world can see if they only know where to look.

JULIE SAID, 'OK, so let's go through this again.'

I had my clothes on now, sitting on Thomas's bed.

Julie said, 'Thomas here sees this picture on the net, manages to get you to go to this address in Manhattan to check it out, which you do, but not really, but you do talk to some lady who lives next door.'

'Yeah,' I said.

'And Thomas calls the landlord and finds out two women used to live in this place, but they've both moved out, and the place has been sitting empty, but the rent's being paid by a guy named Blocker. How'm I doing so far?'

Thomas nodded. 'Excellent.' He looked at me. 'She's doing very well.'

'And within a couple of days of your little mission, the image on Whirl360 is altered,' Julie said. 'That kind of blows my mind.'

I said, 'But it doesn't make any sense. I didn't say anything to the woman down the hall about seeing the image online. Thomas, did you say anything to the landlord about what you saw in the window, on your computer?'

He shook his head. 'No.'

Julie was thinking. 'Did you tell that guy you had lunch with?'

'No. I didn't mention a word of it to him.'

'Think back to when you got to the place on Orchard Street.'

I sighed. 'After the meeting, I found a cab and got out at Orchard. I headed down with the print-out in my hand, comparing the window patterns and everything until I was sure I had the right building. It had the same air-conditioning unit in the window.'

'How'd you get in?'

'Some guy was coming out and I slipped in. I went upstairs, knocked on the door, no one answered. Nothing else to tell.'

'So you had the print-out in your hand the whole time?' Julie said.

'Yeah, I guess I did.'

'So the person heading out of the building saw it, the neighbour lady saw it, and anyone else you walked past saw it.'

'Maybe there was a camera in the lobby,' Thomas said.

'OK, let's say somebody saw that sheet of paper I was carrying. How do we make the leap from that to the image disappearing online now?'

Julie said, 'Maybe when you were waving around that piece of paper, you tipped somebody off about the head in the window.'

'Maybe,' I conceded. 'So, let's say my visit and the doctoring of the image are linked. How the hell would you go online and change it?'

'You'd hack in,' Thomas said.

'It'd be worth calling Whirl360, asking them if anyone has tried lately to break into their system,' Julie said.

Could nosing around backfire, get Thomas in trouble? We'd already had the FBI here. Did we want Whirl360's security people at our door, too?

But I kept those concerns to myself, because I had more immediate questions. 'Thomas, tell me again what the landlord said when you called him. About the women who used to live there?'

'He said the apartment got empty late last summer. I don't think they were sisters or related. They had different names.' Thomas turned to his desk. 'I wrote them down,' he said. 'Courtney Walmers and Olsen Fitch.'

'Wait a second,' I said. 'Olsen Fitch.' Something about the name rang a bell. 'Thomas, let me sit there.' I opened up a new browser on his computer, and conducted the same search I'd done on Dad's laptop of news stories that had mentioned Orchard Street. 'Hang on . . . here we are. Thomas, is it possible the landlord was saying "Allison Fitch" instead of "Olsen Fitch"?'

Thomas thought. 'I guess.'

'OK, so here's a story about the police issuing a statement that they were trying to find an Allison Fitch. She lived on Orchard, and worked at some bar and didn't show up for work. There's just the one story here.'

'That's probably the person in the window,' Thomas said.

'Thomas,' I said, 'why don't you sit back down here while Julie and I talk about how to handle this.'

'Are you going to go finish having sex?' Thomas asked.

I felt my face flush, but Julie was very cool. 'Maybe later,' she said.

Julie and I went down to the kitchen. Julie said, 'Call me crazy, but I think there's something going on here. I know you said you weren't really going to call the New York police like Thomas asked, but that was then. You gonna call them now?'

'None of the reasons that would have kept me from calling before has changed,' I said. I reminded her about the FBI. 'Say we call the New York police, or even the Promise Falls cops. That'll probably trigger some sort of alarm, and the FBI'll be notified. And when the FBI brings everyone up to speed on my brother's activities, just how seriously do you think anyone's going to take him? Especially when what he claims to have seen is no longer on Whirl360?'

'Ray, I get your hesitation here, but I gotta tell ya, this makes the hairs on the back of my neck stand on end. Tomorrow I'm going to call Whirl360 and talk to whoever's in charge of muddying images on the site and ask if someone hacked into it. Or if they changed it themselves for some reason.'

'LET ME HAVE A LOOK at the picture again?'

Lewis Blocker handed the print-out to the woman behind the counter at the art store. It was an image from the surveillance video shot from the door of the Fitch apartment. It was the best image he'd been able to get of the man who'd come with the Whirl360 image in hand.

'So what'd this guy do, exactly?'

'Credit card fraud,' Lewis said. 'Identity theft.' He guessed the woman was around thirty. She had studs in her ears, one through her right nostril, and another just below her lip.

She held the sheet and cocked her head to one side. 'I thought maybe I recognised him, but now I'm not so sure.'

Lewis told her when he believed the man had been in the store. A couple of mornings ago.

'I was on, but I don't remember this guy,' she said. She looked across the store, saw a dark man restocking brushes. 'Tarek, you got a second?'

Tarek examined the print-out. 'I remember him. He paid cash. He bought some airbrush supplies, I think, and some markers. Said every time he's in the city, he pops in.'

'He's from out of town? Did he say where?'

Tarek shook his head. 'I asked him if he was on our email list, and he said he was.'

'Can I have a look at that?'

'I don't think the manager'd want to just turn it over.' He paused. 'He said he was an illustrator. And he said he was going to be doing stuff for a news web site. Some new one. Something political, like the Huffington Post.' Tarek shrugged. 'That's all I know. Good luck.'

Lewis got a booth at a café around the corner, ordered a corned beef on rye with a dill pickle and coffee, and called Howard Talliman.

'You know that HuffPo site?' he asked.

'Of course,' Howard said.

'You know about some new site that's coming out that's similar to it?'

'I could ask around,' Howard said. 'Why?'

'Just ask and get back to me quick as you can.'

Lewis was finishing his coffee when his cellphone rang. 'Kathleen Ford's starting one up,' Howard said.

'I think it's possible she may have hired our man to work for her. You got some contacts for this Ford chick?' Lewis scribbled down a couple of numbers Howard gave him. 'You know her?'

'We are familiar with each other,' Howard said. 'But I wouldn't drop my name. She thinks I'm a reptile.'

Lewis ended the call, thinking maybe this Kathleen Ford was a pretty good judge of character.

ALLISON FITCH so wanted to call her mother. It was like an ache. It had been nine months. She couldn't believe she'd managed to hold off this long. She didn't know for certain, of course, that anyone was listening to her mother's phone conversations. But, assuming they were, was it likely they were still doing it now, all these months later?

Allison could only imagine what her mother was going through. True, she had a history of putting her mom through this kind of anguish. But disappearing for nine months was—even by Allison's standards—over the top.

There was no way to tell her mother it was different this time, that she hadn't called home because she was afraid that if she did, she'd get herself killed. Allison figured it was better to put her mother through hell and show up one day, alive.

Occasionally, she'd borrow someone's computer and do a search on herself, see if there were any news stories about her disappearance. There was one, not long after she'd gone missing, but very little after that.

But there certainly were stories about the death of Bridget Sawchuck. They were short on details, but what few details there were Allison knew to be total flights of fantasy.

If Allison hadn't been convinced before that running and hiding was the smartest thing to do, she certainly was after seeing the stories about Bridget. If the powers that be could cover up the murder of a woman like her, they could do anything. So she kept moving. Starting with her flight from her apartment. The second Allison Fitch saw what had happened in that bedroom, that someone had been sent—clearly—to kill her and had murdered Bridget Sawchuck by mistake, she just ran.

She had had a few hundred dollars in her bag. Enough to buy a bus ticket out of New York.

Her bus ticket took her as far as Philadelphia. From there she hitchhiked. She tacked in a southerly direction, hitching several rides that landed her in Charlottesville, a beautiful college town. She got a kitchen job in a diner. She was there for five weeks before moving on. A couple of hungry weeks in Charleston. Then, farther south, to Jacksonville.

In Tampa, she found work making up rooms at a motel called the Coconut Shade, a place where customers often rented by the hour. No references, no previous work experience required. She said her name was Adele Farmer. Octavio Famosa, the manager, offered her a rollaway bed in a storage room.

Octavio's parents were still in Cuba, and he hoped some day to bring them to Florida. 'Before they are too old to come,' he said. 'I want them to see their granddaughter. What about you?'

'There's just my mom,' she said. 'My dad died a few years ago.'

'Where is your mother?' Octavio asked.

'Seattle,' she lied. 'I haven't talked to her for a while.'

'I bet she misses you,' he said.

Allison cried. She cried so long that she exhausted herself. Octavio tucked her into her rollaway bed in the storage room. He wanted to help her.

When he was sure Adele was sleeping soundly, he took her bag from beneath her bed. In it, he found identification that showed she was not Adele Farmer at all. She was Allison Fitch. And her mother was not in Seattle. There was a tattered letter from her mother dated more than a year ago, in which she told her daughter that she loved her very much and that she was always welcome to move back to Dayton.

Octavio checked the return address sticker on the back of the envelope, wrote down some information, then returned the letter and the ID to the bag and slid it back under the rollaway bed. He went online and found a phone number for Doris Fitch. He got Doris Fitch on the phone.

'Oh my God,' she said. 'She's alive. I can't believe it! I'll get a flight out tomorrow. Tell me where you are.'

Octavio gave her the name of the motel, and the address. 'When you get off the plane, just tell the cab driver. He will find it.'

Adele—Allison—was going to be so surprised.

ELEVEN

I'd made an appointment for Monday afternoon, to meet with Darla Kurtz, the administrator of Glace House, a residence for psychiatric outpatients. I'd left Julie at the house, trying, with very little success, to track down someone to talk to at Whirl360.

Glace House was actually a beautiful, celery-green, three-storey Victorian home in an older part of Promise Falls, with gingerbread trim and a porch that wrapped around two sides. I rang the front bell and a woman held the door open for me. She was wearing a cardigan and a peasant skirt, and her hair was long and frizzy.

She said, 'Ray Kilbride?' and extended a hand. 'I'm Darla Kurtz.'

I got out of there about an hour later. Darla Kurtz was very welcoming, but she had had very specific questions. She also wanted me to bring Thomas in for a visit.

I was getting into the car when my cellphone rang.

'I've been getting bounced at Whirl360,' Julie said. 'The place is in chaos.'

I reached for my seat belt. 'So they have been hacked?'

'No. One of their top people got killed. Yesterday. Him and his wife.'

'Who are we talking about?'

'OK, the guy's name was Kyle Billings, and his wife's name was Rochelle. They live in Oak Park, in Chicago. That's where the company's head office is. Guess what Billings did at Whirl360?'

'Tell me.'

'He's the guy who wrote the program that automatically blurs faces and licence plates and all that kind of thing.'

I had been about to put the key into the ignition but stopped.

'And I just got this off the *Chicago Tribune* web site. Billings was stabbed. Something very long and pointed, like an ice pick, maybe. But the wife—she was suffocated, Ray. Someone put a bag over her head.'

LEWIS BLOCKER WENT ONLINE and read everything he could find about Kathleen Ford and her new web site. She'd lured a prominent columnist from the *New York Times*. Some well-known talking heads from Fox and MSNBC had agreed to be contributors. There was even some mention of an animated political cartoon. Lewis took special note of that.

He wrote down a few questions and then found a contact number for the public relations department of Kathleen Ford's enterprise.

He was put in touch with a woman named Florence Highgold. Lewis explained that he was doing a freelance piece on Ford's new web site for the *Wall Street Journal*. He asked her about the launch date for the site, how many visits they expected it to receive. Would it be a site you had to pay to read?

He made it sound like an afterthought when he asked, 'And what about artists? Does a site like that need a lot of illustrators?'

'Well, you certainly need web artists to come up with a concept for the site,' Florence said. 'You need a distinctive graphic design. We've already said we'd like to do animated political cartoons. Are you familiar with Ray Kilbride's work?'

Even as she said the name, Lewis was tapping it into a search engine. The screen filled with dozens of postage-stamp-sized pictures.

'Yeah, I believe I am,' Lewis said. He clicked on a caricature of noted New York crime boss Carlo Vachon, sticking up the Statue of Liberty. 'And I remember one he did of that mob guy.'

'He's got a pretty comprehensive portfolio.'

'Uh huh,' Lewis said, clicking to a second page of images. One of them was not an illustration, but a photograph. He clicked on it. Up popped a photo of a man leaning over a drafting table, an airbrush in his hand, smiling at the camera. The photograph was accompanied by a short article about Ray Kilbride, who lived in Burlington, Vermont.

'Was there anything else you needed to know?' Florence asked.

'No, I think I've found the answer to my question,' Lewis said.

He ended the call, then went to the online phone directories. He found a listing for an R. Kilbride in Burlington.

He picked up the phone again, dialled Howard.

'Found him,' Lewis said.

OCTAVIO FAMOSA couldn't decide what to do.

Should he tell Allison Fitch—that was how he thought of her now—that he had been in touch with her mother? That Doris Fitch would be flying in today to be reunited with her? Or should he let her be surprised?

One reason he didn't want to tell her was that he wanted to see the look on Allison's face when her mother arrived at the hotel. But as much as he wanted to keep what he had done a secret from Allison, he also felt that as her friend, he had to be honest with her. She was a girl in trouble, he knew that. And a girl in trouble needed her mother.

When Allison woke the next morning, and emerged from the back room, he considered telling her right then. But he lost his nerve.

'Where should I start?' Allison asked.

'Three, nine and eleven are ready for you,' Octavio said.

About an hour later, he found her cleaning the bathroom in unit nine.

'Adele?' he said. He almost called her Allison. 'I need to talk to you for a minute. I need to tell you, first of all, that anything I did was with your best interests at heart. I've been very concerned about . . . about how sad you've been.'

'Octavio, what have you done?'

'Last night, when you were sleeping, I went into your room. I was a total gentleman. But . . . but I looked in your bag and—'

'You were in my bag?'

'Just listen to me. I found the letter from your mother.'

'Oh my God,' Allison said.

'I called her. I told her you were here, that you were OK. Allison, Allison, please, she was . . . she was ecstatic.'

'No,' Allison whispered, disbelieving.

'She is coming,' Octavio said. 'She is flying down to see you. She—'

Allison shoved him out of her way as she ran to the door.

She didn't know how much time she had. Maybe they hadn't been tapping her mother's phone. But she had to assume that they were. And if they were, and if Octavio had spoken to her mother the night before—plenty of time to send someone to Florida. She would grab what few clothes she had, stuff them into her backpack, and get the hell out of there.

She threw open the door to the back room. She dropped to her knees to pull her bag and backpack out from under the rollaway bed. Felt a sudden, very sharp pain in her side.

By the time Doris Fitch arrived that afternoon, the hotel parking lot was cordoned off with yellow police tape.

JULIE MET ME at the house.

'Tell me again,' I said as I got out.

She repeated what she had told me on the phone. I couldn't stop thinking about the fact that Billings was the person who'd created the program that obscured faces on Whirl360.

'You didn't tell Thomas any of this, did you?'

'Hell, no. I think this news might get him pretty agitated.'

'I'm pretty agitated,' I said. 'You find out anything else?'

'I'm going to make some calls about Allison Fitch.'

'OK.' I put my hands on her shoulders. 'Why are you doing this?'

She smiled. 'I like you, Ray. And I like your brother, too. And I have to tell ya, if Thomas really has seen something online, it's one hell of a story.'

'So you're using me,' I said.

'Yes, yes, I am. I'm trying to exploit you sexually *and* professionally.'

'Works for me, I guess.' I slipped an arm around her. As we started walking towards the house, my cellphone rang. It was Harry Peyton's office.

'Hi, Ray,' Alice said. 'I can't seem to find your father's life insurance documents. Would you have those?'

I really didn't need this now. 'Can it wait?' I asked. 'How's tomorrow?'

'I'm taking tomorrow off and Harry's going to be in court.'

'OK, fine. I'll head in shortly.' I ended the call and said to Julie, 'I've got an idea. You want to hang in here till I get back?'

'What else would I do?' she said. 'I've only got a job.'

Ten minutes later, I was in Harry's office with the policy. Wound up as I was, I pretty much threw it onto his desk. 'That's what you wanted, right?'

'Yes. Ray, really, what's going on? It's about Thomas, isn't it?'

I forced myself to sit down. 'Sort of. But not exactly. It started off with Thomas, but now it's something bigger. And I need to talk to you about it.'

He closed his eyes for a moment, as if steeling himself. 'Fire away.'

Harry listened while I told him the whole thing. Thomas's belief that what he'd seen was a murder. My trip to New York. His call to the landlord. The altered image, the murders in Chicago and a missing woman.

I said, 'I feel I've got to call the police. It's reached the point where I have to do something. I thought maybe you'd have some words of wisdom.'

'Let me ask you a few questions first.' He sat forward in his chair. 'How do you know Whirl360 doesn't periodically review the street scenes it's posted, and if the program finds something it overlooked before, it makes a change?'

'I don't know. If what you're suggesting were the case, I still think it's pretty amazing that the change got made within a couple of days of Thomas finding it, and my knocking on the door of that apartment.'

'You may be right. So, Ray, is it possible the image was never there in the first place? Could Thomas have fiddled with the image on his computer, to make it look like the woman in that window was being smothered?'

I didn't have to give that much thought. 'Thomas doesn't have the skills or know-how to hack into Whirl360 and fiddle with the images.'

'OK,' Harry said, nodding. 'But what if he were able to change the image on just his own computer? And then later, when you thought the image had been tampered with, it was actually back to the way it was before Thomas started messing about with it.'

I shook my head slowly. 'I don't . . . I don't think so.'

'Did you ever see this image on any computer other than Thomas's?'

That stopped me. 'No. But the landlord did confirm that there used to be a couple of women living there, and that one of them was reported missing.'

'What else did the landlord tell you?'

'He didn't tell *me* anything. It was Thomas who talked to him.'

Harry Peyton didn't say anything.

'Are you saying Thomas made up all that stuff from the landlord?'

'Ray, I'm only asking you the questions the police are going to.'

I slumped in the chair. 'The thing is, I believe Thomas. And, Harry, Julie did not make up what she found out from the Whirl360 people. Two people were murdered. People who are linked to this image on the web site.'

Harry shrugged. 'Look, I'm not saying you are, but what if you're wrong about Thomas? What if—and please forgive me for this—but what if this thing he saw was something that was pointed out to him during one of his conversations with President Clinton?'

A major storm-front of a headache was moving in. 'I appreciate your caution, Harry. But there's something going on. There has to be a way to get this information to the cops.'

Harry mulled that one over. 'I have a friend. Barry Duckworth, a detective with the Promise Falls police. If, after I explain everything to him, he thinks there's anything worth checking out, he can follow it up with you. Or he can call the NYPD. He'll be able to get someone to listen to him.'

I liked it. Harry had credibility. And Duckworth, in turn, would have credibility with another police department.

'Yeah,' I said. 'OK.' I suddenly nodded with enthusiasm. A heavy weight began to lift from my shoulders. 'I appreciate this, Harry, I do.'

'No problem.'

I stood, but something was holding me there. 'I don't even know whether to mention it,' I said. 'But maybe Dad said something to you about this. Thomas said to me—I'm trying to remember his exact words—but he said something like, "things happen in windows". And then, when he didn't think I'd done a thorough investigation in New York, he said I was acting the way I had before, when someone in a window was in trouble.'

'Sounds like he was talking about himself,' Harry said.

'Yeah,' I said. 'And there's another thing. Len Prentice came by the house when I was in the city. He tried to get Thomas to leave the house for lunch and Thomas refused to go, and he kind of hit Len. Struck him.'

Harry's eyes widened. 'Oh my.'

'Nothing really happened, and Len isn't pressing the point. But he said

Dad told him Thomas had pushed him down the stairs, and when I talked to Thomas about it, he more or less admitted it.'

'Your father never mentioned anything about that to me,' Harry said.

'Thomas said Dad was trying to tell him he was sorry about something that had happened to Thomas when he was thirteen, but Thomas said he didn't want to talk about it, and that's when he pushed Dad.'

'Dear God,' Harry said. 'Did you ask Thomas what it was?'

'I tried, but he's not saying,' I said. 'What could Dad have done to Thomas that he'd feel the need to apologise for, after all these years?'

I WAS WALKING to the car when my cellphone rang.

'Me,' Julie said.

'Thomas OK?'

'Yeah. I went upstairs, asked him to go on Whirl360 and show me my sister Candace's place. She runs a bakery, specialising in cupcakes, in Greenwich Village. Lives over her shop. Anyway, he found it on West 8th just like that. It's called Candy's, in case you ever want to go there. So, how'd it go at the lawyer's?'

I told her how Harry Peyton was going to act as an intermediary between the police and myself.

'Sounds good,' Julie said. 'I know Duckworth. Listen, Ray'—her voice went very serious—'I did a news search on Allison Fitch on your dad's laptop, and I got a hit. Just a short story, out of Tampa. A woman with that name was found dead at a hotel there.'

'HELLO?'

'Thomas, it's Bill Clinton. How are you?'

'I'm very good, sir.'

'Thomas, I wanted to remind you how valuable you are to us. Do you know what the phrase "black ops" means?'

'Those are secret missions?'

'That's right. Covert ops run by the CIA and other government agencies. Operations that the White House has to be able to deny any knowledge of should they somehow become public.'

'OK.'

'When we have operatives in the field, conducting black ops-style missions, they can run into trouble, the kind where they have to slip

away in a hurry. That's why you're so important. Not just if all the online maps disappear one day, or there's another earthquake, or a tsunami.'

'I understand.'

'I'm calling to tell you, again, that there are things in your past you shouldn't be talking about, or the folks at the CIA are going to lose confidence in you. You'll look weak. You understand?'

'I do.'

'Good. That's good to hear.'

NICOLE CALLED LEWIS in the morning from Florida and told him it was done. Lewis told her to catch the first flight north that she could. She'd found Allison Fitch, and he'd found the man who'd paid a visit to her apartment. Together, they were going to retrieve him. A man named Ray Kilbride.

'Retrieve?' Nicole said.

'We have to know what he knows. We have to know why he was there. My employer wants to talk to him. And you're not flying to New York,' Lewis told her. He gave her another destination, closer to where they'd find Kilbride. 'I'm heading up that way now.'

'Fine,' she said, and ended the call.

Then Lewis contacted Howard Talliman.

'She's been found. And she's no longer a problem,' Lewis said. He felt safe discussing these things with Howard, knowing that the man had a security expert who swept his office every morning for listening devices.

'That's a great relief, Lewis.'

'And I'm heading north to deal with our other problem.'

'It's still too early to relax.'

'I agree,' Lewis said.

'We have to know why Kilbride had that print-out. We have to know why he was there. Have you any reason to believe he's anything other than what he purports to be?'

'He's an illustrator. Plain and simple,' Lewis said. 'I've torn his life apart since finding out he's our guy. I've got his Social Security number. He's got $54 charged to his Visa card. He's paid off his mortgage. Last year he reported an income of $73,675 to the IRS. He drives an Audi Q5. Got a brother named Thomas who lives with their father in Promise Falls. That sound like some undercover CIA guy to you?'

'No, but it doesn't make any sense for someone who makes his living doing silly drawings to show up at a murder scene with that print-out in hand. Keep me informed,' Howard said, concluding the conversation.

Howard had always known the Goldsmith matter might still come back and bite them in the ass, even though the man was dead. But did it really make sense that the CIA might be sniffing around Orchard Street? There had to be people at Langley who already knew everything: the plan had originated there. It wasn't as if the whole thing had been Morris's idea.

Was it possible that those left behind after Goldsmith's death were covering their ass by finding a way to lay off more of their troubles on Morris? But, even then, how had they connected Morris to Orchard Street? Had they also been keeping tabs on Bridget? Learned of her link to Allison Fitch? Which could have led them to the web, and the image and—

It did seem far-fetched.

And yet, some facts were not in dispute. This man Ray Kilbride had shown up at Allison Fitch's apartment, presumably led there by an online image of Bridget Sawchuck's murder.

Howard felt he needed to talk to Sawchuck. To sound him out on a few things, without actually telling him about Fitch, or Kilbride, or what had happened at Orchard Street. Morris still had no idea how his wife had actually died. That his wife had not killed herself.

Morris picked up on the third ring. 'Just on my way to lunch. What's up?'

'I've been thinking about what you said, Morris. About how you think it's time. I know you think I'm not listening to you, but I am.'

Morris waited a moment before responding. 'OK.'

'I've been thinking about how you want to move forward, and the only thing that's holding us back is our uncertainty with regard to the Goldsmith matter. I need a comfort level, Morris, that we're done with that.'

'Howard, ever since Goldsmith took his own life, I've felt that the risks have been minimised.'

Howard paused, then said, 'Do you think that people within the agency would have any reason to be monitoring you in the wake of all this?'

'The only one I can think of is those who were close to Goldsmith, who were complicit in what he was doing, would be worried I might come forward. But they'd also know that any such action on my part would be certain political suicide.'

Howard concurred. 'Do you think, before Barton took his own life, he might have had people watching you and, I don't know, maybe Bridget?'

'Why the hell would they be watching me or Bridget? This is crazy talk. Look, forget about the business with Goldsmith. We need to plot our next move. Howard, I hardly need to be telling you this. You wrote the playbook. Let's get together tonight.'

Howard knew what that meant. It had been their routine, over the years, to get together after midnight and work through till dawn, drawing up battle plans. 'Yes,' Howard said. 'That's what we'll do.'

'Good. Talk to you later, my friend. Lace up those boxing gloves.'

Maybe, before tonight's meeting, Howard hoped, there'd be some answers from Ray Kilbride.

BACK AT THE HOUSE, I said to Julie, 'Let's take a walk.'

We headed out of the back of the house and down the hill, to the creek.

'I'm thinking about some things Harry said. About Thomas.' I told her about his speculation, that Thomas might be making some of this stuff up.

'You think that's what he's doing?' she asked.

I hesitated. 'I don't know. I don't think so. I mean, he believes things we know are not true, but he really believes them. Like the online map meltdown, and talking to Clinton. But some things aren't made up at all.'

'Would Thomas deliberately lie to you?'

I'd never really thought about that. 'I guess it's possible. But when I asked him about this thing that happened with Dad, about pushing him on the stairs, he admitted it. Although it wasn't like he volunteered it.'

'He pushed your dad down the stairs?'

I shook my head, like I didn't have the energy to get into it now. 'When there's something Thomas doesn't want to tell you, or own up to, he just keeps quiet. He clams up.' I stopped, watched the creek water trickling past. 'Well, he lied to Dr Grigorin. He told her he'd watched a movie with me when he hadn't—trying to get her off his back, I guess. I just don't know.'

'Are you going to talk to him?'

'I'll try. In the meantime, some other stuff's nagging at me,' I said.

'Like?'

I gestured to where we were standing. 'This is where my father died.' I pointed to the hill. 'That was where the tractor rolled. This is where Thomas found him.'

She looped her arm into mine. 'I'm sorry.'

'I've been thinking a lot about him. About Dad. And about Thomas.

Thomas told me when they had this incident on the stairs, it was about something that had happened to him when he was thirteen. Something he didn't want to talk about. And Dad, according to Thomas, was trying to tell him he was sorry, that he'd understand if Thomas didn't forgive him.' I hesitated, 'There's something more.'

Julie looked at me and waited.

'There was something kind of weird on Dad's laptop.' I told her about what I'd found in the search history.

'Child prostitution?' Julie shook her head strongly. 'I didn't know your dad, Ray. You think he was into something weird?' Then the implications started to sink in further. 'You don't think your dad assaulted Thomas when he was a kid, do you? You think that's what he was talking about when he said he'd understand if Thomas didn't forgive him?'

'It's a huge leap, putting it together like that,' I said, 'but without any real facts, your mind starts going places it shouldn't.'

'Did your father, with you, did he ever—'

'Never,' I said. 'Absolutely never.'

'Then that's not it,' Julie said with finality. 'What else?' she asked. 'I can tell there's something else on your mind.'

I looked down. 'I think there's something funny about how Dad died. It's just the way they say it happened, that he rolled the tractor while he was on the side of the hill here. And that's probably what *did* happen.'

'So what's the problem, then?' she asked.

'They never brought the tractor up. I came down here to see if it would start, to take it back up to the barn. And it did start. But the key was already in the "off" position, and that thing that goes around the lawn-mower blades was raised, like he'd stopped cutting grass.'

'Isn't that possible? That maybe the tractor was acting up, and he stopped it to see what was wrong? Wouldn't you have to lift up that thingie so you could look to see what it was?'

I laughed and said, 'You're a genius. Thanks, that makes perfect sense.'

'What did you think had happened?'

'I was thinking he must have stopped because there was someone else there. So he killed the ignition, and raised the housing. I'd been thinking that someone was actually there and saw it happen, but didn't tell anyone, or call the ambulance, or anything.'

Julie said, quietly, 'Someone like Thomas.'

I nodded, feeling ashamed. 'God, I'm an idiot. Like there aren't enough things to worry about, I have to invent more.'

'Maybe you've been doing the same thing with what you found on your father's laptop. Lots of things have simple explanations.'

I took Julie into my arms. 'I know I keep saying this, but thanks.'

'Wait till you get my bill.' She put her head on my chest. 'Listen, I should get back to the paper.'

'What about later? You want to come back?'

'Why don't I come out around eleven? I've got to cover the evening session of the Promise Falls City Council. After I file my story, I'll bring over a bottle of wine.'

I walked her to her car, and watched until it had disappeared down the road. When I got upstairs, Thomas was exploring Stuttgart. I said, 'I don't know what the hell to make for dinner. How about bacon sandwiches?'

That was when someone started banging on the front door.

TWELVE

Lewis's flight got in ahead of Nicole's, which gave him time to arrange the rental of a white panel van. Two seats up front with an empty cargo bay. When Nicole got off the plane she said she needed to hit a hardware store on the way. She couldn't take ice picks on a plane, and had to buy them as she needed them. Lewis grabbed a roll of duct tape and some moving blankets at the same time.

They pulled up in front of the house. It was still daylight.

'So we're just bringing him back,' Nicole said.

Lewis, behind the wheel, nodded at all the empty space behind them. 'Yeah. My boss has some questions for him.'

Nicole nodded. Finally, she said, 'I know you're not happy with how this went down. But once we bag this guy, that takes care of things.'

'Hope so,' he said. 'Depends on what kind of answers we get from him.'

'Either way, I'm done at that point.'

'Well, after he's been questioned, we're going to have to deal with him. This isn't like when you're fishing and do catch and release.'

Nicole shot him a look. 'But after that, we're square.'

'Sure,' Lewis said.

Nicole looked at the house. 'How do you want to play this?'

'I don't see why we don't both go to the front door.' He grinned at her. 'We look like a nice couple. We need directions. We need the phone. Listen, once he opens the door, we're walking right in.'

Nicole gave the top of the ice pick that was tucked into her boot a reassuring tap. Lewis rooted around between the seats for a backpack.

'Let's go,' he said.

IT WASN'T THE FBI. It was Marie Prentice. She was standing there with a dark blue soft-sided bag the size of a picnic hamper. It looked insulated.

'If I can't get you boys over for dinner,' she said, 'the least I can do is bring something.' There was a warm aroma wafting upwards. Spices, cheese.

'Let me take that from you,' I said. 'It looks heavy.' I took hold of the bag's strap. 'It smells wonderful. Come on in.'

I put the bag on the kitchen table and unzipped it, 'It looks great, Marie,' I said. 'The pan's still hot. Did you just take it out of the oven?'

'I did. Where's Thomas? Is he upstairs? Do you think he'd like to come down and try the casserole?'

'If it's OK with you, I'm just going to leave him be for now,' I said. 'But I'll tell him you're the one to thank for dinner.'

'You see, part of the reason I came by is, I just wanted to apologise to him. And to you. For Len's behaviour the other day.'

'Len and I already spoke about this,' I said. 'It's OK.'

'I heard the two of you talking in the basement and he really shouldn't have said those things to you, about your brother.'

'And Thomas shouldn't have hit Len,' I said.

Marie said, 'I was the one who suggested he try to get Thomas to go out, for lunch, or to come back to the house. Actually, he'd come here to invite you both, but you were gone for the day. Len just doesn't understand why Thomas has to be the way he is.'

'I'm going to put this in the oven to keep it warm,' I said, taking the casserole and putting it on the centre rack.

'He doesn't even understand that I can't do everything he wants to do,' Marie said. 'I mean, you know, like travelling. But I told him, if you want to go away, you go. I didn't think he'd actually go, but off he went once he found somebody else to go with. And he had such a wonderful time over there, I didn't see how I could say no when he wanted to go back.'

'Well,' I said, since I had no comment.

'And not for a second do I believe what Len's been saying about Thomas,' she said.

'What would that be, Marie?'

'Len says your dad always took chances on cutting grass on the side of that hill but, even so, he was the kind of man who always knew what he was doing. He says if the police ever started thinking he got pushed, that someone was there and let that tractor fall on him, well, they'd have to look no further than Thomas.'

Julie's interpretation of things had made sense. But while I didn't hold Len in very high regard, especially lately, the fact that he and I might be on the same wavelength gave me pause. Was it possible Len was trying to make trouble for Thomas? And again, why?

'The thing is,' Marie said, 'Len's always judged people harshly. He's like that. You should hear him go on about the people in Thailand. But it doesn't stop him from going back, even if he has to go without me.'

Thailand.

Over the years, I'd heard friends talk about what a wonderful place it was. One of the most beautiful countries on the planet. Terrific nightlife, a rich culture, spectacular food. But every travel destination had its problems. What was it I'd heard about Thailand?

Prostitution. *Child* prostitution.

'THIS IS THE SORT of thing I'd have thought you might have checked first,' Nicole said, sitting in the passenger seat.

'It was the right house,' Lewis said, through gritted teeth. The van, driving through the night, was doing close to eighty. He figured it would take them another two hours to get to their new destination.

A neighbour had spotted them standing on the porch of Ray Kilbride's house when no one answered. She said her name was Gwen, and that she was picking up Ray's mail while he was away, in Promise Falls. His dad had just died, she said, and he was staying there while he sorted things out. He was looking after his brother, too.

'Wait a minute,' Nicole had said. 'Someone named Ray lives here?'

'That's right.'

Nicole had turned to Lewis and said, 'I told you this was the wrong house. We're on the wrong side of town.'

Lewis had shrugged. 'I'm an idiot,' he'd conceded.

'So you're not looking for Ray?' the neighbour had asked.

They'd said no, got back in the van.

Along the way, Nicole needled Lewis. She wanted to get under his skin. See how angry he'd get. It would be a clue to his intentions.

She said, 'If it was me, I wouldn't have gone up and knocked on the front door. You find a way inside the house, get the jump on them there.'

'Yeah, I guess you're right.' Being nice.

That was when she knew he was going to kill her when this was over. He was being nice so she'd be off her guard.

It would be easy to take him out first. But she needed answers to what was going on as much as Lewis and his people did. Had to find out whether this Kilbride was as big a risk to her as he was to those who'd hired her in the first place. And then she'd have to decide how much of a risk her associates—not just Lewis—posed to her. Whether she'd have to do something about them. Because she was done with this. She was through.

She'd ride this out to its conclusion, keeping a close eye on Lewis. She'd taken at least one major precaution in the event he got the jump on her.

Lewis said, 'Maybe, if we get a second, we can run in somewhere, get some coffee. My treat.'

Oh, yeah, he was definitely going to kill her.

'THIS IS GOOD,' Thomas said, shoving another forkful of Marie's tuna medley into his mouth.

'Yeah, not bad,' I said. But I did not have much of an appetite. The things Len had said to Marie, that she'd repeated for me, were stuck in my head. I couldn't shake the feeling he was up to something.

'I'm going to have seconds,' Thomas said.

'That's fine. And maybe you'd like to clean up after dinner.'

'Is that fair?' he asked. 'You didn't make dinner.'

'So maybe we should both clean up,' I said. 'What about that? You clear the table and load the dishwasher, and I'll scrub out that casserole dish.'

'OK,' he said.

Ten minutes later, we were standing side by side at the kitchen counter. Our shoulders were brushing up against each other, and we actually had a kind of rhythm going. It was the closest I'd felt to him since coming back.

But as he was wiping down the kitchen table, Thomas said, 'You ever feel like someone who was your friend really isn't your friend any more?'

'Yeah, that's happened to me a few times. Who are we talking about?'

He caught my eye. 'The president.'

'Clinton?'

Thomas nodded. 'He's always been nice to me, except the last couple of times we've talked, it's kind of different.'

'What do you mean, different?'

'I don't know. He's been telling me I can't talk about certain things.'

'You want to go in and talk to Dr Grigorin tomorrow?'

'That might be good,' he said. 'I don't like it when the president says I'm going to look weak. Like, if I say certain things, I'll be in trouble. He doesn't even want me to tell you.'

'Tell me what?'

'About when I was in the window. When I waved to you, and you didn't see me. Because you didn't look up.'

'When was this, Thomas?'

'The day you tried to find me. When you found my bike in the alley.'

'I rode all over downtown trying to find you. I even shouted your name.'

'I heard you,' Thomas said quietly. 'That was when I got away, and ran to the window. I wanted to call out but I knew he'd get mad. But if you'd seen me, then Dad would have believed my story.'

'Got away? Thomas, what happened?'

'He hurt me,' he said. He briefly tucked his hand under himself. 'He hurt me back here.'

I put both hands on his shoulders, squeezed gently. 'Tell me what happened. Someone did something to you? Who?'

'Dad got so mad,' he said. 'He got so mad when I told him. He said I had to stop making things up. He said if I ever talked about it again, he didn't know what he'd do. But I knew it would be something awful.'

I hugged him. 'Thomas, I'm so sorry.'

'And I think . . . I think I'm ready to talk about it. But the president says I can't. He says if I tell anyone, bad things will happen.'

'Thomas, who hurt you?'

He looked down into his lap. 'I need to think about this.'

'Would you tell Dr Grigorin?'

'I've wanted to, but haven't. You know who I would be OK telling?'

'Who?'

'Julie. She talks to me like I'm a regular person.'

'She's coming back tonight, kind of late, but I'm sure she'd talk to you. Can I be there, or would you like to talk to her by yourself?'

He looked down, pondering. 'It would be OK if you want to be there.'

'OK. But she's not going to be here for a while, so do you want to watch some TV or something?'

'No. I have to go back to work. But before Julie comes, I want to get some pictures to show her. So she'll know what I looked like then. And what you looked like. The photo albums are in the basement.'

He then left me for his room. I went out to the porch and sat there until it was dark enough that you could see the stars. I was preoccupied. Thinking about Julie. About my father. About Len Prentice. About a face in a window, and two dead people in Chicago, and the late Allison Fitch. About how I wouldn't have to be thinking about a lot of these things if Thomas had a different hobby.

I wondered whether Harry Peyton had had a chance yet to talk to this Duckworth guy he'd mentioned. Why hadn't I heard anything yet?

I went inside, grabbed the laptop, and looked up the Promise Falls Police Department. I found a non-emergency number and dialled.

'Promise Falls Police Service,' a woman said.

'I'm trying to reach Detective Duckworth,' I said.

'I think he's gone home,' she said. 'Who's calling?'

'Ray Kilbride.'

'Let me check.' While I was waiting, Thomas came down the stairs.

'I'm going downstairs to look for the photo album,' he said.

'Hello?' the woman on the switchboard said. 'Mr Kilbride? I reached Detective Duckworth at home for you. Hold on and I'll connect you.' There was a pause, and then, 'Go ahead.'

'Hello?' I said. 'Detective Duckworth?'

'Who is this? Not Adam Kilbride.'

'No, sir. This is his son. I'm Ray Kilbride.'

Detective Duckworth said. 'You're the one from Vermont somewhere?'

'Burlington.'

'And your brother, that's Thomas?'

'Yes.' I was guessing Harry had filled him in pretty thoroughly.

'You'll have to forgive me there a second ago,' he said. 'It threw me, when the girl called, said it was Mr Kilbride. I'm sorry about your dad.'

'Well, thanks. I'm in kind of a mess here, as you probably know.'

'Yeah, your dad and I had spoken,' Duckworth said.

'Excuse me?' I said. 'When was this?'

'A couple of weeks back,' Duckworth said. 'That isn't why you're calling? I told your father, if he wanted to proceed, it wasn't going to be an easy thing to prove.'

'Ray!' Thomas shouted.

'Hang on!' I shouted back. 'Sorry. My brother's trying to find a suitcase in the basement. You were saying, it wouldn't be easy to prove . . . ?'

'Not considering all the time that has elapsed. And the fact that your brother's testimony is going to be problematic. Only spoke to your father the once, but he seemed a decent guy, a good father. With a lot on his mind.'

'Detective Duckworth, you won't believe this, but only in the last minute have I got any kind of inkling what you're talking about,' I said. 'My brother was assaulted, wasn't he?'

'Your father didn't share this with you?'

'No. But since I've been here, since Dad died, some things have come up that have made me wonder whether something was going on. Something my father was worried my brother would never forgive him for. And . . .' I hesitated. 'My father had looked up child prostitution on the computer.'

'Yes, well,' Duckworth said, 'that does figure into it. I'm not sure how much to discuss this with you, Ray, and to tell you the truth, your father held back some pretty relevant information. Like exactly who—'

'*Ray!*'

'Detective, have you got a number where I can get back to you? In a couple of minutes? I really need to talk to you.'

'Sure.'

I grabbed a pencil from a kitchen drawer and scribbled the number down on a pad. 'I'll get right back to you.'

I ended the call and left the phone on the counter. As I approached the basement door, I shouted, 'Thomas, I was on the phone.' I didn't see him as I came down the stairs. 'Where the hell are you?'

'Over here,' he said.

I came around the corner, and there was Thomas. His eyes wide with fear. His arms were pulled back. And he wasn't alone. There was a woman standing behind, and to his side. She was holding Thomas by the hair with her left hand. In her right, she had what appeared to be an ice pick, and she had the tip touching the soft part of my brother's neck, just below the jaw.

The woman said, 'So you're Ray.'

'Yes,' I said, unable to take my eyes off the ice pick.

'And this one? Thomas? He's your brother?'

'Yes,' I said. 'Please don't hurt him.'

I had never seen Thomas look more terrified. 'Ray, tell her to let me go!'

'It's OK, Thomas. I'm going to give her whatever she wants.'

'That's good, Ray,' the woman said. 'So long as you cooperate, everything will be fine.' I noticed she had one of those Bluetooth thingies in her ear. 'You're clear to come in,' she said, like she was talking to her shoulder. 'We're in the basement.'

'Just tell me what you want,' I said.

'Right now I want you to be quiet,' she said, still holding Thomas by the hair, the ice pick dimpling his neck. 'Things'll be moving along shortly.'

I thought I could hear a car pulling up to the house. Then a door opening and closing. About half a minute later, the front door opened, and I heard someone coming down the steps behind me. I turned my head round, and got a look at him. Tall, bald, heavyset, a nose that had been broken.

He looked at me. 'So you're Ray Kilbride.'

'This is the brother,' the woman said. 'Thomas.'

'Hello, Thomas,' the man said, his voice even. 'I'm Lewis. I see you've met Nicole.' I noticed a bulge under his leather bomber jacket that was larger than an ice pick. Slung over his shoulder was a small backpack.

'There's not much here but you're welcome to it,' I said.

Lewis cocked his head. 'You think this is a robbery?'

'They can't have my computer,' Thomas blurted.

'What do you want, then?' I asked.

'I want you to put your hands behind your back,' Lewis said. He unzipped the backpack and took out a set of plastic handcuffs.

'Please,' I said. 'This is some kind of mistake.'

Lewis said, 'If I have to ask you again to put your hands behind your back, my friend's going to let some air into your brother's neck.'

I put my hands behind me. He slipped the narrow plastic bands over both wrists and pulled them snug. They bit cruelly into my skin.

'You good, Lewis?' the woman asked.

'Yeah,' he said, at which point the woman took the pick away from Thomas's throat. She gave him a small shove in my direction.

'I'm scared, Ray,' he said. I could see his wrists were cuffed.

'I know,' I said. 'Me, too.'

'We take them both?' Nicole asked Lewis.

'Good question,' he said. 'Let me think on that. First, I'm gonna do a walk-through of the house. Make sure there isn't anyone else around.'

He was back in two minutes. 'What's the story upstairs?' he asked.

'The maps?' I said.

'Yeah. And the computer.'

'They're mine,' Thomas said. 'I hope you didn't touch any of them.'

'I think we need to move this party upstairs,' Lewis said.

Thomas went up the stairs after Lewis, and Nicole followed me. I thought about spinning round and giving the woman a good kick in the face, and maybe if it had just been her, I'd have tried. But if that bulge in Lewis's jacket was a gun, as I suspected, he'd make quick work of the two of us.

We crossed the living room and went up the stairs to the landing. Nicole had not seen what Lewis had already found. A hallway with maps stuck to the walls everywhere.

'It gets better in here,' Lewis said, pushing open the door to Thomas's room. Nicole went in first, seemingly mesmerised by the walls.

'And look at this,' Lewis said to her, pointing to the computer monitors. 'Where is that?' he asked me.

Thomas said, 'Lisbon.'

'Lisbon,' Lewis repeated. 'This is Whirl360, right?'

Thomas nodded.

'Why are you looking at Lisbon?'

I said, 'He looks at cities all over the world. It's a hobby.'

Thomas shot me a look. Then, to Lewis he said, 'You know, don't you?'

'Excuse me?'

'About the maps disappearing, and how I'm going to help the black-ops people. You're the bad guys.'

Lewis cracked a smile. 'I guess we are. So, which one of you was looking up Orchard Street on here?' He looked at me. 'I thought it was you, since you're the one who came knocking on the door.'

I felt a chill. It was starting to become clear just how much trouble we were in. 'The neighbour?' I said.

Lewis shook his head. 'Motion-activated camera. Got a picture of what you were holding in your hand.'

'Oh,' I said. So now we knew.

'I found it,' Thomas said, a hint of pride in his voice. 'I saw the lady with the bag over her head. Ray went to check it out for me.'

Lewis looked at Nicole and said, 'Well, I guess that answers your question.' When she raised a questioning eyebrow, he added, 'About whether we're taking one of them or both.'

'We should take that with us,' Nicole said, pointing to the computer tower that was connected to Thomas's monitors.

'Good idea,' Lewis said.

'No,' Thomas protested. 'No, no!'

'Thomas,' I said. 'There's bigger stuff at stake here than the computer.'

'But it's mine!' he said. He was horrified, watching Lewis start to unplug the wires that ran out of the back of it. 'Stop it!'

Calmly, Nicole said to me, 'Are you going to be able to control him?'

'Yes. Just let me talk to him a second.'

Nicole allowed us to move a couple of feet away. I faced Thomas, leaned my head in close enough that I was nearly touching his forehead.

'Listen. We're in a tough spot here. I can always get you another computer. But the only way I'm going to have a chance to do that is if we cooperate with them. You hearing me?'

He looked into my eyes. 'You'd have to get me one that's just as fast.'

'I'll get you one that's even faster,' I said, making a promise I knew I was never going to be able to keep.

Lewis pulled the disconnected tower to the edge of the desk and asked me, 'So what were you doing there?'

'My brother was on that site, he saw something funny in the window, and he asked me to check it out when I was in the city.'

'Oh,' Lewis said. 'So, it was just a huge co-inkydink?'

I smiled nervously. 'Pretty much.'

'Yeah,' Lewis said, and came over, putting his face to within an inch of mine. 'When we get where we're going, you're going to need to come up with a better story than that.'

'Where are we going?' I asked.

Lewis reached into the backpack and brought out a roll of grey duct tape. He tossed it to Nicole.

'I'm telling you the truth,' I said. 'We don't know anything.'

Nicole tore off a six-inch strip and slapped it over my mouth.

'Don't do that to me,' Thomas said, as Nicole started tearing off another strip. 'Don't do that!' He was in mid-scream as she applied the tape to him.

Lewis zipped up the backpack, slipped the strap over one shoulder, then picked up the computer tower. Just then, a very faint ringing.

'What's that?' Nicole said. 'That your cellphone?'

Lewis's eyes landed on the old land-line phone on Thomas's desk. It was flashing with an incoming call. He always kept the ring volume very low and he hardly got any calls, anyway. It could only be a wrong number or a telemarketer. But Nicole and Lewis wouldn't know that.

Lewis snatched up the receiver. When he spoke, he adopted the tone of someone sick with a cold. 'Hello?'

After a pause, he said, 'It's Thomas.' A sniff. 'I'm coming down with something. Who's this?'

Then Lewis said, 'Yeah, well, I'd love to chat, Bill, but it's my bowling night with Dubya.' He hung up the phone. 'Crank call,' he said. 'Some ass pretending to be Bill Clinton.'

I glanced at Thomas. I am sure I looked more surprised than he did, because he didn't look surprised at all. Annoyed, maybe, that he hadn't been allowed to speak.

Lewis headed out of the room and down the stairs, the computer tower in his arms. Nicole motioned with her ice pick for us to follow. I wondered whether there was anything I could do now that Nicole was, briefly, without her partner. But she had a weapon, and I had no free hand.

Outside, Lewis and Nicole corralled us at the rear doors of a white, mostly windowless van. Nicole held her hand out for Lewis's backpack. He tossed it over and she produced the tape again, looping it around my knees and ankles. She did the same with Thomas, then opened the two doors at the rear of the van. It was wide open for cargo, with two seats up front. I saw what looked like a small pile of folded moving blankets.

From his backpack, Lewis took out what looked like winter ski masks, with holes for the eyes, mouth and nose. He pulled the mask over my head, with the holes at the back. I heard Thomas grunting as his went on. Someone took me by the shoulders and guided me none too gently into the van.

'OK,' Lewis said to Thomas. 'Shuffle on over here.' I felt the van shift as Thomas fell into it.

Then Nicole's voice. 'We'll be on the road for a few hours. We'll be making stops. Tolls, gas. Don't be stupid and make any noise. That will get you killed. It'll also get whoever hears you killed.'

'We already need gas,' Lewis said.

I heard some ruffling next to me. The moving blankets. Someone was unfolding them. They were draped over us.

The rear doors slammed shut; then the driver's door opened and closed, followed by the passenger's. The key was turned and the van rumbled to life. We rolled on down the driveway, away from my father's house, and then turned onto the road. *We're never coming back here*, I thought.

Just after we left the house, we made a stop for gas. I guessed we were at the Exxon. It wasn't long before I was certain we were on an interstate.

Lying on the floor of the van, one thought kept surfacing through my fear: *Who the hell called Thomas's phone?* It made no sense to me at all. It couldn't be Clinton. *Couldn't* be.

As I was thinking that, another phone began to ring. We were about half an hour into our trip. After two rings, I heard Lewis say, 'Here.'

I struggled to hear his side of the conversation.

'Yeah, we're on the way back . . . no problems . . . yeah, he's got a brother, he's the one found the thing online . . . he's kind of weird . . . Yeah, OK, I'm bringing back a computer they were using to surf that web site . . . Yeah, and one other thing, kinda strange. Phone rang, I answered it, pretended to be the brother. Caller said he was Bill Clinton . . . No, no real accent, but I talked to him only a second . . . I mean, yeah, s'what I figured, too, a crank call or something . . . OK, see ya at the toy store.'

After another couple of miles, Nicole said, 'I got a cop in my side mirror.' So Nicole was driving. 'Coming up in the passing lane.'

And then we all heard a couple of *whoops* of the siren. I could sense Thomas stirring close to me. He'd no doubt been listening, just as I had.

The van slowed. 'Just be cool,' Lewis said. He called back to us, 'Either of you makes a sound, cop gets shot.'

The van went off the edge of the shoulder and came to a stop. Nicole put it into park, left the motor running.

'Pulling in right behind us,' she said. 'Here he—it's a woman.'

I heard a window power down. Nicole said, 'Officer.'

'Licence and registration,' she said.

'Sure. Hon, you want to check the glove box?' Nicole asked Lewis.

'This your van?' the woman asked.

'No, it's a rental,' Nicole said. 'We're just going to his sister's in White Plains, helping her move to Albany. Was I speeding?'

'You have a taillight out,' the police officer said.

'Oh, nuts. Is that my fault?' Nicole asked. 'Isn't it the rental agency's?'

Nicole was good.

'I'm not going to ticket you. But if you're going to have this truck for any length of time, you're going to have to get it fixed.'

'Appreciate that. OK, here's the registration, and here's my licence.'

'I'm going to take these back to my vehicle, ma'am. Please wait here.'

I heard the officer's footsteps as she went back to her cruiser. Minutes later, she was back, saying, 'OK, here you go. Your licence, registration. And you get that taillight fixed, first opportunity.'

'Of course,' Nicole said.

And then the cop asked, 'What you got in there?'

I didn't know about Thomas, but my heart stopped.

But Nicole didn't miss a beat. She said, 'We have a stack of moving blankets so the furniture doesn't get scratched.'

'You mind opening up the back for me?' the woman said.

'Sure,' Nicole said. I heard a seat belt unbuckle and retract. A door opened and it sounded as though Nicole had got out. Two sets of footsteps came down the side of the van, came to a stop around the back.

She's going to die. The cop is going to die.

I was expecting to hear the door unlatch, but instead there was some kind of electronic squawking. Static. Then the cop saying something unintelligible. Then, 'Good night, ma'am. You can go.' Then footsteps running away, the roar of the police car, tyres hitting asphalt and squealing.

A door opened again and the van shifted slightly as Nicole got back in.

'What the hell happened?' Lewis asked.

'She got some kind of emergency call.'

Over the next hour, there was the sound of more traffic. We were clearly in a more densely populated area. Finally, the van lurched to a stop, then backed up, turning sharply. The sound of the engine echoed back at us, like we were in a garage, or an alley.

Nicole killed the engine and the two of them got out. Seconds later, the back doors opened.

'OK, kids, we're here,' Nicole said.

It can't mean anything, Howard thought, moments after he'd finished talking to Lewis. That call to the Kilbride house from someone claiming to be Bill Clinton was, no doubt, what Lewis believed it to be. A crank call. Or it could even be that it *was* Bill Clinton, just not *the* Bill Clinton. Promise Falls probably had half a dozen Bill Clintons.

And as worried as Howard was about the CIA's possible involvement in his and Morris's troubles, it made no sense at all to him that a former president would in any way be involved.

Soon enough, he'd sort it out, once he was able to ask Ray Kilbride and his brother questions face to face. He had every confidence that Lewis, and this woman who'd botched things in the first place, and whom Lewis had brought along, would be able to persuade them to talk.

Howard wondered about that, about why Lewis had brought her in for this. He had a feeling, now that this matter was coming to a close, Lewis was going to settle things. The woman's error had caused them all a great deal of grief. Lewis would do what he felt he had to do. And Howard didn't need to know about it.

Nearly three hours later, another call from Lewis. 'We've arrived.'

'I'll be there shortly,' Howard said.

They'd got into the city late, behind schedule. Howard was not going to be able to have his meeting with Morris Sawchuck. He'd call him from the car.

Howard stepped out onto the front stoop of his 81st Street brownstone. His black Mercedes was parked just up the street. He walked to it and got out his cellphone, and called Morris.

'Hey,' Morris said. 'I'm on my way.'

There were muffled driving sounds in the background. He'd be in his town car, with his driver, Heather.

'I'm sorry, Morris, but I'm afraid I'm going to have to reschedule our all-nighter.'

'What's going on?'

'I'm a little under the weather. Might be the flu. A hundred apologies.'

'Sorry to hear that. You need to take care of yourself.'

'Thank you. I'm grateful for your understanding.' Howard forced a chuckle. 'Our plans for world domination will hold until tomorrow.' He opened the door, slipped in behind the wheel.

'Of course,' Morris said. 'We'll talk then.'

Howard ended the call, pulled his door shut. He keyed the ignition and took off down the street.

HEATHER WAS JUST TURNING the town car onto 81st when Morris, in the back seat, was telling his friend to take care of himself.

Heather said, 'Isn't that Mr Talliman up ahead, sir?'

Morris saw Howard's car pulling away from the kerb.

'Yes,' Morris said. 'He certainly appears well enough to drive. Let's see where he goes.'

Which they did. All the way downtown to East 4th Street.

Howard parked his Mercedes and walked up to the front door of a darkened shop. There was an alley to the left of it, and a white van parked there.

'What is that place?' Morris asked.

'Ferber's Antiques,' Heather said. Even though the display window was unlit, she said she thought she could see a variety of children's toys.

'What the hell is he doing at a toy store in the middle of the night?' Morris said. 'The place is closed.'

'Yes,' Heather said, 'but someone's there. A light came on in the back.'

Morris watched as someone unlocked the door, opened it wide enough to allow Howard to slip inside, then closed it after him. The shop went dark.

'We'll wait,' Morris said.

THIRTEEN

Earlier that evening, the Promise Falls City Council was in a heated debate about whether to sell advertising on city land.

Julie McGill, sitting at the press table, thought she'd rather be making calls about Allison Fitch: who she was, why she'd disappeared, how she'd ended up dead in Florida. She believed there was a story there, but she knew that when and if she got it, it'd be a hard sell with her editors. She'd have to sell them on a local angle. That'd be Thomas, who'd inadvertently uncovered whatever it was that had happened by exploring the planet on Whirl360.

That gave her pause. Would Thomas be OK being part of the story? How would Ray feel about it?

The ads-in-gardens debate ended with a courageous vote to defer any decision at all. Julie grabbed her note pad and her bag and filed her story from the *Standard* office on the premises. Then she got in her car and headed out of town to the Kilbride place.

She was about 200 yards from her destination when she saw a white panel van pulling out of the driveway, heading her way. The van's headlights flashed past. She couldn't see who was driving, and didn't really even try to catch a look. She did catch a glance in her side mirror of the van retreating, enough to notice that it had one burnt-out taillight.

Julie turned into the drive, rolled the car up to the house. Ray's car was there, as was his father's old Chrysler van, and the house was lit up like there was a party going on.

She grabbed two bottles of wine that she'd picked up earlier, got out of the car, climbed the steps to the porch and rapped on the door. When no one came after ten seconds, she opened it and shouted, 'Hello?'

She waited a moment. When she heard nothing, she called out, 'Ray? I can't drink all this wine alone! Well, maybe.' Still no response.

She went into the house, set the bottles on the closest chair, and gazed into the kitchen. No one there, so she went to the bottom of the stairs and called up, 'Anybody home?'

Julie went up the steps two at a time, poking her head first in Thomas's room. *Something about Thomas's room*. A jumble of disconnected wires on the desktop. All three monitors were blank.

The computer tower was gone.

'What the . . .' Julie said under her breath.

She went back downstairs, and she noticed light spilling up from behind the open basement door. 'Anyone down there?' she called.

She went down the stairs even though no one responded. Something on the floor caught her attention. Something more worrying than the missing computer tower. A white plastic wrist restraint. 'No,' she whispered.

She ran back to her car. She'd been here, what, maybe four minutes? A van could cover four or more miles in that time. What kind of chance did she have of catching up with it?

That didn't stop her from spinning the car around and hitting fifty miles per hour before she'd reached the end of the drive. The car skittered and nearly went onto two wheels as she turned onto the road, then floored it in the direction the van had gone.

Once she hit the first intersection, which direction would she go? Left? Right? Straight? She didn't have a clue where the van was headed. On top of that, she didn't know with any certainty that Ray and Thomas were in it.

Why the hell hadn't she just rung Ray's cellphone? She fumbled blindly through her bag until she'd found her phone. She held it, one eye on the road and one on the phone, and called up his number, tapped it.

After the seventh ring, it went to voicemail. 'Hi, this is Ray. I can't—'

'Hell!' Julie screamed, but not because Ray had not picked up. She slammed on the brakes, let her phone fly so she could get both hands on the wheel, and steered the car onto the shoulder. Up ahead, at the Exxon station, was the van. A man was using the self-serve pump to fill the vehicle.

What to do? She wasn't even sure it was the same van that had pulled out of Ray's place. It sure looked like the same one. Should she drive in?

All she could think of was Allison Fitch, the dead couple in Chicago. If the people who'd killed them had figured out Ray had been to the apartment, then . . . The man replaced the cap on the van's gas tank, replaced the pump, and went into the Exxon to pay.

Before Julie could decide what to do, the man returned to the van, getting in on the passenger side. The taillight came on—just one, so this was the right van—as the vehicle braked briefly before pulling out of the station and got back on the road.

The van soon found its way onto the interstate, and got on the southbound. Which, if you followed it for a couple of hours, would take you into New York City. Julie glanced at her fuel gauge. About half a tank. She hoped to God that wherever this van was going, it got there before she ran out of gas.

Once they were on the highway, Julie stayed well back so as not to make the driver of the van suspicious. She unbuckled her seat belt and managed to reach her phone on the floor in front of the passenger seat with her right hand. Glancing back and forth between her phone and the road, she called the Promise Falls police, identified herself as a reporter for the *Standard*, and asked to speak to Detective Barry Duckworth.

'He's off duty,' the dispatcher said.

'Well, get him at home and tell him to call me!' Julie said. She rattled off her number. 'Just have him call me, OK? It's about the Kilbrides.'

'We'll see,' the dispatcher said frostily, and hung up.

Seconds after the call, a police car screamed past Julie in the passing lane, giving her a momentary heart attack.

As it got closer to the van it slipped into the lane behind it, rode there for a moment or so, and then the flashing lights came on.

'Yes!' Julie said as the van pulled over to the shoulder.

Julie did the same, killing her lights, but she kept going along the shoulder, closing the distance between herself and the patrol car a little, then stopping, so she could get a better look at what was going on.

The cop—it looked like a woman—approached the van. She shared some words with the driver, probably asking for licence and registration. Then she went back to the cop car, got in.

A good three minutes went by before the cop got back out of her car and returned the paperwork to the driver. Then—hello, what was this? The driver—it was a woman—was getting out, coming round to the back of the van with the cop. *She wants her to open up the back.*

But just as the blonde had her hand on the lever, the cop turned and ran back to her cruiser, hopped in and sped away. Julie guessed that an urgent call had taken priority. The van continued on its way. So did Julie.

Almost twenty minutes later, her cellphone rang. She answered without looking to see who it was.

'Detective Duckworth here. What's so important, Ms McGill?'

'I think—OK, I don't know for sure—but I think someone may have snatched Ray Kilbride and his brother.' She told him about getting to the Kilbride house seconds after the van pulled out of the driveway. The fact that no one was home. The missing computer, the plastic wrist restraint.

'He was supposed to call me back,' Duckworth said. 'Ray Kilbride called me. Then he was interrupted, said he was going to call me back soon, and he hasn't. Listen, I'm gonna go out to the Kilbride house, see what's going on. You got the licence plate on the van?'

'I'm not close enough to read it. When I had the chance, I wasn't thinking.'

'OK, look, anything happens with the van, call me at this number.'

'I got it.' She stayed with the van.

There was an accident at the far end of the Lincoln Tunnel. Traffic was getting through a car at a time by the mouth. The white van was about five cars ahead. Once it was past the accident, it took off.

By the time Julie's car was past it, the van was nowhere to be seen.

AFTER DRAGGING ME from the van, Nicole or Lewis tore off the tape that was binding my legs. The ski mask stayed on. They led me through a door and guided me down what I supposed was a short hallway. Hands from behind held my shoulders, as though guiding me through a doorway.

Then the hands stopped me, and turned me 180 degrees.

'Sit,' Lewis said, working my bound arms over the back of what felt like a wooden chair, then shoving me down into it. Then he ran a couple of loops of duct tape about my waist, securing me to it. He didn't tape my ankles to the legs. Suddenly, someone grabbed a fistful of ski mask at the top of my head and yanked.

I blinked several times as my eyes adjusted to the light. Lewis was standing in front of me, then moved out of the way as Nicole brought Thomas into the room. He was pushed down onto a second chair a couple of feet away from me, taped in, and then Nicole pulled his ski mask off. He blinked a couple of times, then exchanged a frightened glance with me.

'I'll get the computer,' Lewis said. 'And let Howard know we're here.'

We were in a windowless room, about twelve by twelve, that had the feel of being the back of a shop. In one corner was a heavy, antique desk, on which sat a computer. The walls were almost entirely covered in shelves crammed with musty books, antique clocks, Royal Doulton figurines. But most of all, there were toys. Decades-old tinplate cars and trucks. Pewter toy soldiers. A set of lawn darts and hoops, like we once had and played with in the back yard. But I didn't feel nostalgic, looking at these treasures from yesterday. What I felt was scared.

Lewis returned with the computer tower and set it on the desk. He detached various cables from the computer that was there, then attached them to Thomas's.

Nicole addressed Thomas and me. 'Someone's going to be asking you some questions, so the tape's coming off. If either one of you starts yelling, I hurt the other one. Fast and hard. Are we clear?'

We both nodded. Nicole ripped the tape off me with one short, cruel, backhanded stroke. I winced, licked my lips. When she did it to Thomas, he yelped. 'That hurt!' he said. But then he immediately apologised to Nicole. 'Sorry. I'll be quiet. Don't hurt Ray.'

I said to him, 'You OK?'

'No. My arms hurt, my lips hurt, and I can't feel my hands.'

I couldn't feel mine, either. The plastic cuffs had cut off most of the circulation. I appealed to Nicole. 'My brother's hands, they're probably turning blue. Mine, too. Can you help us out here?'

Lewis went into his backpack for a pair of orange-handled snippers. 'Don't do anything stupid,' he said as he cut my cuffs, then secured my wrists to the chair with duct tape. The blood rushed back into my fingers, and I closed and opened my hands a dozen times to get the tingling out of them. Lewis did the same thing for Thomas, then went back to work on the computer tower, hooking up the last of the cables and pressing the start button. The machine began to whir and the monitor he'd commandeered started lighting up.

Thomas said, 'Anything that's on there is confidential.'

Lewis ignored him. He went on the net and checked the computer's history. Thomas hadn't had an opportunity to clear it, but there wasn't much to look at. Just plenty of locations from Whirl360. He opened up the mail program. He was opening one email after another, no doubt trying to puzzle out what Thomas was up to with all his updates to the CIA.

Everyone looked up when we heard a knock. It sounded as though it was coming from the front of the store. Lewis pulled aside a green curtain that served as a door between this room and the front of the shop. As light spilled into the front room, I could make out more displays of antique toys.

'It's him,' Lewis said as he slipped out of the room. Who was *him*?

I heard a bell jingle as Lewis opened a door. There was some muffled conversation, then two sets of footsteps working their way to the back of the store. I heard a man ask Lewis, 'What is this place?'

Lewis said, 'One of the guys who helped me move Bridget's body owns it. He's a toy nut.'

Bridget?

Then Lewis appeared, holding back the curtain to allow a short, balding man in his fifties to come in. He was wearing a topcoat that looked like it was made of camel hair or cashmere, and an expensive suit under that.

He ran his eyes over Thomas and me. 'So, these are our guys,' he said. Then his eyes landed on Nicole. 'You,' he said contemptuously. 'You're the one who messed this up.'

'Nice to meet you at last, too, Howard,' she said, staring him down.

Thomas and I gave Howard an excuse to break eye contact with her. He said to me, 'Which one are you?'

'Ray Kilbride. That's Thomas. My brother.'

Thomas said, 'Tell that man—Lewis—to leave my computer alone.'

Howard turned to Lewis and said, 'You have it hooked up?'

'Yeah. There's some weird emails on here.'

Howard reached into his jacket for a slender case, from which he extracted a pair of reading glasses. 'Open a few.'

Lewis did some clicking. Howard read quickly through the emails. 'Are they all like this? All addressed to Bill Clinton, care of the CIA?'

'Yeah.'

Howard looked at Lewis. 'Tell me about the phone call again.'

'Someone called the house, asked for that one, said it was Bill Clinton.'

'But you also said it didn't sound like him.'

Lewis shrugged. 'I've never talked to the man, but no, I don't think it sounded like him.'

'People sound different on the phone,' Thomas said.

'What about in the inbox, or the deleted messages. Are there actually any messages from Bill Clinton or anyone at the CIA?'

Lewis did some clicking. 'Nothing.'

Howard went back through the curtain and returned with another chair. He sat it in front of Thomas and me. He looked first at me.

'Ray, I have a number of questions I need straight answers to. I suppose you understand what will happen if you don't provide them?'

'I have a pretty good idea,' I said.

He nodded. 'We'll get back to the Clinton thing. But it makes sense to start from the beginning. Who do you work for?'

'I'm self-employed. I'm an illustrator. I work freelance.'

'I see. You don't do any freelance work that's not related to illustration?'

'No.'

'And how about you?' he asked Thomas. 'For whom do you work?'

'I'm sort of self-employed, too,' he said. 'But I work for the CIA.'

'That's not true,' I said. 'Thomas—'

Howard held up a hand to shush me. 'Thomas, tell me what you do for the CIA.'

'I shouldn't be telling you,' he said. 'It's black ops.'

Howard's eyebrows shot up. 'Black ops?'

'That's what President Clinton said. But that's just part of it.'

'If you don't tell me, Thomas, I'm going to have them start by breaking one of your brother's fingers.'

'Don't hurt him,' Thomas said. But I could see him struggling with whether to sacrifice me to protect the mission.

'It's OK,' I said. 'Tell them.' I decided to play into his world view. 'I would imagine they already know most of it, anyway.'

'Well,' Thomas said, 'I'm helping them for when all the online maps disappear, because that's going to happen sooner or later, and also I'm going to be on call, if there's an agent in trouble. Like, if he's on the run and doesn't know which way to go, he'll call me and I can tell him.'

'Explain that a little more,' Howard said.

'I memorise maps. I memorise cities. I memorise the streets. So when all the maps disappear, I can help.'

Lewis said, 'The computer history's all Whirl360.'

'You memorise streets on Whirl360?' Howard asked.

Thomas nodded. 'That's right.'

Howard gave him a sceptical look. 'OK,' he said, playing along. 'My mother lives on Atlantic Avenue, in Boston. She has an apartment there.'

Thomas closed his eyes. 'Near Beach Street? That's nice along there. Is she in that building with the real-estate office on the first floor? All the sidewalks there are made of red brick. They look nice.' He opened his eyes.

Howard appeared slightly unnerved. I said, 'He's never been to Boston.'

'I got one,' Lewis said. 'The 2,700th block of California Street in Denver. Between 27th and 28th.' He said to Howard, 'I grew up there.'

Thomas closed his eyes again. 'Was it in one of the one-storey blue houses, or the six-storey apartment building across the street with the walls that are kind of white, then go to brick colour, then back to white, and—'

Lewis said, 'It's like he's got a computer in his head.'

Howard took a very long breath, laced his fingers together, and rested his forearms on his thighs. 'How many cities are you memorising, Thomas?'

'All of them,' he said.

'All of them in the United States?'

'In the world,' Thomas said. 'I'm not done. The world's very big.'

'So this is what you do, you memorise these streets,' Howard said, a statement, not a question. 'And what are all those emails about?'

'Updates,' Thomas said. 'On how the project is going. When I memorise new cities, or parts of them, I let the president know.'

'And what's this other thing, about all the online maps disappearing?'

Thomas gave Howard a wary look. 'There's going to be some kind of catastrophic event that destroys all the online maps. A virus or something. This will happen after everyone's got rid of their paper maps.'

Now Howard looked at me. 'Is he for real?'

'Yes,' I said.

'Does this freakish ability of his have something to do with why you showed up at Allison Fitch's apartment on Orchard Street?'

I nodded. 'Thomas was memorising that street, and he saw the woman in the window. With the bag over her head. He wanted me to check it out.'

'How did he know to look for it?'

'He didn't. He just found it.'

'No,' Howard said. 'I don't believe that.' He turned to Lewis. 'What do you think?'

'Seems kind of unlikely to me. Maybe someone asked him to look for it.'

'Is that what happened, Thomas? Someone asked you to look for it?'

'No,' he said. 'Nobody did.'

'Not even Bill Clinton?' Howard followed the question with a laugh.

'No, I send him the progress reports. He's my liaison with the agency.'

'But he never emails you back.'

'He talks to me. Lately, he's been using the phone.'

'What, his voice just comes to you?'

Thomas nodded.

'Thomas,' Howard continued, 'do you see a doctor? A psychiatrist?'

'Yes. Dr Grigorin.'

'And does he have you on medication?'

'It's a she,' Thomas said. 'Yes. It makes the voices go away. For the most part. But I can still hear the president sometimes.'

'With a phone, and without a phone,' Howard said.

'The phone's clearer,' Thomas said.

'No way,' Howard said again. 'There's just no way.'

'You're right,' I said tentatively, making Howard look at me. 'It makes no sense that a former president of the United States would be phoning Thomas and using him for the CIA—his view of reality is sometimes at odds with what the rest of us believe. He was diagnosed with schizophrenia when he was younger.' I continued, 'I mean, this whole thing about all the maps disappearing, and black ops—it's kind of over the top. But let's say you hear of someone with a tremendous gift, and who believes that powerful people are interested in what he has to offer. Do you call him up and say, "Hi, this is Joe Blow, I wonder if you could do a little snooping around for me?" Or do you call him up and say, "Hi, I used to be President of the United States, and I need your help."'

Howard studied me for several seconds. 'What are you saying?'

'That my brother's not working for the CIA. But he is, unknowingly'—I looked apologetically at Thomas—'helping Carlo Vachon.'

'Vachon?' Lewis said. 'The mob guy?'

'And,' I continued, 'they value Thomas so much, there's a very good chance his people are watching this place right now.'

'Preposterous,' Howard said. 'That's simply preposterous.'

'Hang on, hang on, hang on,' Lewis said, shaking his hand at Howard. 'When I was checking this guy out'—he nodded at me—'I came across one of his drawings, his illustrations, you call them. Of Carlo Vachon.'

'That's right,' I said. 'I did it for a magazine, and he liked it so much, he wanted to buy it. I didn't want to take any money for it—not that he offered. But when we said he could have it, he invited me to lunch.'

'You had lunch with Carlo Vachon,' Howard said. 'Where?'

Think fast. 'The Tribeca Grand.' Where I had met with Kathleen Ford.

'What did you have?' Howard asked.

Don't try to lie any more than you have to.

'I have no idea. I was scared and remember almost nothing.' I paused. 'But he asked me about my family, and I got to talking about my brother, and what he does, and Vachon became very, very interested.'

Howard didn't say anything this time. He waited.

But Thomas jumped in. 'You never told me about this.'

'Just hang on.' To Howard, I said, 'Vachon didn't care all that much about the rest of the world, but having a guy who knew New York City, who could remember every street detail, he said he could use someone like that. For some of the same reasons Thomas mentioned, like if you have an agent on the run. Except it's not agents. It's people working for Vachon.'

'I'm not happy about this, Ray,' Thomas said.

'He's not an easy guy to say no to,' I said.

Howard and Lewis were exchanging looks, wondering whether to believe this stuff. The good thing was, it seemed to be buying me some time. I wondered what efforts, if any, were being made to find us. Julie had been intending to come back to the house. What would she have done when she found the house empty, no sign of us, the car still in the driveway?

Howard was about to say something, when his cellphone rang. He took it out, saw who it was, and grimaced.

He put the phone to his ear. 'Hi, Morris . . . No, no, don't worry, you didn't wake me . . . Yes, I'm in bed . . . Yes, sure, I could call him tomorrow . . . No, I don't mind, and again, I'm sorry about having to cancel tonight. I just wasn't up to it . . . Uh huh . . . OK, then . . . You, too, take care.'

He ended the call, put the phone away, returned his attention to me. 'Now, where were we? Oh, yes, your story. I find it implausible at best.'

'What part of everything you've heard so far *does* strike you as plausible?' I asked. 'My brother found, online, a murder you folks carried out. Does that sound plausible? Does it sound plausible that a bunch of professional killers like you would leave yourselves so vulnerable?' I had him there. 'If you don't believe me, why don't you call Vachon?'

Howard laughed. 'Now, there's an idea. I'll give the head of one of New York's most powerful crime families a call in the middle of the night.' Then he got serious. 'Let's say this story of yours is true,' he said. 'Was it Vachon who had him looking for the window?'

Which was the better answer? Yes, Vachon was on to them, or no, he didn't know a damn thing about it? Maybe, if I'd had some idea of who'd actually died in the apartment, I'd know which answer to give. At one point we'd thought Allison Fitch had been murdered there, but she'd died only in the past day. Lewis had said the words 'Bridget's body' to Howard when he had arrived. I had no idea who Bridget was.

While I was thinking, Thomas said, 'I found it on my own. I told you.'

Howard turned so he could look at Lewis. 'If this is some random event, if this *Rain Man* freak here really stumbled upon that image on the web site by chance, then our problems end here.'

'Yeah,' Lewis said.

Howard addressed Nicole. 'Have you any thoughts on this matter?'

She thought a moment. 'I think, if Vachon's guys were keeping tabs on Thomas, they'd have rescued him by now. If you feel your other concerns have been addressed, then all you have left to do is get rid of these two.'

'Yes,' Howard said. 'You may be—'

I think it's fair to say all of us just about jumped out of our skin at that moment. Someone was banging on the front door of the shop. Then, shouting, 'Howard! Howard, I know you're in there!'

Howard's eyes went wide. 'Dear God,' he said. 'It's Morris.'

FOURTEEN

Shortly after putting his phone away, Morris Sawchuck said to his driver, Heather, 'I'm gonna find out what the son of a bitch is up to.'

'I'll be here,' she said.

Morris got out of the town car, stormed across the street and banged on the door of the toy shop. 'Howard! Howard, I know you're in there!' He put his face up to the window and cupped his hands around his eyes.

Inside the shop, a curtain was pulled back and Howard strode towards the door. He turned back the deadbolt and opened the door six inches.

'You're up and around,' Sawchuck said. 'Open the door.'

'Morris, you can't—'

Morris threw his shoulder into the door and knocked it wide open.

'What's going on here?' Morris demanded.

'You have to leave. You don't want to be here. You have to—'

'I'm not going anywhere. You lied to me, Howard. You lied about being sick. And I've got a feeling you've been lying to me for a long time. I swear, if you don't tell me what's going on, I'll—' He looked to the back of the store, and the light coming through the curtain. 'What's going on in there?'

Howard, pleading, said, 'You have to leave. This is what I do for you, Morris. I keep things from you. I get things done.'

Morris made it to the curtain in two seconds, threw it back and stared.

A man he recognised—Lewis, who had done work for Howard for years—and a woman, standing at the back of the room, he did not.

And two men bound to chairs.

'Hello, Morris,' Lewis said.

Howard stepped through the curtain. 'Morris, I told you—'

'Who are these men?' Morris asked.

'I'm Ray Kilbride,' said one. 'And this is my brother, Thomas.'

'Untie these men,' Morris ordered.

Howard said, 'It's not that simple.'

'Oh, I think it is,' Morris spluttered. 'I don't know what the hell is going on here, but this is kidnapping.'

'It's about the murder,' Thomas said. 'On Orchard Street.'

'What murder? What are you talking about?'

The one named Ray said, 'I don't know, but I think it might be someone named Bridget.'

THE MOMENT I UTTERED the words, it was like the air had suddenly been sucked out of the room. Something palpable happened to Howard, Lewis and Nicole at that moment. Their breath was taken away and they didn't know what to do about it.

And this man they were calling Morris, it was like he'd been hit by lightning. Stunned by what I'd said, too shocked to react in any way but to look stupefied. And yet, I could see that wheels were turning. There was something about his eyes, like they were moving around at a hundred miles an hour, processing this latest bit of information.

The moment Morris had walked into the room, I had recognised him. I couldn't place him at first. If I'd been watching the news, I'd have known instantly. But seeing him here, in the back of this toy store, with three very bad people, I couldn't figure out who he was.

So it took a minute or so before I realised this man was the attorney general for the State of New York. Morris Sawchuck. Hadn't there been a lot going on with him a few months back? My mind was racing. Why had he been on the news so much? Why had I seen his picture so often? And in all those pictures, wasn't he usually shown with a beautiful—

Now I remembered the stories. The sudden, unexplained death of Bridget Sawchuck. You had to read between the lines to guess what had happened. She'd killed herself. Except Lewis had said this shop was owned by someone who'd helped him move Bridget's body.

Oh, Thomas, what did you get us into?

Morris was the first to speak. And he spoke to me. 'What did you say?'

'The person who got killed. It might have been Bridget.' Now I realised I was talking about this man's wife. What I didn't know was whether Morris Sawchuck looked shocked because he didn't know, or because I did. For all I knew, the man had had his wife killed.

Morris said to Howard, 'What's he talking about?'

'I don't know,' Howard said. 'He's some kind of crazy person, him and his brother. They're spreading stories that could damage you.'

'No,' I said. 'My brother found out what they did. They brought us here to kill us and—'

'Shut up,' Lewis said.

'No, let him talk,' Morris said.

I took a deep breath. 'Thomas was surfing the net,' I said. 'Whirl360. He saw someone being murdered in the window of an apartment on Orchard Street. I think it was your wife. Bridget, right?'

Morris nodded slowly. His face was becoming flushed. 'What happened to Bridget?' he demanded. 'I want the truth.'

It was Howard who spoke first. 'It was an accident. A horrible mistake.'

'Dear God,' Morris said. 'You didn't.'

Howard continued. 'There was a woman, Allison Fitch. She was blackmailing Bridget. She was trying to damage her, to ruin you. We—I was afraid there were things she knew that could hurt you very badly.'

'Howard.'

'Politically fatal, Morris. Lewis and I talked and we decided we had to deal with the Fitch woman more . . . permanently. But when it came time to do it, to take care of the problem, something no one could have foreseen came up. Fitch wasn't in the apartment.' He paused, swallowed. 'But Bridget was. She was mistaken for Fitch.'

'But . . . but we found her. In her old apartment . . .' Morris said.

'She was moved.'

'But you talked to her!' Morris said. 'You spoke to her on the phone. She told you I was sucking the life out of her! She was going to kill herself!'

Howard had to look away. 'I . . . it was faked. There was no call.'

Morris grabbed Howard and threw him up against the wall. 'You son of a bitch!' he shouted, shaking the man. He made a fist, and drove it straight into Howard's face. Howard yelped and fell to the floor.

Lewis locked arms around him and dragged him off. 'Stop!' he said. 'You can sort this out later, but right now we have to figure out what to do.'

'I'm going to kill you,' Morris said, still in Lewis's grasp, staring down at Howard. 'You bastard.'

'It wasn't my mistake!' Howard said. 'It was hers!'

Now all eyes were on Nicole.

'Like they said, it was a mistake,' she said coolly. 'Sorry. Not much else I can say at this point, really.'

Morris, aghast, looked at Howard, then Lewis.

Noticing that Morris was speechless with rage, Lewis said, 'Howard, I think there's a good-faith gesture we can make with Morris as a way of moving forward. We can't bring Bridget back, but we can help make things right.' He reached into his jacket and took out his gun. He spun around, pointed it at Nicole and pulled the trigger. I was expecting a louder bang, but the gun had a silencer.

Nicole was thrown up against the shelves, then she dropped onto the floor. Two shelves gave way and an avalanche of toys crashed to the floor.

'I was going to get round to it sooner or later, anyway,' Lewis said.

Suddenly, Morris reached into his jacket and now there was a gun in his hand, too. I guessed when you were the attorney general, you packed heat.

Lewis seemed to know instinctively what Morris was going for, so by the time Morris had his weapon pointed at him, Lewis had his pointed right back at Morris. They stood there, guns pointed at each other.

'Let's all try to calm down,' Howard said.

Morris said, 'No one kills for me.'

'It's already been done,' Howard said softly. 'Things have already been done on your behalf. Bad things. Things that, if they come out, you'll never be able to convince people you didn't order yourself. Morris, listen to me. They'll put you away for ever. Not just me, not just Lewis, but all of us.'

Morris and Lewis kept their guns trained on each other.

Howard continued, 'It gets worse. The whole world will believe you killed Bridget. I know you want to do the right thing here, but we're too far past that. And things will come out about Bridget. Although . . .' His voice trailed off. 'They hardly matter now.'

Morris looked down at the floor. As suddenly as he'd raised his weapon, he lowered it. He tucked the gun back into his jacket.

Lewis slowly put his arm down, but kept the gun in his hand.

Morris turned, brushed past Howard, threw back the curtain and started walking towards the front door.

'What the hell's he going to do?' Lewis said.

Howard went after him. Lewis gave Thomas and me a quick look, figured we weren't going anywhere, and followed the two other men.

I figured if Thomas and I were ever going to have a chance, this was it.

I leaned forward in the chair so that my feet were planted firmly on the floor. I waddled myself backwards, with the chair attached, so that I was back-to-back with Thomas. I set the chair down gently, placing it close enough so that my fingers could reach the tape securing Thomas's wrists to his chair.

'What are you doing?' Thomas asked.

'Shh,' I said. 'We're getting out of here.' I was struggling to get fingers from both my hands onto the tape so I could tear it.

'Hurry,' Thomas whispered.

'Just hang on.'

'Ray, you should have told me you had me working for a mobster.'

I whispered, 'I made it up to buy us some time.'

'Oh,' he said. 'That was very smart.'

I could feel the rip I'd started growing. 'It feels looser,' Thomas said.

'When you're free, you untie me, and we're out of here.'

'OK,' he said. 'Ray, I don't even know where we are.'

'Soon as we hit the street I'm sure you'll know.' I tore the tape another half-inch, felt it come apart.

'I can get my wrists free,' Thomas said. 'But there's still tape around me.'

'Just get out of it as fast as you can.'

I could hear Thomas struggling with the tape, then: 'OK, OK,' he said, as he stood, liberated. 'Now you.'

Lewis said, clear as a bell, 'I'll go check on them.'

I whispered urgently. 'Go! Run! Get help!'

I could sense Thomas's panic. He didn't want to leave me.

'Get out of here!'

So he did. He headed into the short hallway off the side of the room that led to the outside door. He ran, pushed open the door, and was gone.

THOMAS BURST INTO the narrow alley, the white van right there in front of him. His eyes adjusted to the darkness, then he looked in both directions, figuring out instantly which was the way to the street. He ran for it.

He came out of the alley, turned right and kept on running, past a bike shop, a tailor's, other businesses. But he wasn't paying much attention to them. All he could think was that he had to get away as fast as he could, and he had to get help. But it was pretty impossible to keep up the pace. So Thomas eased back to a brisk walk. *Get away get away get away*.

He reached a point where he had to stop. He leaned over and caught his breath. He straightened up, looked around.

On one corner, Stromboli Pizza. Next to it, some place offering vegetarian food. Across the street, a shoe store. Without looking up at the street signs, Thomas said, 'St Mark's Place and First Avenue.'

Then he allowed himself to look at a sign, saw that he was right.

'This is New York,' Thomas said. 'I know where I am.'

He walked over to the pizza restaurant, went right up to the glass, and touched it with the tips of his fingers. Thomas could feel the glass. Then he saw something in that window, something he had never seen before, not in any of the world's cities that he had explored. He saw his *reflection*.

Whirl360 had never been like this.

Behind him, a truck rumbled past. Thomas spun around. Here, the trucks moved, made noises. The people walked. And their faces weren't blurred.

He smelled something. Bread cooking. Pizza dough.

His Whirl360 world was noiseless. Odourless. Nothing to touch.

Thomas marvelled at everything around him. It was almost enough to make him forget what he had to do. But not quite.

'Ray,' he said under his breath. 'I have to help Ray.'

He didn't see any police cars around, and he didn't see any phone booths. And even if he did see one, he had no money on him. He didn't own a credit card. Wouldn't know the first thing about using one.

Thomas didn't have a cellphone, either. If he did, he could call the police. But people walking by on the street probably carried them.

Two teenage girls, their arms linked, were coming from the south.

'Excuse me,' Thomas said, putting himself directly in their path. 'I bet you have cellphones. Could I borrow one to call 911?'

The girls stopped abruptly. They unlinked arms and went quickly around him on each side, one muttering, 'Creep.'

Thomas wished Julie were here to help him. He liked Julie. Julie would know what to do. Wait a second. Julie had a sister who lived in the city. She had a place that sold cupcakes. What did Julie say her name was? Candace? That was it. And her store was called Candy's Cupcakes. On West 8th.

Thomas bet if he could find Candace, she'd know how to get in touch with Julie. He walked out into the street, put both hands into the air, and shouted, 'Taxi!' A driver hit the brakes and the cab screeched to a halt.

Thomas walked up to the driver's window. 'Sir, I need you to take me to Candy's Cupcake shop on West 8th Street in New York City.'

'Get in,' the cab driver said.

There was so little traffic it wasn't long before the taxi pulled up in front of the cupcake store. 'Looks closed,' the driver said.

Thomas looked at the first-floor windows, figuring that was where

Candace lived, but he didn't know how to get up there. Maybe the apartment entrance was through the shop. Thomas pulled on the door handle, putting one foot down on the pavement. 'Thank you very much.'

'Whoa!' the cabbie said. 'There's five-eighty on the meter.'

'I don't have any money,' Thomas said. 'My brother has money. When he's not abducted any more, he could pay you.'

'Get the hell out of my cab,' the driver said, and floored it the moment Thomas had closed the door.

Thomas walked to the door of Candy's Cupcakes and banged on the glass. He thought he could see light in the back. 'Hello!' he shouted. 'Candace?' He banged the door continuously, the glass rattling.

Finally, a small, black man came striding through the store, unlocked the door, and opened it a foot. 'I need Candace to call Julie,' Thomas said.

The man yelled to the back of the store, 'Boss! Hey, boss!' Seconds later, a woman in a full white apron, her hair in a net, came to the door.

'What's going on?' she asked. 'Who are you?'

'Thomas Kilbride. Are you Julie's sister?'

'What the hell do you want? What's this about Julie?'

'Do you know her cellphone number? I want her to help me save Ray.'

Candace shook her head in exasperation, stuck her hand into her pocket, and pulled out a cellphone. She called up a number, hit the button.

She looked surprised that someone picked up so quickly.

'Hey, listen, it's me. I'm really sorry to call you but there's this crazy guy here, says he has to talk to—uh, Thomas. He says his name is Thomas. OK.' She handed the phone to him. 'She wants to talk to you.'

Thomas took the phone and said, 'Hi, Julie, they kidnapped me and Ray and took us here and I got away and they've still got Ray and—'

'Are you at the cupcake shop?' Julie asked incredulously. 'I can be there in two minutes. Stay there!'

Thomas handed the phone back to Candace. 'She'll be right here.'

MORRIS SAWCHUCK had his hand on the inside of the front door to Ferber's Antiques, but before he could open it Howard slammed his own hand on it.

'What are your intentions, Morris?' Howard said.

Lewis had caught up to them. 'It's a good question,' he said.

'I don't care what happens,' Morris said. 'Nothing's worth this. I'm going to tell the police what I know. They'll believe me or they won't.'

Morris felt something cold and hard. Lewis was holding the barrel of his gun to the attorney general's temple.

'You think that'll make it easier, Lewis? Blowing my brains out?'

'Maybe,' he said. 'Howard, get his gun.'

Howard reached under Morris's coat and removed the weapon and handed it to Lewis, who tucked it into the waistband of his trousers.

Howard said, 'I know this has all been a terrible shock. I get that. But you have to help us continue to help you, or Lewis here will put a bullet through your brain. And then you know what he's going to have to do?'

Howard tilted his head in the direction of the street. It took Morris a moment to figure out what Howard was getting at. Then he knew.

'Dear God, no.'

'We kill you, then we have to kill Heather,' Lewis said. 'Because sooner or later, she's going to come in here looking for you.'

Howard said, 'I've been where you are now, Morris. When this all started, when I gave Lewis the OK to take drastic action where Allison Fitch was concerned, I couldn't believe I was doing it. I'd never taken that kind of step before. Never, believe me. And then it went horribly wrong, and I felt even sicker. But you know what? You reach a point where you realise there's no going back. You've made your decisions and you have to live with them. That's what you're going to have to do, Morris. You're going to have to make a decision and live with it.'

Morris placed an arm against the door, and leaned his head into it. 'I need a minute.'

'Of course you do.'

'Tell me about that woman,' Morris said to Lewis, who had taken the barrel away from his temple. 'The one you just killed.'

'A killer for hire,' Lewis said. 'She had it coming. She's done a lot of bad things, and the worst of all was screwing up, killing Bridget.'

'I don't want you to hurt Heather,' Morris said.

Lewis glanced towards the curtain and said, 'We should check on them.'

Howard said, 'This Vachon business, I want to know more about that. Do what you have to do to find out if Ray's feeding us a line.'

'Vachon?' Morris said.

'Long story,' Howard said, then to Lewis, 'Once we're sure we have nothing to worry about, then, well, I want them dealt with as mercifully as we can.'

'Yeah, yeah. Don't worry.' Lewis headed for the back room.

'Howard,' Morris said, 'you can't just—'

'Shit!' It was Lewis. He had pulled back the curtain, then called to Howard. 'We got a problem.'

'WHERE IS HE?' Lewis barked at me. 'Where the hell is he?'

'Gone,' I said.

Howard showed up, fixed his eyes on the empty chair. Then he glared at Lewis. 'You let him get away.'

Lewis tore out of the room using the side door, no doubt hoping Thomas had only just left and that he could catch up with him and drag him back.

I just hoped that, having got away, Thomas would have the sense to go to the police, even if that wasn't exactly what I'd asked.

'How did—how the hell did he get free?' Howard asked.

'I told you he was talented,' I said. 'Maybe he's gone for Vachon.'

Howard snapped. He hit me across the face with the back of his hand.

The curtain opened and it was Morris. 'What the hell's happened now?'

'One of them got away,' Howard said.

Morris said, 'It's unravelling. You're unravelling.' He took out his phone and held it up. 'You took my gun but you didn't take this. I told Heather to take the next couple of days off. She's gone. I told her you were going to give me a lift home. You and Lewis.'

'So if anything happens to you, she'll know.'

Morris nodded. 'Let this man go. And you and Lewis would be smart to turn yourselves in. Either that, or you'd better be on a jet to Bolivia by noon with a couple of new identities. You know the best lawyers in the city, Howard. Pick one out for yourself, and one for Lewis. I guess that's basically what I'm going to do, too. Now let this man go.'

I was already working on it. I'd been straining at the tape around my wrists since the moment Thomas had left.

Howard said, 'I wish it were that simple, Morris.'

Lewis reappeared, winded. 'No sign of him,' he said.

'Morris says we should get lawyers,' Howard said. 'He's not going to play.'

'Heather's gone,' Morris said. 'And I'm leaving, too.'

Morris swept the curtain aside and headed for the front door. Lewis, gun in hand, followed him. 'Morris,' he called out.

I heard the same swift sound I'd heard when Lewis shot Nicole. Then a body hitting the floor. Howard didn't even look. When Lewis reappeared, he walked straight past Howard and came up on my right side.

'Where would your brother go?' he asked me.

'I don't know,' I said. 'If I were you, I'd assume the worst.'

Lewis evidently felt a need to let off some steam just as Howard had, so he hit me, too. A gun to the side of head. My right ear exploded in pain and I watched the room spin around for several seconds.

'Great,' Howard said. 'The police may be coming and we've got two bodies to get rid of.'

'There's no time for that,' Lewis said. 'We just have to get out of here. I know people who can hide us until we get the paperwork we need.'

Howard shook his head in defeat. 'Let's finish this and get the hell out.'

'OK,' Lewis said. The gun was pointing at my head. And then he screamed. A horrific, gut-wrenching scream.

There was an ice pick right through his calf.

'WHERE'S RAY?' Julie asked Thomas. 'Think, OK? Think.'

They were sitting in her car, the engine running, out front of her sister's cupcake shop. Candace stood on the sidewalk, watching the two of them.

Thomas said, 'I was running so fast I wasn't paying attention, not until I got to St Mark's and First Avenue.'

Julie said, 'You say you ran out into the alley and out to the sidewalk. What were the first things you passed?'

Thomas thought. 'There was a tailor's, and Mike's Bikes . . .'

'OK.' Julie grabbed her phone. 'I'll see if I can find it.'

'Wait,' Thomas said. Now he had his eyes closed. 'Mike's Bikes. It's next to the tailor's shop.' He was clicking his mouse, in his head. Advancing through the Whirl360 images.

'What street?'

'East 4th,' he said. 'It's on East 4th.'

Julie already had the car in drive. She slammed on the accelerator and tore up the street. 'Just tell me *where* on 4th.'

Thomas closed his eyes again. His head kept jerking. 'I'm at an antiques store,' he said. 'Ferber's Antiques. It looks like it has toys in the window.'

'What's the address?'

He gave her a number. 'I think that's the place. That's where Ray is.'

Julie ran a red light, turned at a cross street, floored it.

'Do you have a gun?' Thomas asked, eyes open again. 'The man had a gun, and the woman had an ice pick.'

'I don't have a gun,' Julie said. She knew she needed the NYPD and the FDNY. What she didn't have was time to explain. Julie pointed to the cellphone. 'Hit 911, then give it to me.'

When the 911 operator came on, Julie adopted a panicked tone and said, 'There's a fire! It looks like it's started in the back of Ferber's! The antiques store on East 4th! And I think I heard shots, too!' She provided a street number, then ended the call before the operator could ask her anything else.

THE ICE PICK had entered the side of Lewis's right leg about five inches below the knee. The tip had come out of the other side.

He dropped to both knees, screaming. He let go of his gun and twisted round so he could get hold of the handle of the ice pick to pull it back out.

Nicole sat up and got her hand on the pick before Lewis could. Instead of pulling it out, she yanked on it sideways. He jerked his leg furiously, the heel of his boot catching Nicole square in the chest.

Lewis was looking for his gun. It was on the floor in a puddle of his blood. He went to grab it, but Nicole had her hands on it first.

She wrapped her hand around the wet, bloodied grip and pointed it at Lewis's head. He had rolled onto his back and was scrambling backwards.

Nicole was on her knees now, both hands on the gun, her arms out. 'I hate guns,' she said. Her blouse was torn, revealing something. *A black vest.*

She pulled the trigger and blew a corner of his head off.

Howard turned, pulled back the curtain, and started to run. Nicole scrambled after him. In the distance, I heard sirens.

I finally pulled my left hand free and started tearing into the tape around my stomach that held me to the chair.

The sirens grew louder. But, even closer, were the sounds of a car screeching to a stop in the alley. Someone shouting. A woman. 'Thomas!'

I broke free of the chair and dived to the floor. I wanted to get over to Lewis. There was a gun tucked into the front of his trousers. Morris's gun, maybe.

In the front room, I heard a *pfft*, and the sound of another body dropping.

From outside: 'Ray!'

'Thomas, stop!'

Julie.

I was reaching for the gun when the curtain was flung back. I glanced up, just in time to see Nicole's boot catch my jaw. I saw stars as my body was catapulted backwards. My right hand had landed on one of the items that had tumbled off the shelves. Even before I looked at it I could feel that it was part plastic, part metal.

Nicole pointed her gun at me. But before she could squeeze the trigger, there was a loud bang from the short hallway that led to the alley.

'I got help!' Thomas screamed. 'I got Julie!'

Nicole's eyes turned towards the voices, and the gun followed. The second Thomas appeared he'd be dead.

I glanced over at my right hand, which was draped across the blue plastic fins of a foot-long, metal-pointed lawn dart. It wasn't exactly a javelin. But I was pretty damn good at regular darts. I grabbed the dart, swung it back over my shoulder, then pitched it forward with everything I had.

'Ray!' Thomas burst into the room.

The dart went into Nicole's neck. It went in far enough that it hung there.

Her mouth opened but no scream came out. Her right hand held on to the gun as her left flew up. She grasped the dart, and yanked it out.

Blood spurted everywhere. She clamped her hand over the wound, dropping the gun from her right, turned, stumbled over to the desk. Then dropped to the floor as the sirens became almost deafening.

Now Julie was in the room, and she hit the brakes as soon as she saw the carnage. A firefighter, running in behind her, nearly knocked her over.

'Ray!' she said.

Thomas was already helping me to my feet. 'Look who I found,' he said. 'I brought Julie.' He smiled. 'I'm back.'

OVER THE NEXT twenty-four hours, Thomas and I, and Julie, had to answer a lot of questions. We were questioned separately, and together, by New York City cops, state police, FBI. One guy was from Homeland Security.

Thomas, when we had a moment together, expressed some concern that there was no one from the CIA. 'You'd think they'd be here, wanting to see how I'm doing,' he whispered. He was hurt.

The blanks started to get filled in, in large part because the fire department and paramedics had arrived in time to save Howard Talliman and Morris Sawchuck, both found bleeding on the floor of the toy shop.

Talliman, whose condition was critical, had not been all that forthcoming so far, but Sawchuck, who'd been shot in the lung, was telling prosecutors everything he knew. He was hooked up to various machines to assist with his breathing, but was answering questions as quickly as he could type them on the laptop they'd brought into the ICU.

A lot of what had happened became clear. Fitch's blackmail attempt led to a decision to kill her. Bridget Sawchuck was killed by mistake. Nicole killed that couple in Chicago as part of her mission to get the image of the smothered woman off the Internet.

Lewis Blocker, of course, was dead.

And the paramedics were not able to save Nicole. Turned out that wasn't her real name. There was talk that in another life she was an Olympic athlete. I didn't feel good about killing the woman. I knew I'd had no choice.

Many of the questions that were put to me, when I was being questioned alone, were about Thomas, and his bizarre preoccupation. By the end, it appeared the various law-enforcement agencies were not only persuaded that Thomas was harmless, but that he was a hero. Bridget Sawchuck's murder would never have come to light without his explorations on Whirl360. What was left unspoken was that it was these same explorations that had led, ultimately, to the deaths of Kyle and Rochelle Billings.

The thing that never came up was the call Lewis took in Thomas's room.

FIFTEEN

Thomas was more withdrawn than usual in the wake of everything that had happened. What we'd been through would be traumatic for anyone. Yet I wondered whether it might have less to do with our recent experience and more to do with what he had seemed ready to tell me just before Nicole and Lewis invaded the house. This thing that had happened when he was thirteen, that had sparked trouble between Dad and him.

He'd said, back then, that he might be willing to talk about it with Julie—but the time wasn't right yet. We needed to decompress. Besides, I had a couple of things on my mind, too.

I'd been debating whether to stay at my father's house, live there with Thomas, at least for the foreseeable future. But, to my surprise, when I proposed the idea to Thomas, he was reluctant.

'I don't think I want to live with you,' he said. 'Look at all the trouble you got me into.' He said he wanted to live at the place I had gone to visit, so long as he could keep his computer.

I SHOULDN'T have been surprised to find a police car blocking the end of the driveway when we got back. Once we'd identified ourselves, the uniformed officer pulled his car out of the way. Julie drove up to the house and stopped. Thomas had got out first.

I called to him, 'Do not touch the phone in your room.'

He didn't argue. He didn't care that much about phones, but the fact he had no computer to return to had upset him. He had asked me ten times on the way home when we would be going out to get him a new one.

I came around to the driver's door. Julie powered down her window.

'Thanks,' I said, bending over, my head half in the window.

'I've got a story to write. Maybe I'll give you a call later.'

'Look forward to it,' I said, then leaned in and kissed her.

I had watched her drive off, then went into the house. I saw the light flashing on the phone, and thought I'd better check the messages.

There were four.

'Hey, Ray. Alice here. Harry needs you to come in and sign a couple more things. Let me know.' *Beep*. I hit 7 to delete.

'Ray? Harry. Alice left a message for you. Right?' *Beep*. I hit 7 again.

'Ray, Harry here, I saw the news, I hope you are OK.' *Beep*. 7 again.

'Hello, this is Angus Fried, from the *New York Times*, and—' 7.

It was time. I didn't know what I was going to learn when I checked the call history on Thomas's phone, on his separate line. Maybe nothing.

I'd started heading for the stairs when there was a rapping at the front door.

Standing there was an overweight, middle-aged man in a rumpled suit holding up a badge for my inspection.

'Mr Kilbride?' he said. 'Our man at the end of the drive there told me you were back. You and I, we didn't get a chance to finish our chat the other night. I'm Detective Barry Duckworth, with the Promise Falls police. It's a hell of a thing you've been through. I've heard all about it. But I was wondering if we could still have a word about your father.'

'Come in,' I said.

Detective Duckworth and I took seats in the living room. 'Are you up to finishing the conversation we were having the other night?'

'I am,' I said. 'It seems like a long time ago.' I rubbed my forehead.

Duckworth settled in the chair. 'Your father contacted me about something that happened to your brother, Thomas, when he was in his teens. But for years, your father didn't believe it had happened, he didn't believe your brother. Because he, well . . .'

'My brother is not what you'd call a credible witness,' I said.

'There you go. So when Thomas came to your father years ago, alleging an assault, your father refused to believe it, because Thomas was pointing the finger at one of your father's friends. He accused your brother of making it up, and told him never to talk about it, never to bring it up again.'

'An assault,' I said. 'Thomas managed to tell me just a bit.'

'A sexual assault,' Duckworth said. 'At least, an attempted one. Your dad did talk to this friend of his, and the man was stunned, shocked by the accusation, denied it completely, and your dad, he believed him. But then, something happened to change his mind.'

'What was that?'

'Your dad wanted a cellphone that would do lots of fancy things, instead of just being a phone. To take pictures.'

I nodded. 'OK.'

'So he happened to be with one of his friends, he told me—this would be the same friend your brother had accused way back when—and he picked up his phone to have a look at it. This friend wasn't in the room at the time, but your dad didn't think he'd mind. He wanted to see how the camera worked on this phone, so he pressed the whaddyacallit, the camera app, and up it came. And then he tapped again, so it brought up pictures that had already been taken.' Duckworth paused. 'He didn't like what he saw.'

I swallowed. 'What were the pictures of?'

'Boys,' Duckworth said. 'Pictures of young boys in provocative poses.'

'These were pictures his friend had taken?'

Duckworth nodded. 'Seems he'd just come back from some trip. A place where a person with those kinds of tastes can find just what he's looking for. He realised that what your brother had said years ago was the truth. A man who would take these kinds of pictures was the sort of man who would have assaulted your brother.'

'Who?' I asked, but I believed I already had the answer.

Duckworth held up his hand. 'So your dad confronted him with it. Said he now realised it had to be true, what Thomas had told him.'

'What did the man say?'

'Denied it to hell and back, of course.'

'What'd my dad do?' One thing I was pretty sure he must have done was a search on his laptop for child prostitution.

'I guess he stewed about it. Finally, he called me. He said he was sick about it, that he'd tried to apologise to your brother, that they'd had a fight over it. He wanted to know whether the man could still be charged, for what he did to Thomas. I told him it was pretty unlikely. It happened so long ago.'

'What about the pictures on the man's phone?'

'Your dad knew he'd probably deleted them right away but, even so, he was asking me, could someone go after him, for paying to have sex with kids in some foreign country.'

'Thailand,' I said. 'I think we're probably talking about Thailand. I know it's not the only country in the world where that sort of thing is available, but one of dad's friends has travelled to Thailand.'

'I haven't answered your question about who the friend is,' Duckworth said, 'because I don't know. Your dad never told me, because he hadn't decided what to do.' He sighed. 'And then he had that accident. And died.'

'Len Prentice,' I said.

'Say again?' Duckworth said, getting out his notebook.

'Dad worked for him for years. They'd been friends a very long time. Thomas has never liked him. Len came by here the other day, tried to force Thomas to have lunch with him. Maybe he was trying to find out what Dad might have told him before he died.' I thought a moment. 'And he takes trips without his wife, to Thailand.'

'Well,' Duckworth said. 'That's pretty interesting, isn't it?'

We were both quiet for a moment. I was the one who finally spoke.

'There's something that's been troubling me from the moment I came home, after I got word that my father was dead. The circumstances.'

'How so?'

'I know it looked like an accident. He was riding the tractor along the side of a steep hill, and rolled it. But he'd been mowing like that for years.'

'A lot of people do the same foolish thing for years, and one day it catches up with them,' Duckworth offered.

'I know. But when I went down to bring the tractor back to the barn—it hadn't been moved since the accident, other than when Thomas pushed it off Dad—I noticed that the key was in the "off" position. And the housing for the blades? It was raised. It was what Dad would have done if someone had come down the hill and wanted to talk to him.'

'No one ever came forward to say they'd talked to your father before the accident. That they were there when it happened.'

'Who would?' I asked. 'If they'd pushed him over.'

'I don't know, but that's an interesting theory.'

'While Dad was debating what to do about Len Prentice, Len Prentice must have been going out of his mind. He comes out to the house one day, trying to talk Dad out of doing anything. Finds Dad cutting grass on the side of the hill. Dad stops the tractor, they get into an argument, Len gives Dad a shove, and he goes back, taking the tractor with him, and it kills him. Len might have had time to get help, or get the tractor off Dad, but he chooses not to. Len's known, for years, that my dad took chances on that hill.'

Detective Duckworth pursed his lips while he thought about all this.

'I suppose,' he said, 'that at the very least it might be worth going over to talk to him about it. See what he has to say.'

'Yeah, let's do that,' I said.

'Whoa,' he said, putting up his hand. 'Just you let me do the talking.'

I nodded. 'First, I want to tell my brother I'm heading out for a little while. And there's just one other thing I have to do.'

'I'll be waiting for you out on the porch.'

Duckworth got up and was heading outside as I went up the stairs.

I went into Thomas's room. He was sitting, staring at his computer monitors and keyboard. 'Are we going to get a computer now?' he asked.

'Not right this second,' I said. 'You'll be OK here for a while, on your own? There'll still be a cop out by the road. I'm going to see Len Prentice.'

Thomas frowned. 'I don't like him.'

I considered asking Thomas, right then, to tell me what had happened to him, who had done it, but decided not to. 'I don't like him, either,' I said.

I turned my attention to the phone on his desk. 'Have you touched this?'

'You told me not to.'

I reached across the desk, pulled the phone closer to me. I hit the button that would give me the call history. There had been no calls to this phone since the night we'd been abducted.

There was a call at 10.13 p.m. that night. It was the only number in the call history. It was, I was pretty sure, a local number.

I didn't think it was smart to dial this number directly from Thomas's phone. I used my cell. I entered the number, put the phone to my ear.

'Who are you calling?' Thomas asked. 'Are you calling the president?'

I held up a hand to silence him. The phone at the other end rang once. Then a second time. A third. Then, finally, a voice.

'Hello, Harry Peyton here.'

'It's Ray,' I said, when I'd found my voice.

'Ray!' Harry exclaimed 'You're back. We called your place a few times, couldn't reach you. At first we figured maybe you'd gone back to Burlington for a couple of days and took your brother with you.'

'No.'

Harry laughed. 'Yeah, well, we know that now. Are you OK?'

'Wrists are a bit sore,' I said. 'Kind of hurt all over.'

'Hell of a thing,' Harry said. 'Listen, these things I need you to sign, we can do that anytime. You get your life back to normal and then—'

'No,' I said. 'I'll be there in a few minutes.'

'Ray, wait. Ray? You know you called me on my personal cellphone. Why didn't you call on the office line? Where'd you get this number?'

'See you soon,' I said, and ended the call.

Thomas looked at me. 'How's the president?' he asked.

I walked into the hall. *What the hell was going on?*

Harry Peyton had phoned pretending to be former president Clinton. Harry knew about my brother's fantasies. He was playing into them.

The call Lewis took couldn't have been the first one. But I also knew, from my own observations, that Thomas had had these conversations when there really was no one on the other end of the line.

Harry Peyton knew about those chats.

And had decided to make them real.

I went back in to see Thomas.

'When you'd get a call, from . . . you know, what would he tell you?'

Thomas blinked. 'He said something bad would happen to us if I talked to you about things. About things that had happened to me, and things that the president was telling me now. He'd say everything was just between us, and he wanted to know about me personally, and about you and Dad. He didn't used to ask those kinds of questions, when he would talk to me without the phone. When I would just hear him.'

'What did he ask about Dad?'

'He wanted to know if he talked about his friends, whether Dad had told me anything bad about them. Because Mr Clinton had to be sure that no one in my circle was an enemy or a spy or anything.'

'What did you tell him?'

'I told him I didn't like Len Prentice, and that I really didn't like Mr Peyton, which was why I didn't go to Dad's funeral, because I figured he would be there.'

'Thomas,' I said gently, 'the thing that happened to you, a long time ago, in the window, it was Mr Peyton who did that, wasn't it?'

'Dad said I wasn't supposed to talk about that. Even after he said he was sorry. He said I couldn't talk about it until he knew what to do about it. But then, eventually, I might have to.' He looked away. 'I didn't think I could do that. Tell the police, or talk about it in a courtroom. No, never.'

I went to my phone, went looking for a number that turned out not to be in its memory. I needed a phone book.

'We'll talk later, OK, Thomas?' I said. 'And go get you a computer?'

'OK,' he said. 'Do you want me to make dinner?' It was such an unexpected offer I thought I might cry.

'We'll sort it all out when I get back.'

I came down the stairs. I found the phone book in a drawer in the kitchen, opened it, looked up a home number for Len Prentice.

'Hello?' It was Marie.

'Hi, Marie. It's Ray.'

'Oh, Ray, oh my, Len and I, we heard about you and Thomas on—'

'I have a quick question for you. When Len went to Thailand, I know you didn't go with him, but did anyone else?'

'Yes, of course. Harry Peyton. Len was a bit disappointed because Harry was always off doing his own thing. Tell me how you and Thomas are—'

I hung up, went out to join Duckworth. 'Change of plan,' I said.

On the way into town in Duckworth's car, I tried my best to explain what I believed had happened. That when Harry Peyton found out Dad knew about his Thailand adventures, and that Dad now believed Thomas's tale of what Harry had done to him when he was a boy, Peyton panicked.

'I think he killed my father,' I said. 'Or at the very least, did nothing to save him. And maybe even before Dad died, and certainly after, Harry started calling my brother on his line, played into his delusion. He was trying to make sure Thomas didn't talk about what Harry had done to him. Figured Thomas would keep quiet about it if it was a presidential order.'

'This is the damnedest thing I've ever come across,' Duckworth said.

'What did Harry say when he called you?' I asked. 'About Thomas, and what he'd seen on the Whirl360 site?'

'What's that?' Duckworth said, his wrist resting atop the steering wheel.

'I went to see Harry, told him about what Thomas had seen online, that I needed to talk to the police but was going to have a hard time convincing them. Harry said he knew you, that he'd give you a call on my behalf.'

Duckworth shook his head. 'Harry Peyton never called me about that.' He glanced over at me. 'You think he knows that you know?'

'Last thing he asked me was, why did I call him on his cellphone?'

Duckworth ran his tongue over his upper lip. 'I'd say he knows.'

We walked into Harry Peyton's law office. Peyton's secretary, Alice, looked up from her desk. She smiled at the two of us.

'Hi,' she said. Then, 'Ray, I can't believe what you've been through.'

'We need to talk to Harry,' Duckworth said.

Alice picked up her phone. 'Some folks here to see you,' she said.

The heavy wood door beyond her desk opened. Harry kept hold of the knob as his eyes landed on us. Me, then Barry. He knew it was over.

'Harry,' Duckworth said, 'I need to ask you a few questions.'

Harry stepped back and slammed the door closed.

Duckworth bolted forward, turned the knob, and pushed, but the door wouldn't budge. He snapped at Alice, 'You got a key?'

While Alice rooted through her desk drawer, I put my mouth up to the door and shouted, 'I know, Harry! I know what you did! To my dad, and to my brother!' I banged on it with my fist. 'He found those pictures on your phone and he knew! He knew Thomas had been telling the truth!'

'Find that damn key,' Duckworth told Alice.

'You're finished, Harry!' I shouted. 'Even if they don't convict you for what you did to Thomas, or my father, you're ruined in this town.'

'Here it is,' Alice said.

'Give it,' Duckworth said, taking the key from her.

That was when we heard the shot.

Alice, still behind her desk, screamed. And kept screaming.

Duckworth took a gun from his jacket and called, 'Harry!'

No answer. Duckworth slipped the key into the lock, turned it, then put his hand on the knob and turned it, pushing slowly on the door.

'Oh, man,' he said.

'I've only been here once before,' Thomas said, as we turned into the grounds of the Promise Falls cemetery. 'When Mom died, remember?'

'I remember,' I said, taking the Audi along the narrow, paved roadway.

The events of the past week had changed Thomas. Changed us all.

But Thomas wasn't like the rest of us. He'd always seemed, certainly to me, incapable of change. And yet, he was not the same person he had been.

A couple of days after Harry Peyton had taken his own life, I bought Thomas a new computer. We got it all set up at home, and he was right back on to Whirl360 as I went downstairs to open a beer.

Twenty minutes later, he was in the kitchen. It wasn't time for lunch or dinner. He just needed a break. He took a Coke out of the fridge, sat and drank it, and then went back upstairs. When I peeked in on him later, he was reading the *Times* online. Wonders would never cease.

He'd been to see Dr Grigorin, and when she spoke to me after his appointment, she said she'd noticed a change, too. 'Let's just see,' she said, careful not to raise any expectations. 'But I think he's going to make the adjustment well. Harry Peyton's death may have been, in some ways, liberating.'

Thomas claimed to be looking forward to his new accommodation. 'Staying in this house,' he'd said, 'reminds me too much of Mom and Dad.' He'd paused. 'And I know you don't want to live here with me.'

'Thomas, that's—'

'You want to live with Julie. So you can have sex with her.'

'Yeah, well—' I'd said.

'I don't want you to get me into any more trouble,' he'd said. A familiar refrain these days. Like it was me who saw Bridget Sawchuck online.

And then he'd asked to be driven to our father's grave, so that he could finally pay his respects.

I'd told him what had happened at Peyton's office. That I had figured out that Peyton had assaulted him back when he lived above a shop on Saratoga Street. That Dad, having seen the pictures on Peyton's phone, had finally come to believe Thomas. Everyone was a believer now. The police, as part of the investigation into Peyton's suicide, had seized all his computers and found images that made my stomach turn.

I did not tell Thomas my belief that Harry Peyton was responsible for our father's death. It was mostly conjecture on my part, but it made sense.

I chose not to tell Thomas, because I felt he'd been through enough.

'They're in the same plot, right?' Thomas said. 'Mom and Dad?'

'That's right.'

'Did you know you can see this cemetery on the computer? There's a really good satellite view of it. I know exactly where to go.' He hopped out of the car and strode off across the lawn. As he approached the gravestone, he stood directly in front of it, and bowed his head ever so slightly.

I came up behind my brother and rested a hand on his shoulder.

'Hi, Dad,' he said. 'I would have gone to the funeral but I didn't want to see Mr Peyton. But I thought I should finally come and see you. Mr Peyton is dead now. Anyway, I miss you. Ray is teaching me to do more things. I'm making meals and learning how to look after myself more, which is a good thing, because I'm moving to this place where you have to help out.'

He stopped talking, but he showed no sign of wanting to walk away. I had the sense there was something else he wanted to tell our father.

'So, I also wanted to say I'm sorry. Not just about not going to the funeral, and not helping out more.' He swallowed. 'I wanted to say I'm sorry about pushing you, on the stairs.' He paused. 'And on the hill.'

My hand froze.

'I'm sorry I got so upset about maybe having to tell the police things about Mr Peyton. I just had to come out and talk to you about it. I never meant to shove you. And I'm real sorry I didn't call for help right away.' Another pause. 'I was really scared.'

I took my hand off Thomas's shoulder.

'I guess that's all,' he said to our father. 'I'll come up again soon.' Then he turned to me and said, 'Can we go and see my new place now? I'd like to figure out where all my stuff is going to go.'

He stepped around me and started walking. I stood there, numb, and watched as Thomas made his way back to the car.

linwood **barclay**

Profile

Home:
Outside Toronto.

Family:
Wife, Neetha; two grown children, Spencer and Paige.

Former career:
Editor and columnist for the *Toronto Star*.

Favourite writers:
Rex Stout, Ross Macdonald, Ed McBain, Tony Hillerman.

Hobbies:
Seeing movies, walking, building model trains.

Website:
LinwoodBarclay.com.

If you love stories that kick off with an absolute humdinger of an idea—something so completely arbitrary and shocking that it seems it can't possibly be true—you're going to love Linwood Barclay's books. Not that he has had first-hand experience of such trauma, happily, but he does know exactly what it is like to live in a peaceful, ordinary neighbourhood, and he uses that familiarity to draw the reader in. 'It's just a case of writing what you know, up to a point. I know what it's like to be a normal person living in the suburbs, so that's the point of view I choose for my thrillers. I try to imagine how someone with no military or law-enforcement experience handles an extraordinary situation. Once you've come up with a premise, you have to work out how it all happened.'

Linwood Barclay was born in Darien, Connecticut, USA, but in 1959, when he was four, his parents moved to Toronto in Canada, where his father, Everett, was employed as a commercial artist. Everett's illustrations of automobiles, before the days of slick, photographic advertising, appeared regularly in prestigious magazines such as *Life*, *Look* and *The Saturday Evening Post*. A few years later, Barclay's parents bought a cottage resort and trailer park in the Kawartha Lakes region of Ontario and moved the family up there. Barclay was only sixteen when his father died and he decided to take over the running of the family business, an experience he has since described in an autobiography called *Last Resort: Coming of Age in Cottage Country*.

At twenty-two, Linwood left home and got a first job on a local newspaper. Shortly afterwards he joined the *Toronto Star*, Canada's largest circulation newspaper. For twelve years he had a variety of editorial jobs, but eventually started a humour column in 1993. In 2008, many, many columns later, he retired, and dedicated himself to full-time writing.

So what first inspired him to become an author? 'I was inspired to start writing, a lot, around the time I was ten years old, and it wasn't a book that did it. It was television. I loved a show called *The Man From U.N.C.L.E.* Since one episode a week wasn't enough for me, I started writing my own adventures using the show's characters. My father taught me to type when I was around that age, so I'd crank out forty- to fifty-page novellas based on the show. For a long while, I thought I wanted to write for television, but that changed over time.'

Barclay's first published works were four comic thrillers featuring a character called Zack Walker. But it was when he began crafting his trademark darker, standalone thrillers that things really began to take off for him. The first was *No Time for Goodbye*, in which a girl returns home from school to find her entire family missing, and it grew into a huge, international hit. Has anything changed about the way he writes, as his success has mounted? 'I'm spending more time on the books themselves,' he says. 'As my readership grows there's a greater sense of "I had really better get this right". And the time spent on promotion—on book tours—has grown exponentially.'

Barclay likes to write in a study that he has created in his home especially for the purpose. 'I am surrounded by kitschy sci-fi memorabilia—a lot of stuff from the old Gerry Anderson *Thunderbirds* shows—various Batmobiles, and works of original art by my late father. When I'm in the thick of a writing a book, I usually start around nine and go on to four or five, with plenty of breaks, some to play nine holes of golf on Nintendo Wii.'

Since retiring from the newspaper business, Barclay seems to have fallen into a career that suits him perfectly. Is there anything else he might have done if he hadn't become a writer? 'I can't imagine. Sometimes I think I'd like to do what Jim Cutter, my hero in *Too Close to Home*, does. He cuts lawns. It's one of those great jobs where you constantly see what you're accomplishing. But seriously, I don't know. I enjoyed being a newspaper editor, shaping material and getting it ready for presentation. Maybe I'd go back to that. It was great to be part of a team that put together a big city daily. It's so immediate. Being a columnist was a very privileged position—my editors left me alone and I did what I wanted. And if it didn't work, you had no one to blame but yourself. Writing books is tremendously satisfying, but you hand in a manuscript and it can be twelve months before you hold that book in your hands.'

Married to his wife, Neetha, for more than thirty years, and with two grown children, Barclay has a recipe for marital success. 'The secret is maintaining a sense of humour, never taking your partner for granted, and resisting the temptation to lift the lid on stuff your wife is cooking, to give it a stir.'

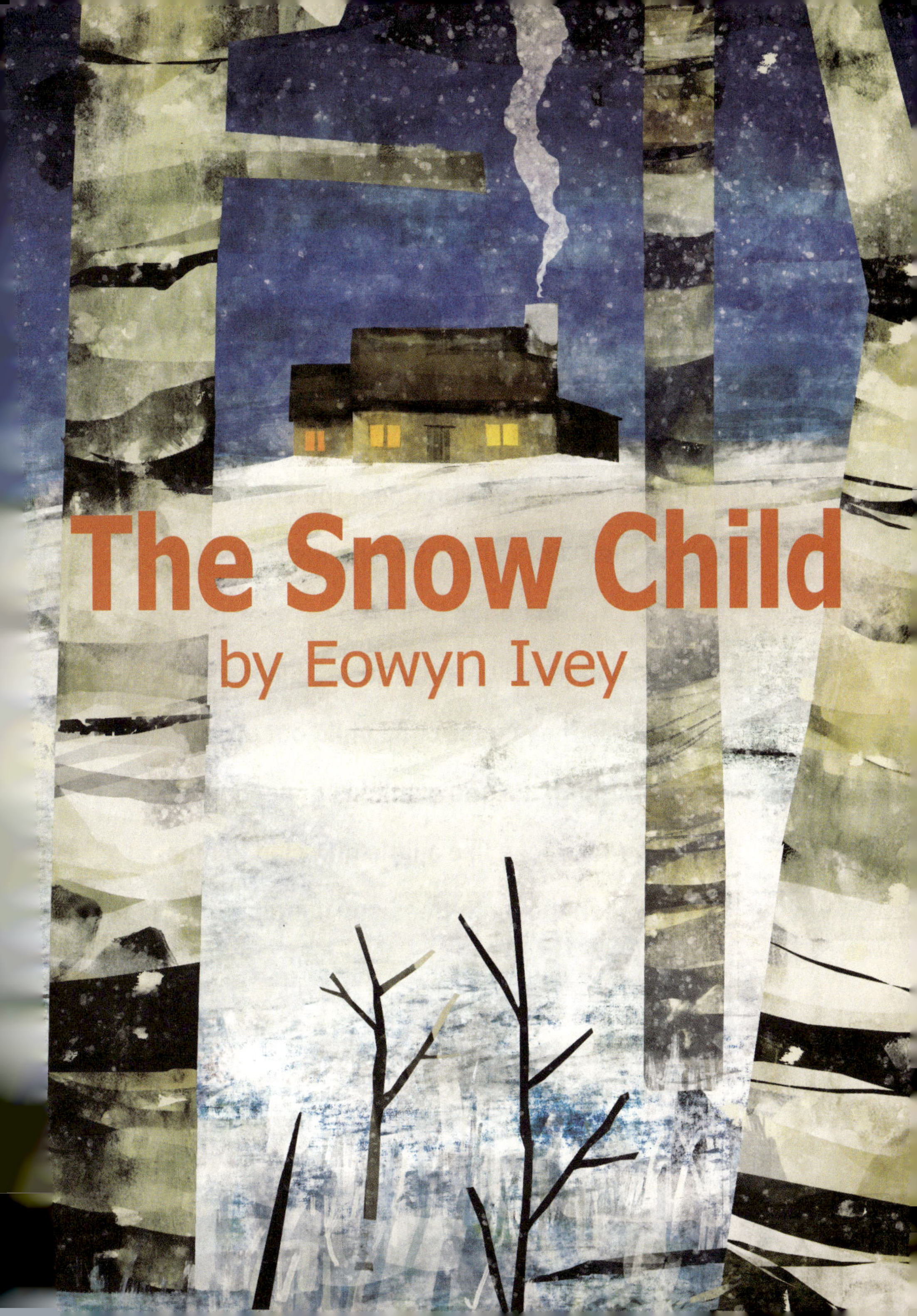
The Snow Child
by Eowyn Ivey

Alaska, 1920. It's a brutal place to homestead, especially for a couple like Jack and Mabel, who long for a child. As winter approaches, they are drifting apart—he buckling under the strain of the work on their farm, she from loneliness and her maternal longing.

Then, in a moment of levity during the season's first snowfall, they construct a child out of snow.

Come morning, the snow child is gone, but Jack glimpses what looks like a little girl, clad in blue, between the birch trees surrounding their home . . .

Chapter 1

Wolverine River, Alaska, 1920

Mabel had known there would be silence. That was the point, after all. No infants cooing or wailing. No neighbour children play fully hollering down the lane. No pad of small feet on wooden stairs worn smooth by generations. All those sounds of her failure and regret would be left behind, and in their place there would be silence.

She had imagined that in the Alaska wilderness silence would be peaceful, like snow falling at night, but that was not what she found. Instead, when she swept the plank floor, the broom bristles scritched like some sharp-toothed shrew nibbling at her heart. When she washed the dishes, plates and bowls clattered as if they were breaking to pieces. The only sound not of her making was a sudden 'caw, cawww' from outside. Mabel wrung dishwater from a rag and looked out of the kitchen window in time to see a raven flapping its way from one leafless birch tree to another. No children chasing each other through autumn leaves, calling each other's names. Not even a solitary child on a swing.

There had been the one. A tiny thing, born still and silent. Ten years past, but even now she found herself returning to the birth to touch Jack's arm, stop him, reach out. She should have. She should have cupped the baby's head in the palm of her hand and snipped a few of its tiny hairs to keep in a locket at her throat. She should have looked into its small face and known if it was a boy or a girl, and then stood beside Jack as he buried it in the Pennsylvania winter ground. She should have allowed herself that grief.

Mabel was too long at the window. The sun had slipped behind a mountain, and the light had fallen flat. The branches were bare, the grass yellowed grey. Not a single snowflake. November was here, and it frightened her because she knew what it brought—cold upon the valley like a coming death, glacial wind through the cracks between the cabin logs. But most of all, darkness so complete even the pale-lit hours would be choked.

She entered last winter blind, not knowing what to expect in this new, hard land. Now she knew. By December, the sun would rise just before noon and skirt the mountain tops for a few hours of twilight before sinking again. Mabel would move in and out of sleep as she sat in a chair beside the woodstove. She would not pick up any of her favourite books; the pages would be lifeless. She would not draw; what would there be to capture in her sketchbook? It would become harder and harder to leave the warm bed each morning. Jack would struggle to keep the animals alive. The days would run together, winter's stranglehold tightening.

She gathered Jack's work shirts and sat down to mend them. She tried not to look out of the window. If only it would snow. Maybe that white would soften the bleak lines, catch some bit of light and mirror it back into her eyes.

But all afternoon the clouds remained high and thin, the wind ripped dead leaves from the tree branches, and daylight guttered like a candle. Mabel thought of the terrible cold that would trap her alone in the cabin, and she stood to pace the floor. She silently repeated to herself, 'I cannot do this. I cannot do this.'

There were guns in the house, and she had thought of them before. The hunting rifle beside the book shelf, the shotgun over the doorway. She had never fired them, but that wasn't what kept her. It was the violence of such an act and the blame that would inevitably come in its wake. People would say she was weak in mind or spirit, or that Jack was a poor husband.

The river, though—that was something different. Not a soul to blame, not even her own. It would be an unfortunate misstep. People would say, if only she had known the ice wouldn't hold her. If only she'd known its dangers.

Afternoon descended into dusk, and Mabel left the window to light an oil lamp on the table, as if she was going to prepare dinner and wait for Jack's return, but in her mind she was already following the trail through the woods to the Wolverine River. She laced her leather boots, put her winter coat on and stepped outside. Her hands and head were bare to the wind.

As she strode through the naked trees, she was both exhilarated and numb, chilled by the clarity of her purpose. She did not think of what she left behind, but only of this moment in a sort of black-and-white precision. The hard clunk of her boot soles on the frozen ground. The icy breeze in her hair. Her expansive breaths. She was strangely powerful and sure.

She emerged from the forest and stood on the bank of the frozen river. It was calm except for the occasional gust of wind that swirled silt across the ice. Farther upstream, the glacier-fed valley stretched half a mile wide with gravel bars, driftwood and braided shallow channels, but here the river ran narrow and deep. Mabel could see the shale cliff on the far side that fell off into black ice. Below, the water would be well over her head.

The cliff became her destination, though she expected to drown before she reached it. The ice was only an inch or two thick, and even in the depths of winter no one would dare to cross at this treacherous point.

At first her boots caught on boulders, frozen in the sandy shore, but then she staggered down the steep bank and crossed a rivulet where the ice was thin and brittle. She broke through every other step to hit dry sand beneath.

When she reached the river's main channel, the ice was black and pliant, as if it had solidified only the night before. She slid her boot soles onto the surface and nearly laughed at her own absurdity—to be careful not to slip even as she prayed to fall through.

She was several feet from safe ground when she allowed herself to stop and peer down between her boots. It was like walking on glass. She could see granite rocks beneath the moving, dark turquoise water. A yellow leaf floated by, and she imagined herself swept alongside it and briefly looking up through the remarkably clear ice. Before the water filled her lungs, would she be able to see the sky?

She set her shoulders, faced straight ahead, and walked without looking down. When she crossed the heart of the channel, the cliff face was almost within arm's length, the water was a muffled roar, and the ice gave slightly beneath her. Against her will, she glanced down, and what she saw terrified her. Only bottomless black, as if the night sky were under her boots. She shifted her weight to take another step towards the cliff, and there was a deep, resonant pop like a massive champagne bottle being uncorked. Mabel spread her feet wide and her knees trembled. She waited for the ice to give way, for her body to plunge into the river. Then there was a *whoompf*, and she was certain the ice slumped beneath her boots, but in millimetres, nearly imperceptible except for the awful sound.

She waited and breathed, and the water didn't come. The ice bore her. She slid her feet slowly, first one, then the other, a slow shuffle until she stood where ice met cliff on the far side of the river. She put her bare palms to the cold shale, then the entire length of her body, until her forehead was pressed to it and she could smell the stone, ancient and damp.

Its cold began to seep into her, so she raised herself up, turned from the cliff face, and began the journey back the way she had come. Her heart thudded in her throat. She wondered if now, as she made her way home, she would break through to her death.

As she neared solid ground, she wanted to run to it, but the ice was too slick, so she slid as if ice-skating and then stumbled up the bank. She gasped and coughed and nearly laughed, as if it had all been a lark, a mad dare. Then she bent with her hands on her thighs and tried to steady herself.

When she slowly straightened, the land was vast before her. The sun was setting down the river, casting a cold pink hue along the white-capped mountains that framed both sides of the valley. Upriver, the willow shrubs and gravel bars, the spruce forests and low-lying poplar stands, swelled to the mountains in a steely blue. No fields or fences, homes or roads, not a single living soul as far as she could see in any direction. Only wilderness.

She turned her back to the river and walked home. The lantern was still burning; the kitchen window glowed as she approached the cabin, and when she opened the door and stepped inside, warmth overcame her.

She took off her coat and went to the woodstove, letting the heat sink painfully into her hands and feet. She had not expected to return here. Once she could open and close her fingers, she took out pots and pans, marvelling that she was fulfilling such a mundane task. She added wood to the stove, cooked dinner, and then sat straight-backed at the rough-hewn table. A few minutes later, Jack came through the door.

Certain he would somehow know what she had survived, she watched and waited. He rinsed his hands in the basin, sat across from her and lowered his head. 'Bless this food, Lord,' he mumbled. 'Amen.'

She set a potato on each of their plates beside boiled carrots and red beans. Neither of them spoke. There was only the scraping of knives and forks against plates. She tried to eat, but could not force herself.

'I went to the river today,' she said.

He jabbed at the carrots with his fork, then swabbed the beans with a slice of bread. He gave no indication he had heard her.

'It's frozen all the way across to the cliffs,' she said in a near whisper, her breath shallow. Mabel looked at his windburnt hands and frayed cuffs, the crow's feet that spread at the corners of his downturned eyes. She couldn't remember the last time she had touched that skin, and the thought ached like loneliness in her chest.

She pushed food here and there with her fork. She glanced at the lantern hanging from the ceiling and saw shards of light stream from it. She was crying. For a moment she let the tears run down either side of her nose. Jack continued to eat, his head down. She stood and took her plate of food to the small kitchen counter. Turned away, she wiped her face with her apron.

'That ice isn't solid yet,' Jack said from the table. 'Best to stay off of it.'

Mabel swallowed, cleared her throat. 'Yes. Of course,' she said.

She busied herself at the counter until her eyes were clear, then returned to the table and spooned more carrots onto Jack's plate.

'How is the new field?' she asked.

'It's coming.' He forked potato into his mouth, then wiped it with the back of his hand. 'I'll get the rest of the trees cut and skidded in the next few days, then I'll burn some more of the stumps out.'

'Would you like me to help? I could tend the stump fires for you.'

'No. I'll manage.'

That night in bed, she had a heightened awareness of him, the weight of him on the creaky bed, the sound of his slow, tired breaths. He lay on his side, turned away from her. She reached out, thinking to touch his shoulder, but instead lowered her arm and lay in the darkness staring at his back.

'Do you think we'll make it through winter?' she asked.

He didn't answer. She rolled away and faced the log wall.

When he spoke, Mabel wondered if it was grogginess or emotion that made his voice gravelly.

'We don't have much choice, do we?'

THE MORNING WAS SO COLD that when Jack first stepped outside and harnessed the horse, his leather boots stayed stiff and his hands wouldn't work right. A north wind blew steadily off the river. It wasn't easy, leaving the comfort of the woodstove. He'd like to have stayed indoors, but he had already stacked Mabel's towel-wrapped pies in a crate to take to town.

Jack climbed up into the open wagon and shook the reins. He did not look back, but he felt the cabin dwindle into the spruce trees behind him.

As the trail passed through a field, the horse seemed to trip on its own feet, and then it tossed its head. Jack slowed the wagon to a stop and scanned the field and distant trees, but saw nothing.

Goddamned horse. It was young and barely broken, but horses were scarcer than hen's teeth up here, and he didn't have much to choose from. Jack was afraid it would be the death of him. Just the other day he'd been skidding logs out of the new field when the horse spooked at a branch and knocked Jack to the ground. He barely missed being crushed by the log as the horse charged ahead. His forearms and shins were still tore up, and his back pained him every morning.

And there lay the real problem. Not the nervous horse, but the tired old man. This was too much work for a man of his age. After a long summer and snowless autumn, he was still nowhere near done clearing enough land to earn a living. He had got a pitiful little potato harvest off one small field this year, and it scarcely did more than buy flour for the winter. He figured he had enough money left from selling his share in the farm Back East to last them one more year, but only if Mabel kept selling pies in town.

As he rode through the end of a half-cleared field, the horse jerked again, tossed its head and snorted. Jack pulled back on the reins. He squinted and studied the fallen trees around him. The woods were silent, not even the twitter of a bird. The horse stamped a hoof on the hard ground and then was still. Jack tried to quiet his breathing so he could see and hear.

Something was watching him.

His eyes caught now and then on a stump or a shadowy spot among the trees. Shrug it off, old man, he told himself. You'll drive yourself crazy looking for something that's not there.

He went to shake the reins, but then peered one last time over his shoulder and saw it—a red fox darting among the fallen trees. It disappeared for a minute but popped up again, closer to the forest, running with its fluffy tail held low to the ground. It stopped and turned its head. For a moment its eyes locked with Jack's, and there, in its golden irises, he saw the savagery of the place. Like he was staring wilderness itself straight in the eye.

He shook the reins, and let the horse gather to a trot, both of them eager to put the fox behind them. For the next hour, he rode hunched and cold as the wagon bumped along through miles of untouched forest. As he neared town, the horse picked up its pace, and Jack had to slow it to keep the crate from spilling out of the wagon.

Back home, Alpine wouldn't have been called a town at all. It was nothing more than a few dusty, false-fronted buildings perched between the train tracks and the river, and some abandoned homesteads nearby.

Jack carried the crate of pies up the steps to the hotel restaurant where the owner's wife opened the door for him. Well into her sixties, Betty wore her hair short and mannish and ran the place with her husband, Roy.

'Good morning, Betty,' Jack said.

'It's ugly as far as I can see.' She slammed the door behind them. 'Colder than hell, and no sign of snow. Got some of Mabel's pies?'

'Yes, ma'am.' He set them on the counter and unwrapped them 'That woman sure can bake,' she said. 'Everybody asks after them pies.'

'Glad to hear it.'

She counted a few bills from the till and put them on the counter beside the crate. 'So I know I'm risking losing a few customers, Jack, but I'm afraid we won't be needing any more after today. My sister's come to live with us, and Roy says she's got to earn her keep by doing the baking.'

He picked up the bills and put them in his coat pocket as if he hadn't heard what she'd said. Then it registered.

'No more pies? You sure?'

'Sorry, Jack. I know it's poor timing, with winter coming on but . . .' Her voice trailed off, and she seemed uncharacteristically embarrassed.

'We could cut the price, if that would help,' he said. 'We need every penny we can get.'

'I am sorry. Can I get you a cup of coffee and some breakfast?'

'Coffee would be fine.' He chose a table by a small window that looked out over the river.

'It's on the house,' she said as she set the cup in front of him.

He never stayed when he brought the pies into town, but this morning he wasn't eager to get back to the homestead. What would he tell Mabel? That they had to pack up and go home with their tails between their legs? Give up, like all those before him? He stared out of the window and saw a white haze shrouding the peaks. It was snowing in the mountains. Soon it would snow here in the valley, too.

'You know, they're looking for help at the coal mine up north.' Betty slid a plate of bacon and eggs in front of him. 'It might get you all through a tight spot. Pay's not bad. They feed you and bunk you, and send you home with a little extra money in your pocket. Just something to think about.'

'Thanks. And thanks for this.' He gestured towards the plate.

'Sure thing.'

A godforsaken job, coal mining. Farmers were born to work in the light and air. Back home, he'd seen the men return from the mines with their faces black with coal dust and coughing up dirty blood. And it would mean leaving Mabel alone at the homestead for days, maybe weeks, at a time.

Cash money is what they needed, though. Just a month or two might be enough to pull them through next harvest. He could stand anything for a month or two. He ate the last bite of bacon and was ready to head out when George Benson came noisily through the restaurant door.

'Betty, Betty. What have you got for me today? Any of those pies?'

'They're fresh off the homestead, George. Have a seat.'

George turned towards the tables and spotted Jack.

'Hello there, neighbour! I'll tell you what—your wife bakes a mean apple pie.' He threw his coat over the back of a chair and patted his round belly. 'Mind if I join you?'

'Not at all.'

George lived about ten miles the other side of town with his wife and three boys. Jack had met him a few times at the general store. He seemed a good-natured sort and always spoke as if they were confirmed friends.

'How's it coming out at your place?' George asked as he sat across from him. 'You got any help out there?'

'Nope. Just working away on it myself. Got one or two good fields cleared. Always more to do. You know how it goes.'

'We should swap a few days here and there—me and my boys come over to your place with our draught horses, and then you lend a hand our way.'

'That's a generous offer.'

'We could help you get some work done,' George continued, 'and your wife could come over and get some girl time with Esther, talk about baking or sewing or whatever. She'd be thrilled to have you all over.'

Jack didn't say yes or no.

'Your kids all grown and gone?' George asked.

Jack hadn't seen that coming. He and Mabel were that old, weren't they, that their children could be grown and having families of their own.

'Nope. Never had any.'

'What's that? Never had any, you say?'

'Nope.'

He watched George. If you said you didn't have children it sounded like a choice, and what kind of craziness would that be? If you said you couldn't, the conversation turned awkward. Jack waited and swallowed.

'That's one way to go, I suppose.' George shook his head with a chuckle. 'Heck of a lot more quiet around your place, I'll bet. Sometimes those boys of mine like to drive me to drink. Hassling about this or that, dragging out of bed in the morning like the pox was on them.'

Jack laughed and eased, drank some of his coffee.

Betty came to the table with a cup and a slice of pie for George.

'I was just telling Jack they're looking for help up at the mine,' she said as she poured hot coffee. 'You know, to get them through the winter.'

George raised his eyebrows, then frowned, but didn't speak until Betty had gone back into the kitchen.

'You aren't, are you? You and I—we're no spring chickens, and those hellholes are for young men, if anybody at all.'

Jack nodded, uncomfortable with the conversation.

'You know why they're looking for men?' George went on. 'They've had trouble keeping crews on since the fires a few years back. Fourteen, dead as doornails. Some burned up so bad you couldn't tell 'em apart. I'm telling you, Jack, it's not worth the pennies they'd pay you.'

'I hear you. I do, but . . . well, I'm backed up against a wall.'

'You need to make it through until harvest? You got seed money for the spring?'

Jack gave a wry smile. 'As long as we don't eat between now and then.'

'You get yourself a moose yet?'

Jack shook his head. 'Never been much of a hunter.'

'Well that's all you need to do. Hang some meat in the barn, and you and the wife will be set till spring. It won't be caviar, but you won't starve.'

Jack looked into his empty coffee mug.

'Those first years are lean for a lot of us.' George said. 'I'm telling you, you might get sick of moose and potatoes, but you'll keep your neck safe.'

As if it were all settled, George finished off his pie in a few huge bites, wiped his mouth and stood. He reached a hand down to Jack.

'Better get going. Esther will accuse me of pissing the day away if I don't get on home.' His handshake was steady. 'Don't forget what I said. And we'd be glad to come over and help you get those fields cleared. Can make the day go faster to have company.'

Jack nodded. 'I appreciate that.'

He sat alone at the table. Maybe it was a mistake isolating themselves the way they had, Mabel without a single woman friend to talk with. George's wife could be a godsend, especially if he went north to work at the mine and Mabel was left alone at the homestead.

She would say otherwise. Hadn't they left all that behind to start a new life with just the two of them? I need peace and quiet, she'd told him more than once. She had shrunk in on herself, and it began when they lost that baby. She said she couldn't bear to attend another family gathering with all the silly banter and gossip. But Jack remembered the pregnant women smiling as they stroked their bellies, and the newborn infants wailing as they were passed among the relatives. He remembered, too, the little girl who had tugged at Mabel's skirts and called her 'Mama', mistaking her for another woman, and Mabel looking as if she had been backhanded. He remembered that he had failed her then, had gone on talking with a group of men and pretended he hadn't seen.

He nodded at Betty as he picked up the empty crate and walked out to the wagon.

Chapter 2

The leaden sky seemed to hold its breath. December grew near, and still there was no snow. For several days, the thermometer held at twenty-five below zero. Jack said people in town were relieved the snow hadn't come—the train tracks were clear and the mine was running. But others worried the deep freeze would mean a late spring and a late start on planting.

The days diminished. Light lasted just six hours, and it was a feeble light. Mabel organised her hours into patterns—wash, mend, cook, wash, mend, cook—and tried not to imagine floating beneath the ice like a yellow leaf.

Baking day was a small gift, a reason to look forward. When it came, she rose early and was taking out the bin of flour and can of lard when she felt Jack's hand on her shoulder.

'No need,' he said. 'Betty told me to hold off on the pies. She's got her sister baking for her.'

'Oh,' Mabel said. She put the flour back on the shelf, and was surprised at the strength of her disappointment. The pies had been a task she took some pride in. And there was the money.

'Will we have enough, Jack, without it?'

'I'll work it out. Don't worry yourself.'

Mabel brought him leftover biscuits and a hard-boiled egg for breakfast.

'George Benson and his boys are coming over later today to help me skid logs,' he said as he peeled the egg. He didn't seem to notice her stare.

'George Benson?' she asked. 'And who is George Benson?'

'I know I've mentioned him before.' He took a bite of egg. 'He and Esther live just downriver from town. They'll be here in a few hours. Don't worry about lunch—but figure three extra plates for dinner.'

'I thought . . . Didn't we agree . . . Why are they coming here?'

Jack was quiet, and then he rose from the table and picked up his leather boots from beside the door. He sat back in the chair, pulled them onto his feet and laced them in quick, jabbing motions.

'What am I supposed to say, Mabel? I need the help.' He tugged the laces tight. 'It's just that simple.' He grabbed his coat from the hook, buttoning as he stepped outside, as if he couldn't wait to get out the door.

GEORGE BENSON and two of his sons arrived an hour or so later. The older boy looked to be eighteen or twenty, the younger thirteen or fourteen. Mabel watched through the window as they met Jack at the barn. They all shook hands, Jack nodding and grinning. The men gathered tools and headed towards the field, leading the Bensons' team of draught horses.

Evening came, and Mabel lit the lamps and cooked a dinner for them. When the men came in from working, she would be gracious, but not overly friendly. She didn't want to encourage this. Jack might need help this particular day, but they were not in need of friends or neighbours. They had come here to find some solace on their own. Hadn't Jack understood that?

When George Benson and his boys returned they nodded politely and said thank you and ma'am and please pass the potatoes, but without ever really looking at her. Mostly they talked loudly to one another about the weather and the crops. They joked about broken tools and the whole blasted idea of 'homesteading' in this godforsaken place and George slapped his knee and asked pardon for his swear words and Jack laughed out loud. Mabel stayed by the kitchen counter, just outside of the light of the oil lamp.

They were going to be partners, she and Jack. This was going to be their new life together. Now he sat laughing with strangers when he hadn't smiled at her in years.

Later, after dinner, George dragged his tired boys to their feet and told them it was time to head home.

'Your mother will be wondering where the devil we went to,' he said. He nodded at Mabel. 'Much thanks for the great meal. You know, I told Jack here that you two ought to come over our way some time. Esther sure would like to meet you. Most of the homesteaders around here are grubby old bachelors. She could stand to have some female companionship.'

She should thank them for coming to help and say she'd be over any day now to meet his wife, but she said nothing. She could see herself through their eyes—an uptight, Back-East woman. She didn't like what she saw.

IT WAS SEVERAL DAYS before Jack mentioned the Bensons again, but he broached the subject as if halfway into an ongoing conversation. 'George said we should come by about noon on Thanksgiving. I told him you'd make up one of your pies. He's missing them down at the hotel.'

Mabel didn't agree or protest or ask questions.

As she flipped through her recipe box, trying to decide what to bake, she thought of Thanksgivings back in the Allegheny River valley, where Jack's aunts, uncles, cousins, grandparents and grandchildren, friends and neighbours gathered at the family farm for the feast. While the men walked the orchards to discuss business, Mabel was trapped in the women's realm of births and deaths. And just below the surface of this prattle was the insinuation of her failure, whispered and then hushed as she entered and left rooms. Perhaps, the whispers went, Jack should have chosen a heartier woman, a woman who had the hips for childbirth. Those highbrows might be able to discuss politics and literature, but could they birth a child, for God's sake? And too proud to take in an orphan child.

Maybe it would be the same with the Bensons. Maybe they would presume her unfit to survive as a homesteader in Alaska or judge her barren and cold and a burden to Jack. She thought of telling Jack she was too ill to go. But early on Thanksgiving morning she rose, well before Jack, put more wood in the stove and began rolling out the dough. She would make a walnut pie with her mother's recipe, and also a dried-apple pie. She might be curt and ungrateful, but by God she could bake.

With the pies in the woodstove oven, Mabel chose a heavy cotton dress that she hoped would be appropriate. Once the pies were done, she gathered wool blankets. It would be a long, cold ride in the open wagon.

After Jack had harnessed the horse, Mabel sat beside him on the wagon seat, the still-warm pies wrapped in towels on her lap. She felt an unexpected shiver of excitement. Whatever happened at the Bensons', it was good to be out of the cabin. She had not left the homestead for weeks. Jack, too, seemed more chipper. As they followed the trail off their property, he pointed out to Mabel where he had been clearing and told her of his ideas for the spring.

Mabel threaded her arm into the crook of his.

'You've accomplished a great deal.'

'I couldn't have done it without the Bensons. Those work horses of theirs put this beast to shame.' He gave the reins a gentle shake.

'Have you met his wife?'

'Nope. Just George and his sons. George used to be a gold miner, when he was younger, but he met Esther and they decided to settle down and have a family.' Jack hesitated, cleared his throat. 'Anyways, he seems like a good man. He's sure been a help to us.'

When they arrived at the Bensons', someone came out of the barn hoisting a flapping, headless turkey. It was George, she thought at first, but this person was short and had a thick grey braid hanging below a wool cap.

'Must be Esther,' Jack said.

The woman raised her chin in greeting, then wrestled with the huge dying bird in her arms. Blood splattered about her feet.

'Go on up to the house,' she called out to them. 'The boys'll help you with the horse.'

In the cabin, Mabel sat alone at the cluttered kitchen table, while Jack disappeared outside with George and the younger son. She wondered where they would eat. The table was heaped with stacks of catalogues, rows of washed, empty jars, and bolts of fabric. The cabin smelled strongly of cabbage. It wasn't much bigger than Jack and Mabel's, except it had a loft where she assumed the beds were. Rocks and bleached animal skulls and dried wild flowers lined the windowsills.

Mabel jumped when the door banged open.

'Blasted bird. You'd think it'd know enough just to give up the ghost when it doesn't even have a head left on its body.'

'Oh. Oh dear. Can I do something to help?'

The woman stomped past the table without removing her dirty boots and threw the turkey onto the crowded counter. A lard tin fell with a clatter to the floor. Esther kicked at it and turned to Mabel, who stood flustered and slightly frightened. Esther grinned, stretched out a bloodstained hand.

'Mabel? Isn't that it? Mabel?'

Mabel nodded and gave her hand over to Esther's vigorous shake.

'Esther. Good to have you out here finally.'

Under her wool coat, Esther wore a flower-print shirt and men's denim overalls. Her face was speckled with blood. She pulled off her wool hat and swung her braid over her back and began filling a large pot with water.

'You'd think with all these men around here I could find somebody to kill and pluck a turkey for me. But no such luck.'

'Are you sure there's nothing I can do?' Perhaps Esther would apologise for her appearance or for the disarray in the house.

'No. No. Just relax and make yourself at home. You could fix us some tea, if you'd like, while I get this damned bird in the oven.'

'Oh. Yes. Thank you. I brought pies. For dessert. I set them on that chair. I wasn't sure where else to put them.'

'Perfect! I hadn't had a chance even to think about sweets. George tells me Betty's a fool to give up your pies. He raves about your baking. Not that he needs any of it. Have you seen the gut on that man?'

Esther looked at Mabel expectantly and gave a loud, startling guffaw.

'I keep telling him he's single-handedly supporting that hotel restaurant, and it's starting to show,' she said.

It was as if Mabel had fallen through a hole into another world. It was nothing like her quiet, well-ordered world of darkness and light and sadness. This was an untidy place, but welcoming and full of laughter. George teased that the two women were 'talking a blue streak' rather than cooking the meal, and it was well into the evening before dinner was served, but no one seemed to mind. The turkey was dry on the outside and half-raw on the inside. The mashed potatoes were creamy and perfect. The gravy was lumpy. Esther made no apologies. They ate with plates balanced on their laps. George held up his glass and said, 'To neighbours. And to getting through another winter.' They all raised their glasses.

After dinner and pie, the Bensons began to tell stories of their time on the homestead, of how the snow once piled so deep the horses could walk over the fence whenever they pleased, of weather so cold the dishwater turned to ice in the air when you tossed it out.

'I wouldn't live anywhere else in the world, though,' Esther said. 'What about you? You both come from farms down south?'

'No. Well, Jack's family owns a farm in Pennsylvania.'

'What do they raise back there?' George asked.

'Apples and hay, mostly,' Jack said.

'What about you?' Esther turned to Mabel.

'I suppose I'm the black sheep. No one else in my family would think of living on a farm, or moving to Alaska. My father was a literature professor at the University of Pennsylvania.'

'And you left all that to come here? What in God's name were you thinking?' Esther shoved Mabel's arm playfully. 'He talked you into it, didn't he? That's how it often is. These men drag their women to the Far North for adventure, when all they want is a hot bath and a housekeeper.'

'No. No. It's not like that.' All eyes were on her. She hesitated, but then went on. 'I wanted to come here. Jack did, too, but when we did, it was at my urging. We were in need of a change and Alaska seemed like the place for a fresh start.'

Esther grinned. 'You didn't fare too badly with this one, did you, Jack? Don't let word get out. There aren't many like her.'

Though she didn't look up, Mabel knew Jack was watching her and that her cheeks were flushed. She so rarely spoke like this in mixed company.

Then, as the conversation began to turn around her, she wondered if she had told the truth. Was that why they had come north—to build a life? Or did fear drive her? Fear of the grey, not just in the strands of her hair and her wilting cheeks, but the grey that ran deeper, to the bone.

Mabel recalled the afternoon, less than two years ago. Sunny and brilliant. Jack was sitting on the porch swing of his parents' house, his eyes shaded from the sun. It was a family picnic, but they were alone for the moment. She had reached into her dress pocket and pulled out the folded handbill—'June 1918. Alaska, Our Newest Homeland.'

They should go, she had said. Home? he'd asked.

No, she'd said, and had held up the advertisement. North, she'd said.

The federal government was looking for farmers to homestead along the territory's new train route. The Alaska Railroad and a steamship company offered discounted rates for those brave enough to make the journey.

She had tried to keep her tone even, not to let desperation break her voice. Jack was wary of her newfound enthusiasm. They were both nearing fifty years old. As a young man he had dreamed of going to Alaska, of testing himself in a place so wild and grand, but wasn't it too late?

Jack surely had such doubts, but he did not speak them. He sold his share in the land and business to his brothers. She packed the trunks with dishes and pans and as many books as they could hold, and they travelled by steamship and train to Alpine.

The first summer he had her stay in town at the dingy hotel while he built the cabin and barn. When Mabel left her hotel room, she found only a muddy, deeply rutted trail beside the railroad tracks. It began in trees and ended in trees. No sidewalks. No cafés or bookshops. Mabel wanted to write to her sister but could not admit she had been wrong. Everyone had warned her the Territory of Alaska was for lost men and unsavoury women, that there would be no place for her in the wilderness.

When at last Jack brought her to the homestead, she had wanted to believe. So this was Alaska—raw, austere. A cabin of freshly peeled logs cut from the land, a patch of dirt for a yard, mountains that serrated the sky. She had imagined the two of them working in the fields as partners, side by side, out from under the shadow of cultivated orchards and expectant generations. Each day she asked, Can I come with you to the fields? But he said no, you should stay.

He returned in the evenings bent at the back and wounded with bruises and insect bites. She cooked and cleaned, and cooked and cleaned, and found herself further consumed by the grey.

Mabel smoothed her hands across her lap, chasing the wrinkles in the fabric again and again, until her ears caught a few of the words around her.

'All you folks have got to do is get a moose in your barn and save your money for spring,' George was saying.

Mabel frowned, not comprehending. 'A moose in our barn?'

Esther laughed.

'Not a live one, dear,' she said. 'Meat. Just to keep you fed. We've done it years past ourselves. You get mighty sick of mashed potatoes, fried potatoes, boiled meat, fried meat, but it'll get you through.'

'Pretty late in the year for moose,' the youngest boy mumbled from where he stood in the kitchen, his hands shoved in his pockets. 'He'd been better off getting one just before the rut. They're different then. Bulls go crazy through the woods. Knock their bloody antlers into the trees.'

'They're still out there, Garrett,' George said. 'He'll just have to work a bit harder to find one.'

The boy shrugged doubtfully.

'Don't mind him,' Esther said, thumbing in the boy's direction. 'He thinks he's the next Daniel Boone.'

One of the older sons laughed and punched him in the arm. The younger boy clenched his fists and a noisy scuffle commenced and Mabel was alarmed. When the ruckus became too much even for the Bensons, Esther hollered, 'That's enough boys!' and they settled down again.

'Garrett might be too big for his britches, but I tell you, Jack, he is a hand with a rifle.' George jutted his chin proudly. 'He shot his first moose when he was ten. He brings home more game than all the rest of us.'

The men were all talking of hunting moose, and once again Mabel had the unsettling sense that they had all conversed on this topic before and, once again, she was the ignorant stranger.

'You got to carry your rifle with you, even when you're just working in the fields,' she heard the youngest son tell Jack. 'Get up in the foothills. Most times, the snow'd already pushed 'em down to the river. But it's late in coming, so they're still up high, eating birch and aspen.'

When it came time to leave, the Bensons tried to insist on Jack and Mabel staying the night, but Jack said they needed to get home to care for the animals, and Mabel said thank you but she slept better in her own bed.

'It's cold out there tonight,' Esther said as she helped Mabel into her coat. She tucked a jar inside Mabel's coat, buttoned it for her as if she were a child, and straightened the collar. 'Keep that sourdough starter warm on the way home or you'll kill it for sure.'

It was clear and windy. The moon lit the ruts of the trail and turned the land and trees to blues. As they rode away, Mabel looked back to the lighted windows of the Benson home, and then she pushed her face down into her scarf. Jack cleared his throat. 'They're quite the family, aren't they?' he said. 'Esther took a liking to you. What all did you two talk about?'

'Oh . . . everything, I suppose.' Mabel was quiet, then said, 'She asked why we never had children.'

'And?'

'She said we can have their boys any time we want them.'

Jack chuckled, and Mabel smiled into her scarf despite herself.

THE NEXT EVENING, the snow fell with dusk. The first flakes clumped together as they twirled and fluttered to the ground. First just a few here and there, and then the air was filled with falling snow, caught in the light of the window in dreamy swirls. It brought to Mabel's mind how it was to be a little girl, kneeling on a sofa at the window to watch winter's first snowflakes filter through the streetlights.

When she returned to the kitchen window later, she saw Jack emerge from the woods and move through the snow. His hunt had been unsuccessful; she knew by his low head and shuffle.

She went back to preparing dinner. She opened the calico curtains over the kitchen shelves and took out two plates. She spread the tablecloth. She thought of the Bensons' cluttered cabin and smiled to herself. Esther in her men's overalls—how confidently she strode into the kitchen and flung the dead turkey onto the counter.

Mabel went back to the window again. The snow fell faster and thicker. As she watched, Jack walked out of the barn carrying a lantern, and the snow eddied round him in the circle of light. He turned his head, as if he had sensed her eyes on him, and the two of them looked at each other across the distance, each in their pocket of light, snow like a falling veil between them. Mabel couldn't remember the last time they had so deliberately gazed at each other, and the moment was like the snow, slow and drifting.

When she first fell in love with Jack, she had dreamed she could fly, that on a warm, inky black night she had pushed off the grass with her bare feet to float among the leafy treetops and stars in her nightgown. The sensation had returned.

Mabel stood spellbound in her apron, a washrag in her hand.

She set down the rag and untied her apron. She slipped her feet into her boots, put on one of Jack's wool coats, and found a hat and some mittens.

Outside, the air was clean and cool against her face. She let the snow float around her, and then she did what she had as a child—turned her face to the sky and stuck out her tongue. The swirl overhead was dizzying and she began to spin slowly in place. The snowflakes landed on her cheeks and eyelids, wet her skin.

Around her feet the snow deepened. She kicked at it lightly, and it clumped, wet and heavy. Snowball snow. She clenched a fistful in her bare hand. The snow compacted and held the shape of her fingers. She pulled on her mittens and balled some snow together, patting and forming it.

She heard Jack's footsteps and looked up to see him coming towards the cabin. He squinted at her. She so rarely came outside, and never at night. She patted the snowball a few more times, watched Jack and waited. As he neared, she threw it at him. The snowball thumped into his leg, just above the top of his boot.

He stopped, looked at the circle of snow on his trouser leg and then up at Mabel, a mix of irritation and confusion on his face, and then even as his brow stayed furrowed, a small smile appeared at the corner of his lips. He bent and carefully lodged the lantern in the snow beside him, then smacked his gloved hand across the trouser leg, dusting away the snow. Mabel held her breath. He remained bent over, his hand down by his boots, and then, quicker than Mabel could react, he scooped up a handful of snow and tossed a perfectly formed snowball at her. It smacked her in the forehead. She stood motionless with her arms at her sides.

'I . . . that's not . . . I hadn't meant to . . .'

And she laughed. Melting snow dripped down her temples, snowflakes landed on her eyelashes. She laughed and laughed until she was doubled over, and then she grabbed another handful of snow and threw it at Jack, and he threw one back, and the snowballs lobbed through the air. Laughing, they chased each other round the cabin, dodging behind the log corners and peeking out in time to see another snowball coming. The hem of Mabel's long skirt dragged in the snow. Jack chased her, a snowball in each hand. She tripped and fell and as he ran to her she flung loose snow at him, all the time laughing, and he gently tossed the snowballs down at her. Then he put his hands to his knees, bent at the back and breathing loudly.

'We're too old for this,' he said. He reached down and pulled Mabel to her feet until they stood chest to chest, panting and smiling and covered in snow. Mabel pressed her face into his damp collar and he wrapped his arms, thick with his wool coat, round her shoulders. They stood that way for a while, letting the snow fall down upon them.

Then Jack pulled away and reached for the lantern.

'Wait,' she said. 'Let's make a snowman. The snow is perfect for it.'

He hesitated. He was tired. They were too old for such nonsense.

'All right,' he said. There was reluctance in the hang of his head, but he pulled off his leather work gloves. He took her cheek in his bare hand and with his thumb wiped melted snow from beneath her eye.

The snow stuck in thick layers as they rolled it into balls along the ground. Mabel made the last, smallest one for the head, and Jack stacked them one atop the other. The figure barely stood above his waist.

'It's kind of small,' he said.

She stepped back and inspected it from a distance.

'It's just fine,' she said.

They patted snow into the cracks between the snowballs, smoothed the edges. He walked away from the light of the lantern and cabin window, into a stand of trees. He came back with two birch branches, and he stuck one into each side of their creation. Now it had arms.

'A girl. Let's make it a little girl,' she said. She knelt and began shaping the bottom into a skirt that spread out from the snow girl. When she stood up, she saw Jack at work with a pocketknife.

'There,' he said. He stepped back. Sculpted in the white snow were perfect, lovely eyes, a nose and small, white lips. She even thought she could see cheekbones and a little chin.

'Oh.'

'You don't like it?' He sounded disappointed.

'No. Oh no. She's beautiful. I just didn't know . . .'

How could she speak her surprise? Such delicate features, formed by his calloused hands, a glimpse at his longing. He too had wanted children. They had talked about it so often when they first married, joking they would have a baker's dozen but really planning on only three or four. How could they have known that twenty years later they would still be childless, just an old man and an old woman alone in the wilderness?

'She needs some hair,' he said.

'Oh. I've thought of something, too.'

Jack went towards the barn, Mabel to the cabin.

'Here they are,' she called across the yard when she came back out. 'Mittens and a scarf for the little girl.'

He returned with a bundle of yellow grass from near the barn. He stuck individual strands into the snow, creating wild, yellow hair, and she wrapped the scarf round its neck and placed the mittens on the ends of the birch branches, the red string that joined them across the snow child's back. Her sister had knitted them in red wool, and the scarf was a stitch Mabel had never seen before—dewdrop lace, her sister called it.

She and Jack stood side by side and gazed at their creation.

'She's beautiful,' she said. 'Don't you think?'

'She did turn out, didn't she?'

Standing still, she became aware of the cold through her damp clothes and trembled. 'Let's go in and warm up.'

Inside, Jack added several logs to the woodstove and the fire crackled. Mabel stood as close as she dared and peeled off wet mittens, hat, coat. He did the same. Clumps of snow fell onto the stovetop and sizzled. Her dress hung heavy and wet against her skin, and she unbuttoned it and stepped out of it. He pulled his damp shirt off over his head. Soon they were naked and shivering beside each other. She was unaware of their bare skin until he stepped closer and she felt his rough hand at the small of her back.

'Better?' he asked.

'Yes.' She reached up over his shoulders where his skin was still cool to the touch, and when she pressed her nose into the crook of his neck, melted snow clung in droplets to his beard.

'Let's go to bed,' Jack said.

After all these years, still a spot within her fluttered at his touch. Naked, they walked to the bedroom. Beneath the covers, they fumbled with each other's bodies, arms and legs, backbones and hipbones, until they found the familiar, tender lines like the creases in an old map that has been folded and refolded over the years.

Chapter 3

Jack woke to the cold. In the few hours he'd slept the weather had changed. He could smell it and feel it in his arthritic hands. He propped himself on an elbow and grabbed at the nightstand until he found a match and lit the candle. His back and shoulders were stiff as he eased his legs over the side of the bed. Not far from the pillow where Mabel slept, frost crept between the logs with its feathery crystals. He swore quietly and pulled the quilt up over her shoulder. A warm, secure home—he couldn't even give her that much. He carried the candleholder into the main room. The heavy metal door on the woodstove clanged noisily as he opened it. A few coals smouldered in the ash.

As he reached for his boots, through the window he saw a flicker. He stood at the frost-edged glass and peered out.

Fresh snow blanketed the ground and glittered and glowed silver in the moonlight. The barn and trees beyond were muted outlines. There, at the edge of the forest, he saw it again. A flash of blue and red. He was groggy with sleep. He closed his eyes slowly, opened them again and tried to focus.

There it was. A little figure dashed through the trees. Was that a skirt about the legs? A red scarf at the neck, and white hair trailing down the back. Slight. Quick. A little girl. Running at the edge of the forest. Then disappearing into the trees.

Jack rubbed his eyes with the heels of his hands. Not enough sleep—that had to be it. He left the window and stepped into his boots, leaving the laces untied. He opened the door and the snow crunched beneath his boots as he walked to the woodpile. It was only as he was returning with an armload of split birch that he noticed their little snow girl. Where it had stood was a small, broken heap of snow. The mittens and scarf were gone.

He pushed at the snow with the toe of his boot.

An animal. Maybe a moose had stumbled through. But the scarf and mittens? A raven or a whiskey jack maybe. Wild birds had been known to snatch things. As he turned away, he caught sight of the tracks that ran through the snow, away from the cabin and into the trees. He bent over them. The silvery-blue light was weak, so at first he didn't trust his eyes. Coyote, or maybe lynx. He bent closer and touched the track with the tips of his bare fingers. Human footprints. Small. The size of a child's.

Jack shivered. His skin prickled with goose bumps, and his bare toes ached cold inside his boots. He left the tracks and the pile of snow and went inside, quickly closing the door behind him. He shoved each piece of wood into the stove. Just his eyes playing tricks. He stayed beside the woodstove until the fire roared again, and then he closed the damper.

He eased himself beneath the quilt and lay against Mabel's warm body, his eyes wide and his brain spinning, until finally he drifted into a restless sleep in which children ran soft-footed through the trees.

When Jack woke again it was late morning, the sun was up, and Mabel was in the kitchen. His body was tired and stiff, as if he had never slept at all. He dressed and in socked feet made his way to the table. He smelled fresh coffee and hot pancakes.

'I think the sourdough starter Esther gave me worked. Here, try them.' Mabel set a plate of pancakes on the table. With a hand on his shoulder, she reached over him to pour coffee from the blue enamel pot into his cup.

'Did you sleep all right?' she asked.

'I don't know. I guess not.' He got up from the table.

'Aren't you going to eat breakfast?' she asked.

'Just going to get some wood. Nearly let the fire go out.'

He put on his coat and some gloves, before opening the door. The snow reflected the sunlight so brilliantly he squinted.

He walked to the woodpile, gathered up more wood, then turned back to the cabin and saw the snow child, or what was left of it. Still just a pile of snow. No scarf. No mittens. Just as it had been last night, but now exposed as truth in the light of day. And the footprints still ran through the snow, across the yard and into the trees. Then he saw the dead snowshoe hare beside the doorstep. He stepped past without pausing. Inside, he let the wood fall to the floor beside the stove, then stared without seeing.

'Have you noticed anything out of the ordinary?' he finally said.

'Like what?'

'I thought I heard something last night. Probably nothing.'

After breakfast Jack left to feed the animals. On the way to the barn, he scooped up the dead hare and held it close to his side so Mabel wouldn't notice from the window. Once in the barn, he looked at it closely. He could see where it had been strangled, most likely with a thin snare. It was frozen stiff. Later, after he had taken care of the animals, he went behind the barn and threw the dead hare as far as he could into the trees.

When he returned to the cabin, Mabel was heating water to wash.

'Did you see the tracks?' she pointed out of the window.

'Those?' he asked. 'Must have been a fox.'

'Are the chickens safe?'

'Fine. They're all fine.'

Jack took his shotgun down from over the door and told her he would go after the fox. He knew now what unsettled him about the tracks. The trail began at the heap of snow and led in only one direction—away and into the woods. There were no prints coming into the yard.

The trail wove among the birch trees, over fallen logs and around bare, thorny wild rose branches. Jack followed the loops and turns. They didn't seem like the tracks of a lost child. More like a wild animal, a fox or ermine. Dashing here and there, running across the top of the snow, circling back and around until Jack wasn't sure if he was still following the original trail. If she were lost, why hadn't she come to the door and asked for help? And the tracks did not lead down the wagon trail, towards the south, towards the town, but they wound north, towards the mountains. The small boot prints were joined here and there by another, different set of tracks—fox, crisscrossing the child's footprints.

He followed the trail for a while longer, then stopped at a fallen cottonwood, wiped sweat from his forehead. The trail meandered down into a dense forest of black spruce. He could not easily fit through those trees so he turned back. Mabel was anxious at the door when he returned. She wiped her hands on her apron and helped him take off his coat.

'I was beginning to worry.'

Jack warmed his hands at the woodstove.

'Well? Did you find the fox?'

'No, just more tracks, all over the place out there.'

He wouldn't tell her about the child, or the dead hare on their doorstep. Somehow, he thought they might upset her.

MABEL NERVOUSLY EYED the trail across the snow as she returned from the outhouse. Never before had a fox come so close to their cabin. She knew they were small creatures, but all the same they frightened her. She stepped over the tracks, but then their smooth, oblong shape caught her eye. They weren't animal tracks at all. Each was a perfect print of the sole of a small boot. She brought her head up and with her eyes followed the trail back to the snow child she and Jack had built the night before. It was gone.

She hurried breathless into the cabin.

'Jack? Someone's ruined our snow child. Someone's been in our yard.'

He was at the counter, sharpening his pocketknife on a steel.

'I know. A child's tracks. And I'm pretty sure I saw her. Last night. Running through the trees.'

'Her? Who?'

'A little girl. She was wearing your red scarf.'

'What? Why didn't you tell me? Did you go after her?'

'This morning, when I told you I was going to look for the fox, I tried to see where she went, but I lost the trail.'

'Last night . . . there was a little girl alone outside in the freezing winter and you didn't see if she needed help? She must have wandered away from somebody's cabin.'

'I don't know, Mabel.'

She went back outside and stared at the little tracks. Just one trail, leading across the snow, away from their cabin and into the trees.

DURING THE NEXT FEW DAYS the skies cleared, a deep cold settled on the valley, and the child's tracks became edged in frost. They trailed sparkling and delicate through Mabel's thoughts, and left her feeling as if she had forgotten something.

Then one morning she woke to a silent cabin and sensed the change before she looked out of a window. Jack had left her a crackling fire before going to hunt moose again. Her senses were confirmed when she looked out and saw a shining new landscape. The snow had come again, and this time it was a driving snow that had erased the tracks across their yard.

She carried a basket of breadcrumbs and dried apple bits left over from a pie to the barn for the chickens. The hens comforted her, the way they roosted along their spruce pole, their feathers ruffled against the cold. When she came in, they hopped to the straw-strewn ground and clucked like old women welcoming a neighbour. She reached into each nesting box. Finally, beneath the soft belly of a red hen, she found two warm eggs.

Mabel put them in her basket as she left the barn. When she turned to pull the door closed, she glimpsed blue in the snow-laden spruce trees beyond the yard. A child, slight and quick in a blue coat, passing through the trees.

Mabel walked towards the forest, slowly at first and then more quickly. She watched for the girl but lost sight of her.

When she neared the edge of the woods she was startled to see the child only a hundred yards or so away. She was crouched, her back to Mabel, white-blonde hair fanning down her blue wool coat. Wondering if she should call out, Mabel cleared her throat, and the sound startled the child.

The girl stood, snatched a small sack from the snow, and sprinted away. As she disappeared round one of the largest spruce trees, she looked back over her shoulder and Mabel saw her glancing blue eyes and small, impish face. She was no more than eight or nine years old.

'I SAW THE CHILD,' Mabel told Jack when he came in for dinner. 'The girl you described from the other night—I saw her behind the barn.'

Jack squinted, as if cross, then hung his coat on the hook beside the door.

'Have you heard anything about someone missing a child?' she asked. 'When you were in town yesterday, did you tell anybody about her?'

'No. I didn't see much point. I figured she'd gone home or they would have got together a search party.'

'But she was here again today. Right near our barn. Why would she come here? If she is lost or needs help, why doesn't she just come to the door?'

He nodded sympathetically, but then changed the subject. He said they would have to kill the chickens as soon as the sack of feed ran out; they hadn't enough money to buy more. The good news, he went on, was that he'd run into George at the hotel restaurant yesterday and had invited the Bensons to dinner the coming Sunday.

It wasn't until this last part that Mabel listened attentively. She was glad the Bensons were coming. Certainly Esther could tell her something about the child; she knew the families in the valley, and maybe she would know why a little girl would be wandering alone through the forest.

AT NIGHT, when Jack closed his eyes to sleep, tree branches and game trails and snowy cliffs were imprinted on his eyelids so that sleep merged with his long days spent hunting. For days now he had risen most mornings before light and gone out with his rifle to look for moose, feeling like an imposter every time. He'd hiked up and down the Wolverine River, into the mountains, back and forth over the foothills, and he was sick to death of it.

He lay in bed longer than usual and considered not getting up at all. But George was right—if he managed to get a moose, he and Mabel could live off meat and potatoes until harvest. They'd run out of coffee, sugar, dried apples, powdered milk, lard.

He got up and dressed. He had until afternoon, when the Bensons would arrive for dinner. He left the cabin with his rifle and pack and walked the wagon trail. The snow was well over the tops of his boots. He'd stick close to home and hope the snow had forced the animals down along the river.

The sky was overcast and leaden, and Jack was weighed down by it. He walked through the field, the snow slowing his way, and entered the woods, but his heart was not in it. He knew how to handle tools and work animals and plough the earth. But this was nothing like farming back home. He didn't enjoy his solitude in these woods but instead was self-conscious and alert, fearing most of all his own ineptness.

When Jack had told his brothers he was moving to Alaska, they'd envied him. God's country, they'd said. The land of milk and honey. Moose, caribou and bears—game so thick you won't know what to shoot first. And the streams so full of salmon, you can walk across their backs to the other side. What a different truth he found. Alaska gave up nothing easily. It was lean and wild and indifferent to a man's struggle, and he had seen it in the eyes of that red fox.

Jack came to a log and made a halfhearted attempt to brush the snow away before sitting on it. He laid the rifle across his knees, took off his wool hat, and ran his fingers through his hair. For some time he sat bent over, head in his hands. Doubt crouched over his shoulder, ready to take him by the throat, whispering in his ear, You are an old man. An old, old man.

It was the quiet that pulled him out of his gloom. A quiet full of presence. He brought his head up.

It was the child. She was before him, just a few yards away. She stood atop the snow, arms at her sides, the hint of a smile at her pale lips. White fur trimmed her coat and leather boots. Her face was framed by the velvety brown of a sable hat, and she wore Mabel's red scarf and mittens. The child was dusted in crystals of ice, as if she had just walked through a snowstorm or spent a brilliantly cold night outdoors.

Jack would have spoken to her, but her eyes—the broken blue of river ice, glacial crevasses, moonlight—held him. She blinked, her blonde lashes glittering with frost, and darted away.

'Wait!' he called out. He stumbled after her. 'Wait! Don't be afraid!'

He was clumsy, tripping over his own boots and kicking up snow. She sprinted ahead, but stopped often to look back at him.

'Please,' he called again. 'Wait!'

A sound came to Jack's ears like wind stirring dried leaves or snow blowing across ice, or maybe a whisper from far away. *Shhhhh.*

He did not call out again. He ducked beneath tree branches and waded through the snow as the girl led him farther into the forest. He had to watch his feet to keep from tripping, but each time he looked up, she was waiting.

And then she wasn't. He stopped, squinted and scanned the snow for her tracks. He saw no sign. Once again he became aware of the quiet, the strange calm of the forest.

From behind him came a high, chirpy whistle like a chickadee's call, and he turned, expecting to see a bird, or maybe the child. Instead, a bull moose stood not fifty yards away. It raised its head slowly, as if the massive, many-pointed antlers were a ponderous burden. Snow sprinkled its long nose and brown hackles. It swayed its antlers slowly from side to side. Never had Jack seen such a magnificent animal. On lanky legs, it must have stood more than seven feet at the withers, and its neck was as stout as a tree trunk.

In his wonder, Jack nearly overlooked the obvious—this was livelihood, and yet he was so ill prepared.

He expected the animal to spook as he chambered a cartridge in the rifle, but it went back to eating the tips of willow branches.

Jack rested his cheek against the wooden stock and tried to steady his grip. His exhalations rose as steam in the cold air and clouded his vision, so he held his breath, aimed for the moose's heart, and pulled the trigger. He never heard the explosion or registered the rifle's recoil. There was only the moment of impact, the animal staggering as if a great weight had come crashing down upon it, and then its fall.

He lowered the rifle to his side and took a few steps towards the moose. It kicked its legs and twisted its neck at a miserable angle. He chambered another round. The moose flailed in the snow, and Jack looked into its rolling, wild eyes. He raised the rifle and shot a bullet into the animal's skull. It did not move again.

Jack's knees were unsteady as he leaned his rifle against a tree and went to the dead moose. Its antlers could have held Jack like a cradle, and his arms could not have circled its barrel chest. It had to weigh more than a thousand pounds, and that meant hundreds of pounds of good, fresh meat.

He'd done it. They had food for the winter. He wanted to jump up and whoop and holler. He wanted someone like George to smack him on the back and tell him well done. He wanted to celebrate, but the woods had a solemn air, and beneath the thrill in his own chest, there was something else. He'd taken a life, a significant life judging by the animal laid out before him. He was obliged to take care of the meat and bring it home in gratitude.

It was something about the child, too. Without her, he never would have seen the moose. She'd led him here and alerted him when, like a clod, he had passed by the animal. She moved through the forest with the grace of a wild creature. She knew the snow, and it carried her gently. She knew the spruce trees, how to slip among their limbs, and she knew the animals, the fox and ermine, the moose and songbirds. She knew this land by heart.

Jack had carved up chickens and a few sides of beef, but this was a colossal, fully intact wild animal sprawled in its own blood in the middle of the woods. He needed to open the gut to let the viscera and heat escape before the meat spoiled, but it would be no easy task. The moose's legs, each weighing more than a hundred pounds, were cumbersome and in the way. He tried to lodge his shoulder beneath a hind leg to expose the belly, but it was too unwieldy. He took a section of rope from his pack and wrapped it round the moose's hind ankle. Using all his strength, he pulled it up and away, and then tied the rope to a tree behind the moose.

He sharpened his knife but wasn't sure how to begin. Daylight was wasting, so he plunged his knife into the belly, remembering he didn't want to puncture the gut sack and contaminate the meat. He was up to his elbows in blood and bowels when he heard something approaching through the forest. He thought it might be the child, but then a horse nickered. Jack stood and wiped his knife on his pants.

It was Garrett Benson, walking a horse through the trees.

'Hello there,' Jack called to him.

'I heard shots. You got one down?'

'Yep.'

The boy tied the horse to a nearby tree. As he neared, his eyes widened.

'Holy Moses! That's one big moose.' Garrett went to the antlers, tried to stretch his arms from one side to the other and failed. 'Ho-ly Moses,' he said again more softly.

'Is he big?'

'Hell yeah.' A boy trying out a man's language. 'Hell yeah!'

'I didn't know. This is the first bull I've seen up close.'

Garrett took off his glove and held out his hand. 'Congratulations! He's a dandy!'

Jack took the boy's hand. 'Thanks, Garrett. I appreciate that. I have to say, I wasn't expecting this.'

'No kidding. I mean, he's a jim-dandy!'

This was an aspect of Garrett he hadn't seen. His boyish face beamed.

'I was riding the river, putting out traps, when I heard your rifle,' Garrett said. The boy ran a hand down the antler bone. 'It's bigger than any I've ever seen,' he said. 'Sure bigger than anything I've ever shot.'

His opinion of Garrett improved. Not many thirteen-year-old boys could win a wrestling match with envy.

'Guess I've got my work cut out for me,' Jack said. 'Maybe you can give me a few pointers, walk me through some of it?'

'It's a lot. But with two of us, it'll go all right.' The boy took a knife from a sheath at his belt. 'Looks like you're starting fine, pulling those guts out.' He drew back the hide and peered inside the rib cage. 'Yeah, see there? You can just cut that away and it'll all come out slick.'

When they sliced away the heart and liver, each broader than a dinner plate, Jack slid them still wet into a gunny sack.

For the next few hours, Jack and the boy worked at the moose. Jack's hands were cold and numb, and several times he nicked himself with the knife. The sun slithered through the trees, the air cooled, the dead animal stiffened, but they kept at it. Sometimes Garrett offered advice about where to make a cut or how to separate a joint. They joked some and talked some, but mostly just worked, and it was comfortable.

When they had cut away the legs and ribs, the tenderloin and backstrap and neck meat, Garrett fetched a handsaw from his saddlebags and they sawed the antlers from the skull.

'You've got to bring these back tonight,' Garrett said, 'so we can show everybody. They'll never believe it if we just tell them.'

Jack would have rather left the antlers and hauled more of the meat home, but he decided the quarters would be safe enough hanging in the trees for the night, until he could come back with the wagon in the morning. He hated to disappoint the boy after all he'd done to help, so they strapped the antlers, and some of the finest cuts of meat to Garrett's saddle.

Bloody and tired, they made their way through the trees, Garrett leading the horse by a rope. Jack hadn't realised how close he was to his field, and from there they followed the wagon trail into the yard. 'I sure am grateful for your help,' Jack said. 'I'd still be out there hacking away by myself.'

'Sure. Sure,' Garrett said. 'Wait till Mom and Dad see it.'

With Jack hobbling after him, Garrett rushed ahead.

'Looks like your folks beat you here,' Jack called out when he saw the sleigh in the yard. Just then, George came out of the barn.

'You're not going to believe this!' Garrett hollered. 'Jack shot the biggest damn moose you ever saw!'

Chapter 4

As she prepared that morning for the Bensons' arrival, Mabel reminded herself of how it had been at their house for Thanksgiving. She would not fret about the stains on the tablecloth or the rough-plank floor that could never be scrubbed clean. Dinner would be well made, but not so much that it seemed she was trying to show them up.

Dusk came and the Bensons arrived on a sleigh pulled by one of their draught horses. George and the two older boys took the horse to the barn while Esther unloaded some things from the sleigh and came to the door.

There was no knock or opportunity to invite her in as Esther pushed past Mabel. 'Thank God, we're finally here.' She tossed a dusty grain sack on the table, nearly knocking a plate to the floor. 'I thought you could use some onions. We ended up with more than we need.'

She took off her coat and unloaded Mason jars from her oversized pockets. 'This one here's rhubarb jam. Terrific on sourdough pancakes. This one is blueberry-raspberry. Might have some currants in there. Hard to tell.'

She laughed and flung her arms round Mabel's shoulders, squeezing her tightly. 'Oh, it's so good to see you. I've been after George ever since Thanksgiving to get us over here. It's no good being a woman in this country, is it? Too many men, in my opinion.'

Esther shook out her long braid. Then she looked around the cabin and Mabel felt a mixture of pride and shyness, sure that Esther was inspecting the curtains and clean kitchen and assessing her skills as a homemaker.

'Nice tight cabin you've got here. George says you've got some problems with the frost coming through, but that happens to us all. Just crank up the woodstove, I say. A sturdy woodstove makes all the difference.'

Esther stood next to the stove much the way Jack did, with her hands spread wide to the heat. Mabel realised she had never really studied the stove before, just as she knew that Esther had yet to notice the carefully set table or the few photographs hanging on the walls.

'Jack hasn't come home yet. He should be here any time, and then we can have dinner. Would you like some tea? I put some water on.'

'Oh, that would be terrific. I'm cold and damp from the ride over. I'm not complaining, though. I've always liked the snow.'

'I do know what you mean. Or at least I can say I am finally getting accustomed to it. There's been a lot to get used to here.'

Esther laughed. 'Isn't that the truth. I don't know if you ever get used to it really. It just gets in your blood so that you can't stand to be anywhere else.'

The women sat at the table, Mabel sipping her tea and Esther talking. Mabel waited for a chance to ask about the child, but Esther never seemed to take a breath. 'I know I'm going to talk your ear right off tonight. It's so good to have a woman to visit with. I don't even care what we talk about.'

She then went on to talk about last year's crops, about the wolves that were running the river and how their younger son wanted to trap a few for the bounty money.

'That boy of mine hasn't showed up yet, has he? He's supposed to meet us here, coming by horse on the river.'

Then Esther asked about the fox Jack had seen in the fields. 'They'll snatch your chickens as soon as they get a chance,' she said.

Mabel was preparing to say that she had indeed seen the fox, with a little girl, right near their barn, but just then the door burst open.

'Well, call it beginner's luck,' George said. 'Jack's gone and shot the biggest moose in the entire valley. Gals, you've got to come and see this.'

Mabel tried to imagine what she would see in the barn as she followed George and Esther through the snow. She expected an entire animal, still in its skin and fur, still a moose. When she stepped into the lantern light and saw the disembodied antlers atop their bloody stump, she drew in a breath.

'Holy Moses!' Esther said.

'That's exactly what I said, Mom. Isn't it?' The boy turned to Jack. 'Ho-ly Moses. Those antlers got to go seventy inches across,' he said, posing behind them like an African hunter with his trophy.

Suddenly Jack grabbed Mabel about the waist from behind, swung her round to face him and for a second lifted her off her feet.

'I did it, love. I got our moose!' He kissed her quick and hard on the neck. He smelled of wild animal and moonshine, and his eyes twinkled from drink. When he set her back down on the straw floor, she was disorientated.

The barn was a garble of talk and cheers while Jack told how he had heard something behind him, turned round and here was this bull moose, and he had shot it, and then Garrett came along and he couldn't have done it without him. A bottle was passed none too discreetly among the men and the two older sons, and each held it up and called out 'Cheers!' while Garrett begged in vain for a swig.

'Not just yet, sprout,' Esther said, and then she took a drink herself, and the men all laughed. Mabel kept quietly to herself. But Esther turned to her and held out the bottle.

'Oh come,' she said playfully. 'Drink a toast to your hunter!' So Mabel took the moonshine and held the cold glass to her mouth. She tipped it back and let the icy-hot liquid splash against her lips, and then she coughed and coughed and handed the bottle back while everyone laughed merrily.

Mabel smiled up at Jack and knew she should be glad, but she couldn't rid her mind of the sawed edge of skull bone at her feet.

The raucous party made its way into the cabin, all of them talking at once and shaking snow from their clothes. Garrett brought in a gunny sack and set it on the kitchen counter. From it Esther took a veined, rounded muscle the size of a bread loaf and Mabel realised it was the animal's heart. Esther began to slice it thinly with a knife.

'Heat up a pan, dear,' she said over her shoulder to Mabel. 'We'll have some of this with dinner. There's nothing better than fresh moose heart.'

Before Mabel could think or move, Esther had a cast-iron pan heating on the woodstove. 'Hand me one of those onions, will you? I'll cut one up to throw in the pan.'

The next hour was a blur to Mabel, her head swimming in the smell of frying meat and onions and the noise of boisterous talking. Someone must have mashed the boiled potatoes and sliced the carrots and opened a jar of onion relish. Before she understood all that had happened, they were crowded at the table, and Mabel was cutting a piece of moose heart with a steak knife and taking her first bite.

'Tasty, isn't it?' Esther asked.

Mabel nodded and chewed and tried not to think about the muscle beating inside a moose's rib cage. It wasn't as awful as she had feared. As the talk dwindled and everyone finished their meals, Esther looked across the table and said, 'Weren't you getting ready to tell me something when George came busting through the door? Something about the fox . . .'

Mabel was flustered.

'I did mean to ask you . . . but it can wait until later,' she said.

'Oh, no one's paying any attention. Out with it, then.' Esther waved impatiently. The men were telling hunting stories and oblivious to them.

'Well, I did mean to ask—do you know if there's a little girl living anywhere near our place? A little blonde girl?'

'A little girl? Let me think. There are only a few families in the valley right now. Most of the homesteads are run by single men who struck out with gold and such. The Wrights have a couple of girls, but they're redheads. And they're nowhere near here. They're the other side of us.' Esther rose and began gathering the dishes.

'The reason I ask,' Mabel said, leaning towards Esther and speaking quietly, 'is we had a child on our place the other night. Jack got up in the middle of the night and he saw a girl run through the trees. The next morning—we had built this little snowman, well, a little snow girl actually—and it was knocked over and the scarf and mittens were gone. I think the child must have done it. It's not that I mind, really. I would have given them to her if she needed them so. I'm just worried she was lost or something.'

Esther stopped gathering the dishes and focused on Mabel.

'Here, at your place, you're saying? You saw a little blonde child just sprinting about? Sure it wasn't just an animal or something?'

'No, I'm certain. We even saw her tracks. Jack tried to follow them for a while, but they just went around and around in the woods. Then the other day I saw her, in the trees beyond the barn.'

'That's the darndest thing . . .' Esther's voice trailed off as she sat down and looked across the table into Mabel's eyes. She smiled gently. 'I don't mean to speak out of turn, Mabel, but this isn't an easy place to get along. The winters are long, and sometimes it starts to get to you. Around here, they call it cabin fever. Sometimes your mind starts playing tricks on you.' Esther reached across the table and put a hand over Mabel's. 'You start seeing things that you're afraid of . . . or things you've always wished for.'

Mabel let Esther hold her hand for a moment, but then pulled away.

'No, you don't understand. We saw her. And we both saw the tracks, and the mittens and scarf are gone.'

'Maybe it was an animal, or the wind. All sorts of explanations.'

The men had stopped talking. They were all looking at her.

'It's true. Isn't it, Jack? We saw her. In her little blue coat.'

Jack shrugged. 'It could have been anything,' he said.

'No. No.' Mabel was angry. 'It was a little girl. You saw her, too.'

She stood and took the dishes to the counter, glad to be free of the table. Jack avoided her eyes as he went to the woodstove and added another log while she busied herself with dessert.

Darkness settled around the cabin and Mabel glanced out of the window occasionally with the thought that she might see the child, but there was only her own reflection in the lamplight.

JACK STARTED WITH A BISCUIT, one of Mabel's sourdough biscuits.

He had risen early to haul the meat home, and after he'd hung it from a beam in the barn and put away the horse, he went in for lunch. When Mabel wasn't watching, he slipped a biscuit in his pocket and told her he was going out to the barn. Instead he went to the edge of the woods. He dusted the snow from a stump and set the biscuit down.

It seemed wrong to bait a child this way. As a boy he had enticed deer and raccoons with morsels of food, and his patience had often paid off. But the child was not a raccoon to bait and trap. He worried about her. He'd felt foolish to admit it in front of the Bensons, but the little girl had come again and again to their homestead. Maybe she was in need but too frightened to knock on their door. Perhaps she needed shelter, clothing, food. The thought preoccupied him, and so he reached out to her the only way he knew.

The next morning, he saw where tracks approached the stump, wove this way and that, the girl must have hidden behind a spruce tree, a bush. The biscuit remained on the stump.

When the sourdough biscuit, bits of peppermint candy from town, even a piece of one of Mabel's pies that Jack had pilfered, had all failed, he was at a loss for what to try next. He wondered if she was cold and in need of more clothes. His brief glimpses of her made him doubt this. She seemed at home in the snow in her furs and wool.

Then, on a trip to town, he saw a miniature porcelain doll on a shelf in the general store. The doll had long, blonde hair, not unlike the girl's, and it wore the brightly coloured dress of a European villager, perhaps Swedish or Dutch. He bought it on credit, and hid it in his coat pocket. When he got home, he took it with him when he went to feed and water the animals.

He brought the lantern from the barn and walked to the stump where the other offerings had gone untouched. He took the doll from his pocket, raised his voice to the cold night and called out as gently as he could manage.

'This is for you. I don't know if you can hear me, but we want you to have this. Just something I picked up in town. Well, then, good night.'

He turned his back, leaving the doll propped up in the snow on the stump.

When he returned to the cabin, Mabel had warmed water on the stove for him to wash. Steam rose as she poured the water into a basin. Jack took off his shirt, put a towel over his shoulders and splashed water onto his face. Behind him he could hear Mabel bustling in the kitchen.

'Oh,' she said quietly.

Jack brought his head up from the basin. 'What is it?'

'The window. Do you see?'

As they watched, thick frost unfurled in swirls across the glass, slowly spreading from the centre towards the corners. Lacy white vines grew in twists and loops, and icy flowers blossomed. Within seconds the window that had been clear glass was covered in patterns like fine etching.

'Maybe it's from the steam,' Mabel said in a near whisper. She pressed the palm of her hand against the glass, and her warm skin melted the ice. She rubbed a small circle in the centre of the window, and looked through.

'Oh. Oh,' she gasped and leaned closer.

'What, Mabel? What is it?'

'It's her.' She turned, her hand at her throat. 'Her little face, right there in our window. She had fur all around her head, like a wild animal. She's there now. Go look.'

Mabel was handing him his boots and coat and opening the door.

When he stepped outside, his wet beard and hair stiffened with ice. He walked round the side of the cabin, but saw only what he expected—snow and trees and night. The child was gone.

The next morning Jack nearly stepped on the basket outside their door.

'Jack? What's that you—'

'I'm not sure.' He set it on the table, and he and Mabel stood over it. It was made of birch bark, its seams crudely sewn with some kind of dried plant root. The basket fitted perfectly in two cupped hands and it was heaped with purple berries. Jack took one, rolled it between his finger and thumb, sniffed it, then put it to his tongue. 'It's a blueberry. Tastes like a blueberry.'

He put one to her mouth and she hesitantly tasted it.

'You're right. They're wild blueberries. Frozen like little marbles,' she said. 'Did she bring these for us?'

'I guess she knew we were having pancakes for breakfast,' Jack said. Mabel did not smile.

'I'll get some wood for the fire,' he said.

Jack followed his old tracks past the woodpile to the stump at the edge of the forest. The doll was gone. The child's small footprints came towards the stump, went once round, and then straight back into the trees. Each track barely dented the snow, as if she weighed no more than a feather.

When he brought an armload of wood inside, Mabel was cooking pancakes. She dotted a few of the wild blueberries in each one, and they ate them at the table. They did not talk about the child, not until the table was cleared and Jack was preparing to go back outdoors.

'I'm going to haul some wood from the east field.'

'How can you?' Mabel's voice was hushed and trembling. 'How can you eat your breakfast and go into the day as if none of this has happened? She's a child, Jack. You might not be able to admit it to the neighbours, but you've seen her out there, wandering around in the middle of winter.'

He sighed. He finished lacing up his boots, and then went to Mabel and put his hands on her shoulders. 'I think she's all right. I think she's warm. And she must know how to get food. Look at the berries, and that little basket. She knows her way out there, probably better than either of us.'

'But she's just a child. A little girl.'

He thought Mabel would cry, and he wanted to be anywhere else. It was wrong and cowardly, and he'd done it before—when Mabel lost the baby and shook with grief, when the relatives whispered harsh words, when the Bensons asked about the child in the woods. But it was like the need to take a breath. The urge was too strong, and without saying another word, Jack left the cabin.

SNOWFLAKES AND NAKED BABIES tumbled through her nights. She dreamed she was in the midst of a snowstorm. She held out her hands and snowflakes landed on her open palms. As they touched her skin, they melted into tiny, naked newborns, each wet baby no bigger than a fingernail. Then wind swept them away, once again just snowflakes.

In the light of day, her dreams were drained of their nightmarish quality, and they seemed whimsical and strange, but the taste of loss remained in her mouth. It was difficult to focus on her tasks and a faint memory emerged again and again—her father, a leather-bound fairy-tale book, a snow child alive in its pages. She couldn't clearly recall the story or more than a few of the illustrations, and she began to worry over it, letting her thoughts touch it again and again. An old man and woman conjuring a little girl out of the snow and wilderness.

A few days after the basket had appeared on their doorstep, Mabel decided to write to her sister, Ada, who still lived in the family home in Philadelphia. Perhaps the book was in the attic along with keepsakes that had accumulated there over the years. She sat down at the table, and was comforted by the act of writing.

Dearest sister, I hope this letter finds you well. We are settling into winter here at the homestead, she began.

She went on to describe the snow and mountains and their new friends the Bensons. She asked about her sister's children, now grown, and the family home. Then, as casually as she could, she enquired about the book.

Do you remember it, dear Ada? It was one of my favourites for some years of my childhood. I believe it was bound in blue leather, but I remember little of the story—not even the title. I am sure it is an impossible task I am asking of you, but it's like having a person's name on the tip of your tongue. I only hope by some chance you know the book I am thinking of, and better yet know where to find it in that jumble in the attic.

Mabel also asked if her sister could send some new pencils, as she intended to pick up her former pastime and had only a few stubs in her drawing box.

She sealed the letter, set it aside and went to the stove. She pulled a loaf of bread from the oven, thumped it softly to see if it was done, then slid it back into the heat. She glanced towards the window and saw Jack at the woodpile. And then she saw the little girl.

She stood in the trees just beyond. Jack hadn't noticed her. He had taken off his coat and was splitting log after log, swinging the heavy maul above his head and bringing it down with a loud crack into the wood. The girl watched and then crept closer, hiding behind a birch tree and peeking round it. She wore the same coat of blue wool trimmed in white fur.

Mabel paced at the window. Should she go to the door and call out to Jack? She was so near she hated to frighten her away. Then she saw Jack raise his head and look at the girl. The child was less than a dozen yards from him. Mabel held her breath. She could see Jack speaking, but couldn't hear his words. Jack stepped closer, a hand extended towards her. The girl stepped back, and then Jack was speaking again. It was difficult to see from the window, but Mabel thought she saw the girl raise a hand in a red mitten, and give a small wave, then turn and run into the trees. Jack stood with his arms at his sides, not moving. Mabel hurried to the door and pulled it open.

'Go, Jack! Go! Go after her!' He startled, then looked from Mabel to the woods and back again. At last he charged after the girl, first at a steady walk, then picking up his pace and trotting through the snow. His legs looked long and awkward as his big boots thumped beneath him.

Mabel waited at the window. Minutes went by, then an hour and another. She considered going after them, but she knew that was not wise. Night came quickly on these short winter days.

As the cabin darkened, Mabel lit the oil lamps, put more wood on the fire, and tried to stop her rhythmic pacing. She finally made herself sit by the woodstove with her sewing and tried to lose herself in the stitches. She didn't know she had fallen asleep in the chair until Jack came in. His beard and moustache were caked with ice and his trouser legs were stiff and snow-covered. He didn't bother to take off his boots but stumbled to the woodstove and held out his bare hands. He hadn't been wearing gloves when she'd sent him after the girl. 'Are you frostbitten?'

'I don't know. Cold, that's for sure.' His words slurred together, either from the ice in his moustache or from fatigue. Mabel rubbed his hands to move warm blood to the tips of the fingers.

'Did you catch up with her? What did you see?'

He pulled some of the ice from his moustache and beard. He took off his boots and then his coat and trousers and without looking at her, he stumbled to their bedroom. 'Nothing. I'm tired, Mabel. Too tired to talk.'

He climbed beneath the covers and was soon snoring softly, leaving Mabel alone again by the woodstove.

JACK HAD ALWAYS considered himself if not brave then at least competent and sure. He was wary of true danger, of flighty horses that could break your back and farm tools that could sever limbs, but he had always scoffed at the superstitious and mystical. Alone in the depths of the wilderness, however, in the fading winter light, disturbing thoughts had whirled around his brain, stories about forest hags and men who turned into bears, and he had discovered in himself an animal-like fear. It wasn't the girl that frightened him as much as the strange world of snow and rock and hushed trees that she navigated with ease.

The girl had deftly jumped logs and scampered through the woods like a fairy. He had got close enough to notice the brown fur of her marten hat and the knee-high leather moccasins that bound her feet. By the woodpile, when he had spoken to her, he had even caught sight of her blonde eyelashes and the intensely blue eyes and, when he asked if she liked the doll, he saw her smile. The shy, sweet smile of a little girl.

But then she had become a phantom, a silent blur. As Jack tried to follow her, an icy fog moved through the forest. Minute crystals of ice filled the air and gathered as hoar frost along the tree branches and on his lashes. He could see only a few feet into the mist. He stopped occasionally, bent with his hands on his knees, trying to silence his heavy breathing. He never heard the girl but he would see her, just ahead, as if she wanted to be seen.

He lost track of how far he had come or how long he had been gone, yet he kept on, past their 160-acre homestead, up into the foothills of the mountains. He followed a ridge that looked down over the snowy river valley and followed her still higher until he crested a rise and found himself in a narrow mountain gorge with steep shale cliffs.

He followed her tracks up the ravine, and then they disappeared. It didn't make sense—her trail didn't continue up the hill or along the creek; it ran into the side of the mountain.

Then he noticed what looked like a small door set into the hillside beneath a dome of snow. Jack crouched behind a boulder, a cold sweat on the back of his neck. He could go to that little door and call out to the girl, but he didn't. What did he expect to find? A fairy-tale beast that holds young girls captive in a mountain cave? A cackling witch? Or nothing at all, no child, no tracks, only insanity bared in the untouched snow. That is perhaps what he feared most.

Rather than face that possibility, Jack turned and set out for home. He expected Mabel would be waiting for him and wanting answers. But he was tired, aching and surely frostbitten, and he had nothing to offer her but an old man who quaked in his boots at a child's door.

Chapter 5

The next morning Jack woke to the sound of Mabel knocking about the cabin. Dishes clattered, a broom swished, bumps and thumps—the unmistakable sounds of irritation. Jack eased himself out of bed.

They each went about their chores, but Mabel's anger seemed only to grow, and her footsteps fell heavier and her sighs more audible. Jack escaped to the barn and the woodpile and left Mabel with her sighs.

For the next few days, he watched the trees and searched the snow for tracks while he worked. If the girl comes back, he told himself, I won't run after her. I won't frighten her away.

So when the girl appeared at Jack's elbow nearly a week later, he did not give chase but instead went about his work as if she wasn't there. He stacked split wood beside the barn, one piece after another. When dusk fell, Jack went into the barn to put away the maul and axe. The girl followed, and stopped at the door. When he came back out, she was there, watching him with her wide blue eyes. He walked past without acknowledging her. Over his shoulder he called, 'Time for supper. Let's go in.'

And the girl followed. Jack held the cabin door open for her. She entered gingerly, as if the floor might fall out from under her, but all the same she came in. As she stepped across the threshold and into the warmth, the thin layer of frost on her coat and hat melted and the frost on her eyelashes turned to droplets. The child's eyes were left wet, as if she had been crying.

Mabel was working at the kitchen counter, her back to them. Jack closed the door.

'I think we might need some more wood on the fire—' she said, turning with a pot of boiled potatoes in her hands. She saw the little girl beside Jack and her mouth formed a circle as if she might make a sound, but instead she dropped the pot of potatoes.

'Oh, oh.' Mabel stared at her feet, soaking wet and covered in bits of potato. 'Oh dear.' The girl had stepped back, startled at the clamour of the pot hitting the floor, but now she let out a little giggle.

Mabel quickly scooped the potatoes back into the pot and used a towel to soak up the water. All the while her eyes never left the child.

'I'll take your coat for you,' Jack said.

The girl took off her mittens, and as he reached to take them, she drew something out of her coat pocket. It was a small animal, white fur and black nose, and Jack was prepared for it to writhe and jump. But it was a lifeless pelt, less than a foot long snout to tail.

'An ermine?'

The child nodded and held it out to him.

'She wants us to have it,' Mabel whispered.

'Is that it? Is it for us? Are you sure?'

A vigorous nod.

Jack hung the ermine from a hook by the kitchen window and smoothed the back of his hand down the white fur. Mabel bent down towards the child. 'Thank you,' she said.

'Here you are.' Jack pulled a chair out from the table. 'You can sit here.'

As Mabel put a plate of moose steaks in the middle of the table, the girl glanced at Jack, widened her eyes questioningly and raised her eyebrows. He shrugged almost imperceptibly.

Mabel set an empty plate in front of the child and fought the urge to grab her hand, to touch her and see if she was real. Never had she imagined the little girl would be sitting before them, at their own kitchen table.

She was even smaller than she had appeared at a distance, and the chair back towered around her. With her coat on, the child had looked almost roly-poly as she sprinted through the trees, but now Mabel saw her thin arms and small shoulders. She wore a cotton dress with tiny flowers on it, but Mabel could see that it was a summer dress for a grown woman. The girl's hair was white-blonde, but woven and twisted among the strands were grey-green lichens, wild yellow grasses and curled bits of birch bark. It was strange and lovely, like a wild bird's nest.

The girl watched as Mabel served moose steaks and boiled carrots onto each plate. Then she leaned forward, as if to inspect the meat.

As soon as Jack and Mabel began to eat, the girl did as well. She picked up the meat with her hands, smelled it and bit into it. When she saw Jack and Mabel watching, she put it down. Jack used his knife and fork to slice pieces off his own steak and eat them.

'It's all right, dear,' Mabel said. 'You eat it any way you want.'

The girl hesitated, then picked it up in her hands again. She didn't devour it the way Mabel expected, but instead ate it daintily, little nibbles here and there, but eating every bit, even a line of gristle that ran through it. Then the child picked up each slice of boiled carrot and carefully ate it. Her plate was clean even as Jack and Mabel continued to cut their meat.

'Would you like some more? No? Are you sure? There's plenty here.'

Mabel was alarmed to notice how flushed the child's cheeks had become. Her eyes had gone glassy as if from fever. Along the bridge of her nose, tiny beads of sweat formed.

'Open the door,' Mabel whispered to Jack. 'Prop it open.'

'What? It's well below zero.'

'Please,' she begged. 'It's too hot in here for her. Go—open the door!'

So he did, and he wedged it open with a piece of firewood.

'There, child. That will cool you. Are you well?'

The girl's eyes were wide, but she nodded.

'Do you have a name?' Mabel asked. Jack frowned. Perhaps she pushed too quickly, but she couldn't help herself. 'I'm Mabel. This is Jack. Do you live nearby? Do you have a mother and father?'

The girl seemed to understand but gave no expression.

'What's your name?' Mabel asked again.

At this the child stood. Her coat was on before she reached the doorway.

'Oh, don't leave. Please,' Mabel said. 'I'm sorry if I asked too many questions. Please stay.'

But the girl was already out the door. She did not seem angry or frightened. As her feet hit the snow, she turned back to Mabel and Jack.

Thank you, she said, her voice a quiet bell in Mabel's ear. And then she slipped into the night with her long blonde hair trailing down her back.

THE GIRL APPEARED and disappeared without warning, and it unnerved Jack. There was something otherworldly in her frosty lashes and cool blue stare, the way she materialised out of the forest. In some ways she was clearly just a little girl, with her small frame and rare, stifled giggles, but in others she seemed composed and wise, as if she moved through the world with knowledge beyond anything Jack had encountered.

Jack was certain her visits were driven by more than just curiosity or hunger. It was something akin to sorrow or weariness.

Only a few times did she venture into their cabin, and always she refused to stay the night. But she brought them her little gifts: the ermine pelt, the basket of berries, an arctic grayling cleaned and ready for the pan. Jack came to see that the snowshoe hare—strangled and left on their doorstep—too, had been a gift. He regretted throwing it into the woods.

Then the day came when she appeared without gifts but instead with questions in her eyes. She arrived early, just after he had finished breakfast, and she followed him around the barn and yard like a shadow. As he closed the barn door, he felt her small cool hands clasping at his wrist. She tugged at his arm so that he bent to her.

Will you promise? Her voice small and frightened.

And before he knew the implications of such a promise, he was following her through the snow. The child ran as if pursued, but when Jack fell behind, she slowed and led him up the alpine slopes towards the mountains.

He followed as best he could. He was a huffing, slow-footed oaf next to her. Her steps were so light and sure. They continued higher, to the next ridge, and on again. The snow was deeper than before and he slogged through while the girl seemed to float across it. He sensed her impatience.

Are you well? she said. We're almost there.

Fine, he said. I'm fine. Lead the way.

The girl seemed to make an effort to go slower, to show him where he could place his feet.

Then he saw rocky cliffs ahead of them and heard the trickle of a creek beneath the ice. He followed the girl up the ravine. Soon they were among a clump of large spruce trees that seemed out of place so high up the mountain, and the large boughs and immense trunks gave a sheltered feeling to the narrow valley. She stopped and pointed towards a snow-covered heap beneath one of the trees.

What is it?

The girl didn't answer. She only pointed, so Jack walked past her to the heap. He brushed away some of the snow and uncovered a canvas tarp. He looked at the girl again, questioning, but she turned away.

When he pulled back the tarp, a dozen voles scuttled away into the snow, and he saw a man's neck where blond hair met a woodsman's wool coat. Jack's heart beat loudly in his ears. He put his hand to the broad shoulder, and it was like shoving a cottonwood log, cold and frozen to the ground. Jack stepped around the corpse. He saw now where the voles had made their small tunnels through the snow, spreading in a maze in all directions from the dead man. He dusted the snow off the face and head. He was a big man, much taller and broader in the shoulders than Jack. His milky eyes, sunk back into his skull, stared blankly ahead. His skin was a ghastly blue. Ice crystals grew on his face and clothes and along his blond hair and long, bushy beard. The rodents had begun to gnaw away his frozen nose and the tips of his fingers, and their droppings were everywhere.

Jesus. Christ almighty. Who is he? Jack asked.

My papa, she whispered.

What happened?

I tried. I tried and tried.

Jack looked into her eyes, and it was like watching water gather on lake ice. No sloppy dribble, no sobs. Only a quiet pool on the blue.

I pulled on his arm and said, Please, Papa. Please. But he wouldn't come. He only sat in the snow.

The girl's chin trembled as she spoke.

He told me Peter's water kept him warm, but I knew it wouldn't. I wanted to make him warm. I held his hands and then I held his face, just like this. The girl reached down and cupped the dead man's cheeks in her small hands with the tenderness of a daughter's touch.

I tried, but he was colder and colder and colder.

Jack went on one knee beside the corpse and caught the smell of liquor. A green glass bottle was clenched in a frozen claw of a hand. Jack's stomach turned. How could a man drink himself to death in front of his child?

Still on one knee, Jack reached out and took hold of her small shoulders.

You aren't to blame. Your papa was a grown man, and no one could have saved him but himself. This is not your fault.

He pulled the canvas back over the dead man.

When did this happen?

The day the snow first came, the child said.

He knew when. It was the night he and Mabel had built the little snow figure in the yard. Nearly three weeks ago.

Why didn't you ask for help?

I kept Fox away. I threw stones and yelled. And I wrapped Papa so the birds wouldn't peck at him. But now . . . the voles are eating him.

He stood and dusted the snow from his knee. I might have to get some help, from town, he said.

The girl's eyes flashed with anger.

You promised. You promised.

And so he had. Jack sighed. This was more than he'd bargained for.

I've got to think about this, about how we're going to take care of . . . your papa.

All right.

The girl was tired and calm, the fight drained out of her.

You will stay with us until we can sort things out.

The girl stood straight, her eyes sharp again. No. This is my home.

She stood with her head high. The mountain wind blew through the spruce trees and stirred her blonde hair.

This was her home. Jack believed it.

IN ALPINE HE ASKED AROUND, saying he'd seen axe blazes on several trees, signs of marked trails. Had anyone been trapping near his homestead over the years? Anybody living up towards the mountains?

'Yeah. Funny you ask 'cause I haven't thought of that fellow in an age,' George said. 'We called him "Swede" and he never told us different. More likely Russian, I'd guess—judging from the way he said his words.'

'What did he look like?' Jack asked.

'Big, strapping man. Built like a lumberjack. Light-coloured hair. A beard. A little off, if you ask me. Not the friendly, talkative sort. You think he's trapping around your place?'

Betty remembered the man, too. 'Oh, he was an odd duck, that one,' she told Jack as she poured him a cup of coffee. 'He panned gold in the summers, trapped in the winters. Couldn't understand him half the time, always mixing another language with his English.'

'You seen him lately?' Jack asked.

'Nope. Can't remember the last time he was in here. But then he only came into town a few times a year. Spent all his spare time drinking with the Indians upriver, from what I heard.'

'You recall him having any children? . . . Or a wife? I was just thinking Mabel might want to get to know her.'

'Can't say that I do. Seemed a pretty solitary type to me.'

A tired sadness settled over Jack as he rode back to the homestead. The horse trotted sharply and tossed its head, as if invigorated by the brisk weather. He thought of the girl on the side of the mountain with her dead, frozen papa and wondered if he was doing the right thing. She had made him promise not to tell anyone, especially Mabel, and Jack understood. The girl feared being yanked away from what was familiar.

And Jack was fairly certain she could look after herself. She knew the woods and trails. She found food, shelter. Besides, he had promised. He made few promises, but those he made, to the best of his abilities he kept.

The secret clung to Jack in the scent of black wood smoke. At night, Mabel pressed her face into his beard and touched his hair with her fingers.

'What have you been burning?'

'Just some of those stumps from last summer. Good weather to burn.'

'Yes. I suppose so.' She didn't seem altogether convinced.

THE GROUND WAS TAKING LONGER to thaw than he had predicted. He had dragged the dead man out from under the tree and cut it down. Then he cut up the wood where it lay, and built a fire from its tinder-dry branches. The girl watched the tree burn. She stood well back and the flames flickered in her eyes. When night fell, he piled the wood high then climbed down the mountain. Behind him, the fire crackled and flamed in the night.

The next day he scraped at the frozen earth beneath the smouldering wood, digging as far down as he could with a shovel. A December grave was hard earned in this place, but it would come. He left the man beneath a tarp, far from the fire. He didn't want the body to thaw.

On the third morning Jack returned to dig in the softening earth and build the flames back up. He was drenched in sweat and coated in charcoal from the half-burned logs. The girl was nowhere to be seen, but at times Jack felt something watching him from the trees and wondered if it was the girl or the red fox he had seen slip now and then between snow-covered boulders.

By midafternoon the pit seemed deep enough to bury a man. Jack scraped the last coals out of the hole and then leaned on the shovel, his cheek resting on his hand. He called for the child. It's time, he said. Time to put your papa to rest.

She appeared from behind one of the spruce trees.

There was no coffin. He didn't have the lumber to build one so the tarp would have to do. Jack dragged the body to the grave.

Have you said your goodbyes?

The girl nodded. It didn't seem right to Jack, burying a man without notifying the authorities or signing a piece of paper or at least having a man of the cloth read something from the Bible. But he didn't see a way out. The worst that could happen to this child, besides her father dying in front of her, would be for the authorities to be involved. She'd be shipped off to some orphanage far from these mountains.

Without another man to help him lower it slowly, Jack shoved the tarp-wrapped body into the hole where it fell with an ungodly thump.

Shall I cover him up then? he asked.

The girl nodded.

He began shovelling in dirt and black, dead coals, shovelful after shovelful, the girl silent behind him. He wondered if he had the strength to finish. Occasionally he stamped his feet on the dirt to settle it and the girl joined him, hopping up and down on the grave, her small face frowning, her marten-fur hat hanging down her back by strings tied at her neck.

So it's done, Jack said, scraping a few last piles of dirt over the grave.

The girl came to Jack's side. When he spoke, his voice was hoarse from the smoke. Maybe we can plant some flowers in the spring, he said.

The girl nodded and then wrapped her arms round his waist, pressed her face into his coat. Jack stood motionless for a moment, awkward with his arms at his sides, and then he slowly reached round her and patted her softly on the back, smoothed her hair with his rough hand.

There, there. All right. It's going to be all right. It's done now.

IT WAS UNEXPECTED, to look forward to each day. When Mabel woke in the mornings, happy anticipation washed over her and for a moment she would not know its cause. Was this day special for some reason? A birthday? A holiday? Then she would remember—the child might visit.

Mabel was often at the window, but it wasn't with the melancholy weariness of the previous winter. Now she watched with excitement and hope that the little girl would appear from the woods.

The child came every other evening for a week or so, but then for two or three days she wouldn't appear. One morning she came and stayed with Mabel in the kitchen instead of following Jack around the barn. She watched Mabel mix bread dough, and it was as if a songbird had landed on a bedroom windowsill. Mabel did not want to frighten her away by moving too abruptly, so she emulated Jack's quiet, accepting manner and spoke softly to her.

That evening, the girl stayed for dinner. Jack came in from the barn, and Mabel and the child joined him at the table. Jack seemed in an uncommonly good mood, making jokes and talking about his day's work as they passed the food around the table. At one point, he turned to ask the girl to hand him the salt. She was focused on her own plate and didn't notice. Jack cleared his throat, then tapped lightly on the table.

This is getting silly, he announced.

The child startled. He quieted his tone.

We must call you something. Will it be 'girl' for ever?

The child was silent. Jack reached over her for the salt, apparently giving up on getting a name from her. Mabel waited, but Jack went back to eating.

Faina, the girl whispered.

What's that, child? Mabel asked.

My name. It's Faina.

Will you say it again, more slowly?

Fah-EE-nah. Each syllable a quiet whisper.

What does it mean? Mabel asked.

The girl bit her lower lip and frowned.

You must see it, to know. Then her face brightened. But I'll show you. Some day I'll show you what it means.

Faina. It is a lovely name.

That night, after the child left, they said her name again and again. It began to roll easily off their tongues, and Mabel liked the way it felt in her mouth, the way it whispered in her ear—Isn't Faina a beautiful child? What will Faina bring next time she visits? They were like children pretending to be mother and father, and Mabel was happy.

Dawn broke silver over the snowdrifts and spruce trees. Mabel was at the kitchen table trying to sketch the birch basket the girl had brought them. She had it propped against her wooden recipe box and she tried to remember how it had looked full of wild berries. It had been too long since she had drawn, and the pencil was awkward in her hands, the shading and angles all wrong. Frustrated, she put a hand to the back of her neck and stretched.

At the sight of the girl peeking in the window, Mabel startled, but then smiled and raised her hand in greeting. When the child waved back, affection surged through her.

Faina, child. Come in, come in.

The child brought the smell of snow in with her, and the air in the cabin cooled and brightened. Mabel unwrapped the scarf from her neck, took her mittens, fur hat and the wool coat.

What were you doing?

The child stood at the table with one of the pencils in her hand.

I was drawing, Mabel said. Would you like to see?

She set the child's outdoor clothing on a chair and left the door cracked open, so a draught could move through the cabin and cool the girl. Then she pulled a chair out for her and sat beside her.

This is my sketchpad. And these are my pencils. I wanted to draw a picture of the basket you gave us. See? Mabel held up the drawing.

The child skimmed her fingers across the paper surface and rounded her lips in wonder. I think it's nice. What else can you draw? she asked.

Mabel shrugged. Anything I set my mind to, I suppose. Although it won't necessarily look the way it ought.

Could you draw a picture of me?

Oh, yes. But I must warn you, I've never been very good at portraits.

Mabel put the child's chair near the window so the winter light shone on the side of her face and lit up her blonde hair. For the next hour, Mabel glanced from sketch paper to child and back again, and waited for the girl to protest, but she never complained or moved. She was stoic, her chin slightly raised, her gaze steady.

With each stroke of the pencil, it was as if Mabel held the child in her arms, caressed her cheek, stroked her hair. She drew the gentle curve of the child's cheekbones, the peaks of her small lips, the inquisitive arch of her eyebrows. Self-contained and wary, innocent and knowing . . . something in the turn of her head hinted at a wildness Mabel wanted to capture, too.

Would you like to see? She turned the sketchpad towards the child, not knowing what reaction to expect.

The child took in a breath, then clasped her hands in delight.

Do you like it?

Oh, yes! Is that me? Is that what I look like?

Have you never seen yourself, child?

The girl shook her head.

Never? Not in a mirror? Well, I have just the thing.

Mabel went to the bedroom and came back with a hand mirror.

Do you know what this is? It's a glass, and you can see yourself in it.

The girl peered into the mirror, her eyes wide and her face sombre. She reached out and touched the shining surface with one fingertip, then touched her own hair, her face. She smiled, turned her head from side to side, brushed her hair away from her brow, all the while watching in the mirror.

Would you like to have the picture I drew of you?

Faina smiled and nodded.

Mabel folded the portrait until it was a square small enough to fit in the child's pocket.

WHEN THE LITTLE GIRL was gone and dinner was finished, Mabel knitted by the woodstove. Outside, the wind tore down the river valley and she thought she could hear another sound, too. A mournful baying.

'Is that the wind, Jack?'

He stood at the window, looking out into the blackness.

'Nope. I think it's those wolves upriver. I heard howling the other night, too.' He put more birch logs to the fire, the flames catching on the papery bark and flickering light against the cabin walls.

'Is she safe?' Mabel asked. She continued to knit though her eyes burned and her hands were tired.

'I expect she's all right.' Jack went outside several times to get more wood, despite the stack of logs just inside the door. Finally they could stay awake no longer and crawled into their bed together. They fell asleep to the sound of the wind blowing down the valley.

Chapter 6

It was mid-February when a parcel addressed to Mabel arrived, wrapped in brown paper and delivered via train to Alpine. Jack brought it from town, along with a few supplies bought with the last of their credit.

Mabel waited until he went back outside before she sat at the table to open it. Could this be it at long last? It seemed ages ago that she had written to her sister to ask about the book, and she had assumed her sister hadn't been able to find it.

She was tempted to tear open the package but felt the need to be calm and collected. She sat at the table and unknotted the packing twine and carefully unfolded the paper. Inside were two separately wrapped packages. The smaller one contained several drawing pencils as well as sticks of charcoal. She turned to the larger package and unfolded the brown paper slowly.

The book was just as she had remembered it—oversized and perfectly square, a shape unlike any children's book she had ever seen. It was bound in blue morocco leather. An exquisite snowflake design was embossed in silver on the front cover. She placed the book flat on the table in front of her and opened it. 'Snegurochka, 1857' was written lightly in pencil in the upper corner of the blue marbled endpaper. 'The Snow Maiden.' It was her father's neat writing. He had collected many books on his travels, and some he had brought back especially for her.

Mabel turned the first page. On the left was a full-colour plate overlaid with a sheet of translucent paper, on the other the story, written in blocky, illegible letters. It was in Russian! How could she have forgotten? Although this had been one of her favourite childhood books, she had never actually read it. Her father had told her the story as she'd looked at the illustrations. Now she wondered whether her father had known the words or had invented the story based on the pictures.

It had been many years since her father had died, but now she recalled his voice, melodic and rumbling. 'There once was an old man and woman who loved each other very much and were content with their lot in life except for one great sadness—they had no children of their own.'

Mabel shifted her eyes back to the illustration. It showed two old people, a man and a woman, kneeling in the snow at the feet of a young girl who seemed to be made of snow from the ground to her waist, but to be a real child from her waist up.

The snow child's cheeks glowed with life and jewels crowned her blonde hair. She smiled sweetly down at the old couple, her mittened hands held out to them. Behind her the snowscape was framed by a stand of black-green spruce trees and, in the distance, snowy, sharp-peaked mountains. Between two of the trees stood a red fox with narrow, golden eyes.

She turned the page. The next illustration had always been her favourite.

In a snowy clearing, the girl stood surrounded by the wild beasts of the forest—bears, wolves, hares, ermines, a stag, a red fox, even a tiny mouse. The animals sat on their haunches beside the girl, their demeanour neither menacing nor adoring. It was as if they had posed for a portrait. Did they love the little girl, or did they want to eat her? All these years later, Mabel still could find no answers in the wild, gleaming eyes.

She closed the book and traced the embossed snowflake with her fingertips. She began to gather the brown wrapping and it was then that she saw her sister's letter, tucked into the folds of paper and nearly discarded.

Dearest Mabel,

What a joy to read your letter and know you are alive and well. It must sound terribly outlandish to you, but to all of us here it is as if you have been banished to the North Pole. It was a relief to know you are warm and safe and even have welcoming neighbours.

As to your request for this book, it is a pure stroke of luck that I was able to send it to you. A student from the university, a Mr Arthur Ransome, has been sorting through Father's collections and was particularly enamoured with this book. He cautioned me that it was a rare find and should be treated with great care. He was appalled to learn that I would be mailing it to you in the farthest outreaches of civilisation.

I asked him to tell me something of 'Snegurochka', the Snow Maiden, and he told me that like many fairy tales, there are many different ways it is told, but it always begins the same. An old man and an old woman live happily in their small cottage in the forest, but for one sorrow: they have no children of their own. One winter's day, they build a girl of snow.

In the most traditional tale, the snow child comes and goes with winter. One day she loses her way in the woods and encounters a bear, which offers to help her find her way. She looks at the bear's long claws and sharp teeth and refuses his assistance. Then along comes a wolf, which also promises to lead her to safety, but he is also ferocious looking and she again refuses.

But then she meets a fox. 'I will take you home,' he vows. The child decides the fox looks friendlier than the others and she takes hold of his fur scruff and he leads her back to the old couple's cottage. When they arrive the fox asks for a fat hen in payment for her safe return. The old people are poor and so decide to trick the fox by giving him a sack with their hunting dog inside. When the fox opens the sack the dog lunges out, chases the fox and kills it.

The snow child is angry and sad, saying that since the old couple do not love her even as much as one of their hens, she will return to live with Father Winter and Mother Spring. When the old woman next looks outside, all that remain are the child's red boots, red mittens and a puddle of water.

What a tragic tale! I think if I ever tell it to my grandchildren, I will change the ending and have everyone live happily ever after. We are allowed to do that, are we not, Mabel? To invent our own endings and choose joy over sorrow?

CARRYING THE BIRCH BASKET Faina had given them, Mabel waded through the deep snow near the cabin. The late February weather had warmed to just below freezing. The sky was blue, the air was calm and it was surprisingly pleasant to be outside. The cranberries were tiny red rubies scattered among the bare, spindly branches, but Mabel was beginning to fill the basket. She planned to make a savoury relish with the berries, Esther's onions and spices. Maybe it would make the moose meat taste like something other than the same meal they'd eaten every day for weeks on end. She was smiling to herself, thinking of how necessity truly is the mother of invention, when she looked up to see the child and the fox.

Faina never ceased to startle Mabel. It wasn't just the way the girl appeared without warning, but also her manner. She stood with her arms at her sides in her wool coat, mittens, scarf, fur trim and flaxen hair. Her brown fur hat was dusted in snow, as were her eyelashes. Her expression was calmly attentive, as if she had been waiting, for minutes, perhaps years, knowing it was only a matter of time before Mabel came to this place in the woods.

Just as startling was the fox. It sat beside Faina with its silken red tail curled round its feet and its ears pricked forward.

Is he your friend? Mabel asked the child.

Faina shrugged her small shoulders. We hunt together, she said.

Who does the killing? Mabel asked.

Both of us.

Do you ever pet him?

The girl shook her head.

Once I did, she said. When he was a kid, he took pieces of meat from my fingers, and he never bit me. At night he sometimes slept beside me. But he is too wild now. We run and hunt together, but that is all.

As if to show the truth of what she had said, Faina reached her mittened hand down towards the fox. It swiftly ducked and darted around the child's legs and into the trees. The girl watched, and Mabel thought she saw a look of wonder and longing on her face.

Have you picked many berries? Faina turned back to her.

A few, Mabel said. Not as many as I should have. But it's a lovely day. I don't mind that it has taken me most of the morning.

The girl nodded, then pointed past a stand of spruce.

There are more just over there, she said.

Thank you. Won't you come with me?

But the girl was already running away, towards the cabin. Mabel was alone again in the forest. Sunlight sparkled on the snow and she could hear the wind blowing down from the glacier, but here it was quiet, so quiet Mabel was left to wonder if she had always been alone. She walked through the snow and into the spruce trees.

IT TOOK SOME TIME to identify what she was hearing. Her basket was full to overflowing with the cranberries Faina had pointed her towards and she held the basket carefully as she didn't want to spill a single berry. When she neared the cabin, she thought she heard shouts. Or maybe it was singing. As she broke through the trees, she heard it clearly—laughter.

Jack and the child stood side by side, their arms outstretched and their hands nearly touching. Then, without warning, they threw themselves backwards into the deep snow.

Come see! Come see! the child called out to Mabel.

We're snow angels, Jack called out, and the girl giggled.

Mabel walked to them, the basket in her hands, and looked down. Jack had sunk nearly a foot into the snow and he was waving his arms and legs like a drowning man. He grinned, and Mabel saw that his beard and moustache were caked with snow.

Nearby, the child lay on top of the snow, smiling, her blue eyes wide.

She saw now that they were surrounded by angels in the snow—Jack's large, deep-set figure and the child's, smaller and lighter. A dozen or more were sprinkled across the yard two at a time, and they shone in the sunlight.

Jack struggled to his feet. Then he reached down to Faina and grabbed her hands.

Watch, the child called to her.

Jack plucked Faina from the snow, both of them laughing.

What Mabel beheld in the snow took her breath away. The angel was so delicate, and its wings perfectly formed, like the print left on snow where a wild bird has taken flight.

Don't you remember doing this when you were a little girl? Jack said. You just wave your arms and legs around. Come on. Give it a try.

Mabel hesitated, held up her basket of berries.

Oh, please. Won't you? the child begged.

Jack took the basket and handed it to Faina.

I don't know. With my long skirts and all.

But he took her by the shoulders and, before she knew his intentions, gently shoved her backwards. She expected it to hurt, but the powdery snow was like a thick duvet that softened her fall and muffled all sound. She saw Jack and the child grinning down at her and above them the brilliant blue sky. Go on then, Jack called down to her. You've got to flap your arms to make the wings.

Mabel swept her arms up and felt the drag of the snow, then back down again. Then she moved her legs from side to side.

All right? she asked.

Jack reached down and pulled her to her feet.

Oh, look! Look! the child cried out. Isn't it perfect?

Mabel looked down at her own snow angel. Like Jack's, it was set deep into the snow and the wings weren't feathery. But it was lovely.

Yours is the most beautiful of all, Faina said. She threw her arms round Mabel's waist and hugged her tightly, and Mabel felt as if she were falling again, tumbling, laughing, backwards into the powdery snow.

The snow angels remained in the yard, even as the little girl came and went from the forest, and Mabel smiled at them. It wasn't just their whimsical presence, dancing from barn to cabin. It was also the memory of Jack flinging himself back into the snow like a boy, and giggling Faina at his side. And the child's arms round her, hugging her as a daughter hugs her mother. Joyfully. Spontaneously. The most beautiful of all.

When Esther sees them, she will know it's true; the child is real. How could she and Jack make a dozen little angels the shape and size of a little girl?

Though the child had at first been a source of gentle teasing, as winter progressed Esther had become kind and cautious in her doubt. She asked if Mabel was getting enough fresh air, if she was sleeping too much during the day. She encouraged her to come visit, and when Mabel said she wasn't comfortable driving the horse alone, Esther had begun to show up regularly, often on a Sunday afternoon.

THE NEXT DAYS were bright and calm. Mabel guarded the snow angels, and they didn't fade. They glittered and shone beneath the blue sky as the days lengthened. It wasn't until Sunday morning that the wind began to blow down from the glacier and gust along the riverbed. Please, Mabel thought. Come quickly, Esther. Come see, and you'll know she is real.

Mabel did not hear the horse trot into the yard that afternoon—the wind was blowing too violently. She didn't know Esther had arrived until the door burst open and she came tripping into the cabin.

'Look what the wind blew in!' Esther said. She laughed boisterously and slammed the door closed.

'Oh, Esther! You came. And in this weather! I'm so glad. Wait! Don't take off your coat. I want to show you something.' She wrapped a scarf round her face and pulled on a hat.

True to her adventurous nature, Esther didn't ask why, only turned on her heels and followed Mabel back out into the blustery afternoon. Although the sun was still shining and the sky was clear, the wind swept the powdery snow off the ground, swirled it through the air.

'Over here,' Mabel called to Esther, as she headed towards the barn. Maybe on the lee side the snow angels would be protected.

When they arrived, however, only the faintest suggestion remained, just a few shapeless dents in the drifting snow.

'Do you see?' Mabel pointed to where the snow angels had been.

Esther shook her head, then raised her eyebrows and held up her hands questioningly. 'No, Mabel. What am I supposed to be seeing?'

'It's just . . . They were here.'

'What was here?' Esther spoke quietly, concerned.

Mabel forced a smile.

'Nothing. It was nothing.' She hooked her arm into Esther's. 'Come on. Let's get back inside, before the wind begins to blow again. I want you to try my cranberry relish.'

JACK HAD SHOVELLED a path through the snowdrifts and was splitting kindling when Garrett rode into the yard with a dead fox slung across the front of his saddle. Jack stood beside the chopping block and watched the boy ride in. Garrett swept his hand overhead in greeting, and then pointed to the dead fox.

'What did you bring in today?'

'Isn't it a beaut?' Garrett said as he jumped down from the horse, grinning. He reached up and took the fox by the scruff and lifted its limp head. 'A silver fox,' the boy said with some pride.

Jack walked to the horse. The fox's ears and muzzle were as pure as black silk, but along its back and sides, the fur was a frosted silver.

'It's splendid all right,' Jack said. 'You catch any reds?'

'About a month ago, pulled a cross fox out of a snare. You ever see one of those crosses? They're a mix of red and black, and they've got a black cross along their back.'

Jack shook his head. 'What'll you do with this one?'

'I was thinking of a ruff for mom's parka. Don't mention it though. I'd like it to be a surprise.'

Jack was ready to go back to chopping kindling, but the boy wanted to talk, so he let him. While he set another spruce log on the block, the boy stacked kindling and told him about the tracks he'd seen that day—a pile of rabbits, a porcupine, a few lynx and a lone wolf heading upriver.

'You like that life, do you?' Jack said and picked up another log. 'Trapping wild animals.'

The boy shrugged. 'Beats dirt farming,' he said. His look was quick. 'No offence.'

'Ah well. I'm none too keen on it myself sometimes. But it's a living. Trapping, though—that's got to be tough work. Kind of lonely, too.'

'I like it. Travelling the river. Just me, the wind and the snow. When I get older, I'm going to build myself a cabin up the river. Buy myself a team of dogs and push my line all the way up to the glacier.'

'You won't stay on and farm?'

'Nah. My brothers—they can have it.'

Jack felt for the boy. It wasn't easy to make your own way with brothers already busting ahead of you.

'Guess I'd better be going before it gets too late,' Garrett said. 'Do you think your wife might like to see the fox before I go?'

'Maybe another time,' he said.

Garrett nodded, pulled himself up into the saddle and rode towards home.

'What did Garrett bring to show you today?' Mabel asked when Jack went in for the night. She was setting dinner on the table.

'A fox.'

She stopped what she was doing.

'I know what you're thinking, but it wasn't Faina's. This was a silver fox. Nothing like that red one she runs with.'

A bit of quiet, and then, 'But he could catch Faina's, couldn't he? He could kill her fox? Can't we tell him to stop?'

'Stop trapping? Don't see we have that kind of authority. And Garrett's not the only one out there. Up and down this river, men are trapping.'

IT WAS A TANGLED, sickening kind of vigil. Mabel watched for the boy, but it was the fox and the little girl that occupied her thoughts. Any sound that could be horse hooves in the snow brought Mabel to the window. Sometimes she even walked to the river to look up and down the ice.

If Garrett were to ride onto their homestead with a red fox dead in his arms, Faina would be lost to them. That was how the story was, there in Ada's lovely handwriting—the fox is killed, the one that brought the child safely out of the wilderness and to their cabin door. Love doubted. Boots and mittens abandoned. Snow melted in clumps. Another child gone.

At last, when March came and Jack said the boy would soon pull his traps, Mabel began to breathe more freely. The first signs of spring arrived, snow melted and then rain and snow again. The drifts in the yard dwindled to small patches, but in the woods the snow was still deep.

Mabel was dozing by the woodstove just before noon one day, a book propped open in her lap. She woke to a small, cool hand atop hers and opened her eyes to Faina.

I have something, the girl said and pulled at Mabel's hand.

Oh, child, you surprised me.

Please hurry, she said, tugging at her, pointing out the window.

Outside? All right. All right. Let me get my boots and coat.

Your pencils, too?

Is it something to draw? Yes, yes. And my sketchbook.

When Mabel opened the door, the falling snow amazed her. The first week of April, and it was snowing.

Faina took Mabel's hand again and together they walked into the yard. Even with the snow, it smelled of spring, of thawing creek banks and moist earth, of old leaves and new leaves and roots and bark.

Will you draw? Faina said quietly.

The snow? I wouldn't know how to go about it.

Faina let go of Mabel and put her palm to the sky, her mitten hanging from a red string at her wrist. A single snowflake lit upon her bare skin. Faina turned and held it to Mabel.

Now can you draw it?

The snowflake was no bigger than the smallest skirt button. It sat in the child's palm like a tiny feather when it should have melted.

There in the child's hand. A single snowflake, luminous and translucent. A sharp-edged miracle.

Please, will you draw it?

What else was there to do? Mabel fumbled to open her sketchbook. She took the pencil into her weak fingers and began to draw. Faina stood motionless with the snowflake in her hand.

I have never been any good at symmetrical drawings, she said more to herself than to the child. I'm too impatient. Too imprecise. She began drawing with broad strokes and filling the entire page with the single geometric shape. Snow began to land as wet spots on her paper. Mabel worked faster and let out frustrated sighs. If only she were a better artist.

It's perfect, Faina whispered. I knew it would be.

Mabel looked from her drawing to the snowflake in the child's hand. I can always work on the details later. Shall we call it finished for now?

The child put the heel of her hand to her lips and blew on the snowflake and it fluttered into the air like dandelion down.

Oh, Mabel said. Tears came to her eyes, and she didn't know why.

The snow fell heavier and wetter. Faina pulled on her sleeve. Mabel leaned down, expecting her to whisper something in her ear, but instead Faina put her cool, dry lips to Mabel's cheek and kissed her.

Goodbye, the child said.

When Faina let go of her arm and ran into the snow that was now rain,

Mabel knew. She tucked the sketchbook under her coat and stood in the rain until her hair was dripping wet and her coat was soaked through and her boots were in mud. She stood and stared through the rain and tried to see into the forest, but she knew.

Chapter 7

Winter had been a foolish waste of time. He had tinkered in the barn, sorted tools, plucked chickens, played in the snow. It was true what they said about this land—all the work was done in a few frenzied months. The only reason a man could farm here at all was because the sun lasted twenty hours a day during the height of summer, and vegetables grew enormous overnight. But here it was May, and Jack couldn't till a row without the horse nearly drowning in mud.

This season the homestead had to support itself. He was banking on the fact that several farmers had given up, even as the market seemed to open up with the railroad expansion. He would throw everything into this year. He'd plant not just potatoes but also carrots, lettuce and cabbage, and sell the vegetables to the mining camps.

He and Mabel talked little, but when they did, they argued. He mentioned that he needed to hire a crew of boys from town to help plant, but they had no money for it. 'I'm not a young man,' he said. 'My back aches and I can hardly make a fist in the morning. I need help.'

'Who says you have to do this alone? What am I?'

'You're not a farm hand, Mabel. And I won't let you become one.'

He walked out, but kept himself from slamming the door.

A damp, mouldy dreariness had settled over the homestead. Jack counted the days—nearly three weeks since the girl's last visit, the longest absence since she'd come into their lives.

The child's name had gone unspoken. Her chair sat empty, and Mabel no longer put a plate in front of it. Jack worried as much for his wife as for the girl. Instead of watching out of the window for her, Mabel was often found gazing into a basin of dirty dishwater as if she'd lost track of the hours. The past winter had been so different. They had looked forward to their meals together; they talked, even when Faina wasn't there. Their joy had gone with the child.

He walked past the barn towards the new field. The land was naked without snow or summer greenery. At his feet, fiddlehead ferns unfurled and tiny shoots pushed up through last year's dead leaves. He followed a path that led away from the field. He climbed for some time, and when he arrived at the cliff face he followed a game trail along the base of the cliffs, ducking under alders, until he heard rushing water. The sound led him to the creek, swollen with spring run-off.

He walked up the creek until he crested a rise and saw the familiar stand of large spruce. There was the stump of the tree he had cut and burned. A heap of rocks had been arranged on the man's grave. Faina must have brought them from the creek bed.

'Faina?' His shouts were lost to the roaring water. 'Faina? It's Jack.'

He recalled the door in the mountain where he had watched the girl disappear. He scanned the hillside several times before he saw it. It was made of rough-hewn boards cut short enough so that a grown man would have to stoop to enter, and was set into a grassy knoll. When he rapped with his knuckles, the door swung inwards on leather hinges.

'Faina? Dear child, are you here?'

Inside it was not as dim as he'd anticipated. Daylight came from somewhere overhead.

'Faina?'

There was no answer. His eyes adjusted. The walls around him were made of logs that had been squared off with an axe. Above him was a wooden ceiling, with a small, square opening to the sky. Directly below this hole, a large fire pit held the cold, charred remains of a few logs.

The builder had dug into the side of the hill and framed the room inside, then replanted sod over the top. The effect was that the small cabin looked like a grassy knoll on the mountainside. The air was musty, but as he walked around the small room he caught specific scents—wood, dried meat and fish, tanned furs and wild herbs.

The door behind him swung shut with a thump. 'Faina?' He pushed it open again, but no one was there. He paced the small quarters. There was a bunk made of peeled spruce logs, with caribou hides and other tanned furs for bedding. One corner formed a makeshift kitchen of sorts, with a counter and shelves lined with jars of beans and flour. The opposite wall held wooden pegs from which hung snowshoes, axes, saws, woodworking tools and a few items of clothing, including a fur-ruffed parka that would have been too large even for Jack. It was hard to believe a young girl had ever lived here. There were no toys, no child-sized clothes of any kind. The fire had been out for days, if not weeks.

He headed towards the door, then remembered the doll. It could be here somewhere. He tossed aside the furs on the bed but found nothing. Then he noticed a wooden box underneath the bunk. He got on his knees and pulled it out. Inside were scattered a few black-and-white photographs. One showed a nicely dressed couple standing on a dock, suitcases and trunks stacked beside them, as they embarked on a journey. He didn't recognise the man at first—in the photograph he was much younger, with a dapper haircut and clean-shaven face. The woman wore a stylish dress, and in her fine-featured face and blonde hair Jack saw Faina. These must be her parents, perhaps leaving for Alaska. Another showed the man posing with snowshoes, parka and a lopsided grin. He barely resembled the grizzled corpse Jack had pushed into a hole in the ground, but it was him. How could a man abandon his daughter to the wilderness?

Jack put the photographs in the box and slid it under the bed. Standing up, his knees creaked and he felt old and afraid. The girl was gone. This place had swallowed her. It was small comfort that wherever she was, whatever had befallen her, the doll had been with her.

THE NEXT DAY, when afternoon came and went and Jack did not return from the fields, Mabel was only vaguely puzzled. He must have worked through without a break. When evening came and dinner sat cold on the table, she knew something was wrong. Panic constricted her throat, but she dressed calmly in her coat and boots and took the shotgun down from the wall.

Her hem dragged in the muck as she followed the trail to the fields. She scanned the first field she came to, but she saw no sign of Jack or the horse. Evening shadows darkened the edge of the forest and in the sky a handful of stars were scattered across the pale blue. A flock of sandhill cranes rose up from a meadow, their calls as ghostly as their grey, slow-beating wings. The mud was beginning to stiffen in the cold. Mabel followed the trail and trembled uncontrollably.

Through the trees she heard the horse whinny. The trail circled round to the new field, and there she could see the silhouette of the horse, lifting one hoof, then another, still harnessed to the overturned plough.

'Jack? Jack?' she called.

She made out only shapes in the gloomy half-light, but she walked towards the horse. There was a muffled groan.

'Mabel? Here, Mabel. Here.'

She followed the sound, her head bent towards the ground until she nearly stepped on him. He lay flat on his back, his face to the darkening sky.

'What happened?'

'The horse. Dragged me along. Hours ago.' His words came through a slurry of dirt and blood. Mabel knelt beside him and with her sleeve tried to wipe the mess away from his mouth.

'How did this happen?'

'Black bear. Over by the woods. I busted a bolt on the damned plough, was trying to fix it. The horse saw the bear first and started prancing.'

Mabel looked towards the forest.

'Gone now. Don't think it meant us harm. The horse spooked and flipped around on me, caught my leg up in it. Pulled me through the dirt, till I fell free.' Jack tried to sit up, but grimaced in pain.

'Where do you hurt?'

'Damn near everywhere.' Jack tried to laugh, but it came out as a gravelly cough. 'It's my back.'

'What can I do?'

'Unhitch the horse. No, don't be nervous. He's all run out now. Then we've got to get me on him so you can walk us home.'

'Can you stand?'

'I don't know.'

She unhitched the horse and led it to where he lay. Slipping her arms beneath his, she tried to help him off the ground but sank in the cold mud under his weight. He wrapped his arms round her shoulders and, groaning, got to his knees, squinting tears from his eyes.

'I should go for help. I'll get George.'

'No. We can do this. Here.' He held her round the shoulders again. 'Easy. Easy there. Grab his bridle.'

With one hand Mabel tried to hold the horse steady. Jack fell from her and leaned into the animal's side. He grabbed the mane and cried out as he hauled himself up, sprawling belly-down across the horse.

'Whoa! Whoa!' Mabel fought to keep the horse still. Jack eased one leg round so he straddled the bare back, his head against the animal's neck.

'Easy. Easy does it,' he whispered.

The way home was long and disorientating. Mabel carried the shotgun in one hand and led the horse with the other. Whenever the horse stumbled, Jack cried out. Several times the animal yanked the halter strap from her hands, and she feared it might throw Jack to the ground and bolt home.

'It's OK, Mabel. Just take it slow.'

She led the horse to the cabin door and helped Jack slide slowly to the ground. 'Take the horse to the barn,' he said. 'I'll get myself inside. Go.'

As she led the horse away, she looked over her shoulder to see Jack crawling on hands and knees up the doorstep.

A focused composure came over her as she heated water and helped Jack out of his clothes. She put a wool blanket on the floor in front of the woodstove so he could lie there while she washed the blood and dirt from his skin and hair. He grunted in pain occasionally, especially as she dabbed at the abrasions across his shoulder blades. What concerned her more was the deep purple that had begun to well up across his lower back.

'I should go for help.'

He shook his head. 'Just get me into bed.'

She slid a clean shirt over his head and Jack went on hands and knees into the bedroom. Mabel helped him onto the bed. Later she brought him a bowl of broth and tried to spoon it into his mouth, but he gritted his teeth in pain.

She sat up late that night with a candle on the table and a cup of cold tea in front of her. She knew the pain would worsen by tomorrow. She thought of the empty fields and the frantic pace he had been working. Even if he healed quickly, this could ruin them.

Mabel never really slept that night. Her agitated mind worked in relentless circles of planting days and calculated earnings. Occasionally she nodded in the chair, only to startle awake at the sound of Jack's cries.

Her prediction was correct—his pain doubled up on itself through the night, and by morning Jack could hardly speak.

'My feet are numb, Mabel.' His whisper was desperate.

She gave him a kiss and said she had to go out and feed the animals.

She did not want to leave Jack alone but she would go for a doctor.

The horse would be faster than the wagon, so after a wearying two-hour ride, Mabel dismounted and walked into the general store in Alpine.

Jack had always spoken well of Joseph Palmer, the owner. The old man seemed embarrassed on Mabel's behalf when she asked after a doctor.

'No doctor around here. Nearest one would be in Anchorage.'

'You must be joking? No doctor? Isn't this a town, for God's sake?'

Mabel took a slow breath, tried to find some small reservoir of strength inside herself. Mr Palmer nodded as she told him of Jack's injuries. He'd known men who'd twisted up their backs and doctors never could do much anyways.

'You've just got to let time take its course. It'll either heal, or it won't.' Mr Palmer could offer her only a brown glass bottle. 'Give him a bit every few hours. It'll ease the pain and help him sleep,' he said.

Mabel paid and thanked him. As she turned towards the door, he spoke again. 'You could consider getting him a few jars of drink. Ted Swanson, on the other side of the tracks, down by the river. He could help you. It might do Jack some good, mix a bit of that in alcohol. It sounds as if he's in need.'

Laudanum and moonshine—all this place could offer her injured husband. She mounted the horse and galloped towards their homestead, too angry to be frightened.

STICKY COTTONWOOD BUDS cracked open beneath blue skies and the mud in the fields turned to moist, rich soil, but Mabel's grief seemed beaten over and dusty and all too familiar.

She was alone. The strong husband who had cared for her was a crumpled man who sobbed in the night and begged her to leave him, to go back home and find a new life without him. The little girl she had begun to love had vanished, another child lost. Sitting upright in the chair, she slept in brief, intense bouts at odd hours. Fatigue distorted her sense of time, and often she did not know whether it was day or night, dusk or dawn.

One afternoon she went outside and blinked against the sun. She threw bread scraps to the chickadees and went to the pasture and stroked the horse's soft muzzle. She wandered into the trees and picked the boughs of highbush cranberries. She let her eyes search for the girl, but the woods were silent. She had only to get Jack well enough to travel, and then they would leave this place. There was nothing for them here.

'Hello! Hello! Anyone at the homestead?'

With the sun in her eyes, she couldn't make out the figure on horseback. The man dismounted and removed a burlap sack from his saddlebags. It was George. Relief nearly buckled Mabel's knees.

'So the old man is laid up, eh?'

He led her indoors to a chair and began taking clinking Mason jars from the sack. He lined them up on the table, each jar sparkling with clear liquid.

'Now, don't give me that look, Mabel. Never been a better excuse than a broken back. So where is he?'

Mabel pointed to the bedroom where Jack slept.

'He can't walk on his own yet,' Mabel whispered. 'And when the laudanum wears off, the pain is unbearable.'

George shook his head from side to side and clicked his tongue softly.

'Damn. He's not up to snuff, is he?'

'No, George. No, he is not. As soon as he is well enough, I'll schedule our travel,' she said. 'And I know he will want you to have any of our tools and equipment. We can't take any of it with us.'

'You're leaving the homestead? For good?'

'We were barely keeping it going as it was, George. It has been a fantastic adventure, coming here. But now it's time we went home.'

'You can't just walk away. You've done so much work with the place. How much had he got done on the fields before he got hurt?'

'He was still just preparing them but nothing's been planted.'

'Goddamned— excuse the French. It's just a helluva blow, isn't it?'

'Yes, George. It truly is.'

He was unusually quiet as he mounted his horse.

'We'll say goodbye before we go,' Mabel called to him from the cabin door. 'Tell Esther thank you, for everything. You were truly the most wonderful neighbours we could have hoped for.'

George glanced back at her, shook his head, and rode off without a word. Mabel was certain his look was reproachful.

She was emptying the basin behind the cabin later that afternoon when she heard a wagon approaching on the dirt road. She hurried indoors and began to hide the linens and underwear she had been washing.

'Don't do that on our account.' Mabel heard Esther's laugh at the door.

'Oh, Esther!' She was surprised to find herself hugging her, then pressing her face into her friend's shoulder and sobbing.

'Go on. Go on. You have yourself a cry.' Esther patted her on the back.

Mabel pulled away, smiled and wiped her face. 'Look at me. I'm a mess. What an awful way to greet a visitor.'

'I wouldn't expect anything else. Poor woman, here for days on your own caring for a banged-up man. Strong as they are, they're like children with pain.' Esther looked Mabel straight in the eye when she said this, and there was no wince of regret or embarrassment.

'Where the hell am I supposed to put this?'

Garrett stood in the doorway, glaring over a heap of parcels in his arms.

'Watch your mouth. And put it wherever you can find room.'

'What is all this, Esther?'

'Supplies.'

'But we don't . . . didn't George tell you?'

'About your plan? Oh, he told me all right. We finally get some interesting friends and you think we're going let you go without a fight?'

'But we are leaving, so we don't need any of this.' Mabel dropped her voice to a whisper. 'And Esther, we don't have the money to pay for it.'

Garrett stomped by and dropped another armload onto the table. As the boy marched by, Esther pretended to slap him on the back of the head. Despite herself, Mabel smiled.

'Don't worry about the money. Everybody heard about your predicament and threw some stuff together. Nothing fancy, but it'll keep us for a while.'

'I don't know what to say. It's too much . . . too generous.'

'Well, we might not have a doctor around here, but we do have a few kind hearts among us.' Esther began unloading boxes and sacks. 'Garrett, put those bedrolls over there, behind the woodstove.'

'Bedrolls?'

'Didn't I mention? We're moving in. The boy and me. We might be a bossy, ill-tempered pair, but you can't complain about free help. You've got us for the rest of the season, or until you get sick of us.'

'Esther—No, no. We can't allow this.'

'Can't allow it? I don't think you understand who you're up against here, dear heart. We'll be planting those fields, Garrett and me. You can either help or get out of the way, but we'll be doing it. Garrett, have Mabel take you out to the field so you can see if the plough needs fixing. Go on, Mabel. Some fresh air will do you good, and I'll take care of things here.'

The boy was sullen and unresponsive on their walk, and Mabel soon left him in the field, working on the plough. Despite a niggling guilt, she took the long way back to the cabin. She inhaled the green scent of new leaves and studied the sharp line along the mountain tops where white snow met leafy forest. Then she remembered she had missed Jack's dose of laudanum.

'Back already? You should have stayed gone a bit. Your water's not done yet.' Esther dipped a finger into a giant pot on the woodstove. Mabel hurried to the bedroom. Jack's hair was damp and combed, and he smiled meekly up at her from the pillow.

'She gave me a bath,' he said.

'Esther did?'

He nodded as well as he could. Pillows and blankets propped him up in a peculiar position, with his knees bent and separated.

'Are you comfortable?'

He squinted self-consciously and then nodded. 'Believe it or not.'

'I'm sorry I missed your dose of medicine.'

'Esther gave it to me, with a nip of something stronger.'

'Hurry on out here,' Esther called from the other room, 'before the water gets cold or that adolescent son of mine comes back.' She was dumping the pot of steaming water into a horse trough Garrett had hauled into the cabin.

'Usually it'd be the other way around, ladies first, but I wanted to get those wounds clean as possible.'

Mabel wanted to tell Esther she had done too much, but she stripped and climbed into the knee-deep hot water. Beside the makeshift tub Esther had placed a bar of milled soap and a bottle of lavender-scented shampoo. Mabel let herself sink until even her head was submerged and her untied hair floated around her. When she got out, Esther wrapped her in a towel and fluffed her hair.

'There. Now we're getting somewhere. Dinner will be ready soon. Get some comfortable clothes on. Just something to sleep in. I expect Garrett will be gone until late, looking at the fields. He's not keen on bunking with two old women, but he'll get tired eventually.'

With both of them wearing nightgowns, Esther served Mabel black bear stew and fresh biscuits. Then she spread out three bedrolls.

'I figured you'd been sleeping in a chair for days now. I know how it is when you've got a sick one tossing and turning in your bed. Come on now,' and she crawled beneath her covers and patted the bedroll beside her.

Mabel found it an unexpected relief to rest her head on a pillow, to be clean and fed and not alone.

'So, do you really think we can manage this?' she whispered from beneath her covers. 'You and Garrett and me? Planting our whole farm?'

'I wouldn't be here if I didn't think we could do something.'

'But what about your own place?'

'George's got Bill and Michael there to help, and we've got a good portion done already.'

'I don't know how to thank you.'

'We're not there yet.'

The two women were silent a while, and then Esther spoke gently.

'And what of your little girl?'

'She's gone, Esther.'

She reached over and found Mabel's hand and squeezed it once.

'Sweet Mabel,' she said. 'I suppose now that you're getting some sunshine and fresh air, she isn't coming around any more.'

Chapter 8

Esther insisted on being Jack's nurse, slowly reducing the laudanum doses and increasing the length of his daily walks. First, to the kitchen table. Then to the outhouse so he wouldn't have to use a chamber pot.

'You're too easy on him, Mabel. He's got to get up and move. It's the only way those muscles can start to work again.'

So while Garrett showed Mabel how to cut seed potatoes so each piece had one eye, Esther spent the morning walking Jack around the fields. Mabel couldn't bear to watch his slow shuffle. When his foot caught on a root or rut, he would grunt and stand in one place, his eyes closed and his jaw muscles clenching and unclenching. She would have been ashamed to admit it to anyone, but she was glad to sit in the yard with Garrett, cutting seed potatoes rather than escorting her husband on his agonising walk.

And the boy wasn't such terrible company. Mabel observed Garrett's resentment: he stomped in and out of the cabin and sulked when his mother ordered him around. But when she was alone with him, the boy was less petulant. He was, actually, patient and instructive.

The sun climbed higher in the sky and warmed the top of Mabel's head while she tossed the cut seed potatoes into the burlap sack between them. When it was lunch time the boy followed her inside and helped her fix a meal of moose steak and yesterday's bread. After Esther helped Jack back into bed, the three of them ate quickly and went out to load the wagon with the seed potatoes. It was only as Mabel handed a heavy burlap sack to Garrett on the back of the wagon that she appreciated what she was doing—farm work. The boy grabbed the bags and hopped down. As Esther drove the wagon towards the field, Mabel and Garrett followed behind.

Esther dropped sacks of seed potatoes up and down the field, then harnessed the horse to a cultivator to form the rows. Garrett and Mabel followed. The boy showed her how far apart to plant and how deep to dig the hole before dropping in the cut potato, following her to scoop dirt over the top and lightly pat it.

At the end of the row, Mabel stood, put her hands to the small of her back and stretched. Her hem was soiled, her hands dusty and tired. She looked down the field and saw how much they had done. Garrett slapped his hands on his trouser legs.

'One row down,' he said. ''Bout a thousand to go.' And the boy gave her a half-smile, his eyebrows raised as if to ask 'Are you still in?'

Mabel nodded. 'Onward ho?' she asked.

Garrett raised a hand, like a conquering explorer. 'Onward ho!'

As Esther rounded a row and headed back down the field, she slowed the horse and gave a wave to the two of them. Mabel raised her hand and waved back. A breeze stirred the loose strands of hair around her face and licked away the sweat. The sky overhead was cloudless and brilliant. In the distance, beyond the trees, she could see the white mountain peaks. She lifted her skirts and stepped over the row they had just planted. Garrett pulled the burlap sack to her and they started again.

They worked until dusk and arrived back at the cabin well past dinnertime. Jack had lit the lanterns and was frying steaks.

'What's all this?' Esther said. She inhaled deeply and grinned. 'Something smells mighty good.'

'Can't do much. Thought the least I could do is feed my help.' He smiled.

The next days were a blur of potatoes, earth, sun and aching muscles as each row of planting went by. Jack did what he could but mostly stayed in the cabin and fixed meals. By the time night fell, Mabel was numb with fatigue. Yet for all the sore muscles and monotony, the days of working in the fields filled her with a kind of pride she had never known. She no longer saw the cabin as rough, but was grateful at the end of the day for warm food and a bedroll. She didn't notice if the dishes went unwashed or the floor unswept.

'I think we've done it, Jack,' Esther announced one afternoon, hands on her hips. 'I know you had plans to do more this year, but I was thinking, we've got the potatoes in the ground and we'll see what happens.'

Jack nodded in agreement. Maybe it would be enough to get them by.

'We wouldn't be here if it weren't for you two.' His voice was gravelly and genuine. 'I don't know how we'll ever repay you.'

Esther waved him off impatiently, and said she planned on going home that evening.

'It's been a hoot, but I'm ready to sleep in my own bed, snoring husband and all. You're shaping up, Jack, and I think Garrett can manage the fields. George and I have talked about it. He works better here than he ever did at home, and our planting's done. You can fix him a place in the barn and then you two can have your place back to yourselves.'

It was time, yet Mabel dreaded it. Jack was a different man, unsteady and unsure. She could not forget how, during the worst of it, he had cried and begged her to leave him. With Esther gone, she and Jack would once again share a bed, and she wondered if it would be like sleeping with a stranger. Jack looked at her sadly, as though he could read her thoughts.

After dinner, Esther left and Mabel showed Garrett to the barn loft. He brought his bedroll, and she overturned a wooden box for him to use as a nightstand. There she set a lantern, as well as an alarm clock and a book.

'*White Fang*, by Jack London. Have you read it before?'

'No, ma'am.'

'Please, just call me Mabel. I think you'll like this one, but if it doesn't suit you, I've got dozens of others to choose from. Come inside if you need anything, even if it's just company.'

'Yes, ma'am . . . I mean, Mabel.'

It was a cold night, and Jack had started a fire. The dirty dishes were left piled in the kitchen, and Mabel sat in a chair in front of the woodstove and stretched her feet to the warmth. She was more tired than she could ever remember being. Her muscles ached and hummed.

'Mabel. You're falling asleep. Come to bed.'

Jack rubbed her shoulders. 'This has been too much for you.'

'No, no.' She looked up at him. 'It feels wonderful, to share in the work, to feel like I'm doing something. Today might well have been one of the best days of my life . . .' Her voice trailed off as she understood what she was saying. Jack nodded without speaking.

She put on her nightgown and got into bed. Jack, stripped to his long underwear, sat on the edge.

'Jack? We are going to be all right, aren't we? I mean, the two of us?'

He groaned as he eased his feet onto the bed. He rolled onto his side to face Mabel, reached to her and ran his hand down her unbraided hair. Mabel saw tears in the corners of his eyes, and she propped herself on an elbow. She leaned to him and kissed him on his closed wet eyelids.

'We will, Jack. We will be all right,' and she cradled his head in the crook of her arm and let him cry.

THAT SUMMER was a farmer's blessing. At perfect intervals the skies rained and the sun shone. Of his own accord, Garrett planted rows of vegetables to supply the railroad, and the plants flourished in the fields.

Jack's back still gave him trouble, and there were mornings when he had to slide out of bed to the floor and crawl to the bureau to pull himself to a standing position. His hands and feet sometimes went numb, and other days his joints swelled and ached.

But in the evenings, when the snow-capped mountains went periwinkle in the twilight of the midnight sun, he would walk the fields alone, and his step was lighter. He would go down the perfect rows of lettuce and cabbage, their immense leaves green and lush. The earth was soft beneath his boots and often he would scoop some of the soil in his hand and marvel at its richness. It hardly seemed the same stretch of lifeless ground the horse had dragged him across last winter.

He owed this to Esther, he knew, and the boy. Garrett staggered the lettuce and radish crops so they were ready when the railroad needed them week to week. He weeded and hilled the potatoes. He knew which kind of fertilisers worked, and which didn't, so Jack didn't have to trust the salesman in Anchorage.

Even at just fourteen now, the boy was a dependable farmer, but his heart wasn't in it. With permission, Garrett would leave for days at a time, taking his horse, a rifle and a knapsack. Sometimes he returned with the pack full of rainbow trout or spruce grouse for dinner. Once he brought Mabel a beaded moose-hide pouch sewn by an Athabascan woman upriver.

One evening, the summer sun glinting down the valley, Garrett asked to join Jack on his stroll around the fields.

'I'll bring a gun. Maybe we'll run into a grouse or two.'

Jack didn't care much for the boy shooting game on the farm, so he said nothing in hopes the boy would take the hint, but Garrett dashed to the barn to get his shotgun.

'We'll be back in a bit,' Jack said over his shoulder as he walked out the door, but he doubted Mabel had heard. She was bent over the table, working on a sewing project and he felt a rush of affection for her.

It had humiliated him at first, knowing she was working the farm in his place. But now, with summer mostly gone, he knew she was no longer a lost soul—she was right there beside him, the same dirt on her hands, the same thoughts on her mind. How many rows of reds should we plant next year? Do we need to lime the north field? When the new hen starts laying, should we let her hatch a dozen or so? The fate of it all, the farm, their happiness, was no longer his alone.

Shotgun in the crook of his arm, Garrett trotted down the dirt road and caught up with Jack. 'We'll probably never see another year like this,' the boy said. He shook his head in disbelief as he looked out over the field. 'Can you believe it? We want rain, it rains. We want sun, the sun shines.'

'It's been good.' Jack bent and pulled two plants. He handed a radish to Garrett. They both wiped them on their trousers and silently ate them, then followed the trail that led to the new field.

Jack noticed that Garrett had shot up several inches during the summer. He had lost some of the boyhood softness in his face, and his jawline and cheekbones were more prominent. He looked Jack in the eye, spoke his opinions clearly, and rarely had to be asked to do something.

The trail ran along the edge of the field and past a swath of black spruce. It was such a thin line that separated the forest from the tidy green of the field, and Jack was thinking of the work that had gone into it when Garrett stopped, broke down his shotgun and thumbed a cartridge into the barrel. Jack looked past him. It took a moment for his eyes to focus.

'No! Wait.' Jack put his hand on the boy's back. 'Don't.'

Garrett looked at him out of the corner of his eyes, and took aim.

'I said don't shoot it.'

'That fox? Why not?' Garrett squinted in disbelief. The fox ran out of the woods and crouched in the trail.

'Leave it be.' Jack shoved the gun barrel down.

The animal took its chance and darted into the potato field. Jack glimpsed the fluffy red tail between the plants and then it was gone.

'Are you crazy? We could have had it.' Their eyes met, and Jack saw a flash of irritation, maybe even contempt. 'He'll be back, you know.'

'Let's just say I know that one. He used to belong to somebody.'

'Belonged? A fox?' They walked back to the barn and Jack wanted the talk done and Garrett off to bed, but the boy stopped in front of the door.

'Who did it belong to? There's nobody else around here for miles . . .' His voice trailed off and he turned to the barn, then back again. 'Wait. It's not that girl, is it? The one Mabel says came around last winter?'

'Yep. That was her fox, and I don't want anyone shooting it. Is there a problem with that?'

'No. No, sir.' He shook his head. 'It's just . . . there wasn't really a girl, was there?'

Jack was tired and he wished he had stayed at home in front of the woodstove. But he faced Garrett.

'Yes. There was a girl. She raised that fox from a pup. It still comes around sometimes, but it's never done any harm.'

Again there was the shake of the head and a soft snort.

'There's no way. A girl, living by herself around here, in the woods. In the middle of winter? She wouldn't stand a chance.'

'You don't think a person could do it? Live off this land?'

'Oh, somebody could. A man. Somebody who really knew what he was doing. Not many,' he said. 'Certainly no little girl.'

Garrett must have seen a look pass over Jack's face, because his confidence seemed to falter. 'I mean, I'm not doubting what you think you saw. Maybe there's just another way to account for it.'

'Maybe.' Jack walked slowly towards the house. As he neared the door he heard him call out, 'Good night. And tell Mabel good night, too.' Without turning round, Jack held up the back of his hand in a brief wave.

'Nice walk?' Mabel's eyes were on her sewing.

Jack eased off his boots. 'It was all right. Quieter on my own.' He added a log to the woodstove. Nights were cooler now as autumn approached. 'So what have you been sewing on over there?'

'Oh, just a little something. It's for Faina. A new winter coat.' Mabel stood and held the pieces of the coat in front of her, laying the blue boiled wool across her front. Then she picked up a few strips of white fur.

'For Faina?'

'Yes. Isn't it beautiful? This is rabbit fur. Snowshoe hare, actually. I asked Garrett for it.'

He wanted to yank the thing from her hands and throw it to the floor. He felt sick, light-headed even.

'Don't you like it? You see, I noticed last time we saw her, how her coat was frayed and worn. And she had nearly outgrown it last winter.' Mabel spread the coat on the table and picked up some spools of thread. Her face was radiant. 'It'll be lovely. I just hope I can finish it in time.'

'In time for what?'

'For when she comes back,' she said as if it were as plain as the nose on his face.

'For Christ's sake, Mabel, she's not coming back. Can't you see that?'

She stepped back, her hands at her cheeks. He had frightened her, but then her temper flared in her eyes. 'Yes, she is.'

She folded the coat and began sticking pins in a little pincushion, her movements quick and angry. 'She is coming back. And damn it, Jack, I won't let you or anyone else tell me differently.'

She carried the lantern with her into the bedroom, leaving Jack alone in the dark.

WHEN MABEL WOKE the next morning and looked out of the bedroom window, she saw snow. Just a dusting across the distant peaks, but with the snow came hope.

The child did not have to die. Maybe she wasn't gone from them for ever. She could have gone north, to the mountains, where the snow never melts, and she could return with winter. Mabel had only to wish and believe.

And so, as autumn hardened the land and snow crept down the mountains, she sewed a coat for a child she was certain would return.

The lining would be quilted silk, and the hood and cuffs would be trimmed with white fur. It would be sturdy and practical, but befitting a snow maiden. The buttons—sterling silver filigree. She had saved them for years in her button jar, never finding a purpose for them until now. Snowflakes, embroidered with white silk thread, would cascade down the front and back of the coat, each stitch a devotion, each snowflake a celebration of miracles.

A week later, the last of the potatoes were in burlap sacks and they woke to a skiff of snow across the land. It was early and thin and by midday, it would be gone. All the same, Mabel was delighted by the sight of it.

It was Garrett's last day. He was going back with his family for the winter. She meant to let him choose a book to take with him.

Garrett had grown and changed these past few months. He had taken on much of the responsibility of the farm, and in the evenings they talked about crop varieties and weather patterns, books and art. Mabel no longer sat outside the circle of conversation. She was as eager to discuss the type of turnips they would plant as to describe the museums she had visited in New York.

Who would think that an adolescent boy would have anything to teach an old woman? But it was Garrett who had led her into the fields and closer to the life she had pictured for herself in Alaska. She could think of no way to explain that to him.

'Garrett, I was thinking you could borrow a book to take home with you. Only if you would like to, of course.'

'Could I? I'll be real careful with it.'

'Of course you will. That's why I'm offering.' Mabel led him into the bedroom and knelt on the floor to pull out the trunk.

'Here, I can get that.' He easily tugged it out from under the bed. 'This is full of books? This whole thing?'

'That one, and a few others as well.' She laughed at Garrett's surprise. 'You should have seen my father's library. A room nearly the size of this cabin, lined with shelves of books.' She opened the trunk and Garrett began pulling books off the stacks inside.

She stood and dusted off her skirt. 'Take your time. Your mother isn't expecting you until dinner.'

She was at the door when she heard Garrett say, 'Thank you, Mabel.'

She thought of expressing her own gratitude, of trying to explain what he had done for her.

'You're welcome, Garrett.'

WINTER CAME HARD AND FAST at the tail end of October in a sudden, grainy snowstorm blown by a cold river wind. Just after dinner it was already midnight dark, and Jack and Mabel listened to the storm knock against their cabin. Jack looked up from greasing his boots by the woodstove and Mabel paused in her sewing at the kitchen table. The knock came again and again, louder. Jack went to the door and opened it.

He had the momentary notion that what stood before him was a mountain ghost, a bloodstained, snowy apparition. Faina was taller and, if possible, thinner than he remembered. Her fur hat and wool coat were covered in snow, and her hair hung like damp, fraying rope. Dried blood streaked her hands and brow. Jack could not speak or move.

The girl took off her hat, shook the snow from it, and looked up.

It's me. Faina.

She was slightly breathless, but her voice, even and cheerful, broke his spell. He took the child in his arms and held her, rocking on his heels.

Faina? Faina. Dear God. You're here. You're really here.

He pressed his beard into her hair and smelled the glacier wind that blows over the tops of the spruce trees and his knees nearly gave way. He pulled the girl into the cabin and closed the door.

My God, Mabel, and he knew he sounded shaken. Faina is here.

Oh, child. I wondered when you'd come.

Mabel, calm and smiling. How could she stand so assuredly when he, a grown man, was staggered by the sight of the girl? Mabel's eyes glistened but she did not shriek or bawl.

Faina began to unbutton her coat, and Mabel helped her out of it, shook off snow.

There. Now let me see. She held the girl at arm's length. I knew you'd have grown.

Grown? Surely Mabel had lost her mind. No talk of the blood, the child's desperate appearance, her long absence.

Jack touched the girl's chin and turned her face up to his.

What's happened to you, Faina? Are you all right?

Oh, this? The girl looked at her hands. I was skinning rabbits.

Her eyes were wide, expectant. I'm here, she said. I've come back.

Of course you have. Mabel said it as if there had never been a doubt. I knew it would be soon. That's why I've hurried so. I just finished tonight. But wait. You need to wash up and get settled, yes?

Faina smiled and held out her hands. They were cold-chafed and stained with blood, but Mabel merely clucked like a mother hen, as if it were a bit of dirt smudged on a boy who had played in the mud.

Well, let's see, she said. I had water on the stove already for tea. There should be enough to wash with.

Faina smiled shyly. Before long, Mabel was sitting with her, washing her hands in soapy, lukewarm water, wiping her face with a washcloth. Jack stood beside the woodstove, bewildered as much by his wife's calm as by the child's appearance. When Mabel left to get something from the bedroom, Jack strode to Faina's side, knelt at her chair.

Where have you been? What has happened to you?

Jack, don't pester her so, Mabel said from behind him. She's tired to the bone. Let her rest.

It was true. The child was alive and well, here in their cabin. Jack felt a rush of pride in her. She had survived, against all odds.

What do you think? Mabel asked Jack, turning Faina to face him.

The child stretched out her arms and gazed down at the new coat. Jack had never seen anything like it. It was the cool blue of a winter sky, with silver buttons that glistened like ice and a white fur trim at the hood and cuffs and along the bottom edge. But the coat's splendour came from the snowflakes. The varying sizes and designs gave them movement, so they seemed to twirl through the blue wool. Its strange beauty suited the child.

Lovely, he said, and he had to choke back his emotion at the sight of the little girl in the snowflake coat, come home at last.

You did this? the girl whispered. You made this, for me?

Well, yes. But it's nothing but fabric and a few stitches.

The girl smoothed her hands down the front, over the snowflakes.

Do you like it?

In answer, the girl leaped to Mabel's arms and in the child's smiling face Jack saw such affection.

I love it more than anything, she said against Mabel's arm.

Oh, you couldn't make me happier. Mabel stood and held the child's hands in her own and looked her up and down. It does fit well, doesn't it?

Mabel was giddy and talkative as she cooked dinner, not allowing Jack or the child to speak of anything except the joy of being together. It was only when the cabin became overheated, with the woodstove and steam from the cooking, when the girl seemed to wilt in her chair, only then did Jack sense some fear in Mabel's desperate happiness. She dashed to the door and brought in a handful of snow. She dabbed it to the girl's cheeks and forehead.

There, there. It's much too hot in here. There, there.

Jack put the back of his hand to the child's forehead, but she was cool to the touch.

I suspect she's just tired, Mabel.

But she continued with the snow, putting some to the girl's lips.

Too hot, too hot, Mabel murmured. Please, get some more snow.

Jack opened the door to the swirling storm, driven in all directions by the wind off the river. It was a miserable night. He would not let the girl leave, not to go back to that cold, lifeless hovel in the mountains.

You'll stay here tonight, he said as he brought in another handful of snow. He spoke with more confidence than he felt.

The girl sat forward in her chair, her blue eyes narrowed and fierce.

I will go, she said.

Not tonight, he said. You will stay here, with us.

Oh yes, you must, child. Can't you hear that wind blowing? You can sleep in the barn. We have a little bedroom made up, for the boy who helped us this summer. It's cosy and out of the wind.

But Faina was on her feet. When she looked at Jack she didn't speak, but it was as if she were shouting. You promised. You can't keep me here.

He wondered what he could do. Physically hold the child, force her to stay against her will?

Faina had already fastened the shining silver buttons on her new coat. Please don't be angry, she said.

The child was already at the door. He waited for Mabel to protest.

All right, she said. If you must go, you must. But you'll be back, won't you? Promise always to come back.

Solemnly, as if swearing an oath, the child said, I promise.

JACK WATCHED HER LEAVE, and it seemed like a disturbing dream, the child with her twisted blonde hair and snowflake coat, and his wife, composed and accepting. He stood some time at the window, staring into the night while Mabel bustled with the dishes.

'How could you have known she was coming back? Now? Ever?'

'It's the first snow. Just like the night when we built the snow child. Snowflakes as big as saucers. Remember? We threw snowballs at each other. Then we made her. You carved her lovely face; I put on her mittens.'

'What are you saying, Mabel?'

She went to her shelves and brought back an oversized book bound in blue leather, adorned with silver gilding.

'Here,' she slid it across the table towards him. 'You won't be able to read it, though. It's in Russian.'

Jack flipped through the illustrations, impatient.

'What is this?'

'It's a storybook . . . It's about an old man and an old woman. More than anything they want a child of their own, but they can't have one. Then, one winter night, they make a little girl out of snow, and she comes to life.'

Jack felt a stomach-turning sinking. 'Stop,' he said.

'She leaves each summer, and comes back when it snows. Don't you see? Otherwise . . . she would melt.'

'Jesus, Mabel. What are you saying?'

She opened the book to an illustration of the old man and old woman kneeling beside a beautiful little girl, her feet and legs bound in snow. 'You see?' she said. She spoke like a nurse at a bedside.

'No, Mabel. I don't see at all.' He slammed the book closed and stood. 'You're telling me you think that little child, that little girl, is some sort of spirit, some sort of snow fairy. Jesus. Jesus.'

He stomped to the other side of the cabin, wanting to escape but unable.

'I know it sounds implausible, but don't you see?' Mabel said. 'We wished for her, we made her in love and hope, and she came to us. She's our little girl, and I don't know how exactly, but she's made from this place, from this snow, from this cold. Can't you believe that?'

'No. I can't.' He had the urge to take her by the shoulders and shake her.

'Why not?'

'Because . . . because I know things you don't.'

Now she looked frightened. She held the book to her chest, her lips pursed and trembling.

'What do you know?'

'Jesus Christ, Mabel, I buried her father. He drank himself to death in front of that poor child. She begged him to stop. She put her little hands to his face, trying to warm him even as he was dying in front of her. All those days I was gone? Where did you think I was? I was up there, in the mountains, trying to help her. Digging a goddamned grave in the middle of winter.'

'But you never told me this.' As if he was lying, inventing this awful tale to prove her wrong.

Jack clenched his jaw again and again, felt the muscle work as he bit back his anger.

'She made me promise not to tell you or anyone else.' It sounded so weak. A grown man making a promise like that to a girl.

'What about a mother?'

'Dead, too. When she was a baby. I think it must have been consumption. Faina said she died of a coughing sickness, in the Anchorage hospital.'

She stared blankly. Her head nodded slightly, all the blood drained from her face. He went to her, knelt beside her chair, took her hands gently in his.

'I should have told you. I'm sorry, Mabel. I am. I'd like it to be true, that she was ours, that she was a wilderness pixie. I would have liked that, too.'

She whispered through her teeth, 'Where does she live?'

'In a sort of cabin dug into the side of the mountain. It's not that bad really. It's dry and safe, and she has food.'

'By herself? Out there?'

'Of course, Mabel,' he pleaded. 'What could you have thought, that when she wasn't here with us she was some kind of snowflake, a snow child? Is that what you thought?'

She yanked her hands from his and stood with such force she knocked her chair over. 'Damn you! Damn you! How could you?'

Her anger startled him. 'Mabel?' He put his hands on her shoulders, and he could feel the heat of her fury through the fabric of her dress.

'How could you? Let her live out there, like a starving animal? Motherless. Fatherless. Starving for food and love. How could you?' She shoved her way past to the coat hooks.

'Mabel? Where are you going?' He took her by an arm, but she pushed him away. She wrapped a scarf round her neck, pulled on gloves and a hat, then took the oil lantern and slammed the door behind her.

He stood there in his socked feet. It was night, and it was snowing. She couldn't go far.

But the silence of the cabin unnerved him. He lit another lantern, paced at the door. Finally, he put on his coat and boots and took the lantern. Outside the snow was thick. It fell so densely that he could see no more than a foot or two in front of him, and Mabel's tracks had disappeared.

Chapter 9

Mabel ran without seeing, her face wet with tears and snow, her feet tripping. The small circle of lantern light swung wildly among the snowy trees. For some time all she did was run towards the mountains. Her skirt dragged in the deepening snow, spruce branches raked at her face, and more than once she nearly fell, but she felt neither cold nor pain. All she knew was the rush of blood in her ears and a hot rage that with each step began to cool to a sort of grieving stupor.

At last the ground climbed slightly and Mabel again found herself among spruce, birch and scattered cottonwood. She stopped and held the lantern high. Where the light spilled ahead of her, Mabel saw that the snow was disturbed. She ran to the tracks. They led over a fallen birch tree, and she wrestled with her long skirt as she climbed over it. By the time she cleared the log, she was drenched with sweat and her legs trembled with exhaustion. She followed the trail to her left, half running. She would find the girl and make this right.

It was only when Mabel came again to the fallen birch and saw where she had already climbed over it that she realised her mistake. She was a mad old woman, running in circles, chasing herself through the woods at night. When she began to walk again, she no longer searched for trails. Everything was strange and unknown and she could see only a few steps in front of her. Hot and thirsty, she scooped up snow in her gloved hand and brought it to her mouth, letting it melt down her throat. She hoped to find a trail again, any trail, and let it take her where it would, perhaps to the mountains, perhaps to the river, maybe back home. In her fatigue she shuffled and her boots caught on bushes and roots.

When she fell, it was so hard, so sudden, it was almost as if something had shoved her from behind. She plummeted to the ground, and the blow forced the air from her lungs. At the same moment, the lantern dropped to the snow in a clatter and hiss. The blackness was now so complete that, except for the touch of cool air, she could not tell whether her eyes were open or closed.

She tried to stand, and hit her head on a branch. When she reached out, her hands brushed something hard. She took off her gloves and felt, the way a blind person might feel a face. It was a tree trunk. She had stumbled beneath the branches of a great spruce tree. She felt the ground at her feet and was surprised to find a bed of dry needles. She sat at the base of the tree and leaned against it.

The chill approached along her hairline, damp with sweat and melted snow. It crept down the nape of her neck and up the backs of her wet legs. As it made its way beneath her clothes, along the skin of her ribs, down the curve of her spine, she knew it for what it was—a death chill. As if to confirm her suspicions, her teeth began to chatter.

'Jack.' The name came as a whisper from her cold lips. 'Jack?' Only a bit louder. He would never hear her. Who knew how far she was from the cabin. 'Jack!' She yelled and cried until she was hoarse and her voice a noiseless screech. 'Pleasc, Jack. Please.' Finally she curled up, her clothes clinging wet and cold, her body racked with tremors.

She woke to the breaking of twigs and the flash of fire in the darkness. Her body ached and she couldn't move. Something bound her. It was heavy and smelled familiar. Like home. Out of the corner of her eye, she saw movement in front of a fire. A figure bending over, putting something to the flames. The figure turned towards her, blocking the light.

'Mabel? Are you awake?'

She couldn't speak. Her jaw seemed sealed, the muscles stiff. She tried to nod, but it hurt. Everything hurt.

'Mabel? It's me—Jack. Can you hear me?' And he was beside her, kneeling, brushing her hair back from her face.

'Are you warmer? I've got the fire going good now. You feel it?'

Jack. She could smell him, the scent of cut wood and wool. He reached round her, pressing at her sides like he was tucking a child into bed. She was wrapped in blankets. She was confused. Was she home, in her own bed? But the air was so cold and overhead there were branches.

'Jack?' It was only a whisper, but he heard. 'Jack? Where are we?'

She heard him clear his throat. 'It's all right. This is going to be all right. Let me get that fire bigger, and you'll warm.'

Mabel closed her eyes. He was angry with her. She remembered the child, the snow, the night. 'How did you find me?'

He was feeding the fire, building it higher and higher until she could see his face and feel its heat. 'I don't know.'

'Where are we? Are we far from home?'

'I don't precisely know that either. But it's going to be fine, Mabel. In a few more hours the light'll come, and we'll find our way.'

His voice faded. Mabel drifted, sank into the warmth, and it was like a childhood fever, dreamlike and nearly comforting.

'Can you sit up?' Jack held a canteen.

'I think so.' He grasped her round the shoulders and helped her to sit. When she reached for the canteen, the blanket fell open to reveal her bare arm. She was naked.

'My clothing? Why on earth . . .'

He pointed towards the fire where her dress hung from a branch, along with her undergarments. Her boots were propped open near the flames.

'There was no other way,' he said, almost as if apologising.

She tried not to gulp the water, but to take small sips. 'Thank you.'

'Sometimes I thought I could hear you calling my name,' he said. 'Then I tripped over the lantern and I knew you had to be nearby.'

Jack went to the fire. He took down her dress and shook it out.

'It stopped snowing,' he said as he crawled under the tree with her. He groaned softly as he leaned against the trunk and put his arm round her. She thought of his barely mended back. 'You were soaked through.'

Mabel leaned her head against his chest. 'How does she do it?'

'She's got something different about her,' he said finally. 'She might not be a snow fairy, but she knows this land. Knows it better than anyone I've ever met.'

She cringed inwardly at the words 'snow fairy', but knew there was no malice in it.

'I'm not angry any more,' she said, 'but I can't bear the thought of something happening to her. She may be lovely and brave and strong, but she's just a little girl. If something were to happen to her, I just don't think I could stand it. Not again. Not after . . .' She expected Jack to shush her, to pull away, to go back to the fire, but he didn't.

'I've always regretted that I didn't have courage enough to hold our baby and see it for what it was.' She turned to look up into his face. 'Jack. I know it's been so long. My God, ten years now. But tell me that you said a proper goodbye. Tell me you said a prayer over its grave. Please tell me that.'

'His grave. It was a boy. And before I laid him in the ground, I prayed for God to take our tiny babe into His arms, to love him and keep him safe.'

Mabel let out a sob and hugged Jack with her bare arms. He tucked the blanket round her and they held each other.

'A boy? All that time the baby was inside me, I thought it was a girl. But it wasn't. It was a little boy. Where did you bury him?'

'In the orchard, down by the creek.'

She knew exactly where. It was the place they had first kissed, had first held each other as lovers.

Jack got up to feed the fire and when it was burning well he sat again with Mabel under the tree. 'Are you warm enough?'

'Yes,' she said. 'But won't you come in with me?'

'I'll only make you cold.'

She insisted, helping him strip out of his damp clothes and opening her blankets to him. She burrowed more tightly against him, rested her head on his chest and watched the fire flare up into the cold night sky.

MABEL WOULD REDUCE THE CHILD to the shabby clothes and slight frame of a flesh-and-blood orphan, and it pained Jack to watch. Gone was Mabel's wonder and awe. In her eyes Faina was no longer a snow fairy, but a feral child who needed a bath.

'We should enquire about schooling in town,' she said just days after Jack had told her the truth. 'We'd have to take her by wagon each morning.'

'Mabel? I just don't know if . . .'

'And those clothes. I'll get some fabric and sew her some new dresses. And some real shoes. She won't need those moccasins any more.'

BUT THE CHILD was not so easily tamed.

I don't want to, she said when Mabel showed her the tub of hot water.

Look at yourself, child. Your hair is a mess. You're filthy.

The child backed towards the door. Mabel grabbed her by the wrist, but Faina yanked it free.

Mabel, Jack said, let the child go.

Faina's eyes darted from Mabel to Jack and in the quick blue he saw that she was afraid.

I will no longer allow you to live like an animal, Mabel said. Starting right now, you will stay here with us. This will be your home. With us.

No, the child said.

Jack waited for her to fly away. Mabel, can we talk about this later?

Just look at her. She needs a clean home, an education. How will she find her way in this world if all she knows is the woods?

She belongs out there. Jack said. Can't you see that? It's her home.

He reached up to Mabel, took her hands in his. Her fingers were slender, and he rubbed his thumbs along them. How well he knew those hands.

I'm trying, Jack. I am. But she chooses to live in dirt and freezing cold, tearing apart wild animals to eat. With us she would be safe and loved. Mabel let go of his hands and turned to the child.

You will stay here tonight, she said.

She took hold of the child's shoulders, then smoothed her hands down the girl's arms and spoke more gently. It's in your best interest. Tomorrow we will go to town to ask about school classes.

The girl's cheeks flushed and she shook her head no, no.

Quickly, quietly, the child was nearly away, already wearing her hat and coat. Mabel stepped towards her. It's for you, don't you understand?

But the child was gone.

Jack went to the open door. It was a clear, calm night, the moon shining through the branches. He saw the child at the edge of the forest. She had stopped and was looking back at the cabin. Then she turned away and, as she began to run, she shook her hands out from her sides in a gesture of frustration and then vanished into the forest.

'THE BOY'S BROUGHT YOU something, Mabel.'

Jack opened the cabin door wider so Garrett could follow with his bundle, wrapped in leather and tied with a string of rawhide.

'Well, good morning. Come in. Come in.' Mabel wiped her hands on her apron and tucked a few strands of hair behind her ear. 'Would you like something hot to drink?'

'Yes, thank you.'

'So how's trapping?' Jack asked.

'I'm just getting the sets out now. But Old Man Boyd said I could have his marten line. He's retiring down to San Francisco.'

'Is it a long trail, his trap line?' Jack asked.

'It'll take me two days to check it. I've got a wall tent I'll put up so I can stay overnight when the weather's bad.'

'Are you frightened?' Mabel asked from where she stood at the window.

The question seemed to confuse the boy.

'No. I can't say that I am.'

Mabel was quiet.

'I mean, I suppose I've been scared a few times,' Garrett said. 'Fall before last, I had a black bear act like he was hunting me. Followed me all the way home, but most times a bear will hightail it in another direction.'

'But are you lonely?' Still Mabel did not face them as she spoke.

'Ma'am?'

'Lonely. When you are all alone in the wilderness, there must be something terrible about it.'

'Well, I don't spend all that much time in the woods by myself. Longest I've been gone is a week, when I went salmon fishing last summer. And I liked it just fine. I fished all day and sometimes all night 'cause the sun never went down. I smoked the fish on alder poles. That was the first time I saw a mink. It tried to steal a whole salmon right from under my nose. I was laughing too hard to take a shot at it.'

'But you have a safe, warm home, why would you want to be out there?'

The boy hesitated. 'I don't know,' he said with a shrug. 'I guess maybe I don't want to be warm and safe. I want to live.'

'Live? Isn't this living?' She let out a long sigh.

No one spoke again until she came to the table with the coffee, and it was as if the boy had just arrived. 'So what's this you've brought?' she asked.

Garrett's face brightened, and he turned bashful. 'Well, I uh, well . . .' and he pushed it across the table towards her. 'It's for you.'

Mabel untied the string and folded back the leather. Inside, Jack saw fox fur. Silver and black.

'It's a hat. See?' The boy took it from her and lightly punched it from beneath, so the crown stood up. 'Betty sewed it for you. It's got earflaps you can pull down and tie it under your chin. I hope it fits.'

He gave it back to Mabel, who turned it slowly in her hands.

'I can't . . . I can't accept this,' she said.

The boy's face fell. 'It's all right,' he mumbled. 'If you don't like it.'

'It's not that,' she said. 'It's too fine. I have no place to wear it.'

'But it's nothing fancy,' the boy said. 'Trappers wear them. You don't have to save it for trips to town or anything. It's warm.'

'Try it on, Mabel,' Jack said quietly.

He wasn't ready for the effect. As Mabel pulled it down and tied the strings beneath her chin, the dense black fur, tipped brilliantly in silver, framed her face, and her eyes shone grey-soft and her skin looked like warm cream. She was stunning. Neither he nor the boy said a word.

'Well! The way you two gawk, I guess it must not suit me,' she said and tugged off the hat in an angry fluster.

'It suits you fine,' Jack said.

'You could be in one of those fashion magazines from Back East,' the boy jumped in. 'And I'm not just saying it either.'

'He's right. It suits you better than fine.'

'It does fit well,' she said, 'as if it were tailored for me. And it is warm. I guess I'll be the finest-dressed farmer's wife you ever saw.'

Mabel sent the boy home with several books from her trunks. When he had gone, Jack went up to her and softly touched the nape of her neck.

'I think the boy was smitten with you in that hat.'

'Don't be silly,' she said. 'I'm an old woman.'

'You're still beautiful. And you don't seem to mind it being made of fox. I'd thought you'd object.'

'It is practical. I'll be warmer with it.'

WHERE WERE YOU, child?

I was at the river. That's where I found this. In her hand, Faina held a dried salmon skull. Mabel was trying to draw it, first this way, then that.

No. Not just now. Always. This past summer. Where did you go then?

To the mountains.

Why? What is there for you?

Everything. The snow and the wind. The caribou come. And little flowers and berries. They grow even on the rocks, near the snow, up by the sky.

You're going to leave us again, aren't you? This spring, you will go back to the mountains.

The girl nodded.

And tonight, when you leave, where will you go?

Home.

What kind of home can you have out there?

I'll show you.

THE NEXT BRIGHT DAY, the child came for Mabel and led her away into the forest, along trails Mabel alone never could have seen or known—snowshoe hare runs beneath willow boughs, wolf tracks along hard-packed drifts. The day was cold and peaceful. Mabel's breath rose around her face and turned to frost on her eyelashes as she stumbled in Jack's wool trousers and snowshoes; ahead of her Faina strode in ease and grace, her feet light on the snow.

They climbed out of the river valley and up towards the blue sky until they were on the side of a mountain.

Everything was sparkled and sharp as if the world were new that very morning. Willow branches were cloaked in hoar frost, waterfalls encased in ice, and the snowy land speckled with the tracks of a hundred wild animals: coyote and fox, fat-footed lynx, moose and dancing magpies.

The trail led across a frozen swamp and then up a steep bank and back into a forest of broad white spruce and twisted, knotted birch. They came to a pole with a trap, but it held only an animal's foot, ragged edge of bone and ripped tendon, brown fur frozen to steel. Faina put the trap to her knee, released its hold, and tossed the paw into the woods.

What was it?

A marten's foot. A wolverine stole it, the child said. She pointed to tracks in the snow. It ate the marten out of my trap.

Faina seemed unburdened by this knowledge. She walked on, her steps as quick and easy as they had ever been. Mabel followed without speaking, eyes newly alert for tracks and her chest filled with the rhythm of her own heart and lungs. And then she realised they had come back round to the river and were travelling towards their homestead.

But wait—we can't go back yet. You haven't showed me your home.

It's here. I've showed you.

Here? Maybe the place where she slept and ate wasn't worth seeing.

But Mabel knew the truth. The snowy hillsides, the open sky, the dark place in the trees where a wolverine gnawed on the leg of some small, dead animal—this was the child's home.

The sun was disappearing behind them and the girl pointed across the valley to the mountain slopes aglow in a cool purple-pink. Silhouetted against the sky, tendrils of snow unfurled from the peaks, whipped by what must have been a brutal wind. Here on the rise, though, the air was still. The colours were distant, impossible, untouchable.

That's what my name means, Faina said, pointing. That light. Papa named me after the colour on the snow when the sun turns.

Alpenglow, Mabel whispered.

She felt the awe of walking into a cathedral, the sense that she was being shown something powerful and intimate.

We should go, Faina said. It will be night soon.

The child led Mabel back to the homestead, to the warm cabin where Jack waited with hot tea and bread he had baked in a Dutch oven.

HOMESTEADERS CALLED that bittersweet season when the river ice gives way and the fields turn to mud 'breakup'.

Jack watched the sun climb higher above the mountains each day. Water ran along the surface of the river ice. And then one night the skies cleared and cold fell like a fog over the valley. Jack awoke to find the windows frosted inside and out. After kindling the fire and pulling the quilt over Mabel as she slept, he set off for town.

Jack had paid for his supplies and was preparing to leave the store when he caught sight of the ice skates, their blades gleaming in the sunlit front window. He had not thought of them since he was a boy skating on the cow pond. It was a crazy whim, but he went home with three pairs.

The next evening Faina came and they settled into their familiar habits of preparing dinner and gathering at the table. When Faina yawned, Jack stood and announced, Get your coats. We're going out.

What? Going out where? Mabel asked.

Down to the river.

The child jumped to her feet, her eyes alive. Will we all go? she asked.

Jack nodded. Get dressed.

He rarely gave orders so bluntly, and Mabel seemed surprised into submission. They got their coats and boots, and Jack grabbed a canvas bag from beside the door.

What's that you're bringing? Mabel asked.

He merely raised an eyebrow comically and grinned.

I don't think I trust you. Not one little bit.

It was cold outside, clear and still, with a nearly full moon shining just above the mountains. With the fresh snow and moonlight, they didn't need the lantern, but it gave a comforting glow. They followed the trail down to a small side channel of the Wolverine River. The wind had blown the ice clean of snow and it glistened black beneath the moon. Jack found a driftwood log and had Faina and Mabel sit side by side.

For heaven's sake, Jack. What are you doing?

Jack pulled the skates out of the bag. Mabel started to stand.

Oh no you don't, she said. Have you lost your mind? I'll fall flat on my back, or I'll break through the ice and drown.

Jack laughed and knelt down, grabbed her feet, and buckled the blades onto her boots. Mabel spluttered indignantly.

Quick, Faina, Jack said. Do you know what these are?

The girl shook her head, her lips pinched tight in fear and excitement.

They're ice skates. You put them on your feet and slide on the ice.

He showed her how to put them on, then he led them onto the ice.

The river's still frozen thick, he said. All this last thaw did was smooth the ice to a perfect shine. And even if we did fall through, this isn't the main channel. The water's only a foot deep. We'd just get cold and wet, but even that won't happen. I promise.

Mabel was hesitant, but soon her childhood came flying back to her and she slid confidently across the ice. The child, on the other hand, seemed to have left her braver self, the one who slayed wild animals and slept alone in the wilderness, back on solid ground, and she surprised Jack by clinging to his arm like a toddler.

It's all right, he told her. Even if you fall, it only smacks your bottom a bit. No harm done.

Mabel joined them and the three held hands and slowly skated in a circle. The riverbed echoed with the sound of their whoops and laughter and their blades carving into the ice.

Mabel let go and skated farther up the channel.

Will she be all right? Faina whispered, still holding on to his arm.

Yes. Yes she will.

Eventually Faina grew comfortable on the skates, and Jack set the light in the centre of the ice. Mabel returned to skate gracefully round and round the lantern, while Faina followed like a long-legged fawn learning to walk. Jack skated in the opposite direction and caught Mabel by the hand.

We used to skate like this together when we were young, he said as they passed Faina. Do you remember?

How could I forget? You were always trying to kiss me, but I could outskate you, so you never got the chance.

She laughed, pulled her hand free and skated upriver. Jack pursued her across the ice, the night-blackened trees and sky flying past him.

Faster! Go faster! Faina called out, and Jack didn't know who she was cheering on, but he skated as fast as he dared and prayed his blades would not catch in a crack or rough spot. Mabel stayed just out of reach, until she slowed and swung round to face him. Hand in hand they skated back to Faina. Without a word, Jack and Mabel each took one of the child's hands and skated up the river, following the curves of the bank. Faina squealed in delight as they glided fast enough to create a breeze against their faces.

As they neared the corner, where the small channel rejoined the main river, they slowed to a stop and the three of them stood arm in arm, Jack and Mabel gasping for breath. The moon lit up the entire valley, gleaming off the river ice and glowing on the white mountains.

Let's keep going, Faina whispered, and Jack, too, wanted to skate on, up the Wolverine River, round the bend, through the gorge, and into the mountains, where spring never comes and the snow never melts.

Chapter 10

They said goodbye to the girl each year just as the bog violets bloomed purple and white along the creeks and cow moose nuzzled their newborns. The land softened and warmed and the farm thrived. Most Sundays when the days stretched long, Mabel and Jack shared a meal with the Bensons, sometimes here, sometimes at their homestead. Esther would bring potato and beet salad; Mabel would bake a fresh rhubarb pie and spread a white tablecloth. Then the two women would walk together arm in arm and pick fireweed and bluebells. When Mabel set plates and silverware, Jack would sometimes come up behind her, softly pull back the wisps of her hair, and kiss her neck. 'You've never been more beautiful,' he would say.

Then, when the days shortened again and the first frost came, they whispered their blessings and prayed for snow. Mabel would try to guess how much Faina had grown since they had last seen her, and she would sew wool stockings and long underwear and sometimes a new coat, always blue wool with white fur trim and snowflakes embroidered down the front.

Each time the girl arrived, she was taller and more beautiful than they had remembered, and she would bring gifts from the mountains. One year it was a sack of dried fish, another it was a caribou hide, tanned supple and scented with wild herbs. She would hug them and kiss them and say she had missed them, and then she would run off into the snowy trees she called home.

Winter after winter, Faina returned to their cabin in the woods, and in all that time, no one else ever saw her.

GARRETT WATCHED THE FOX through his iron sights. It was still a few hundred yards away, but its gait did not falter as it travelled up the river towards him. It wouldn't be long before it closed the distance. Garrett leaned back into the cottonwood log, and steadied his rifle.

He knew it could be the one. For years, Jack forbade him from killing the red fox that hunted the fields and riverbed near their farm. He said it belonged to a girl who lived alone in the forest, hunted in the mountains, survived winters that killed grown men. A girl no one ever saw.

Garrett's rifle gently rose and fell with his breaths, as he let the fox come. When it was less than 150 yards away, he sat forward, put his cheek to the rifle stock, and lined the iron sights on the fox's spine. But the fox veered behind a willow shrub, headed for the nearby poplars. It moved quickly. Garrett lowered the rifle. He'd hesitated a moment too long.

Then he saw that the animal had stopped and sat watching him from the forest's edge. Garrett leaned again into his rifle, squinted down the barrel and pulled the trigger.

It took only the one shot. The impact was enough to flip the small animal onto its side, and it did not move again. Garrett ejected the shell, then with his rifle at his side, he walked until he stood over the dead fox. The animal had thinned to a scruffy frame, but there was no doubt. It was the one.

All these years, Garrett had obeyed Jack's command. But now that he had killed it, he regretted it. He should take it to Jack and Mabel's door. He should confess. He shouldered his rifle, picked up the fox, and carried it into the trees, where he arranged the animal in the snow at the base of a spruce tree. He broke off evergreen boughs and laid them over it.

As he turned to walk home in the dusk, he no longer felt like a nineteen-year-old man, but instead a shameful little boy.

'GARRETT.' JACK GREETED HIM at the cabin door and shook his hand. 'We were hoping you'd make it this evening.'

At the kitchen table, Mabel smiled up at him.

'Mom said you all wanted me to come over.'

'Have a seat,' Jack said. He held out a chair.

Garrett sat and looked from Jack to Mabel and back to Jack again.

'We've been wanting to talk to you about the farm . . .' Jack began. 'You know we couldn't have made a go of this place without you.'

'I don't know about that. Just been a hired hand. Could have been another one.'

'That's where you're wrong. These past years, we haven't been able to pay you near what you're worth.'

'And you were never just a hired hand. You've been so much more, to both of us,' Mabel said. 'What would I have done without you to discuss Mark Twain and Charles Dickens with?'

Garrett's shoulders relaxed some and he let out a slow breath.

'You know what this is?' Jack gestured towards some papers spread on the table in front of them. 'These are legal papers that make you a partner in this farm. And they also lay out that when we are both gone, this place will become yours. Now, hear us out before you start shaking your head. You know we don't have a son of our own to leave this place to. And the truth is you made it what it is today.'

'I don't know . . .'

'We understand farming hasn't always been your aim,' Jack went on, 'but maybe you'd be able to run this place along with your trapping and such in the winters.'

'Or,' Mabel added, 'you could be free to sell it. After we're gone.'

'I wouldn't . . . I don't know.'

'Well, think it over if you'd like,' Jack said. 'We aren't rushing off to the grave yet, are we, love?'

'No, not any time soon. But Garrett, whatever you decide, we want you to understand how proud we are of the man you've become. We wouldn't be here if it weren't for all your hard work. We don't have much in this world, but we want to offer you what little we do have.'

'Are you sure? I mean, isn't there anybody else, from your family?'

'Nope. You're the closest we've got. And we've never been more sure,' Jack said, and he reached across the table and shook his hand again.

MABEL AND FAINA were cutting out paper snowflakes to decorate the little spruce tree in the corner of the cabin when the Bensons showed up unannounced with Christmas gifts. Esther shoved the door open without knocking, and Faina bolted to the opposite side of the room, her eyes wide with fear. For a moment, Mabel feared the girl would try to break out of the glass window. She went to her and gently took hold of her wrist, hoping to calm her with her touch.

Esther, Mabel said. I would like you to meet Faina. Faina, this is my dear friend Esther.

Just then George and Garrett bumped noisily through the door behind her and Esther waved a hand and shushed them as if they were about to startle away a woodland creature.

It's the girl, George, she whispered without taking her eyes off Faina. She's here. She's right here, in front of me.

George laughed out loud, but behind him Garrett was silent.

The boy's eyes were wide, until he caught Mabel looking at him, and then he stepped back behind his father. Mabel nudged the girl. Hello, Faina said quietly.

My God, Esther said. Your girl is flesh and blood.

The next few hours were awkward. Esther tried to include Faina in the barrage of gifts and treats, as if she'd known all along she would be there.

As the two families gathered for dinner, the tension eased. Faina remained quiet, but she was well mannered, carefully passing dishes when prompted and giving a small smile here and there. Garrett, however, seemed incapable of speaking or looking at anyone, particularly the girl, and for the rest of the evening, the boy did not utter a word.

After dinner Mabel cleaned up and paced behind Faina. The girl was shrinking in her chair, beads of sweat gathering on the bridge of her nose. Mabel fanned her with a napkin and wiped at her temples.

Too warm, much too warm, Mabel whispered to herself.

At last the Bensons said their goodbyes, and Mabel was relieved to usher them all out of the door—George, Esther and Garrett to their horses and wagon, and Faina to the snowy forest.

GARRETT CURSED AND URGED his horse up the steep hill to follow the footprints. He ducked to avoid a low spruce branch, but still managed to get covered in snow. When he reached the top of the ridge, he reined in the horse and leaned from the saddle. The tracks were old, shapeless indentations beneath several inches of snow, but they were hers.

Garrett followed the tracks as they wove among the spruce trees. He was tired of the girl. For six years he had listened to Jack talk about her. Faina, Faina, Faina. The angel from the woods. And yet, for all the talk, never once had Garrett seen hide nor hair of the girl.

So how was it that this winter was different, that everywhere he went the forest snow was riddled with her tracks and he couldn't be free of her?

Everything about the girl filled him with guilt. He had shot her fox and told no one. As he pursued her he told himself he was going only where he wanted—towards the mountains, towards the wolverine. And it was true. Wolverine roamed higher in the alpine country, closer to the glacier. He would never catch one in the lowlands, where he trapped coyote, fox, beaver and mink. But it was wolverine he had his heart set on. It was the one animal that every winter eluded him.

He followed the tracks up into a narrow ravine. The horse stumbled occasionally, and finally Garrett dismounted and led the animal. Although getting on in years, the gelding was still steady and sure-footed. Garrett's traps and chains clanked in the burlap sacks strapped behind the saddle.

At any moment he expected to see the stout, bearlike paw prints of a lone wolverine. Instead he saw small tracks, this time fresher. The girl again. Garrett paused, hands on his knees, to look at the trail. Bare traces on top of the snow, like a lynx or snowshoe hare. The girl was nearly as tall as Garrett, so how could she be so insubstantial as to not sink into the snow? Irritated fascination twisted in his gut.

She was near. He was certain. Something in the air had changed. It was the same when he stalked a moose—abruptly the woods quieted and his senses sharpened. When he looked ahead, he saw the girl standing just out of the trees, her blue coat decorated in snowflakes, her hair an unearthly blonde. He could turn back, but surely she'd seen him, too. She waited for him. He continued up the ravine, trying to walk slower than his heart raced.

She did not move or speak until he was within several feet of her.

You are the one who killed my fox.

For a moment Garrett could not make his mouth work. How could she know? Yes, he finally choked.

Why did you come here?

He could have asked her the same. He had no reason to feel inferior.

Wolverine, he said. I'm scouting for wolverine. There's got to be one on this creek. I'm sure of it.

The girl turned her head from side to side.

What do you know? he asked. You know this whole valley?

She gave a short nod. Then turned her back and bent to the ground. In the snow was a woven birch-bark pack he hadn't noticed. She stood it up at her feet and began to pull something from it. When she faced him, she held a dead wolverine by its front paws. Its head was like that of a small bear, its body compact, legs short and powerful. It was close to forty pounds, Garrett guessed, but she easily tossed it at his feet.

What's this? he asked.

A wolverine.

I can see that. What are you doing with it?

I'm giving it to you. So you can leave.

Garrett was speechless for a moment.

I don't want it, he said crossly. Not like this.

I'll skin it for you, said the girl, and she turned again to her pack.

What? Hell, that's not what I mean. Why should you give it to me?

I don't want it. You do. It was stealing marten and bait. Take it.

Garrett had never been so mad in his life. To think of the years he had tried to find a wolverine to trap, and here was this girl throwing one at his feet. He turned back to his horse, grabbed the saddle horn and mounted.

Won't you take it with you? The girl's voice was higher pitched, more childlike than before.

Garrett didn't answer. He shook the reins, and the horse began to work its way slowly down the ravine.

Take it with you, she called. So you don't have to come back.

I don't want your blasted wolverine, he yelled over his shoulder. And I'll be back if I want to. You don't own this land.

GARRETT'S NIGHTS were haunted by the girl. He lay in his bed and thought of her blue eyes and the delicate features of her face, but they were always veiled by falling snow or covered in the fall of her blonde hair, and he could not recreate them clearly in his mind. He tried to remember the shape of her lips. He wondered what it would be like to touch them.

He returned again and again to the foothills to find her trails skimming across the snow. He told everyone that he was trapping, and yet for days he did not put out a single set. He no longer thought of wolverine, but only of her, and he grew weary of watching for a flash of a blue coat or white-blonde hair. He suspected that she kept herself hidden, but still he went back.

Soon the snow in the mountains was too deep for his horse, so he snowshoed. Sometimes he siwashed, sleeping beneath a canvas tarp and cooking on an open campfire. He was sure the girl was watching him from the trees, and sometimes he found her footprints the next morning. But still she did not reveal herself to him. Not until the day he stood desperate beside her fresh trail and called out her name.

Faina! Faina! I just want to talk with you. Won't you let me?

The trees were silent.

Faina! I know you're there. Won't you come out?

I'm here, she said and she stepped from behind a snow-heavy spruce branch. What do you want with me?

I don't know. Garrett was surprised at his own honesty. He was reckless and emboldened. I don't know, he repeated.

She narrowed her sharp blue eyes but did not retreat.

Have you seen any more wolverine? he asked, only because he could think of nothing better to say.

The girl shook her head. And you? Have you found your wolverine?

No. Never, actually. I've never caught a wolverine.

Is that why you're here?

No, it isn't.

Why then?

You. I think.

The girl shifted, wary now, but she stood her ground.

I'm sorry about your fox. I shouldn't have shot it. Wait. Don't leave. Won't you talk with me? I've never met anyone like you before.

She shrugged. A peculiar expression passed over her face, and he thought she smiled.

Do you want to see something? she asked. She darted round the spruce tree and was gone. Afraid to lose sight of her, he ran as well as he could in the snowshoes. They made their way above the tree line, where the snowy slopes rose over their heads into rocky mountain tops. Although he was damp with sweat and his lungs ached, the girl seemed tireless. She waited on a wind-blown rock until he managed, huffing, to climb to her.

Instead of leading him higher up the mountain, as he expected, she began to traverse the slope. Where her feet touched, tiny snowballs formed and rolled down the hill, leaving dotted trails. Covering the steep ground in snowshoes was difficult, but Garrett knew if he removed them he would sink well past his waist in the snow, so he slogged on. Soon they descended into a steep-sided ravine thick with alder bushes.

At the base of a small knoll, the girl went down on one knee and gestured for him to be quiet. Deep snow covered the hill except for a spot no bigger than a man's head. Come closer, the girl said with her hands.

It was a gloomy hole in the earth, part of a much larger entrance mostly buried in snow. Recognition sank in as a cold shiver up his neck and along his scalp. She had led him to a bear den.

Garrett squatted in his snowshoes beside her and leaned into the hole. He thought he could make out roots and black dirt, but it was so dark he couldn't be sure. He expected it to be cavernous and foul, but all he could smell was snow and earth and maybe damp leaves and fur. He could hear nothing but his own breathing.

He pointed and raised his eyebrows at the girl as if to ask, is it in there? She nodded, her eyes lively and her mittened hand on his shoulder in warning. Even through his heavy winter coat, he could feel the pressure of her hand on his skin, and it left him light-headed. They slowly backed away from the den and walked in silence down to the creek bed.

Is it in there? he whispered. Now?

Yes. I watched it dig the den from up there, and the girl pointed to the slope on the opposite side of the creek.

Brown bear? Garrett asked.

A mama, with two cubs.

No animal in the wilderness more dangerous, Garrett thought. He had watched brown bears on mountainsides, seen their muscles ripple across their humped backs, their fur undulate in waves. Each time he caught even a passing glimpse of one, he was awestruck. But never had he been this close. Snow alone had separated him from a sow grizzly, heavy with sleep, her cubs nursing at her side, her long claws trailing from her padded feet.

THE BOY WAS AT MABEL'S DOOR, covered with snow and leading a half-grown puppy on a rope leash.

'Faina? Is she here?'

'Why, no, Garrett. She isn't. But come on inside.'

He paused in the doorway and looked down at the black-and-white, floppy-eared pup.

'I suppose you can bring your new friend in as well,' Mabel said, gesturing them through the door.

The puppy wagged its tail furiously and, when Mabel bent beside it, tried to jump into her lap. She laughed and let it lick her face before she stood.

'So you got yourself a new puppy?'

'Naw. You know Mom and Dad won't let me have any sled dogs,' he said. He remained near the door, shifting awkwardly in his boots. 'No, actually, well, I brought it for her.'

'Not for Faina?'

'You don't think she'll like it?'

'Well, yes. Most any child would adore a puppy, but I'm not sure . . .'

'She's not a child.' His tone was irritable, even a little defensive.

'No, I guess she isn't a child any more, is she?'

Mabel had noticed a change in Faina. Her cheeks had thinned so that the bone structure was more striking and her limbs had gracefully lengthened. Close to sixteen or seventeen years old, Mabel guessed.

'Are you expecting her tonight maybe?'

'I don't know. We can never be sure when she will come. And I'm sorry, Garrett, but I'm not sure she could care for a puppy on her own.'

'She could.'

'Well, let's see what Jack thinks. He'll be home in a few hours.'

Garrett took the puppy outside to romp in the snow, and Mabel was left to muddle through her thoughts. She doubted the girl would even come into the house if she knew Garrett was there. Faina never visited when strangers were around. How long would Garrett stay, waiting to see her?

'Garrett's here?' Jack said when he returned just before nightfall. 'Saw his horse is in the barn.'

'Yes. He's come with a gift for Faina. A puppy.'

'A dog? For Faina, you say?' He grinned broadly. 'It'll be good for her. She's lonesome. I'll bet she's never been around a happy-go-lucky pup.'

WHEN FAINA KNOCKED at the door later that evening, Jack, Mabel and Garrett were on the floor with the puppy, tossing a knotted rag around the room. At the sound of the knock, Garrett stumbled to his feet.

Mabel opened the door, wondering if Faina would sprint away when she saw they had company, but the girl stood just inside the door without removing her hat and coat. When she saw Garrett, her eyes widened.

Here, child, Mabel said. Let me take your coat. Has it started snowing again? You remember Garrett, don't you? Esther and George's son? He . . . well, he has brought you something.

Garrett had been holding the puppy by its leash, but now he slipped the rope from its neck. The puppy charged towards Faina, tail wagging, tongue flapping. The girl backed away, until she was pressed against the door and the puppy was jumping at her.

It's all right, child. It's only a puppy, Mabel said. And I'd say it's already quite fond of you.

He won't bite. I promise, Garrett said. He knelt at Faina's feet and put his hands on the dog to settle it. See? He only wants to play. He reached up, took Faina's hand and brought it down to the dog's head. There. You can pet him.

The puppy lapped at the girl's fingers, and Faina giggled.

So, you like him? Garrett asked. Faina nodded, smiling and letting the puppy lick her fingertips. Because he's for you.

The girl looked at Mabel, then back to Garrett, her brow furrowed.

I know he's not like your fox, Garrett said. I thought about trying to live-trap one for you, but then I thought a pup might be better.

Faina put her palms to the puppy's cheeks, and the puppy leaned into her touch so that it seemed to be grinning.

You'll have to feed it regularly, Jack spoke up for the first time. That's a sled dog you've got there, you know, Faina. A husky. He'll carry a pack or pull a sled. And these dogs love the snow. He'll go everywhere with you. Take him out in the yard, you'll see what I mean.

Jack opened the door then, and the dog bounded out into the snow. Faina and Garrett followed, buttoning their coats as they ran. Jack closed the door after them and went to the window to watch with Mabel. The cabin's lantern light spilled outside and near the trees she could see Garrett and Faina tossing snow at the puppy and running as it chased after them.

OVER THE NEXT FEW WEEKS, Garrett and Faina and the puppy cavorted through the snow outside their cabin. Often Garrett would come early in the day, with some excuse of bringing a jar of his mother's jam or an axe handle he had mended for Jack. Then, inevitably, Faina and the dog would emerge from the forest. The girl's blue eyes were alight with joy, yet Mabel was apprehensive. She tried to enjoy the afternoons when they all came indoors, the young dog sprawled beside the woodstove, Garrett and Faina eating pie at the kitchen table. This had been part of a life she'd once hoped for herself—children dancing outside her window, children safe at her table.

Garrett soon hatched a plan to train the dog, and Mabel teased that this had been his motivation all along, to have a hand in raising a sled dog. He laughed but said he knew this pup was born for the snow. The next time he came, he brought a small wooden sled he had built and a harness he had fashioned out of leather. Since the dog was far from fully grown, he said, it would pull the sled empty. Mabel watched as the puppy charged towards the river, the sled bumping along behind it, and Garrett and Faina running behind.

Garrett returned alone just before sunset. 'Tomorrow we're going to take the dog for a long run, up the river. We're meeting here in the morning. Can I sleep in the barn for the night?'

'Sure,' Jack said. 'Looks like you found her a good husky.'

The next morning, as Mabel gave Garrett a lunch she had packed for the two of them, she could no longer keep her silence.

'Garrett, promise me something,' she spoke in a near whisper.

'Sure. What?'

'Promise me you won't build a fire? When you stop for your lunch. Promise me you will never let Faina near any kind of fire, even just a little one of twigs. I know it must sound like a strange request, but will you promise?'

Garrett looked down at her kindly, and for a moment she wanted to tell him the truth. Maybe she and Garrett could laugh at the improbability of it, and then it might never come to pass.

'I don't understand, but I promise,' Garrett said earnestly. 'And I would never let anything happen to Faina. You must know that.'

And in his face, she could see that he believed his own words.

THE BEAR DEN was a gift Faina had given him deliberately and with some understanding of his heart. It took Garrett time to think of a gift of equal significance, and at first he worried the puppy was a mistake.

Weeks later, he was more confident in his choice. The puppy was thriving under her care, its black coat thick and shiny. And Faina—where she had been quiet and serious around Garrett, she now laughed and danced. She and the puppy would chase each other in tighter and tighter circles until the girl fell giggling to the snow and the puppy bounded on top of her.

Now, they headed up the Wolverine River, sunlight flashed off the snow and every branch and dead leaf glittered with frost. The air stung Garrett's lungs, and his face burned in the cold. When they stopped for lunch Garrett thought of starting a campfire but then remembered Mabel's plea. They ate sandwiches and fed the puppy some frozen moose roast Mabel had packed.

We could head back now, Garrett suggested when they finished eating.

No, just a little farther. Please?

So they continued north, sometimes crossing the frozen channels, other times weaving through the trees along the shore. The riverbed was blown clear of snow and Garrett could see where the white-blue ice had buckled and frozen into great swells and dips. As they came to a bend, Garrett realised this was the farthest he had ever travelled upriver. Round the curve, the valley opened up and, in the distance, spires of blue ice glowed. It was the river's source—a glacier cradled between white mountains. From so many miles away, the craggy peaks seemed to waver in the sunlight like a mirage, close and distant, real and unreal.

Come on! Faina called, and she and the dog darted across hard-packed snowdrifts and into a stand of willow along the river bank. Garrett tried to follow but he could not weave so easily between the frost-encrusted trees. Stumbling through the brush, he did not see the girl until suddenly she was in front of him. She had hooked her arm round the trunk of a small willow and it bent gently under her weight. She leaned out from the sparkling branches and leaned closer until he felt her breath cool on his skin. Like a startled snowshoe hare, Garrett didn't move, not until her lips touched his.

Her cheeks were so smooth, so cold against his, and she tasted of the fragrance that all winter had haunted him—mountain herbs and wet stone and new snow. He slowly circled his arms round her and pulled her closer still. He shook off a glove and put his bare palm to her hair. Pressed against his, the entire length of her body was delicate but steady, alive and cool.

You are warm, she whispered against his lips.

Garrett let his mouth follow her jawline down to her neck and back to her ear and he knew he could lose himself in the place where her blonde hair met her soft skin. He could lose himself in her pale smoothness, in her gentle fingers, in her wide blue eyes.

He wanted to let his knees give way and pull them both down, to lie together in the snow, but he didn't. He stayed on his feet, one arm round her waist, the other at the back of her head, his face against her neck.

It was her—she reached up and began unfastening the silver filigree buttons of her coat.

No, no, Garrett mumbled. You'll be too cold.

She continued unbuttoning her coat. Garrett shook his other glove to the ground and slid his hands beneath the wool, his rough skin catching on the silk lining. A wave of guilt shuddered through him, that somehow what they were doing was wrong, but it was too late. There, along her delicate rib cage . . . there, against her beating heart . . . there, he was lost.

'I'M TROUBLED, JACK.'

'Hmmm?' He ladled some beans onto his plate. Why she always waited until mealtime to make her worries known he had never been able to figure.

'I'm concerned about the children . . . well, that's it, isn't it? They aren't children any more. A young man and a young woman, I should say. They spend so much time together, just the two of them, and I'm not sure it's appropriate. Considering their age.'

'They're just kids. It's good for her to have a friend.'

'But Jack, they aren't children any more. Don't you see that? Faina must be sixteen now, Garrett nineteen.'

'I suppose you're right, Mabel.' It did surprise him, how time had passed. Faina had been a child when she'd first come to their door. 'But Garrett isn't one for chasing after girls. And courting is a long ways off for those two.'

'You're wrong, Jack. My sister was married when she was Faina's age.'

After that Jack watched the two of them, the way they stood so their arms touched as they talked, the way they squeezed hands when saying goodbye to one another. Jack said nothing but couldn't put his finger on why it unnerved him.

The sun came and the snow began to drip, first from the eaves and tree branches, then down the mountainsides. Spring came fast and warm, and the river broke up in a great crashing rush. Jack told Mabel he was going to watch the ice flow past, but in truth he was following Garrett and Faina. The boy was already staying in the barn, though planting season was far off, and he met Faina and the dog in the yard. They hadn't even come to the cabin to wish Jack and Mabel a good morning before they walked down the trail towards the river.

'I'll be back in a bit,' Jack said as he put on his work jacket. Mabel looked at him as if to say something, but just kissed his cheek.

While the yard and main road were muddy, the trail to the river was more pleasant as it meandered among spruce trees. The ground was dry and mossy and webbed with roots. Soon he heard the roar of the river, and when he neared the water, he saw soft, silvery pussy willows budding.

He hoped to find them at the shore, throwing rocks at rotten river ice or tugging a stick from the dog's mouth. They weren't there, so he followed the trail along the river and through the willow shrubs until it eventually led him back onto higher ground and into another spruce forest. Here the trees were taller and thicker, and the land had a hushed, shaded quality. The trail dwindled to nothing, but he heard voices. He could call out, alert them to his presence, but he was here to spy on them, and he was sick with it.

He found them finally, tucked under one of the largest evergreens, their coats spread beneath them like blankets. It was a beautiful place; the sun shone through the needled branches and dappled the ground, and the air was scented with sharp, clean spruce. He watched through the trees only long enough to understand what he was seeing, and then was so overcome by shame and rage that he could barely see to find his way home again.

It seemed such a terribly long time that Jack was gone, and Mabel realised that she had made a mistake, telling him. She should have set aside her own uneasiness and talked frankly to the girl herself. Now it was too late. When Jack walked back into the yard she was at first relieved. He was alone. Then she noticed how upright he strode towards the barn, went to the woodpile and picked up the splitting maul. My God, she thought, he is going to kill him. But he began splitting logs, one after the other, and she was nearly as distressed. Jack wasn't doing a chore—he was unleashing his fury. Despite everything Jack had always said about Faina not being their daughter, he was viewing this all through a father's eyes.

Mabel didn't notice when Garrett came out of the trees, but when she no longer heard the rhythmic crack of wood, she looked out of the window and saw the two men standing beside the woodpile. She couldn't hear their words but they were speaking—first Jack, then Garrett. Jack waved his hands and she saw the young man's shoulders slump. Then he stood straight again and spoke more animatedly. Mabel was at the window, one hand against the glass pane. And then, seemingly without warning, Jack punched Garrett in the jaw and sent him sprawling to the ground.

She had never seen Jack strike anyone. When Garrett sat up, he rubbed his jaw with the back of his hand. Jack reached down, perhaps as an offer to help him stand, but the young man refused and stumbled to his feet.

When Jack came into the cabin, neither he nor Mabel spoke. She led him to the washbasin where she soaked his swelling knuckles and wrapped them in a cold wet cloth. Outside she heard Garrett's horse gallop from the yard.

Chapter 11

This summer we'll go down the river, towards the ocean. We'll catch salmon fresh from the salt water, when they still shine all silver. We'll make a bonfire and sleep in the sand. Maybe we'll go all the way to the ocean.

I've never been there.

You know what else we'll do?

Faina turned her head against his chest. No, she said. What else?

We'll swim in the river. We'll take off all our clothes and swim naked in the river.

Won't you be cold?

Nah. There's little ponds on the riverbed, where the water gets warm from the sun. They're clear and blue. You'll see. We'll float on our backs and when we put our heads under the water, I'll kiss you. Just like this.

It was like a terrible thirst. He could drink and drink her in and it was never enough.

When they were together, wandering the riverbed or hiking up a creek, they shared everything they knew. They studied the mud in the trails, pointed to tracks and named them. Garrett tried to teach her how to call like a lovesick bull moose. Faina tried to teach him the songs of wild birds. Then they would laugh and chase each other through the trees until they found one with wide boughs and a bed of spruce needles beneath it. There they would huddle together and taste each other's lips and eyes and hearts.

And when they were apart, he felt as if he were dying of thirst.

'SO I GUESS THAT'S THAT,' Jack said. He smacked the soot from his hands. At his feet was a pail of ashes he had cleaned out of the stove. 'I guess we're through with him. We won't be seeing that boy around here again. Planting time, and I'll be out there breaking my back, trying to get the fields done.'

'I think you underestimate him.'

'We'll see.' He knocked on the stovepipe and listened to the creosote fall. Then he shovelled it from the stove into the pail.

'He's the same young man we've always known. He's just in love.'

The horse still wasn't there. Jack walked through the barn and out into the pasture and saw, on the far side, that the gate was open.

He had been late coming out to feed and water the horse. He'd meant to be working the fields just after daybreak. But his back had been stiff this morning and he'd stayed in the cabin. He shut the gate and followed the trail towards the nearest field. Blinded by the sun, at first Jack couldn't see. He stood at the edge of the field and shielded his eyes with his hand.

Garrett was at the plough, tilling along the outside edge of the field.

He thought the boy nodded at him, but from this distance it was impossible to be sure. Jack started to wave at him, then stuffed his hand in his pocket. He turned on his heels and walked home.

A MISTY CHILL hung over the spring morning, but they left the cabin because the girl was like a caged animal, tense and fidgety. Mabel knew something was wrong and that Faina might tell her if they went for a brisk walk, just the two of them. They followed the wagon trails around the fields, striding side by side, until the words poured out of her.

Am I dying? the girl asked without looking at Mabel.

Why would you say such a thing?

I was bleeding. For months it came and went, and I doubled over in pain. Then I thought I was better, because it stopped and didn't come back. But now I wake and eat and can keep nothing in my belly. And all day I just want to lie and sleep.

Mabel understood at last; she led the girl to the picnic table and sat on the bench.

You will have a baby, you and Garrett. You are carrying his child.

The fog lay low along the riverbed, and their breath was visible in white clouds from their lips. Rigid and straight-backed, Faina stood and stared towards the distant mountains.

I know you are frightened, child, but you can do this. I believe in you.

How can I? What do I know of babies? The girl turned to Mabel and her eyes strained in a desperate grief. But you, she said suddenly. You must know something about babies. Please. You must. Take it and be its mother.

Mabel folded her hands in her lap.

For years, her arms had ached with longing. It was a self-indulgence she didn't often permit herself, but sometimes she would sit in a chair, her eyes closed, her arms crossed against her breast, and she would imagine holding a small baby there—its trusting warmth against her body, its tiny head smelling of milk and talcum powder, its skin softer than flower petals.

So now an infant, or at least the potential of an infant, was unexpectedly placed before Mabel, and she was tempted to accept it as a gift. Perhaps it was fate. And it was the right thing to do, wasn't it? She and Jack were equipped to raise the baby. The child would have a clean bed to sleep in and warm food on its plate. When the time came, the child could go to school in town.

Mabel allowed herself this brief daydream, then pushed it away. As much as she had ever wanted a baby, this one wasn't hers to take. It was Faina's, and she at last told her so.

The girl was poised to run, the way she had so many times before. But Mabel reached up and took one of her hands, coaxing her to sit beside her.

You can't run, child. Not from this. It is within you.

Faina's thin fingers, like the pale bones of a bird, rested in Mabel's hand.

You will have help, Mabel said gently. From all of us. Me and Jack. Esther will be only too eager to help. And there's Garrett, too.

The girl cast her eyes down.

You must tell him, Faina. Now that you understand what is happening, that you two have created a child and it is growing inside you.

He will be angry.

No. He won't. He'll be scared, like you, but he won't be angry. He loves you. And I believe in him, just as I believe in you.

Faina left her sitting alone at the picnic table, and Mabel shivered inside her coat and crossed her arms tightly. Faina, a frightened wisp of a thing, disappeared into the forest, and Mabel was angry at the injustice of it—that she should have wanted a baby so dearly and be denied one, and that this young girl should be cursed with one as a burden.

'FAINA IS PREGNANT.'

Mabel knew it was a terrible habit, waiting for dinner to tell Jack bad news, but it was one of the few quiet moments they had together. This time, though, she feared she might have unintentionally killed him. He was choking, coughing until his face was a horrid reddish purple.

Mabel waited for him to speak, but he didn't. 'She's pregnant, Jack.'

'I heard you.'

'Well, don't you have anything to say?'

'What is there to say? It's entirely our fault. She was more innocent than a child has ever been, and we were the only ones who could protect her. We let this happen.'

'Oh, Jack. Why does it always have to be somebody's fault? Sometimes these things happen. Life doesn't go the way we plan or hope, but we don't have to be so angry, do we?'

He pushed his plate away.

'There'll be a wedding, I suppose?' The disgusted expression hadn't left his face.

'Oh. Well. No one has spoken of it.'

'There will be a wedding.' It was a hard, clear statement that left no room for argument.

'We'll have to share the news with Garrett and Faina, then.' She gave her husband an ironic smile. 'But I agree. It's the only way.'

JACK WAS CALM. He could undo nothing, but at least he had a plan of action.

It began when Garrett came to him a few days after Mabel's news about Faina. The young man came with his hat in his hands.

'I'm here to ask permission to marry Faina. I don't have much to offer her, but we're bound together now and I mean to make the best of it.'

It was like a blow to the chest, and Jack had to sit down in a kitchen chair. Garrett stood by, shifting on his feet and clearing his throat.

He hadn't seen this coming. He was sure they would marry; he had assumed Garrett would take responsibility. But the boy came to him—Jack—to ask permission.

Fatherhood had arrived quietly, gradually, over the course of years, and he had been blind to it. And now, just as he understood that a daughter had been flitting in and out of his life, he was being asked to let her go.

'I'll do good by her. You have my word.'

Jack's focus returned to the boy, and when he looked up at the earnest face, he saw what Mabel had tried to tell him—Garrett did love the girl. Jack eased himself out of the chair until he stood eye to eye with Garrett.

'You will do good by her,' Jack said, and it wasn't an agreement but a command. He reached out to Garrett, and they shook hands like two men who had only just met and weren't yet certain of each other.

That night Jack's plan came to him, and he woke Mabel. 'We'll build them a cabin down by the river. That way Garrett will be close to the farm, but they'll have their own place.'

'Hmmm?' Mabel was half-asleep, but he went on.

'Faina and the baby will be close to you, so you can help. We'll start building right after planting. Maybe we can even have the wedding there.'

Jack let her drift back into sleep. He was satisfied.

He noticed the way the clean morning light slanted in through the window and lit up the side of Faina's face, and he wondered if it was always so hard, being a father. They'd finished a pot of tea and a few slices of bread with blueberry jam and he was left with no other way around the conversation he'd promised Mabel.

Jack cleared his throat, hoping to sound fatherly.

Faina? Is this what you want? Your life is going to change. You won't be able to disappear into the woods for weeks at a time. You'll be a mother, a wife. Do you understand what that means?

Faina tilted her head to the side in a half-shrug, but then she focused her blue eyes on Jack and their clarity seized him. Her face carried the same look he had seen many times before, a startling blend of youth and wisdom, frailty and fierceness.

I do love him. And our baby. I know that.

So you want to marry him?

We belong together.

Jack had expected to be happy. Isn't that what a father should feel? Joy?

But something weighed on him. Faina would never again be the little girl he had seen darting through the winter trees, her feet light on the snow and her eyes like river ice. She had been magic in their lives, coming and going with the seasons, bringing treasures from the wilderness in her small hands. That child was gone, and Jack found himself mourning her.

JACK LED GARRETT DOWN the wagon trail and out into a meadow within sight of the river. 'It's yours,' Jack said. 'Consider it a wedding gift. We'll build the cabin right in here, facing towards the mountains.'

'It's a fine place.'

The next evening, after they stopped planting for the day and ate dinner, he supposed Garrett had gone to sleep in the barn. He told Mabel he was going out for some fresh air, and he walked to the meadow. There he found Garrett with a shovel rough-sketching the outline of a cabin into the dirt.

THE WORK had a rhythm and purpose, and Jack and Garrett fell into it with ease, even relief: the back-and-forth pull of the two-man saw and the thunderous crash of trees falling, the slide of the draw knife along the spruce logs, the bark peeling off in long strips, the chop and slice of the sharpened axe, each notch hand-carved.

By the time planting was done, they had the log walls up waist high and it went faster now that they had all of each day. Jack let Garrett do the heaviest of the work. Mabel often came with lunch in a basket and sometimes she would stay long enough to discuss where a window should go or what kind of front porch they should build.

Faina was nowhere to be seen. Jack assumed she and Garrett met alone sometimes, but the girl did not come to Jack and Mabel's for dinner. For once, it was Jack who worried.

'Shouldn't she be resting, eating regular meals?'

'She's fine,' Mabel said. 'She's where she needs to be. Her life is going to change soon. Whatever else happens, she won't be able to run through the woods like a sprite. Everything will be different.'

FAINA CAME on a warm June day. Garrett was straddling the unfinished wall as Jack used a pulley to raise another log into place. Tall and lean, she showed no signs of pregnancy yet. She ran to them in bare feet, her arms and legs bronzed, her long hair bleached white by the sun.

She and Garrett gave each other shy smiles, and Jack felt like an intruder. Garrett jumped down from the log wall and led her through the rough-cut doorway and into the roofless cabin.

I know it's hard to see, with just the four walls, but over here will be the kitchen and the window will look out to the river. Won't that be fine?

Faina nodded, but her gaze was distant.

Garrett seemed unnerved by her silence. Don't you think, Jack? It's coming together?

Jack started to say that yes, he thought it would be a dandy little cabin for a family starting out, but then he saw the girl smile up at Garrett, a tender, reassuring smile. Jack was struck with the notion that perhaps she was the wiser and stronger of the two.

Faina stayed while the two men worked. She threw sticks for the dog. She ran through the tall, green grass around the cabin and picked bluebells and wild yellow asters. The dog ran, barking, to chase a squirrel into the woods, and Faina followed. When she reached the edge of the meadow, she looked over her shoulder and gave a small wave back towards the men.

'SHE'S LEAVING,' Garrett said. 'She'll be back but sometimes I wonder if this is the best for her—a baby. Me. If it's the right kind of life for her.'

'Too late to change that now,' Jack said. He regretted his anger.

'Maybe she doesn't have to give up everything,' Garrett said. 'You know. We'll run traps together this winter, after the baby comes. I'll take her out in the woods and she can put out her little snares.'

'Everything will change. It will. But you'll do the best you can.'

Chapter 12

There's no way in hell that cabin is going to be done in time for the wedding.' Esther's hands were on her hips as she stood looking up at the honey-coloured logs. '"Just a few more days, Mom." That's what he says to me. "We've almost got it wrapped up." Why is it men always overestimate their own prowess?'

Mabel smiled in spite of herself. 'They have done a great deal.'

'Ah well. When you're young, everything is romantic, right? Even a cabin without a roof.'

'It's lovely. I've sewed some curtains for the windows. And George tells me you're making them a quilt.'

'Yep. And it will be done by Sunday.' Esther laughed at herself and added, 'I might not sleep much this week, eh? But how's the dress coming?'

'It is finished, but Faina has secret plans. She's been working on it these past few nights at our house. She waits until we go to bed, and then she stays up at the table doing something, but she won't tell me what.'

'She is an odd duck, isn't she?'

Mabel had never thought of Faina in those terms, but the girl was peculiar, and even unconventional Esther could have misgivings about her son marrying her.

'It is true—I have never met another person like Faina,' Mabel said, choosing her words carefully. 'But then, I've never met anyone like you before either.'

'All right. All right. I'll give you that one. And I know I should count my blessings that someone is willing to put up with that son of mine.'

'She doesn't just put up with him. I think she's quite taken with him. They have a great deal in common. They love this place, and each other.'

'But who is she? She's a wild thing from the mountains. When she's saddled with a screaming brat and a sink full of dirty dishes, what then?'

Mabel's throat was swelling shut. She walked round the corner of the cabin, pretending to inspect the other wall. Esther was instantly at her side.

'Oh, Mabel. I meant no offence. I know she's like a daughter to you, and my son surely loves her. That'll have to do for the rest of us, won't it?'

Mabel smiled and nodded and blinked away tears. The two women hugged and hooked arms to walk back to Jack and Mabel's.

THE DAY OF THE WEDDING CAME, and Esther was right—the cabin wasn't finished, but it was all the more lovely, like a cathedral sculpted of trees and sky. Mabel walked there in the morning and was grateful to be alone with the sound of the river, the fragrance of the freshly peeled spruce logs, the blue sky, the green meadow. The cottonwood trees were blooming, and the downy white seeds floated on the breeze like feathers.

Jack was back at their own place, loading the wagon with tables and chairs to haul to the cabin. George and Esther were coming just before the ceremony so they could bring the food for afterwards. Garrett's oldest brother Bill would marry them. He wasn't a pastor but Garrett had wanted him to perform the ceremony. The brothers, who both had wives and families of their own now, would be the only other guests at the wedding.

They had curtained off a section of the unfinished cabin with white sheets so that Faina could put on her dress and prepare herself. She had not yet appeared this morning, and she had the wedding gown with her.

Mabel had sewed the dress from raw silk Esther had given her, leftovers from her oldest daughter-in-law's wedding gown. The ivory-hued silk had been shipped from San Francisco and had certainly cost more than Mabel and Jack could have afforded. The fabric was exquisite, weighted and fine and textured.

She had to be creative with the odds and ends of raw silk but she had sketched and sewed and embroidered for days on end. The skirt was straight and ankle length, the sleeves long, and the bodice fitted in a style that reminded Mabel of European brides in country chapels, of alpine beauties, of Russian maidens.

The dress itself was easy to sew; it was the embroidery that kept Mabel up late each night, bent over the kitchen table. Along the sleeves, across the narrow bodice and scattered down the skirt, Mabel used white silk thread to embroider tiny flowers and loops of thin vines and pearl-drop leaves. When the light caught the white stitches on the ivory silk, the flowers could be mistaken for snowflakes, the vines for eddies in snow.

Still, Mabel had yet to see the gown on Faina.

It's a surprise, Faina said. Wait and see.

Mabel had sewn it herself, so how could it be a surprise? But all she could do was make the girl promise that if it did not fit perfectly, she would bring it back in time for alterations. She had not seen Faina since.

Garrett wasn't to be found this morning either, and he had the wedding rings. Again secrecy. Garrett had asked Mabel to weave a wreath of flowers.

'For Faina's head?' Mabel asked.

'Nah. Not for Faina,' Garrett said. 'It needs to be bigger. About this big,' and he held his arms in a circle the size of a large mixing bowl.

Mabel had waited until the day of the wedding, knowing wild flowers would quickly wilt in the summer heat. And it was hot. Barely past eight in the morning, and already the arctic sun burned over the mountain tops.

Flowers for Faina's veil and flowers for her bouquet, flowers for the

Mason jars and flowers for the wreath Garrett had requested—Mabel longed to be consumed by them, as she had been by the embroidery. She wanted to escape the sense that fate was rolling in over the mountains like thunder.

Careful not to rip her newly sewn cotton frock, Mabel took her metal pail and walked the edge of the meadow to gather fireweed, their tall stalks just beginning to bloom fuchsia; bluebells with their sweet nectar; wild roses, simple with five pink petals and prickly stems; geraniums, their thin petals lavender with deeper purple veins. Farther into the woods, away from the harsh sun, Mabel plucked delicate white starflowers, dwarf dogwood with their fat white petals, oak ferns and lady ferns, and, at the last minute, a few wild currant branches with trailing vines of ripe red berries translucent as jewels.

The Bensons came just as she was arranging the fireweed and oak ferns in glass jars filled with cold river water.

'Well, look at us,' Esther said as she jumped down from the wagon.

'My goodness, Esther, I don't think I've ever seen you in a dress before!'

'Don't get used to it. I've brought my overalls for the reception.' The two women laughed and hugged. 'So where's the happy couple?'

'I haven't the slightest idea. I hope Faina arrives soon, though. I need to help her with her dress and hair. What time is it?'

'Nearly high noon. Time's a wasting.'

Just then they all turned towards a strange rumbling sound coming from the wagon trail. From round the corner appeared a shiny, bouncing automobile, a stream of dust kicked up behind it.

'That'll be Bill.' Esther made a disgusted face at Mabel. 'It was a present from his wife's family. Must be nice to be rolling in the dough.'

The automobile came to a grinding stop in the grass just short of the picnic table. The Bensons' oldest son opened the door and he and his wife and two small children piled out looking as if they had stepped off the streets of Manhattan. The children were dressed in ruffles and bows and the wife was wearing a stylish flapper dress in mauve silk.

'They don't even look like they're part of the family, do they?' Esther whispered in Mabel's ear. 'But I guess you can't kick them out just for that.' And, in fact, Mabel was surprised to find them all warm and charming.

The Bensons' other son, Michael, arrived next with his wife and three daughters, the youngest still in her mother's arms.

'Is she here yet? I can't believe none of us has even met her before,' Mabel heard the two young wives whispering.

As she helped Esther spread white tablecloths over the picnic and kitchen tables, Mabel tried to concentrate on the billow of fabric and the feel of the linen over rough, splintery wood as she smoothed out the wrinkles.

I'M HERE.

The voice was a whisper over Mabel's shoulder, but when she turned, no one was there.

Here. Inside the cabin. Will you help me?

It was Faina. Her voice came through the empty window frame of the cabin. How had she got past without anyone noticing? Mabel excused herself and stepped through the cabin door. The log frame overhead broke the sunlight into sections and dazzled Mabel's eyes.

Have you put on the dress?

No. You can't see it yet. But will you help me with my hair?

Faina stood in bare feet, wearing the cotton slip Mabel had sewed for her. There was the slightest rounding in her belly, just enough to pull the slip tight, and across her breasts as well. Faina was no longer a child, but a tall, beautiful young woman, and she had never seemed so substantial, so full of life. Mabel quickly let the curtain fall closed behind her.

Faina swept her hair across one bare shoulder. Will you plait it for me?

That would be perfect, child, with the veil I've made for you.

So Mabel brushed Faina's long hair, so blonde it was white. Once it was as smooth as silk, Mabel braided it into two plaits, one on each side. Just as Faina looked away, out of the empty window frame, Mabel pulled a tiny pair of sewing scissors from a pocket in her dress and snipped some hair from one of the plaits and slid it into her pocket. Then she set the veil on Faina's head, securing it with hairpins, and weaving the wild pink roses and white starflowers into the lacework above Faina's braids and across her forehead.

You will leave now, so I can put on the dress.

Are you sure? It will still be a surprise.

Please. Faina reached out for Mabel's hand and squeezed it. Her touch was strong and warm, and Mabel squeezed back and then impulsively brought the girl's hand to her lips to kiss it.

I love you, child, she whispered.

Faina's face was quiet and kind.

I wish to be the mother you are to me, she said so softly Mabel doubted her own ears. But those were the words she spoke, and Mabel took them into her heart and held them there for ever.

WHEN FAINA STEPPED ACROSS the cabin threshold and onto the green grass, a hush fell across the small gathering. Even the children quieted and stared up at her, and Faina bowed her head down to them and smiled as if she had known them all her life.

At first, Mabel could not see what was different about the dress. It fitted her perfectly and moved with a soft rustle against her skin. Faina wore leather moccasins beaded in shimmering white beads and tied with white ribbons up her calves. The veil flowed down her back and she held the bouquet of wild flowers, ferns and currant vines.

Then, as Faina stepped closer, Mabel saw the feathers—white swan feathers, stitched along the neckline of the dress. They lay flat against the fabric so that they seemed part of the raw silk, a mere variation in the texture. Mabel could see the pattern now, how the feathers went from smaller to larger at the centre of her chest. Other feathers were sewed along the hemline, and not one covered her embroidery of snow flowers, but each seemed part of the design.

Mabel heard someone take in a breath, perhaps one of the young women, but then Faina was walking past her to Jack's side and she could see the back of the dress. Pure white feathers fell down the centre of the skirt and fanned out into larger and larger sizes until along the hem some were as long as a woman's forearm, all laid flat against the fabric and moving gently with the silk. Like the fabric, the feathers gleamed ever so slightly, a sort of luminosity that came from within the filaments themselves.

Jack, wearing his best and only suit, took Faina's arm and they began to walk slowly towards the river where the jars of wild flowers sat on tree stumps. Everyone followed without speaking and the rustle of Faina's gown became the gentle roar of the river. They arranged themselves near the shore, the jagged, snowy mountain peaks behind them.

'Where is Garrett?' Mabel heard someone whisper. The sun was unbearably hot on her head and shoulders and her eyes ached from the piercing brightness. When she looked up at Jack, he nodded at her and gestured with his chin back towards the wagon trail. She turned and looked over her shoulder, and there was Garrett, riding his horse at a gallop across the meadow. He, too, wore a fine suit; with one hand he kept a black hat on his head and with the other he held the reins. At the horse's feet, Faina's husky sprinted, his tongue flapping at his mouth.

Garrett slowed the horse as he neared the cabin and dismounted even as the horse was still trotting. He loosely tied a lead rope to a nearby cottonwood, wiped his forehead with the back of his hand, and walked towards the gathering. Mabel was surprised when he came directly to her.

'Do you have the wreath?' he whispered.

Mabel pointed to the table where the circle of roses and ferns lay.

'Thank you,' Garrett said, and he kissed her on the cheek.

Curious, she watched him pick up the wreath and then tap the side of his leg with one hand. Faina's dog ran to him. Garrett held up a hand, and the dog sat. He slipped the wreath over the animal's head, and then what looked like a loop of ribbon and a small pouch. Again he held up his hand, and the dog stayed sitting while Garrett walked to the wedding gathering.

As the ceremony began, Mabel held on to Jack's arm, but it was as if she were floating and spinning. The hot sun blurred her vision. She would faint, or already had. Words swam and dodged, and she could not tell if they were spoken aloud or only in her head . . .

. . . Hope is the thing with feathers . . . perches in the soul . . . to have and to hold . . . Do you? . . . Do you? . . . until death do you part . . . until death . . .

I do . . .

I do . . .

There was a whistle, and Faina's dog trotted past as Mabel's eyes focused again. Faina was calling the husky to her, and Garrett was grinning proudly. The dog, the wreath of wild flowers round its neck, sat obediently at the bride's feet, and Garrett knelt beside it and untied the ribbon from its neck. He opened the pouch and poured two gold rings into his hand.

Then all sound was lost to the river's roar, and the ground shifted beneath Mabel. She saw Garrett and Faina, face to face, the flicker of the gold rings in the sun, and then they were kissing and everyone was cheering.

'Are you all right, Mabel? Mabel?' Jack held her from behind, his arms firmly beneath her elbows. 'Here, let's sit down at the table. It's this heat. It's got the best of you.'

Someone brought her a glass of water and one of the young women swept a fan back and forth in front of her. At last she could breathe and think.

'Faina? Where's our Faina?'

'She's over there.' Jack pointed to one of the big cottonwoods where the girl stood, white and shimmering, beside Garrett.

'But . . . is it snowing?' and she heard someone laugh beside her.

'Goodness no, dear.' It was Esther. 'Just cottonwood seeds.'

The air was filled with white down. Some floated up and over the trees, while other seeds drifted lazily to the ground. Faina looked at Mabel through the falling white and held up a hand, a little wave, like when she was a child.

'They're married?' Mabel whispered.

'Yes, they are,' Jack said.

Chapter 13

The night was cool and pale blue, and Faina lay naked atop the wedding quilt. She was on her side, her long legs askew, one arm beneath her head, the other curved below the slight round of her belly. Garrett took off his suit jacket. His white shirt was clammy with sweat and his feet ached from the dress shoes he had worn all day. He undressed and left his clothes on the rough-cut plank floor. As he walked towards the bed, he let his hand skim across the wedding gown where it had been thrown over a chair, as if a giant wild bird had shrugged off its skin and cast it aside.

After the ceremony, as they had eaten fire-grilled salmon, potato salad and an extravagant white cake with white frosting and candied rose petals, as the voices ebbed and flowed and the sun danced off glasses of homemade elderflower wine, again and again Garrett let his hands touch the small of Faina's back where the feathers lay flat against the silk, and he knew they had come from a wild swan she had snared the past winter.

Aren't you cold? Garrett whispered as he lay beside her. She shook her head and slid her arm round his neck to kiss him. Overhead, a few stars shone in the gloaming. It could rain, the bugs could be ferocious, he had told her, but she had insisted on sleeping in their unfinished cabin.

It's our home, she had said. So he hauled their wedding bed to the cabin, along with the quilt his mother had sewed for them.

As they made love beneath the summer night sky, he tried not to think about the child in her womb. He wanted to think only of her.

DURING THE NEXT WEEKS, as Jack and Garrett worked beneath the endless sun to put the roof on the cabin, then add the doors and woodstove and cupboards, Faina disappeared into the trees, her dog trotting beside her. She was gone for hours, sometimes the entire day, and Garrett did not know what to make of it. He politely dismissed invitations to Jack and Mabel's for dinner, not wanting them to know how rarely Faina joined him for meals.

Where do you go every day? I thought you wanted to be here, with me, in our home.

I do.

So?

We love each other, don't we?

He didn't want his voice to whine.

She came to where he sat, held his face up to her and kissed him hard. That night she stayed.

It was the end of September and cold. He smelled burning wood one evening as he walked the wagon trail home. As he got closer, he saw smoke rising from their chimney and then Faina was standing in the doorway, her hands on her swollen belly. Garrett had never seen anything so welcoming.

You're home, he said.

So are you.

Inside, rows of large birch baskets crowded the floor, each filled to overflowing. I, too, have been working, she said with a small smile.

She led him through the rows of baskets and paused to put a leaf to his nose, a berry to his lips. Some he knew—Eskimo potato root, blueberries, tender spruce tips. A few of the plants he had seen before but did not know their names; others, like the mushrooms and lichens, he would have been afraid to eat if he'd come across them in the woods. He trusted her, though, and carried her baskets up into the tall-legged log cache he had built.

Still she returned to the forest with her birch baskets. She wore a long wool skirt and full-cut blouse Mabel had sewed for her, and she held the small of her back against the weight of her growing belly. She brought home grayling and salmon, grouse and rabbits, which she skinned and cleaned and dried in strips on racks by the shore of the Wolverine River.

Each night, as the windowpanes turned darker with the coming winter, she was home. She served Garrett strange-smelling soups and bowls of nameless mush. His mother noticed he had lost weight and smelled of smoked meat and wild plants. She wanted to know what Faina was feeding him, but he would pat his stomach and tell her he was faring fine on her meals. Then he would sneak a few of his mother's buttery cookies.

GARRETT WASN'T PREPARED for the screaming. Faina's voice had always been clear and serene, like a glacier pond, but now it was ripped from her throat in a beastly, tortured growl. He went again and again to the curtained-off door, but Jack put a hand on his shoulder.

'It's no place for you.'

'Is she all right? What's happening in there?'

Jack looked tired and old, older than he ever had. 'It's never easy.'

Just then Esther pushed aside the curtain and Garrett could only stare at the blood covering his mother's hands and arms.

'We need more rags.'

'Is she OK? Is the baby OK?'

'I said more rags,' and she turned back to the room where Faina lay on their bed. Before the curtain fell closed, Garrett caught a glimpse of her legs, her bare feet in the air, and blood, everywhere blood.

'Jesus Christ. Is this how it's supposed to be?' Jack pushed by him with a bundle of dishtowels in his arms. The smell of blood and sweat and something else, something like a salty marsh, overpowered Garrett and he stumbled to the door.

Outside it was dark and cold. He gulped the fresh air and walked towards the river. Then he heard Faina cry out again. He went back indoors and asked Jack if he should fetch more towels or heat more water.

At some point in the night Garrett dozed in a chair and when he woke to the absence of screaming, he jumped to his feet. He went to the curtain. 'Is it here? Has the baby come?' he whispered loudly through the fabric. His mother came to him and put her hands to his shoulders.

'Not yet, Garrett. Not yet,' and her tone, gentle and kind, was so unlike his mother that it terrified him all the more. 'We're letting her rest up a bit, before she pushes some more. She's asking for snow, of all things. You could bring her a cupful. It can't hurt.'

He packed a pitcher with fresh snow and gave it to his mother.

'Tell her I love her. Will you do that?'

It was hours later, when the voices rose again. 'There you go. Come on, dear. The head's crowning. Come on now. Don't give up on us, girl.'

And then there was a cry like the bleating of a calf, and Garrett didn't understand what he heard. He looked at Jack, who stood beside him.

'It's your baby, Garrett. It's here.' Jack guided him towards the curtain.

'Faina, are you all right? Can you hear me?' he called.

'Yes, Garrett,' and it was the voice he loved. 'We're all right.'

Then there was the child's cry again, racking and tiny.

'There we go, little one,' Esther said. 'Time to meet your daddy.'

Mabel stood beside the bed, tears streaming down her cheeks. Faina was propped up in the bed with pillows behind her. Her face glistened with sweat and her hair was a ragged mess. She looked up at Garrett and then down into her arms where a blanket was bundled.

'Go on. Don't be afraid,' Esther said. 'Go meet your son.'

'Son?'

'That's right. As if there weren't enough of you around here.'

When he got to the bedside, he put an arm round Faina's shoulder and looked down into the blanket where a small, wrinkled and red face looked up at him. Garrett bent and put his lips to the baby's cheek, and the skin was so soft he could barely feel it. Then he turned to Faina and kissed her damp forehead.

Chapter 14

The days became fragile and new to Mabel, as if she had only just recovered from a long illness and stumbled outside to discover summer had passed to winter while she slept. Her entire world was held in the little clenched fists of the newborn baby.

Each morning she walked the snowy path to Faina and Garrett's cabin. In a basket, she brought hard-boiled eggs, bread or slices of bacon left over from her breakfast with Jack, along with a sack of diapers, washcloths and clothes that she had washed at home and dried by the woodstove.

How are you today, child? she would ask Faina, and Faina would smile and look down at the baby in her arms. I am well. And so is he. See how he looks at you when you speak. He knows you are here.

The infant did indeed seem to be thriving. The first few days of nursing had been a trial, but now, two weeks later, he slurped noisily as Faina covered herself with a blanket of muskrat furs she had sewed. She cooed to him as he drank, and closed her eyes contentedly while he dozed, and Mabel took out her drawing pad and pencils and made little sketches.

When he woke, Mabel changed the baby's diaper, his legs bending and straightening as he screamed a protest. He doesn't get any more used to that, does he? Mabel said, as she pinned the clean diaper.

But Faina wasn't listening. She had gone to the window and was looking out over the bright snow.

You can go outdoors for a bit. I'll stay here with him.

Faina did not speak as she put on her blue wool coat and her knee-high moccasins, but when she opened the door, she glanced back at Mabel and her son. Mabel could not read her expression.

Whether because of the gust of cold air or the sudden absence of his mother, the baby fussed in Mabel's arms, so she stood and walked to the window, patting the newborn and humming into his small ear. Out of the corner of her eye she saw the blue coat against the white snow.

Faina was walking across the meadow and towards the trees, but she struggled in the snow and stopped frequently to rest. Mabel watched and was troubled by what she saw. The labour and delivery had taken a terrible toll on her body, and she needed more rest. She considered going to the door and calling out for her to come inside and lie down, but then Faina was no longer walking. She simply stood, a single, forlorn figure in the snow, the wilderness stretched out before her, her long blonde hair shining in the winter sun. And then she turned back towards the cabin, towards her son and home, and followed her own deep trail back.

MABEL WOKE with her pulse racing, sat bolt upright in bed, and waited to understand what had startled her.

'Mabel? Are you awake? It's me, Garrett.' A hoarse whisper from the bedroom door.

Mabel scrambled over Jack and pulled a sweater over her nightgown as she walked into the main room of the cabin. Garrett's presence was making her trembling old heart sink into the pit of her stomach.

'I'm sorry to wake you . . .'

Mabel held up a hand to Garrett. She was weak and nauseous.

'Let me sit.'

Garrett pulled a chair out from the table and put a hand on her shoulder to steady her. She sat and inhaled deeply. 'Faina's not well,' Garrett said, and just then Jack came from the bedroom.

'What is it? What's going on?'

'All day she was restless and not herself. She kept going outside, as cold as it is, and I tried to stop her. But I couldn't. I should have . . .'

'And now?' Mabel asked, trying to help the young man focus.

'She got worse. She said she hurt and her cheeks were red. She didn't want to get out of bed, and she wouldn't eat a thing. But she nursed the baby and they both went to sleep, so I thought I'd wait until morning and see how she was. But then, just now, I rolled over and my arm touched hers and she's burning up hot.'

'She should have had the baby at the hospital in Anchorage,' Jack said.

'She didn't want to go,' Mabel reminded him. She went to the bedroom and got dressed by candlelight. When she returned, Garrett was sitting in a kitchen chair with his head in his hands.

'Where's the baby?'

'I left him at home, sleeping in his cradle. I didn't know what to do. It seemed too cold to bring him.'

'In the morning, we're taking her straight to Anchorage,' Jack said as he laced his boots.

ON THE WAY, the same kind of calm determination settled over Mabel as when Jack had injured his back.

The baby was still asleep in his cradle, and Faina was in bed curled up on her side, arms wrapped round her middle, moaning softly. She rolled over onto her back and Mabel could see her face. Droplets of perspiration ran down her temples and her skin was flushed and blotchy.

Mabel put a hand to her forehead. It was hot to the touch. Then she felt burning fingers round her wrist and heard a dry-throated whisper.

Mabel? You are here?

Faina was holding on to her. At first she thought rivulets of sweat were gliding down her cheeks, but then she saw they were tears.

What is happening to me?

Shhh. Don't be frightened, child. You have an infection in your blood. That is what causes the fever. But there is a medicine you can take that will make you better.

I won't go to the hospital. I won't leave my baby.

Mabel was relieved to see that defiant jut of the chin.

Let's not fret about that now. Here, I brought you water. You must drink it. It will cool you, and it will help you make milk for the baby.

Mabel held the glass to Faina's chapped lips and she drank and drank until it was empty. When Garrett came to the bedroom door, Mabel asked for a basin of snow. She dipped a wet cloth into the cold snow and wrapped a clump inside it. When she pressed this to Faina's skin, the girl sighed in relief. Her cheeks began to cool and lose their ruddy colouring.

There. There. Is that better?

Faina nodded and took Mabel's hand and held it to her cheek. She closed her eyes and rested her head against her arm. Only after Mabel was certain she was asleep did she slide her hand out from under her cheek.

It was three in the morning when she heard Jack putting more wood into the stove. The two men had alternated sleeping in chairs and busying themselves with contrived chores. The baby woke for his feeding then, and Mabel carried him in to Faina.

Your little one is hungry, dear.

Faina rolled to her side but never seemed completely awake, even as she slid her breast from her nightgown and held the baby against her. Once again her skin was hot and blotchy. Not until the baby was back in his cradle, fed and changed and fast asleep, did Faina awake and begin to plead with Mabel.

Please, she whispered. Take me outside. I feel so hot, and I feel as if I can't catch my breath. Please?

No, child. You must stay in bed and rest. Perhaps there was hope there, in the winter night. But what would Garrett and Jack say?

'SHE WANTS TO GO OUTSIDE.'

'What? Now? In the middle of the night?' Jack said. 'Are you mad?'

'It's so stuffy in here. I think she feels as if she's suffocating.'

'We could prop the door open,' Garrett suggested.

'She wants to be outside, under the night sky,' Mabel said, and Garrett nodded, understanding.

'OK,' he said finally. 'We'll take her outside.'

MABEL EASED FAINA into a sitting position on the edge of the bed. She laced the girl's moccasin boots and pulled her blue wool coat on over her nightgown. Then she took the red scarf and mittens Garrett had handed her, and as she wrapped the scarf round Faina's neck she recognised her sister's dewdrop-lace stitch.

I've always meant to ask you . . .

But she stopped herself and slipped the mittens over Faina's hands.

Mabel helped her lie back on the bed. A short while later Garret returned to the bedside and he and Mabel helped Faina to her feet. Garrett put her marten hat on her head and tied the straps beneath her chin.

Come and see the bed I've made for you under the stars.

Faina smiled up at her husband as he helped her walk outside. Not far from the cabin, he had laid several logs side by side, and on top of these he had piled caribou hides and beaver pelts until they formed a thick mattress.

The night was calm and cold, perhaps the coldest Mabel had ever known. The snow squeaked beneath her boots, and the air was sharp. Mabel hesitated. Perhaps this was a mistake. But then she heard Faina's long, easy breaths and imagined the cold air against her feverish brow. With each of them holding one of her arms, Mabel and Garrett led her the short way from the cabin to the makeshift bed. She let out a long sigh as Garrett spread a beaver-pelt blanket over her. Mabel had brought the wedding quilt from their bed, and she laid this on top, too.

Look at the stars, Garrett whispered. Do you see them all?

Yes. They're beautiful.

He stayed with her, sitting in a kitchen chair at her side, while Mabel went in to the cabin. A short time later, when the baby awoke wanting to be held, Mabel asked Garrett if he would like to come indoors for a while. She could sit with Faina.

Do you want me to stay? Garrett asked Faina.

No, she said gently. Go inside. Hold our son.

Mabel leaned over Faina and tucked the wedding quilt around her. Then she wrapped herself in a blanket and sat in the chair.

Are you well, child?

Oh, yes. Out here, with the trees and the snow, I can breathe again.

It was like an extraordinary dream: Faina's quiet sighs and the occasional pop and crack of river ice and tree branches snapping in the cold, the stars everywhere in the broad, deep night, broken only by the jagged horizon of the mountain range. Illumination behind the peaks shot up into shards of light, blue-green like a dying fire, rippled and twisted, then spun circles into ribbons of purple that stretched up and over Mabel's head until she heard an electric crackle like the sparks from a wool blanket in a dry cabin at night. She looked directly up into the northern lights and she wondered if those cold-burning spectres might not draw her very soul into the stars.

'JESUS, MABEL, you're buried in snow. Where's Faina?'

She did not remember falling asleep. Who could doze in such cold? But she was warm in her cocoon of wool and blanket, her nose nuzzled into her coat, and she did not wake until she heard the men's voices.

'She must be in the cabin, tending the baby.'

'No. She isn't there.'

Stiff and sore, Mabel stood and wondered at all the snow covering her blanket. The night had clouded over and it had snowed several inches. She went after the men, could hear Garrett calling in the cabin.

'Faina? Faina?'

'Where is she, Mabel?' Jack turned to her, nearly accusing.

'She was just there, beside me. She must be near.'

Garrett came from the cabin with a lantern.

'Where is she?' There was no anger in his voice, only desperation, and he ran towards the river. 'Faina! Faina!'

Among the caribou hides, Mabel saw the wedding quilt buried in snow. She picked it up to shake the snow off, and caught sight of blue wool.

'Jack?'

He came to her side, looked down where she pointed, then knelt and with his bare hands swept away the snow. Faina's blue coat, embroidered with snowflakes. Her scarf. Her mittens. Her moccasins. He picked them up one by one, shaking off the snow, then draped the clothes over his arm and carried them inside. Mabel followed with the snow-dampened quilt, and they set them all on the table.

'I'll go after Garrett. Care for the baby,' he said.

'But Jack . . . I don't understand.'

'Don't you?'

'She's gone?'

He nodded.

'But where?'

Without answering he left the cabin.

When the baby woke, crying for his mother's milk, Mabel dipped the end of a clean cloth into warm, sweet tea and put it to his mouth. He sucked frantically, then turned his head and cried. She walked him back and forth in front of the window until he cried himself to sleep. She sat in the chair and swayed from side to side with the sleeping baby and prayed this night was not real, that indeed it was a nightmare. But then Jack came through the door. She raised her eyebrows at him, and he shook his head.

'Nothing?' she asked.

'Not even a set of tracks.'

'Where's Garrett?'

'He won't come in. He says he'll find her. He's gone to saddle his horse.'

'Oh, God, Jack. What have we done?'

He didn't speak for some time, but sat to unlace his boots. Then he reached to Mabel, to take the baby.

Surprised, she stood and gently slid the bundle into his arms. Jack swaddled the blanket more firmly and ran a finger along the baby's cheek, his head bent so low to the newborn that at first Mabel could not see the tears streaming from his eyes.

'Jack?' Mabel reached out and held his face in her hands. 'Oh, Jack.' She took the baby from his arms and set him in the cradle, rocking it slowly until she was certain he was asleep. When she stood, Jack was behind her. Mabel went to him and pressed her face into his chest, and they held each other like that for some time.

'She is gone, isn't she?'

Jack clenched his teeth and nodded as if his entire body pained him.

Grief swept over Mabel with such force that her sobs had no sound or words. It was a shuddering, quaking anguish, and she wept until there was nothing left in her. She wiped her face with the tips of her fingers and sat in the chair, expecting Jack to go out the door and leave her alone. But he knelt at her feet, put his head in her lap, and they held each other and shared the sorrow of an old man and an old woman who have lost their only child.

Maybe it was only the wind, or her own terrible grief, but Mabel was certain she could hear Garrett's voice. Sometimes it was like a shout, down by the river. Other times it was a deep, mournful cry that seemed to come from the mountains themselves.

She and Jack stayed with the baby that night, waiting for Garrett to come home to his cabin. Mabel dozed beside the cradle, where the infant slept quietly, but again and again she was jolted awake.

'Did you hear that?' she asked.

Jack stood beside the woodstove, his face drawn. 'Wolves, I think.'

But she knew differently. She knew it was Garrett, riding and searching and crying into the starless night sky. Faina. Faina. Faina.

Epilogue

Hello. Anyone home?' Jack rapped on the cabin door, and then slowly opened it. 'Hello?' Using his cane, he stepped into the cabin, stood for a moment in the doorway. There, on a shelf near the woodstove, as always, was Faina's porcelain doll, its blonde hair still in neat braids, its red and blue dress as bright as the day Jack had set it on a stump for her.

'Garrett?' he called out again, knowing there would be no answer. He left and closed the door.

He wasn't far down the trail, walking at his slow, awkward gait, leaning on his cane, when he heard the boy calling through the trees.

'Papa! Papa!'

Jay ran down the trail towards him and not far behind him lumbered Faina's old husky.

'Papa! Look what I caught.' The boy held up a willow branch with one small, dusty grayling hanging from it.

'Well done. Well done.'

'Maime said we could eat it for dinner.'

Jack took the stringer from the boy and inspected the fish. 'As I recall,

Grandpa George and Grandma Esther are coming for dinner, too.'

'And Daddy?'

'He's still out riding. But he'll be home soon.'

'He says this year I can come on his long trap line, and maybe we'll catch a wolverine.'

'That would be fine, wouldn't it?'

But the boy was already dashing ahead.

'Jay?' Jack called to him. 'Do you think we might catch a few more fish, to make sure there's enough for everyone?'

'Sure, Papa. We can catch some more.'

The boy disappeared round the next bend in the trail.

'Just me and you, old man,' Jack said and patted the dog's greying muzzle. 'Think you'll find my pace suits you better.'

The autumn day was chilly, and the trail was littered with yellow birch leaves. Along the mountains, clouds gathered. 'Smells like snow,' Jack said, and the dog held its nose to the air as if in agreement.

Jack made his way past their cabin, through the brush and down to the stream in time to see Mabel reel in a grayling as it splashed through the shallows. The boy pranced excitedly on a nearby boulder.

'Maime caught the biggest one ever! Look, Papa. Look.' The boy jumped to the shore, unhooked the fish from the line, and held it up.

Mabel smiled at Jack, the fishing rod still in her hand. Her hair had gone completely white now, and wrinkles folded softly round her eyes and mouth, but there was a youthfulness in her gaze.

She spent many an afternoon out of doors with the boy, teaching him to catch fish and listen for birds and watch for moose. Some days she would tell Jay about his mother, how he had her blue eyes and how she had come from the mountains and snow and knew the animals and plants as well as she knew her own hands. And sometimes she would open the locket at her throat to show the boy the twist of blonde hair.

'Little Jack could have had that big fish,' Mabel said and kissed the top of the child's head. 'He just let it get away.'

Little Jack. That's what she always called him. Garrett had asked permission, nearly a month after Faina was gone. Would it be all right if I named the boy after you? He's your grandson, after all.

George and Esther arrived before nightfall, and as always Esther was talking even as she came in the door and her arms were loaded with jars and towel-wrapped goodies. As they were flouring the grayling and frying them in a buttered cast-iron pan, Jay ran to the window.

'It's Daddy! Daddy's here!'

Jay was in his arms before Garrett could take off his coat and hat.

'What did you see, Daddy? What did you see?'

'Well, let me think. Oh, yes. I saw . . . a wolverine. I was way up high, above the tree line, in this little valley I once visited a long time ago. There used to be a wolverine there, but there hasn't been for years.'

'But you saw one?' the boy asked.

'I did. I'd tied the horse off to a tree and was hiking up over these rocks when, on this ridge, a wolverine was looking down at me. I thought it might jump on my head. He had claws this long.' Garrett held up his index finger and thumb to indicate several inches.

'Were you scared?'

'No. No. He just looked at me with his yellow eyes. Then he turned, real slow, and sort of loped away and over the ridge.'

'What else did you see, Daddy? What else?'

'I guess a wolverine's not enough,' Esther said and chuckled.

'Well, not much else. Except for those clouds over the mountains. Bet you anything the snow will come tonight,' Garrett said.

All through dinner, the boy kept looking out of the window, even as they commended him on the good-tasting fish he had helped catch.

'Settle down, Jay,' Esther said. 'You know a watched sky never snows. Go sit with Grandpa George. Maybe he'll share his piece of cake with you.'

George playfully scowled at the boy, then grabbed him in a bear hug and tickled him.

After dessert, George and Esther began to gather their belongings and talk of going home, and the boy looked crestfallen. He always protested when these gatherings ended.

Mabel helped Esther put on her coat, Jack shook hands with George, and Garrett said he and Jay would come out to hitch the wagon.

'Put your hat on, Little Jack,' Mabel called after him, but the boy had already run out the door.

Jack was stacking dishes on the table when he heard the wagon begin to creak down the dirt road, and then he heard another sound—yips and whoops of laughter. Mabel was at the kitchen window.

Jack peered over her shoulder. At first he could see only their reflections in the windowpane, but then he began to see past their two old faces to make out the figures in the night.

Garrett stood near the barn with a lantern in his hand and nearby the boy was leaping and throwing his arms up to the sky. The dog bowed playfully beside the boy, barked, then jumped and ran in circles, too.

As Jack's eyes grew accustomed to the darkness, he saw the ground covered in white and, in the light of Garrett's lantern, snowflakes spinning and falling.

He took hold of Mabel's hand, and when she turned to him, he saw in her eyes the joy and sorrow of a lifetime.

'It's snowing,' she said.

eowyn **ivey**

Profile

Born:
Denver, Colorado.

Name:
Eowyn (pronounced A-o-win) . Her mother named her after a character from J. R. R. Tolkien's *Lord of the Rings*.

Family:
Husband and daughters, Grace 13, Aurora 5.

Education:
BA in journalism and creative writing through Western Washington University's honours programme. Studied creative nonfiction through University of Alaska Anchorage's programme.

Favourite Book:
The Hobbit.

You live in Alaska where *The Snow Child* is set. What do you love most and least about it?

I love the wildness. There is still a great deal of wilderness here, and it's a very humbling, awe-inspiring place to live. There is little about Alaska that I don't like, but mid-February is dark, cold and dreary; the holidays have come and gone and spring seems far away. The wind howls and temperatures often fall well below zero degrees Fahrenheit. This is when I think, Hmmm, a tropical island might be nice.

What's your favourite time of year and why?

What I love is the change of seasons. I love the extremes of the midnight sun in the summer and the near complete darkness in the winter. I love that in the summer it is incredibly lush and green, and then that gives over to barren whiteness in the winter.

How did you meet your husband?

We grew up in the same small town here in Alaska, after my family moved from Denver when I was three or four years old. We started dating when I was fourteen and he was sixteen. We just celebrated our nineteenth wedding anniversary. I know how rare this is—somehow we lucked out and discovered in each other a best friend and lifelong companion.

You wrote a newspaper column for a time, dedicated to outdoor adventures. Is this something you do a lot?

I do enjoy the outdoors, and it is very much a part of our family life. When we take our daughters on holiday, it is usually on a hunting or fishing trip. I love to spend an afternoon hiking into the mountains to pick blueberries, or cross-country skiing out of our backyard, but I particularly relish the longer trips we go on. Each fall we spend weeks on the tundra, sleeping in tents and hunting caribou; other trips we camp along a river so we can catch our salmon for the winter. These times, when life is stripped down to basic necessity and I am surrounded by the wilderness, make me feel very alive and peaceful.

You work now in a local independent bookstore. What's best about that job?

I have always loved to read, and I am so completely at home among books and other readers. It is a wonderful gift to spend the working day talking about books, learning about new titles, recommending books to customers. It really is a dream job for me.

Tell us about the origins of *The Snow Child*—your inspiration came from the bookstore originally, I believe?

Yes, I was working at the bookstore when I came across a children's picture book that told the *Snegurochka* fairy tale. In the story, an old man and woman build a little girl out of snow and she comes to life. I had never come across this Russian fairy tale, and it lit my imagination on fire. I abandoned another novel I had been working on for nearly five years and started writing and researching *The Snow Child*.

If you were hosting an Alaska-inspired dinner party, what would you serve?

Oh, this sounds like fun! Let's start with smoked salmon on toasted homemade bread for an appetiser, and maybe a glass of ale brewed by our neighbour. Then, for dinner, barbecued moose ribs, grilled Copper River sockeye salmon, potato salad with fresh basil from our greenhouse, and sautéed broccoli, carrots and leeks from the garden. For dessert, rhubarb pie and a glass of homemade crème de cassis made with wild currants.

Would you describe the interior of your home for us so that we can imagine the setting?

Our house is in the middle of a twenty-acre parcel, so out any window you see spruce and birch trees and mountains. Our main living area features a well-worn couch and two comfy chairs, the woodstove, a set of moose antlers on one wall and a lovely quilt made by a friend on the other wall. Out through the large picture windows, you can see our deck with pots of summer flowers—yellow and purple pansies and nasturtiums, and then down to our garden and chicken house. Not far off are the Chugach Mountains, where snow still lines the deepest valleys even in July.

And your next book?

I am part-way into my next novel, and it will share some similarities with *The Snow Child*—set in historical Alaska with some mythological elements. But I'm hoping to continue to branch out with my imagination and writing. I think this next one might be more adventurous and epic in scope.

COPYRIGHT AND ACKNOWLEDGMENTS

Spine: Rick Lecoat @ Shark Attack. Front cover (from left): © Roy Bishop/Arcangel Images; (centre left): © Zia Soleil/Getty Images; (centre right): © Clover/Superstock; (right): © www.blacksheep-uk.com. 6–7: illustration: Rick Lecoat @ Shark Attack; 160: © Alexander James. 162–3: photo: Lisbeth Hjort/Cultura; illustration: Lisa Christophi@velvet tamarind. 274–5: illustration: Kessell Direction & Design. 436 © David Cooper. 438–9: illustration: Richard Smythe. 574 © Stephen Nowers.

Every effort has been made to find and credit the copyright holders of images in this book. We will be pleased to rectify any errors or omissions in future editions. Email us at gbeditorial@readersdigest.co.uk

Printed and bound by GGP Media GmbH, Pössneck, Germany

020-280 UP0000-1